Please return/renew this item
by the last date shown.
Books may also be renewed by
phone or the Internet.

www.tameside.gov.uk

Take nothing but pictures. Leave nothing but footprints. Kill nothing but time.
Anonymous

Nigel Jay Robson has been a TV and radio broadcaster (as Nigel Jay) for over 20 years, mainly with the BBC in North West England and in the Midlands, with additional appearances on national TV news and BBC Radios 1, 4, 5, the World Service and Children In Need. He directed for television *Another Pakistan*, which has been transmitted around the world, from the USA to the Middle East and beyond.

In a career which has spanned writing fifteeen-second news clips, half-hour documentaries and presentation scripts for three-hour magazine programmes, this is his first novel.

*

AND NO WINGS combines, adventure, intrigue, science (fiction?) and humour to present a possible, if improbable, answer to the crisis facing Twenty-First century planet Earth, whilst exploring some fundamental human dilemmas. If God exists, does He take sides? Why is *avarice* at the core of our behaviour? And is Gabriel right? Are we just cretins?

AND NO WINGS

Nigel Jay Robson

impressions
Joint

Published by Joint Impressions 2009

A CIP catalogue record for this book
is available from the British Library

ISBN 978-0-9561833-0-9

Printed and bound in the UK by
CPI Mackays, Chatham ME5 8TD

Joint Impressions
275 Deansgate
Manchester
M3 4EL

ACKNOWLEDGEMENTS

I am Indebted to Sandy Lindsay, Tris Brown and Jane Hargreaves for accepting the task of reading through the first manuscript of this book. I feared the worst but their reactions - a mix of enthusiasm and constructive criticism - encouraged me to continue. Following their comments, I embarked on a series of revisions - some major, some minor, including a whole new chapter - to produce the final version here. But I am most deeply grateful to my Denise who, as editor and proof-reader, read and re-read the manuscript more times than is healthy for any mortal and her detailed observations and corrections have made the book as complete as it can be. I should also like to thank McKay's, Waterstone's, Gardners and Nielsens, whose expertise and patience has provided invaluable guidance. There has to be mention, too, for Zac, into whose care I passed the charred remains of three computers, containing the almost completed manuscript, after my canal boat fire. Somehow, miraculously, he rescued the file. Thank you Zac. I would never have remembered so many words, and definitely not in the right order.

Nigel Jay Robson
2009

For my sister Alison

Who would have been
so proud

Part One

PLAN

PLAN

Gabriel

"On second thoughts", murmured God, now that He considered the situation, "I'm not sure that actually *appearing* is really necessary."

"Yes, Guv", grunted Gabriel, hunched at His side.

There were two things God did not much like about Gabriel. One was his smell. Nowhere in the Bible, or in any related scriptures, was there any reference to the *stinking archangel*. God regretted that he had not hinted at it when providing material for Moses and other loyal scribes. The occasional passage like, 'And lo, the angel of the Lord appeared before them, and half of them passed out with the stench', might have given Gabriel pause for thought about his personal hygiene.

It was not as though God had the kind of relationship with Gabriel which allowed Him to broach the subject in conversation. He could not bring Himself to say something like, "Listen, Gabriel, my old mate, why don't you have a wash?" It was more like the famous advert, in which his best friend never told him. Not that Gabriel was God's best mate or anything. God did not have mates as such. Friendship was not something that went with running the universe, although he and Gabriel did go back a long way. Even so, any familiarity, if such it was, did not extend to the more intimate personal topics like body odour.

Which was why He sent Gabriel away quite a lot, on errands and various missions. That was how he got packed off to Bethlehem. "Look after those shepherds for me", God said, "and see they go down to the inn. We need word to get around afterwards and you know what shepherds are like for gossiping." Actually, he knew very well word would get around without any help from Him, Gabriel or any shepherds. It was not every day babies were born in the stable at the inn, even at Bethlehem crawling with people at census time; especially not to a woman who kept telling everyone that not only was her old man not the father, no-one else was either. Still, He could not be sure.

God had pondered on whether to really get drawn into this whole thing, while He was putting all of Creation together. Christianity was preordained to flourish up to a point, without His intervention; but this Jesus character was going to be a bit of a maverick. It was a manifestation of that 'self-determination' factor He was building into future humanity, along with a number of the other planetary species. Jesus was going to change the course of history but he might need a few 'fatherly' (not really) nudges along the way. So off went Gabriel at the very start of the Bethlehem bit, with instructions to nudge as required.

Anyway, at least it got Gabriel from under His nose - as it were - for a while. Even longer when it transpired Gabriel had nipped off to the desert at the same time (even angels can almost manage *two* things at once) to grab the three camel kings. Where they were going, God only knew, but as soon as Gabriel appeared, off they went, following the bait. What made Gabriel show up as a *star*, God never asked; he just assumed Gabriel realised that any three kings on camels, even remotely wise, would have simply fallen about at those ridiculous wings.

God never found out what happened to the gold, frankincense and myrrh, either. Gold and myrrh apart, obviously Gabriel had not kept any of the frankincense for himself ... if only! Not that a couple of touches under the armpits would have made any difference to the pungent aroma which emanated from his trusty companion. Angelic it was not. It always seemed worse when Gabriel returned from one of his interstellar trips, especially if he had been to Splong (this is a translated name, of course, as the Splongies are largely telepathic and transmit thoughts which are well-nigh impossible to transcribe, including the names of them and their planet). Much as he loved the Splongies, just the same as all the myriad beings which inhabited the furthest reaches of His universe, God tended to conduct His relationship with them at a cautious distance. A wasted exercise when, lo and behold, Gabriel would turn up from every Splong mission smelling as though he had brought the entire planet back with him. It was how he seemed to absorb it to the very core of his being. Just a smell would surely have wafted away after a while. Slow wafting in a vacuum, to be sure, but waft it certainly should. Not from Gabriel it did not. It must have infiltrated his every particle, to subsequently escape by a kind of horticultural slow-release mechanism. God thought His garden analogy particularly apt, since few manures could be as putrid.

The other thing about His well-loved and loyal mercenary was his tendency to adopt the mannerisms of whichever planetary population had most captivated his imagination while visiting them. For some reason which even God could not fathom (despite fathoming being His speciality), Gabriel was most impressionable when in the company of the 'lower orders'. Not that God was in any way class-conscious, of course, or prejudiced against the less intellectual members of His immense flock, but it did get on His nerves when Gabriel adopted one of those *accents* and addressed Him as 'guv' or 'boss'. (These , too, are just recognisable translations from all the similar variants across the mighty cosmos). And the way he would not look Him in the eye, all kind of shifty and a bit rebellious and offering opinions which did not necessarily coincide with God's own. Discussion he welcomed; He was not the kind of God to order his angel about willy-nilly without consulting him; but neither did He like a lot of aggravating argument, with His observations subjected to tiresome challenge and debate. He was God, after all, and He did know everything. Well, more than any angel, anyway.

These two combined charms of the angel at His side - actually, not that close, as God was keeping a bit of a distance between the two of them - should have deterred Him from entering into conversation on the delicate subject of 'appearing'. This, though, was one which God, even after several thousand years (Earth-time), was having great difficulty resolving on His own. If it meant taking a chance on drawing Gabriel closer in intimate discussion, with its accompanying whiff and attendant possibility of contrary opinion, so be it. Gabriel was no particular help, though, mused God, when he was in one of his 'yes, Guv' moods. The Almighty looked across at him, utterly absorbed in *that* occupation.

Yes, there was a third thing. He tried to ignore it, preferred
not to think about it. On its own He could tolerate the recalcitrant
servant stuff (tolerance being another of His strong suits); and
His own brand of aroma therapy - moving away a little, or even
a lot - was usually sufficient to dispel the mild wave of nausea
which overtook Him when too close to Gabriel. But this was
something else. Perhaps most people, let alone gods, would
scarcely have noticed. Probably regarded it with some disdain,
especially when it was not preserved for moments of privacy, but
would have become used to it to the point of ignoring it. God just
could not. Okay, He told Himself, people - angels, even - have
their idiosyncrasies, those little things which are all part of their
personality. That's who they *are* and we should be grateful for
individuality. That is what he tried to tell Himself. It was the
intensity, though, which made Him feel giddy looking at it; the
studied application, the single-minded devotion to a task, with
which Gabriel picked his toes.

Answer

"And ... ?" Gabriel glanced up from some serious foraging in the
space between the third and fourth toes on his left foot and
looked down again to examine the results as he spoke.

God knew, from long experience, that He could never get very
far down an avenue of thought when in reflective mood before
Gabriel would interject to break his reverie. Not one for sustaining
lengthy silences, his faithful archangel.

"Pardon?"

And Gabriel was expecting that. The Lord's regular gambit to
play for time, in the hope, Gabriel always suspected, that his
aide would have forgotten what he was saying and would not
therefore draw Him into a conversation. No such luck.

"And..." muttered Gabriel without looking up "...appearing is
not really necessary, and...?"

For a moment there was silence.

The answer to everything was, of course, God. Theoretically,
anyway.

God had woken up that day and...

Well, He did not 'wake up', exactly, because he is 'awake' all the time, omnipresent - everywhere - day and night.

Not that He has any day or night; He just *is* all the time. So God did not actually wake up that day ...being always awake - or, rather - just being *always.* Outside time, no day no night.

It suddenly dawned on him -

That, actually, is not a concept particularly appropriate to God, either, since dawn is a function of time the same as day and night. It implies that God started off not having a particular idea at a particular point in time and then - at a later point- had the idea. This would, of course, explain why it took seven days to create the world but does not square especially neatly with the instantaneous Big Bang, which concerned the entire cosmos rather than just one world in it. Would have been more of a long slow rumble, even if God had a lot of ideas very quickly. Tricky for non-supernaturals to understand but God, Time and Ideas do not fit together into the same box. God and Ideas are there but Time is not. *However,* since it is impossible for any other inhabitants of the universe to grasp the concept of things simply existing and occurring in a permanent condition, without being governed by the passage of time, there is no way around giving God's activities a temporal reference; just like there is no way around explaining where you have been all night.

So, whether or not it dawned on Him in the literal sense, God found Himself contemplating the conundrum of revealing Himself, from a new perspective. Perhaps, He pondered, He should have been and done it already. Because could it be that, while He had been waiting for people to believe in Him *before* He revealed Himself, *they* were all waiting for Him to reveal Himself before they *believed* in Him. A neatly balanced state of affairs that could continue to infinity; which would not be a problem for His Timelessness if it were not for the fact that any species - and in particular the Humans of Earth - were highly unlikely to get very far down the road to infinity before expiring *en masse*, most probably in a conflagration of self-destruction. So no God worth his salt (and He was worth at least a pillar of the stuff) was going to let things go very far before stepping in to help out, was He? Or should He? Had the 'time' - that vehicle of change, changing attitudes, changing opportunities, beliefs, fashions, acceptance - passed? At any rate, for now. Appear? Perhaps ...but on the other hand-

The disadvantage from God's viewpoint, of there being just the two of them together, was there being no-one else Gabriel could strike up a conversation with instead.

"I was thinking", volunteered The Lord, reluctantly, and paused, hoping that would be enough.

"About...?" came the persistent voice.

God sighed inwardly. "About ... about going there."

"There?" Gabriel's question was a sort of aggressive grunt, voice and forefinger both pursuing their quarry.

"Down there", God offered in hounded explanation.

"Down?" Gabriel flicked a bit of something peremptorily from his finger, matching the sharpness of his tone.

God often marvelled at the quantity of malign matter emerging from the gaps between Gabriel's toes; and sometimes wondered if it was His fault. After all, He had created everything hadn't He? So presumably He was responsible for Gabriel's feet as well.

"Down, up, sideways: you know what I mean", God responded, patience slightly stretched. Spatial references were, strictly speaking, irrelevant as well, with God's ability to be everywhere all the time, with time itself being devoid of meaning. For God could be at any and every point in the cosmos, at any point in time - past, present or future - simultaneously. Really, that is what being God is all about. That said, He did find it a bit disconcerting. Being on every planet, with every life-form, in its past, present and future simultaneously meant that everything tended to become a bit of a jumble. Wherever this quaint theological theory came from that He was everywhere all the time! Okay, so it was true but it was also very confusing. The Lord found it much more practical to focus on one or two parts at once, at the most, and preferably in their present.

The fact that He could not only see the future but be in it was no particular help to anyone, anyway. All right, so He had created the future along with everything else. That did not mean He could change it. Well, He could in theory but where would He begin? By the time He had changed one action, which had altered another event, each of which had caused a series of changes, all of which had numerous side-and-knock-on effects, He might as well have gone back to the Beginning and started all over again. So He decided it was best to leave the future well alone, in which case He largely ignored it, whether He was there all the time or not. At least, that is what He had decided until now.

Everywhere had different timescales, too. They were all more or less a function of a planet's revolution around its sun: bigger, smaller, longer, shorter, for simplification. The Splongies, for example, would be shocked at the brevity of the humans' lifespan, who themselves would be deeply envied by the Thxxws. Even focusing on one at a time had its pitfalls. God tended to become absorbed in that portion of the universe, forgetting the different timescales elsewhere. That was one of the main reasons behind the Joan Of Arc debacle, though He had never admitted as much to Gabriel.

"We've been through that a hundred times", retorted Gabriel: "(a) would anyone take any notice; and (b) what would You go as? You can hardly go as some ordinary workman. Look what happened to the lad."

The 'lad' was how Gabriel usually referred to the carpenter.

"Precisely", replied God, "I was beginning to think about the alternatives."

"What", chuckled Gabriel darkly, "Go as something completely unexpected? Like a politician? Or a reformed arms dealer? Or a *woman!*"

"No ...." The Lord spoke in one of his measured, I-am-God-and-I-am-not-stupid tones, ".... the alternatives to not going at all."

"Oh ... Is that what some of them call 'chickening out'?"

"Gabriel." The measured tone had changed to mildly admonishing.

Gabriel looked up, flicked something, and looked down again, with just enough contrition in his expression.

"Sorry, Boss."

There was a silence, God musing, Gabriel picking away quietly, unusually concerned not to break the serenity of Heaven. After some moments, the angel took stock of a job well done, for the time being at least, and brushed his hands together, curling his legs underneath him. He looked up again.

"What alternatives?"

The Lord hesitated again. "I think", He pondered aloud, "I think perhaps we could help from here."

He paused again.

"Yes ......?" The terrier was refusing to let go.

"I ...." The Almighty was drawing His words out slowly, painfully, almost as though they were the slaves of thought, like one of those ordinary mortals, "... there may be things we can do to ... to change ...."

"Change? Change what?" Gabriel looked up abruptly.

And then a look of shocked realisation began to spread across the angel's face.

"No!" Gabriel's feet shot into view again as he fell back on his hands, staring up at The Lord. In all the aeons (if you count it in time) they had existed together in Heaven and the cosmos, this had been taboo. This was all accounted for at the Beginning Of Everything and that was that. Set in stone (to use one of their metaphors, there not being any stone in heaven). "You're not seriously suggesting -?"

The Lord shifted slightly uncomfortably, even though He managed to remain fairly deific as He did so, being God.

Gabriel was still staring. "You're talking about changing the future, aren't you!"

God struggled to regain His usual Omniscient bearing, only partially successfully in the withering gaze of his servant.

"Are You?" Gabriel added, almost querulously, as though waiting to be told he had got completely the wrong idea, thank goodness.

"Just ...perhaps ...just some nudging ..here and there", God forced out the words, hoping they sounded like a justification for contemplating the uncontemplatable.

"Nudging", Gabriel repeated the word. He had, true, done a bit of nudging himself before now, but just small-scale stuff, shepherds nudged down to the inn, that sort of thing. But what was this? What kind of "nudging"? A whole world? A whole planet? Where would they begin. What would they try to achieve? He realised his thoughts were racing well ahead of anything God had even hinted at. No reference to what, how, where. Why should his whole head be spinning just at the mention. Silly, no. He looked at the silent, beneficent, all-wise Lord. Silly Gabriel. Why should he get all panicky all of a sudden. They had nudged before. Just a bit. It turned out all right. More or less. Okay, maybe a few million dead a bit sooner than they might have expected but it was not always easy to control. That was the trouble. He looked at God again.

"How much nudging are You thinking of? One or two", he suggested hopefully.

God now looked troubled but said nothing.

Gabriel spoke hesitantly. "You mean quite a lot of nudging."

"Not a lot", God rejoined, a little too hastily, "but ... but it might have to have significant effects; to..to make any difference", He added. And then, for the first time Gabriel could remember, and that was a very long time even where time did not exist, God looked and asked Gabriel a question almost plaintively, almost as though relying upon his angel for an answer which He - the Lord God Almighty - could not supply.

"If we are to do anything at all .. if we accept that any difference is required .. if I am to accept any responsibility .... what else can we do?"

Suddenly, to Gabriel the idea of God Himself going there after all, as something - anything - was appearing (joke) a whole lot more attractive than any 'alternatives' He might have up His proverbial sleeve.

Blackout

"Find the lighter! For Christ's sake, find the lighter!" Walt took a step forward and struck a tender part of his thigh on the hard table corner. "Shit!"

There was the sound of a drawer sliding open in another room and the scuffling of contents: cutlery, some things that sounded like small boxes, kitchen stuff.

"Christ, just ... It's there, in there!" Walt wailed, rubbing his sore leg.

"Jesus, I'm looking!" came a female voice from another room. "Can't you see it's dark in here!"

"I can't see because it *is* dark!" Walt shouted back. "When did you move the goddam table, for Christ's sake!"

"I didn't move it! Whad'I wanna move the table for?" There was the sound of the drawer slamming shut, with the rattle of cutlery and other contents. "Have *you* had the damm lighter? ...Oh, shit! Oh Jesus! You left your damm toolbox here! ....Ooooogh ...!" The sound of a woman's groan, and a little sob: "Ooooh ... aah!"

"Sorry, Hun, I thought it was our power box." Walt's voice had softened as he called out. "Here, stay there, find a stool, I'll come through. Gee, for Chrissake ...!"

Walt edged gingerly around the offending table in the pitch dark, feeling ahead with his hands as he headed more or less towards the connecting door to the kitchen.

The whole of North America was dark. Yes, it was night, but this was really dark. Not a light shone anywhere, except maybe here and there some folks had groped around and found a generator but not many had one of those tucked away in a cupboard. Scarcely a light on the highways, either, because no-one was venturing out. What would be the point of driving from one dark house along an unlit road through blacked-out townships to another dark place? Here and there, just one or two lonely sets of headlights threaded their way through the black, like stray cats with nowhere to go.

"Hun? ... Olivia?"

"Here." The voice still bore the trace of a sob.

"Okay, stay there, Hun." Walt was feeling his way between the door jambs into the black hole of the kitchen. At least the last big blackouts had begun during daylight, like the one in teatime in summer, time to get organised before nightfall; bad enough no-one could cook a meal, but this! Same time, of course, peak power-burning in early evening, but now it was nearly winter. Everyone, like them, had been caught in dungeon-like homes, or stumbling along streets suddenly transformed into open-air tunnels, or subways become *real* tunnels, forbidding and frightening. Walt had searched out his toolbox from the store cupboard in the dark, climbed perilously onto a stool with his flashlight at the power box - just in case it was only a fuse! - wobbled on the stool, dropped the flashlight (which broke on impact!) and inched his way through to the breakfast room, bumping and cursing as he went, to seek out the other torch, while Olivia made her way from bathroom to kitchen to ... find the lighter for him! Huh.

At last he reached out and felt her arm, then clasped her fingers and pulled her to him in the dark. They held each other.

"No torch?" she whispered.

"No lighter."

"No."

"You okay?" Walt's tone had become tender and concerned. He hated losing his rag, especially with his beloved wife. He breathed in her subtle perfume: she had just been completing her regular transition from daytime work to evening woman.

"You smell gorgeous."

She broke into a giggle. "Oh well, that'll probably make up for having my bra on back to front."

His hand reached blindly, but accurately, to fondle her. "I don't think so", he breathed into her invisible ear.

"Walt, love ...hey .." She lightly kissed his cheek, just a shape, even though her eyes had adjusted to the dark. "This isn't no time ...and anyway .."

"Yeh ... anyway ... race you to the bedroom."

They both laughed in each other's arms, each hugging a familiar but more or less unseen form.

"Come on", she said, reaching down his arm for a hand again, "let's get outa here." Five years, and she still loved the way they could both be sexy and funny anywhere, any time, any circumstances. She knew he did, too.

"Yeh", he agreed, "can't do anything in here ...except go to bed."

"Walt!"

"Okay - we'd break our legs trying to get there."

They were making their way hesitantly out of the kitchen, holding hands, into the hall where, at last, there came just the faintest light from the front door window panes at the far end: the night sky, naturally not quite black - no moon but stars, maybe - and a very dim flicker of yellow or orange. Walt's hand found the latch.

"You got keys?" He asked.

"No, no, in my bag upstairs."

"Ah, Jeez, dropped mine in the dark when I came in."

"Walt, we can't go out and leave the door open; looters ..." Her voice faltered.

"Gee, I know", he replied. Okay, there had been very little looting the last three or four times: a spirit of community and camaraderie seemed to have taken over, with such unity, it appeared, that regular thieves must either have been infected with it, too, or simply kept at bay by the powerful sense of mutual support against any wrongdoing. Nevertheless, like Christmas in war, you couldn't expect that kind of truce to last indefinitely, least of all here in the big bug-eaten Apple. "But we won't go out of sight of the door", he added, "leave it off the latch, it'll look shut. We can't just stay inside."

"You sure?"

"Yeh, we'll just stick around out here."

They went down the five steps of the Manhattan town house, thankful to actually make out their feet in front of them for a change, down to the sidewalk below; she first, he carefully pulling the door closed behind them. A strange sight greeted them, although with an uncomfortable sense of *deja vu* following recent repetitions. It was almost a Victorian scene, like those old mock-up postcards of yesteryear sold for tourists in gift stores, except without the street lanterns, which were as off as anything else that required power. People dimly-perceived, standing in huddles, some sitting on walls, railings, or even on fold-up chairs they had somehow managed to find and bring out with them.

So was this the way things were going to be now? The collective sins of their present forcing them to revisit the miseries of their past? There was just enough light to see most of the way up and down the street, about a hundred and fifty metres each way. Enough to make out the big-coated figures, some hats, puffs of condensed air from mouths, catching the eerie bluish light; but not enough to recognise faces, even nearby. That faint yellowish-orange flickering had emanated from barbecues, several scattered here and there along each sidewalk, though mostly the flames had now gone, with just the dull glow of charcoal remaining. Oh, for a real good bonfire with big warm flames, thought Olivia, as she peered to see if she could recognise neighbours among the huddles. They stood, still holding hands, not quite sure what to do next. Walt marvelled at how much more prepared for this some other people were.

"Well, that's your conference", Olivia remarked.

"Yup", agreed Walt, "can't see this clearing up by morning."

"Tonight, you mean."

"Yeh, sure, tonight." Walt was due to fly from JFK to Washington on the 22.35 American Airlines. Typical cloak-and-dagger school-boy stuff coming from some federal office, he thought: travel at night to meet with shadowy figures in the morning. "Time is it?" he asked, peering unsuccessfully at his wrist.

"Must be after six-thirty."

"Yeh. Yeh, that's it, I guess." Last time, all flights were grounded even for hours after the power came back on, such was the disruption caused to timetables and air traffic control. Trains all stopped where they were - chaos for all those travellers - and it had been utterly pointless driving a car from one power-less city to another.

"What's funny?" She could just make out his smile in the uncertain gloom.

"Thinking."

"Yeh?"

"Seeing eight or nine of us sitting around a table in low generator light, all staring at blank screens, trying to have a high-security conference on energy." He chuckled at the irony, she smiled. "Mm", she said, "don't think you'll be the only one not there."

"*Burger*?"

The woman's voice came from right behind them. Tall, a broad, friendly face just caught at an angle in the light, and a shock of dark - could be any colour in daylight, Olivia supposed - curly hair, and with both hands thrust forward, each clutching a giant beefburger.

"Oh, wow!" exclaimed Walt.

"Oh, you're so sweet", smiled Olivia.

"You folks just about to cook, were you?" grinned the woman, through big cheery lips.

"Gee, yes", Olivia smiled again, "guess we're all the same."

"Yup", the woman chuckled, "my Dirk just happened to have the barbie by the door the whole time since last time. Coulda killed him for the dust but - hey! - guess he was right!"

"Right enough", chuckled Walt in return. "These spare?"

"Not spare - for you! Saw you come out."

"Wow!" He grinned again and reached for both burgers, handing one to Olivia.

"All relishes included!" the woman added. "You like mustard? - you got no choice - enjoy!"

She was sweeping away, back to the barbecue, no doubt.

"Hey." Olivia reached for her arm as she went. She knew she recognised her but only as a regular fellow-resident somewhere nearby. "You're ...?"

"Joan."

"Ah .. Olivia ...and Walt", Olivia explained in reply.

"Ah, yeh. I guess we aint all great neighbours till there's a crisis. But nice to meet you."

"And you!" exclaimed Olivia, "and thanks ...really ... thanks, a whole lot!"

"Yeh", Walt mumbled through a mouthful, cramming bits of bun back with his fingers, "sh'really great ...great! ...thanksh!"

"You're welcome!" called Joan, cheerily, disappearing into the shadows.

Thinking

"Have You thought this through?" muttered Gabriel, shaking his finger irritably, as he tried to disengage whatever had adhered to it.

"Have I ...?" began God, incredulously. He, who had created *everything* with the power of super-supernatural thought (much, much bigger than thought, really) and had somehow squeezed it all - *all* - into a minuscule little blob that was too small for anyone other than Himself to even *imagine*. And then exploded it. Had *He* thought this through!

He looked at Gabriel from His safe distance and was relieved He was not close enough to distinguish sufficiently clearly the object of the angel's disgruntlement. Thank the Lord, He might have said, if He had been anyone else. Gabriel glanced up and noted the gathering clouds in the Almighty's expression. "Well, You know", he remarked, sounding slightly more conciliatory, which was probably wise in the circumstances, "You know what they're like. You think you're doing them a favour. I mean, look at when you stuck that road down the middle of the sea -"

"Parting the waters", God corrected him, with rather exaggerated patience.

"Yeh, yeh, whatever ... anyway, didn't work, did it?"

"They were my people", breathed the Lord, a little heavily.

"They're all your people, aren't they? That's what You sai-"

"They -" the Lord rumbled ominously, "Yes. As you well know. But *they* were bearing my message for their future - all 'mankind'. That was their role. They had to be saved."

"My point exactly", returned the archangel, wiping the now unadorned digit on a piece of loose garment. "Eventually they went back and they've all been fighting each other ever since."

God wondered where He could take a conversation in which the only other participant insisted on reducing thousands of years (their time) of deific endeavour and subtle nuances of divine intervention to -

"And that was all from a nudge", Gabriel grunted, breaking into the Almighty's ponderings, again.

"All we need", said the Lord, ignoring his aide's contrariness, "is someone to be a 'messenger'."

"Oh, not that one again", Gabriel groaned.

"May I remind you", responded the Lord - and had it come from any being less benign or passing all understanding it might have sounded a little testy - "that there were two, in particular, who have had quite a lasting influence, quite apart from others."

"A bit different, though", retorted Gabriel, turning his attention to the other foot, "the carpenter was already going on about being the son of God, what with his mother still claiming he didn't have a proper dad; and so You thought -" (resisting the temptation to add 'and may I remind You') "okay - let's go along with this and back him up a bit."

God sighed, as four whole gospels and reams of other scriptures and testaments were reduced to 'back him up a bit'.

True, He lent a hand with the 'miracles'; to save the lad from drowning on one occasion, to be sure. But He had realised that the whole chartered course of civilisation could have been squandered by a few rash promises about feeding five thousand people from one family's picnic, or making a terminally lame beggar walk. So he stepped in. Fair enough. "Christianity has been something of a success story", he remarked, chidingly.

"Sure", agreed Gabriel, cautiously, adding under his breath, "tell that to the infidel."

God heard that, of course, since he is everywhere all the time, and so on, but He had to pretend not to pick up everything Gabriel said, or He would seem like Big Brother, or Big Father in this case. Instead He added, "And Islam."

"Oh, yeh", commented Gabriel, "that cave."

"Cave?"

"That cave where I went to give Muhammed his instructions. And then chasing him around all over the place after that. That went on for over twenty years! I never knew why You couldn't tell him all at once. Not as though he was thick."

"They are people", God sighed. "If it takes them years to learn to count their change while shopping, how could they possibly understand the Koran in one go?"

"Well, okay", Gabriel conceded, "but I got fed up with looking for him all the time. .... Anyway, what I'm saying is", as he resumed some more picking, "those two were both on a mission, already, *spreading* Your Word -"

God wondered why Gabriel always made it sound like jam, rather than a code of ethics and way of life.

" - and You - we - just smoothed the way a bit. The ones like that down there now are just nutters, aren't they?"

Zealots, bigots and false messiahs had always been a problem, God was only too aware, but He had to accept it went with the territory. The future of the human race - and He had created it, after all - meant that distortions and paradoxes would arise in every sphere of their development; and their variable, and sometimes unsavoury, attitudes to His existence and His message were no different.

"We don't need another messiah, necessarily, another messenger in quite that way, perhaps."

He paused.

"So?" Gabriel was leaning forward now, attentive to what the Lord might be suggesting. "You're talking about alternatives? To going down there?"

"To *Me* going 'down', yes", the Lord acknowledged quietly.

Gabriel's hands fell from what they were doing as he stared blankly back in reply. He felt the air chill around him (or would have, if there was air in Heaven) and observed the Almighty in silence, while his heart sank even more silently. His misgivings had been real. Earth. He tried to prevent the sense of resignation from revealing itself on his face. Shepherds, caves, nudges. Oh, yes. I see. Here we go again.

Elroy

They watched as Joan's shape merged with others in the gloom and Walt gave a sudden start, surprised by the vibration in his trouser pocket, followed by the muffled twang of the *Stars And Stripes*. The last thing he expected right now was his phone to ring. He tried to thrust one hand into the pocket, bits of burger crumbling to the ground.

"Here - ." Olivia took the remains of the burger from him as he yanked the cellphone to his ear.

"Hi?"

"Hi Walt?"

"Yeh."

"Elroy."

"Hi El."

"Guess it's off, eh?"

Elroy sounded quite cheerfully relieved, which did not surprise Walt much at all. Elroy Fitzgibbon. Genius. More or less. Co-opted, like Walter Brown, to LOTUS - the LOngTerm Unexploited energy Sources group - and increasingly troubled, or so he confided only to his fellow co-optee and friend, Walt, by what was expected of him. Walt's own view of the group, initially, had been to wonder at whoever obsessively contrived to invent an acronym which missed out the initial letter of the most important

word in its title; then, he considered more darkly, such a
carefully unpublicised 'committee' might distract attention
from itself even further by having a five-letter conundrum for a
label. More recently, he too had begun to reflect on quite where
this covert, apparently unaccountable group of unelected
professionals was ultimately heading.

For himself, he was only the provider of back-end information - the stats, if you like, on which to base future action - but
Elroy, well it was becoming evident how pivotal he was to the
whole thing. The fact he was deeply religious did not help, not
in terms of the morality of the project. You would have
thought, Walt had considered more than once, that they would
have turned that up straightaway in the vetting. 'Course they
had. So Elroy must sure be one helluv an important element if
they knew that about him and were still prepared to push him
to the sharp end.

"Yeh", replied Walt, hushing his voice with a meaningful
glance at his wife - he shared more with her than he would have
admitted to anyone who asked - "guess there'll be no flights and
no power when we get there anyway. You had any calls?"

"No, but you'd get one first - you're the official guy."

Yes, true, although they were both co-opted, Walt already
worked on contract to a Government department - Energy - as a
top dog in forward energy planning. His field was 'energy
requirement prediction' - the official jargon - serious roulette, as
he sometimes joked to colleagues: what kind of future demand
there might be for all types of energy, though mainly, of course,
oil and electricity. A whole host of other experts and statisticians
were available to him, ranging from population prediction and
demographic shifts going decades into the future - birth rates,
migration between states, between town and country, between
types of jobs and so on - to estimates of demand in anything from
household appliances and electronic gizmos, computers, toys,
God knows what, to automobiles and other forms of transport,
though mainly - in fact mainly above everything else right now -
automobiles, the dreaded, beloved, indispensable, all-consum-
ing power monster, the motor car. Thank you Henry Ford, the
jury is still out. So, yes, Walt would likely get the call first, saying
group meeting tomorrow is off.

"No, no-one called yet", replied Walt, "but I guess they're all like us, just trying to grope around some place. But no point in aiming to get down there. Not till someone calls and sends a car, maybe."

"Or the shuttle!" came the jocular response, *"guess it'll be the only thing still working - rocket fuel!"*

"Oh yeh, good one", Walt laughed down the phone. "Tell you what, I'll suggest it. I'll call you if they call me. Don't move till then, in case we can't find you."

There was a guffaw in his ear. *"Ha, ha, who'll find me in the dark anyway! Speak soon. Stay cool!"*

A lot of people did not know the fun guy inside Elroy. They just saw the brilliant techno wizard. Though that description belittled his talents, reducing them to the limits of what ordinary minds could comprehend. To Walt, and indeed a number of other professionals working with Elroy, he was the Beethoven of advanced covert surveillance technology, the Dali of transmission frequencies, the Shakespeare of molecular electronics, and a bit of a dab hand at nano-technology on the side. A wild mind only just on the leash, working at the very edge of the remotely possible and, Walt suspected, requiring only a nudge from the right quarter - some unopened hatch in his own extraordinary brain perhaps - to tip him beyond that edge into the wholly improbable. All this in a dapper six-foot-two, forty-two year-old, ever so slightly greying, sometimes bespectacled, today withdrawn, tomorrow wisecracking, two hundred and twenty pound, black guy from Minneapolis. No wonder some people could not get a handle on him.

Walt envisaged the others who would have sat around that table tomorrow: a pair from the State Department (one an 'observer'), two from Energy, plus himself co-opted, one or two from the military - still not explained precisely which area - a physicist and/or a geologist - sometimes just one but usually both (resource identification, analysis and extraction - officially, anyway) - another 'observer' (department unnamed), someone high-up in the automobile trade - obviously, when you thought about it - and Elroy. Walt had his own suspicions about the two 'observers', one a woman - the only female in LOTUS. Neither ever said anything much, except ask some banal questions. Just for cover, he guessed, since he reckoned they were both probably

CIA. Or even more undercover than that. Keeping an eye on what? Or whom? Waiting for poor, brilliant Elroy to come up with just precisely the most appropriate, penetrating, long-distance eavesdropping, and counter-surveillance systems, to enable activation of a darker plan?

He and Walt were in the same boat. When the Federal Government - the President, effectively - comes along with a co-opt request, you do not turn it down. Then suddenly you are sworn in and you are walking down unidentified corridors, making solemn undertakings to very senior, very important people you never knew existed, and you are in. Up to the neck. And then you are thinking, so they are admitting to themselves now that Iraq was just a very clumsy rehearsal. But you do not say that, not even to Elroy, and certainly not to Olivia. Lovely, beautiful, understanding Olivia. He had told her too much already and she had enough problems to deal with at NSA.

"Thinking about?" Her voice broke in at his side.

" ... About ... I'm dying of thirst", Walt replied, swiftly switching himself back to the gloomy sidewalk with one of those harmless little pale milky lies, of which even the best marriages are made.

"And me", she agreed, handing him the clammy remains of his burger. He munched it down quickly, since it was better than nothing, and nothing was what he was otherwise likely to eat between now and daylight.

"I guess someone will be out selling drinks, coke, beer, whatever; let's go see", suggested Walt.

"Walt", Olivia spoke nervously, "we can't leave the door."

He looked back; they had already moved twenty metres or so, drifting involuntarily towards the nearest huddle and glow of charcoal, where Joan had been heading. Their front door could barely be distinguished even at this distance. "No, okay", he agreed. "Hell, we'll just have to find the fridge! Come on."

They turned back and up the steps, groping their way through the hall, bumping with the occasional 'ouch!' into the pitch dark kitchen. Walt felt around to the fridge, saying 'stay there', while he pulled at the door.

"Hell, what now?" Walt spluttered after downing a coke can in the dark, some of it down his chest - "shit!"

"Watch TV in bed?" Olivia offered, brightly.

"Oh yeh?" said Walt.

"Oh ...yes.." came the rueful reply, dissolving into a giggle unseen beside him. "Everything's electric, isn't it?"

"Yup. The whole of goddamned life", remarked Walt.

"But I guess there's nothing else we can do."

"What", he said, "watch an invisible switched-off TV in the dark? Spot the telly?"

"No", she murmured in amusement, "go to bed."

"Oh, yeh, I guess", he concurred, reaching out to where her voice came from and touching her waist with a brush of his hand. They fumbled their way upstairs, stumbling into each other at moments and clutching for support. Walt started to struggle out of trousers and shirt as they edged around the bedroom, just about avoiding disagreeable contact with bed-posts, dresser corners and the like. He found his way to the en suite.

"Where are you?" Olivia called softly.

"Bathroom", he called back.

"Don't miss!"

She heard his chuckle and then a distinct absence of the sound of water hitting water. "I said 'don't miss'!" she called again as she pulled off jumper, jeans and underwear, leaving them wherever they invisibly lay.

"You not going?" he asked, as he slid under the duvet and nestled up to her, seeing nothing at all but a dim, dark shape.

"Can wait until I can see ..unlike whatever you've done in there", she mumbled into his chest, giving him a jab in the ribs. "God", she added, "what's the time? I bet it's not even eight o'clock!"

"Haven't a clue." Then he breathed into her ear, "So you won't be tired."

"No ... I guess ...." She turned herself up to where his face was and suddenly felt a familiar prod against her thigh. Their mouths met. After some moments, she pulled away. "I might have a headache." He heard the twinkle in her voice, if he could not see it in her eyes.

"You might in about an hour", he murmured, his hand snaking lightly over a breast and he felt her breath against his lips again.

"I've told you about wearing these shorts in bed", she admonished, mockingly, her warm moist air spilling with her words, over his mouth.

"Oh, yeh ...what?" His lips opening.

"About ... ahh..." Her words were lost in their next kiss, as each hooked a finger over the elastic and pulled down.

Beijing

A cock crowed. Solitary. Then a few minutes later another - different timbre. A short pause, then the first again, as though reasserting itself. Then, at a distance, another, a response perhaps, joining the exchange of early calls. Further away still, after a brief lull, another; and then continuously, all of them, and more, one after another, pulsing at intervals: strident heralds spreading their cacophony across the night's end.

Cock-a-doodle... A-cawk! ...Cawk! ... a-a-a ...cawk! ...Cawk-a! ... Do-o-o-o-o-o... A-cawk! ... A-ooh-ooh-ooh ...cawk! ...a-a-a...!

Brown earth outside, barely first light: the rough pebbles and scrub littering the ground were still indistinct, colourless shapes among the spartan trees, whose dark outlines were just being transformed into leaves and crooked branches by the first glimmer of dawn.

Hoi Fong Choi turned face up on his pillow, as his eyes cracked slightly open. Through slits he picked out the familiar shadow of cotton patterned curtains and the chink of sky that was just lighter than the dark of the bedroom. The slits widened full open and he pushed back the lightweight sheet and duvet, slipping, silk-pyjamered, from his side of the bed. He guessed it was about six o'clock. Who needs an alarm clock with the concert party outside? He picked up the TV remote in the dark, without needing to grope blindly to find where he last put it down, on the low polished marble table by the bed. He felt with his finger and jabbed a button: CNN, the last channel he had been watching the night before, as usual. He glanced back across the well-proportioned room, softly illuminated by the television pictures, and noted, as usual, the other side of the bed was already empty.

The TV time-check announcement said it was five o'clock - 1700 hours - in New York, midnight in LA, 4pm in Chicago and Detroit. That meant Beijing: 6am. He smiled slightly. In New York, LA, Chicago, Detroit and various US cities 'flashing' up on the screen it was very, very dark. Especially Detroit, in contrast with its customary night-time blaze of factory, street and automobile lights. In fact, the CNN presenter admitted they had to electronically enhance the Detroit city outline, and some others, for the TV screen, just to see the buildings. And the factories. The smile stayed where it was, not so much inscrutable, the Chinese smile of myth and legend, as just a plain, ordinary, satisfied smile with a hint of anticipation. If these blackouts continue like this, thought Hoi Fong, the carmakers of Detroit and elsewhere in the States will be so undermined, their delivery times and product development rendered so unreliable, they will lose all credibility in the world trading markets. Especially here, here, in the Chinese Republic, where dependability and reliability were fast becoming mantras for the country's surge towards a fully-industrialised, technological economy. Space flight was merely the spectacular manifestation of the nation's hunger for the more mundane, but desirable, trappings of modern society - like driving one's own motor car.

"And then", Hoi Fong was musing as he completed his shave before donning the crisp white shirt and smartly creased dark trousers left out for him, "I won't have the Americans muscling in on my territory." It made him smile again to think of his own plans to carve a niche in the vulnerable British market and the ease with which the agent had made the first inroads. All the more convenient if the Englishman turned out to be eager as well as greedy. He tucked the shirt over the neat red triangle imprinted in the small of his back - a mark he tried to forget about now - and drew back the curtains, revealing the rapid transition of Far Eastern night to day, already well established this clear morning.

Despite his burgeoning wealth as one of Beijing's new breed of private car manufacturers, they had chosen to remain living on the outskirts, in the country. The dry, crumbly, ill-nourished soil, the stones, pebbles, scrub and plaintive trees were all familiar friends from both their childhoods. It was home. Hoi looked down from the second-floor window. Second floor! That was the difference. Long gone was the house on stilts, the rickety steps, the plain wooden boards of a single-level shanty house. Now it was a two-storey concrete dwelling, with pipes buried in channels around the gleaming white walls, to carry the wet season flood water; not wooden stilts to allow it to rush in a torrent underneath. A man of substance does not live in a wooden house on stilts.

Hwee Lo, his pretty, dainty wife, passed by on the dry ground outside the window, scattering morning corn for their hens beneath the first golden glow of sunrise. Habit! he thought. In former days, with his parents, and she with hers, they had no choice. Protein - meat and eggs - had to be running around your own bare scrap of land or you would not eat any. Then, when as a small boy, his 'education' was to help ensure they did not starve. Families could not live on a few chickens alone. The long, hot dreary days of just picking, picking, picking rice in the paddy fields; and staggering, he and the other five-to-fourteen year-olds, boys and girls, with the enormous bundles to be piled onto frames made of sticks - bamboo rucksacks! - then carried home or to the nightly street market for a few pathetic yen to keep the family alive. And the hot days of shimmying up the tallest trees to shake bundles of nuts from the uppermost, flimsiest branches - which would only support a child - to be gathered from the donkey-track below. All that before school provided its escape and challenge to the future.

Habit! To keep chickens, though they could buy all the poultry and eggs they ever wanted now, yet these hens, too, were 'home'. A Chinese, he thought to himself, will savour the past, enjoy the present, work for the future. Yesterday nourishes today; today feeds tomorrow: experience is worn as a lifetime of lessons. The man whose today includes no yesterdays, his wise old Cantonese father used to say to him, will never discover tomorrow. The news had switched to Beijing: CNN's global reach, leaving no corner of the world with its secrets. It was a multi-car pile-up, on an urban highway into the city. Not even quite yet 'rush hour' but the pictures showed many, many cars crushed, battered and slewed across the road. Several dead, intoned the report, numbers to be confirmed. Not usually even worthy of the news except that this was the third of its kind in Beijing in a week.

Hoi Fong shrugged inwardly, He only made the cars, he did not teach people to drive. He did not teach them to be idiots, either. Death, destruction, congestion, pollution? Nonsense. The bleatings of the West. He loved the sight of automobiles crammed nose-to-tail on every highway. It was visual poetry. It warmed his soul. He would love to count how many were his, how many - fewer, he hoped - were of other manufacture. If the Americans lost their grip, confounded by their own greedy consumption, it would open up so much more of the market, here in China and overseas. He thought of the Englishman he was negotiating with on behalf of the car dealer in London; nice if the Americans would - what do they say - shoot themselves in the foot and leave the door open for him.

The smile still played faintly about his features, as he contemplated the potential of this new future. So, his fellow Chinese kept killing themselves and each other in his motor cars. He sold them the cars, he did not turn them into goddam fools! Ha, he chuckled a little. That word, 'goddam'. It came from America, too, like the automobile society, like strong houses: it all seemed to come from America somehow. The United States. Huh, he mused again, united in darkness right now, or most of them. Goddam! Why did they damn their God when things went a bit wrong? Was He not supposed to be the benevolent being, caring for them, looking over them, not to be questioned about the glitches here and there, in His long-term cosy, rosy plan for their souls! He, Chinese, he worshipped, yes, the earth, his past, tradition, respect, the ground from whence he came and would one day return. And he worshipped, for now, his millions of automobiles. Shining, gleaming, desired possessions of Chinese, more and more so every day. He did not wish to rule the earth. Ruling the highways would suffice.

Hwee Lo met him in the kitchen, with a basket of eggs held lightly over her stomach. She was eight years younger than his forty-one and they had decided it was time to take their entitlement in the one-per-couple population programme. It would be a single, unique gift in their lives; great care must be taken of his Hwee Lo. They embraced lightly and he sat, picking up the Beijing Times, as he waited for his foo jong, beansprouts, bacon, rice and green tea.

The television in their smart, modern kitchen was on the same channel, showing the half-hour headlines. The Beijing pile-up pictures again, fourteen dead, thirty-six injured, at least five critically. It again failed to move him. The top headline - recap- was two-thirds of North America still plunged into darkness. The Detroit production lines motionless and silent. He smiled again. This time not inscrutably at all. This time his smooth, olive features were split by a full, open, delighted smile. Hwee Lo turned from the hot-plate with the wok. She had learned not to enquire about mysterious smiles for she was usually rewarded with the remark, kindly, that he could not possibly retrace all the thoughts which had led to that particular, singular expression upon his face. So, as usual, she let it be, and served breakfast.

List

"Where shall we start?" Gabriel was leaning forward, clasping an ankle in each hand, staring up at the Lord.

"Where shall we begin", breathed out God in thoughtful response, although he found Himself rather more reluctant to breathe in again, as His companion had just returned from an interplanetary flit - to Crsnax, of all places. Thank you, Gabriel, He thought, for visiting it during the mating season when you could have gone at any other point in its long elliptical year. The planet was so huge and irregularly shaped that time bent as it reached it, causing a part of the year to pass more quickly than the rest and at that period stimulating the brief but passionate annual mass reproduction orgy. And with it, that smell, exuded from each globular Crsnaxite's 'love ventricle'. It was an odour instantly recognisable and to be avoided at all costs, unless You were unfortunate enough to be in the company of a certain angel who just happened to have been there - recently.

"War, famine..." He continued softly to Himself, moving a little further away.

"Could You speak up a bit", interjected Gabriel, "You know, from where You are over there."

God was unaccustomed to receiving instructions, even from his loyal angel, but He swiftly weighed up His options and decided that raising His voice was preferable to drawing closer.

"War, famine, pestilence", He proceeded more loudly.

"What?" Gabriel butted in.

"...famine, pestilence -"

"Pestilence? That's a bit biblical, isn't it, for the twenty-first century?" Gabriel was sounding unusually forthright but he was aware he had a personal stake in the outcome of this dialogue.

The Almighty would have liked to point out that He was perfectly entitled to quote from His own Book but He desired a constructive, indeed vital, conversation, not one of those downward-spiralling arguments at which Gabriel could be so adept when he wished.

"Disease, if you like", He continued, "and genocide, terrorism, corruption, pollution, criminality..." His voice trailed off, the list of Earth's ills mounted inexorably as he spelled them out.

"Of course You started it all." Gabriel was feeling emboldened by the hesitancy in his Master's voice and conscious of where this was all leading, or leading *him* anyway.

"I beg your pardon." The Lord looked at his angel, not altogether amused.

"Preordaining it all", added Gabriel decisively. "It was there, packed into that minuscule little dot of everything before the big ...."

"Bang."

"...Yes." For a moment Gabriel had been halted by the thought he might be going too far but, well, he was saying it now. "It was up to You whether it all happened or not." With that, in a truculent tone, he looked away and down at his feet.

God sighed and there was a silence. Trusted, faithful, loyal, if at times smelly, Gabriel had never quite grasped the central paradox of Creation. The paradox of combining the opposites of predetermination and self-determination. True, He could have preordained everything in that single dot of matter: every life from its beginning to end, every planet from birth to destruction, every smile, every tear, every Broog's grunt, every Tryxxx's slithery slurp, all could have been fixed in the cement of evolution - for eternity. But what kind of a universe would that have been? No single creature capable of independent thought? Only *thinking* they were. No member of any intelligent species able to make a choice of action in any circumstances? Only *believing* they could. And there, the other paradox, of course. If they thought and believed they were behaving independently of any control, that their decisions and actions were not preordained, then what was the difference? Precisely, they would never know the difference, just running around like little toys under remote control.

No, the difference, the Lord had determined at the start of it all, had to be their ability to decide. Otherwise, He would have simply lit the blue touch paper and sat back - for ever. Quite apart from there being little point to a universe like that, He did not fancy an eternity of doing nothing Himself. Even where time does not exist, eternity can drag.

"Wasn't it?" Gabriel could only endure so much silence, especially in the infinite hush of Heaven.

"Wasn't what?", the Lord felt compelled, despite Himself, to enquire.

"All up to You."

Yes and No, the Lord wanted to say, but Gabriel was not particularly receptive to contradictions. There had been occasions when He had attempted to explain how, in the Creation of all Things, yes He had predetermined everything, *including* the capacity of all the intelligent species to exercise self-determination, *without knowing when*. Tricky to understand. Well, impossible, actually, except for God Himself, because every time any Human, or Splongie, or Crsnaxite, or whatever, made a decision, they would not know whether it was predetermined. Hence, the paradox. Whatever the consequence of any action, 'good' or 'bad', whether simply to go shopping or, more controversially, declare war, the instigator would believe it had been an independent decision, as indeed it might, but it might alternatively have been predetermined from the Start of All Things.

Apart from anything else, this avoided the convenient excuse, "Oh well, it's all been predetermined so I might as well do it anyway." Perhaps of little consequence to the shopping trip but deserving of some pause for thought prior to going to war, or any other form of slaughter. The final paradox, though, was that, having predetermined the ability to make unpreordained decisions (this was where it began to lose Gabriel), even God Himself could not know in advance what those decisions would be. Thus, contrary to the original rule about not meddling with the future, there had been those bits of nudging at certain times to adjust the course, on Earth at any rate. Jesus had needed a bit of help. Having declared himself the son of God, there had been no harm in backing him up on that, a little assistance with miracles and so forth; it strengthened the loyalty of his disciples and enabled Christianity to become a major world religion, with all the benefits it bestowed on the human race. ("And killing", Gabriel persisted in reminding Him).

And then there was Islam and Muhammed and all those visits to the cave and other places and sometimes some considerable nudging on God's part to draw Gabriel back from one of his favourite destinations in the cosmos to 'do Earth again' as the angel was in the habit of putting it.

But now the big decision. The big nudge, or nudges, as the time (on Earth) had come to do something. Appear? No, an alternative. "How long have they got?" Gabriel had asked. God was unable to say, since only the paradox could determine that, but the signs were not good. No other species seemed bent on destroying their own habitat, their home, each other, their entire planet, in the way the humans were.

"Yes, but", Gabriel had commented, anxious to demonstrate how surplus he was to Earth's requirements, "they're trying to do something about it, aren't they? I mean, changing their ways?"

Were they? God had pondered. If that were the case, perhaps all the more reason to encourage their faltering steps before they, according to habit, undermined their own well-intentioned efforts. And if it were not, well, their own history was littered with declarations of good intent ultimately usurped by their own nature. So if their new-found determination to 'save the planet' turned out to be no more than a pebble obstructing their lemming-like charge to the cliff, it would scarcely be a surprise.

"You want to give up on them?" Gabriel had added. No, not that, not now. Not yet. They deserved - surely as a species - they deserved more.

"Gabriel." The Lord looked kindly at his angel and this allowed Gabriel to meet His gaze. "Whatever was determined at the Beginning", He continued, "we may help them now. We are able to."

"We?" Gabriel could not disguise the suspicion in his voice.

"We", the Lord emphasised, with a look that meant 'We, but you get the away-days'. "So", he continued, "war, pestil...disease...famine, corruption, greed -"

"Greed", repeated Gabriel, thoughtfully.

"Avarice", God concluded.

"Does it all come down to that?" Gabriel looked up at Him.

"All?" It was not as though God did not know all this from the Beginning but, like any good boss, He tried to ensure that Gabriel felt he was making some original contribution. Call it heavenly psychology.

"War, famine, pestil - disease - murder ... torture ..." Gabriel paused, uncertain what more to add to the list. Wasn't there enough already?

"Terrorism ... Genocide..." added God, helpfully.

"Yes, genocide." Gabriel scowled in disgust: "power, corruption?"

"Congestion, pollution ..." It was a list without end. They fell silent.

Gabriel spoke: "They've really messed up, haven't they?"

The Almighty offered no response.

"Should we just forget it?" the angel suggested brightly, seeing an opportunity to call the whole hopeless venture off.

"Avarice", pondered The Lord.

"Eh?"

"Wanting more, sharing less", God was musing, "inspiring jealousy, resentment, hatred and, in turn..."

" - So which bit of war, terrorism or genocide", cut in Gabriel as huffily as he dared, since his suggestion to abandon it all had been ignored, "are we nudging, exactly?"

"...Avarice", continued The Lord and then, turning to look at his not-always-angelic lieutenant, added "none of those."

"Oh well, then", chirped Gabriel, "Splong it is", and jumped to his feet.

"Gabriel." God fixed him with one of his 'sit-down-Gabriel' sort of looks.

"Guv?" Gabriel sat down again.

"We cannot influence events", said The Lord, feeling He was stating the oft-repeated obvious.

"No, Guv. Well, I'll be off then." And Gabriel started to get to his feet.

"Gabriel!"

"Guv?"

He always deserves full marks for trying, reflected The Lord and then explained, "Not directly", considering it unnecessary to go through everything about changes, knock-on-effects and eternally-spiralling consequences all over again. "But", He continued, "we may address some of the causes."

"Avarice?" enquired Gabriel, thinking he had better start playing ball or this could go on for ever (literally, it being Heaven).

"Precisely", agreed The Lord.

"Wanting more, sharing less", the angel pondered, seriously, now that he was taking part.

"Indeed."

Visions of a jolly excursion to some happier corner of the cosmos were fading pretty rapidly so Gabriel began to feel they might as well get on with it.

"So where do we start?"

Bar

Walt still felt uncomfortable. They were out of the LOTUS meeting now, postponed three weeks because of the blackout, and its after-effects, and the need to co-ordinate everyone's diaries: not his, Walt had noticed; he had just been given a date, no argument, 'now the other guys are sorted'. Huh. Nice to be important. Only upside, the transfer to 'HQ', New York. For someone else's convenience, no doubt, not his. They were walking towards the city, uptown Manhattan. Two New Yorkers walking! And not even looking for a pickup fag!

They had emerged from the building together and each had eyed the yellow cabs waiting and both - almost simultaneously, Elroy first - had said, "Let's walk", "Yup, let's." It was that kind of a feeling. Needing air, needing space, needing time. Anyhow, early afternoon traffic - even worse these days - likely made it quicker on foot. Walt had been to five LOTUS meetings so far, Elroy the same, or so Walt had thought. But at the previous session, about seven weeks ago now, the observer guy, forty-ish, connection unnamed, with the slick black hair and glint of gold tooth, had glanced at Elroy at one point and said something along the lines of 'like you told us, Mr Fitzgibbon' Told him? Told him what?

Walt could not make any connection at the time with the subject being discussed so let himself forget it. Then just now, this morning, the same guy, said something to Elroy about 'how you been the last coupla weeks?' Two weeks since they last met, not two months? His big friend had not replied, looked like he was pretending not to have heard. And then, between times, Elroy saying nothing in particular to Walt but - that was it - saying nothing really at all about LOTUS when they spoke on the phone, just kind of going quiet.

Walt's attention was jerked back to the sidewalk as Elroy clutched at his elbow, pulling him to a halt as they paced through the gathering gloom between already glowing street lights.

"They can bug us!" The big guy's voice was an urgent whisper, his look was fretful.

"What?" Walt was taken aback by this sudden halt to their progress.

"*On* us", hissed Elroy, "like cars."

"Whaddya mean?"

"Like under the trunk, or the door sill."

"We're not cars." Walt defiant tone hid his unease.

"No, no", breathed his friend, "like, you know, in our shoes, our coat linings."

"What? You think we got bugs on us?" Walt began feeling around his coat, pressing for hard objects against his body. "Could they?" he added.

Elroy shrugged and tapped his heel against the gutter.

"What are you doing?" Walt queried.

"See if the heel's loose."

"Eh?"

"See if they coulda slipped a bug in there?"

"What!" exclaimed Walt loudly in alarm.

" - Shuddup!" hissed Elroy, "Keep ya voice down!"

"Well, you left your shoes off someplace?"

"Nope, not as I remember." Elroy shrugged again.

"Well, I guess you'd know if they put a bug in while you were wearing them. 'Scuse me, man, can I have your foot a minute while I slip this here little feller in there'." Walt laughed out loud and slapped his friend on the shoulder.

"Shuddup! Shuddup!" Elroy half-raised a big black hand, as though he might have clamped it over his companion's mouth to silence him, then obviously thinking better of treating a best friend like a naughty child. "Just speak down", he growled in soft urgency, "A bug'd easy pick that up!"

Walt checked Elroy's expression as they passed under a street light, the big man frowning, lines drawn tight over his brow.

"Hey, man, you serious?"

"Dunno, dunno", muttered Elroy.

"Well, you should know, man, you're the expert." Walt realised he was still talking in the exaggerated whisper forced on him by his friend.

"Exactly, man", Elroy acknowledged.

"They could do it?" Concern was beginning to show in Walt's voice.

"They can do anything, man."

"What? Like there could be bugs on us now?"

"You kept that big coat on all the time in there?" responded Elroy, darkly, jerking his head back to the office block receding behind them.

"Course not", Walt retorted; and then continued as he began to figure what the sharp Fitzgibbon was getting at. "You mean...?"

"Yeh, could be."

"What? A bug in this coat? Now?" Walt was feeling all over the garment, starting to run his hands again up and down his chest, pressing his fingers over the little bumps and undulations from the seams, the stitching where the lining ended, the pocket seams. The whole damned coat was full of lumps. Christ, and it cost a fortune!

"They're tiny, man", said Elroy, observing him, "I mean real, real small. You know how they can fly a jumbo with a chip this size?" He held up a thumb and forefinger, curled together to form a hole, a dime across.

"Yeh", Walt acknowledged.

"Well, imagine how small it can be just to pick up your voice right here, and transmit it. There's no way you could ever feel it in there." He glanced at the coat and Walt's hands still patting over it. "It's like a communion wafer - for a toy priest."

"You're joking", Walt spluttered with an nervous chuckle.

"Were we all joking in there?" Elroy jerked his head back at the ordinary-looking office block that had receded behind them: 'Apex Insurance, N.Y.' on the outside and in the polished wood customer reception area beyond the automatic glass doors; LOTUS somewhere deep down below.

Nope, thought Walt, that was no joke.

They had resumed walking as they talked, still in hushed tones. Elroy put a finger to his lips and murmured, "Now shuddup, no talking!". He quickened their pace, covering a few hundred metres along the damp streets until they had put some turns and intersections between themselves and 'Apex Insurance, N.Y.' and were crossing into another district, uptown away from the commercial buildings. Offices had given way to shops and bars, more cars, more lights, more noise.

"Here", Elroy spoke suddenly, steering his friend by the arm into a bar with atmospheric coloured lights, some chart-type music inside and plenty of people making up a lively, busy atmosphere. Not one of those sombre, dull-lit dives where the likes of Humphrey Bogart used to lean over and order many a bourbon in the abandoned gloom.

"This'll be good", said Elroy when they had jostled their way to the bar. Several office schedules were clearly surrendering to the advancing festive season. He ordered a bourbon on the rocks each, which actually made Walt think of Bogart, danger, and conspiracies floating through the smoke-hung air.

"At least they got rid of all the goddam smoke!" exclaimed Elroy, as though reading his friend's thoughts. "Sling your coat -

sorry, place that expensive piece of cow hide! - over there on the shelf." They were sitting in lounge seats in an alcove, with a broad window ledge behind them, heavy red curtains already pulled across the fading light. "There - right there." Elroy was prodding Walt's arm and pushing it, holding the coat, along the ledge. Walt realised they had sat near one of the music speakers and his coat was right beneath it; Elroy's too, as he placed his own there.

"They'll just hear a lot o' big bass thudding, now", he chuckled, his face breaking into one of its familiar broad grins. The old Elroy was back.

"You're sure of this, aren't you?" remarked Walt.

"No, not sure at all. Could be nothin'. But, like I say, we can't know: they can do anything..except -" he glanced at the loud-speaker, "kill the music." Still smiling, he raised his glass; Walt did likewise and smiled with him.

After they had each taken a swig and sat back, relaxing in the social atmosphere, Walt leaned towards Elroy, now that they had to speak up against the music, instead of being hushed by the 'bugs'. "But that coat thing. You had me worried but it's ridiculous, isn't it? They can't take the coat, unstitch it, slip the bug, stitch it up like new again!"

He stretched behind to his coat and flipped over one side of it. The stitching appeared as perfect as when he had bought it. Elroy pulled Walt's hand back before he could proceed to subject the entire garment to close inspection.

"Listen, man", he looked him in the eye and then away again, staring into the chunky glass slung between two big black hands. "like I said, they can do anything. They need seamstresses to sew up bugged coats - they got seamstresses. They need shoemakers to slide the heel off a shoe and put it back like perfect again - they got the shoemakers. I don't know whether they got them there all the time or just fetch them on-call when they need them but there aint no stopping what they want.

"I tell you - you know what I do - I do surveillance, don't I? I do electronics. I do radio signals, I do covert communications, I do the things aint no-one supposed to know about. Couple of years back, we were setting up surveillance in a country" - he glanced across at his companion - "can't even tell you which one. And there was this interference; couldn't get the goddam signal out;

tried everything; tell you, it was busting Fort Knox to get the right equipment. Steam coming out of CIA's ears, and the rest of them, crucial to nail down this surveillance. Big league, I tell you.

"In the end, I figured out there was a counter-signal about half-a-mile away, getting right in the way, jamming our frequencies. Had to send in a 'Stealth' to spot it - that spoiled the White House Christmas, a hundred million bucks of AWAC just to find a TV set! Yeh, that's what it was! This guy had about every TV gizmo you ever knew, to pick up signals from anywhere in the world; and not just that but amplify them like crazy and then beam them out to his friends across a hundred-mile radius. Like a one-man international TV network. Whole house was full of electronics. Anyway, he had to go."

Walt looked up sharply.

"Well, gee, no, not him, exactly", Elroy explained, "but all that kit. So they sent the Government in."

"The what?" Walt had visions of a massed attack of grey suits from the Pentagon.

"It all went. Gone", carried on Elroy, simply. "You know what they do? Turned out they faked up a whole government department in that country - not the building, just the name, just for this one guy. Sent a party of officials to him, all guys from that country - our plants - not a group of obvious Yanks. So it all looked just the business. Heavy metal. Told him he had a load of highly illegal equipment, playing havoc with the country's defence systems.

"But then, they're cleverer than that, they don't just rip it all out. They replace his wonderful gear with a crappy little TV and hi-fi that doesn't look quite right. Different shape than in the shops, see? Tell him, the only way he gets off without losing a hand or something - yeh, that kinda country - is sit tight and say nothing 'cos - you see - this strange-looking TV is actually part of the Government's defence system now, 'cos his house happens to be in just the right position - like, that figures, see, with what he'd created for himself - and if he only gets crappy TV signals from now on, it's 'cos that TV is really working hard to receive and relay defence signals with some extra tiny highly advanced chips inside. The latest thing - no, the *future* - in military communications. But, man, if he ever meddles with it, tries to take it apart, they'll know straightaway from the signal.

Or if he ever tells anyone about it - anything at all - they'll find out. Either way they'll get him and it won't just be his hand."

Elroy sat back, a grim frown on his features, gazing at Walt. "So?"

"So now he has this crappy TV set, a few local channels, lousy signal, and shit-scared to even imagine doing anything about it."

"All because..." wondered Walt.

"All because", concluded Elroy, "I needed my signals." He looked again at Walt, with a serious expression. "You think I'm proud of that?"

"They coulda just moved him out."

"Like I said, they're a whole lot cleverer than that", commented Elroy darkly. "This way, he's so dumbstruck, so convinced by the whole thing - so terrified - he's never going to tell a soul. And anyhow, he probably feels kinda proud that he's in on a government thing. Makes up for the lousy telly."

He continued examining his glass, talking at the rich brown fluid: "Not only that, most important, their Government never knows a thing. Nobody's disappeared. No-one's complaining about anything. No neighbours see anything different. Even the people he'd been transmitting to: I'm told to fix a transmission from him saying that all illegal TV reception will be identified and punished. Flashes up on their screens about every half-hour for a week. So they all get rid of their receiving gear. Sheer terror. And silence. I tell you, man, there are things you can do in those countries. And us - our lot - we just carry on doing our thing, my thing, like nobody gets in the way." He grimaced bitterly as he lifted the glass.

"All that for one man", Walt shook his head, "A whole team, fake officials, fake TV, whole fabricated story, total subterfuge - and an AWAC for Christ's sake!"

"So you see", said Elroy after a silence and another sip of bourbon each, "when it comes to just needing a seamstress or two ...."

Walt gazed at his friend. The music beat thudded away in the bar. They were close in a way he couldn't quite pin down. Something about 'chemistry' maybe. They didn't socialise a lot, not like every other night in bars or weekends fishing, that kind of thing. They'd call each other from time to time, every couple of weeks or so, for a drink, or just a chat on the phone. Their wives knew each other, as they had foursomes for dinner at each other's homes, and all four got along fine.

It was a friendship, the two of them, that had begun nearly twenty years before; a chance meeting at one of those specialist conferences - something like 'communications and the energy industry' - each arriving at the coffee service at the same time and just exchanging pleasantries. Elroy had recently completed his PhD and was a highly-qualified but junior representative of an electronics research outfit; he, Walt, held a youthful high-flyer's middle-management position in Enron - oh, wow, little did he know! - and was already wondering if big corporation was his 'bag'. They were both a bit revolutionary, maybe, in similarly unpronounced ways. Both were too young to openly express doubt but found themselves discussing the negatives of big Uncle Sam as much as the obvious benefits he bestowed on them like everyone else.

Then it was cheery 'see ya's', exchanged phone numbers and - unlike so many promises - a succession of lunchtime drinks, occasional golf, in which Walt was persuaded to adapt his experience of holiday 'pitch 'n' putt' to the real thing (only to be shamed by El The Elbow, as he was known at the club), and then those unexpectedly successful double-couple dinner evenings.

The surprise was that they had both got involved in LOTUS, quite separately, and without each other knowing until Walt had mentioned it to Elroy a couple of weeks before the first meeting. "Wow, you as well!" Elroy had exclaimed over the phone. When they considered it, it was perhaps less surprising to both of them now they were both out of 'corporate America', Walt having long since left to work in Government departments and Elroy - well, he never really knew quite who Elroy did work for, since 'Research Electronics Inc' meant absolutely nothing to Walt and Elroy only vaguely described it as a 'publicly funded company' but he 'wasn't allowed to say too much'.

So here they were, some years on from that conference, some months on from those daunting inductions into LOTUS, in a bar chosen for its noise in case they were being bugged by the very people Walt thought they were teamed up with. His friend had still not looked up from his glass.

"What is it, man?" asked Walt, tentatively, leaning towards him to be heard.

The big guy looked up slowly and met his eyes.

"Yeh?" Elroy's expression was wary, not wishing to engage.

"You're in deeper than me, aren't you?" Walt enquired, keeping his eyes fixed on the other.

"Whaadya mean?", breathed Elroy uncertainly, turning back to his glass, so Walt could only just make his voice out above the din.

"Look, El, you don't have to tell me. This whole shit is classified. Christ, your drink could be top secret for all I know." He gestured his elbow at Elroy's glass and the otherwise ordinary-looking bourbon lining the bottom. "But I guess you been to meetings that I've not - that's okay, I'm not complaining; you know me, I'm not the big 'how come I'm not involved' kinda guy - but ... I only just realised tonight really ..and maybe it's why you been, I don't know, quiet."

His friend looked up at him again, opened his mouth as if to speak, then looked away.

"Well, I guess I don't mean quiet. I mean 'worried'."

This time Elroy didn't stir. He seemed to examine his almost empty glass even more intently for several long moments then abruptly slung its remaining contents down his throat.

"More?" The big man was already moving to the bar as he spoke and returned minutes later with replenished glasses. He sat down closer to Walt and turned his head to speak so their faces were almost touching. Just like the movies, Walt found himself involuntarily thinking.

"You know why we're in this thing?" Elroy began.

Walt knew why *he* was in or it seemed pretty obvious. He was the leading expert in future energy needs analysis. What the USA would need beyond immediate predictions and LOTUS was the quasi-federal organisation set up to plan ahead and match up oil capacity. In other words - the words of the senior energy department man at the table - 'get the damn gas'.

"Well, yeh", responded Walt., remembering at that moment that, whatever LOTUS quasi-was, it was also a total secret. No-one knows about it. 'That clear?' had been said to both of them Right. Too clear.

"Yeh?" continued Elroy, "you know what L-O-T-U-S is really about?" He had hissed the word out in its separate sounds, not as letters but as an entity drawn from the air around them. Walt just returned his gaze. He could not imagine what on earth Elroy was attempting to tell him.

"It's about long-term *theft* ." The way Elroy enunciated that single word, Walt reckoned a half-trained lip-reader could have seen it from a hundred paces. He looked nervously at the crowded room but no-one seemed aware of anyone beyond their own immediate companions.

"What?" Walt breathed back at him, as though they were two conspirators in that corner plotting the downfall of the land of the free.

"I tell you what I do -" Elroy looked fiercely at him. Walt wondered if the bourbon was having too much influence.

"Elroy", he broke in earnestly, "look, man, don't tell me anything. Christ, man, you've sworn your life away on this, even to me. I don't expect this. I'm not your friend for this. You can keep this, man, you don't *have* to tell me, not anyone." He was telling his worried friend it would break no bond not to share a confidence like this. But he knew he was also telling his friend that if he needed to share it with any living soul then he was sitting with him right now. The way the brown eyes stared back from under the knitted grey-flecked brows and the lightly sweating deep brown skin told him his friend understood.

Elroy moved his face even closer.

"We're stealing oil. And that's the plan for the future. And, man, I'm the one they've hooked to do it."

"Steal oil? What do you mean, man?" Walt breathed and almost made a joke that would have involved a bucket, a torch and the turning of a small tap but realised just in time that it would not be funny.

So Elroy told him. And Walt somehow heard beneath the music and the thudding bass and the chatter of voices that his genius friend had invented 'systems'. He had developed the Iraqis' new highly sophisticated communications network for analysing and reporting oil reserves, extraction and supply, transmitted by broadband between oil wells, pipeline distribution points and central government offices. Part of the US post-occupation contribution to the country's new, ultramodern oil industry, with pinpoint data accuracy, critical for a sophisticated balance between controlled exports, dollar yields, financial stability and stable oil reserves. Only it wasn't. It wasn't accurate.

Elroy was speaking more rapidly as he spilled out details that Walt scarcely understood, about intercepting microwave transmissions, 'doctoring' the data, then re-transmitting it back into the system but leapfrogging the firewall barriers in the network by 'stitching' X-rays into the microwaves. "What!" Walt exclaimed. "One's short, one's long, see, one fits nicely into the other", explained Elroy as if it was common knowledge, "kinda marry them together, confuse the systems." "Where didya get the idea?" hissed Walt, incredulously. "Didn't. Don't reckon anybody discovered it before." There was no real pride in Elroy's tone, more regret. The genius regrets, maybe there was a song in there somewhere.

"But why? What's it for?" Walt leaned back a bit, still keeping his voice subdued.

"The pipeline, of course."

"Eh?" This was losing Walt.

"All these figures -" Elroy was starting to speak rapidly again, muttering through his teeth " - these *new* figures - are so they don't know how much oil they're losing. Poor goddam fools." The slicked-hair guy in LOTUS would not have liked the bitterness in those words.

'The pipeline', Walt learned - and indeed he thought he should not be learning any of this - was the secret pipeline, constructed as a branch line off one of the main pipes leading to the sliver of Iraq coastline where the tankers waited. Built during 'reconstruction', behind specially-made dunes - great barriers of piled-up sand in the desert - 24-hour military guard, all under the auspices of anti-terrorist security. Oil piped to other tankers at another, heavily-protected part of the coastline, just over the Kuwait border, and shipped away in vast quantities. For free, to the oil barons across the pond. Except the 'stats', thanks to big El, did not reveal any of this at all.

"Kuwait?" asked Walt, puzzled.

"Done the opposite there", explained Elroy, with a shrug. Then added, seeing his companion waiting for more, "fixed their

figures, too, so it looks like they're selling a load of oil to us when
they aren't. Same thing in reverse. So off sail the tankers into
the big blue sea, full of Iraqi oil ..."

"... Which the Kuwaitis think is theirs", continued Walt in
quiet astonishment.

"And nobody's paid a single dime", Elroy finished.

"Kuwait. They're going to notice, aren't they?" Walt broke the
silence after a moment. "I mean, even if they don't notice they've
still got the oil, they'll miss the money."

"Listen, man", Elroy leaned closer to him, "if the figures tell
them they've got the money, there's no way they're ever going
to count it. They're drowning in cash. You think our guys don't
know this?"

"And who knows?" Asked Walt

"No-one. Except this lot." Elroy frowned even more deeply.

"This lot?"

"The ones behind LOTUS", explained Elroy.

"And the President", added Walt.

"Nope."

"What!"

"You know the war?" Elroy looked up at him.

Well, Saddam's overthrow and all that aftermath was going
back a bit now but Walt was hardly likely to forget, no more than
any American, except a hermit perhaps.

"Well, yeh", responded Walt cautiously.

"Dubious intelligence reports to set it off, but convincing
enough for a trigger-happy President?" Elroy was still looking
him in the eye. "All concocted by these guys, just so the country
would get smashed up a bit and they could go in and do the
reconstruction - *their* way."

Walt looked dumbfounded. A whole war just a set up?

"Look", Elroy continued, " you know about oil supplies. That's
your job. You know it's running out. Who do you think cares
most? The President with feet up on radiator in the White
House? Nope. The guys making their fortunes out of it. But show
the big chief some dirty dictator who might also have some
nukes and nasty substances pointing our way and - hey - you just
try stop old Uncle Sam kicking ass."

"But these - 'oil barons' - they're rich already!" protested
Walt. "And they'll be dead before the oil runs out!"

"And their sons? Their daughters? Their *dynasties*? Did the old slave-owners release all my people on their death beds? Did they shit."

"But ...but .." Walt was struggling to get his thoughts straight, "you're saying all this stuff, war, LOTUS, your corrupt signals, diverting oil, is all done covertly, on a vast scale, and either it fools the President - and the whole government - or they don't know about it at all."

"Yup. That's it." Elroy finally straightened up in his seat and finished off the glass, staring ahead at the crowd of fresh young Americans chattering and laughing.

"But they'd have to have people in all the right places for a start." Walt still could not believe there could be a kind of 'alternative power' behind the running of the greatest democracy in the world.

"They *are* the people in the right places", replied Elroy in a stubborn tone. "What do you think rules the world. Justice? Politics?" He looked directly at his companion again. "Or money?"

"But", Walt heard himself spluttering in protest, "it can't go on. Somebody will rumble it. They can't just take the oil indefinitely. They'll notice."

"Notice what?" challenged Elroy, guilt-lines drawn on his face. "Empty holes in the desert? It ain't like a car, you know. They don't poke a goddam long stick down it to see how much is left."

"No?"

"No, man, it's all done with figures, stats, that's the point. Once they're fiddled, they stay fiddled. Whatever quantities they tell, that's what everyone believes."

"Empty wells showing like full ones", said Walt, wonderingly.

"Well, no", corrected Elroy, "there's a helluva lotta oil down there: just a bit less of it than they think there is."

"So what difference does it make?"

"The difference", declared Elroy, the bitterness returning to his voice, "is they stay poor, 'cos we don't buy their oil anymore. Leastways, not nearly as much as we would if we weren't stealing most of what we want."

"So it could go on forever, you're saying", pondered Walt, still absorbed in this revelation.

"Yup. As long as no-one blabs."

"Who knows?"

"Me, you now, them."

"Around that table", Walt jerked his head back in the general direction of 'Apex Insurance'.

"That's why ..." Elroy began after a pause.

" - You think we're being bugged." Walt finished his sentence for him.

"Yup."

"Clothes?" Walt glanced at his folded-up coat again.

"I don't know that", Elroy shrugged again, "that's just a precaution. But hell, man, I'd be mighty surprised if we're not bugged someplace - home, work, car -"

" - and followed?" suggested Walt.

"Mebbe." His big friend looked resigned, glum, defeated almost.

Walt looked at him. "Christ, man", he exclaimed, forgetting his companion's sensitivity to that profanity, "it's not your fault. How were you to know? We were told it was an honour to work for the White House."

"Oh, yeh", Elroy responded ironically, "if only the White House knew about it."

"Jeez, man, they didn't rope you in 'cos you're a bad guy. You just happen to be brilliant at your job."

"Yeh, thanks", Elroy grunted without looking up.

"Actually, probably the only one in the world who could do this", Walt added.

"Thanks again."

They finished their drinks. There was too much to take in for Walt. Gone was the honour of a privileged position in a secret Federal group working for America. In its place, ethical doubt, insecurity, even physical fear. He felt sweat in his palms.

"We could get out", he muttered, as they both sat staring at their empty glasses.

"Oh yeh?" Elroy raised an eyebrow at him. "And how do you want to go?"

"Uh?"

"Remember Alan Cargill?" Elroy looked meaningfully at him.

"Cargill? ...Wasn't he with you?"

"That's right", affirmed Elroy, "doing surveillance. I never knew quite what. But I found him crying in his empty office once.

Was going to tell me something, then clammed up. I got the feeling *he* wanted out."

"Didn't he die in a car...?" Walt's voice tailed off as he tried to recall the event.

"Car crash? Yep. Brand new out of the showroom. Brake failure. How original!" Elroy snorted and lifted his glass to see if there was anything left to drain from it. "Wanna get out?" He fixed his friend in the eye.

Walt sat in silence. He had heard too much. He had never considered himself an innocent; how could he, working for the government? But which government? Shadowy figures behind the scenes, possessing untold wealth and power which was never enough but always enough to exert an influence beyond the wildest conspiracy theory? Or the 'real' government, with the label on the tin? Either of them, always leaning on others; the genius conveniently at hand, like Elroy, or just some ordinary guy in the way.

"It's dirty", he grimaced at last, frowning.

"Dirt?" Elroy looked sharply at him and retorted bitterly: "Dirt! What we do, it's like the dirt under a car mechanic's fingernails. You can't ever get rid of it."

They donned their coats and stepped towards the door. As they passed outside, Elroy patted his coat at his chest, glanced at Walt and put a finger briefly to his lips again. Walt nodded. They walked on in silence, it almost dark now, Walt brooding on the uncertainty of privacy, the potential invasion of his life, the realisation that being part of that team meant you were actually *more* vulnerable, not less so. After a few blocks, it was time to part company. Walt looked out for a cab and only just noticed the scattering of white snowflakes that had begun falling, glistening against the street lights as they walked.

He stopped suddenly, leaned towards Elroy and muttered half under his breath, still mindful of bugs, "That pipeline, that's just a one-off?"

"That's just the start", his friend mumbled back, hardly moving his lips, his voice half-submerged by the laughter of passing revellers. "Why do you think we're hooked into this thing? You're telling them the oil they need, they're looking for the next country to do it all over again."

"Again? Where?"

Elroy looked at him: "That's obvious, isn't it?"

Walt studied the sidewalk beneath his feet. Things that even his best friend could not spell out to him. But, yeh, he could guess. This was how the chatter of politics and the rasp of aggression added up.

"You going home?" he asked.

"No", replied Elroy.

"Family?"

"All out. Christmas shopping, I think." Elroy flipped his eyes skywards with an ironic grin that said 'yet again, more spending, oh boy'. "Seeing Santa, I guess", he added.

"You?"

"Chapel."

Walt looked querulously at his friend. This was where they went their separate ways. Walt did not share his God. He doubted the declared belief of many of his fellow citizens and preferred to reject the deity outright, rather than put on an outward show, church on Sunday, curse on Monday, as the saying goes. Not Elroy, though. Walt respected his devoutness, just could not accept what the big man believed in. It never came between them, they just never discussed it, not beyond the occasional remark, never an argument. No point in that, Walt knew: Elroy simply believed in it all, absolutely, and that was that. He felt glad it had never been an issue between himself and Olivia. Well, he guessed they would never have 'clicked' if she had been religious; the differences between them would have been too transparent.

"I need to pray." Elroy responded to his companion's unspoken question, evident in the expression on his face. Walt smiled slightly and took his hand, to demonstrate he understood, or tried to. They shook, clasping each other's forearms, firm smiles to match. Walt saw a cab through the lightly falling snow and hailed it down.

"Call me in a couple of days", he said as he climbed in. "We'll talk again, sort it." He sounded unconvincing. The door slammed shut.

Elroy waved and smiled at the departing cab. He turned and walked a few steps to hail one for himself, brushing wet white crystals from his cheeks.

Begin

"Avarice", Gabriel repeated.

"Yes", agreed God.

He was reminded of a popular human saying, 'money is the root of all evil'. He had an idea it might even have had a biblical reference but He could not remember where. It was a big book, after all. However, money, no. Not as simple as that. Avarice was more acquisitive, more encompassing, as though the original desire for wealth had been subsumed by an overwhelming desire to *acquire*. Just acquire what was available, regardless of need. Sucking it all in.

"It won't cure everything."

"No", agreed The Lord again, although they (well, He, actually but He had allowed Gabriel to believe a lot of it was his own idea) had determined that it might remove the root of a number of ills.

It was not as though God did not want it all to work out. But hearing it spelled out in front of Him, by an angel hitherto markedly sour about further missions to Earth, made it sound as though it might not hang together quite as He had hoped. However, they were pretty much on their way, bar a few crossing of 'Ts' and dotting of 'Is' (this would be slashing of '(//*s' on Zlarog and splitting of '"-<^s' on Chtmpl but, thought God, fortunately neither of them presented the same problems as Earth). Now He just had to remind Gabriel who was actually going there.

"Are You sure You wouldn't rather go Yourself?" Gabriel asked, after a sequence which had gone: 'discussion ...pause...objection...reminder of Who's Boss ...protest about other pressing duties millions of light-years away ... further reminder of the Boss thing...further pause followed by suggestion to rethink whole plan ... severe knitting of deific (and metaphorical) brows .. sudden recollection of urgent request for immediate help at opposite end of the universe ...additional recollection of required attention to personal hygiene (the Lord was nearly persuaded) ... pathetic plea ("they're all cretins") ... quiet but formidable reminder of Who is actually God'.

"I am quite sure, thank you", was the Almighty's predictable response but, singularly, He did not look Gabriel in the eye. Not go Himself? He was not sure, that was the trouble. Was he delaying the inevitable? Could He indefinitely assume the role of 'strategic planner', leaving his angel to undertake the missions, to do the 'appearing'? Surely, yes, He sighed inwardly.

"I mean ... maybe -" Gabriel considered one last throw of the dice "we don't need to rush in just yet."

The Lord wondered what his trusty lieutenant was up to this time.

"I mean," continued the earnest angel, earnestly attempting to avoid the inevitable, "they are at least having a go now, aren't they?"

"Are they?" posed the Lord, sceptically, hesitating to nip anything in the bud.

"Yeh, You know, agreeing to change their ways, save the planet, and so on .. You know ...?" Gabriel faltered, unable to look or sound any more convincing. "You know?"

The Almighty looked at him in a 'Do I?' sort of way. Then he sighed, just a little, and thought, but didn't say, 'Yes. Perhaps. If they stick to it. But even so, too little too late'. He knew He did not need to say it. He would be understood.

"Oh all right", sighed Gabriel, in resignation. "But I can do it my way as usual?"

"Of course", God replied. What else could He say? He would just try not to watch, although He felt obliged to make the point about wings not being very 'twenty-first century' and might 'undermine' the mission through 'ridicule'. He was issuing a friendly instruction, not friendly advice, Gabriel noted without comment. In fact he had never used wings very much. They had become the stuff of legend and of countless works of art but in fact he had more often appeared as a blinding light, a thunderclap, lightning, an ephemeral shape - sort of moody and misty - and, of course, a star. Really, he brooded somewhat resentfully, he only kept the wings for special occasions.

"When then?" asked the angel, a superfluous question where time does not exist.

If they had already been on Earth, God would probably have looked at his watch and tapped it meaningfully, glancing up at Gabriel as He did so. As it was, He was able to cut out the watch bit and just look meaningfully at the angel instead.

Gabriel sighed again. "There's just this little job I need to do on Splong first", he started hopefully, "and -"

"Gabriel!" God interrupted. Somewhat sharply for the Lord, Gabriel thought.

"Okay Boss. But what about that problem on Tryxxx -"

"Gabriel!" God almost thundered now. Very noisy for the Boss, thought Gabriel.

"Oh, okay Guv", he said contritely, "I just thought -"

"Gabriel..." This time the voice was quieter, more intense. This was the voice Gabriel did not like. End of discussion sort of voice. He looked at the Lord and saw his gaze steadily returned.

"Okay, Boss, okay."

Gabriel moved slowly towards the edge of Heaven. Oh well. Won't last forever (ha, joke, while still with one foot in eternity). And after all, a lot of this was his idea (mm?) so it has got something going for it. His enthusiasm was beginning to return and he started to slip gently over the side, as the Lord watched him leave. God took a breath of the freshness already flowing through Heaven as the angel was departing. Much better that his aide did the missions, it reminded Him. Remarkable, he had thought before, that this welcome aroma could so penetrate a vacuum. Some dislocation in the universal laws of physics somewhere but He was blessed if He could work it out, despite having invented it all. Anyway, Who's complaining, He considered as He turned away. He was not too absorbed, though, in His sense of well-being, to turn back for a moment and call out to the departing angel.

"Oh, and Gabriel..."

The angel looked around, half over the edge.

"Yes, Boss?"

The Lord viewed him sternly.

"No wings."

Best

"Chilli sauce?"

"No thanks."

"You don' like chilli sauce to warm you on this cold winter night, sir?" The guy was beaming at him, eyes wide open, big swarthy smile flashing between thick black moustache and grey-flecked, frizzy beard. That familiar appearance of old man's facial hair on younger man's head. The hand was poised with a plastic bottle of the menacing dark red fluid tilted above his kebab.

"No, no thanks, That's fine."

"Okay sir, you're the boss."

Paul Best had been burned alive by their 'authentic' chilli sauce once before, and once was enough. He did not mind occasionally giving in to a fast- food stop on the way home - indeed, it seemed to be becoming more regular these days - but he'd leave the Asians to their more suicidal culinary tastes. And keep his tongue intact.

"Thanks. Perfect." Coins and hot paper bundle exchanged hands and he stepped out into the wet London night, but not before he glanced back to acknowledge the jaunty proprietor, who was bidding him goodnight. Those big wide dark eyes. He had noticed them before when calling for a takeaway. And always smiling. Always polite. Cheerful. Pleasant. As though somehow the world could do him nothing but good.

Yet all he had was a small, drab kebab house on the corner of an unprepossessing London suburban street. It had not even been modernised like many of them. Wooden window and door frames where others had plastic; old 'formica'topped serving counters, where most now had mock polished marble, or glass with shiny aluminium edging. And his two or three staff always seemed more sullen than he, or at least reticent, doing his bidding but with few words other than 'sauce?' or 'salad?" for their customers. Even other Asians, Paul had observed, did not get much more than a nod and a brief exchange in their shared language. He picked his way between the puddles, pins of rain glistening in the orange lamplight, pulled the car door shut and drove away.

Asif Hassan had already turned back to the kebab spindles, still smiling. It was an inner peace, if his customer but knew. Something inside Asif that kept him at ease, in good humour, in equilibrium with the world about him. He glanced up at the clock and then briefly back to the fat fryers and the hot plates, issuing a swift, quiet instruction to his two young assistants. It was nearly time for prayers, the fifth and last of the day. He stepped through the hanging strips in the doorway, to the gloom behind, catching sight of himself in the darkened glass of the back door and wondering, as he did so, if it was true, as they always said, that he seemed to have something of the prophet about him.

Paul Best drove through the busy streets, munching on his kebab. No different to holding a phone to your ear, he thought, but one was illegal, the other not. Good job, or busy people like himself might starve. He felt the pitta and meat-of-dubious-origin slip down his gullet to the larger than average stomach eagerly waiting below.

The line of traffic slowed to a halt. Damn! Even going home at this time, mid-evening, you had to sit in bloody traffic! Well, this Chinese car seemed okay, anyway. More comfortable than he had expected. And the guy had sent it all the way from Beijing - *free gratis* - on trial. He had been a bit sceptical but the agent was very persuasive and so committed to the product. Paul, as a salesman by nature himself, had appreciated that. He was beginning to believe this might be one of his 'best' decisions. 'Best Cars' might become the first main dealer for the leading Chinese independent motor manufacturer.

It was a good name, 'Best'. For him, anyway. His father had not made anything of it, just working in a Post Office sorting-room most of his life. But son Paul, with something of the entrepreneurial flair about him, suited the family name perfect-ly. 'Driving a Best Car, the Best Thing You Can Do'; 'Buying a Car? Buy The Best'. The permutations of sales catch phrases were endless. Of course, it was his own name but, sadly, he did not own sole rights to the word itself.

If he could have bought a monopoly on his entry in the English language, he doubtless would, as many friends and acquaintances had remarked. Not that he had not tried. He had taken a rival to court for using the phrase 'best cars'. Lost the action, of course, but the publicity had been worth ten times the legal bill. And where was the rival now? Went out of business years ago. Shortly after that demise, Paul had blazoned the line on every possible advertising medium: 'Drive The Best Because

Where Are The Rest (our case!)'. Sales rocketed. Well, he had reflected, he did not need anyone to like him, only his cars.

Or a Chinaman's motor cars. Hm, indeed. His fingers pushed the crumbling remains of the kebab between his lips and he wiped a podgy hand across his mouth. Who would have thought, eh? An ordinary London lad selling a Chinaman's cars - exclusive. Well, he was driving it and if he was a punter he would spend good money on it; unlike some on his forecourt. Wonder what the guy looks like. Never been to China, his thoughts rumbled on; done the Med, the States, Caribbean, South Africa - safari. Never attracted to the far east. Could you trust them? Those slinky eyes.

"Dunno", he muttered aloud, watching the windscreen wipers flick to and fro on 'intermittent' in the crawling traffic. I'd probably trust a guy who made a car like this, even this cheap. Respect. In the trade. Probably never meet him, though, Paul thought. All done through the agent; and he's just another Londoner. Good car, though. Get the order shipped over. Should sell well. Fucking traffic! So bloody late again! He grimaced at the chill welcome awaiting him. He could hear that hard New York voice in his ears. Once it had seemed only warm and voluptuous. Now it was all Brooklyn bite.

Eight thousand miles away, Hoi Fong stirred in his sleep, felt the warmth of his wife beside him and the comfort it infused in him. They could not have come this far without the Society, he kept telling himself; it would prove to be no harm in the long run. It helped to soothe his unease as he lightly caressed her, ripening taut and smooth, before she rose to another cockcrow dawn.

Trap

Chapel had been a help. His work and most of his social life kept him chiefly in the company of all colours of America. A natural, cosmopolitan way of life along the eastern seaboard, if not everywhere in the States, even now. In chapel, though, it was different. Among the almost entirely black congregation Elroy felt a sense of homeliness. The relationship with God, the relationship with the act of worship, whatever it was; a kind of simplicity and joy, maybe. Maybe from the times when the only solace for his forbears, the only source of hope and joy, was in the celebration of faith in the Lord and His power to overcome the ills of humanity. Even though the manifestation of this power seemed at times a long time coming.

Being there, in that holy place and among his fellow-worshippers, was like a soothing palm passing over his brow. It calmed some of the turmoil inside. This evening, though, in prayer for an hour alone, except for a couple of other silently bowed souls, it could not ease his guilt, it did not absolve him of the responsibility he felt, nor his feeling of helpless entrapment. "You're in a very privileged position", Slick-Hair had remarked at their last private meeting. Elroy wondered whether 'obligation' should be substituted for 'privilege'.

He had to draw his coat-collar up around his neck as he walked home, the big soft snowflakes starting to find the gap between hair and clothing, causing him to wince at the cold drips on his skin. It was a mile or so from chapel to home. Maybe he should have called a cab. He had reckoned, though, by the time he had found one prepared to come way out of the city, struggling through all that traffic for one short ride at this time of night, amid worsening weather, he would be home already. He might have felt safer, though. Despite the roar of vehicles - with horns blaring, angry faces at windscreens contemplating dried-up dinners, missed appointments, wasted theatre tickets, children long a-bed - the chaos of the town street was the pedestrian's protective wrapper. Once he had turned down the quite local back road, he could not help glancing around behind him at any sound or hint of movement in the long unlit stretches.

He had to tell himself there was no-one following, just shadows, tricks of the dim light in the darkness. How could he be sure? He knew his step was quickening as he drew closer to home. Would it be obvious? Slow down! Don't advertise guilt! Surely, surely, why should they follow him? Could they have heard anything he said? Bugged? His hands were feeling up and down his coat, just as he had mocked Walt for doing. He smiled grimly to himself. And shuddered. He pulled his coat around his throat.You're shivering because you're cold, you fool, he told himself.

What would they do, anyway? Leap out at him in the dark? A silent assassination? Why? He could see the headlines: 'Government top-techno hacked down in the dark". Questions would be asked. LOTUS might be exposed. Surely! They would not take the risk! He could not be sure. There was a sudden rustle to his side. His breath caught as he spun to look. He peered, for a moment frantic, but there was only darkness. Then he saw the black shape of a dog scampering away from the sidewalk through the trees that lined the road. Elroy realised his heart was pounding. Get a grip, man!

All at once he was among some glimmers of light again, street lanterns partly-masked by trees separating the discreet and well-spaced executive homes. But light there was. Sanctuary. He felt like a small child, chased by hobgoblins through the night. There were no nightmares. He had simply walked home through the dark and the snow, and now here he was. In the portico porch, he slotted the key in the lock and in a moment was inside. The house was dark and silent. Everyone out, still doing the pagan side of Christmas - which he enjoyed as much as anyone else. The vision of his customarily warm family home flicked across his mind: wife, two young children, smiles, comfort. He had sometimes wondered if Walt and Olivia missed that: just the two of them. Maybe choice, both in second marriages, maybe not. He never asked. They were deliciously in love, though.

He flicked the hall lights switch and allowed himself an unChristian curse under his breath - another blackout! He flicked it up and down again, as people do as though expecting the friction to ignite a spark. Dead. Dark. He sighed. It was becoming so commonplace now, it was not a particular surprise. He took another step inside, without turning to look behind him. He did not see the warm glow filtering from all the other windows in the close, their drawn curtains closed across well-lit rooms, with flickering television screens and the glint of coloured Christmas lights sprinkled around window and door frames. No-one else was blacked out.

Elroy shut the door behind him and peered ahead as his eyes adjusted to the darkness. Candles and a lighter were somewhere but he could not anyhow remember where. Kitchen, probably, and he needed a drink. He stepped carefully across the spacious square hallway, walls and doorframes starting to materialise faintly out of the night now. He gradually made his way to the outline of the open kitchen door ahead on the left. A few more cautious steps and he had pulled open the fridge door in the dark. No fridge light, of course, but he fumbled inside and drew out an invisible can. A fizz and pop as he opened it sightlessly and tasted - ugh - that sickly stuff the kids drank. Oh well. He turned to feel for a surface to put down the can and something caught his eye. A narrow beam of light slanted across the hall floor. Odd. How had he not noticed that? He shuddered slightly. The light looked as though it must be coming from underneath a door, out of sight of the kitchen.

He felt sweat on his brow and was aware of it in the palms of his hands. Come on, he grimaced. The light must have been on all the time. Not been switched off when the family went out. He had simply not noticed it as he concentrated on getting to the kitchen in the dark. The dark! The blackout! He had forgotten the blackout! How could there have been a light at all? Or had the power come back on? Confusion gripped him. He felt along the wall to the light switch and eased it down. Nothing. Still dark.

The sweat was trickling. He could feel it. It was behind his knees, too, and under his collar. He knew he was a big man. Big enough to be a match for most others. But even big men can feel fear. He was aware of a sharp stinging in his hands and unclenched his fists, freeing the nails that had been digging into skin.

Intruders? Burglars? Then the thought struck him: bastards! God forgive him! This was it. He and Walt *had* been bugged and overheard. This was *them* lying in wait. This was the Alan Cargill treatment. Only this time it wasn't car brakes fixed by a faceless assassin, it was face to face confrontation in his own home. They must have their own flashlight. He felt a cold droplet of sweat trickle down the side of his nose but avoided the movement of raising a hand to wipe it away. It dripped to the floor. So. This was it. His jaw was tightening in the gloom and his whole body tensing with anger. So, a few misplaced remarks in the street, confidential exchanges with an old friend - another of their poor suckers - and they wasted no time in ...*wasting* him. Of course - they'd had plenty of time to get here before him: he had spent that hour or more at chapel. Thank the Good Lord the family had gone out, he breathed inwardly with gratitude to the Almighty.

He steadied himself for a moment then slowly, silently, turned around to reach for the knife rack where he knew it was hanging in darkness on the wall. Careful, careful! Like a blind man! He knew the knives would rattle if he was clumsy. His fingers grappled for the largest, the meat cleaver, and sightlessly unhooked it. Perfectly quiet! Cleaver in hand, he began to take the few steps from the kitchen towards the streak of light on the hall floor. He could see the source now - the crack under his study door. Huh! The irony of using his own study as the snare! Bright light. Almost eerie in the darkness.

Slowly, slowly he crept towards it. Then he stopped. A sound? No, none. His breath had caught in his chest and he had to force himself to let it out soundlessly, not in a sudden gasp. By heaven, they were cool. Not rushing out to charge him down, plug him with bullets or dispatch him silently with blades. No, just waiting for him. Well - he tensed with angry determination again - they were not going to find it so easy. He was bristling with mounting fury at the outrage of this invasion into his home, this assumption that, from a few careless words he was a traitor and had to be despatched.

His skin was stretched taut over the knuckles grasping the cleaver. More sweat was dripping off his nose and he could feel it running down his back. Slowly, carefully, silently, step by agonising step. Step then pause, step then pause. He had almost reached the study door but something halted him. The light. What was it about that light? It no longer appeared like a streak spilling under the door but a glow, almost suffusing the whole door itself in front of him. Some powerful flashlight! Was this an interrogation cell they had turned his study into, like they show in the movies? He was momentarily struck motionless with fear. He must escape. Crazy to take them on. Mad. Turn and flee. Safety outside. Sanctuary. Phone for help. Call Walt. Call the cops. Anyone.

But he stood still. Anger overcame fear. Anger at this intrusion. Anger at the whole scheming subterfuge and violence. And fear, too. Fear that 'they' would still come and find him. No. Confront it now. Here, where surprise, a charge, might be his best chance. The sweat was going cold on his skin. Still there was silence. Uncertainty held him back for a moment. Then he made a move. He put his hand to the door. It was not latched and began to swing open.

Everything, all the sights, the impressions, the images, all happened at once. And the sounds, of his breath sucking-in, the heaving of his chest and the thundering drum his heart. All, as he lunged forward, pushing the door with one hand, raising the cleaver in his other. The intensity of the light. The unnatural brilliance. Interrogation lamps! No. The door opened wide to reveal ... nothing! No leering hoods. No flash of weapons. No menacing inquisitor with devilish smile. In the blink of his eye Elroy saw his empty study. The wall lined with bookshelves. The portrait of his great-grandfather freed from slavery. The corner of his desk and a chair. Until he turned to face them, where they could only be concealed, behind the door. That light! That awesome, unreal glow of golden light. Where had they got this light from!

Sweat poured from every part of him His eyes were smarting, sweat and glare dazzling him. He clutched the cleaver even tighter, afraid it would slip in his hand as he struck. Now! He pivoted around the door, raising the weapon above his shoulder to bring it crashing down through the blinding light. He saw the blade glint past his cheek to its target, anticipating the ghastly crunch of impact. But then he froze. Like a statue he hovered immobilised, transfixed in the blaze of light, cleaver glinting in space. For one more instant there was silence. Then it was broken by the sob rising from his throat and spilling through his stiffened, sweat-soaked lips.

For it was at that moment Elroy Fitzgibbon thought he had died.

Found

"Have you tried to talk to him?"

"Only once", she faltered, and tears were welling into her eyes. "He just stared ...and stared."

Mariana Fitzgibbon began to sob very quietly. They both knew she was a strong woman but this was about as much a shock as she could take.

"The doctor?" enquired Olivia, gently.

Mariana shook her head. "Busy", she replied, tearfully, "all busy. Too many emergencies. Try later."

Snow. Blizzard. Inevitable road accidents. They knew that would be the problem.

"Honey." Olivia squeezed her shoulder more tightly.

"Then ...then .." Mariana continued, "I just had to call you ..and ... and ..I've just watched him."

She was weeping fully, tears flowing down her burnished cheeks, Olivia holding and hugging her.

They had rushed from their apartment as soon as they got the call, around ten o'clock, and driven almost blind through the swirling blizzard. It was Walt clutching the wheel, knuckles tight, eyes peering through the dark; Olivia anxiously prompting at his side.

"Walt, darling, slow down - please."

"Sure, hun. We just gotta ...."

"I know. We've got to get there. But we've got to *get* there.." Not adding. 'Alive'. Not wanting to.

"Okay, hun, sure."

Headlights were reflected back in a glare from the big soft flakes, blurring a montage of black tar, brown slush, white snow, bright light and intermittent road markings, the screen wipers piling up a white border around the glass.

"She didn't say he's hurt", Olivia had soothed, attempting to steady their slithery progress.

"She didn't say he isn't", Walt muttered. "How do we know? He's said nothing. Could be ...."

"Be?" she had repeated nervously.

"...Critical ... internal."

"Oh!" Olivia gave a sharp intake of breath.

There had been near-misses; horns blaring, headlights flashing, white lines impossible to follow, wheels skidding and sliding.

"Not, surely not badly injured. She didn't say anything about pain, did she?"

"Nope." Walt's thoughts had been on Elroy as much as the road. Had 'they' got to him already? The sobs on the phone had said nothing of harm; nothing even out of place, only a kitchen cleaver lying at his feet; and a sheet of paper. "Just staring. Like a doll."

They had found the turning more by instinct than by sight, a familiar route suddenly alien in the white-out. Walt steered around the few hundred yards of gently curving roadway from memory, the boundary between tarmac and grassy verge under a blanket of snow in the night.

"There she is", Olivia had whispered, the small knot of executive houses appearing in the dark behind a curtain of snowflakes. The proud figure of Mariana Fitzgibbon could be seen waiting for them, sheltered under the twin-pillared entrance portico. They were prestigious homes: neo-colonial, but red brick not white wood, big tall windows bordered with white stonework, and that impressive portico over the front door. Reward for reaching the top, Walt had mused in the past, whether by selling your soul or retaining a troubled one, like Elroy.

The polished oak door between the pillars humbled even Mariana, thought Olivia, as they drew up; or perhaps it was the circumstances tonight. Puerto Rican, tall - five-eight at least - burnished bronze and an 'hour-glass' figure, reminiscent of the golden age of Hollywood legends, Mariana Fitzgibbon defined beauty for many, with her wavy copper-tinted hair, deep brown eyes, kiss-shaped lips and, as more than one man had wishfully described, a powerful pair of nutcrackers for thighs. Not for Walt, though. No woman could compare with his adorable Olivia: her allure of peach and tan, misty hazel eyes, a smile like a rose and the willowy figure of a fashion model - but with rather more substance!

Right now, though, it was the proud woman in tears, the distraught friend, gratefuly meeting them at the door, no more than a shawl flung over her shoulders against the night. Walt had briefly clasped Mariana's hand and pecked her cheek, while Olivia hugged her quickly as they all brushed inside, Mariana shutting the door behind them.

She had directed them to the study, melting snow shaking from them as they went.

"The children?" Olivia asked.

"Ma has them" was the whispered reply. "They were too upset."

Olivia nodded in understanding.

Now Walt faced his friend, slouched in his chair, hands hanging by his sides. The features were expressionless, mouth slightly ajar, eyes wide open and staring blankly ahead. Walt turned to follow Elroy's gaze which fell only on the empty wall and curtained window behind the desk. He looked hard at the big man's face to discern from his expression what had happened, what might have paralysed his mind. If he could interpret anything through the glaze, it could have been wonder mixed with fear; like someone who had seen a ghost. Some ghost, grimaced Walt to himself: the bastards!

He scanned the man's face again, and his neck: no evident bruises or marks. He felt some relief. Clothes seemed unruffled as well, no signs of a struggle. He placed his hands on Elroy's shoulders and stared intently at him but the distant gaze that returned passed right through him. Walt glanced swiftly around the room. As Mariana had described, tearfully on the phone, everything was in place: curtains neatly drawn closed, desk accessories tidily where they should be. Just one out-of-place sheet of paper with something written on it. He looked down. The cleaver lay beside the chair; he peered closer, thank God no blood stains!

"Bastards!" he suddenly hissed between his teeth. Olivia and Mariana had stepped silently into the study after him and were halted by his bitter tone. Mariana gave a little gasp and Olivia clutched at her hand. Bastards, he thought again to himself, they can do this to him without leaving a mark!

"Christ!" he swore softly again

"Wha - !" Mariana exclaimed fearfully in the doorway.

Walt looked up hurriedly, aware of their presence, and raised a consoling hand. Olivia clasped Mariana's shoulder to comfort her.

Walt stared intently into Elroy's eyes again.

"Hey man", he said softly to him, "what did they do to you, man?"

There was no response, not even a flicker of the eyes.

Walt looked across at Mariana.

"The cops?" Olivia inquired gently.

"Walt said no", Mariana whispered.

Walt looked up at Olivia.

"They could all be in this", he muttered, darkly, "best leave them out."

"Oh", responded Olivia, wondering how much she did not know.

Walt was feeling churned up inside and turned again to his friend, desperate to get through.

"Hey, man, It's me, Walt." He took him by the shoulders again, urging him to react, anything, just acknowledge he was there. "Chrissake, Elroy!" He felt a surge of anger at whoever was responsible. "What have they *done*, man! Chrissake, man, say *something*!" He looked again at Mariana. "Has he been like this all the time?"

"Yes", she faltered through tears.

Walt began to lean forward, about to grasp the big brown head between his hands, maybe shake it in sheer frustration, just shake the goddam evil bug outta him! Then, suddenly, the wide brown eyes were looking at him. Focused on him, seeing him and recognising! Walt pulled back sharply, not quite taking it in. He was watching a broad smile spreading across Elroy's features, eyes and mouth lighting up together. The grin broadened even further as the eyes became sharp with their familiar twinkle. Elroy beamed at him.

"Walt!" he drawled in delight, "Hi, man! What you doing here? You okay?"

There was a gasp from the women just inside the door and Mariana took a step forward but hesitated, still fearful.

"Christ, El", breathed Walt, unable to smile in return, "it's not *me*, man, what about you? You hurt?"

"Hurt?" Elroy was still smiling hugely. "Gee, don't think so. Did I fall or something?"

"Dunno, El, dunno", replied Walt, continuing to examine his expression, "you tell me. You okay?"

"Why, sure!" The smile was one of almost infant delight. Walt felt slightly unnerved by it, as though he were a stick of seaside candy being held out to the child.

This time Mariana moved to her husband and wrapped her arms around his neck, gratefully sobbing and kissing his cheek. Elroy held her arm.

"Hey, Mariana, honey. What is it?" He spoke gently to her, still with the broadest of smiles. "I just been thinking, y'all... You know?"

Walt and the women glanced at each other, worried.

"El", began Walt, "you been sitting here for hours. Mariana says, just staring into space, man. You have to tell us what they done to you. I mean, did they give you anything. A drink, you know ..."

He looked helplessly at his friend, whose smile only altered to include a hint of puzzlement.

Olivia stepped to his other side.

"Or a needle, Elroy, can you remember anything?"

They all knew without spelling it out between them that his condition had to have been induced by something. If not a violent beating, then - the horror of it! - injected with something? Walt was seized with the growing realisation they must have used drugs to get him to talk, to reveal his misgivings about the project. Christ! Turning the man's mind to jelly! The bastards, the bastards! He must have been bugged, like he said, they both must have!

Olivia could see the rage working in Walt's face. She moved over to hold his hand and looked around at Elroy.

"Elroy, darling." She cast a sympathetic glance at Mariana, knowing it was beyond his wife to penetrate his mystery at this moment. "Elroy", she continued softly, "if they've given you anything, please remember, we need to help you."

"Christ, man", choked Walt, despairing at the vision of his genius friend reduced to a blankly grinning idiot for the rest of his life.

"Hey Walt ...Livvy ..Mariana", beamed Elroy, smiling at each of them around him, "whaddya mean, 'they'?" He looked puzzled but still with the enormous, joyful grin. "I just been sitting thinking awhile, you know." He looked at Walt and a purposeful tone entered his voice, behind the constant smile. "I got it, man."

Walt's heart sank. Now the man was talking nonsense. The bastards! This is what they did!

"Elroy, what happened here. Try to bring it back, man. Something happened, eh? You aint just been sitting here doing nothing. Who was here. Who was here, man?"

The women heard a savage edge to his voice as he wanted somehow to force the night's events out of the big beaming friend in front of him.

"My darling", coaxed Mariana, at last finding voice as she held him to her.

"Elroy", Olivia was imploring him.

"Oh ye-e-h", said Elroy expansively through his smile, as though finally realising there was something he knew that they needed to share. The words almost spelled themselves from his lips, slowly, precisely, in an orderly line: "It ... He ...came! He was here."

He looked around at the three of them again, with his wondrous smile. "He came to *me!*" It was as though the vision glowing on his face would light up the whole room. "And I got it, Walt ...I *got* it!"

Walt was feeling numb, drained.

"Got what, El?" was all he felt capable of asking.

"The answer, man." The smile was at last relaxing in his face but only to leave the wide-eyed expression of wonder in its place. "He showed me!"

Mariana was hugging him ever more tightly, as though to squeeze him to his senses. Olivia just stood, feeling a quicksand of incomprehension shifting beneath her feet.

Walt did not know whether he was witnessing mental collapse or the vacant meanderings of a man still half-drugged.

"Who, man?" asked Walt. "Showed you what?"

There was triumph in the returning smile.

"This."

Elroy leaned slowly forward to put his big hand on the stray sheet of paper on the desk and slid it around so it faced Walt the right way. There was only one word on the entire page, scrawled in handwritten ink: 'Piggyback'.

"He showed me", added Elroy, still beaming.

"He ...wrote that?" said Walt, slowly, picking up the idea of a 'he' who had been there. Some hard information perhaps, at last.

"No", Elroy smiled at him, "I did. He showed me."

Walt did not know what to say, what to ask. Who? If not the heavy mob, or the white-coated inquisitors, who? And inducing the ramblings of a dummy in the process. Bastards.

Olivia spoke for them.

"El, who do you mean, who was this?"

Elroy gazed back at her, and at all of them staring blankly at him. Momentarily, a shadow seemed to pass over his expression. He looked at Walt and spoke seriously to him.

"I thought he had come for me, you know. I thought it was my time...but ..."

"But?" Walt leaned forward in consternation. The threat had returned.

"But ...no." The big wide smile reclaimed its owner once more. "Gee", he breathed in wonder, "it .. He ..was so bright...so bright!" His voice trailed away as he appeared to relive something only he could see.

Walt feared Elroy was about to collapse back into the trance as his eyes gazed distantly ahead, wide with their inward-looking vision. He moved closer to him, not knowing what to say.

"Bright, Elroy, darling? What do you mean, bright?" Olivia's voice was soft but perplexed.

Elroy's eyes turned to her, and to each of them in turn, transmitting his fervour.

"And you know", he almost sang the words, ignoring the question he had just been asked.

"Yes?" responded Walt, urging it from him.

Elroy stared into his eyes and clutched Walt's wrist with an intensity that caused a small stab of pain.

"It had ... he ...had ...wings!"

Return

God was not happy. Gabriel had been with Him long enough - about as long as time itself - to know when he was in the company of an Unhappy Almighty; and an Unhappy Almighty was One, in Gabriel's experience, to steer clear of. Or, at least, not One to deliberately strike up a conversation with. especially when he, the loyal but not altogether obedient archangel, was the likely source of this deific discontent. Not that Gabriel was in danger of suffering any divine retribution. No more than the Good Lord's myriad creatures scattered around his cosmos.

That was all part of the mythology. Fire, brimstone, earthquakes, ammonia storms (on Axgthe), plasma plagues (Splong), even pouring rain on summer weddings (Earth): none of these had anything to do with sin and punishment. They were all preordained and were going to occur anyway, whether you behaved perfectly (which, on Axgthe, included spitting foul orifice-extrusions at each other) or horribly.

"I wish they were all rather less inclined to take it so personally", God sighed at times. To which, Gabriel responded, "Well, You haven't exactly worked hard to put them right on that. I mean, look at the liquid telepathy Divine missives on Trryxxx" (which Gabriel did not pronounce that way but it is as close as we can get, here), "full of dire warnings about apocalyptic zincquakes. And Earth, well, the Bible and the Koran, all that stuff about the wrath of the Lord and all that. Not exactly predicting a little tap on the head: 'there you go, my children, try to do better next time'."

"Thank you, Gabriel", God murmured on such occasions, wanting to add that all the intelligent members of his universal flock ("and that includes humans, Gabriel, if you don't mind") had to be allowed their own interpretation of his 'signs', within the context of their own cultures and their freedom of self-determination. However, He kept that remark to Himself, to avoid a lengthy discourse about how social conditions changed over time and could He not have found a way to bring some of these 'interpretations' up to date a bit.

This kind of circular argument, in which Gabriel habitually failed to see, or wilfully ignored, the fundamental precept of neither meddling with intellectual development nor with the physical universe, was a discussion with the potential to continue indefinitely. Even where time was not a factor, this, to God, was an extremely tedious prospect. So the fact that the 'wrath of the Lord' was a human misunderstanding which He could not just step in to correct, was a subject left unbroached if at all possible. Running the universe was a bit more subtle than that.

"I mean, how about 'The Bible - The Remake' or 'The Koran - The Sequel'", chimed in Gabriel after a silence. "Here you are my flock, or whatever, now you've grown up a few centuries and have got a bit of science behind you, here's an update: if a load of you get squashed under an earthquake it's not 'My' way of punishing you for being trash, you do that to yourselves enough with all your wars and killing each oth -"

"Gabriel!" God had thundered on more than one occasion during such conversations, just to bring him to a halt. He sometimes considered that, if it were left to Gabriel, there would be tablets on mountains, visitations in caves and strange stars in the sky about two or three times a decade. Meddling to the point of creating abject boredom: 'Oh here's something from God again; will you open it or do I have to?' And, actually, interfering to the point of making a nonsense of the twin pillars of preordination and self-determination.

Right now, though, the issue of non-existent Divine retribution apart, the Lord was feeling not entirely sure how to engage the subject of the angel's deviation from instructions, since those orders themselves had included a significant degree of hitherto prohibited 'meddling'. Gabriel was conscious of the Lord's quandary and, with a smugness he was studiously trying to conceal, considered he could tactically wait for Him to speak first. He applied his attention to the recently neglected gap beside the little toe on the left foot, frowning and grunting with exaggerated concentration.

After a lengthy silence, in which it became clear to the Lord that Gabriel was not going to volunteer an explanation, despite being confronted with evident Holy disquiet, He remarked drily, "So you thought it appropriate to scare the living daylights out of him. An imaginative approach, wouldn't you concede?"

Gabriel shuffled slightly and muttered, truculently, "Only same as on the Damascus road, boss."

"And did I not tell you then about going over the top?" came the frosty reply.

"It worked", Gabriel grumbled into the offending gap, while jabbing a finger into it.

"Worked? If you mean you bludgeon them into obedience by putting the fear of ...." The Lord hesitated.

"God."

"Precisely ...into them." The Lord was troubled. Like 'divine retribution': so much emphasis on fear!

"I just .." began Gabriel. "I mean, it has to work, doesn't it. Can you rely on love alone? For the love of God, and all that. How could we be sure? Look at all they've accomplished on Earth 'for the fear of God'."

"Yes, indeed." If sarcasm were at all a Holy virtue, which of course it is not, one might have detected an element of it in the Lord's response. He was about to proceed with the retort, 'how many millions dead?' but, not unusually, Gabriel was cantering along ahead of Him.

"Okay, maybe not fear, exactly, not terror" (though he could not help recalling the expression on Elroy's face), "but awe - you know, love and awe - the shepherds, Saul, Joan of Arc -"

"Please do not mention her", the Lord winced.

"All of them", the angel was making a blinkered charge down the back straight, "a bit of both, isn't it, enough love to make them want to do it, enough awe to .. to ..."

" - Terrorise them?"

"No, not terrorise. None of them looked like that. Just ...just... they feel they have no choice. I mean, that's the plan, isn't it?" Gabriel had passed the winning post. God breathed deeply. Love and fear, or love and awe. Like dogs. Did He wish to subjugate his civilised creatures like dogs? A kind of panting, tongue-lolling, cringing, fearful love? The love that obeys because it also fears. What kind of a relationship is that? What happens when the fear fades? When choice emerges. When the alternative to 'right' is 'wrong'. When the preference to 'good' is 'bad'. When children start smoking. When greed leads to theft. When power enables control and - that word again - subjugation. And the 'fear' itself had been wilfully manipulated like a tool: 'Fear God and may He have mercy upon your soul'. The crackle of the fire, the thunder of guns, the turn of the rack, the twang of the rope, for the fear of God.

The Lord brought Himself and His musings back to the immediate discussion. "Plan?" He queried.

"The plan: they have to be shown what to do and be certain to do it."

"And will he?" enquired the Lord.

"I shone", replied Gabriel, simply.

"Yes, I did notice", said the Lord, "you have a habit of nearly blinding them."

"Just a bit of a glow", protested the angel, "make a bit of an impression. Has a big effect, all that light, especially when they can't see where it's coming from."

"I sometimes think", mused the Lord, softly, "We're lucky they don't just end up in a lunatic asylum."

"I don't think they have those, anymore, Boss. Not there, anyway."

"You know what I mean." What could He say? He - they - had set it in motion. Gabriel's enthusiasm was not something easily curbed. Perhaps it was the key to success; the shepherds, after all....

"However..." The Lord's tone changed, it was cooler, less benign, as he remembered the real reason He had felt 'unhappy', almost annoyed, had that sentiment been at all possible in the Supreme Being, which of course it was not. Nevertheless, the reason He had wanted a word with Gabriel as soon as he returned from the mission.

"Guv?" Gabriel looked up a little cautiously as he wiped a finger down his chest.

God observed his less than obedient angel. "I thought I said 'no wings'!"

"Aw, boss", Gabriel replied with a pained expression, "they were the icing on the cake!"

PARADIGM : CONCEPTION

He - shining bronze and carved like the statue of gods; she - the gold and silken curves only of imagination.

They lay side by side on a single flat stone, naked except for the light whisps of garment which yet were slipping from them as they moved. Gazing through fading sunlight across the rippling blue-green sea, to the distant curving horizon, his rich hair falling loosely to his shoulders, he turned his head to look deep into her grey-brown eyes.

"You know I love you", he said, and his full lips widened slightly into a quiet smile.

"I know you do", she smiled back at his expression of concern, seeing frown and smile playing together like lithe cats across the gleaming brown plain of his face. "Yet one day you shall kill me", she added, simply.

"No, no", he recoiled, "How could you -!"

"Sshh." She lay a soft finger on his lips, smiling at his shock, soothing his dismay. Then he felt the warmth of her hand slide over his thigh, between his legs, and the moist heat of her lips pressed to his, then moving lower, caressing, pressing, and lower, as they turned to each other. And they lay back across the stone to make the new life which would one day burst from them, as the sun slowly dipped behind the shimmering glint of gradually darkening waves.

Part Two

ACTION

ACTION

Stranded

"It just stopped on me, I tell you! ... Yeh, that's right! Just seized up! Whaddya think I'd pull that old trick!"

The irate, disbelieving tones from the other end could be heard well beyond the cellphone, despite it being jammed to Tony Delgardo's ear.

"I was just giving her a ride home, for Christ's sake! Whaddya think! .... Whaddya mean, 'some brawd'!"

Ten years in Virginia had not softened the Italian Bronx accent which whined into the cold afternoon air. He was leaning with his back to the big white Chevvy, stuck dead as a doornail on the bleak highway and, inside, Suzy Rose beginning to shiver. More muffled invectives were crackling through the phone.

"My fucking secretary, for fuck's sake!" Tony was screaming back into the phone.

"Exactly!" Any passer-by - of which there were none- would have quite distinctly heard that response, as Delgardo suddenly pulled the phone from his ear and glared at it, as people inexplicably do when someone hangs up, as though the explanation were somehow scrolling on the screen display in front of their eyes.

"Martha! ... Shit!" He thrust the phone in his pocket and jerked open the driver's door. Pretty blonde Suzy Rose leaned over, wrapped up in a fur coat, and not much else, by the looks of things.

"Sweetie!" she pleaded in a faltering voice, "Sweetie, I'm cold! Hold me!"

Her dewy eyes gazed at him. She shivered and huddled close as he sat down and fiercely tugged the door shut.

"Hold me", she whimpered again.

He curled an arm over her shoulders and pulled her to him but it was an absentminded gesture as he stared out of the frosted windscreen and wondered how to get out of this fucking fix. Christmas! Jesus Christ, they'd only just got over Christmas and fucking blackouts! - bar, party, shopping, club, everywhere you went, blackouts!   Cussing, swearing, bruises, drunken punches you couldn't see, nowhere to go but home. Everyone bitching. Christmas in the fucking dark! Blown again for half this morning as well! - and now this!

"Turn the engine on so we can get warm" she simpered into his cheek.

"Honey", he breathed with scarcely disguised irritation, "if we could run the goddamned engine we wouldn't be fucking stuck here, would we?"

Bella

Paul Best could not be accused of being a 'news junkie'. He was one of those - more common than the news media would like to believe - who more or less allowed most significant contemporary events to pass him by, at any rate until they became impossible to ignore or otherwise materialised as crude and unforgiving jokes in the pub. Tragic Princess Diana had been the butt of many of those, not to mention 'Nine-Eleven'. He picked up the occasional tabloid (popular not heavy) when pausing to buy cigarettes but these could only be relied upon to indicate whose torso had been publicly revealed recently, or indeed with whom that same torso had been entwined according to rumour, innuendo and jealous speculation. Thus, it was a few days, and courtesy of a better informed customer, before he became aware of the 'Virginia standstill'. It amused him. Bloody Yanks (with no due deference to his dear wife). Serve them right. Cars that big. All show-off. Of course they'll run out of fuel if they use that much. Only, it wasn't fuel, according to the customer as he peered at the unusually small print in the 'Best Cars' contract. They just stopped. Not all of them but quite a few. Enough for it to be a strange coincidence.

Back home, where the chill silence tended only to be broken by staccato exchanges like, 'dinner's ready' and 'I'm going out', it was an opportunity to create something more resembling a conversation to enquire further about cars seizing up in the States. Where had it all gone wrong, this relationship? Not infrequently, he tried to trace back from those heady moments when she had appeared out of nowhere at Doug's party. A smart north London lounge, quiet leafy suburb and all that, all the usual people milling around. The glam ones, the gold watches, heavily-ringed fingers (men), bejewelled necks (women), flashy earrings (both); and the very middle-aged-looking, whether they were or not, huddled over conversations about DIY and holidays and the 'bloody government', who's cheating on whom, all of which held an intrinsic interest until you had heard them from the same people a dozen times before.

Then there she was, this tall woman with the crazy hair, all dark rings of natural perm cascading down her cheeks and neck and a slight, hesitant smile that told of an inner confidence even though she clearly knew not a soul there. Ah, one, she knew one. He remembered the tinge of disappointment as Doug himself, a rabid loner of disrepute, moved over to her. But then, all of a sudden, it was "Here, meet Paul. Paul, this is my friend from New York, Isabella. Paul's going places. Just opening his new showroom, aren't you, Paul? Anyway, leave you to it."

All of eleven years ago. He also had to wonder now what she saw in him then. He was slimmer, sure, but never an athlete. Huh! That he could never be accused of, always a good build on him. People used to tell him he was good looking, in those days when maybe he was at that eligible age. "Oh no", she'd grinned and drawled, yankee-style, at the notion she and Doug might have been an 'item', "met him a coupla years back, been a good friend when I'm over the pond here." Turned out he had rescued her from some dippy guy at a casino. Him - Doug - flashing rings, notes and a cigar as usual; her guy from the bank taking her on an adventurous night out, to impress her no doubt, and completely out of his depth. She was on some management exchange with the bank at the time and now here she was again, same thing. "Yeh, sure he did", in reply to Paul's inevitable question about Doug not having made a pass at her. "Flash Brit!" she chortled behind her glass, surrounded by his friends at that party. "Love him, though! He's just so cute." Cute, thought Paul at the time, was one word he never expected to hear applied to friend Doug. Certainly not by any of the many women he had bedded.

That was it, though. She hadn't been looking for the archetypal rich Brit. The swanky lay. She could get that, and more, Stateside, except for the Brit bit, maybe. Later, she confided she hadn't been looking for a man at all. Fed up with relationships and things not working out. She was nearly thirty, had plenty of time left and was focusing on her career. But they got along. Paul took her to dinner the following week. Other dates but nothing more. But they were hooked. Then she went back home. Then, the next year, she was back again, on top of all those letters, phone calls, texts and e-mails, having wangled another secondment to London. And that was it. This time she stayed. Mr and Mrs Best eighteen months later. Ah, he sighed inwardly, she did, she did see something in him then.

"Jesus, Paul!" Bella's voice was a mixture of sharp and genuinely incredulous. "Where are you all the time! It's been all over the goddam news!" Well, it hadn't actually. People tend to exaggerate in uncomfortable relationships, just to 'get one over' the other partner at times. Just because all points are worth giving the heaviest possible emphasis if it underlines a simmering antagonism. Nevertheless, true, the 'seize-ups' had not been ignored in the British media, although without much comment except a general conclusion that American workmanship had always been suspect.

What had she seen in him? That thought rumbled around her thoughts, too. He had been unlike the others. Neither as predictable and conformist as the bank tribe, nor as brash as that crowd Doug had introduced her to. Ambitious, though, with the expanding motor business and cutting a bit of an image in that part of town. And he was good looking, yes. A bit on the heavy side but not fat. And, yes, an inch or so shorter but women of sixty-nine inches don't all insist on six-footers. Anyways, tall guys were nothing special, in bed or anywhere else, unless they had the personality to go with it and, well maybe she had been unlucky, but she had yet to find one. What had gradually crept up on her since those happy times was Paul seeming to approach middle-age with a complacency that belied his mere forty-one years. And with a burgeoning stomach to go with it. She forgave him his receding hairline, not his fault. Okay, so she still had the same hair-do and, in some respects, even more rebellious attitudes but no-one, not that she knew of, was accusing her of being mutton dressed as lamb (quaint English expression!). She was just not growing older, as he was.

"Well", he called out from the comfortable drawing room, "I'm busy."

"All the time", she muttered without him hearing.

"So what else?" he called again, wondering why all their 'conversations' had to be conducted between separate rooms. "What happened?"

"How should I know?" She appeared through the doorway, carrying her drink. Just hers, he noted. The usual vodka. No, no. No drink problem, he knew that; except the increasing inability to carry more than one.

"Well, you seem to know all about it", he added gruffly.

"Not *all*", she said. "But you never even heard of it."

He looked up at her. He wished he could smile but doubted so strongly that it would be returned. She was still gorgeous, still so suited to that mad hair.

"Well, maybe", he suggested mildly, so wanting to avoid another of their verbal hostilities, "you could e-mail New York."

"Hate e-mails."

Well, that was new to him.

"Phone, then", he continued in his conciliatory tone.

"Maybe ...well, okay, then." She realised she was as intrigued as him to find out more. Cars halted at random. Some reports, even, of appliances like washing machines and refrigerators breaking down. No connection made but she felt too detached from it all. Too detached from home altogether, these days. Okay so she would phone Olivia. As had become her custom, she moved out of the room to make the call. Privacy had acquired a life of its own.

He waited, flicking through TV channels and the usual early evening garbage. The twenty-four hour news channels were trying to make something of the Virginia problem but it was taking third or fourth billing against another terrorist bomb in

the Middle East, a bank rate hike and another flood warning.
Pictures of stalled American automobiles, stranded at intervals
along bleak Virginian highways could only excite so much interest.

She came back. "Busy", she declared. No reply from the
Browns.

"Engaged", he muttered in response.

"Busy", she repeated firmly and shot him a sideways glare.

Oh God, he thought, when does language become a barrier ..
when the foundations are already built? "Busy" hung in his mind.

"I'm going out", she said.

Phone

Hoi Fong reached from his favourite bamboo chair to pick his
phone from the polished wooden side-table. He was enjoying
the entertainment, provided by television scenes, of his rivals'
products inert and immobile on the American highways. Just
like the covert glee with which Chinese TV conveyed coverage
of the blackouts in the States, this odd occurrence was being
given top news billing. How is the mighty American Imperialist
fallen! Okay, only random vehicles in one US State, but we
Chinese can still gloat!

Hoi Fong held the phone to his ear. He did not like evening
calls, not on his mobile. He made it clear to all who should know
that this was effectively his work phone, his office in his pocket,
not to be called after hours. Calls on the domestic phone, at any
time, that was different; even though, halfway through the
evening, it would as like as not be someone such as Cousin Wu
phoning on a pretext to call round for a Singha beer and a bit of
leftover fried chicken. Poor cousin Wu. Over fifty, never married,
never in a job that paid for a decent apartment; a shack in a
shanty village, always hungry, never embarrassed to make the
most of his cousin's affluence. Families, wondered Hoi, are they
the same in America? Always there, always dependent. Yet, of
course always reliable; and you never knew when you might
need them more than they needed you.

Wu, now, he would phone and make it sound as though he was the one doing the favour: "I'll just pop round to bring your hat back." As though cousin Hoi, owner of several hats, was desperately clinging to the hope that this particular headpiece would make a rapid return in the hands of cousin Wu. "Won't you stay for a beer?" He would hear himself saying. "Oh!" Wu would start in affected surprise, looking at his watch as though life might be too short, "Oh, all right, then." "And there might be some chicken", Hoi would hear himself add just as, right on cue, Hwee Lo would appear in the room, bearing a bowl of tasty morsels freshly fried for their visiting relative. Sometimes a 'thank you', sometimes not. That's what families are for.

Hoi answered and listened. His hand tightened around the phone, as did his fingers clutching the armrest of the chair. He said little, while the lines narrowed at the corners of his mouth. "Yes", he nodded into the mouthpiece. "Indeed", it was surely a good time. "Of course", if the Americans were having trouble with their manufacturing and reliability was letting them down. "Naturally", he understood: this was the opportunity to capitalise on their failings. "No", he agreed, he could not expect the Society to tolerate unnecessary delay. "Yes, yes", he was aware that his expressions of gratitude would only be acceptable for so long, results were what were expected from this investment. Always so polite, we Chinese.

The man of substance trembled slightly as he laid the phone back on the table. The TV pictures of automobiles stranded on the American highway had made him smile a few minutes ago. At this moment, a smile did not readily spring to his lips, even at being reminded of those circumstances. However, he thought grimly, if this helped him emphasise Chinese dependability in the London connection, things might move faster. Hwee Lo had entered the room and broke him from his musing. She noticed his sallow features seemed even paler and his eyes darted before settling upon her; an anxiety that was unfamiliar to her. She could not ask but it troubled her.

"Would you like some tea, my dear, or some beer?" she enquired gently.

He visibly collected himself.

"Some tea, my dear, please. And a little vodka."

She inclined her head slightly and did not demur from this unusual request but moved to softly touch his cheek with her delicate white fingers. He stroked them lightly with his own and managed a reassuring smile, resting his head for a moment on the rounded swelling of her stomach. She turned to bring tea and vodka from the kitchen.

Six

It was driving him nuts. Six days! Nearly a fucking week! Tony Delgardo couldn't even remember the last time he went a week without a car. Probably when he was fourteen and his Dad banned him from even going near the family car after he had scraped it twice and nearly written it off the third time. That was when his mother made his uncle Mario come round and teach him to drive properly. Out on that old abandoned parking lot in the Bronx - that was before every tiny scrap of spare ground got snatched up to provide prized and lucrative parking space for any and everyone who was prepared to pay through the nose just to hole up their pile of aluminum and plastic for the day while they sat in their anodyne offices. Six days! He felt like a junkie with serious withdrawal symptoms.

Almost as bad withdrawal as not seeing Suzy Rose all that time. Not only did he have nothing to drive her in, he'd had to cool it just for safety's sake. No escape from the house and Martha and fucking blackouts. Christ! It was bad enough the tow-truck driver knowing exactly who they both were - shit this small-town outback America! - but who else but poky-nose Annie Jones just happened to be passing Suzy's house when they dropped her off! Like, you know, it was dark and it should have been safe and, anyhow, what's wrong with giving a girl a ride home and, so what, it's a breakdown truck, so, like we broke down and, like, she's my secretary, you know, nosy face.

Not that he said any of this. He had just groaned inside as sweet Suzy alighted from the truck and blew a kiss which he wished could have been swallowed up by a passing hurricane, just as nosy Jonesy tripped along the sidewalk. If there was a

God he could have sworn He must have planted her there, just out of spite. So now the whole town was looking at him, he swore it. Except for Martha, who hardly gave him a passing glance. Unless it was soaked in venom.

It had almost made him forget the strange sight on the drive home. God, they had froze that afternoon! Could he get through to a breakdown company! Could he Jesus! Phone call after call, all the numbers he could get. Either busy or 'Sorry sir, our trucks is all out'. Typical that at last when it was almost dark he remembered Jose from down the street; his friend had a truck he only used sometimes. Sure enough - well, lucky enough - once he had tracked down Jose's number, no-one had thought to call the guy, whose occasional job was fetching goods into town from the railroad depot. Friendly local business - cost him a fucking fortune! "Sorry, friend, times is hard and your need is great." Anyways, at least they got home before Suzy Rose turned into an icicle (which would have taken a lot of doing in normal circumstances). But all those other cars! And trucks. And all sorts. It seemed like anything that should have been moving, wasn't.

Actually, plenty were. Other cars were passing them on the highway but it was just that every quarter mile or so there was another stuck at the side, and another. Breakdowns normally occur sporadically. For every few thousand vehicles in motion there may be the odd one that's bust. Not one out of every four or five. Or so it seemed. It was a bit like an automobile graveyard, just very spread out.

Just added insult to injury that next door - who hardly ever spoke to them! - her washing machine broke down, with kids and that, all needing clothes for school - thick warm stuff for winter - and Martha, well hadn't she just crashed in and offered to do their washing for them! Washing! What about his fucking shirts! "Oh, you can make them do an extra day", she says, with a smirk! Good job he wasn't getting close to Suzy Rose just now, what with stinking shirts, and all! Not that he was minded to put it quite like that to Martha.

Well, pissed, that's what he was. He walked disconsolately out to the front of their white duckboard house in its nice bit of yard off the main street. Another phone call and it had still been,

"Sorry, Tony, cain't book yer yet. Full up. Cain't work out what's wrong with these others anyhow. Stopped and jest won't start." Well, not as though it was more than a score or so cars and trucks to deal with in the whole town but - shit this small-town America! Thanks to Martha for bringing us here! - the guy could only handle four or five at the best of times. And that's when he could fix them right away.

Tony pulled open the car door, sat inside and unhappily fumbled the key into the starter slot. He turned it almost without thinking - and it started up! He thumped his foot on the pedal to make sure it was really alive and then gave a loud whoop! Yep! No more rides with morose Albert just to get to work. He was back on wheels! He dared stop the engine and then turn it to start again. Maybe it wouldn't work. He had better know now. But yes! Ticker and vroom! The lady was turning again! Not the only one , before long, flickered through his mind. Well, well. Then he cursed. How many fucking days ago could he have tried it and it would have worked! Oh well, shit, too late now. Anyhow, on wheels again. Yippee!

He went back in.

"Bill's been on." That was all Martha said and that was a kind of hiss.

Tony called Workshop Bill.

"Hi, Tony, can do yer car now. Wanna tow in?"

"'S'okay, Bill. It's fixed."

"Fixed?"

"Yup. Just started her up."

"No kid?"

"No kid."

"Jeez, Tony. This aint half pekoolar." No-one in town ever knew why Workshop Bill couldn't say 'peculiar'.

"Yeh?" Tony was losing interest in this conversation now he had his wheels back.

"Yeh, Tone. You and all the others."

"Eh?" Interest rising again.

"Yeh, man. All's I called to bring 'em in, they's all okay. Cars all fixed."

"How?" Tony could not help taking part, since he was receiving various statements without explanations attached.

"By theirselves."

"*Eh!?*"

"Well, how's yourn fixed, Tony?"

Tony paused for a moment.

"Well, I guess -"

"By itself?" Bill's voice almost had an edge of sarcasm, since this was one helluva trade bonanza suddenly wiped away in front of his eyes.

"Well, yeh, I guess." Tony was trying to figure it now. In his exuberance he had overlooked an explanation as to how one highly dead automobile had suddenly resurrected itself without the aid of expensive and mysterious mechanical surgery, as had always been the case previously. "What about the ones you got there?" he added, having seen Bill's yard chock-full of all the disabled vehicles he had managed to tow in and make room for.

"Well ...."

The fact was, Bill had been going round all of them, incessantly, incapable of working out what was wrong with any of them. Once he had exhausted all the possibilities with one, he moved on to the next, and so on. He had been round all of them at least four times in the past six days. Same thing today - and suddenly one of them fired up! Natural thing was to go to the next that needed fixing - and that started up, too! And the next. And all ten of them! What to do? Try diagnostic analysis to work out what had got them going? Or call it quits and phone down the line to tell other folks he could tow 'em in now? Business was business. He didn't get paid for explaining why cars worked. He earned a living from ones that didn't. So on the blower. And every goddam one: "Thanks, Bill, but 's'okay now."

Every goddam one! He had already planned his week in Vegas on the proceeds. Goddam it! It weren't jest a blown away holiday. It was downright spooky. Cars don't mend theirselves! Like dead people don't climb out of graves. Except in horror movies. Well, this was his own goddam horror movie. Fine for the rest of them but this was his living. But he just knew he could not get away with pretending he had suddenly mended them all at once. Not even if he tried to let them out one by one, as though he was repairing them two-a-day or summat. Especially as everyone else in the town would know about all the cars that were 'fixing theirselves'. In the end he just wouldn't get paid. Same result and more hassle.

"Well..." he continued, "they done the same, Tony, they done the same."

"All of them?"

"Goddam all of them. Started all up jest fine, jest now. Never known it before, Tony." There was a kind of despair creeping into his voice. Okay, so nothing lost, nothing gained. In the normal run of events he would be just dealing with the odd repair here and there, day by day, eking out a living. Suddenly he thought he had won the lottery. You can't lose what you never had. He sighed.

"Don't yer think yer might need an oil-change, now it's not been running a week?"

"Six days, Bill. Not a week, yet. Nope. Thanks. I'll call in some time. Stay cool."

Stay frozen to pieces, thought Workshop Bill. Nothing changes.

Tony Delgardo mused a bit on this but he was not into conundrums. Car was fixed, that was that. Other people can be engineers with or without explanations. He sold things. And there was a certain 'secretary' he needed to do some sales analysis with.

There were a number of towns through Virginia, right across to the West and the Blue Ridge Mountains, where they talked about the 'cars that fixed theirselves'. The bigger repair stations and the main dealers, they were more concerned. They wanted to know what was going on. They had engineers dissecting models that had suddenly, inexplicably sprung into life - vehicles that had represented a few hundred dollars apiece in repair bills (and still culled a fair bit of that just for 'inspecting'). It also moved up to the State office, where it got bogged down in arguments about which category of experts might be detailed to look for an answer. It filtered up to Federal level as well but became even more vague there. No-one knew.

Basically, everyone wanted to blame the manufacturers for an inherent fault. It was just not too easy to see what kind of fault could result in approximately twenty per cent of all motor vehicles in one State juddering to an unexplained halt, all at more or less the same time on the same day. All makes, all ages. And then all being okay at the end of the sixth day after that. Someone was heard to joke about God and seven days - since it was actually six days He took to create the world and then had a nap on the seventh. Some people, especially in Virginia's own bible belt, did not think that was funny.

After a couple of weeks it was all either fizzling out or stuck in bureaucracy, depending on whether you were driving your car or watching the memos pile up on your desk. By then, some experts were seeing if they could pin it on electrical discharges in the atmosphere, that kind of thing.

Tony called Suzy on the seventh day. He'd had enough rest.

Joke

"I fail to understand ..." Which was stretching the truth slightly, since there was pretty well nothing He failed to understand, although with the exception, perhaps, of some of Gabriel's inner workings; and some of his outer ones, come to think of it.

"I fail to understand", continued the Almighty in one of his level, quiet tones, "why you have to invest everything with one of your 'jokes'."

He looked down at the archangel, who remained studiously focused on another pedealogical dig.

"If that is how you see it", added the Benign One

Gabriel tucked his head down further towards his knees in a vain attempt to conceal the half-supressed grin. The Lord wanted to utter a parental kind of admonishment - "I can see you, you know" - but this would break the confidence between them that, despite being All-Seeing, All-Knowing, and so on, He had to pretend this did not apply to the archangel. Most of the time, anyway. Otherwise, Gabriel would be afforded no privacy in the entire cosmos (although there would be some advantages in that, the Lord considered).

There were times when the Almighty was enormously tempted to bend this little rule, if not completely break it. But then, wasn't resisting temptation something He was supposed to set as an example to all His myriad flocks (or the 'flock' counterpart on Tryxxx, Splong, and the like)? So He suffered a little bit of Divine sacrifice - well, compromise, let's call it - and turned a blind eye, or appeared to do so.

Gabriel was not fooled, anyway. He knew God knew. For his part, though, it also served their relationship if he managed to avoid openly grinning in the face of the Lord's disapproval. Therein had lain their equilibrium for most of eternity.

"Joke?" he mumbled into his knees, fighting to suppress an untimely giggle.

God observed him, aware that He was having to draw on some of the reserves of patience that passeth all understanding.

"I trust you are keeping an eye on things", He observed.

"Things?"

Gabriel was still finding it difficult, apparently, to lever his head into vertical alignment with the rest of Heaven. For a fleeting moment, had He not been God, the Lord might have considered it would serve a certain angel right if he remained stuck in that position. Being God, however, means being denied the satisfaction of such thoughts. Holiness is not everything it's cracked up to be, He sometimes reflected. Nevertheless, indulging Gabriel's sudden bouts of 'incomprehension' was not, He considered, a required attribute of being Holy.

"Keeping an eye? Oh, sure", acknowledged Gabriel, once he realised the Lord was not rising to the 'things?' bait and felt perhaps he ought to look up at last. "Just waiting for the jelly to set." He looked down again, as well he might.

"Gabriel..." Sometimes, a distant and foreboding rumble of thunder in the summer sky may be mistaken for the Lord addressing his devoted angel in this manner.

"Guv?"

"I think you know I am not enquiring about the Long Sleep on Qkyyyssfvv." (Sorry, there is no way to pronounce this one).

"No, Guv? But I'd better get over there to check, eh?"

"Not before", rumbled the Ever-Loving One, "you are sure of the Plan."

Gabriel was about to mumble 'plan?' from between his knees but had the uncomfortable feeling this might be one unconvincing expression of ignorance too many. The consequence of such was unknown to him, since there was something about their relationship, extending through all eternity, which had always stopped him short of stepping over that mark. He looked up again with a sort of 'plan'do-I-really-have-to pleading kind of expression on his face. The Lord, reading him like a book, simply murmured:

"Yes. I'm afraid you do."

"More nudges", Gabriel muttered resignedly.

"Indeed", agreed the Lord, adding, "if circumstances demand."

Gabriel suspected, morosely, that circumstances might well demand, however much he wished they would not. Earth. A bundle of laughs.

"Okay -" he began but the Lord interjected, not being One to let One's angel so lightly off the hook.

"And as I was saying..."

"Yes, Guv?" Gabriel felt an all-too-familiar sense of divine disapproval hovering over him.

"Perhaps we might be a trifle more sparing with the jokes." God was masterful at saying 'we' whilst meaning totally, absolutely, no-one else but 'you'.

"Jokes?" repeated Gabriel, feebly, and before he could stop himself.

"Six days, six days", drummed the Lord, "Was that really necessary?"

"Why?" sulked the angel under his breath but with his mouth still contorted to suppress a grin. "Didn't they get it?"

The Lord had to let that one go. If He picked on everything, they would be there for ever.

Society

Hoi did not hear the door open, only click shut. His smart but modest office overlooked the line of cars being assembled on the factory floor. His insistence on being able to view any portion of the assembly area at a glance compromised the elegance of an owner's suite. Instead of being sealed from the rattle and hum of the production line, the dividing wall was glazed floor to ceiling - single-glazed so he could hear the noises and feel closer to the action. It meant that, if someone got past his secretary in the outer room, they could gently slip open the heavy polished wood door at the opposite side to the flimsy factory window-wall, unheard above the muffled sounds from below.

Hoi turned around. He had been watching the London cars go through final interior fittings before pre-delivery checks.

"Brother Teng!" he exclaimed softly, "how..." And he was about to say, 'how did you get in?' But swiftly changed it to, "... How good to see you", as he inclined his head politely to his uninvited visitor, forcing a weak smile as he did so.

"Brother Hoi" greeted Teng in reply, smiling and inclining in turn. The two men stood facing each other for a moment, almost identical in height at around five feet six inches, and quite similar in appearance, each dapper with tidy straight black hair, neat and slim, Teng just the older of the two by a few years. Teng also bore a small scar on his chin, not matched by any such blemish on Hoi Fong's features.

"I have come with the arrangements, brother", said Teng, business replacing the polite smile in his expression.

"Arrangements?" repeated Hoi, uncertainly.

"The women ... and the gifts."

"Women, brother Teng?" Hoi felt it had been difficult enough getting this order finalised so quickly - an extra heavy discount to the London man, through the agent and his commission - without complications he had not even been told about. He felt Teng's sharp glance go through him like a needle, querying any doubt which might be about to surface. It reminded Hoi that the loan to get this whole expansion going, a *guangxi* payment through the Beijing network, which he knew deep inside was more than just Chinese brotherhood but must have Triad connections, did not come without its price. The red triangle on his back was enough to remind him of that, etched for mutual allegiance, so they impressed upon him.

He had reflected on his other option at the time: to make what progress he could in the face of stiff international competition and perhaps never reach his dream, but it was too late now. The offer had been so tempting, the terms so flexible. The terms, that is, concerning finance. The quiet but menacing pressure to push through with the London connection in unseemly - and disadvantageous - haste had been a different matter. It made Hoi nervous. He wondered if he had actually become afraid. If he was afraid, he had to fear not just for himself but for his beloved Hwee Lo, too, and their expected child. And now this. Women? Gifts?

"The women, brother Hoi", Teng was saying, "who will present the cars, and the gifts, to our London friends. I have the details." He drew a sheaf of documents from a black attaché case, the papers carefully bound into a plastic clip folder. "They will fly on a schedule flight to Heathrow, to arrive a few hours before the cargo. Time for them to meet with the transporter."

Hoi was bemused. There seemed nothing objectionable about all this but he just had no clue what it was all about and it was the very first he had heard about it. They were his cars, after all, going to his client. Shouldn't he have been a bit more included?

"How many?" he murmured, not really sure what to ask.

"Many?" asked Teng, looking up from the documents he was checking through.

"Women", explained Hoi, weakly, beginning to visualise a delivery charabanc not unlike a visit by the Chinese State Circus.

"One for each car." Teng stated it in a matter-of-fact manner, as if it were obvious.

"Fifteen?", concluded Hoi, reluctant to comprehend and turning the spectacle over in his mind.

"Precisely, brother. And a gift with each car. The details are all here. Some people will arrive to put the gifts in the cars tomorrow. They will be ready, I trust?" Teng remained exceedingly polite, with his slight, intermittent smile, all the time he spoke. But his underlying tone was of a man who was dictating exactly how things would be done, and that was that.

"Gifts", murmured Hoi to himself, and adding "women", even more quietly, conscious it might appear he was dwelling unduly upon this detail. Then he began to regain his usual demeanour. Brotherhood or no brotherhood, this was his company, his cars, his deal. All right, aspects of it were being organised without consulting him, but just the frills. It sounded as though the others were intent on making a bit more of a splash of this breakthrough into new territory than he would have considered necessary but it might have its benefits.

"We thought you should be bold and proud of we Chinese bringing your new products to London", smiled Teng, as though reading his thoughts, "and there will no doubt be publicity. Let us not underplay our virtues, eh brother?" He might have added, 'unlike America and cars that stop in their tracks, eh brother?' but they both understood without the words being spoken.

"Not at all", agreed Hoi, bringing himself to smile in return. Perhaps this would be no bad thing for them all: the London dealer, himself, the Society. It was to all their advantages to make English customers aware of modern Chinese quality, so that his cars - and then more and more - would be sold, and so he could realise his dream, not to mention pay the money back. "Thank you, brother", he added, still with a smile.

"Brother Hoi", returned Teng, inclining his head once again with a smile and retreating, still half-facing him, through the door. That last vision, had anyone observed it, was of the dominant manager dismissing his humble supplicant with an indulgent smile. Very subtle, very Chinese, wondered Hoi, left alone in his office.

Argument

A 'Best Car' was not the best place to be right now, Paul was thinking. Bella sat in the passenger seat, scowling.

"You're part of all this", she muttered, eyes glowering at the stationary evening traffic ahead.

"Meaning?" He shot a brief sideways glance at her then back at the road.

"You. Cars." Her tone was blunt. "You're adding to this - all this goddamned chaos."

"Oh yeh", he replied sardonically, "my few hundred cars a year, a big difference. They'd hardly fill Piccadilly." However, he thought to himself, this Chinese order, finally due in a couple of days, might double that number if they catch on. Wow. Wads of notes danced in front of his eyes.

"You're just encouraging it", she retorted stubbornly. "Look at this - cheap .." She gestured at the plastic facia. "Just making it easier to buy, with this cheap Chinese shit."

"It's not shit!" he snapped. "I don't sell shit. This is better than some nearly twice the price. Cheap labour, that's what. I bet they don't pack up like American garbage." She bristled inside and was about to hit back that it was maybe just what London needed, fewer cars on the road. "And anyway", he added sullenly as they edged forward a few metres, "you don't complain about what you get."

"Yeh?" Her response had a defensive ring to it. She knew what was coming.

"The house. Clothes, things. You want to stop going out?"

This was her weak spot. He didn't need to press it too hard. He was not callous enough to go on to point out who was earning and who was not; who depended on whom for a comfortable way of life. She had given up work because they did not need both incomes and she was told at the surgery to relax her lifestyle to give herself a better chance of conception. Well, it worked to a degree but only for a succession of three distressingly late miscarriages. She had hated it so! She, feisty, sexy, strong, how could she not accomplish such an elementary female function? After that, the warning was to give up which, as it happened, removed the only remaining incentive for sex.

Three years now, bar the occasional drunken fumble (he, the drunk). But it had changed her. Most of all, she could not face going back to work. At first it was the self-consciousness of failure but then she realised she had become detached from the work politic itself. Disenchantment. Almost a reversion to adolescent doubt: 'what's it all about?' Then without a child, too, her attention seemed to refocus. She attended local planning meetings; spoke at some. Surprising herself even more, she joined a protest march, cajoling a friend to accompany her for mutual safety in the jostling throng. Then another march. The environment, global warming, pollution, the planet. These were becoming her concerns. 'Going green', Paul had remarked with disdain, and even 'ageing hippy' under his breath, though he still adored that shock of hair.

"See!" she exclaimed as they halted again. "What *is* the point!"

And then, "oh no!" they both groaned involuntarily together. Street lights, shop lights, traffic lights ahead, all suddenly extinguished.

"All the goddamned time", hissed Bella through clenched teeth.

Paul flicked on the radio to provide relief from their own voices barking at each other.

"... *Power stations should have been built years ago ... Ah* (Presenter), *another cut, generator kicking in, hope you're still with us ... mothballing power stations* (Expert again) *... plundering them for spares ... knew oil and gas were going ... consumer society ... no forward planning ... using more energy ... indecision about energy generation ... pressure ... too much demand ...*"

"See!" cried Bella again, punching the radio off.

"I'm in cars, not power", countered Paul with some venom.

"It's all the *same*", she retorted heavily. "Same oil. Same energy. Same result!"

"Well you can get out and push if you like, save a bit."

With that she did. Not to push, though. He watched her storm off into the darkness.

Customs

"Checking 'em all out, Andy?"

"Yeh." Grunt from the other end of a pair of overalled legs protruding from the open car door.

"Open everything up, mind." The first voice was thrown across the cavernous shed floor, topped with a peaked cap, from beside a second car.

"On all of 'em?" queried Andy.

"Well, no, mebbe. Thorough on that one, then see what we reckon about some more."

Gordon Pierce was senior officer on shift in the London Heathrow Customs vehicle shed. Andy, contract engineer on regular Customs inspection duty, was pulling up the running board on the front passenger door sill, a row of screws placed neatly at his side. The panel eased up in his hands.

"No", he called, "clean." He ran his fingers along the exposed channel in case his eyes had missed anything. On the driver's seat lay the air bag panel cover, the driver's door sill panel and more screws. There were fourteen other cars identical to this one, in two rows awaiting inspection. Other vehicles, either already cleared or allocated to another inspection rota, were parked around and about in groups and rows. Gordon had left Andy to randomly select one of the Chinese cars for a Class A inspection: a 'going-over' they called it. He had picked the third car in the first row, using his usual mental eeny-meeny-miny-mo method, always starting at a different point in the row. It was the only way he felt he was making a truly random 'pick'.

So far, the dogs and the electronic meters had registered no reaction with all fifteen cars but they knew that sophisticated chemicals could neutralise giveaway smells, whilst treated coatings had been developed to fool the meters. They were mainly on the lookout for heroin, especially from Asia.

"Gee, these dolls don't half pong!" Andy was extricating himself from the car, feet first, after replacing all the panels and screws, exactly like new. He had been forced to breathe in the pungent scent from the bright red, gold and silver Chinese doll suspended from the rearview mirror, while he worked. It was quite a luxury item, not much short of thirty centimetres in length and a solid weight. He had knocked his head on it a couple of times: "heavy little bugger!" They had checked them out, naturally, one in each car. Blank in the X-ray, solid wood or something, inside each richly-coloured traditional Chinese costume. The dog had turned its head in disgust at the perfume.

"Chassis?" called out Gordon.

"Done that. Clean", replied Andy, "Watcha reckon? Another couple?"

"Aw, pick one for a quick once-over, they're all clean with the dogs and the clicks." Gordon tended to term the meters 'clicks' because of their audio response to contraband goods. Andy went through his silent selection routine again and picked number four in the second row.

"Anyways", Gordon was saying, "with all this show - " (each car was bedecked with miniature Chinese lanterns and paper chains) " - they'd know we'd take a look. Just rising to their bait if we go through every one." He was aware, at the same time, that it could be a double-bluff to encourage them to react precisely this way but they were stretched as it was, without second- and triple-guessing every blamed exporter, wily Orientals or the rest. Sometimes you had to wait for clearer signals, like the dogs or a tip-off or a 'click'.

It was not long before Andy emerged with 'clean' for the other car.

"Okay, let 'em all through", instructed Gordon and looked at his watch. Nearly eight o'clock and give way to the night shift. "G'night", he called to Andy, as he headed for the internal door.

"Coming", Andy responded, joining him. "Fancy a jar?"

"Nah", said Gordon. "Not eaten. Should be something waiting."

"Okay. See yer tomorrow." Andy let the door swing shut behind him as they headed off in their separate directions.

A quarter of the way around the M25 to the north, and a few miles in, Paul Best thought he might as well stop at the kebab house, seeing as the atmosphere at home would be unlikely to provide either a ready meal or a dinner companion for going out. He could see through the window as he parked that there was no-one serving at the counter. He'd sensed before that the proprietor was the devout sort who would often slip out to the local mosque at prayer times. However, a train of people were arriving at the private door round the corner of the building; dark figures in the night, hurrying in from the cold.

They looked furtive. Well, anyone would, hunched up against the chill. On the chime of the doorbell as he entered, one of the regular Asian lads appeared from the back, with a hurried glance behind him, perhaps confirming his visitors were in, with the door closed behind them. Paul took a regular 'doner' with relishes (but declining the chilli), then drove half a mile before pulling in at a precinct parking area. It was a big day tomorrow, he did not want to be emotionally churned up the night before. He would eat before driving. He was in no hurry to get home.

Bella half-sat, half-knelt on the soft hearthrug by the glowing coal-effect fire and gazed slowly around the room, a vodka glass on the polished tiles in the Georgian fireplace. Her eyes took in all the trappings: luxurious cushioned suite; rich, elegant curtains; rosewood, pearl-inlaid lounge table with two matching display cabinets; cut glass and silver in the cabinets; fifty-four-inch HD TV in another custom-made cabinet; expensive ornaments discreetly placed here and there; elaborate hi-fi; stacks of cds and dvds; some beautiful paintings on the walls. She took a sip of vodka - her first and one glass of the day - and settled back on her heels, glass in hand, motionless. Tears rolled gently down her cheeks.

Cars

Such a commotion!

The Chinese dragon pranced and twirled along the street, the many legs of its bearers seen trotting beneath its bright green and yellow skirt. All varieties of trousers, jeans. boots and jogger bottoms; a dragon clothed for London in February! It rolled its great head with the flame-red eyes lolling this way and that, young children grabbing at the fluttering fire-strips hanging from its felt-toothy jaw. Mums with pushchairs and prams stopped with their shopping bags to look, people paused in doorways, the hairdresser turned to see and came within a whisker of removing an ear, cars slowed - mostly they had to - and windows were wound down in the crisp winter air. At the dragon's side stepped fifteen beautiful Chinese mannequins, clothed in the finest red, gold, silver, blue and green traditional dress and headgear, each deftly waving a Chinese fan.

A substantial gaggle of onlookers trailed along, half on and off the pavement on both sides, whilst ahead and behind marched the band, all drums, cymbals and xylophones, ribbons fluttering from each. The press and radio were there, and a camera crew puffing all around the scene to get their pictures from every angle. Discordantly, occasional car horns honked from front and rear, as some unamused drivers demanded the road be freed for the usual traffic jam.

And behind came the transporter. Fifteen spanking new cars, their rows of mini-Chinese lanterns and decorations bobbing between door-handles and hanging from bumpers. Stacked on the twin ramps, cars one above the other, some of the gift-dolls could just be seen, dangling inside. The dragon, with a wave from a 'Best Cars' salesman, veered left into the showroom forecourt and swayed uncertainly this way and that, divesting itself of its human escorts; until the front-and-rear band merged into one and led the beast off to the side. The transporter wheeled slowly in pursuit, with Paul Best himself taking charge to direct it to a prominent strip right between showroom windows and the road, for a public unloading of its consignment of Manchu Mets, on Chinese New Year's Day.

Paul's new banners were already stretched across the showroom frontage above the display windows, some of them causing his staff to cringe but he would brook no argument when it came to publicity and promotion. 'Don't buy the bUSt, buy the Best' exhorted one, Paul neatly confusing seized-up American cars with American-owner car manufacturers in the UK. Still, the banner looked good and it was repeated in posters and handbills scattered around the showroom and forecourt, along with: 'Test-drive Your Best Little China Doll today!' and 'Buy it Now and Bank the Rest - Brilliant Beijing and Bargain Best!' The crowd of onlookers did not represent Paul's choice of buying-public on a chilly Thursday lunchtime but he could not pick the delivery time, which had to be in daylight and, anyway, the main event was this evening.

By evening, the cars had all been moved inside the showroom, all other models relegated to the forecourt outside for the occasion. The place bustled and was healthily filled with all the right kinds of people this time: men in suits straight from work (wine, cheese and other titbits enticing them from their own meal-tables), their wives plus other women together in twos and threes - smart-casual and independent, Paul noted with satisfaction - older couples more casually dressed, in the market for the smaller economical car - and even a few curious twenty-somethings, there to see if 'small' meant 'sport'. They were the most likely to be disappointed, Paul realised, but that was to be expected.

The show was a whirlwind. First, the dragon took to the floor, this time its legs clothed in matching green and gold. It ducked and twisted and turned, while the same band struck the tune and beat that commanded its moves. It swirled breathtakingly close by its audience, glasses and canapés in hands, causing them to sway and laugh, it flung its great head high in the air then lunged down to the floor, whilst its fin-barbed tail zig-zagged behind it, green and gold feet scuttling to maintain its flow.

Then forward stepped the mannequins, smiling and bowing, fans to faces as demurely as you will, uncovered hair in buns and pins and posies, as they engaged in a complex flowing dance, dipping and turning and pivoting around one another, smiles fixed, turning this way and that in a mesmerising figure-of-eight, with wide eyes that occasionally met an onlooker's stare, inducing a blush from the man and a sharp look from his partner.

Suddenly each girl made for one of the cars, which were spread in an arc facing the audience, doors akimbo. They all delicately stooped and lifted a doll from where it hung and then swept together, whirling and spinning like dervishes, a dazzling flash of movement and colour, passing the dolls between them, sometimes tossing them in the air to each other, while the dragon cavorted around them.

Then, in a dancing column, the girls abruptly flew beneath the dragon's skirts, all at once and together and vanished from view, and the dragon became a writhing, churning monster, bulging with the distorted shapes of the dancers inside. As the frantic music drummed and jangled to fever pitch, hands reached out from under the dragon and the dolls were flung high into the air, instantly followed by the mannequins who miraculously caught them before they fell to the floor. Smiling and bowing and holding the dolls aloft, they and the dragon eddied to a halt and finished with a curtsey, remaining motionless as the dragon sank to the floor on it skirts, like a hovercraft powering-down on dry land.

The music concluded with a fearsome crash and applause broke out wildly in the showroom, people turning and bending to rid themselves of glasses so they could do full justice to the performance with both hands. The girls held their pose and their smiles, scarcely a hair awry nor the hint of breathlessness.

A small Chinese man emerged from the crowd, neat in dark suit with mute-coloured tie and, bowing, turned to address them. "Friends, may we wish you a Happy - Chinese" (he chuckled sagely) - "New Year." There were grins amongst the audience and another ripple of applause. "You have seen us banish the dragon evil from the China dolls", he continued, smiling, "so you may possess gifts from our land -" and he gestured broadly to the cars behind him and the dolls still held aloft by the girls - "with plenty of Chinese good luck. Thank you." He gave another little bow and retreated behind the girls to the rear of the showroom to more, vigorous applause.

The remainder of the evening was a riotous success. Sales staff scarcely knew which way to turn, badgered from every quarter for test drives, information, prices, and even a handful of orders there and then. Paul himself was scurrying from place to place, providing 'personal attention' as the boss, wherever it looked likely to lead to a sale. He was astonished by the whole occasion. When the agent had phoned to say the Chinese wanted to make a bit of an event of the delivery, he said okay, why not, no harm, and when the dapper Chinese man - Mr Sing - appeared a couple of days before to explain about the dragon and the girls, well, it should attract some punters but this, this was like his own West End premiere.

He could not believe his luck. And as for the coverage he would get in the media tomorrow! He sought out Mr Sing at one point to congratulate and thank him and surprised him carefully tucking a couple of dolls into a large suitcase on top of some others, padding wrapped between them. The little man was slightly ruffled, almost dropped one. Hardly surprising, thought Paul, heavy damned things, he had held one in a car earlier. These must be secret spares, for he had already checked that all the 'gifts' had been returned to the cars. Anyway, the two men parted with smiles.

When at last, flushed and beaming - despite the cloud hanging above every return to the domestic threshold - he stepped out of the taxi, replete with several celebratory glasses of wine with his staff, he hardly noticed what Bella was saying. He marked it as a bit of an upturn that he managed to plant a peck on her cheek before she could turn away, although the response was as fixed as those mannequins' smiles - without the smile.

"Sorry, what was that?" he asked in a bit of a haze, as he headed for the lounge to collapse and recover.

"I said", she called out from beyond the door as she set foot up the stairs, "I hope they're not like the cars in the States."

"Eh?" He mumbled with an effort to project his voice from a slump in the sofa.

"The States. They're all stopping again."

"When?" He was puzzled. This had nothing much to do with his triumphant day.

"News today." Her voice was disappearing across the landing. "While you were at your 'do'. Stopping like the last time." A door clicked shut and the voice was silent.

"Hmph", thought Paul, wondering whether to stagger to the coffee-maker (since the usual one had gone to bed). "Chinese ones won't stop."

PARADIGM : EXPECTING

It was a golden dawn.

He - striding through the shimmering haze as it gave way to the radiant light of a new day - saw her waiting for him. She sat with the sun's first rays caressing the locks cascading to her shoulders. Her face, uplifted, snared the beams that flew through the world to bring warmth, life, comfort and the means to live. Cheeks glowed and shone in burnished bronze and her smile to greet him sparkled like a shower of gems in his path.

He bore the morning's hunt, a brace of game slung from his belt of hide, swinging against the ripple of his thighs as he loped towards her.

"We shall eat", she smiled to him

"We shall always eat", he replied, those lips dancing into smiles like hers. Their eyes shone in one another's gaze and he softly touched her silken cheek, then let his strong brown fingers - the hunter's hand - slide slowly down her neck and across her naked breasts to rest upon the blooming of her stomach below.

She clasped his hand and pressed it, firm but gentle, against the taughtness of her skin.

"We shall all eat", she smiled again and a lightness of laughter flowed between them.

"Yes, we shall all eat", he said and made to kindle their fire as the warmth of the day advanced to embrace them.

Stopped

"This is WPPJ One-Zero-Three-Point-Five in Chattanooga Tennessee this fi-i-i-i-ine and sunshiny Thursday morning, brought to you by Sally's Sodas - The Can That L-i-i-i-i-fts Your Day. You jest feel that fi-i-zzy fun when you take a s-i-i-i-p of Sally's Soft Cream Soda - jest like your ol' mamma made. And it's a h-i-i-i-gh of one above zero on a c-o-o-old winter's day but you jest stay close and warm with Jerry's morning show. Get yer fingers on them dials fer four-two-three, six-four-two, two-two-two, on the Chattanooga Two-Two Show!" The right hand, that belonged to the voice that belonged to the long lanky legs that were attached to the baggy khaki trousers that sat on the wobbly swivel chair in front of the sparse selection of knobs and dials on the rickety wooden table in the duckboard and corrugated iron shack just off main street Chattanooga, flicked the button on the CD-player (something modern anyway!), while the left hand reached for the opened can of beer (a mile or more from Sally's Sodas) at Jerry Corrie's side.

He looked through the facing glass panel at the engineer on the other side.

"What we got, Al?"

The voice came back through his headphones.

"More o' them car calls, Jerry!"

"Aw, lawdy", sighed the town's most popular DJ-cum-newscaster-cum-phone-in host, "put 'em through."

The music, something suitably Country, like just about ninety-five per cent of WPPJ One-Zero-Three-Point-Five's repertoire, ended.

"Hi Marjorie", came the friendly greeting from JC, fed the caller's name by Al through headphones, "How y'all today?"

"I'm swell, just swell, Jerry ...well, no, I *was* just swell till my car stopped, Jerry, just with my bags on the way home an' all."

"Lawdy, Marjorie, you an' all them others", sympathised Jerry, managing a swift gulp from the can before adding, "Jest where were you?"

"I was in my car, Jerry."

"Yes, Marjorie, but where *was* you *and* yer car?"

"I was with my shopping, Jerry."

The eyes of the most popular radio voice in town rotated upwards as he engaged that warm encouraging tone so loved by all his listeners: "Well, sure thang you don't deserve that, Marjorie, the La-a-awd only knows. Have a nice day!" At that, drawing a finger across his throat with his eye turned to Al and taking another swig from the can, all pretty much at once.

The rest of the morning calls were mostly the same, some with more information to impart than Marjorie's, some not. And they were all over the place, on other shows. Bob and Phyllis Hanks on the way from Tulsa to Broken Arrow Oklahoma to see their daughter and grandchildren. Blake Morrison taking a very important client from his paper mill in Clarksville to catch the train back to Little Rock, Arkansas. The Governor of Texas, no less, halfway between Fort Worth and Dallas to address a meeting of Oilmen's Charity Wives. Bud and his girlfriend Penny in her dad's brand new SUV, just sneaked the keys while he wouldn't know, only he'll soon find out when they're stranded forty-five miles from nowhere except nearest town Orangeburg, South Carolina.

It had begun without warning. Right after yet another blackout but drivers were not so much aware of that unless they were at traffic lights. Vehicles coming to a halt. Lifeless. Dud. Useless. It began with only a few here and there, not enough to raise suspicions at first. People kicked frustratedly at tyres and slammed driver's doors. It was when repair stations said they 'can't get to you a while, too many others calling' that word travelled to indicate something strange was afoot. Then people started remembering Virginia of three weeks before. Nobody was counting but through that morning it could have been up to a quarter of cars in some places that stopped and that is quite a lot when you think about it.

Mothers with children. Travellers between appointments. A jailbreaker in a stolen car. People going to the late shift. People coming from the early shift. Women with dinners to cook. Men looking forward to eating them. Bankers and biscuit-makers, thieves and pastors, lovers on promises, mistresses waiting, buyers, sellers, doers, thinkers, winners, losers, rich, poor (but rich enough to own a car), old, young (and a few too young to drive), and all ages inbetween. Singles, couples, triples, families, and as many as you could fit in with the doors closed. Stopped dead. Alone on the highway, or in a crowded city street, at traffic lights, in a one-way street, on a bridge, in a tunnel, at a 'no waiting sign', overtaking in the third lane, at a drive-thru burger bar, in an automatic car wash, doing a three-point turn just before the lights change, on the slipway in a multi-storey car park, boarding the river ferry, just speeding up, just slowing down, cruising along just fine an' dandy thank you. Stopped. No reason. Halfway through a cold Thursday in February.

State Governor's office, Jefferson, Missouri. "You're kiddin' my ass!" Governor not using the language of the office. "Cars, what! Where? All over the State? Get me the Police Department!"

Police Department, different one, different State, Atlanta, Georgia. "You can darn well get the crap off-of this line with your stoopid shit! Eh? Where? Waddya mean, everywhere? You better get me summat to see or your job's a gonna, officer! Where? Okay, bud, you got it ... I'm looking right outa this window right now! .... holy shit.... Well, don' hang on this line, get them off the goddam street!"

Washington, federal office, transportation. Emails and phone calls tracing lines between every official in the building. What's going on? What can we do? This is the states' problem. Not FBI, no crime is there? The Governors want back-up? Just move the cars. Does the President know? Does the President care? Where *is* the President? I'll give you one guess.

"Look!" A hand slammed down on the polished maplewood table, care taken to make heavy contact with the sheaf of papers not the solid wood itself. Nevertheless, a mighty thud. "Our cars don't just stop!" The collection of six 'suits', hastily summoned to the emergency meeting around the boardroom table, twenty-third floor, at the Detroit car plant, looked up from their seats at Max Drummond, chief executive, standing over them. An imposing six-footer, two hundred-plus pounds, he made it seem as though it was all their fault.

"We're still testing the samples from last time. Max, but with them fixing themselves -"

Drummond's eyes swivelled skywards as he muttered, with despairing irony, "Jesus ... fixing theirselves!"

"Yeh, Max", said another one, head of various things to do with engineering, "the boys don't find it easy looking for faults in cars that are fine. I mean, as soon as one breaks down again-"

"Yeh, well", cut in big Max, "looks like we got plenty broken down now ... Plenty! Just pull some in and find out what's wrong - fast! Christ, this could kill sales for a year!"

"It's not just us, Max. Ford, Chev, they're all reporting it. Maybe it's not the cars -"

"Christ, Tom! What is it, the little stones off the road?" Drummond had not got where he was without blowing the hair off people's heads before they had a chance to finish what they were saying.

"Max", Abe joined in, "it's too big a coincidence. Okay we can check some cars at random, and we'll hope to track the fault -"

"Fault?" Max snapped.

" - well, whatever", continued Abe, unruffled, "but the *cause* may not be in the cars themselves. Could be ... well, some of the 'brains' are already trying to identify atmospheric changes. Electrostatic ... whatever."

Drummond was silenced and thought for a moment.

"Yup, okay", he pondered, "let's see. Just get the tests done as fast as we can. We gotta get these products back on line, back on the road - and before the other guys, if we can. Meeting over."

"I can't believe there's so many of them, Abe", Tom murmured on the way out. "We're talking about *faults* in cars. Some places are saying there's about one in six or seven cars gone dead. All in the same way, just stopped. If this is a fault, there's something mighty wrong all of a sudden or, like you say, something else is interfering. All these blackouts, you know. Do you reckon ...?"

"I don't know, Tom. Let's find the fault first."

Drummond was leaving the room at the same time and gave them a 'Hmmph' and a sharp look on the way out.

Friday

All Friday, the phones were alive. Lines jammed to the carmakers in Detroit and elsewhere; to every car dealer and repair shop; to every police department; to the state offices; to the federal offices; to television, radio and the newspapers. Talk shows could talk of nothing else. TV programmes showed stranded cars on every highway, every street in every town. Some local weekly newspapers could not wait, they rushed out special editions full of pictures. Cars that still worked were seen weaving carefully in and out, picking a path between junk metal. Tow truck drivers clapped hands to foreheads, wondering where to start next. Still no-one was counting but it was maybe creeping up to one in five now and that is a mighty few breakdowns on a busy high street. On the open road, it looked more like too many people had forgotten to fill up with gas, abandoned automobiles dotted at intervals along the way.

It could not be mechanical. Thousands of cars just do not suffer a mechanical breakdown, give or take a few minutes, simultaneously. Or maybe they could. Maybe, in a particular set of circumstances - temperature, static electricity, components a bit too reliant on intricate computer technology - the same fault strikes them all together.

"Get them goddam tested!" rang out in car plants.

"I just don't understand", muttered the scientists to each other. Already the universities and the research labs were beavering away at the Virginia problem of three weeks ago. Now they had more data to work with but were no nearer an answer. It had to be atmospheric. Or maybe it was something electrical combined with the extra carbon dioxide in the air. Global warming! 'Oh, Christ' groaned the coalmen, the oilmen, the factory men, in fact anyone who burned or produced anything to make something, or heat something or cool something else down or make a goddamned car move along the goddamned highway - if it could still move, that is - or, basically, to keep America going around and around and churn the by-product up into the air. 'Here we go', they moaned.

They all wanted the President to say something, make a pronouncement, calm things down. People were getting mean in some places. 'Can I hitch a ride', from the guy with the broken-down automobile. 'You and who else, jack?' Or a good excuse not to go to work for some. Only one day so far but business-owners already getting nervous. A few folks were starting to make the best of things, though, sharing rides. It spread a bit further when they discovered some of the washing machines would not work when switched on. Some had broken down full of clothes and water already. Some cookers stubbornly stayed cold when it came to evening mealtime. And microwaves. A few folks on Friday night unexpectedly spent it in each others homes, just to eat. And watch TV, since a few of those were broken down, too. If you were really unlucky, it happened to your cooker and your microwave *and* your TV. And if you were really, really unlucky, your neighbour was the same. A few 'lucky' homes were quite busting full with other folks that Friday evening.

Saturday, it was all much the same. A few more things breaking down. Get to the shops instead of work. And the ball game. And the kids clubs. And if you had three cars, with one bust, or two cars with only one that worked; or only one in the first place, life was suddenly one big swamp you could only move around with great difficulty. Some folks felt quite resentful of the ones that still had enough wheels to get them and their families where they wanted. And many could not. There were some bitchy remarks when folks drove by without asking. But there was a kind of feeling growing that maybe you shouldn't do that.

The President. Well, no-one heard a word out of the President. Well, we know what the President'll be doing, is what everyone said. And then there was God. Where was God in all this? Why's God doing this to us? Is it a punishment? they wondered out loud. For what? What have we done? We're good, law-abiding folks, we look after our own. Our cars, our cookers, our washers, our televisions, we work hard for these. These are our 'things' and we have all the things we want if we work hard enough. It couldn't be a punishment from God. God punishes the bad, not the hardworking. When they were part of these discussions - much of it in supermarket queues and on golf courses and in bars all that Saturday, and some in cars that were giving a ride

- a few began to wonder if all that sounded quite as right as it should, although amongst some others there had begun to be a simmering resentment, a sense of betrayal. No-one, however, well hardly anyone, actually questioned God. This was the South, after all.

Then it was Sunday.

Piggyback

"Hoh-oo-hoh", chuckled Olivia softly, eyes wide with amused astonishment. They were in Elroy's expansive lounge, Walt and Olivia on one sofa, El on the other, the plasma TV screen glowing in front of them with an extended evening's roundup of the seize-ups across the South.

"Phew", breathed Walt, leaning forward with elbows on knees, "Virginia was just playing at it!"

"Yup", grinned big El, stretched back across the sofa, arms spread to either side, "sure was."

Six days. It had not been lost on him. He had even smiled - the big El grin back again - as he had watched it all unfold, especially when everything was back to normal on the seventh day. Just as planned. Then - just as planned, and when everyone was starting to think it was just a one-off, a freak event, confined to a single State - it began all over again; but more prolonged, more substantial. They had seen the 'rehearsal', watched Virginians struggle with it. Now, through the whole of the South, they all had to cope with it, adjust to it, adapt. This was real. And this time it wasn't going to conveniently end on the seventh day.

Piggyback. He still felt overwhelmed. Humbled to have been chosen. Awestruck at the enormity of it. Dazed that he should have been afforded the revelation of genius. Something from outside him presented like a gift. Was this how Michelangelo received his vision of the Cistine chapel? Did Shakespeare discover all those unique creations like implants lodged by another power in his brain? Yet this was more. This was actually impossible, if you were to define 'impossible' as beyond science that had yet been uncovered.

What he was doing could not be done, because it was as yet unknown. But it happened. The equation had appeared in his mind as though he had opened a hitherto concealed door. Yes, it was his, he had formulated it but he was fully aware that the inspiration - the genius? - was the gift he had received during those moments that had seemed like eternities, in the terrifying, awesome, wondrous manifestation in his study. What had passed there, he did not know. He was given no recollection of how any communication took place. There was the light, the enveloping, edifying brilliance of it. Somehow within the dazzling blaze of gold there was that vision, as had been depicted in so many paintings and church windows over the centuries, but real, three-dimensional, alive!

There was an overpowering sense of being embraced, without any physical contact, an outpouring of communion from another being. No words nor sounds he could recall. No transmission of thought as though he might have been penetrated by the mystery of telepathy. He was only aware of being shown that hidden door in his mind, as though it had always been there, he just never could find it. And while the brilliance enveloped him, he saw through the door, and in a flash he understood, and knew if he wrote that one word it would bring back the revelation when later he needed to formulate it for action. And then it was over. He had no memory of it ending, only Walt's face in front of him and those worried frowns, and poor Mariana, in his study. Piggyback

Mariana glided into the room, trundling a silver trolley laden with cups, plates, glasses, coffee pot, fruit juice, beer cans and a pile of sandwiches, samosas and salads.

"Gee", she exclaimed with a puzzled smile, "you done all this?" TV crews had spread like a rash across a dozen states to show the whole story. She pushed the trolley between the sofas, within everyone's reach, and seated herself beside Elroy. He let his arm slip from the sofa-back to curl around her shoulder and hugged her to him, pecking her on the cheek and grinning, "You impressed?"

"Gee ...." she murmured again, "I guess ... yeh ..." and her voice tailed off , engrossed in the TV pictures.

"So..." Walt sat up to pick a can and a sandwich, "what next?" He still wondered whether this wasn't quite it, a kind of limbo to be resolved one way or another. This was not his game, he could not even see the ball. It didn't make it any less unnerving that Big El was permanently enveloped in this serene rapture that never seemed to leave him since his 'revelation'. Jeez! How had he and Olivia got wound up in this thing! Elroy seemed almost to have hypnotised them both with his fervour. Yeh, they saw it the same way, sure; especially after that talk in the bar, the whole stuff about bugging and Cargill and the oil scam.

Yeh, he'd been wondering where the hell America was going and the blackouts, the violence of the hurricanes, the floods, the chaos, they both had. They both saw it close up, too, in their different jobs. He, in the constant chase to keep ahead of this crazy consumption - find the gas! - and she, overseeing worldwide nose-poking. In the interests of national security? No way. In the interests of keeping all the other noses in the dirt.

And then this big, beaming black face looks up at them and says he has the answer! Been given it. Been 'visited' for Christ's sake! It's so simple. So beautiful - he says. A formula no-one could ever imagine, way beyond our times. And so he goes on, crazy guy. Except they both somehow feel he's not crazy. He's their same genius pal who's discovered something they're never going to understand - maybe *he* won't either. It doesn't make sense but he's so intense, *seized* with such powerful persuasion. Like when you're kids and your friend has big wild eyes, telling you the monster really is just around the block, you gotta believe him, honest! And you have to follow, you're compelled to believe, no matter how crazy it sounds.

If you just stood still a moment and were rational about it, you'd see it was mad, impossible, but you don't, you follow because this zealous power of persuasion has gripped you so tight! It's not just a gleam in the eye, it's a pouring from the soul. Possessed. And it possesses you, too. And that's he and Olivia, the two of them. Possessed by Elroy's passion. He told them he had seen ... seen ... no, Walt could not take that in. It was beyond his capacity to believe; but he could not question his friend's conviction, however it might improbably be explained.

What next? Elroy frowned as they watched the TV scenes of abandoned cars, stranded travellers, clothes piled up beside dud washing machines, families dining on chilly winter salads. What next? He was a bit nervous, too. Not that anyone could trace it back to him. Lord! They would have to understand it first! However, this was so enormous it could not simply stay as it was. Maybe there would be riots. Surely that was not what it was about. Ours is not to reason why, he thought to himself.

That was how he had felt when he and Walt met in the visitors' car park of the drab, unprepossessing building a few weeks ago to set Piggyback in motion. The place was a natural choice for government surveillance activities yet had probably taken months, if not years, to hunt down. Lower East Side Manhattan, with a view across the Hudson River but only a quick cab ride from city life so staff would not drift away complaining of distance from shops, bars and the rest. NSA, the National Security Agency, had these anonymous quarters scattered around the whole country and nobody knew: just the few who worked in them, not even staff in other centers. The Federal Oath saw to that.

This one, this square Sixties block of greyish concrete, could be anybody's. Plain rows of glass inset in the concrete slabs to create a monotonous pattern, a main entrance porch that almost looked like another double window, occasional black shuttered doors around one corner and the near side. The kind of building where you couldn't tell how much was office space, how much was storage or even some unexciting low-tech workbench manufacturing. It might be struggling to survive the hi-tech age or it might have made its owner a multimillionaire from an anonymous niche in the broad industrial fabric. Or maybe not. It said 'Housteads' over the plain entrance doors but it had not long ago been 'River Designs' (named from location, naturally) and, previously, 'NuFlair', 'Isaac Marks' and 'Trek Tech ... something', fading with local memory that no-one could now recall.

For most of those years all its six floors had been devoted solely to the business of one or other of its occupants until, more recently, the top floor - with its clear line of sight above its lower-level neighbours - had been leased through an agency. The satellite dishes and antennae discreetly placed behind the balustrade surrounding the flat roof, went unremarked in an age when it was unusual for roofs *not* to sport such furniture. NSA had found it tougher in some parts, like Kentucky for instance, where the operations building ended up separated from the signals unit by half a mile of dusty township street, with the dishes and all being concealed atop a disused windmill.

This was all post-nine-eleven and the other atrocities and the awareness that if the very public NSA HQ in Maryland was taken out, even with the all the safeguards and subterranean backups, international surveillance had to be maintained, indeed even more crucially so. 'Housteads' and other sites were effectively dormant sub-NSA sections, ready to be activated at a second's notice and in the meantime a skeleton technical staff was administered by local non-technical managers like Olivia Brown. A clever idea in contrast to the very public spotlight on Maryland: the whole of NSA operations could be replaced by just half these clandestine support centers and no-one would even know they were there. Not 'would not': did not, not now or any time.

Inside, in front of the array of computer terminals, power units, and vdu screens in the small, windowless room, Elroy had seated himself at the centre keyboard with Walt and Olivia standing either side behind him. His fingers hit the keyboard. A blistering parade of alpha-numeric characters blipped into rows across the screen, mingled with other special characters, the preserve of computer cognoscenti. It was done. "There", he had declared, leaning back, satisfied and excited.

He had glanced then, from the large monitor and its mass of moving dots, at Walt's puzzled features, and allowed himself a brief grin. Yup, he had felt he owed it to his great pal to explain but it was pretty difficult to explain the incomprehensible. This formula came from within him but was not solely his, not sole ownership, so he did not fully understand it himself. 'Piggyback' was not much more than an acronym that functioned like a trigger in his own memory: Pi (ah, that elusive value that no mathematician had yet pinned down to an absolute number) over Double-Gamma multiplied by Y (where Y equals the property of the string) equals Back, or: Pi/Double-Gamma x Y = Back. The 'Back' was not strictly part of the equation, more a symbol of what was to occur: Piggyback.

Put simply, the flush of characters still spreading across the screen would cause an adjusted - or 'corrupted' - radio signal to be emitted, which would 'catch' gamma rays entering the earth's atmosphere. This joined-together, or 'piggybacked', radio+gamma wave would be redirected by satellite to Earth below, utilising NSA's surveillance transmission systems. Upon reaching the surface, the Piggyback waves, encountering any microwave 'leak' from any man-made source - motor car, TV, oven, washing machine and so and so on - were programmed to latch onto the microwave in a second 'piggyback' - hence the 'double-gamma' - and hitch a ride into the heart of the source - car, fridge, or whatever. Then ... oh boy ... then this uniquely corrupted wave - radio/gamma/micro - hits the strings -

"Strings?" Walt had interjected in utter bewilderment, an image of white lengths of stuff in balls penetrating his mind.

"Strings", affirmed Elroy. "You know the theory that's been knocking around a while now, that atoms aren't the smallest particles but they're made up of strings, the minutest possible things beyond imagination?"

"No", was all Walt could say.

"Well, man, it's right, they exist. That's what everything is made of: you, me, Livvy -" He had glanced up at Olivia, looking tense in her position of vulnerable responsibility. " - this keyboard", he continued, "everything!" Elroy could only imagine the astonished response in scientific journals if this proof of a decades-old and hotly-argued theory could be laid out within their pages. He remembered his own boyish enthusiasm as he had proceeded to explain to Walt and Olivia together how these infinitesimally minute particles - strings - became corrupted by the incoming 'piggyback' wave and, being the particles of which the entire object - car, fridge, TV - was made, caused instant failure.

Not only that, a separate part of the program had scooped up protein atoms in its journey and deposited them in amongst the atoms of the affected object. That's when nanotechnology kicked in. "Savvy?" He had said to the two of them, to be met by two dumbly shaking heads. Well, he had summed up, the protein atoms immediately set about repairing the strings in the affected atoms and when they are finished - hey presto! -

"It's working again!" Olivia had broken in, delighted at seeing it.

"And is it possible?" Walt had asked in the NSA room, as the signal was being transmitted.

"Nope", replied Elroy.

"So why are we doing it?"

"Because", replied Elroy, his manner becoming distant as he recalled the beginning of all this in his study, ".... Because we'll just have to wait and see." But there had been a faith in his voice which conveyed a certainty that persuaded them also. Even after it took effect, that first time, and cars, TVs, dishwashers and the like, in Virginia, suddenly stopped working, Elroy could not have fully explained why. He knew it was strings, he had been given the knowledge of what was happening, and how to make it happen, but the intricacies of parts of the formula were beyond his understanding. Some of the equations seemed to spawn other combinations of characters which bore no relation to his own thought process.

He understood the random-and-percentage quality - only a percentage of vulnerable cars and domestic equipment would be affected and their geographical location, age , make and so on would all be random. He controlled the actual geographical area - hence the first, limited trial just in Virginia. He had no overt control over the rate of recovery, it was locked into the program.

He saw it must be more than coincidence that everything was back to normal at the end of six days and assumed it was all part of the Divine message. Ha. Neat. Then came the next phase, again buried mysteriously within the formula, starting all over again, across all the southern states of the US.

"Now, just the timing", Elroy had said at the keyboard. The morass of characters in lines on the screen suddenly vanished and were replaced by 'System Test Operating'. Olivia and Walt smiled at each other, 'System Testing' being the cover under which she had authorised their visit (Walt really being there for physical support should it be necessary). Elroy leaned forward again to another small keyboard console to his left and tapped in a series of characters, checking satellite co-ordinates on the big screen as he did so.

"At precisely ten-thirty-three and fourteen-point-eight-two seconds to ten-thousandths atomic accuracy. Two days from now." He had leaned back again, a slight smile on his lips.

"Why that particular time?" Olivia had queried.

"Don' know", Elroy shrugged. He had that specific date and time lodged in his brain. He did not know how it got there, nor why it was there. It was fixed with all the other information received during the glory of that other day in his study. Later, he was aware that the Virginia 'piggyback' seemed to have more or less coincided with the end of a power cut in that part of the States but he thought nothing of it at the time, being so excited by the immediate effect to be seen all around. Brilliant! Reducing the number of cars and all kinds of domestic appliances that could function, at a stroke. Dramatically cutting the need for energy - oil, electricity, all types (hah! Eat your heart out, LOTUS!). And the next time it would be a whole lot bigger, covering a wider area and continuing perhaps indefinitely because, although he did not understand why, there was a randomisation built into it that was missing for Virginia. "Which could make it impossible", he grinned at them, "to work out any pattern to it! Total confusion!"

"And is that it?" had remarked Walt, doubtfully.

"How do you mean?" asked Elroy, the grin fading.

"Well", continued Walt, "is this all that happens?"

"Don' know", replied Elroy again, with a frown. Somewhere buried in his subconscious was an awareness that there was indeed more to all this than the humble part he was playing. Lodged there with all the other material conveyed to him during his 'revelation' but he could not remember the details, nor even whether it was something he was required to know. And now here was his friend again, while they watched the television in triumph, asking, 'what next?' What now? Was this not enough, what they saw before them? Did there have to be more to it than this? Why?

"I don't know", he spoke out loud in reply to Walt. "I guess .. something .. I guess I just did what ..." He found it difficult to say.

"What you were told?" Walt looked at him quizzically and so did the two women.

"Yeh. I guess so." And Elroy beamed that broad smile at them again that said he was so sure, so very sure, that he was content to be given questions without answers. Those were for a higher authority. They all turned to continue viewing and it proved to be a richly entertaining evening.

Smug

Gabriel looked smug. Despite his earlier misgivings, he was beginning to enjoy himself. At any rate, smug was what it looked like from a distance. It was at times like these (where, of course, time does not exist) that God appreciated the infinity of Heaven. Gabriel had just returned from an unscheduled trip to Splong. God was using the infinity of Heaven to put more of it than usual between Himself and His loyal but questionably aromatic angel. The Splong trip had obviously been made when His back was turned, since He had no knowledge of it. God did not have a back, of course, any more than he had a front or indeed any number of sides. He just *was.* However, He did occasionally allow His attention to be diverted - 'refocus' He preferred to describe it to Gabriel - which might mean, at a particular time, He was not entirely 'focused' on Gabriel's whereabouts.

Gabriel chortled half to himself, rocking to and fro on his haunches.

"Strings ...."

The Lord pretended not to hear. A wasted exercise.

"Strings..." chuckled Gabriel again, this time looking across to the Lord, whom he could just more or less make out in the distance; and then added, "Are You all right over there?"

"Perfectly, thank you."

"I mean", carried on Gabriel, a bit louder, just in case, and still chortling, "good, isn't it?"

"Good?" The Lord vaguely hoped the conversation might be suffocated by His minimalist responses.

"Yes. I mean, only a few of them even think they exist."

The Almighty was aware that Gabriel's childlike delight - and smugness - was due to his belief that all this was his idea. Well, so be it. It appeared to have yielded a quite unheralded level of enthusiasm in the archangel. Not so much of the 'pah! Earth!' now.

"Well, it's ironic, isn't it?"

"Is it?"

"This whole nudge using strings - that they mostly don't even believe in!" And the angel began rolling even more vigorously backwards and forwards, laughing out loud as he did so.

Well, the fact of whether humankind would eventually unravel the mysteries of this or any other facet of science was preordained, just as the Akrungites (there, that one is quite easy, isn't it) had known about the fundamental particles of matter for a couple of millennia (their time). 'Big deal', was their reaction so much further down their history. Manipulating those particles, now that was something else altogether. Still worrying away at that one, they were.

However, not everything was preordained, including what they had begun on Earth and what was planned next, as the Lord was only too aware. Perhaps they could just call a halt now. A bit of unexplained turbulence in the course of human history, logged but soon forgotten. A tempting consideration, He mused. But no. Why begin now and go no further? Besides, the need was now and, if ignored, would either remain or arise again.

"I trust", He called to His mirthful aide, "you are not overlooking matters."

"Boss?"

"Requirements", added the Lord, by way of explanation.

"Guv?"

Oh, the Good Lord, thought God, or might have if He was anyone else, do I have to spell it out?

"Oh ..oh.." came the angel, "no Guv ... not overlooking matters." Sometimes he wondered if the Lord gave him any credit for thinking for himself. And how could he miss this one anyway. This was going to be the best since ...since that time on Earth when -

"Gabriel?" The Almighty expected a response.

"Yes, Boss, I'll be off then."

"Well, well, not quite yet", interjected the Lord, hastily. "In due time." (Earth time, naturally).

"Yes, Boss, right." Just checking, was He, the Almighty? Well, yours truly wouldn't be under such close scrutiny once out of Heaven. The smug look returned. God noted it but said nothing. As long as the archangel stuck to the plan, that's all.

Sold

"Brother Hoi."

"Hah ..." Hoi Fong spun round. "Brother Teng!" He felt he could become quite unnerved by these sudden appearances. He had been looking down onto the assembly line from his office window again, absorbed in his own thoughts. He forced his welcoming smile.

"Very good, Brother Hoi, very good indeed, do you not think?"

"Indeed, yes, Brother Teng. Better even than I could have anticipated", failing to add, 'and at that price, who could resist a bargain?' Yet, he could scarcely complain at the impact they were having. The agent had phoned immediately on Friday to recount how sales were going and in particular to convey the success of the arrival and the show. Hoi had known little of all this beforehand; he had simply been told that the delivery would be 'ceremonious' and the London dealer would be provided with some spectacular entertainment for his 'product launch'.

"So much so, Brother Hoi", Teng was saying, "that we suggest you waste no time in securing an even bigger order. After all, the Society..."

"Yes, yes", Hoi hurriedly agreed, "but -" and he suggested how it might be wiser business practice not to appear too eager, considering the heavily-discounted price for the introductory order and might it not be in all their interests to wait for the dealer to make the first contact - "though far be it from me to prolong my obligations to the Society."

"Quite so, Brother Hoi. But a good time, also, to emphasise the reliability of our Chinese technology." It was a slight but meaningful smile.

"Certainly, Brother Teng."

We might suggest tripling the order?"

"Triple?"

"Brother Hoi, do you not think the vehicles are worthy?"

"Of course, Brother Teng", Hoi acquiesced with dignity. He was inwardly disquieted at the unseemly haste being pressed upon him.

"Well, no doubt you will have some news in a day or two. Then we can make arrangements for the women and the gifts." Teng made his crablike departure with assumed humility. Hoi stood and reflected. This was becoming more like an emperor's coronation than trading in automobiles.

The cars had all been sold by the end of the weekend, with half a dozen more deposits paid and as many test drives requested but with no cars remaining to drive! Nevertheless, Paul was going to play it cool, excited though he was within himself. He had done well up to now but not attained his dream, of expansion into at least another showroom and then perhaps more after that. Competition was stiff, the car trade susceptible to the ups and downs of the national economy. Each time he felt ready to go for it, a blip in the trade made it seem too much of a risk. This might be his opportunity. These appeared to encapsulate much of what people wanted in a car now. Neat, small but not 'mini', zippy, comfortable and roomy inside, low fuel consumption. And the price, wow!

That was mainly why he was determined not to make the first move if he could possibly avoid it. Yes, he could sell them three times over but just hang on a few days, keep the Chinaman on the back foot. And make sure they provide that show again, along the street and at the showroom. With the girls (he grinned to himself: beauties). And those stupid heavy dolls. The punters seemed to think that topped off the deal. Personally, he'd keep them for panel-beating.

Sunday

Sunday morning. The church in the heart of bible country, Louisiana, was packed as usual. This, despite so many folks being without their regular limos, people-carriers and sports utility vehicles. Old Hank and Adele were in their pew, right by the centre aisle, four rows from the front; the Brents - six of them, aged six to sixty-two - were there, and the Slomans, the devout if rather supercilious Williams spinster sisters, young Jim and Jilly Hogan, recently wed in this same church, the Abrahams. And all the rest. They had got there by hook or by crook, by plenty of neighbours offering rides and packing friends and neighbours into every seat, and some where the dogs usually went in the back. Same as in all the states where the cars had 'just stopped, darn it!'

Churches and chapels from Georgia to Kansas, from Texas to Virginia, all filled with folks who had given a ride or taken a ride, exchanging gossip and sharing views - most particularly about the 'cars and other things' gone broken - with an intimacy and familiarity they had rarely experienced with each other before. If some had made sure of getting there to offer a question in silent prayer to the Good Lord, and maybe a spoken one to the preacher, too, they did not show it.

In Louisiana and most of the way across the South it was a brilliant blue crisp morning and the light shone through the huge stained glass window depicting Jesus with four of his disciples, shining from behind the congregation and onto them seated below. In front, as they waited, was the preacher's platform and pulpit, a simple smooth maplewood plinth bearing the bible lectern and a small microphone hidden from view.

There was a keener air of anticipation than usual. This had been no ordinary week and could be no ordinary day of worship. In times of trouble, who to turn to but the Almighty? Some privately considered that a bit of help with a dud automobile was the least they could ask for; some others were not entirely at ease with the notion of supplication to revive a dishwasher which defied all mortal attention, rather than feed the poor. Perhaps it would be acceptable to request both.

Jesse Martins at the electric organ - it was merically spared the fate of other appliances - struck up the rousing opening chords of 'Jesus Is All The World To Me' and the murmuring congregation hushed. From a door at one side, in swept Pastor Dirk Donahoe, immaculate in dark suit with polka-dot gold and black tie, dark hair brushed sleekly back over his head, and strode to the central pulpit. He raised his arms outstretched in the air, palms facing the eager assembly. "Praise be the Lord!", his amplified voice resonating around the lofty space above them.

"Praise be The Lord", cried the people in response.

"Praise be The Lord", he boomed again, louder, and in turn they cried even louder to him, "Praise be The Lord!"

"Friends! Brothers! Sisters!" he declared to them all, "In our troubled times, let us give thanks to the Lord!" And, with the hymn number indicated boldly in a list on the wall, the organist led the ignited worshippers in 'The Lord Is My Shepherd'.

As the service progressed, with the opening prayer, another hymn, the Lord's Prayer, bible reading and another hymn, thoughts were floating around regarding what the pastor would say about the crisis - if it were to be labelled thus - how would he confront the Lord with this consuming perplexity which was none of their making? This was not starving children in a foreign land, nor even 'our boys' protecting freedom in some other distant place. This was at home, this was personal, this was crippling daily life right here. Would Pastor Donahoe be seeking a Divine explanation?

"Friends, brothers, sisters," the pastor intoned, in lower, more measured tones, as he began his sermon, "where is the Lord?"

"Where is the Lord, where is the Lord", rippled the echoing whisper around the church.

"He is here!" The reverend Donahoe confirmed for their ears.

The echoing, "He is here", once again.

"He is here amongst us", repeated the sonorous preacher. "Is He here to judge us?"

"Yes .. Yes", came the awed response from many voices.

"Is He here to punish us?"

"Ye ...." a few voices began in response, then faltered as they wondered whether they should be inviting yet more Divine retribution, considering what they were already suffering.

"Friends," the preacher Donahoe picked up their unease, leaning earnestly across the pulpit towards them, "the Lord does not wish us ill, perhaps the Lord entreats us to be bolder-" and with that his voice assumed a brief crescendo - "in striving for the rewards of life, to *scorn*" - and his voice bit upon that word - "those among us who cannot *defeat* their difficulties, not to be cowed by adversity but, oh Son of God to -" and he raised his eyes to the sacred window "to .... to ...."

And then the strangest thing happened. Those who saw it would never forget it to the end of their days. As they watched the reverend Dirk Donahoe, his face lifted to look over their heads, they saw his features begin to glow. It was as though - they described it - light was radiating from him and, as it did so, his voice stuttered to a halt.

There followed an unearthly silence, while the pastor stared in a kind of trance over their heads to where the window was above them. None dared turn to follow his eyes but were rooted on him as he appeared to be listening to an unheard voice, nodding almost imperceptibly, lips moving all but indiscernibly in awed acknowledgement of something they could not hear, even in that stillness until, at length, he began to speak once more, now without that authoritative drone but suddenly humbled: "... to ... to ... *share*? ... Oh Lord? ... not to desire more than .. we need ..."

Then his speech became firmer and fluent again, while he continued to mouth words he might be repeating from another source, his features almost bleached with radiant light, "Is that it, oh Lord", he began a question, gazing in such supplication above their heads that now, gradually, in ones and twos and threes, they took their eyes off him to turn around and look above at the window behind them. To their undying astonishment they saw the light was not radiating from the preacher's face at all, but from the face of Jesus in the stained glass window, pouring from it in rays of gold and pink and bronze, and it was not the light from the day outside but a stream of dazzling light as though from a search-beam, striking and reflecting from the face of the pastor staring up at it and creating a golden aura all around them. The whole figure, but most especially, the stained glass face of Jesus was bathed in its own light and showering it down upon them.

And then, as the reverend Dirk Donahoe continued with his question, all of them now facing around and transfixed by the outpouring of light from the image of Jesus, they saw what none of them really believed, yet knew it was what they saw.

"...is that it, oh Lord", continued the pastor, "what you require of us ... to ... to... share?" And his face not only glowed even more strongly but became wreathed in a huge, childlike smile, and he stood, just beaming up at the image in the window, smiling and beaming and softly repeating the word until it became louder and more powerful: "share .. yes .. share ... yes ... *share*...!"

But not one of his congregation saw him, for they were all still staring at the window, while some began to weep and others sank back into their seats, disbelieving what was before them yet knowing it could be nothing else, mouths gaping open, eyes wide and filling with tears. The face had moved!

Not long afterwards, the people walked, drifted, stumbled from the church into the brilliantly sunlit street, the organist playing behind them, pounding the keys and pedals as one possessed and extemporising variations and harmonies she would never ever be able to repeat. The Reverend Donahoe remained in the pulpit, gazing at the window until, as the golden light faded from it, he dropped his eyes to watch the remnants of his congregation departing through doors before him.

Outside, most of the people were too stunned to say much, if anything at all, except perhaps to mumble, "share", echoing the preacher as they climbed back into their shared transportation to return to their technologically dysfunctioning daily lives. Each had one thing in common as they departed, and it remained with them all for the rest of that day and, at times and sometimes irrationally, beyond. Each face was lit with the most rapturous smile.

Smile

"You did what -!"

"Made him smile", said Gabriel matter-of-factly. "Well he always looks so serious."

"He was bearing an important message to all my people", the Lord felt He should remind him.

"Yeh, okay", rejoined Gabriel, "But a bit of a laugh wouldn't do any harm sometimes."

God was about to make the point that establishing moral laws and codes of ethics amongst a species like the humans did not lend itself to including jests and quips along the way; but Gabriel was getting into one of his unstoppable modes.

"I mean –" the angel continued, "I mean, religion down there, it's not a bundle of fun, is it?"

"Gabriel...", the Lord sighed.

"Look at the Bible", the trusted one went on, "You show me a joke in it. And that's a very big book."

Well, the Lord considered, books don't all have to have jokes in them. Even big ones. What about Proust? And The Illyad. And countless works by former world leaders: pompous, interminable and entirely humourless. Even Lord Of The Rings, almost presenting an alternative religion to some; compelling, fantastic, convoluted and scarcely a chuckle anywhere.

"I think you are being somewhat selective", He observed. "The Koran, Islam –"

"Hah!" Gabriel snorted, leaning forward to check a couple of crevices with his fingers as he did so. "That whole religion is a joke-free zone!"

He did have a point, the Lord admitted to Himself. Buddah, though, now there was an icon not infrequently depicted with a big cheerful grin. And the humans in the East, where the Buddah was their 'God', a lot of smiling individuals there. Must be a connection. Perhaps other religions should have taken a leaf out of that book. Well, Buddhism did not have a book in quite the same way. Maybe that was the answer. A bit late, now. Perhaps the Bible would have been a little easier to read if it had contained the occasional rib-tickler. He should have encouraged the scribes to think along those lines at the time. 'Why does Moses' missus always have a headache?' .... 'She keeps taking his tablets'....No, no, He reflected. No guarantee it would have worked. Virtually impossible to read but at least the Bible was taken seriously. A weighty tome. What carries its weight with more dignity, the book you can't put down, or the one you can hardly pick up? Hm, yes, His inner musings became almost audible amusement ...

"Guv?"

"Mm?" as He returned to the immediate concern. "So you made him smile? In a stained glass window?"

"Yes, Guv." There was just the hint of conceit in the angel's reply. "I mean, you know, same as the tears from the statues. And the mirac-"

"Yes, Gabriel, I know." God wondered how the archangel had pulled this one off without allowing it to look like one of those television cartoon shows seen regularly on weekend mornings. However ... it seemed to have worked.

Part Three

DISLOCATION

DISLOCATION

PARADIGM : HOPE

In the still morning, there was a mist rising. Hovering at first, it clung to the limpid sea, then lifted slowly, in swirls and veils, as it was beckoned by the warming sun above.

"I felt a movement", she smiled at him, her enchanting smile. It could not be told whether it was the sun's reflection in her face or her very glow, shining to challenge the mastery of their fiery, golden orb. Their life-giver.

"A movement?" His eyes gleamed in delight. He sank lithely to his knees before her, rippling bronze in the vibrant morning light.

"He kicked." Her lips played with a satisfied smile.

"He?" He leaned to place strong, firm fingers on her blooming curve.

"Our son", she smiled again.

"Or our daughter", he smiled, too, and let his fingers slide and linger on her, feeling the tautness, as if he might sense the beat of a drum beneath.

"We shall love him. Or her." Her eyes were twinkling in the bright sunlight, the cloying mist dispelled and shunned by the warmth of the new day.

"Yes, it shall be our love, each of us." He gently caressed her lips with his, touching her cheek with the hand which could love or kill.

"I shall bear our needs", he declared and rose, simply, to face the sun. She watched the supple snaking of his limbs as he strode away to tend for her, and her unborn.

Donahoe

Two things happened. Well, three, actually, but the third - the collapse of the American economy - began just afterwards. The first involved Gabriel in rather more work than he had anticipated. "Did you know it would be like this?" he grumbled as accusingly as he dared. "Gabriel..." God warned him in *that* tone of voice. "Tchk", Gabriel tutted in a minor display of petulance, returning to the matter in hand (as it were), the petulance bit being Benignly ignored.

Paul Best was neither particularly aware nor particularly interested, understandably perhaps. He was gleefully finalising details of two more tranches of Manchu Met deliveries, at just the right price, having successfully held out for the call instead of phoning first himself. Yes, he assured the agent he would provide the publicity and the trimmings for another special performance to announce the arrival of each delivery (exactly what he wanted himself, anyway); The Chinese, moreover, seemed almost as anxious about their dragon and dolls as selling their cars.

Hoi Fong, eyes and ears glued to CNN News, was well tuned to circumstances on the other side of the world and the favourable image they might help induce in his own product: 'reliable Chinese'. However, he was torn between helpless resentment and a quivering anxiety. Teng had sidled into his office once again, to remind his 'brother' of the importance and urgency of effecting further sales, "to build upon our success, surely, Brother Hoi?" "Indeed", Hoi had murmured impotently, not wishing to add that early repayment to the Society might be compromised by adhering to the same low profit margin as before. Between a rock and a hard place, neither delay nor failure, to sell or repay, would be welcomed by the Society, he knew that.

Brother Teng's demeanour did not suggest he was receptive to such argument. Besides, he had brought a taller, more sturdily-built companion on this occasion: "Brother Cho Hey, I'm sure you must have made his acquaintance already", Teng smiled. No, he had not, thought Hoi, and he did not wish to. The exaggerated outline of muscles beneath the tight black T-shirt, rubber-banded ponytail and thick-lipped grin were not qualities of endearment to him. Hoi found himself clasping Hwee Lo the more protectively to him in their living room and in their bed, her expanding abdomen soliciting his care.

Isabella failed to express the delight which might have been expected of one on the threshold of a new level of affluence. On the contrary, it was as though she was retaliating, in Paul's judgement, with more carping comments about traffic, congestion, pollution. It was the only downside for Paul, but not enough to deflect his ambition. She kept her growing excitement about events 'back home' to herself but was disappearing to more rallies and meetings in London, despite the very congestion and blackouts she was campaigning about conspiring to prevent her. He even discovered banners tucked away in the kitchen cupboard, as her involvement grew.

To avoid the twin alternatives of a cold stove and an icy atmosphere at home, Paul was more frequently stopping at the kebab house in evenings. Oddly, he thought he saw the Chinese man, Mr Sing, on one occasion enter by the side door, as he got out of the car. But he dismissed it as a trick of the streetlights. Highly improbable for a Chinaman to choose to eat at an Asian kebab house, never mind go in by the private entrance. He could not somehow see the wily little Oriental befriending the kebab house proprietor, who appeared increasingly lost in a world of his own, in smiling serenity. Shrewd Sing and otherworldly Kebab Man? The image of such a twosome made Paul smile.

So, the first thing? Pastor Donahoe's church could not cope. Word got around like wildfire, even if people could not. The following Sunday, despite even more cars having given up the ghost, not only was the church jam-packed the minute the doors opened, nearly an hour before the service, there were as many would-be worshippers stretching in a line outside. Mostly, the ones inside were the regulars but some interlopers got there early, too, leaving a handful of Donahoe's regular flock gnashing their teeth in righteous fury down the stone steps and into the street. "Where they goddam come from?" "Whose church do they think this is?" "Go drag 'em out, Wilber!" It did not get that far but some of the utterances were less than Christian on the Lord's Day.

People had abandoned their own churches and driven from miles around - all stuffed into the cars that still worked - only turning back when they saw the numbers already crowded outside, otherwise even more would have been waiting. All had come, either to be astonished or in disbelief, to witness the 'smiling Jesus'. As it was, it did not happen. Not at first, anyway.

"Lost? What do you mean, 'lost'?"

"Well, you know", mumbled Gabriel, not looking in the general direction of the Lord.

"No, I do not know", breathed the Lord God Almighty and, had annoyance been a Divine characteristic, which of course it is not, He would have found difficulty containing it.

"They all look the same", shrugged the angel, burying his chin in his knees as he fiddled with a couple of toes, separating them to examine the gap between.

"What do?"

"Those churches. I mean ..."

"Yes?" God's insistence upon an explanation was bearing down on His angel.

"Well, I mean", continued Gabriel, evasively, and still keeping his eyes well away from the Lord's simmering (and rather unGodly) glare, "they could have shown a bit more imagination, couldn't they, painted them different colours or something. You know, there I was -", warming to his defence.

"There you were *not*, as it happens", the Lord interrupted, a trifle icily for the Good Lord, Gabriel felt bound to think (to himself).

"Well, I was, in the end", the archangel struck up defiantly, "just missed the first showing, that's all. Anyway, most of *them* had already seen it."

"Are we, by any chance", (and saying that without sounding sarcastic takes some doing, even if You are God), "talking about the same thing or is one of us referring to a visit to the cinema?" The Lord actually made it sound like an innocent query regarding sharing a pot of tea or its heavenly equivalent but his loyal if not entirely reliable aide did not require inflexions of the voice to get the Lord's drift.

"Yeh, okay, Boss." Meaning, 'fair cop, I'll miss out the Splong trip on the way next time'.

Thus it was, in the appropriately biblical phrase, the second service bore witness to the 'smiling Jesus', Gabriel by that time having found the right church. Before that, Dirk Donahoe had striven to summon the previous week's miracle for the assembled congregation, most of whom, as has been noted, were the same regulars but with a sprinkling of 'strangers'. No matter what energy he poured into his look of supplication, the stained glass window remained sublimely unmoved and he was forced to fall back on 'God moving in mysterious ways', and all that, to counter the air of deflation and disappointment which descended upon them all. However, his powers of evangelical exhortation were more than sufficient to persuade the crowd waiting outside to join him in a repeat of the service and, sure enough, this time the phenomenon rewarded and amazed them.

The regulars afterwards quickly learned that 'he smiled' for the visitors so the following Sunday both lots turned up nearly two hours in advance, along with as many again. By the time Pastor Donahoe had gone through four consecutive services, during all of which the miraculous wonder blessed and enthralled them (Gabriel did not fancy having to explain himself a second week running), he was spiritually and emotionally drained and had to profusely apologise, to the large crowd still waiting outside for a fifth service, that the Holy Lord had commanded him to withdraw into prayer. Gabriel, who could have told them the Lord could not be relied upon to actually be watching all that closely, was nevertheless relieved, since the novelty was wearing off and he had had enough himself for the time being.

The long and the short of it was, the Reverend Dirk Donahoe could see a whole day of services stretching through the following Sunday and spent all of Monday and Tuesday on TV and radio shows, which were clamouring to have him anyway, explaining that he could not, however much he was in awe of this Divine revelation and the wondrous sign from the Lord Jesus, conduct services from morning till night in his church for all those who wished to attend from far and wide.

It backfired on him. They took him at his word, from Georgia to West Virginia, from Tennessee to Arkansas, the pastors and the congregations invited the Reverend Donahoe to preach at *their* churches instead. Something in them seemed to say that it was not a window which was blessed with the holy sign, it was the pastor himself. And they were right. To Dirk Donahoe's own astonishment, and a little dismay, the following Sunday when he visited a township chapel in Texas, invited there for the presence of a similar stained glass window looking down upon the preacher and flock, the miracle occurred just as before.

With remarkable acumen and not a little forward planning, other churches in the state announced they would delay their Sunday service if the Reverend Pastor would honour them with his spiritual leadership; and accept a ride in a fast car - triple-checked to ensure it worked - and the occasional helicopter that arrived remarkably speedily at the door. His feet scarcely touched the ground all that day. By the end of which, approaching ten o'clock at night, he had conducted eight services spread around a large portion of Texas, the last couple of them blessed with the miracle occurring after nightfall and the most celestial showering of wondrous light and that 'smile'.

Gabriel was blessed if he could face doing any more as well, hence the, "Did you know it would be like this?" The Lord allowed him to grumble away to himself, knowing full well that it was not as though *he* had to clamber in and out of cars, or do without meals, or try to remember his words time after time. He just had to be at the right church at the right time which, seeing as neither space nor time held any restrictions for him, did not seem too much to expect.

"I trust ..." assayed the Lord, mildly, when the angel had finally slumped down beside him at the end of it all.

Gabriel looked at Him and was inclined to feign a weariness which, being an angel, he could not possibly carry off, especially in the face of the Lord, when he broke out in a broad smile instead. Actually, it was all going rather well and, he had to confess within himself, all according to plan. Which meant he was quite prepared to put up with the next bit.

"Yes, Boss", he continued smiling, "every one a treat."

The next bit took him, and Pastor Dirk Donahoe, all over the South, which was a great deal easier for Gabriel than for the

Reverend Dirk, not that the angel would admit it too readily to the Lord. Everywhere the pastor preached where there was a stained glass window of the appropriate design, so he evinced the 'smiling Jesus'. Sunday by Sunday, state by state, service after service, as many as he and his hosts could organise in a single day, there they - the two of them - travelled.

For Dirk Donahoe, although he knew the routine off by heart, it constantly sent such a shiver through him that the spiritual shock never diminished and it meant the message he imparted to each congregation was always as devout and as mesmeric as that first time in his home church in Louisiana. For him it always *felt* like the first time and that is how he conveyed it; and that is why it was so powerful and convincing. Gabriel was particularly proud of that although he could never boast as much to the Lord, since he knew, inside himself, that it was not necessarily all his own idea.

Anyway, that is why the second thing worked the way it did.

Friends

"Olivia?"

"Yea."

"Hi! It's Bella!"

"Isabella!" It had been weeks since they had spoken. Bella's number had been on her phone a couple of times and there was an email that all she had written in response to was 'Hi ... we're fine ... busy but speak very soon'. A rather abrupt deflection of her one-time best friend but Olivia felt too preoccupied, and confused even, to answer what she suspected would be a torrent of questions from Bella marooned the other side of the Pond. She did still think of her as her best friend but had seen her so rarely in the last few years, the last time when she and Paul came to New York about three years ago, when Bella admitted her problems, she and Paul arguing more and inexorably drifting apart. The two women had been at NY State University together, firm friends from the first week and afterwards for the years before Bella made her big move to London. She remembered how they all, the students, wanted to call her 'Izzy', the popular abbreviation of the time, and how Isabella would erupt and bite back that she hated 'Izzy', would refuse to speak to anyone who used it, was not too keen on 'Isabella' either, and warmly encouraged, indeed ordered, them to call her 'Bella', cascading curls shaking around her cheeks. Sometimes, like just now, Olivia could not help herself addressing her by the full 'Isabella' because she had always felt it was such a waste of a beautiful name never to utter it.

"Livvy! What the fuck's going on there?"

Olivia smiled at the phone. She could just see those curls quivering again as the mouth contorted for the expletives she always reverted to when excited, angry or any of those other Bella emotional extremes.

"Bella, darling, how are you?"

"I'm fine, Livvy. Well, no, shit I'm not fine. You know that. But here - I'm not calling about that - what's all this back home?"

"What do you mean, Bella?" Olivia suddenly became cagey, trying not to let it sound in her voice.

"Christ, Olivia! You know, all that cars stopping and stuff! I've been trying to call you and text -"

"Yea, I know Bella. Sorry, so sorry. I've been trying to get back to you but there's a lot going on. I didn't want just a short call, you know -"

"Oh, I know, I know, Livvy, darling. You and me, you know, I don't take it hard. I know you'll call. But I couldn't wait. All I got is this stupid stuff in the papers over here about cars in the South, like something peculiar in the air, or something. I mean, what is all this? Reads like science fiction over here."

"Yea, it is a bit like that." Olivia was trying to think what else she could safely say to her friend.

"And - what else?" Isabella chimed in again, "Is that all you know?"

"Yes. I mean ... listen Bella, I was just going out, can you call me straight back on my cell. I'll talk on the way out."

"Yeh? You sure?"

"Yes, yes, honest, straight back. On my cell. Please, Bella, I want to talk."

There was something about the way Olivia said that which caused Bella to check instantly for the cellphone number and make the call, all in less than thirty seconds.

"Livvy?"

"Yea, I'm here."

"You all right?" Momentarily, she had forgotten her own reason for making the call, uneasy at the strained sound of Olivia's last few words.

"Yea, I'm fine", which was not quite how Olivia sounded. Then she continued, "Listen, Bella, I had to get off that phone. We're not sure about taps." She was outside by now, not going anywhere in particular except to avoid being overheard.

"What? Whaddya mean, 'taps'? You got a leak or something?"

"Might have", replied Olivia cautiously.

"Might have? What ... Livvy, what the Christ are you talking about? You got water in there, or what?"

"Wha - ? No ... leak -" Olivia smiled nervously to herself, as she walked down the street, " - no, I mean *phone* taps." Olivia was almost whispering into her cell.

"Eh? Livvy? What are you talking about?"

"Elroy warned us, that's all. Not to say anything we'd not want to be heard, on the house phone."

"Elroy? Phone? Christ, Olivia, you joined the FBI or something? Livvy ... hey, Livvy .. you serious? What *is* going on?"

Isabella's voice had also dropped from the near- shout it had risen to, in her perplexity, to an intimate tone of concern.

Olivia gathered herself and injected some energy into her voice.

"Yea, Bella, it's amazing. Loads of cars just stopped - broken down - all across the South; and other things, washing machines, TVs, kitchen things. And ..and... What they're saying is, they're all having to borrow each other's, share rides to work, do their washing, and all."

"Share!" Bella's incredulity bawled in Olivia's ear. "You mean, like the old days, take washing next door and all?"

"Yea, seems."

Bella burst out laughing in huge guffaws down the phone. Olivia wondered if it might be as much because she'd not laughed out loud for a while. Then the voice dropped again.

"Yeh, that's sort of what they're saying here in England but they don't go into it much. Like it's only the American South, sort of thing. But, Livvy -" her tone was serious "What do you mean about phone tapping, hun? Where are you?"

"In the street?"

"Going out?"

"Not really. Just ..just... getting out of the house."

"What? You scared of something, honey?" Bella felt nervous but powerless to be of any help so far away. "And who's Elroy?" she added.

"Bella", Olivia began, "Elroy, he's - did you never meet him? - Walt's friend, the electronics guy. He was in a bar one time."

"Black? Big guy?" Isabella was casting her mind back across a few years and three thousand miles.

"Yea." Olivia nodded into the phone.

"Oh ... yeh", said Bella, remembering, "fit."

Olivia grinned.

"Maybe."

"Oh-oh", Bella chortled, "well, I know, you only *see* Walt. Normal women ..." And she laughed again, bringing another smile to Olivia's unseen tense features. "But, hey, phone tapping, so he's the expert and all? Livvy, what the fuck's going on? You ain't got your phone tapped? What for?" She was shaking her head, her face creased with lines of bemusement and worry.

"I don't know. Bella", Olivia's voice hesitated as she attempted an explanation of sorts, "We're part of it."

"Part of what?" crackled the voice from London.

"This cars thing." And cutting off another incredulous response from Isabella, she hurried on. "It's Elroy. He had some kind of .. experience -"

"Experience?"

"I don't know. He called it, 'revelation'. Listen Bella, honey, I don't know, but they - him and Walt - they've got me involved at work. I mean, I wanted to help, El's so ..so ... persuasive, like some kind of missionary. And it's all for a good purpose. Bella, you just look at his eyes, you just believe him. But ...but now there's this ... problem."

"Problem?" In her mounting alarm, Bella only wished she could beam herself across the Atlantic to be at her friend's side instead of trying to understand and visualise her expressions and what she was trying to explain.

"Well, I don't know, Bella. Danger." Isabella heard Olivia emphasise that last word and then falter.

"Danger?"

Olivia tried to speak calmly but her voice was breaking.

"We - Elroy, he's started all this, some secret code he's got - I can't explain it all but we, Walt and me, we're in it too. Oh, Bella."

There was a silence followed by a long, low exclamation from the other end.

"Jeeeezus Chri-i-i-ist! Olivia!" Isabella really could not understand what her friend was talking about, except she sounded frightened, even from so far away. "Are you crying, hun?" she added in a tone of concern.

"Bella, honey, and are you okay?" Olivia sniffled the words, wishing to deflect attention from herself while she wiped away the moisture trickling from her eyes.

"What, me? Hun." Bella had to pause to accept this reversal of the conversation. She thought for a moment. "No, I'm not, Livvy. Like I said." She paused again. "It's ... awful." And there was a catch in her voice, too. They were suddenly joined in mutual distress, for their different reasons, across the distance that separated them. "I said are you crying?"

"Bella, honey," Olivia was wiping her fingers on her coat to dry them, "do you want to get away?"

"Honey?"

"Do you want a break, I mean, over here?" explained Olivia.

"Oooooh", Isabella gasped quietly. It had not occurred to her. She suddenly pictured a brief escape, a respite from the tension and bickering. "Would you want me there?" she asked.

"It would be nice ... cool", Olivia gave a little girlish giggle through her drying eyes, knowing she had used a word that Bella would have smartly added to her own contemporary lexicon.

"Hey, honey", Bella was smiling, too, all those hours and miles away and, like close friends, they could precisely visualise the amused expression on each other's faces. "It would be great ... cool dude." They were laughing together; they felt close. "I'll think about it. I mean, sort something real soon. As long as you don't make me share the neighbour's bath!"

Olivia was still smiling.

"Oh no", she said, "It's not happened here, in New York." And then, realising what she had said, was unable to prevent herself adding, "not yet."

Sharing

The second thing was: sharing really took hold. It gripped the whole South. You did not have to look far, it was there in your street, next door, everywhere. Linda Ross in West Virginia is taking Annabelle's two children to school ('Oh thanks, Linda, you're a peach! I just can't get this car to start'). Chuck Morgan's hitched a ride to work with neighbour Ezekial, even though Zeke has to go ten miles out of his way ('Gee, Chuck, this ain't no easy time! You an' all them others.' 'Thanks Zeke, saved my life!').

And so on, in towns and cities and tiny cut-off places where even three cars aren't enough to get Pa to work *and* Ma to the school with the young'uns *and* son Joey to his job, when one of the vehicles is just dead as a doornail and when you live nowhere near a rail station. And as for the buses! *What* buses?

And not only that. Molly Waites has a week's washing to do and the machine doggone broke and the repair man scratches his head, with all the inside bits out on the floor (the machine, not his head) and says it looks fine. Looks fine! So why don't it work, then? And the whole family wanting clothes for the week and all. But Rachel, good Rachel, three doors down - a hundred metres and more to walk with all them clothes in a basket - she takes *all* Molly's washing for her, *and* Karen's, and Belinda's, from up and down the street. All their machines broke! *And* cookers.

Folks even cooking other folks dinners for them. Here, there, Louisiana, Georgia, the Carolinas, Missouri, all over the South. Sometimes someone had a cooker working and a busted car, next door it was the other way around. Seemed obvious what to do. "It's what the Lord wants", they would say, or "It's how God wants us to be". But, as they became accustomed to it, more folks kind of found they enjoyed it as well. They wouldn't have to put up with it for long, of course, but there was a community spirit developing in the whole process of giving and taking, while somehow managing to do without exclusive access to some of life's essential accoutrements.

Those who had not seen the 'smiling Jesus', and listened to the Reverend Donahoe's words themselves, either heard it reported in other church services by preachers who had studied

the phenomenon on the internet and at hastily convened conferences and conventions, or listened agog to the accounts of those
who had been there. Everywhere was alive with talk of it. In a
part of the country famous for deeply held religious beliefs, high
church attendance and widespread acceptance of the influence
of the church on secular daily lives, an evangelistic fervour was
spreading like a prairie fire. The fact that the 'miracle' was
occurring on a weekly basis, wherever the ardent but exhausted
Dirk Donahoe preached, made it difficult to disbelieve, even for
the minority who were inclined to.

There were some heretical mutterings about overkill. The
affected churches swarmed with electronics experts and particle
physicists; that is, where the local pastor allowed and did not
regard it as challenging Divine authority. Dirk Donahoe himself
at length, after a month, permitted a televised truth test and
hypnosis - which he detested the notion of - and was duly cleared
by both. No-one could find any 'rational' or scientific explanation, nor uncover a hoax.

When anger began to rise, where congregations felt both
their faith and integrity questioned, the bevy of experts relented
and withdrew. They still sought an explanation but attention
became focused upon atmospheric particles, whilst motor engineers continued in their attempts to identify a common vehicle
fault that would unravel the entire conundrum.

"Look!" The big hand did its dramatic thump onto the boardroom table (connecting with the protective sheaf of papers laid on
top) and half a dozen pairs of eyes swivelled up to confront those
of Big Max Drummond blistering down at them. "There damn well
is something wrong with them, one helluva fucking thing, or
they'd *go*, wouldn't they! You know - vroom, vroom - eh, Abe?"

"We think", began Abe.

"You think! You think! If I goddam thought anyone in this
company was thinking, I'd ..." He halted, unable to conceive of
the reward, prize, bonus or any appropriate benefit he would
bestow in the unlikely event of discovering an elusive thinker
lurking somewhere in the building. "Nearly three weeks now -
and that's after we had three weeks to cure it in Virginia . And
now, where is it? Ten states?"

"Twelve", someone corrected him.

"Twelve!" exploded Drummond. "And how many cars?"

Tom looked up.

"Ours, Max?"

"Of course, ours! What do I fucking care about anybody else's! Ford can go hang. I hope they never start a car again!"

"Just over five thousand, Max."

"Five fucking thousand!"

They each managed to peer intently at the documents in front of them rather than look up during the deafening silence that had descended on the room. Drummond glowered like thunder and waited for the first who would have the temerity to raise a head and meet his eye.

"Max."

"Dawson?" Drummond succeeded in effortlessly reminding colleagues of their place in the pecking order by addressing certain of them only by their surname.

"Some of the cars", continued the insulted Dawson (Victor, as it happened) slowly, "have fixed -"

"Fixed theirselves?" broke in Drummond, a sarcastic gleam in both voice and eye.

"Well, Max, it's just a fact", Dawson finished, knowing he had nothing to lose in the pecking order of things so why not just say it.

"Is it?" Drummond breathed deeply, lowering himself into the chair at the top of the table. "Is it?" he breathed again, looking around the figures sat at the table. "And how is this possible? Fairies in the middle of the night?"

Company debates of this type, with many of the same intimacies, naturally, found their way into the media and, amongst all the many who read, heard or saw these reports, reached Elroy, who grinned. He was understanding more of it now. There had been that tiny part of the coded formula which had puzzled him because it indicated a circular activity, causing a repeating cycle. He couldn't see how he had missed it now, wondering when he first clarified in his memory how it would be logically necessary to disable any piece of equipment - car, TV, vacuum cleaner, and all - more than once. In the Virginia trial, his brief was to omit that section of the formula. Now he realised. It was indeed a self-repeating effect. Once the strings had been 'repaired' and the car or whatever worked again, apparently of its own accord, there was an unspecified time delay before the whole disabling formula kicked in again. Hey presto, busted car all over again, just when you thought it was fine!

When he told Walt, they were both spluttering over their double bourbons enough to nearly get chucked out of the smart New York city bar. Not only that, the formula included randomisation so the whole stop-start sequence was unpredictable over a period of up to two weeks for any individual item of equipment. Enough to drive more than just one Max Drummond bonkers. What about all the folks trying to plan driving, washing, cooking; in fact, plan life?

Not everyone was ready to share what was theirs. Some folks were saying, 'no way, not in *my* car!' 'Use my iron? Can't you get it mended?' 'Gee, sorry Julius, we got this dinner gonna take the whole evening to cook' (not entirely true, since they have to eat it before bedtime), 'Ain't yer got nothin' in the freezer? What, yer freezer broke?' So some folks just had to get along without their neighbours' help. Maybe it hurt a bit; maybe they understood. The ones that held back, some excused themselves by thinking: it's weeks already, surely things'll be fixed pretty soon. Motor mechanics, domestic appliance engineers, TV repair men, they were all doing a lot of head scratching but no fixing. No fixing at all.

Gradually, more people got accustomed to sharing what they had kept to themselves before. They were getting to know each other, too. Half-acquainted neighbours were all of a sudden sitting talking in each other's cars, chatting in each other's kitchens over one another's washing, cooking and ironing. Coming around for a drink, and a bite maybe, to watch TV or something.

Except Tony Delgardo. He wasn't sharing his wheels with anybody. Not anybody. Final. What's with the bus? Or legs? Anyways, a lot of times he was either fetching Suzy Rose or taking her somewhere or bringing her back, or maybe stopping somewhere quiet along the way. Giving other folks a ride? Huh. Just lucky *his* car was okay this time.

It had all happened over such a short period, nobody thought to do a count, nobody official. But it amounted to thousands and thousands of cars out of action, most of them eventually towed back home - rich pickings for the tow-truck operators - with no help but fine words from the manufacturers ("we're working on it as hard as we can") and a keen but utterly thwarted desire amongst all the car repair workshops to make a fortune, except that not one man-jack of them could put a single car right. A great many Workshop Bills spending a lot of time for no return.

Plus all the domestic appliances, TVs, hairdryers, you name it, that no longer functioned. Not reliably: for they started working again at different times, after a while, but only to pack in again a couple of days, or maybe a week or more, later. It got so you never knew whether something would work or whether it wouldn't: car, cooker, TV or anything else.

On the East Coast, where they were much more sophisticated, in their own esteem, they were bemused and amused. Whatever caused the problem at least it was confined to the South. They saw it all on TV and in the newspapers: stranded vehicles, comatose appliances; and all the good-neighbourly stories. All the radio phone-ins, too ("Gee folks, you're sure swell the way you're seein' this through", said the phone-in hosts). The New Yorkers and the New Englanders just smiled condescendingly: those poor simple southern folks.

While, in the mid-West and through to California they just shrugged and got on with life; if it wasn't happening to them, it wasn't happening. Nevertheless, many on both sides of the country were unable to entirely ignore the message that the behaviour, if not the technical breakdowns, was declared to be a response to a unique 'message'. That astounding factor escaped no-one's attention. This was God's own country and few, when the chips of faith were down, were prepared to deny it. Then, little by little, the complaints diminished. The state government offices, the police departments, even the car repair shops, received fewer calls. They no longer spent all day tearing their hair. People had given up on them and, also, had been finding their own way around this new, awkward life with so much success that they were adapting to it. This is what eventually led to the third thing. Before that, however, someone in a meeting somewhere deep in the White House finally said, "Where's the President? This is a crisis."

As Olivia had inadvertently hinted to Isabella, it was a crisis destined to spread.

Changing

What was taking place, it occurred to Elroy, was almost surreal. Across whole swathes of the southern states people were adjusting to a different way of life. 'Sharing' was being promoted as an evangelical mission in the churches but it was also becoming the only practical manner of accomplishing a range of ordinary day-to-day objectives: travelling, eating, laundry and the like. He had exclaimed in wonder to the others when he first heard about the Louisiana pastor, when they were together again one evening, this time at Walt and Olivia's apartment in New York.

"Don't ya see! I'm getting it now. This has gotta be the other part!"

"How do you mean?" asked Walt, quizzically.

"You know when you said, 'Is this it'?" replied Elroy, recalling his friend's scepticism about the outcome of their mission at the NSA site downtown. "This must be it." His eyes were rolling in awe. "He ... It ... He's going to the churches!"

"Elroy?" Walt was looking at him, features screwed up in puzzlement.

"You mean", Olivia joined in, "What you ... saw ... is in those churches?"

"The same?" He turned to her. "I dunno that. But something like ..." He shrugged and smiled.

"Honey." Mariana smiled in return and reached across from her chair to clasp his hand. All three looked at him for a moment, still unable to truly comprehend what he told them he had experienced.

Whatever it was, whatever the incredible connections between a brilliant mind with a vision and a pastor who could induce miracles, a profound change was in motion. At first, folks were taking the smaller items - coffee blenders, hairdryers, dvd players - to repair shops. They were getting them back still broken, only for them to work for a while then break again; or they'd get them back 'repaired', and charged for, only to break again and 'I'll have my money back, please'. But it was all so unpredictable that they soon stopped bothering. The larger items - washing machines, plasma TVs, ride-on mowers - mechanics would come round hoping for big paydays of continuous work, only to spend fruitless hours achieving nothing but a series of bitter squabbles about 'trying to charge for doin' nothin'!

That's when they started to give up, too. Might just as well stay home for nothing. Elroy noticed there were few, if any reports, of damage to particular items, perhaps where there might be implications for community health; so there appeared to be no broken fridges. Nor indeed did a single airplane fail while airborne, though a number refused to start up on the tarmac. Someone, mused Elroy to himself, must have thought this through. Someone ... or some other authority. Almost as though it were possible to identify the characteristics of individual strings within the atoms of particular appliances. Almost like each of the human genes, out of the sixty to eighty thousand, were preselected to perform unique tasks, or uniquely malfunction. He shuddered slightly when he realised all that, indeed, had probably been predetermined a very long time ago.

The media were, predictably - if anything could be predicted these days - of enormous assistance in accelerating the momentum. Give a bandwagon the slightest push and the media would spot its motion a mile away and run so fast to jump aboard that their sheer impetus would propel it headlong at ever-increasing speed. "Why, y'alls doing so fine for one another!" from jocks like Jerry Corrie on Chattanooga Two-Two-Two, swiftly transmuted to, "Why, what a fine gesture from y'all!" when folks called the shows to offer the use of appliances which still functioned - an ever-changing scenario, as quickly became evident. So it was no time before the radio shows cottoned on to acting as go-betweens, setting up 'share shops' and 'share lines' which identified a need and available supply, to match sharer to borrower.

It was the new craze. Forget the shock jocks - most of whom were canny enough to adapt rather than die - now it was the 'borrer jocks'. It was already as socially-acceptable to borrow as to lend, since it was inevitable the roles would be reversed on a daily, sometimes hourly, basis. In fact, if you were not sharing something with somebody, people started to talk.

TV and newspapers were onto it like dogs after a rat. Neither enjoyed the immediacy of live radio programmes but newspapers and magazines were able to report the tales and set up 'share pages' (though frequently superseded by the pace of changing circumstances), whilst TV could show it in pictures and reinvent daytime shows in the blink of an eye. Reporters with camera crews infested streets and homes, exposing the secrets of next-door's undergarments as they emerged from the shared washing machine.

Hundreds of friends and neighbours traipsed nose-to-tail through TV studios to proclaim their new-found familiarity and comradeship, almost entirely displacing the existing shows where many of the same sort of people had previously been insulting and abusing each other over extramarital relationships and similar outrages. And all the time, meanwhile, most people never knew if their car would start up, or break down, or where, or when. If they were getting used to it, actually, collectively, managing with fewer cars on the road at any one time, the car-makers and repairers certainly were not.

Biscuit

"Biscuits", grunted Gabriel, engaged in some unsavoury deep mining enterprise.

There being no biscuits in Heaven, the Lord felt obliged to pause in His ruminations on matters celestial and wait to see if there was to be further elaboration on matters biscuit.

"Is that what You meant," continued the angel, glancing up in mid-scoop (the Lord tried not look: difficult for One who is All-Seeing and All-Knowing and everything), "about if someone down there would decide to have a biscuit or not?"

Ah, pondered the Almighty. The predetermined biscuit conundrum. The paradox. He had, indeed, attempted on one occasion to explain the paradox to Gabriel in terms of coffee and biscuits but, He had concluded, with a marked lack of success. An archangel can be very clever with wings and equations but still have trouble with eternal contradictions, even when spelled out in terms of coffee and biscuits. Simple for God, of course, and He recognised that. If God couldn't grasp it, who else stood a chance? How the course of history or, at least, a series of events making up part of history, could be changed just by deciding to have a biscuit. More accurately, choosing the cup of coffee immediately preceding the biscuit.

Ingenuously (ingenuousness, surprisingly, being an occasional characteristic of the Supreme Being), He had considered the coffee and biscuit explanation would finally get it through to Gabriel. Wherein (and that's a divine-sounding word for a start) if someone chose 'coffee please' instead of 'tea thank you', it might be an exercise in self-determination ultimately leading to the child being killed by the bus. The 'tea thank you' might have been predetermined at the Beginning Of All Things but 'coffee please' was the choice actually made: self-determination exercised on a whim, at an unpredicted point in time. Perhaps a sudden change in the light; a leaf espied floating past a window; an internal passage of wind from a few too many forkfuls consumed the night before; a faint aroma of cheese; the colour of the hostess's hair. Any one of those might have minutely diverged from its preordained destiny since the Very Beginning, thus unexpectedly triggering 'coffee please' instead of 'tea thank you'. A whim. A decision unforeseen. A change.

The biscuit was accepted because it happened to be enjoyed with coffee, whereas it would not be taken with tea. Hence, the hostess ran out of biscuits a little sooner than had otherwise been ordained and thus went to the shop for more biscuits on a day other than that which had been predetermined. And on that particular day, in the company of young offspring - because it was a Saturday, not the preordained school day - happened to encounter an old friend just outside the shop, who would not have been there had it been the otherwise predetermined biscuit-shopping day. And, while distracted in happy conversation in this unpreordained encounter, while in the company of child who would otherwise have been at school, mine biscuit hostess let loose both her grip and her attention on the child, just as a bus – which itself would not have been there at that precise time on the *preordained* biscuit-shopping day – came throbbing by.

Escaping child and large heavy bus collide at an exact time and place only resolved by the previous exercise of self-determination or self-will – perhaps as much as a week or two earlier – to choose not 'tea thank you', as had been predetermined at the Beginning Of All Things, but coffee please'; and 'oh, yes, a biscuit, that's nice'. One dead child. Yet somehow during that apparently simple elucidation, the Lord had sensed the angelic mind wandering, the attention faltering, and a frown deepening on the brow. When the foraging resumed, God knew he had lost him.

"Yes, that is what I meant", responded the Lord. "The consequence of an unpreordained decision which we can neither predict nor alter."

"Mm", nodded the angel, attention obviously divided between this enlightenment and other more organic revelations, "I see."

But the Almighty was not at all sure he did.

Departure

There was no way Bella could have known the next occasion was to be the following day. Olivia could not confide anything like that. What she had told her friend on the phone already was enough and she had not elaborated on the details of the NSA exercise, enabling Elroy's access to the satellite signalling. Nor could Bella have predicted the time of the next power cut, frequent but unpredictable as they were. Only the Good Lord could know that. Neither could she have foreseen Paul's reaction. Surely not even the Almighty would have got that one right.

She had delayed telling him until the last possible minute, packing her bag while alone in the house, unsure whether it would spark a row, of which she'd had more than enough lately. It was only going to be a few days, after all, although she doubted it would feel like enough by the time she was due to return. She was about to phone for the taxi to take her to Heathrow for the Thursday afternoon flight and thought she ought to at least give him that much notice. He did not explode. He did not argue. Neither did he shrug, with a more expected 'okay if that's what you want' attitude. He did not make what she anticipated would be a complaint about not having meals cooked (when did she do that now anyway?), or bed made, or shirts ironed (she had made sure there were several in his wardrobe;

she did not begrudge him that part of the bargain; he earned the wage).

No, he just stood there, while she waited to pick up the phone. In his eyes there was a look she could not remember seeing for several years, one that passed deep into her without bearing any expression she could define. Once, that look used to mean love, when she learned to recognise it. It bore no question, no acquiescence to her desires, no dispute, but seemed to carry him into her soul for her to do with as she pleased. It used to be his way of giving himself. Now here it was again, as if he was saying, 'Why have we fallen apart? We have forgotten how to be together'. He merely said, with that look in his eyes, "Okay.. okay", and nodded quietly, adding, "Say hello from me."

It made her pause, her whole intention for a moment suspended in time. It all took place in an instant: that look, her meeting his eyes, and the flicker of a shutter, up-down, inside her head, that was the instant of doubt - shall I, shan't I go? - all in no more than two seconds. A pause. It was not the decision of whether or not to go that made the difference, for she would have gone anyway, whether she realised it or not. It was those two extra-seconds pause. Did all the years, hours, minutes, seconds in his life lead inexorably to that look? Did all the time in hers lead to that pause? Or was there a momentary displacement in the predetermined order of things?

In that moment, the moment when she would have picked up the phone for the taxi, it rang. It was nothing but Ruth and the next rally. Would she get a banner made - they'd pay out of the donations - and could it be ready in time? Not only that, would she organise her section of the march and make sure everyone knew the rendezvous and where to take their places? And more. And more. Yes, yes and yes. Usually, she would have happily chattered along for ever but she kept looking at her watch and calculating the time.

Ruth finally rang off twenty minutes later, by which time Paul had nodded his way past her to go out. After which time, also, three taxi firms said they were struggling to meet demand but they could be with her in half an hour. Thirty minutes! Okay, all right. She worked out the time. Even with security, check-in would probably let her through a quarter of an hour late. Just.

Then came the power cut, moments before the taxi was due. Earlier, and she would have been well on her way. Twenty minutes later the driver was apologising as she clambered in. Thursday afternoon was bad enough but - power cut - chaos! Creeping in stop-start lines to negotiate road junctions, dead traffic lights and roundabouts. They both agreed, as they got under way, the ratio of traffic speed to traffic lights not working was completely illogical. Like rain. Why is it always *twice* as slow in the rain. Same number of cars, aren't there?

However, even if everyone in a car grumbles and curses, it does not make the traffic move any faster. It was nightmarishly slow. She dashed out, left the change, ran and bumped her way into the terminal and up to the desk. Sorry, madam. Missed it. She waited until the evening flight, phoning Olivia to tell her she would be later than planned. It had only been a two-second pause. And for nothing you could predict. Just that look.

Eye

"Oh no!" The cry came from behind the bathroom door. Walt groped his way upstairs in the dark.

"You okay?" he called out.

"Yes", called Bella's voice, "but I've dropped the torch ... hang on ... okay ... shit ... it's broken." She had felt around and found it, pushed the switch, but no result.

"Wait a minute..." Great, thought Walt, edging his way up, hand against the wall, feeling his way. We finally get back at one in the morning just in time for a power cut, and now this. If she'd arrived when she said she was going to, we'd all have been in bed by now and no aggravation.

So friend Isabella was going to be late, Walt had learned on arriving home from work, and it would mean going to JFK around ten o'clock at night to meet her. Marvellous.

"Didn't you *tell* her what we're doing tomorrow?" Walt had asked his wife, over dinner.

"How could I?" Olivia had responded in alarm, "I can't tell her that. Can't tell anyone." Her brows had knitted, knuckles tightening on her fork.

"She's your best friend", Walt had observed, "You said you've told her about this."

"Only that we're involved. That's all, no details, nothing about what we're doing." She said nothing about admitting 'danger' to her friend. But she was relieved only she and Walt, with Elroy, knew what was going on and she felt safer for it, no matter how high her regard for dear Isabella. "What are we going to do with her?" Walt had demanded; and Olivia mildly scolded him, "She's not a bag of garbage, Walt." So okay, she would settle down with books, magazines, dvds, TV. "She won't be offended, Walt, she's not a child, you know. We'll just say we've got a lunch engagement."

Lunch engagement! Olivia felt she would like to sleep through the whole of tomorrow and wake up on Saturday. The subterfuge unnerved and unsettled her, however Walt and Elroy tried to assure her there was no way anyone would find out. And Isabella would be late but at least she would be here. "You want her here?" Walt had checked. "Of course, she's my friend." A friend at her side, even if to be kept out of the loop. Best for all of them, Olivia considered. Keep danger within the tightest circle. It was only fair. Not her fault she was late. Power cut and traffic in London. Same everywhere. "Tell me about it," Walt had grimaced. Out of their control.

Except there had been that one look. Something Gabriel knew as a 'biscuit'. An event outside the preordained order of things, leading to an act of self-determination. An unscheduled pause in a sequence of events. A delay. Changing the future. From just one look.

"The torch - it's probably not broken", Walt called to Isabella from the pitch darkness. "It's a bad switch. Stay there, I'll be with you." He continued feeling his way upstairs.

"You all right there?" came Olivia's voice from the lounge, where there was already a flicker of light as she found candles and matches.

"Yeh, okay", called Walt, "just the torch." And then spoke to the invisible Bella as he reached the top of the stairs, "Here I am."

"Oh, thanks, here's the torch." Bella pulled at the door then pushed, since it was, in order to create more space, an outward opening bathroom door. It flung open sharply, as she stretched a hand to pass the torch through in the dark.

"Agghh! Christ! Agghh! ... Agghh!" Walt staggered back as the leading edge of the unseen door struck him in the face. "Agghh! Christ!"

"Oh God!" exclaimed Bella, dimly seeing the shape collapse on the floor in front of her. "Livvy!" She screamed. "Quick! Oh Jesus, God!"

Walt was lying muttering, "Christ! Shit! Ooohh!" And groaning, almost invisible below her.

Olivia had found the other torch in the darkness downstairs and was running up to see what had happened. Walt was lying on his back, a hand held tight to one eyebrow, blood seeping through his fingers, groaning and cursing.

"Oh, Livvy, I'm sorry", faltered Isabella, "It was the door ... I didn't know..." And then she was suddenly shaking and sobbing. "Oh-oh Livvy, Oh Walt, I'm so sorry. Oh if I'd got here earlier .. This wouldn't have happened! ... It was the phone, you see ... I was held up ... It rang .. Oh-oh .. Walt, I'm so sorry.. Please, are you all right ...?"

Just a look, and a pause, that's all it had been, that delay. Changing the order of things.

"Would You know?"

This is not a question you sensibly address to He Who Knows Everything. The Lord refrained from speculating upon what it could be He might *not* know.

Gabriel raised a shifty eye at Him then lowered it again.

"Would *we* know?" he corrected himself, "Would *we* know?" A compromise he considered did not suggest blank ignorance confronting absolute knowledge. Angels, as much as anyone, need their self-respect.

"I mean", continued Gabriel, features screwed up in concentration at the enigma, "after the very first time there is a change -"

"Self-will?" queried the Lord.

"Mm", nodded the angel, "after that, that first change in the Order, nothing afterwards is preordained. Is it?"

"As if," murmured God, half to Himself, "once the first independent decision has been made - the very first act of unpredestined self-determination, the paradox - the whole of predetermined future has been altered. So, from that point, nothing is as it was originally preordained."

"Yes," Gabriel agreed, earnestly. "So would we know about any *other* change? How do we recognise if they've gone off their predestined path, if nothing has *actually* been predestined since ... since the first time they -"

"Went off it?" suggested the Lord

"Yes", concurred the angel and looked at Him, his everlasting Almighty, as if to say, 'so what's the point in being God?'

The Lord looked on him benevolently, with deep understanding at his confusion, a confusion which had simmered within the angel for most of eternity in spite of His periodic attempts to explain it.

"It doesn't work like that", He said at length.

Gabriel eyed Him dubiously.

"Any act of self-will", proceeded the Lord, "merely transfers the future from one preordained path to another. Think of it as railway lines", He explained, utilising an Earthbound analogy, since that was the location of their present engagement. "If you are travelling along a railway line - with consideration", He added, before Gabriel could butt in with one his unhelpful objections, "for the fact you are an angel, not a railway train - if you slip, by means of a set of points, from that line to another adjacent to it, you proceed in that, alternative, direction. The line, though, has always been there, as has the one you have, until that moment of change, been travelling on. Both lines have begun at different places, which have not altered, and are heading towards different destinations, which have remained fixed. Only your position has changed: you are now travelling in one fixed and predetermined direction instead of another. And you will continue to do so until you change to another line which, like the others, is waiting in its fixed position to carry you to *its* predetermined destination. It is the directions and the destinations of the lines - in both directions, past and future, which are predetermined. You merely make decisions which transfer you between them. Eventually you will remain on a line until you reach its destination."

"Your end", summed the angel.

"Precisely."

"And it might not even be a concious decision?" wondered the angel, "A deliberate act of self-will?"

"Indeed no", agreed The Lord, "perhaps a mere whim, a change in the pattern of thought, the briefest pause in the preordained order. Enough to dislocate it. Sufficient to change-"

"from one line to another", pondered the angel. "So You..."

"I predetermined all the possibilities, all the lines, allowing intelligent species in the Cosmos -"

" - including humans", interjected the angel, as if to be sure.

"Yes, including humans, Gabriel -   to make decisions to transfer between - "

"Lines", Gabriel finished.

"Exactly."

"Millions of them!" The angel shook his head.

"That would be an understatement."

"For all planets, all species, all individuals -"

"For the Universe", God interrupted him.

Isabella was still shaking and sobbing as Walt eased himself up on one elbow in the torchlight.

"It's okay, Bella," muttered Olivia, kneeling with the torch to examine the damage. "How are you, hun?"

"Dunno ... Oooh! ... "Walt squinted up at her. He felt dazed. "Where are we?"

The torch shone on a deep cut in the eyebrow and forehead. Next, Olivia had found a bandage in the gloom of the bathroom and the two women were somehow staggering downstairs, supporting most of the weight of the injured man between them. He 'felt sick'. "Concussion", decided Olivia, and, "Hospital for you." "But tomorrow!" he groaned. "Tomorrow nothing!" was her retort. "But who will go with Elroy? It *has* to be tomorrow. He *said* ... He *said* ...!" Walt mumbled as they stuffed him into the car for the drive to Emergency.

"Tomorrow?" sniffled Isabella, wiping a hand across her tear-stained face beside Olivia, Walt slumped in the back seat. "Lunch? With Elroy?"

"Not lunch, Bella dear. Oh Lord."

"How many are there?"

"What?"

"Lines", Gabriel explained, "'railway lines'."

"To count would be to separate the inseparable", the Almighty recited to him, "to quantify would be to divide the indivisible. For every choice there is a line, upon every line lies a multitude of choices."

Gabriel thought for a moment.

"So we still wouldn't necessarily know which change has made a difference. Here, now, when it matters. If any of them have started on a new ... line ... the cause might not be here where we can see it. It might have been something not very obvious -"

"Indeed."

" - at any point in their past."

"There might be one single instance which led to this point in their time but itself may only have arisen as a result of another change of course previously, and another before that", the Lord said.

"And so on back through their history", concluded Gabriel

"Exactly so", said the Lord. "All we can do is identify the course they are *now* pursuing, in order to influence it - if we believe that we may. And if we believe that we should", He added.

"Because it's no longer the original Plan", replied the angel.

"Quite." The single affirmative disguised a sea of deific doubt.

"It's like cause and effect", considered the angel.

"Self-will and predeterminaton." agreed the Lord.

"Biscuits and railway lines?" suggested Gabriel.

"An interesting juxtaposition."

"Chicken and egg."

"If you say so."

"You can't say which came first because you can never trace it all the way back."

"Well, One can, actually", remarked God,

"It must have been a very big bang", mused Gabriel.

"Indeed it was."

And it's not as easy as it looks, being God, thought the angel to himself.

Bones

"So Isabella will have to come instead of Walt, Elroy".

"What!" Elroy's voice on the phone betrayed alarm, concern and doubt all rolled into one, at Olivia's statement. *"It's gotta be Walt!"*

"I know, Elroy, but he can't!"

They had spent half the night at Emergency: six stitches, moderate concussion, back at five in the morning, the two women helping woozy Walt into bed. Three hours fitful sleep and Olivia was up again, on the phone, out in the street with her cellphone (a security measure she now adopted automatically), not knowing what to do.

"Gee, Olivia."

"Yes, I know, Elroy, but he just can't get out of bed. It's a kind of twenty-four-hour concussion, they said. If he's on his feet for more than five minutes he starts to sway about."

"Where is he now?"

"Sound asleep."

"It has to be today, Livvy."

"I know." Olivia would not have minded if this was the grand excuse not to go through with it but she understood very well it had to be done. This, Elroy said, was the big push. He'd been 'told'.

"Can't you get someone else", she asked.

"Yeh, if we were the genuine guys, no problem. But we aint.'

"Can't you do it on your own?"

"No way. It has to be two. Security. Both witnesses to each other if anything aint right on the 'systems check'. Huh", he chuckled ironically. *"They all know that. Can't you just get him on his feet, pump him some pills or something? Anything?"* He was beginning to sound desperate.

"Elroy, he'll just collapse on us." She paused. "So - Isabella. We can trust her, Elroy. You remember her?"

There was a slight pause at the end of the phone.

"Yeh, Sure. Sure." Elroy was nodding but frowning. *"Trust her with your life, Livvy?"*

A brief shiver of fear ran through her.

"Yes, I can. El, do you think - ?"

"No, Livvy, no. But you know what I mean. This is real, this aint the movies, this aint no game."

"I know that", she responded with a quiet resolve, "I would trust her with anything. But I'll have to tell her a bit, you know, I can't expect her to come in blind." She wondered whether Bella would remember her faltering reference to phone bugging and danger. "What about her security clearance", she added.

"I can do that now. Just need her details. You sure of her?"

"I'm sure, Elroy. Can you fix all this in time?" Her anxiety was no more than seeking practical assurance by now. The game was on.

"Of course, Livvy. This is what I do."

"You would know. Wouldn't You?" insisted the archangel, looking on. *"You* would know: if it's not what you preordained? You would remember what You had preordained and what You hadn't? If it was going to affect the Plan?"

The Lord wanted to say, "Yes. Of course." But, really, was He supposed to remember *everything* He packed into that infinitesimally tiny dot of matter? Every nuance, every nod, every wink, each pause, all the merest, briefest, most subtle shifts in expression and changes in decision, amongst all the myriad species populating all corners of the Universe, which might now be recognised as having been preordained at the Beginning Of All Things, as opposed to those that, here and there, arose as expressions of self-determination, dislocating the preordained order of things, changing the predetermined future? Was He supposed to have remembered all that?

Instead, He said, "Mmm. We shall soon know. We shall soon see if anything has distorted the Plan." And Gabriel thought, 'well, anyone could say that. You don't have to be God to say that'. But he held his tongue.

If you pressed the button for the sixth floor at 'Housteads', the elevator stopped at the fifth. No matter how much you pressed it again, hit it, thumped, kicked, it would not budge any further. However, very few ever tried. No-one who was not supposed to go to the sixth floor generally got as far as the elevator. Nothing sinister. That was another clever bit. You just got politely halted at ground floor reception. If you were for 'Housteads' you were directed to one of the first five (including ground) floors. If you were expected on the sixth floor, someone came down to meet you.

This was guaranteed because the receptionist, at the rather unprepossessing - even scruffy - desk in the entrance lobby, was not 'Housteads', she was NSA. Although, naturally, no-one knew that, except sixth floor staff, and then not all of them. There were also a couple of fairly large, bulky but fit gentlemen in black leather jackets in a booth just out of sight of the reception desk, in case anyone, unjustifiably, persisted in demanding Floor Six.

Occasionally, one would make it to the elevator only to discover the unhelpful Sixth Floor button. Eventually, they would come down; or try various other lower floors before finally re-emerging at ground level. (There were no stairs. Just a suspended fire escape at the back). None of this occurred more than once or twice every few months and the leather-jacketed gentlemen were permanently bored. Mostly, when it did occur, it was an honest mistake so they did not even get to exercise the special qualities of their trade.

Olivia Brown, and the handful of others who worked anony-mously on Floor Six, did not even give the Floor Six button a second glance. They just spoke their names. The receiver was not programmed for their names - it didn't care who they were - it only recognised voices. If there was a match, a small circular panel glowed, the size of a war medal, and an instruction, 'touch here'. The owner of the voice then pressed lightly with a thumb. If the thumbprint matched the voice, you went up to Floor Six. If it did not, you just stayed at Floor Five until you gave up and went back down.

If a movie scenario took over - or a nine-eleven - and you were genuine but had a gun to your head, you touched with your left thumb. The prints are different. The left thumb sent the elevator plummeting to ground level, simultaneously sounding an alarm in the security booth. In that event, the leather jackets would be flung open during the charge to the elevator door, revealing weaponry adequate for most contingencies. It had never happened, devoutly though the two gentlemen had wished for it. The principal safety valve was still intact: nobody knew NSA was there.

Olivia, being in charge and totally security-cleared, could vet and admit visitors using standard procedures. Actually, they were supposed to acquire HQ low-level clearance first: basic ID with photo match. Elroy, though, had tapped into that system from somewhere else - he wouldn't say - and got a bypass for both himself and Walt, on their previous visit, and now Isabella.

Barely three hours since Olivia had clicked the phone off and hastened to her duties at NSA, Elroy had collected Isabella and brought her with him, exchanging reintroductions and delivering a briefing in the car. She did not have to do anything, she was just another 'body' so it all looked up front and official. He was concerned she seemed anxious despite his reassurances and wondered what the Browns may have told her. They stepped through the elevator doors onto the sixth floor and through a set of glazed double doors to a small entrance lounge, where Olivia was waiting for them.

"Good morning again, Missah." A scrawny black guy, in a dull blue brushed cotton suit that hung on him like he was a coat-hook, emerged through the double doors behind Olivia, peering at them all through thick, round social-issue glasses.

."Hallo, Charlie", breezed Olivia with a smile This is Mr Jones again, and Mrs Watkins", indicating the new 'Systems Analyst' at her side. Bella smiled at the scrawny black man with his goggle eyes.

"Ah yes, massah, nice ter see ya again. Yah. The ol' systems again, yah?"

"That's right", acknowledged Elroy with a slight frown. The geezer must have ears like a donkey and picked up a snatch of conversation. Still, no harm done. Systems check was their cover so it was almost a bonus the more who were aware of it. Anyway, the guy was security-cleared like the rest.

"Charlie Bones", Olivia had chuckled the first time. "Security-cleared if that's what you call it. Poor guy worked here before, therapy-cure from a community home. Main security is he basically doesn't understand much of what goes on around him. But keeps the place spotless and fixes lightbulbs and things. It was more 'normal' just to keep him on. Did the checks on him but of course nothing there. .. in more ways than one." Slightly cruel for the gentle Olivia, had thought Elroy, but people are usually a bit different in their working environment. He allowed her to lead himself and Bella to the signals room, with Charlie Bones shuffling rather superfluously behind.

In that small, windowless room, about four metres square, three walls were completely lined with grey and black computer hardware, top to bottom, some plain, others with display panels, of which about half flickered with green, blue and orange metering, the rest dark. The rear wall was filled with the electric power and connection stacks, the kinds of thing offering nothing but bafflement except to electronics engineers. There was just space for the door in the corner. Elroy sat in front of the large display monitor and its moving dots again, with Olivia and Isabella behind him, having ensured Charlie the caretaker was left outside.

He touched a key on a small black box adjacent to the main keyboard and looked up to check the result: the moving dots were each replaced by a set of digits and characters. Each denoted a satellite somewhere in the heavens above Earth, the characters were each satellite's ID. Elroy touched a second key and the characters were each substituted by another set: x,y,z co-ordinates. He touched a third key and the dots returned. He grunted quietly, as if expecting nothing less. All set to deploy Piggyback. Big time.

It never seemed quite clear, afterwards, where exactly it went wrong during what followed; quite what they could pin down to their change of plan and what was already in motion. Elroy had tapped in the code, then the satellite co-ordinates - three sets this time - and then Bella, watching him with nervous fascination from behind one shoulder, suddenly perceived an incredible opportunity.

"Elroy." She leaned over and spoke conspiratorially, close to his ear. "This is amazing. Is this what makes the cars stop?"

Elroy grunted and half looked around at her with the hint of a mischievous smile.

"Elroy", she breathed, as Olivia looked across at her in concern, "Elroy, can you do London?"

Her graphic complaints about traffic and power cuts had punctuated their conversation continuously as they drove nose-to-tail through mad Manhattan. She'd had no hidden agenda, merely prompted by the familiar mayhem around them. Suddenly, though, she saw the solution being enacted in front of her. The antidote. The answer.

The excitement rose in her voice as she pleaded, "Elroy, please, can you do it?"

Something stirred in Elroy. He glanced at Olivia, who had stifled a startled exclamation at Bella's words but now regained her impassive bearing, her features displaying only her anxiety at the danger she felt for herself, her job and the companions she had conspired to admit for this enterprise.

"Gee", Elroy whistled through his teeth. Now he, too, could envisage how this might spread. He had no 'instructions' for this but if it was the right thing here then it must be right everywhere. It was his mission. He could feel the shiver down his spine whenever he recalled the visitation. He felt it now.

"Yup." He gave a determined smile as he swung back to the keyboard. Bella gave a shudder of delight. Olivia frowned nervously and almost intervened to hasten them away but Elroy was already tapping at the keys. He could pick his own date for this.

"It'll have to be later", he muttered. "Might start to ask questions if they're all at the same time. Leave it a month, maybe."

"Okay", whispered Bella, tense with excitement. She watched as the formula reappeared on the screen, then he was tapping the satellite co-ordinates. Neither of them heard the click of the door. Olivia did.

"Why, Charlie", she exclaimed. "You again! How long - ?"

"Sorry, missah", came the thin-voiced apology, as Elroy swivelled abruptly around to see the goggle-eyed odd-job man. "My, you's just doin' them same figures as last time, massah!" he exclaimed ingenuously, as a child delighted at viewing a favourite sketch drawn for him on the blackboard.

Elroy was taken aback, as if the unannounced presence of the man wasn't enough.

"How did you know - ?" he began. Then realised he had not completed his task. But in the confusion of the interruption, his mind for a second went blank. He could not remember precisely which point he had reached in the program. Bella was staring at Charlie Bones. There was something uncanny about the way he stared back at them and at Elroy's fluttering fingers on the keyboard. She wanted to get out, her excitement had drained away, replaced by the undercurrent of fear fuelled by Olivia's hesitant admission of 'danger'.

"Let's go", Bella moved impulsively but caught Elroy's chair as she did so and stumbled into him. His fingers were retyping co-ordinates, repeating moves he was unsure whether he had completed the first time. He looked up, startled at Bella bumping into his chair, and lifted his eyes, but not his hands, from the keyboard.

There was a brief, semi-articulate exchange of "Wha - ?" "Sorry, Elroy", then "Hell!"

"What, El?" Olivia turned her attention back from Charlie Bones to Elroy, who had suddenly stiffened in his chair, switching his gaze from keyboard to screen and back again.

"Hell, that's not right!"

"What, El?" from Olivia again.

"I've hit the wrong key. Oh … shit." He breathed the last word in a hush, staring intently at the screen of moving satellite dots, then switched it into co-ordinates mode. "Oh, shit", he breathed again, slowly exhaling the words through half-open lips. "Oh, holy shit."

There was a knock and the door swung open, causing Charlie Bones to shuffle out of the way. A man appeared partway through the doorway.

"Mrs Brown."

"Yes, John," responded Olivia to her subordinate, trying desperately to maintain her managerial calm.

"Head office called just now. Said they want to fix a day for systems check."

He looked at Elroy at the computer console, and Isabella near him, in puzzlement.

"Isn't this the check now?" He addressed the question to Olivia, the silently blinking Bones shifting from foot to foot beside her.

"Yes, yes," replied Olivia, hurriedly. "A mistake, I guess, I'll get back to them. We're finished now."

Bella was already edging towards the door, uncertain what was going on around her, forgetting entirely the thrill of the moments before.

"Yes, we're going", she nodded to John at the door.

"Wai -" Elroy began but Olivia cut in with, "You *have* finished, I think you said, Mr Jones?" and cast her eyes at the screen, still showing satellite co-ordinates parading across the black background.

"Yes ..er .. Mrs Brown", Elroy hastily agreed and, seeing what she meant, turned to add a few key-taps, whereupon the 'System Check In Progress' caption appeared, replacing everything else.

Bella was hurrying through the door. Olivia summoned enough self-control to wait to usher out Elroy and pass through the door held for her by the uncomprehendingly obliging Charlie Bones, and ensuring John headed back towards his office.

"Come on", Bella was taking charge of their departure despite herself and found she was glancing back nervously at the shuffling figure of Charlie Bones peering blankly at the three of them as they made for the elevator. She couldn't wait for the door to open. She suddenly felt she was in the wrong place at the wrong time but could not work out what had changed from a few moments before. They stepped in and Olivia spoke her identification. The dial lit up and Bella, seeing it, said, quickly, "Here?" And pressed with her thumb.

"No - !" cried Olivia but too late to halt Bella's nervous impulse. Bella and Elroy started in alarm and all three sensed the elevator plummeting with unnatural speed.

"It's okay", uttered Olivia, swiftly, knowing what was happening, and braced herself facing where the door would open. "Don't say a thing", she said grimly to the other two, "I'll deal with it."

"With what?" queried Elroy in concern but his question was halted by the rapid bump of the elevator as it made its emergency halt at ground-level and the door opened for them to be faced by the two heavy men directing automatic weapons at their faces.

"Stop! And raise your hands!" one of them barked, as they both squinted down their gun barrels, legs splayed and braced to fire.

"It's okay, guys, it's okay", Olivia spoke with supreme calm, without moving from behind the opened elevator door. Bella was rigid with shock immediately behind her, Elroy frozen in helpless fear at her side.

Olivia slowly raised the ID card hanging from her neck and held it towards the guards. It was an unnecessary gesture as the one who had spoken lowered his weapon and addressed her.

"Sorry, Mrs Brown, we got the alarm." He raised his gun again and aimed it past her towards Elroy. "You okay, ma'am? These with you?" He added suspiciously.

"Yes, Drake, it's fine. Just a mistake in the elevator. Systems Check. The visitor -" she indicated Bella - " was not aware of our security. Pressed the button for me." She gave a little shrug and a smile and Drake the security guard followed suit.

"Sure, ma'am. Easy done."

"I'm sorry for the trouble", Bella smiled weakly at him as they stepped out into the lobby.

"Not at all, ma'am, we just sure have to be ready, that's all." He smiled in return and the two of them withdrew to their room, disappointed again.

Olivia ushered Elroy and Bella outside.

"Oh my God", she breathed.

"Look, don't worry about that head office call", said Elroy when they had each recovered their composure. "I got this all sanctioned through the security system. These IDs all check out, so does the firm we're supposed to work for. We do this all the time, Livvy, it's our usual dirty business. Your head office will do a check then make a call to verify and they'll get the answer they want. Don't worry, hun."

"You sure?" Olivia looked earnestly at him.

"Yup. Honest."

"But in there", broke in Bella, who had regained some of her composure, "what were you saying?"

"Oh, yeh, oh Lord", muttered Elroy. "That guy coming in, threw me, and then you bumping into my chair, I was just hitting the satellite co-ordinates again to make sure. But it knocked my hand."

"But you did London?" Bella asked with concern.

"Yeh, yeh, I'm sure I did. I'm sure I did the first time, now I think about it. But that second time, I was repeating to make sure but my hand was knocked .... Oh holy shit."

Olivia knew very well this kind of language was normally well out of order for Elroy, even if Bella did not.

"What do you mean, Elroy?"

"I think I've set it up for somewhere else as well."

The two women stared at him.

"Where?" Bella was the one to ask.

"Not sure", replied Elroy, "Not sure but, I think, China."

"China!" both women exclaimed in unison.

"Yup", replied Elroy in a tone that was resigned more than troubled.

None of them could think of anything else to say. Let's face it, thought Elroy to himself, we don't really know what it's all about here, never mind the other side of the world.

He and Bella went through formal handshakes with Olivia, for the benefit of anyone who might see, and set off. Olivia returned to the main doors, deep in thoughts that refused to put themselves into any rational order.

From a sixth floor window, a black guy in blue overalls was gazing at them as they parted company below. He had removed his thick-lensed spectacles and was methodically cleaning them with a soft yellow cloth. His frame seemed less meagre and his eyes sharper and more focused than when masked by the glasses. He was not smiling and was holding himself uncharacteristically still.

"She shouldn't have been there, should she?" muttered Gabriel, from their vantage point in Heaven.

God said nothing. It had only been one look. Just one look. And the pause that followed. Now He remembered. That pause. The slightest delay. The merest dislocation. He remembered, now, it was not in that dot of matter. It had not been preordained. But then, He sighed inwardly, what could He do. That was the whole idea. Their ability to step outside the predetermined order of things. He had granted them that. So what, now, could He do? He was only God, after all.

Gabriel was muttering to himself. "Biscuits. Railway lines. Earth. Didn't I just know it."

Spreading

"ABC News ... Good morning ... southern seize-up spreading ... and west to California..."

"CNN twenty-four-hour news ... all western states ... cars breaking down ... domestic equipment ..."

"WBGH Boston ... has the seize-up spread east? ... cars ... washing machines, vacuum cleaners ..."

"New York CBS news ... no answer to the systems bug ... car makers ... engineers..."

It was difficult to believe there was still no solution. Over a month it had been, nearly two if you counted back to the first time in Virginia. How come modern technology was stumped for an answer? No part of any car or domestic appliance appeared damaged in any way so could not be effectively 'repaired'. Replacement of individual parts made no difference. The only way was to replace every single moving part. That was only reached by trial, error and despair.

That, though, was tantamount to replacing the whole god-damned thing, or all the parts that made it work: a whole engine and every other part in a car, the whole motor and accessory functions in a washing machine, all the filaments, microchips, circuitry, connectors, resistors, and the lot in anything relying on electronics. In other words, apart from the body or the casing, new-for-old.

First of all, hardly anyone was prepared to pay for that, just on the say-so of the mechanic who wanted to charge a fortune for it. Secondly, no company on the manufacture or repair side of things had the resources to become involved in a wholesale replacement of absolutely everything that failed to work - which was a helluva lot of items - with all the hassle of whether or not people were prepared to pay, especially when most items managed to 'fix theirselves', if only temporarily. More-over, they did not feel inclined to give in just yet. There must be a reason.

Theories were emerging, almost entirely unhelpfully, from the scientific quarter. The favourite one was the surge in electricity, and accompanying static, when power resumed at the end of a blackout. On its own, it could not be the cause, but there was talk of the increased sensitivity of modern microchip technology and heavy reliance on computer circuitry. Was there also a possible conflict with the additional carbon dioxide in the atmosphere? Global warming! Gamma rays were posited as the 'wild card' in all this; immediate research was needed to discover whether gamma pulses may have increased, emanating from a cosmic explosion. It all seemed far-fetched but, then, so did the problem itself but there it was. It was real; and everyone was searching for any explanation.

Elroy and the others were lapping it up. A three-day gap between the West and East sides, plus another strike in the South to 'top it up' - that was Elroy's three sets of co-ordinates - soon the whole country was in the grip of the 'bug'. People had

started calling it that and it stuck. It defied diagnosis. It possessed a quality of the unknown. What was it? Where did it come
from? You couldn't see it. You couldn't get rid of it. 'Bug' suited
it perfectly.

Elroy especially liked the reference to power surges after
blackouts. He wondered if that really could be why both
'piggyback standstills' had occurred shortly after a blackout had
ended. Just as a red herring. Surely not. Who could have predicted the blackouts? Only someone who knew most things, if
not everything. Indeed.

'A 'smiling Jesus' in New York', proclaimed the New York
Times on the first Monday. It was true. In the Church of the Holy
Name in uptown New York City, where Dirk Donahoe was
nowhere to be seen. The 'enlightenment' befell Father Daniel
Peck. He was not the only one. It soon became clear the miraculous
phenomenon had descended upon a few more churches scattered
across the United States, now taking in the Mid-West, West,
New England and the eastern seaboard, where they had only
heard about it up until now. It had spread beyond solely
Donahoe's Louisiana church to some others in the South, too. It
had become a blessing shared.

Gabriel wished he had a map.

"Some in the morning, some in the evening, a few in the
afternoon", soothed God later, "Nicely spread out."

"Nicely", grumped Gabriel, "I've hardly finished one when the
next one's opening his mouth", he protested.

"Well?" the Lord remonstrated mildly, observing that doing
shepherds and wise men on camels at the same time had not
been too much trouble.

"Yes, but", argued the angel, "not absolutely simultaneously.
Not like Some I know Who could have managed it a lot easier",
he humphed under his breath.

"Gabriel." On this occasion the Lord considered it was
appropriate to quietly remind the angel there were not many
things he could say which would not be overheard.

It even provoked Brother Teng into cracking a joke, if that is
what you call it, of the Confucious-he-say variety: "He who can
still drive an American car, drives a still can." It took the thirty
seconds or so of Teng's silently shaking frame, as he revelled in

his own mirth, uneven teeth revealed in a split grin, for Hoi to work it out. He smiled in response; in fact he managed to force a chuckle for his 'brother'.

"Very good, Brother Teng", he lied.

"Well, well, Brother Hoi, we have certainly chosen the right moment to consolidate our new market. The cars are ready, I trust?"

Hoi nodded politely.

"Good. Very good. People will be here tomorrow to prepare them and bring the gifts."

"Those dolls, Brother Teng?"

"Quite so, quite so." Teng smiled and nodded, performing his slight ritual bow and crab exit.

'Confucious', Hoi grunted to himself when alone. And those dolls, for goodness sake. He scarcely believed the London man would refuse the cars without them. It was the price he was being persuaded to sell them at that was the lure. Yes, precisely, he frowned. He had no desire to rub his hands over the accounts on this particular deal. Perhaps he could allow himself a consoling gloat over the Americans instead.

"Philadelphia WBED, the morning show! Call two-one-five, two-zero-four, eight-five-three-nine, with what you need and what you got ... And let's sha-a-a-a-re it all around!"

It had not taken long for the pattern in the South to be imitated everywhere else.

"Hi y'all this fine and dandy afternoon! Randy Waller, your borrer jock ...!"

"Sacramento KFBD. Hokey Burns is a-giving a ride from LA to Vegas tomorrow morning. Call nine-one-six, seven-six-six, six-one-zero-one! And call that same number if *yo-o-o-o-o* got anything for other folks!"

Some resisted. Especially some busy people anywhere from Manhattan across to Seattle.

"I'm not giving a ride in *my* car! I got places to go! Let some other guy!" (meaning 'stupid sucker').

It was different the next day, though, when the busy person's car refused to start.

"Hey Myro", he wailed on the phone, "You going my way today?"

Elroy and Walt could not resist sharing their delight on their mobiles every couple of days. What legitimised the new behaviour in most people's eyes was the extraordinary display of the same miracle in church-after-chapel the breadth of the country. After a while, few places remained untouched. Where a church itself remained 'less blessed', (sometimes only because Gabriel could not find it or, to give him his due, because it did not possess the right kind of window), it was emptied as its congregation headed for one known to have 'the light', piling into any available vehicle that worked: friends, neighbours and sometimes even sworn enemies, all crammed together.

"There seems to be", a leading social psychologist solemnly declared on a TV talk show, "a collective spiritual awakening among American citizens." Being a social scientist, the words 'religion' and 'faith' stuck in his throat before reaching his lips but people knew. They just knew. In God's own country, this was some kind of a new dawn. Not only that, it was something practical you had to adjust to. If it don't work and no-one can fix it, complain, yes, complain until you and the poor guy who sold it to you or tried to repair it are blue in the face. After that, you have to get used to managing without it.

Managing without it.

A Detroit car company tried virtually giving away a couple of car-lots-full of brand new models in a new-for-old deal; and, 'friends, you don't pay us a dime'.

"Okay. Do it for the first thousand who apply!" barked Drummond. He made it sound convincingly like his own idea. Actually it was Victor still-only-Dawson who had suggested it.

"How about -"

"Yes, Dawson?" snapped Drummond.

"How about giving some people free part-exchange. A good-will gesture. It will both get a lot of our new cars on the road - high profile - and give us a lot of cars to work on to find this fault."

"Fault?" glowered Big Max.

"Whatever it is we have to find out, Max", interjected Abe. "Sounds like a good idea of Victor's."

"Who?" was Drummond's abrupt query, followed by a furrowed glance across the table at Dawson and, "Humph. Oh yes. What do you mean by 'free part-exchange'."

"We just take their car - provided it's ours - and give them a new one closest to it, no price difference to pay."

"Jesus", breathed someone.

Drummond thought.

"The other thing, Max -" Abe spoke up quietly.

"Yes?"

"Sales are falling. People are losing faith. They're concerned if a fault's not found it will be endemic in new models as well."

"Right", declared Drummond, "This is a good idea; gets us back on the road. First thousand and we'd better goddam find the problem amongst that lot! We'll win this goddam ball game, eh guys? Meeting over."

But the sheer logistics meant it would take a while to shift the cars out to their eager exchange-happy 'buyers': long enough for the first ones to start breaking down before too many had reached their new owners. The scheme collapsed barely two weeks old.

"They're what!"

"Breaking down, Max", was a cowed mutter beneath eyes reluctant to raise any higher than the voice.

"For Christ's sake!" A mighty hand did a mighty thud on the table high up somewhere in the car city. A mighty unhappy collection of faces around the table. "Find the fucking fault!"

"Max", a low sigh from a patient but worn-out associate, "we don't think it's a fault."

"Oh no?" A sneer from behind tightly-pursed lips. "It's perfect but broke, eh? Perfectly broke?"

The other car makers got wind of the idea before it was too late, scared stiff of losing yet more of the market to a mistrustful but car-adoring public, and all got *their* vehicles out on the same deal. And the same result. The result? No-one trusted any new car because all makes had joined the same race and all had tripped over on the starting blocks. Not only cars. For a while, people were buying new cleaners, washers and cookers; but not many and not for long. Word got around they were just liable to break down.

"The strings in the atoms were penetrated before the components were even manufactured!" chuckled Elroy to Walt. "How clever is *that*!"

Managing without it. Had anyone but the poor ever heard that phrase before? "What ya doing Al?" How ya going on, Jean?" Whaddya got Louise?" Howse y'all making out, Joel?" "Why, Philly, sugar, didya get along all right now?"

"Same as you, Mandy." "I guess, like y'all, Elma." "Why, I aint really thinking about it, Jesse."

"I'm managing without it."

Managing without it. Even in those high class neighbourhoods where everyone has everything and don't expect to share what is private. Like Elroy. Ho, ho, he was having his morning chuckle when Mariana cried out her car wouldn't start. Children to get to school, job to go to. Elroy was on a deadline, had to hurry to work in the opposite direction. What to do? Phone a neighbour. Yes, he ruefully saw the funny side. He had no special dispensation.

Neither did Walt and Olivia when their vacuum cleaner stopped vacuuming, just after one of them had spilled crumbs all over the carpet. Walt had to laugh when he told Elroy Olivia had sent him next door to borrow one. You know, he said, he knew all about what was going on but, even so, it felt quite natural to go around and knock on the door to borrow a vacuum cleaner! Like they said about the old days when they went next door with a cup for sugar. So the old folks used to say.

Managing without it.

Some tried not to take part. There were instances here and there of petty violence. People forcibly having their cars taken from them by those they refused to offer a ride. There were examples of plain, ordinary theft, under the guise of 'sharing'. Society is not Utopia, whether undergoing change or not. Quite understandable, the not sharing, quite natural. Except, things were not natural. The repeated 'smiling Jesus' emphasised that.

The sole topic of conversation everywhere - bar, office, home, bed, beach, car (!), party, Congress when not passing laws - everywhere, was the way things were changing, how parts of life were being lived differently. Sharing? Managing without it? Like all 'religions', it was not universally followed. Worship is rarely universal, except by order. But this 'religion', or way of living, suddenly pasted onto a new awe - thank you, 'smiling Jesus' - of the other, 'true' religion, meant most people were thinking much the same way and getting on with it together.

"Let's face it", as Gabriel put it when unable to conceal his grudging satisfaction at the unfolding outcome, "they're thinking quite a lot about You."

"Mm", murmured the Lord. So far.

Bella was back home, glowing. She could tell Paul nothing. She had sworn not to tell anyone. Anyway, she was scared. Perhaps she might have felt compelled to confide in Paul just to relax the tension inside her. There was a space between them, though, across which confidences could no longer reach.

Paul was scarcely interested anyway, until it occurred to him that the increasingly damaged reputation of American car-makers might filter into the American-owned share of the UK market and enable him to focus more attention on these new, reliable Chinese 'Manchu Mets'.

"Better and better, is it not?" smiled Teng to Hoi, who smiled weakly in return, "Yes, indeed, brother Teng", more worried at the way the accounts were not quite adding up as a result of the Society's determination to push the cars into London at any price. His customer must be rubbing his hands in glee; as, indeed, Paul was.

Bella risked one phone call to Elroy. "No, hun", he said, "I don't know exactly. I got confused with that caretaker guy, you know, like I said, I think London is in about a month. Not sure."

"And China?"

"Gee", he whistled softly, "Don' know. Just don' know. I wish ..." But he did not know what he wished that might spoil everything right now.

"Retail sales in sharp fall!" proclaimed the Herald Tribune.

A warm Spring was giving way to the start of a hot Summer, all the forecasters were predicting. And the start of the third thing which, up to now, they were not.

"Wall Street down!" shouted the Washington Post, an organ of the media not given to shouting but this was not looking good.

"People just aren't buying the goods", moaned more than one senior executive gazing out at an unchanged landscape of high-rise offices, towering above lower profits, quieter streets, fewer people, emptier shops. Well, the appliance and electrical stores which sold things with motors, chips and circuits, they were emptier. That is a lot of shops. Most clothing stores, they were all right for now, until the third thing really got under way. It was happening too fast for anyone but economists to make the connection.

There was a sense of missing leadership. People wanted to be reassured this was the right way to go. It felt good but was it right? The President. The President had said nothing but brushed away questions, saying people were making the best of things, the experts would soon have it sorted out, no crisis.

"No fucking crisis!" Drummond's reaction echoed a thousand others in the higher echelons of big business.

In fact, managing without and sharing many of the customary trappings of modern life no longer presented too much of a problem, let alone a crisis. Remarkable how people adapt; like during a war. Like wartime, they felt the need for endorsement or, if it were appropriate, rebuke. Someone above, saying it. The Lord, yes He had spoken, as it were, in that strange and wonderful manner. But what about the President? What are Presidents for? The President, huh! Everyone knew what would be occupying the President. No change there.

That was how the President ran the country. Foreign governments had quickly come to realise it would be advantageous to send emissaries who were young and good looking; handsome, well-built men who were less capable of subtle diplomacy than considerably more besides. They were not too sure who came out best from it, that was all. The emissaries got an audience all right, no problem there, but the diplomacy not infrequently became muddled. 'Securing good relations' would be the bland diplomatic phrase, as the President gently patted the departing supplicant on the buttocks.

Nevertheless, this was a President who commanded as much respect and admiration as any other in recent history and certainly enough to smother any hints of disdain. The popularity of this antidote to the historic parade of grey-hair-dark-suits-narrow-minds in the Oval office was not threatened by personal predilections, however thinly veiled. On the contrary, the dalliances behind the closed doors of the White House served to underline America's diplomatic supremacy over jumped up nations who expected to 'get one over' this unlikely holder of the highest office.

The landslide election victory had been testament to the people's canny ability, on this occasion, to get it right. That was why, as much as anything, they were beginning to feel abandoned by the occupant of the House on the Hill, who might just forget about attractive young men for a moment, if you don't mind.

Meetings

"Come along, boys, we have customers!" Serenity of spirit made Asif Hassan a stranger to such base sentiments as irritation. He remembered how he used to have to exercise conscious self-control to overcome the petty anger and jealousies of youth and he had not always been successful. Latterly - and he was still only in his mid-forties - the infusion of inner calm, which he sensed was more than just maturity, enabled him to accommodate most adverse circumstances with a benign, if sometimes resigned, smile.

He never cursed - not even to invoke the aid of Allah - he rarely frowned and no-one could recall the last time he raised his voice in anything but an attempt to make himself heard above the roar of London traffic; or, indeed, to summon his staff from their pursuit of indolence at the back of the shop. Frustration, though: he could not entirely suppress that. It was frustration which caused him to feel edgy and under pressure as he was attempting to cater alone for the queue of customers at the counter.

"Meetings, always meetings", he smiled ruefully across the service top, as he handed over a carrier bag of paper-wrapped bundles in one hand, change in the other and turned his eyes to the next in line to take the order. "Boys! Come along!" He threw the command in English to the doorway behind him, with a half-turn of his bearded face.

Paul Best pushed open the door, with its jingle-jangle bell, to hear the slightly anxious tone in the voice, as he joined the queue of half a dozen or so. The proprietor smiled briefly in recognition and raised a pair of eyes to the ceiling with a smiled, "meetings", again. There were footsteps on stairs from behind him somewhere and two young men emerged through the coloured plastic strips hanging in the open doorway, wispy jaws - scarcely true beards yet - and introverted smiles greeting the clientele.

At Paul's turn, it was the owner who served him.

"Kebab again, sir?" beamed Asif.

"Yes, thanks", Paul responded with a slight smile of his own. He was tired, as always, by the middle of the evening at the end of a long day but the warmth of the man's welcome was endearing.

"Glad you like to come back, sir", smiled Asif, as he turned the skewer on the grill. "You should try something different one day. I'll recommend ..."

"Thanks, I will", Paul replied. True, he was a bit unadventurous with takeaways and not always confident about what he was asking for if he had not tried it before.

"You finish late, a lot?" chattered Asif over his shoulder from the grill.

"Yes", acknowledged Paul, adding: "Cars."

"You sell cars?" Asif was returning to the counter and adding portions of salad to the meat in the pitta bread.

"That's right", Paul confirmed, "some new ones coming tomorrow. Chinese."

"Oh?" Asif raised a pair of bushy eyebrows. "I didn't know they sent cars here."

"First ones - second batch", explained Paul. "First private, you know, not Chinese Government."

"Ah", nodded Asif in understanding. "A good thing they aren't American, eh?" He grinned, tapping a knowing finger to the side of his nose.

"Uh?" Paul did not follow the reasoning.

"All breaking down", added Asif, still grinning confidently.

"Ah." Paul smiled in acquiescence. "These won't break down."

"Buy British, eh?"

"Buy Chinese", countered Paul, still with a smile.

"Of course. Just so", agreed Asif. His two assistants had both paused in what they were doing, apparently interested in this account of the Chinese motor trade, until Asif directed a meaningful glance at them and they turned their attention to their duties.

"A busy day tomorrow, then?" suggested Asif to Paul, as bundle and money exchanged places over the counter.

"Yeh", nodded Paul, "a bit of a show as well."

"Oh?" The eyebrows made half an ascent. "Well, enjoy your meal."

There was another rumble of footfalls on stairs at the back, as Paul pulled open the door. He was aware of a group of three or four figures appearing around the corner of the shop as he stepped outside, presumably departing by the private side door. They hurried past as he made for his car at the kerb.

"Huh!" Paul exclaimed as he nearly bumped into one of their number, trailing behind as though he was not part of the main group but setting off on his own. "Oh, Mr Sing. Hello." Paul greeted the little man in surprise, as he recognised the organiser and 'compere' of his Manchu Met presentation show.

The slightly-built Chinese man looked up at him with an expression of similar surprise and hint of a frown, which he swiftly replaced with a polite smile and a nod before he scuttled away along the pavement.

Strange, thought Paul. Perhaps it *was* Mr Sing he saw here a few weeks ago. Unlikely companions, surely, Chinese and Asians. Huh, don't think so, he reflected as he settled into the driver's seat. Just a coincidence, walking by at the same time. Could hardly imagine Sing and those lads and their friends sharing a joke over a cup of coffee; or whatever else they might do in that back room. He chuckled as he drove off, the improbable image in his mind. Maybe he's flogging them Chinese mushrooms! And he laughed out loud at the wheel, for a moment, as though highly entertained by the crawling traffic.

Lotus

The atmosphere was cool, tense. Elroy felt it as soon as he entered the room. He would have preferred not to go alone. He would have liked to be in the company of his friend, and now 'partner-in-crime', Walt. But it was one of those LOTUS meetings restricted to members and co-optees strictly associated with 'research into new markets' or, in Elroy's private definition, which country 'we're going to crap on' next. He knew he was an outsider himself in this context but they had to include him for his observations on preparatory surveillance and the probable subsequent method of communications subterfuge.

These meetings were reduced to a hard core of six plus himself. He was sure there were other instances of even fewer conferring together, not necessarily at formal meetings, from some of the remarks and asides which bore no obvious connection with the subject under discussion. Some oblique references escaped on occasion, such as indications of the type of misinformation which might trigger the next 'liberation and reconstruction' campaign. 'Nuclear threat' and 'endemic terrorism' were notable examples.

The others were already gathered round the table, as though they were just concluding a prior meeting. Slick-Hair raised his eyes and gave Elroy a nod as he arrived. The Federal guy, chairing at the head of the table, greeted him with a curt 'Fitzgibbon' and vaguely waved him to the two or three available chairs. Elroy was aware of several pairs of eyes being raised to view his entry. He was granted a couple more nods and a grunt, otherwise expressionless responses as he lowered himself into a spare chair down the left side from 'Fed'.

"Unusual times, Mr Fitzgibbon", the chairman addressed him, with hands clasped beneath his chin, resting it on two index fingers and staring at Elroy through narrowed eyes from the end of the table.

"Yeh", agreed Elroy, glancing briefly around the others, each looking at him, except Slick-Hair, who was examining notes on the table, and the 'observer' woman who was looking impassively at the chairman. "Yeh", Elroy repeated, sensing that something more by way of a contribution was expected from him, "nobody seems to know what it is, eh?"

"No, Mr Fitzgibbon", agreed the Fed chairman, eyeing him thoughtfully.

"We wondered", the single 'State Department' man (Elroy doubted he really was a *bona fide* government man) joined in, "if you had any ideas about these atmospheric theories, you know, gamma rays and all." He, also, fixed Elroy with an intense stare, as if to drill the answer out of him.

"No", Elroy shrugged and wanted to run his finger around the inside of his collar, where it suddenly felt tight, but resisted any gesture that might indicate discomfort. "No, it's not my field", he added helpfully, "I can't see what could cause it. I guess the guys working on these theories'll work it out soon."

"You think so?" murmured the chairman, drily.

Slick-Hair indicated the white screen set into the wall at the bottom end of the table.

"We've had a computer model programmed", he said, his eyes taking in all of them but dwelling momentarily longer on Elroy, or so it felt. He struggled to maintain his composure. Walt and he had already discussed this type of scenario, where it would be all too easy to appear compromised even where there was no logical basis for suspicion. "Guilty conscience gives you away", Walt had warned, without any more confidence in his *sang-froid* than his friend. Mind over matter. How could anyone possibly know? It is too improbable to believe. Keep telling yourself that. Elroy was silently telling himself now and hoping he looked calm, assured and as unenlightened as the rest of them.

Slick-Hair had clicked the remote control and a graph was displayed on the screen, showing two irregular lines descending in parallel from left to right.

"This is what", he explained, "it predicts. One: mistrust of all technological products - mainly anything that uses electricity, but not exclusively those; cars, especially, and a whole range of domestic equipment - washers, televisions, cleaners, you know the kind of thing. Two: people stop buying new. As we know, this is already widespread, and getting worse. It's fuelled - and I apologise", he grimaced and looked swiftly around the table again, "for my choice of the word - but it's *fuelled* by this 'sharing' craze."

"Jesus wept", muttered the chairman, rubbing a palm across his brow and clearly unaware of the contradiction in what he had said. "You understand this, Fitzgibbon? You're a religious man?"

"Sure", Elroy shrugged again, taken aback at this casual reference to his personal faith which suggested it was common knowledge amongst some who scarcely knew him. It was not as though it marked him out particularly, except in present company, perhaps. "Sure. But I only see what everyone sees." And he managed a wry smile, adding, "my wife's car won't start and we're hitching rides with other folk. Ain't got much choice." He hoped he was not placing too much emphasis on being as much a victim as anyone.

"Yes", the chairman acknowledged, unable to contradict the obvious that most people were encountering the same problem in one form or another; it was not collusion to seek similar solutions.

Slick-Hair continued.

"This -" moving the screen to the next chart " - reduction in demand leads to a general downturn, falling sales - which is occurring already - leading to falling demand for raw materials; shop closures; short-time working; layoffs; falling incomes and - well, you know the cycle -"

"Slump", muttered the automobile executive.

"The thirties?" broke in the 'State Department' guy. "Depression?"

"The issue is", interjected the chairman, "and I'm only spelling out what we know, when people aren't driving, or buying, cars, not using half their electrical goods, not earning the money to buy things which they're scared will break down anyway, *we* don't sell the oil - *or* the coal -" he directed a courteous glance at the newcomer on his right, whom Elroy had not recognised, "because", and he lowered his voice for maximum impact, "nothing is moving, working or being manufactured anymore."

He stopped and passed his gaze slowly around the faces looking back at him, down one side then up the other, pausing a fraction longer on Elroy, two seats away.

"And what makes it more of a goddamned problem", the words spitting now from barely moving lips, "is they're all *sharing* everything instead."

Elroy felt a sudden thrill of excitement inside and it was all he could do to prevent his face breaking out in a satisfied grin. He heard his voice participating in the deprecating discussion which followed, while his mind was racing with the implications of what had just been revealed. Of course! This was it! He could only dimly see it but it began to make sense. The 'sharing' brought on by Piggyback, reinforced by the phenomenon in the churches, it had reignited a sense of community and all that.

Fine. But why? Of course, that was not the point. It might enrich communities but it was only a means to an end.

He bet to himself that, if the computer model had been developed further, rather than halted at the diminished demand for oil and coal - ah, he realised now, the new guy must be one of the coal magnates stripping the tops off mountains to get at the shallow-lying black gold - the program would have revealed far wider consequences. For starters, the global climate -

"Oh, they'll kiss their goddam asses over that", the 'CIA' observer was growling, "but they'll soon shuddup about clean air and no more global warming when it means no job, no dollars, no auto, no fine clothes, no ...life!"

"The bottom line is", declared the chairman, levelly, "we got wells and tankers busting with oil - *and* mountains of coal -" someone laughed ironically at the *double entendre* " - and if we can't do something about it, that's exactly where it's going to stay. And that's *before* the next project, which I guess we may not be getting on to today."

"The fucking President", someone muttered, to a ripple of ironic chuckles and a couple of "yehs."

"We need", announced the observer woman, in a tone that lacked amusement, "some young guy to go in there and *persuade* -" and she looked meaningfully in the direction of the laughs " - the President to get our message out: this whole sharing thing is just stupid and is going to wreck us all - and all them damn fools, too."

"Yeh", agreed the chairman, "You got the guy in mind?"

"No, I sure don't", she bit on the words and a few of them wondered just what kind of guy she did have.

"Well, we could work on that", the chairman picked up on the momentary awkward silence, "could be our best shot. Send me any ideas, soon as you got them. Get our guy in there, play this right and the President could turn this whole thing around. They listen to this President", he grimaced, as if he were admitting the 'runs' was good for you.

"It won't fix the cars", commented someone.

"Sure, no", conceded the chairman and he shot a penetrating glare at Elroy. "You *sure* you got no suggestions on that, Mr Fitzgibbon?"

"Why, I really wish I did", replied Elroy, fixing an honest gaze on the Fed man in return.

"We just had reckoned maybe," came Slick-Hair's voice, which had remained largely silent except for his exposition of the computer prediction, "you might have worked it out." And the way he looked at Elroy caused a trickle of sweat to slip down the back of his neck beneath the constricting shirt collar.

"Just racked my brains", confessed Elroy, "and got no explanation. I'll sure keep trying."

"We sure hope you do", said Slick-Hair with a thin smile and looked away.

The meeting was declared over. It had got to the point when it could not end soon enough for Elroy. In a rational world, he would not have been surprised by their assumption that he, the wizard of the technologically unfathomable, would be ready with the answer they wanted. And he would have experienced no discomfort in protesting failure. In this unreal world he now inhabited, every nuance and frown aimed in his direction was translated as suspicion and doubt.

Nobody knew. No-one *could* know. It was not just unbelievable, it was *unknowable*. He was safe.

"Good-day."

"So long."

Courtesies exchanged as the group departed. Elroy felt the sweat begin to dry and his collar loosen. The Fed guy, chairman, followed behind Elroy and paused to nod briefly at Slick-Hair, who remained seated at the table. As soon as he was left alone, he pulled a phone from his pocket and dialled.

PARADIGM : BEGINNING

The tiny thing lay on its patchwork bed of leaves and dried seaweed woven on the rock. Puckered creases caught tints and shadows from the sun as she gently bore it from under a shaded ledge to show him. It rested with its shrivelled features screwed shut against the brightness, some streaks upon it, of ruby red, drying to mahogany, trapped in the wrinkled crevices of its skin. It was beautiful.

"He is beautiful", she whispered, gazing on it with her liquid smile.

He dropped to crouch beside her, the hunter's wary poise, but his face was soft, his stretched limbs relaxed.

"He is ... beautiful", he murmured.

The entrail was at her feet, where she leaned on the same rock, her hands stained dark red and brown from drawing it out of her; the last act of birth, the first of a mother. Crouching, he took her streaked hands in each of his, kissing them lightly, one each after the other.

"I shall feed it to the beasts", he smiled.

"And the birds", she smiled , too.

"They will feast upon you." His voice was light with the joy of a father, the humour of the hunter with a new son.

"And then perhaps we shall feast upon them", she laughed softly.

"We feed upon each other." His eyes twinkled in his amusement, yet there was a wisdom in his eyes. "They are for us, and we are for them."

"My love", she murmured, still with her smile and clasping his hands more tightly before pulling away to caress her newest love, her baby boy.

"Ah", he nodded, "one day indeed we shall die and they shall feed on us. Life for life."

She gently lifted the naked thing to place it once more in the cool beneath the ledge of rock. He rose to his feet, proud and with a full heart, feeling pureness in the air around them and basking in their sun of life.

Repeat

Elroy drove home as night gathered. Hours after the LOTUS meeting, he was a maelstrom of emotions. Excitement, at what he was beginning to comprehend. Anxiety, unable to shake off the unease which had stalked him since departing the portals of 'Apex Insurance'. Regret, as the realisation grew that his role in this awesome enterprise was now over. It was a turbulent mix. The fear which curdled unforgivingly in his gut was like the troubled water upon which the tremor of anticipation, the oil - hah, a fitting metaphor! - was poured. He could not quite work it out. Practical surveillance was his game, not soothsaying. He could discern a shape in the mist, though, the unravelling of a riddle.

The key was the disquiet amongst the LOTUS cabal. To use less, to share more. To thwart the ambitions of the corrupt and powerful? No, that was a sideshow, surely. To spite the few might be a justifiable cause in this instance but scarcely a noble one. Such a thing could not be driven by petty motives, not if the source was what he understood it to be; what, indeed, had visited him.

He shuddered. He remembered what else was churning inside him: the knowledge that he had stepped outside the manifest; broken ranks. He felt sick. Whatever had possessed him to listen to Isabella! Possessed? Was he? Everyone knew about being possessed by evil - spirits, the Devil, drink - but possessed by good? So much in thrall to a benign force that you lost your independent reason just like you were high on cocaine? He had never taken coke so he could not square with that one. He only knew he had leapt at her suggestion as though he had been given control of the wheel.

What? A naive seaman taking the helm in a storm! But he could recall no captain hollering from the bridge, "Hey, you, Fitzgibbon! Set a new course, just as you please!" He wished he had heard such a voice, to validate his decision. In cold reflection, he only wondered if he was no longer in command of himself. Possessed? Who said London? Bella did. Was that enough? Touch his elbow, whisper in his ear, light a gleam in his eye, and he was off, charging riderless into the fog. London.

Well, whether it was prescribed or not, he could not stop it now. And China! Oh, the Good Lord, which was as near in most circumstances as he came to blasphemy.

At least no-one would find out. The formula deleted itself within seconds of the program's completion. Simple enough: a novice programmer could do it. There was no trace in the NSA system and no signature left in the transmission. He relaxed somewhat. He had felt better earlier, having detoured on the way home to stop for nine holes and then a drink in the club-house. The Elbow had been a bit shaky, someone had remarked; and someone else had laughed, 'bent El'. It was the sort of joshing his friends could venture with a man confident in himself, although this evening they noticed his laughter in return did not bear its usual heartiness. In these lighter evenings towards summer, they could play quite late - "hit the goddamned thing, it's white isn't it!", they mocked each other - and enjoy a drink on the veranda looking out at the sunset.

He remembered that walk home at night, that other, cold, snowy night. No reason why he should recall it now, driving through a warm early summer night, except maybe the hollowness of the feeling that, for him, it was over. Regardless of his maverick actions with Bella at his side, there was no way he could take it upon himself to 'play God' around the world.

Besides, it was odd, but he was having difficulty repeating the formula. He had tried bringing it to mind, just in case it might be needed, though he was convinced the occasion would not arise, but it would not piece itself together in his memory. He reckoned perhaps he was just tired at the time and it would return when he was more alert. But he sensed it was fading away, its job done. Was he programmed to fail, too? At any rate, this vital and complex program, part inspired from outside him, part invented by him, was it designed to disintegrate after a certain time? The strings of his atoms programmed like those in a vacuum cleaner? If so, something told him they would not, in this instance, 'fix theirselves'.

On no account, it had been made clear during the miracle, was he to write it down. Sadness infiltrated him as he sat at the wheel, nearing home in the dark. The glory would live within him always, he was changed by it. But never to experience it again.

He yearned now for that visitation, more ever than a lover bereaved. Just a glimpse. Yet he knew in his heart it was a betrayal even to hope for such consideration. Even once, it was a vision denied to almost all others.

He turned into the sweeping arc of his entrance drive. The house was dark. Mariana and the children were staying overnight at her mother's: one of the reasons he could dally at the golf club. He often made a bit of a boast of it in advance, in general conversation: "My night on the tiles tonight!" They all knew the regular family man would spend the night happily in his fidelity bed, not on any tiles. He flicked the hall light switch. Nothing. Power cut? He flicked it up and down again a couple of times.

Blackouts were more unusual just lately, with lower demand on the electricity grid: half of all appliances were not working at any one time. Must be a fuse this time, he thought, and noticed lights glimmering through the trees from other homes. He closed the door behind him, thinking about groping for the torch, finding the fuse box or, alternatively, just going to bed and fixing it in daylight. Then he noticed it. The light gleaming from under his study door. His heart leapt; and then welled. After all! After all: he dare not think it, he dare not hope it. No, this could not be. Why now? Then, in terror, it struck him: was this the visit of remonstration for his wilful act at NSA? Or, worse, retribution? No, not from the Benevolent, All Beautiful, All Wise. He was almost singing the hymn aloud.

He had no choice but to move forward. He allowed himself a sardonic, suppressed grunt: would he have gone to bed and left this just to .. to go away? His inner confidence was returning, as he recalled the experience of just a few months ago; a confidence that, whatever the reason for this second visitation, it might not be to congratulate him - oh vanity! - but surely not to admonish him. His heart was leaping. Perhaps, after all, it would be instructions for a new phase, an episode he could not even imagine. He was already at the door which, again, was off the latch, the light spilling out onto the polished wooden floor, bright as he remembered it. Ha, he had thought then it was spotlights - the interrogation. No, it was more. Much more!

A smile was spreading across his features in the half-light, a smile of delight, warm with welcome, almost ready with recognition as one greets the unexpected visit of a long-lost friend. There was no hesitation now, none of that perspiring summoning of will with which he had thrust open the door that other time. He pressed against it firmly but smoothly, allowing it to swing gently open as he entered and turned to face across his desk, as he did before, at the brilliant light bathing him in its glow.

He blinked for a moment, adjusting to the glare, then slowly felt his body go tight. He stared ahead of him, disbelieving.

"Do sit down, Mr Jones."

Elroy blinked again and a bead of sweat trickled down his cheek. The spotlight standing by the wall was shining directly into his eyes, as he tried to avert them. The man stood immediately to the side of the lamp so that, at first, Elroy could only distinguish him in silhouette. He was puzzled by the name, 'Jones' and the manner in which it had been articulated, with heavy, almost sarcastic emphasis. His emotions were a confusion of distressful disappointment and fear; anticipation supplanted by dismay. The figure in front of him was acquiring more detail and an arm was raised to turn the glare away a fraction, out of his eyes. Features were appearing on the face, and skin colour - brown - and a slight smile.

Elroy gave a jolt. Did he recognise this man? The face had acquired intelligence, the body was no longer scrawny and huddled, it was wiry, sinewy with strength, the bearing had authority in a frame which seemed to have grown a couple of inches and the eyes, the eyes were sharp and penetrating now they were not bloated behind thick lenses and, surely -

"Charlie Bones!" Elroy gasped in a half-whisper, now dropping into his chair.

"Mr Fitzgibbon - or would you prefer '*Massah* Jones'?" Bones smiled a crooked smile. "We do apologise for calling so unexpectedly."

We? Elroy looked round from the glare of the light and saw there were two other men in his study, standing by the wall behind him: big, blank-faced, black-coated, it was obvious what role they played.

"So...?" Elroy began.

"Yes", Bones smiled humourlessly again. "You guess all those nice, cosy NSA units are just left to themselves, nobody looking after them?"

"Looking after?" Oh, God, thought Elroy, so it was no idiot caretaker creeping into the transmission room. Oh, God, had he understood what he was seeing? "Who are you?" he added.

"Me? Oh I just do the looking after, places here and there. Like when folks arrive to do systems checks - three times. What's wrong? You messed it up the first two times? Or maybe not no system check, eh?" Bones was as far removed from the scrawny caretaker as Elroy could imagine, without actually changing his body for another. No shuffles of the feet, no deferential tilting of the head, no obsequious smile, but more the lithe athlete on the home straight, cool and confident of victory. "Anyways", he added, "I guess you'll have more to say about that later."

"Later?" Elroy mumbled.

"Yeh, Mr Fitzgibbon, *suh*", and Bones grinned, "we have to go now. It was just so much quieter meeting you at home than in some other place with all them people around."

"I aint going nowhere", muttered Elroy.

"Oh?" Bones raised his eyebrows and looked over Elroy's shoulder. Elroy glanced behind and was aware of the two men each taking a step towards him. "Well, we could have a kinda little *discussion* about that and this place" - indicating the furnishings around them - "might look kinda untidy afterwards and your good lady might be worried about what happened" - he looked steadily at Elroy - "or we could just walk outa here, nice and friendly and your nice lady can get a call from you in the morning, saying you're outa town on business. Either way", he added casually, "we're all leaving."

The same Bones eyes that had gazed ingenuously outside the elevator, accompanied by the foolish grin, now glinted hard and uncompromisingly at Elroy. He was aware of body movements behind him, as of men setting their stance for physical confrontation. He thought of Mariana entering a study with chairs knocked over, books scattered, maybe blood spatters on the wall.

"Okay", he mumbled tensely, "where?" At least he could use the time to think about his story. They surely could not know the truth and the formula itself had gone, even from his memory should they possess the drugs to wheedle it out; they would only get a useless parade of disconnected characters.

"Just a place downtown", replied Bones and Elroy felt a prickling under his skin as his abductor added, "somewhere private, ya know."

Outside he had to give away his car keys to one of the 'heavies' while he accompanied the other two men to a limousine parked discreetly away from the nearest house, under some trees. It flashed through his mind to make a run for it; but if he got away they would lie in wait for his return or, worse, for the family. Whenever he got back to the house, they could call again. He could phone for help but who? Who were these guys working for? Who would it be safe to phone? Police? The company? Friends? Endanger Walt and Olivia even further? The notions had come and gone in seconds. He remembered the family returning tomorrow, at least to the appearance of normality.

"The lights?" he grunted to Bones, with the bulk of the other man walking close to his side.

"Oh", chuckled Bones and indicated the third man getting into Elroy's car way back in the driveway, "Brad put your trip switch up just now. Everything fine."

"Why the dark?" muttered Elroy, puzzled now he pictured the whole charade and ruefully recollected what he thought it had been.

"Jest one of them things", replied Bones in amusement, "put the lights out and they always do that - come to see what the only light is first. Can't resist it." He looked at Elroy as if to say even the cleverest will do the same dumb thing. "Like moths to the flame."

Part Four

PRESIDENT

PRESIDENT

Dolls

"**H**ey! Guess what *I* got!"

Andy loitered into Gordon Pierce's office by the Customs shed. He was holding out a Chinese doll, colourfully attired in national costume.

"Oh?" Gordon looked up. "One of them we checked?"

"Yeh", grinned Andy. "A mate bought one of the cars. Didn't want the doll. Got two boys. Brought it in the pub. I said your little girl might fancy it."

He handed it to his boss. Pierce turned it over and stood it on the desk in front of him holding it by its two arms and lifted it off its feet a couple of times.

"Yeh. Thanks. She'll be chuffed." He raised and lowered it again. "Yeah", he added, thoughtfully, still smiling, "not as heavy as I thought they were. Good thing. You half cracked your head on one, didn't you?"

"Yeh." Andy touched his head as he remembered. "Heavy buggers. What's it made of?"

"Dunno." Gordon tossed it between his hands. "Hardwood or something." He flipped it over to Andy. "Whadyer think?"

"Yeh, I guess", agreed Andy, weighing it in each hand. "Some of them are heavier, though."

"Whadyer mean?" Gordon watched him checking it between his hands.

"That second batch we did the other day. They were heavy buggers."

"I thought we were going to leave them, for time: they were clean on the scanner again?" Pierce was concerned how they were getting complaints about delays and suggestions they might be missing some drugs hauls by focusing on the wrong goods.

"Yeh, sure. Left 'em all", acknowledged Andy, "but I moved one or two so I didn't get me head cracked again while I was working on the car. Heavy bugger, I tell you."

"Heavier than this?" Gordon held out a hand for Andy to toss the doll back to him.

"Yeh, I guess so. Well, I've not got them both to compare, have I?"

Pierce frowned for a moment, looking closely at the doll and turning it over. He pulled up its tunic at the back and ran his finger around the hard wooden body. There were no joining lines, the body was a single carved piece. He was skilled in examining items for places at which they might been opened up for insertion of something else. Some of their easiest 'hits' were from 'finding the join' in anything from toys to steel ingots and revealing what had been hidden inside. He tapped it: it was solid anyway. He shrugged and smiled again at Andy.

"No. Fine. Thanks for thinking of Laura. Just wouldn't want her scooping up any white 'sugar' powder, eh?"

"Hey, no." Andy recoiled. "I never thought -"

"No. Joking." Pierce grinned. "Good job it's not too heavy, like I said. They're probably all different. Only Chinese, you know - cheap."

They both chuckled. Anyway, it was free. Not as though you'd actually go out and pay good money for some lump of Chinese doll, however good it looked. Probably fall to bits in a fortnight.

Hoi Fong looked across at Hwee Lo and smiled. The tiny baby cradled in her arms was peacefully asleep. They had named her Soo Wong, one name from each of their families. His wife smiled in return and then at the infant face, screwed tight in repose. The evening sun was shining red through the haze outside, bathing all three of them in its glow as they sat in the lounge, he in his bamboo chair, she on the sofa, babe wrapped in soft linen.

"You are quiet", Hwee Lo spoke softly across the room.

"Mm?" He shifted in his chair and continued to smile, reassuringly. "I am looking at you and our beautiful daughter."

"Are you content?" she enquired, aware that prosperity was tempered with caution, these days.

"Content?" he replied, preferring not to elaborate upon his inner thoughts, if it could be avoided.

"The Society?" she added.

"It is well", he nodded to her, "it is well."

She lowered her eyes again to their child and stroked its sleeping forehead. She would not probe. He told what he felt she should share, protected her from what might trouble her. She knew enough to know they might have chosen a different path had all the conditions been clear from the start. A tremendous challenge, a wonderful opportunity, he had explained to her and she had agreed. She would not, could not have stood in his way, not like these young modern Chinese girls who declared independence in the marital home from the outset. She was still traditional in her outlook, as she had been in her upbringing. Perhaps that was why Beijing was right for her, and for him, rather than the brash, frantic thunder of life and business in Shanghai.

Here, modernising retained a character of old China, even though that was a quality eroded day by day, little by little. She knew he had business friends who laughed at their life of chickens and scrub in the countryside. "Live in the city!" they admonished, "then we can drink you under the table, Hoi Fong!" She doubted he was much tempted, except perhaps for an occasional overnight stay, and then he would return the next evening, bleary-eyed and flopping into his chair after kissing her lightly on the cheek and muttering with a sheepish smile, "that'll do till New Year." She did not mind if it was sooner than that. Mostly, they were here, together, in a land they both loved. Such a pity it was clouded with uncertainties just now.

Hoi watched her caressing their baby girl and stifled a sigh, lest she was troubled by it. They would overcome these trials. Eventually the deal would pay off, and so the Society would be paid off, too. The third delivery, the largest, was already on its way by sea. Where they were getting all these *dolls* from, he had no idea! It did not concern him. Maybe they were right: this whole paraphernalia of dancers and dolls was attracting the interest leading to these rapid repeat orders. Low profit margin but a healthy turnover. Once the trade was really established, he would be able to continue on his own without any of their support. Just live with it for now.

He was happy, at least, that 'opening up' meant he was actually allowed to compete privately with the Chinese state car deals being struck with foreign manufacturers around the world. Count himself lucky. He grunted in his musings, causing Hwee Lo to look up at him again.

He anticipated her question.

"It is well", he repeated. "It is fine."

The sun had dipped out of sight and the evening gloom sank into their home, as he reached to switch on a lamp.

Friendly, mild-mannered, even-tempered, Asif Hassan would not, in the English colloquial phrase, say boo to a goose. However, he was tiring of the Chinaman's visits delaying his 'boys' from attending the counter at opening time. His staff knew very well what time it was and that at least to make an appearance at the beginning would ensure prompt service to any waiting queue.

They were good boys, good devout Muslims, said their prayers most times, if not every time he said them himself. He did not mind their belligerence towards other faiths; they would mature and grow out of that. He understood their outrage, youthfully expressed though it was. The Western alliances, dominated by the Americans, had stepped roughshod over nations of Islam until all too recently and, even now, while both ideologies were combating the same adversaries, seemed incapable of dealing with Muslim partners as equals, rather than with condescension. Most of the boys had never even been to an Islamic state but their citizenship of a country like England had the effect of making them feel isolated in the land where they lived and strengthened a sense of allegiance to the nation of their religion and ancestry. He regretted it. It was not their fault. Think of all the British youths of a previous generation who took up the cause of Communism: and that was on behalf of nations they had no birthright in at all. Disaffection.

Asif sighed and wiped his hands on a cloth hanging from the counter. It was all very well. You can have your beliefs, your religion, your politics; he had all these himself but he also had a shop to run. This was a brief lull. No customers. Probably soap opera time on telly. He checked the clock: yes. He locked the door and hung a sign that read 'back in five minutes' - five minutes starting when, he knew people would say - and went through the plastic strips to the back. He trod softly up the stairs in his moccasined feet and pushed open the door at the top. He knew the Chinese man had gone, he had heard his footfall on the stairs earlier, but the boys - his two staff and two companions - were sitting around on armchairs and the settee.

"Abdul, Mohammed, come along. We have been busy. Why do you not come down?" They were all startled by his entry, the sound masked by low music playing from the hi fi. He cast his eye around them, as he beckoned his own two and then noticed a large canvas bag of the sort he had seen on occasional visits to warehouse retail stores. The kind of bag you bought to carry away smaller goods like table settings or cutlery. It was partially folded over at the top but protruding from the gap were the arms, legs and heads of dolls. Dolls in multicoloured Chinese dress, from what he could see at a glance.

"What are these?" he enquired, mildly.

"Nothing, Asif." The smaller, stockier of his two assistants leaned forward hurriedly and pulled the bag towards him, folding the top over further so the contents were concealed.

"You boys buying dolls?" asked Asif, puzzled

"No, no", stammered Mohammed, "Well, yes, yes, presents - you know - for Eid."

"Eid is a long time away. Customers are waiting now", said Asif, sternly, believing he did not have to remind them the festival at the conclusion of Ramadan would not be upon them until long after tonight's abandoned customers had dispersed to other takeaways. "Come", he commanded. The lads got to their feet. They were all in their early twenties except for one of the visitors, who was clearly a bit older and had a sullen air. Hmph, thought, Asif, regarding him briefly before he turned back to the door, he's behaving as though I've invaded his private space - in my house!

The older one glanced at Abdul and then at the bag. Abdul nodded and mouthed, 'safe'. They all followed Asif downstairs,

Mohammed opening the side door for their two companions to leave, before joining Abdul and boss Asif in the shop. Asif had opened the door to allow the half-dozen people waiting outside to enter. He apologised to each one in turn and was met with reluctant smiles of acknowledgement, as he silently thanked Allah for detaining them, while wondering how many he had lost. He had already forgotten about the dolls.

The phone rang. Paul answered.

"For you", he called to the next room and heard Isabella pick up the handset. He was not really interested, it was Olivia in New York, but the doors were open between the rooms so he heard snippets of Bella's voice:

"Oh? .... When? ... Never? ... No, nothing, just asked him about London ... Yes ... Nothing else ... He wouldn't tell me that, anyway ... What about you? ... No? ... Gee ... Yeh, okay, speak soon." The phone clicked off. Paul knew the way things were, he could not ask her about an overheard conversation but she drifted into the lounge, deep in thought. He felt he could make a bland enquiry.

"Okay?" He looked over to her from where he had sat down.

"It's ... You know that Elroy guy? ... No, well, this friend of Livvy's, well, Walt, her husband's friend .. I met him ... family guy -" she shot a quick glance at Paul to say whatever their problems, this was not a secret Manhattan fling she was having. "He's stayed out, just phoned next day to his wife. Never does that, apparently ... Livvy thought maybe he'd told me."

"You?" Paul had never felt part of her New York life, even during occasional visits, and now he was conscious he might be excluded from a whole circle of friends, of both sexes.

"I called him."

"Eh? You know him that well?" Paul flushed a soft pink round the base of his spreading neck.

"No, heck, only met him coupla times." She was sullenly on the defensive. "But I went on a visit with him and Livvy to her work - computer inspection." She realised she was having to invent these details fast, to explain how she knew Elroy without revealing anything else, especially about the London connection. Subterfuge and double-talk were not her game; her style was to talk as she thought, shooting from the hip.

"He asked me about a London bank address and I called him with the details."

"What about email?" asked Paul, quelling his suspicion.

"He said he doesn't trust the security."

"Uh", Paul nodded. "So what did you say to your friend Olivia?"

"Couldn't help", she shrugged, relieved the lying was finished, "he's not going to tell me about his work or when he's staying out, is he? Hardly know him."

Paul realised there might be any number of things he hardly knew about his own wife now. Meetings and rallies in London with people who were only names and phone calls; friends in New York he barely remembered; and now new names cropping up, as though she were reclaiming her former life without him. If this wasn't the guy, it might be the next. He wanted to push it from his mind and picked up the motor magazine lying at his side on the sofa. Front page picture was a colourful shot of the dragon ceremony in his showroom, with the cars arced to the rear and the Chinese dancers in the foreground in the act of catching the dolls falling through the air. It was a highly professional photograph. He must ask them for a copy, great promotional material. Bloody dolls. He'd even had people phoning up to ask if they could buy one, disappointed at his impatiently ironic response that they cost several thousand pounds each, but you got a free car. Bloody dolls.

Gay

"What would You say if I was gay?" enquired Gabriel, blowing something off his fingers and ceasing maintenance works for a while.

Had the Divine One been permitted the occasional wisecrack, in the gift of almost all the intelligent species in his cosmic flock, He might have riposted - what with there being only the two of them - 'You're out of luck here, my friend'. However, not that He was devoid of a sense of humour but Deity does require a certain *gravitas* generally speaking, He drew a long deep breath (whoops, the orbits of several stars thrown into reverse) and said, quietly, and with not so much as a hint of amusement, "Pardon?"

"Gay. Me, gay. What if I was?" pressed Gabriel, with customary disregard for the deific frown cast in his direction. "Never mind gay bishops. What about 'gay Gabriel'? I mean", he continued earnestly, while the Almighty began to wonder if the infinity of Heaven wasn't just a bit too small for the two of them sometimes, "I mean, it might help, mightn't it?"

"Help?" repeated God, faintly, thinking he could do with some of that Himself.

"Yeh, see", the energy mounting in the angel's tone, "You could say to them, 'Look oh My children, and so on, no need to be in a tizz about gay bishops and priests and all that because my mate Gabriel's gay, you know, the archang -' "

Gabriel broke off suddenly, aware of the silence enveloping him: more silent, even, than the habitual hush around them. He looked up.

"Er .. servant", the angel corrected himself uncomfortably and looked away again from the disquieting expression that bore down on him. There were times, for all his devotion and loyalty, when he rankled a little at the term, 'servant'. He felt there were occasions when he acted on his own initiative, when he was more than just a servant, they were a team. Not equals, of course - heavens, no! - but himself not just an odd-jobber, an artisan, more a general, executing Divine strategy among the galaxies. All right, though, not a 'mate'. Slip of the tongue. Not even the fallen Dark One had been a 'mate'. 'The Lord hath no mates' could even have been included in the Big Book, just in case anyone got ideas.

" - Servant", Gabriel picked up his momentum, erasing the lapse and moving on, "My archangel, he's gay, so - all this bother about gay bishops and priests - what's the problem?" Gabriel was rocking to and fro, clutching his feet, engrossed in the argument.

"I mean -" he continued again.

"Gabriel."

"I mean -"

"Gabriel!"

"You see..." The angel's voice faltered into silence this time, as he looked up at a less-than-usually-benign Almighty.

"You are not gay." God's tone was heavy with emphasis.

"But -"

"You are not gay", breathed the Lord, heavily again, "You are not anything, you are an angel."

His love for this Gabriel in front of Him did not prevent Him delivering His words like a dull drumbeat, thudding around the cosmos about them:

"Angels ... do ... not ... have ... gen -"

"Genitals?" cut in Gabriel eagerly.

"Gender!" thundered the Lord, shaking the very heavens (and a few planetary climate changes, besides).

"But -" (Would he never give up?)

"But what?" simmered the Good Lord.

"They don't know that, do they?"

Twigg

"Visitor coming through."

There had been a few changes since the last occupant had departed the White House, tail between legs, humbled in land-slide defeat. It had been a vote in which the usual bickering of party politics had been transcended by something else: the vigour of personality, individuality and a new declaration of self-confidence. All this embodied in the victor, as the van-quished old guard, with its defeated values, limped to the side-lines. America had been a nation confused; one whose self-esteem had taken a battering over recent years. For a population the majority of whom regarded foreign travel as traversing the country east to west, or vice versa, or a holiday adventure to Mexico, it was discomforting to be so *disliked* in parts of the world most of them had difficulty pinpointing on the map.

They had saved the world from the Nazis, hadn't they? And Communism? And brought peace to such alien climes as the Balkans, the Middle East, Vietnam. Well, okay, forget Vietnam. Try to forget. But now try to forget Islam. That was the problem. There are some things a nation cannot forget. Until this nation, seeking now only reassurance, had found itself rewarded with much more: a triumphant declaration of 'self'. Americans, famously generous beyond measure to visitors in their own land, had nevertheless been deemed selfish abroad. Self-seeking and brash in pursuit of their own material gratification or, worse, their own definition of the common good.

Was it not an unjust decree from an ungrateful, mistrustful world? Now, with one mighty, collective lunge at the ballot box, the decades of grey-suited solutions to a malaise of self-doubt had been banished in favour of, 'This is me! This is us, this is who we are, we don't have to prove anything!'. 'Self': not selfishness but confidence in who you are.

It was, however, easier to admire in another than to demonstrate in yourself, which was why the best person to exemplify it was your leader. A leader, moreover, who broke the mould. Unmarried, for a start, which was unheard of! However, that excused - no, glamourised! - the fabled private life acted out behind the very public White House walls.

"Okay." Renee Fleck, the President's personal secretary, responded with an air of resignation. One of the new commands had been to modify security procedures. Any guest still had to make it through all the customary protocols of identification and the series of physical barriers at outer gates, main doors, security screens, body scanner and so on, but escort to the inner sanctum was different. It was assumed, correctly, that anyone getting that far was either completely harmless or mortally wounded and therefore posed no feasible threat. It was then a disconcertingly casual passage through to Ms Fleck's unguarded Reception, adjacent to the Oval Office itself. A prudent courtier, armed, but discreetly so, was the only attendant to accompany the visitor. And for good reason: privacy. Confidentiality is the more reliable when confined to just the one or two.

"Don't tell me", groaned Renee to the intercom, from her first floor office in the converted 'Chief Usher's room', "young?"

"Naturally", the sardonic reply.

"Tall?" Fleck again with that 'don't-tell-me' tone.

"Whaddya think?"

"Hmm." Fleck wrinkled her nose at the intercom speaker grille, not in disdain but suppressed envy. "Yeh, sure", she added knowingly. "Looks - ?"

"Drop dead -" crackled the female confidante.

"Bitch", muttered Renee and clicked off, as the guest stepped through the door held open from the other side.

"Good-day", smiled Renee, politely, eyeing him with candid admiration. "The President is waiting for you."

"Good-day", he replied. He possessed a serious air but was athletically proportioned and - ooh - yeh, d-d-gorgeous. "I apologise," he looked at her directly, "I did not realise I was late."

"You're not." Renee returned his gaze with undiminished appreciation. "The President is well ready for you, that's what I mean."

He lifted his well-formed hands from his sides, in a light gesture of enquiry.

"Go right in." Fleck indicated the large dark wood double doors, with a sideways tilt of her head, and felt a brief quiver down below as he moved smoothly past her, hesitating a fraction before knocking. There was silence.

"Just go in", directed Fleck, watching him. He turned one of the handles, pushed open the door and walked through. She only looked away when the door had closed behind him, sealing off the modest grandeur of the famous room and the secrets it would not betray. She knew the visitor's eyes would swiftly flick from side to side, taking in the chamois-coloured wallpaper behind historic Presidential protraits; the white Georgian fireplace to one side and matching dark wood connecting doors to left and right; the carefully-arranged eight or nine antique beechwood-and-gold-braid armchairs with their silky blue backs and seats; his eyes could not help but fall upon the neat, round, marble-topped table in the centre of the room, before they rose to scan the bay of floor-to-ceiling windows at the far end of the large, elliptical room, framed by their exquisite sapphire blue, satin-and-braid drapes.

At that point, Renee Fleck knew, the visitor's roving gaze would halt on the official resident and sole occupier of the Executive Residence, poised to welcome another victim to the Blue Room. "Bitch", she muttered again and turned to the papers lying on her desk. The closed doors emitted no sound. She did not need to hear; she was pretty sure she could write the script.

"Hi-i-i."

The greeting was delivered in a rich oyster-sauce drawl, spreading across the room, lapping at his senses before enveloping them with its subtle embrace. He was uncertain of the reply being solicited by this familiarity as he gazed back at the ruby smile beneath the window. He stood watching, and waited. This present Incumbent had declined to adhere to the modern convention of the Diplomatic Reception Room, downstairs, for such international representations. The preference was to revert instead to an earlier tradition of the similar-shaped, but less formal oval room above, with its predominantly blue furnishings and the feel of something a little less 'restrained' for receiving well-presented 'guests'. It usually had the desired effect.

President Victoria Twigg leaned languidly against an invisible pillar in front of the middle window. It was a statuesque pose she had perfected to display the Amazonian outline of her six-feet-one-and-a quarter, or one-metre-eighty-six, frame. She called it 'lounging to attention' and it unnerved most who observed that it was achieved with no visible means of support except her two very long, very shapely, partially exposed and athletically bronzed, bare legs. It was a pose she deployed at what might otherwise have been politically awkward meetings or on occasions when the argument could be difficult to win on intellectual grounds alone.

Twigg possessed a powerful intellect but rarely needed to employ it in support of her equally powerful sexuality. She was a snatch over one hundred and fifty pounds of pure, solid woman and you sure as heck knew it, whether you were in the next room, the next country, watching on television, gawping at her on the steps of the White House or, my quaking friend, right here in the same room like a mouse transfixed by the snake. And that was most probably at the root of the admiration, going on adoration, she inspired across the country. It was raw honesty, whatever else it was besides. It was what people had yearned for, for longer than they could remember. Not a leader who was 'one of us', not demeaned by such a hollow accolade but, rather, one whom most could never equal yet might aspire to emulate in the manner of an ordinary mortal. A Catherine or a Cleopatra.

Hah, where had she been until now! For such elusive qualities are many foibles forgiven, or even quietly envied.

Twigg continued to hold the visitor in her gaze. Unlike many who had preceded him, he retained his composure of calm, unflinching silence which, although she did not show it, caused an unsettling motion within her.

"And may I ask your name?" she purred, with the light of sun and sky behind her, tinging her figure and her dark, dark hair swept back across her cheeks, in a silver outline.

"Gabriel", he replied.

"Gabriel", she murmured, scrutinising him.

"Gabriel", he affirmed, politely, wondering if he was going to have to say everything twice and if she always stared like this. He had, however, done a good job on himself. He had checked out how 'Adonis' should be represented and was quite pleased with the outcome. He was not altogether delighted with some of the necessary appendages and the clothes felt like a prison but it made a not disagreeable change from flashes of light, stars and, well, he did consider including the wings but conceded to himself (he was wise enough not to ask the Lord's advice first) they stuck out rather oddly at the back and so, yes, this was a change from wings as well.

Altogether 'handsome', confirmed by the admiring looks he had attracted on his way through the various levels of security, although they had been looks of a somewhat lobotomised nature, consequent upon the mental paralysis he had temporarily induced in anyone whose job it was to prevent him getting any further. He tried to suppress contempt at how too easy it was and how it would have required considerably more effort to achieve the same result on, for instance, Splong. Cretins.

"*Mister* Gabriel", Victoria Twigg repeated, as if turning it over in her mind, whilst maintaining her fixed stare upon her guest. "And what is your first name, if you don't mind my asking?"

"Gabriel", he said again.

"Gabriel Gabriel", she reiterated, tempted to comment upon the lack of imagination displayed by his parents but deciding to remain courteous for the moment. "And do you have a middle name?"

"Gabriel", was the undemonstrative response.

"I see", she mused, wondering if she was absolutely in command of this exchange but becoming more determined not to be misled, even by this most attractive of guests. "Gabriel Gabriel Gabriel. Well, now, many Americans have two middle names, either to distinguish them from other members of the family or perhaps to reflect their ancestry. Do you have such a name?"

"Gabriel", was the stoically polite reply, as he tried to imagine what number they might eventually stop at.

"Well, indeed", Twigg breathed a little more deeply, as there was just a suggestion of her wide brown eyes narrowing their beam at the visitor before her. "Gabriel ... Gabriel ... Gabriel ... Gabriel. Your parents", and now she could not resist it, "do appear to have struggled for ideas."

He smiled - it was a strain to render it a neutral, pleasant, not sardonic smile - and said nothing. Most of the responses which sprang to mind would have sounded disdainful and, reluctantly, he kept them at bay. Earth. It was bad enough being adorned like this. He felt like calling out to the Lord (Who was never likely to be far away), "You think wings are ridiculous! Have You seen some of their stuff?" However, apart from disconcerting his present host if he appeared to talk into thin air, the Almighty needed no enlightenment, since He had been the One to invent all the unseemly lumps and bumps on the human form in the first place.

Feet. Gabriel did not mind feet. He had become quite attached to feet, as it were. So much so that he retained them for long periods in Heaven, only allowing them to metamorphose into the alternative appropriate appendages when setting off to Crsnax, or Tryxxx, or wherever. Feet were a whole lot more interesting than some of the slithery - aesthetically-pleasing but slithery - bits in some other species. Feet absorbed one's attention. No bad thing when confronting eternity.

He felt he ought to say something.

"Nice place you have here."

Not only a man with a repetitive line in names, considered Twigg, but one disconnected from normal diplomatic language. A bit of rough, in the image of a god. She quivered. The gleaming, light brown hair, beautifully-proportioned frame discreetly outlined within the perfect dark grey suit; broad shoulders, slender hips, confident stance. And that smile. She usually instilled a smile of awe, or suppressed desire, not this enigmatic glint of the lips which had nothing to declare. She was challenged.

Regular protocol demanded that some formalities were initiated in which the visitor's purpose was broached before her own designs were entertained. She realised she was unaware of any briefing documents, nothing laid on the desk before her which informed of the origins of her guest and the diplomatic gains he might be aspiring to win. This was not helpful. She would rebuke Renee later. However, the diplomatic niceties had better be observed, for appearance sake.

"And what brings you here?" She was aware this was a somewhat lame question issuing from the President of the mightiest power in the world but it was one delivered with such haughty authority as to submerge the complete lack of political research it disguised.

"I've come about the world." Gabriel felt there was no point in extending this interview any further than necessary. He knew exactly why he had come and was in no mood to beat about the bush. Not in this get-up, anyway.

"All of it?" Victoria Twigg, President, USA, attempted to hide the surprise in her voice. Most visitors were selfishly content to solicit her aid for some pathetic corner of the globe, just because America was rich and powerful enough to annihilate their mutual enemies and then pump them with wealth. This was the first request she had heard for global conquest at a stroke. The whole goddamned world. Who was this guy?

"Yes, all of it." Gabriel wondered if all conversations on Earth were conducted along these unnecessary question-answer lines and then remembered it was not dissimilar to some of the conversations in Heaven between himself and the Lord God Almighty. And, after all, these people believed - or some of them - they had been fashioned in the image of the aforementioned Lord so maybe their conversations were, too. He was mighty glad God was not privy to these thoughts he was having. There was a certain freedom of expression available when he was not up there in Heaven, always assuming the Good Lord was not doing one of His everywhere-all-the-time personifications, right here, right now. No. He deserved some privacy. They had a deal. He had to depend on that, otherwise he might just as well be a puppet.

"Hmm. I see." Twigg contemplated her guest, without yet having moved from her statuesque pose by the window. She was accustomed to witnessing emissaries falter in her gaze, stumble over their replies; however assured in their bearing, avert their eyes, if only momentarily, and maybe shift their stance, adjust a tie, smile deferentially. No matter how the lustiest of them secretly fermented before her, her will was the iron grip in which they were held, until she chose to release them, and then it was merely to serve her bidding. But not this one. He stood before her calm and self-assured, unmoved, looking coolly at her while articulating the most preposterous notion, delivered from God knew where, some tinpot dictatorship, no doubt, seeking ratification for hideous atrocities in - well, in this instance, apparently - in every accessible corner of the planet.

"The whole world", she murmured, silken dusky eyelashes rising and falling as though curtseying serenely in front of her eyes. She moved. Easing herself forward, she began to glide round the desk from the window, the hardness of her thighs clinging to the sheen of knee-length black skirt, slit halfway to her left hip. Gabriel was surprised at the tingle at the top of his spine and the wholly unfamiliar sensation of warmth below his stomach. He knew why he had come but there was something here he was unprepared for. He was conscious he might be slipping out of his depth.

She stood now in front of him. He wondered if he had been too casual in his preparation: she was two or three centimetres taller than him, an advantage which could easily have been avoided if he had paid more attention. Too late now. The insidious workings of this human metabolism were beginning to take on a life of their own. Her eyes studied him from their marginally superior elevation, just sufficient to emphasise the predatory glow of her smile. She was too close. He felt the aura radiating from her. She was arousing sensations which were definitely not part of being an angel. Being a man - not the hologram he had rejected as too insubstantial an alternative - was implying intimacies he might not be able to control.

"And where is it exactly," her hot breath rolled over him from half a metre away, "you come from?"

"Heaven." He was not of a frame of mind to make things up, however discomposed he might be feeling.

"Yeah", Twigg smiled appreciatively, "I guess it must be." She held out a hand and he remembered this was the formal greeting. He reached to accept it. Her hand was strong but soft and warm and gripped his firmly, then slid away, the fingers caressing his palm as it did so. She smiled into his eyes. "And must be such a long way to travel", she twinkled seductively. "You need to sit down."

He glanced past her at the elegant occasional chairs placed informally about the room but she turned smoothly behind to the desk and took up a small remote control key pad and touched a button. There was a quiet swish to his left and a section of painted wall opened sideways, allowing a deep-seat, softly up-holstered sofa, in the style of a double-arm chaise-longue, in red and gold, to slide out into the room, its high back filling the space in the wall behind.

He looked questioningly at her.

"One of my personal additions", she drawled and gestured him to it, waiting for him to be seated, then sat against the opposite arm, eyeing him and smiling, drawing her richly tanned legs onto the seat, one almost wholly exposed by the slit in her skirt. Gabriel felt warm prickles in his back and an uncomfort-able motion between his legs.

"Are you comfortable, Mr Gabriel?" Twigg purred.

"Quite." He looked steadily at her. "Thanks."

"Good. I like to make my visitors comfortable." This was her regular entree, heavily laden with innuendo. The leonine smile, the exposed silken skin, the muscular curves, the musk of desire. Generally, by now, there was an issue of diplomacy to be des-patched before being forgotten in sensual oblivion. Today, such formalities were of no consequence; she was charged by this 'god from heaven' who matched her allure with masterly compo-sure. Moreover, he was challenging her customary dominance. This was a nut to crack.

"Do you like this?" she asked, and parted the top of the loose silk jacket she wore, to withdraw an icon hanging from a silver chain around her neck.

"Yes." he replied simply.

"You will have to some closer", she breathed, holding out the chain so that it stretched its full length, only six inches from her throat.

Gabriel edged along the seat and leaned forward to examine the icon. It was a small silver cross, studded all along both lengths with tiny sparkling diamonds.

"Mmm?" Her voice was so close the warm moistness of her breath touched his lowered forehead. He raised his eyes and met hers, inches away. He felt her legs move to press against his and saw her glistening red lips move, almost touching his own. "Now what is it you have really come for?"

The heat was rising in him. He felt his control slipping. So. The knowledge of why he was here was being fused with this new experience. It was not part of the plan but he could accommodate it and regain the initiative. It would be now, in this manner, in his present form. He could not complain the circumstances were unexpected, he could only protest the experience was unforeseen. She would get her desire. He looked into her eyes, then slowly rose until he stood, looking down on her, spread languidly on the couch.

"I have come for you", he said slowly.

"Ahh." She smiled up at him and reached below the seat to touch a hidden button. The chaise longue moved outwards further into the room, carrying her on it and, as it did so, the back tilted away to double the length of the seat until it all lay flat, forming a large triple bed. Victoria Twigg, President, United States of America, rolled languorously over until she lay along the length of the bed on her back, facing up at him, fingering her clothes as if to remove them.

Gabriel stood at the end of the bed, staring down at her lying spreadeagled before him. She felt a glow flow through her. In all this time, she could not recall a sensation quite like it. She breathed deeply, willing him to succumb, as her senses flooded with expectation and desire. Yet it was not quite right. She commanded the greatest nation on earth. She inspired her fellow-countrymen to reach *beyond* greatness. She commanded respect and awe in all who met her. But not now. This man, this god, held her in his vice, enveloping her even before touching her. Somehow, he seemed to glow with his own light. She was gasping. She was the one supposed to be exercising power. It was not she who should be seduced. Her loins were pounding. So - terrifyingly - was her soul. Gabriel felt his own power and let it take control. It was now, here, together, the two of them.

"Come to me, you angel!" she cried.

Outside the doors, Renee Fleck was all ears as usual. Not much sound escaped until things got exciting, then she knew events were following the familiar pattern. She strained to hear. She frowned. There was none of the usual melody of laughs, giggles, groans. Just silence then, suddenly, a long drawn-out moan; female, yes definitely female. And something that sounded like a cry of exultation. A cry that gradually grew to a panting climax which seemed would never stop. From outside, Renee could hear it pulsing behind the walls and the doors, expanding to a crescendo as though it would break through and engulf the corridors with its passion. She sat stiff and upright, staring wide-eyed at the double doors. Then swiftly the cry faded, withdrawing into the space behind the doors and finished with what sounded like an exhausted sob of joy. Fleck hit the intercom to downstairs.

"Jesus Christ, Alice, who is this guy!"

"Whaddya mean?" came the instant reply.

"I never heard her like this before!" exclaimed Renee, hissing into the box in case she was overheard now that silence had descended.

"Like what, Renee?" Alice's intrigue came through sharp and clear. "Like what?"

"Shaddup, shaddup!" Renee snapped suddenly and hit the 'off' button just as one of the two double doors began to open. The visitor stepped through, urbane, calm, unruffled. Fleck looked in astonishment. He must have dressed in five seconds; or never taken them off. What is this freaky guy, she thought as she watched him, some kinda perv? Gabriel closed the door behind him, looked at her and smiled, walking past with a nod. She reached out automatically for the buzzer so the opposite door would be opened and the guest politely escorted away. Unbeknown to her, he could, of course, have disappeared without leaving the Oval Office by the door at all but he wisely chose not to cause any additional confusion.

Renee looked at the doors the guest had just walked through from the President's office. There was no sound of movement beyond. She felt a sudden chill. The President was so much in command of herself and all who met her, it never occurred to her staff that any visitor who was vetted to reach her might actually do her any harm. Renee shivered. Some minutes passed. By now her boss would normally have emerged from the room, her face lit up with a triumphant smile and, more often than not, herself accompanying her conquered and shaken prey to the door.

She hesitated. It was not up to her to make an uninvited entry, especially not immediately after one of the President's 'diplomatic receptions'. She touched the Oval intercom button and called into it, nervously, "Madam President?" There was only silence. Fleck knew she should really call for security assistance but she did not know in what condition - clothed or otherwise - their employer might be discovered. She headed tentatively for the doors. Best to sneak a look inside first. If anything was awry she could instantly sound the alarm. Otherwise, 'personal assistant' incorporated this and many other undisclosed duties.

Fleck slowly opened the door. At first all she saw was the empty desk by the sunlit window. Then she peered round to where she knew the secret bed would be, now probably restored to 'chaise longue' mode if not already returned to its hidden position; but the bed was still a bed, dominating the left side of the room. Fleck drew a short intake of breath. The President lay motionless on the bed. She hastened swiftly to it and pulled up sharply at its foot, gazing down in a mixture of dismay and astonishment. President Victoria Twigg lay stretched full length, arms and legs spread wide, eyes staring open and her features bathed in an ecstatic smile. She was fully clothed.

Late

"President tied up again?"

Joe Kirk of CBS News allowed his lips to twitch into the subtlest of sly smirks as he cocked an eye at the White House Press Secretary, Will Jerome, hovering by the bottom step.

Jerome looked sharply in return at Kirk.

"Shuddup, Joe. You wanna stay at the front?"

Media pecking order ensured that craggy Joe Kirk was always in the front row outside the White House with his cameraman alongside, next to CNN and ABC, no matter who else managed to insert themselves at the front of the grid for press conferences. Jerome wielded absolute power in these circumstances. He could demote anybody he wanted to the back, even though both he and Joe knew the cameraman would be apoplectic if his pictures suffered by it and the Network would go ballistic. Nevertheless, while no-one could remember the Press Secretary's authority ever being exercised in this manner, it was real and therefore, like the pristine school cane of old, could always be employed the first time.

Joe smiled, so did his cameraman beside him. They both habitually squinted, at these opportunities, at upstairs windows in the vain hope a compromising bare torso would flit by or, happy days, the flash of an uncovered breast. Cameramen had been know to hallucinate over such visions. It never happened. For no other reason, probably, than the main office and private quarters were all round the back. Still, you could wish and hope, like winning the lottery.

In the meantime, Will Jerome frankly had no idea whether the President was tied up, tied down or double-wrapped in packing tape and still struggling to break free. The handsome, urbane young visitor from - well, scratch my head, Will could not quite recall which country the guy had claimed to represent - from somewhere, had departed best part of two hours ago. And, to be honest, he had not really looked that type. Not that Will truly believed those sorts of deviations carried on in the hallowed office. Plain, ordinary, red-blooded stuff, yeh, but nothing most regular folks did not do. Like all the White House staff, he appreciated the Boss for being perfectly 'straight'. Straight in all things: what she said, how she behaved, the way she treated staff, politicians, diplomats, people she met wherever she went, everybody. He knew, they all did, that was what got her elected.

Victoria Twigg did not have the prescribed presidential background. She was not rich. For how many years, decades, a century or two, had the people been faced with no choice but to vote for one super-wealthy candidate or another, the triumphant of whom would then mount the podium and spend the next four years claiming to represent the 'American people'? So, okay, sometimes it was someone who had successfully pursued the American Dream and climbed from rags to riches first but it still meant wealth was the predeterminate to attaining the Highest Office.

Where were all the 'ordinary Americans' then? Well, as it happened, one of them had been lurking in the wings for a while. Not that Victoria Twigg was 'ordinary' but then who else was? In a country peopled with strange stories, hers was just another of them. Cuban mother and baby daughter Viaz plucked from homeless poverty in the streets of Miami by handsome, romantic altruistic French American Albert Tigue, who was captivated both by the mother's beauty and the tragic vulnerability of the infant. For him it was love at first sight; romance and lust for the woman, doting paternalism for the child. Next it was back to his home in Baltimore and an upbringing of ease and love, just the three of them.

There were two things Victoria never knew: one, why she never had any brothers of sisters but remained the only child; and two, that she had first been named Viaz in the stinking gutters of the Miami slums, by a young mother abandoned to her child and her fate. Her flamboyant Parisian father, who had migrated to the New World, never told the young Victoria he had persuaded her mother to cast off her sad association with the past and rename his adopted daughter in the spirit of the Old World and a 'victorious' new beginning. He might have told her one day but there was another day before that when he suddenly vanished, swept off by another new romance, leaving nothing but a note, some money and the roof over their two heads.

As the turbulence settled once again in their lives, her mother was too wise to dig up buried roots, and let things be. Perhaps one day she, too, might have told an older, maturer Victoria, just for interest's sake and in case she might wish to reclaim her birth name. But the mother, too, was taken, by a tuberculosis which must have festered within her from those very streets of her rescue, all those years, until ambushing her before either she or modern medicine recognised what was happening. At twenty-three years of age, Victoria - erstwhile long ago Viaz - was alone.

That was when she changed her name. Her surname. She had always considered the combination of anglo first name, which she had no objection to with its triumphal associations, and franco surname, Tigue, an ugly coupling. With both her parents gone and an independent, some already considered headstrong, free spirit, she simply sat in front of the mirror one night and mouthed her name, watching her lips move until they had phonetically translated French into English. Tigue ... Twigg. Nothing if not pragmatic, our Victoria. Never Vicky, mind, and beware anyone who should attempt to abbreviate or diminish the connotations of conquest. Few tried; and no-one dared a second time. Beauty, strength, character, in whatever conjunction she had inherited them from mother and two vanished fathers, one by blood and one by love, and her stature: she was equipped at every stage of her development to dominate all who confronted her.

Of such histories, and their sadder counterpoints, is America made. The difference for Victoria Twigg was, without becoming wealthy first, she became President. A brief story. Loves and heady days and nights, before and after first class graduation. Some work in commerce, some in industry, gaining from them an understanding of how national economic and fiscal policies take effect and acquiring, too, her disdain for the designs and foibles of men. Disdain with desire, a paradox of passion, to become a hallmark. Then there came radical politics, out of nowhere except a reaction against 'the establishment'. And then a disappearance of two years or more, no friends quite knew where, abroad perhaps or far up north, or south to work with the poor, perhaps back 'home', all rumours, yet to be confirmed.

The media dug and dug but so many people wished to link their past to that of the President, there would have been six of her. There was a marriage, too, brief and failed, and then, without warning, mainstream politics, in Wyoming. Wyoming! No-one knew why she turned up in Wyoming, Maybe just to go somewhere without an association with any part of her life. Never explained. Local prominence, independent views, policies which were aimed at the people, not the politician's future career. Intentionally or otherwise, she was popular. Congress. A seat in the House. Flamboyant, like her adoptive father, but reliable; straight but strident.

She did not seek a State Governorship, nor the Senate, the usual formal routes. It was not clear if she really had her eye on the White House but, suddenly, there it was. Twigg for President. Vote for Victoria. You know what she was? Then and now in the White House? She was Superwoman. She was someone you can never be. The girl who flies without wings. The boy who does that *and* never grows up or dies. She was Joan of Arc, inspiring respect and allegiance without her followers being able to answer why. She was the person all the children - *all* the children - dreamed of being, with powers they long to possess, until they grow up and dream no more. Victoria Twigg inspired because no-one else could have coped with being her but it was awesome to see her being herself, an elevated spirit you could aspire to, without feeling obliged to match. The thing was, it made people bold and confident to go through unfamiliar doorways themselves, if she opened them first. To boldly go ... formerly only a catchphrase in the nation's mythology.

Will Jerome was not the only one on tenterhooks. His problem was where the hell was she? For the captains of industry, Max Drummond and many a seething counterpart in highrise strongholds, it was let's get the President out on them White House steps and kill this whole sharing farce stone dead, before we aint got no economy left to get mad about. All these weeks of waiting for the President to take it a bit more seriously than the next 'climax of diplomacy' (some clever newshawk's coinage, that), and now at last we are going to get a pronouncement. A Presidential statement to set things straight and maybe, rumour had it, even an announcement on solving the seize-up enigma.

With all due respect to the evangelicals (but less respect from some), people need a kick up the ass and stop thinking it's just fine to swap things with neighbours and not go shopping any more. No-one else knew, except Will Jerome and the media posse, the President was in danger of failing to appear on schedule to say all this but they would soon know she was 'otherwise engaged', if he did not get her butt out there pretty damn soon. He looked anxiously at his watch, while Kirk and others leered knowingly at him. Jerome turned his mouth to lapel to speak into mini-radio. Surely Renee Fleck, who had banned anyone else from entering the Oval Office for the last two hours, must have roused 'VT' by now. 'Sleeping off a sickness', 'must be left alone', were the messages.

"Okay, okay", he muttered in reply to the words in his earpiece, "soon as you can, Renee, just get her damn ass out here!"

The President lay quite still, staring up at the ceiling, quivering almost imperceptibly from head to toe. Fleck could only gaze at her, as she had done for nigh on two hours, except to stall demands from Jerome and others to be informed what was going on. Renee began by being worried; then, when it appeared her President was physically unharmed and, evidently, 'unviolated', if one could deem such a personage 'inviolate', she was concerned as to what she should do. Calling doctors would only set off the alarm, all the more so when they saw her perplexing condition. While one might describe her smile as 'serene', another might panic and term it 'vacant'. Word would get out. Opponents were always ready with sharpened knives; if they suspected part of her brain had been immobilised they would be all too eager to lunge in and finish the job - politically, that is.

Renee had been contemplating all this, pacing to and fro, moving to the bedside, bending over her boss to see if her proximity would attract some attention, wondering if food or drink might be the antidote to whatever was afflicting her, frightened at how long she could keep this to herself and everyone else at bay. Then all at once the President's eyes moved, found Fleck hovering halfway across the room, and the smile broadened further, losing its dreamy air for one of delight and recognition.

Twigg let out a deep, long drawn-out, "Wo-o-ow!"

Then she observed her own unseemly sprawl across the bed and drew in her arms and legs.

"Oh, Renee", she declared wide-eyed, "Oh my God. My God. Oh, Renee!" And she seemed to thrill with elation.

"Some guy, eh?" Renee allowed herself to observe, discreetly, enviously.

Twigg looked seriously at her personal assistant.

"Hey, Renee. No, not like that; not like that at all, d'ya hear?"

It was not a rebuke, more an experience being recalled to mind, and shared with her private assistant. "It's not what you think, Renee", she drawled softly, "it's something else. Wow. Something else..." Her voice faded into the memory that was seeping back.

"Like what, ma'am?" Renee sensed her contribution was expected, mingled with her own curiosity. This was not the Victoria Twigg she thought she had come to know quite well.

"Like.." Twigg replied, dreamily, gazing up at the ceiling again, before swinging her legs to the side of the bed and sitting up. She looked up at Fleck again and stopped speaking, as though unable to articulate precisely what 'it' had been 'like'.

Fleck's earpiece emitted a light buzz. She turned her face to her lapel: "Yeh?"

She was being urged by Will Jerome to get the President out there. She was certain Twigg would have completely forgotten she was scheduled to give a press conference to cast some reassurance concerning the crisis of technology, 'sharing' and imminent economic collapse.

"What is it, Renee?" enquired Twigg, some of the natural authority restored to her voice.

"Your press conference, Madam President." She paused, recognising this information was not fully registering. "About the crisis", she added.

"Ah, yes. Of course", Twigg assented reflectively, as she took to her feet.

"What will you be saying?" asked Renee, wishing to encourage the President to collect her thoughts and get swiftly back on stateswoman track.

Twigg looked at her.

"Mm?" It was as though the President was wanting to check whether she was being offered gin or brandy.

"Your message", urged Renee, fretful that this stormy intellect and passionate communicator was going to disintegrate before the nation's press, if not on the way to meet them. "What will you be *saying*." Renee felt the same as when she had desperately tried to remind her nine-year-old daughter of her speech at school prize-giving, moments before the terrified mite mounted the platform.

"Why, Renee", and Twigg smiled a broad, understanding smile, delivered to a fellow soul who had yet to be enlightened, "like ... the answer."

"The answer?" Fleck was unsure who was beyond help, herself or the proud, statuesque lunatic standing before her.

"That's what it was." And Twigg gazed wonderingly around the room, her eyes settling on the bed, before turning back to Renee. "Like ... the answer."

Twigg smiled again as she straightened her jacket, gave a little tug at her skirt and swept some hair back behind her ears, before gesturing to the door.

Renee walked numbly to hold the door open and watch her President, glowing with anticipation, stride through.

TV

In their quiet home on the Beijing outskirts, Hoi Fong settled himself into one of the chairs he reserved for visitors and leaned forward eagerly to watch the television. The President of the United States was about to make a much-anticipated announcement. Ruefully, Hoi expected it would reverse the economic downturn, condemning the 'sharing' craze and setting America back on track as the world's foremost industrial power. He shrugged. After all, competition was the norm; anything else a bonus.

Hoi shrugged again as he glanced across to his favourite bamboo chair, occupied by a contented Cousin Wu. Wu had turned up some hours before Hoi arrived home from work, ostensibly to return a plastic pot; a pot amongst many surplus to the Choi household requirements, which had gladly been disposed of in the direction of Cousin Wu. As on many another occasion, delightful and caring Hwee Lo had gratefully welcomed back the returning pot before conjuring up an appetising supper for her cousin-by-marriage. That same cousin now stretched his satisfied limbs in the coveted bamboo chair and smiled.

Ah well, reflected the sanguine Hoi Fong, it was less of a disappointment than having arrived home too late to play with his beloved Soo Wong, being forced to make do with a peck on her sleeping cheek. Curse this pressure of work imposed by the

Society and its deadlines! However, at least he was in time to catch the broadcast. Every twitch of the American leviathan's economic tail could send shock waves to all corners of the earth, even China. Hoi frowned as he watched the regal figure of the maverick President Twigg emerge in the sunlight onto the White House steps.

In a motel room with the sunlight filtered through closed curtains, Tony Delgardo frowned too.

"Crap!"

He rolled over, snatched up the remote control lying on the bedcover and zapped the television off.

"Crap", he repeated, chucking the remote on the floor and rolling back again to wrap a strong, tanned arm around the soft form at his side. The shower of blonde curls fluttered and the silky, firm body shuddered with delight, cuddling closer.

"What?" giggled Suzy Rose, sliding a hand between his legs and caressing with a stroke and a squeeze.

"Crap", Tony repeated with a small moan of pleasure and licked her ear. "Fucking President."

"Ooh", she thrilled, and squeezed harder.

"Ouch!" he exclaimed and reached to squeeze a breast in return. Suzy squealed with relish.

"Fucking *me*, if you don't mind, honey", she reproached and snuggled to bury her lips in his, mouth open wide, while her legs separated in unison. Delgardo, not by any means the most popular guy in town, or any of the towns he visited to ply his trade or his Suzy Rose. Still blessed with wheels which continued to rotate whilst many others were stalled; but still bluntly refusing to "goddamned share! ... Fuck that!" He was not the only one to respond in that manner but one of the most blatant about it, driving by folks who were obviously stranded, making transparent excuses when someone asked for a ride, calling up maybe, or knocking on his door. All the worse in contrast with Martha, who behaved like most ordinary people, sharing and borrowing by turns. Not Tony. No more than he would dream of sharing Suzy Rose. Checked in a motel, once again telling Martha he was stopping over for a sale. True enough, except no mention of his 'secretary', required for 'personal assistance'.

"Okay, fucking you", he growled in her ear.

"Ooh, baby", she wriggled against him, "please."

Announcement

In a windowless basement, probably somewhere in Manhattan - he had been blindfolded but heard traffic all the way and the journey had not been long - Elroy fiddled disconsolately with the TV buttons. Up to now, he hadn't bothered. He was still unnerved by the new incarnation of Charlie Bones, his tightlipped, sardonic abductor. Where was the myopic, shuffling, obsequious 'caretaker' now? He had not seen the treacherous guy since being led down here last night. It was a plain but tidy apartment; unprepossessing old brown leather three-piece, of sofa and two armchairs; kitchenette through an archway; small bedroom with single bed through one door, cramped bathroom through another; and another door, locked, with a keyhole revealing nothing but blackness beyond.

The television was on a small wooden table facing the chairs. He found the power button and pressed. He quickly skipped through a Simpsons repeat, using the remote control from the table, a couple of daytime game shows and a Harrison Ford movie with familiar ironic grimaces, and then took his thumb off the button at an image of the White House. It cut to the CNN news presenters in the studio. Then back to a closer shot of the White House and a throng of news crews at the bottom of the steps, on the lawn. There was a tone of urgent excitement in the news commentary.

Elroy looked at his watch. Coming up to one o'clock in the afternoon. At least they had fed him, if sparingly. A plate of waffles with maple syrup and coffee had been brought by one of Bones's henchmen after their arrival. A fitful, fretful night with little sleep had been followed by fried eggs and more waffles and coffee, delivered by a second minder at around eight-thirty this morning. He was unsettled all the more by having no windows, no natural light, no indication of day or night. He was consoled they had not taken his watch. It was troubling enough to have been relieved of his belt and shoelaces. He shuddered. What might they be expecting of his state of mind?

He looked away from the television and around the room. Was this a prison? And who were these people? Who was Bones, and who was he working with, or for? Or was he the Number One? But what could he know? What could he have seen, even less understood, in the NSA transmission room? There was no way he could have linked the array of symbols and characters with the 'seize-up' phenomena. Here, today, he could only wonder who wanted him so badly. FBI? CIA? And why? Had someone, improbably, worked it all out? He shuddered again.

They had taken his phone, of course, after his call to Mariana, lying to her for the first time he could recall: "Away on Federal business, hun, not sure how long." He had tried to think of a code which would enable her to alert others but he conceived of nothing which would not cause the phone to be grabbed from him, call halted and Mariana worrying herself sick. His attention was caught by heightened tension in the newscaster's voice. Elroy looked at the screen. The tall, imposing President Twigg was treading down the White House steps to the white podium placed at their base. Elroy was still distracted by his own thoughts, only half-hearing phrases in the commentary, such as 'now we'll find out', 'bring some sanity'. Then a key turned in the lock and the apartment door opened.

"Good-day, Mr Fitzgibbon."

Elroy felt his knees give way. He tried to steady himself but lost his balance and sank backwards into the armchair in front of the television, his eyes fixed in astonishment on the purveyor of the greeting, his gut wrenching. Slick Hair! LOTUS!

"Do accept our apologies for bursting in on you", Elroy heard the sneering voice continue, as his mind fought to make sense of what was happening. LOTUS! So it was them! Slick Hair! But Bones? Where was he? The same humourless tone that had accompanied the computer diagram of economic decline resulting from the 'seize-ups' and 'sharing' was echoing in his ears: "But Mr Winston and I thought we should see this with you. And", he added, glancing at the television, "you got it on already", he finished with a cold smile, before adding, "See, Mr Winston?"

Slick Hair turned to Charlie Bones, coming through the door behind him.

"Winston?" choked Elroy, "Bones? With *you*?"

"Ha-huh", Slick-Hair emitted a dry chuckle, "I think you already know that Mr *Winston* is not a genuine ..er .. caretaker."

Bones - Winston - grinned his sly, very unBones-like grin again at Elroy. LOTUS, Slick-Hair, Bones, the unnerving triangle was complete. Images and conclusions flashed through Elroy's mind: the frigid atmosphere at that recent meeting before his abduction; the fixed stares in his direction, the chairman's persistent requests for his expert guidance. What could they possibly know? So he was here because Bones - Winston - had been some kind of spy on their behalf but where did it go from there? There was no way anyone - whoever Bones-Winston might really be - could have seen that formula and interpreted its function, Even he, Elroy, in the grip of a Divine revelation, had been manipulating equations he could not wholly define.

"Do help yourself to some lunch." The insincere smile indicated an aluminium trolley being wheeled in by a minder. It bore some plates with sandwiches and a coffee pot, with mugs, milk and sugar. Elroy shook his head dumbly, whilst the smile turned to a smirk and Slick Hair, Bones-Winston and the three henchmen now in the small room each took something to eat, one of the minders pouring coffee. Elroy nodded to accept coffee, aware he needed something to freshen his tangled thoughts.

"*Now.*" Slick Hair abruptly gestured at the television. "Sit, please." He dropped onto the sofa, ranging a leg along it, leaving the two single chairs and waving a hand at them for Elroy and Bones-Winston each to take a seat. The minders remained standing, two by the door, the third hovering behind the chairs. Elroy felt a prickling of hairs at the nape of his neck. "Sshh", Slick Hair urged needlessly, as they silently watched Victoria Twigg begin to speak, "let's hear the bitch."

At first Elroy wasn't taking it in. A Presidential address was the least of his concerns while surrounded by the menace of minders, LOTUS and the turmoil of not knowing why he was captive and what they wanted from him. But a snarl from Slick Hair focused his attention. Something jumped inside him and he had to suppress a gasp. The whole nation had been waiting for the President to pronounce on the 'sharing mania', as the corporate establishment termed it; and all that establishment, along with most of its supportive press, were anticipating Presidential condemnation of the 'madness' and 'folly', which threatened the whole economy and American way of life. This capricious but influential President would kill it stone dead, inject some commonsense into the population and restore normality. Just a few words would do. A few words! Yes! But the wrong ones!

"Fucking shit!"

Slick Hair swung his leg onto the floor and leaned forward, glaring at the TV set. Elroy's heart was in his mouth. He dare not show it, dare not reveal one iota of his mounting excitement. He wanted to hang on every word but he was too stunned, the speech becoming a blur, just key phrases being cauterised onto his brain.

"A time for the United States to take a lead ... a new path for the developed world to follow ... selfish consumption ... we have begun to learn a new way ... do possessions mean happiness? ... scarce resources ... the world's climate ... friends and neighbours ... sharing together ...halting the spiral ..."

This was the President outdoing even herself. She was not condemning 'sharing', she was celebrating it! But more than that, Victoria Twigg was making reference to economics, something about a 'controlled slowdown' in which no-one suffered: everyone worked less, required less, spent less. The President was making it sound like a kind of Utopia.

"Crazy fucking bitch", snarled Slick-Hair again.

Elroy wanted to cry out in triumph and had to screw his fists tight, furrow his brow, to conceal his emotions. Because there was more, more than merely the words. It became a talking point as much as what the President had *said*. How she *looked*.

"Use less, share more ... we have been shown the light .." And it really was as though Victoria Twigg was lit by an inner radiance. There was an eery, ethereal aspect to her expression, as if powered by an unseen energy. People said she *glowed*. Elroy felt a thrill. He knew how she felt. He felt a bond with the President. He dared not imagine why.

"... Many of you have witnessed the Lord's sign ..." It was not known whether President Twigg had attended a service visited by the 'smiling Jesus' but she would know all about it. "... sharing what we have, without always wanting more ..."

And then, to Elroy it was akin to those famous recordings of Great Britain's Winston Churchill exhorting a nation to expend all its 'blood, toil, tears and sweat' or, more profoundly, Martin Luther King's "I have a dream!" He could almost hear the nation listening in silence to the President's final words.

"The Lord has chosen America to lead the world."

It was much contested afterwards that this had always been the nation's role and destiny. But not with this complete reversal of the objective. Albeit, if the course had been set in motion by the consequences of seize-ups and breakdowns and had been blessed by the visions in the churches, this was the endorsement the nation had waited for. The nation, that is, with exceptions such as LOTUS, Max Drummond, Tony Delgardo and their like.

Elroy found it difficult to conceal his rapture and excitement. It was all falling into place. Not quite, though. He was here, not knowing what might happen next. Slick-Hair regarded him keenly. Elroy hoped fervently that his demeanour was blank and calm.

"As I said at our meeting", remarked Slick-Hair, coolly, "we thought you might have worked this out."

"What do you mean?" replied Elroy, levelly. He had prepared for this, without anticipating these particular circumstances. Straight down the line, no savvy, that had to be his line.

0"The source of all this ... insanity", proceeded Slick-Hair, "things stopping, breaking down. Don't you have a theory?"

"Like I said", replied Elroy, feeling the sweat again, "just wish I could make something of it."

"We wish you could, too, Mr Fitzgibbon."

Slick-Hair was regarding him very steadily. Elroy glanced at Bones and met a fixed stare from him, too. His defence was slipping. He turned back to Slick-Hair and was a trifle too hurried as he said, "Why did you think I could work it all out?"

Slick-Hair rose from the sofa and Bones got to his feet at the same time.

"I'd like to give you one more opportunity to 'work it out' if you can, bearing in mind Mr Winston was with you at NSA."

Elroy felt a tingle of nerves behind an ear and short hairs stiffening at the nape of his neck once more, as he looked swiftly again at Bones. Bones offered a thin, unfriendly smile.

"Our systems check, you mean?" he managed to respond, innocently.

"Was it?" asked Slick-Hair. "Perhaps you'd like to spend a little time recalling it. As I said, I'd like to give you the opportunity."

The two men left the room. Elroy sank down onto the sofa. It was not possible. Even if Bones was a scientist in disguise, he could not possibly have linked what he saw to the seize-ups. Elroy himself did not fully understand the whole formula and now he had forgotten most of it anyway; he could not tell them even if he was left with no other option.

All he could do was think and wait.

Prediction

Chattering voices. Rippling phrases. Ideas, notions, concepts snaking across newsprint, airwaves, public and political forums. It began immediately, the moment that regal figure radiated one final smile and turned back up the steps through the White House doors. 'What do you mean?' 'Are you suggesting?' Reversing growth?' What about the poor?' And so the questions tumbled over each other from the stupefied, sceptical, cynical hacks. The answers came back: "Surely" ... "This is the new way" ... "We can do this together" ... "This is the answer." Not one of them believed it, not while standing there at the foot of the steps and having expected to file reports to the effect, 'Twigg denounces sharing', 'Let's get America back on track', 'President calms crisis', 'Seize-ups to be solved'. But no, instead, they were invited to join her in cloud-cuckoo land.

Will Jerome found himself declaring, in a dozen different ways, "No, I wasn't aware the President planned to say exactly that but she's the President, not me!" And by the time he had put that in as many variations as he could, without risking the sack the same number of times, he stomped off, reflecting bitterly holding down a job where you take the flack for everything your boss says, even when you had no idea what the goddam fuck she was talking about. At times like these, he could personally wring the neck of every individual voter, no matter how long it took. In fact, the longer he could spend on it the better.

"Hi, Derek." Gordon Pierce was on the evening shift, a quiet one, and thought he would see if his counterpart at Folkestone docks was on duty.

"Gordon?"

"Yeh. How's things?" Gordon knew Derek from when they both did service at Gatwick Airport.

"Fine. What's up?"

"Not much", Gordon responded, then recalled something that had amused him a few moments ago: "Hey. You seen that crazy Twigg on the box?" He had the TV switched on in the corner: legitimate to keep updated on weather forecasts, international industrial disputes and flight delays on teletext so he could avail himself of programmes at other times. "Says 'sharing is good for you'!" And he laughed. "Crazy Yanks! But we could do with things slowing down, eh?"

"No, mate, didn't see it", came Derek's voice, "too busy. Bleeding Chinese dolls, amongst other things."

"Dolls?" Gordon exclaimed.

"Yeh. Shipload of Chinese cars with dolls in 'em."

"Oh", laughed Gordon, "we've had those - twice."

"Yeh?"

"Yeh, some promotion or other. They're clean."

"Yeh? Sure, they're okay in the scan", agreed Derek. "We were going to bust open one or two of 'em."

"Don't bother" advised Gordon, "they're genuine."

"Heavy buggers", remarked Derek.

"Yeh, I know, my guy cracked his head on one", Gordon chuckled again. "Solid wood. No joins - the dolls, I mean!" They both guffawed. "I'd leave them. Go after the real stuff. Anyway", he added, "we checked Beijing. Top private manufacturer. You know how we're supposed to only lean on the Chinese if we're reasonably sure. Sensitive relations."

"Yeh, good, we'll leave 'em", said Derek. "Pong, don't they? Chinese scent? Handy you've gone through 'em first. Heavy buggers", he added.

With that they rang off with the promise of a drink when one was in the other's patch, Derek thankful for being spared another wasted forensic exercise and the subsequent complaints about vandalised merchandise.

Gordon picked up the doll he had still not remembered to take home to his daughter. "Not as heavy as all that", he muttered. "Huh, maybe I'm just used to it." He weighed it in his hand, momentarily, then put it down, where it was about to be forgotten again. Laura might be too old for dolls if he did not remember it soon.

Gabriel nonchalantly flicked something the Lord would rather not have seen, in the opposite direction which, when you think about it, is not really possible when God is everywhere, including the opposite to where you think He is.

"Oops, sorry." Gabriel would not normally have overlooked the eternal truth of God's multiple presence but he was too cheerful to be paying attention to such detail. A whole cosmos beckoned. "That's it, then", he announced with an air of finality and a brisk brush of his hands.

"That's what?" enquired the Almighty, mildly.

"It", explained Gabriel, as if stating the obvious..

"It?" He repeated, wondering if He might have to redefine Eternity in order to get to the end of this.

The prediction was startling and almost unanimous, including among those who welcomed it least and, in some cases, whose calculations had been designed to rebut it but yielded the same result as the rest. It was hedged with 'ifs' and 'buts' and fundamentally depended upon human behaviour. However, this was the reason it raised such profound echoes across the United States and was seriously noted elsewhere in the world: people were *already* behaving this way. Six months ago, it would have been unthinkable, laughed out of every bar and off every street corner. Now things were different. From necessity, reinforced by the 'Divine message', people were already scaling down their material possessions, had become used to relying on each other, not just themselves, and were glad, not embarrassed, to do so.

The prediction, reached by a variety of computer programs from sources with markedly divergent political and economic philosophies - rightwing think-tank, centre-ground conservative, left-of-centre liberal, Yale, Harvard, Stanford, Keynesian, Fried-manite, all of them - was that this might just conceivably develop the way it had been so passionately proclaimed in the Washington sunshine a few short hours before. All had been eager to test this astounding declaration as fast as they could and be the first to uphold or demolish its validity.

"You mean", the famously tenacious television host leaned forward in his seat, unable to maintain his habitual cool composure, "we could lead the world in reversing the upward spiral of growth?"

"We are already", came the sanguine response from one of the score of experts, "it's a question of whether the world will follow."

"Or will want to", persisted the host.

"Indeed", consented his studio guest, drily.

Millions of viewers gawped at the graphic display of the collective predictions, all pointing to the same conclusion that *if* most people continued sharing as they did now, and *if* the fall in purchases and energy consumption remained at about the current two-thirds of previous levels, and *if* people did not attempt to dispose of their income in alternative material ways, and *would*, if necessary, accept some reduction in working hours and therefore reduction in pay that was already surplus to their requirements -

"Because they're not buying things like they used to", interjected the TV man.

"Precisely", acknowledged the boffin.

- because the whole economy was operating at a lower capacity - then we could settle into a new way of life, without anyone suffering as a consequence. On the contrary, we'd all be better off. Better off? How?

"Mad!" stormed Max Drummond. "Fucking raving mad!" The hand crashed down on the maple-topped, leather-trimmed desk, unprotected by loose papers; he flinched as his palm stung. He was staying late in his office, watching the early evening News, accompanied by Abe and a couple of other senior colleagues. These two glanced nervously at Drummond and nodded in agreement, muttering "You're right, Max" and "Mad." Abe held his tongue. There was a disquieting logic underlying all this, which would be better left unmentioned.

If there was any doubt amongst what was already a significant majority of the population, it was dispelled each Sunday at church. Although the 'smiling Jesus' phenomenon had become much less frequent and more random in its appearances (Gabriel having persuaded the Lord that the effect was enduring and only required sporadic reinforcement, and even *that* he adopted as a somewhat haphazard commitment), the combination of memory, message and fearful expectation was a potent force. Congregations had surged if they were not already healthy, even if voyeurism had been, for some new converts, the original motive. For most of the rest, the stay-at-homes, by now a shrinking minority for the first time in living memory, it challenged their scepticism more than ever; and the lack of a code by which to lead their lives.

It had only come this far because it was believed to be no more than temporary. A succession of state, federal and industry pronouncements had provided assurances that the seize-up crisis would soon be resolved, a solution found. Modern science could not be confounded for long, and so on and so forth. These pledges were utterly without foundation but vital to uphold the authorities' credibility and, to a diminishing extent, the stability of the nation. To a diminishing extent, because people adapt. Tell someone it is forever and they will devote every sinew to finding a way out; say it is just until tomorrow and they will make the best of it today, not suspecting that tomorrow may never come.

It is how a child, by and large, learns to behave: short-term reward leads to lifelong custom and habit. Only in this instance, not just children. In fact, children were the most resistant until they got used to it. "Ma, the TV's bust again!" "Well, go next door, darling, Joe came here yesterday!" Grump, huff, why can't it be fixed! But, okay, next door it is. "Dad, can I have a ride to school?" "Car's bust, son, hitch a ride with Susan." "Yuk, Susan!" Mutter, grumble but, shucks, maybe she wasn't so bad when we gave her a ride last week. "Okay, Dad, see ya."

Adults - parents, singles, couples, old, young - began changing their ways as soon as it became clear it was that or do without the normal things: shops, cinema, work, sport, just visiting or going out somewhere; as well as all the domestic chores and leisure activities, from laundry to hi-fi. At first it had been a challenge, people versus technology. Now it was very nearly a way of life and today, this warm sunny day, the President had at last bathed it in an official glow of approval. Those who did not go along with it, resisted sharing and sacrificed borrowing, and there were a number of them in every town, were increasingly perceived as curmugeonly and antisocial.

Beyond this, many Americans were making a remarkable discovery: legs. It turned out you could actually walk to the store and bring back the provisions, provided you did not purchase six bags of siege supplies but were prepared, instead, to go back again in a couple of days. Where the store was too far to walk - speaking of miles not metres - you could share rides with a friend and maybe just bring back half a siege each. The old, the infirm, they never had so many offers of rides as now, or just have things brought to their door. "Mine's bust, can we use yours?" was a phrase employed without embarrassment; just as, "Sorry, can't help today", caused no offence because it was genuinely meant, not a lame excuse.

It was all absolutely, entirely improbable. But it was happening. Even in car-only cities like LA, where the walking American had previously been assumed to be an escaped mental patient, there were complaints about the absence of sidewalks. In New York, people started ambling across Fifth Avenue and Forty-Second Street as though cars should feel privileged to share the same stretch of tarmac and would just have to wait their turn. They were becoming heavily outnumbered anyway. Insurance companies, scarcely the fairy godmothers of automobile owners, had already begun offering new discounts for up to six named drivers, so you could all be on each other's insurances. It was not charity; just one of the companies thought of it as a great sales gimmick so they all had to follow suit.

Olivia met Joan again. Joan, who had miraculously appeared out of the gloom in that power cut way back before Christmas, handing them each a burger. It turned out she lived about ten doors up the street, strange how you hardly knew your fellow-residents before. They chatted about other blackouts and how they were much less frequent now - half the electrical appliances not working most of the time! - and yeh, sure, Joan's hairdryer not working and she going out tonight and sure don't want to buy a new one that'll be bust by the weekend and, hey, borrow mine, says Olivia, "but friends often call me Livvy." "Gee, thanks Livvy, you're swell." Walt laughed, "Why, course I remember her, seen her once or twice since but wasn't sure enough to say 'hi'; it was dark that night." And he added, "Wonder what El makes of Twigg. Sure puts the seal on it. Working out of town; did you say Mariana's worried?"

"She says he never stays away or, if he does, gives her plenty of notice, for the kids an' all." Olivia recalled the fretful tone in Mariana's voice earlier that day.

"Aw, things come up suddenly", declared Walt reassuringly, "he's just fine. Working like a dog, probably."

Elroy's heart was half up, half down. He had devoured the interviews and computer predictions, the most astonishing of which had projected forward to demonstrate how the pattern in the US could influence all the industrialised and developing world. That world always depended on the American economy: US goes down, everyone goes down; US flourishes, so does everyone. In this model, if the whole States economy adopts a slower pace, buys less, sells less, uses less - of everything - the other economies are forced to fall in line. Slow down, everyone! Yet, he could not jump for joy, quite apart from the fact Slick-Hair or Bones-Winston might enter at the wrong moment, he was a captive and he did not know what they wanted from him, although he suspected it was something he could not supply. His stomach tightened when he considered what their response might be. What was it about them that made him afraid? He had tried the locked door a couple of times, thinking of escape, but wherever it led, it was not going to let him through.

"Yes, *it* ", repeated Gabriel emphatically; almost, but not quite, allowing impatience to creep into his voice. "Done. Finis." A master of tongues, the archangel.

"Quite what", pursued the Lord, likewise resisting a measure of weariness in his tone, "is 'finis'?"

Gabriel judiciously avoided repeating the word 'it' again, although that summed everything up, as far as he was concerned.

"Everything working out", he asserted, with the glint of a self-satisfied smile.

"It is?" queried the Lord and then added, circumspectly, "Perhaps."

"Biscuit?" asked Gabriel, uncertainly, afraid that visions of a happy jaunt to somewhere warm (spiritually) and rewarding (intellectually) like Dryx were going to be a touch premature.

The Lord's silence was enough..

"Yes, well", riposted the angel, "it's up to them to deal with that, isn't it? We've given them a start." Surely he was not going to be deprived of his anticipated excursion at the last, so to speak, minute.

"Consider", mused the Lord, "if someone is in danger because, originally, he is in circumstances which have only arisen because We .. We -"

"Because we started it in the first place", broke in Gabriel.

"Quite", the Lord nodded, "and if he is in even greater peril because of a dislocation not of our making -"

"Their fault, You mean", cut in Gabriel, resentfully, seeing where this was leading, "something unpreordained happened. A biscuit. Out of our control."

"Quite, quite", assented God again. "Yet even so, even if it is not our 'fault', as you say, not part of the Plan, that he is in such desperate circumstances -"

Gabriel groaned. So just because we started it, we have to sort out the problems they create for themselves along the way: their unplanned 'dislocations' to the predetermined order. Why is Earth never simple?

" - We shall have to intervene to rectify the situation," the Lord finished.

"You didn't with Joan of Arc", grumbled.the archangel.

"Pardon?" responded the Lord, knowing very well what the angel had said.

"Joan of Arc", repeated the aggrieved archangel, mental galactic brochures being returned to their cerebral shelves, "You didn't intervene there."

The Lord paused, unwilling to enlarge on the whole issue of decisiveness, amnesia and any temporary conflict between the two.

"That was different", He replied.

"*You* gave her those signs", retorted the angel, "*You* started it."

"She was inspired, anyway", responded the Lord, unaccustomed to being on the defensive with his aide, "She just needed a -"

"Nudge?" sniped the truculent angel.

The Lord declined to respond.

"Like the carpenter, You mean", pressed the angel: "nudges."

The Lord felt obliged to elucidate now, or anything that would get Gabriel off His back.

"We cannot change events themselves but We may be obliged to reverse a side-effect such as unforeseen personal danger if We have ourselves initiated the original imbalance." He hoped that would be enough but added, "even if additional dislocations were not our 'fault'."

"So You could have made it rain", grouched Gabriel.

"Pardon?"

"Joan of Arc. You could have made it rain."

Elroy tried to analyse what had led to this. Bones was present during the previous visit - Piggyback for the southern states - and there had been no adverse outcome. Likewise, he had taken them all by surprise the next time but ... but ... was it that mishap with Bella, the stumble into his chair, his fluster over the keyboard? Something, enough to arouse suspicion. The look on his own face, had it betrayed guilt? So if Bella had not been there ... no, he could not retrace history in order to invent an alternative 'just suppose...' No point. Whatever the cause, here he was. There she had been. Life is full of 'if onlys'.

Like, if only Slick-Hair, Bones and all three minders had not entered the room at just that moment.

Pause

Bella was on the phone to Olivia.

"Any news of Elroy?"

She had been struck by a sudden pang of guilt. Her mind had flashed back over events in New York. Did her presence there have any connection with his uncharacteristic absence? No, of course he had said nothing to her, just that reference to London on the phone. Nothing that would be picked up in a phone tap. Her unease had been aggravated by the recollection of Olivia's caution and her reference to 'danger'. Was it something in that computer room? She had been so excited, thrilled by what she saw and its potential right here in England. Had she complicated things? No, she had only watched. Except ... except ... it was she who had persuaded Elroy to type the formula in a second time, prolonging their stay in the room. She remembered Olivia's anxious glances, as though willing Elroy to complete the task and leave. Then - of course - she had forgotten that stumble into Elroy, and his alarm, tapping at the keyboard to rectify the error.

All delay, delay. And that queer little black caretaker guy, with his peculiar grin. How long had he been watching? Did he understand what he saw? How could he? He was only a caretaker, for Christ's sake. *None* of them understood, except Elroy. Her initial excitement had become tempered with concern, the more she thought about it all. How come she had been there in the first place? Oh yes, the bathroom door, Walt, the injury and, according to Elroy, someone had to go in his place, so as not to arouse suspicion.

"No, hun", replied Olivia down the line, "no more news but Walt says Elroy'll just be involved in his work like, focused, ya know? I've told Mariana not to worry."

A few words more and they hung up. Bella turned the vodka glass in her fingers. took a sip and looked around the room. It reminded her of that day she had left for New York. Her late arrival there, that blackout, that clumsy accident with Walt. She grimaced now with regret at not having been more careful. It was her fault, Walt's cut eye. Why had she been so late at all, was that her fault? Her thoughts shifted to the flight, check-in, missing the earlier departure. She had forgotten that, the reason why she had arrived late in New York: the London power cut, delays in the taxi, her late departure from the house. Why? The phone call from Ruth about the march. Why had she not left before then, that ridiculously endless call? Why had she not already phoned for a cab and was on her way? She would have caught the earlier flight.

No. It meant nothing. Nothing that made sense of those lost moments in time, somehow winding up with her and Elroy and

Olivia in the computer room. She heard the phone ring in her mind - Ruth - and then it reminded her of Paul's look before she left, that afternoon. She rotated the glass in front of her eyes, gazing at its twisted distortions of furniture and decor. She could see his expression again. The way he had been looking at her before wishing her well on her trip. That look. Something about it. She remembered how it made her pause, time somehow halting, if just for a moment. She was aware of a tear in her eye now. It had only been a second or two, that was all. A phrase came to her. Where had she heard it? Was it just one of those things people say? 'A mere pause in the fabric of time'. Just that look.

"Gabriel."

"Boss?" The archangel saw he was being treated to one of those 'Isn't it time you went?' looks and thought better than to argue over conflicting concepts of Eternity in Heaven and Time on Earth. It was one of *those* looks. "Okay, Boss", he shrugged.

God watched him leave. After all, it wasn't just a rescue, it was to maintain an agent of the Plan in active service. That would be little consolation, He was aware, to all the countless others who had at one time or another begged to be spared, in the face of preordained history.

Chair

"Good for the planet, eh?"

Elroy remained impassive, pretending to think about it.

"You agree, surely?"

Slick-Hair was eyeing him sidelong, with a slight smile as if to encourage him they were all of the same opinion and was merely seeking Elroy's endorsement. Elroy acknowledged with a brief smile of his own but kept his counsel, trying to maintain an appearance of neutrality while he was giving it due consideration. They had been watching more television, a condensation of the later news briefings.

"Well, it's obvious, don't you think?", continued Slick-Hair with sly confidence, assuring him they were all of one mind.

Elroy guessed his host would utterly abhor the conclusions of various panels of experts that had thrilled him as he watched. Slick-Hair, though, was doing his best to be convincing. "We all benefit, don't we? Less pollution, less congestion, lower demand on energy, reduction in global warming. And a blow against the blight of poverty." He opened his arms with a gesture of accomplishment, the results unarguable.

Indeed, Elroy had been dumbstruck at the projections based on President Twigg's exhortations from the White House steps. Almost as an afterthought to one of the journalist's questions, she had suggested that surplus income, now unspent on so many of the material trappings of life, could be channelled towards charitable donations, particularly where they would help the poor. Even more telling was her smiling silence in response to another suggestion, posed as a question from cunning Joe Kirk of CBS, that such surplus spending power could be available as tax, enabling the government to address the crisis of poverty rather than wait for the goodwill of the people. Victoria Twigg had already established a tradition of enigmatic smiles which could often mean, 'just what I was thinking'.

"All from a surprising accident of atmospheric conditions, eh? How remarkable. Oh, and of course, not forgetting the appearance of our good Lord quite by coincidence. How fortunate." And Slick-Hair continued to look with his head half-turned to Elroy, peering from under hooded eyelids as they sat at an angle to each other, Slick-Hair on the sofa, Elroy on the armchair. Bones was casting shifty glances between the two of them, from the other armchair; two minders stood by the door, the third was facing them from the kitchen area, perched on a stool.

Elroy returned a nervous smile and realised he would have to break his silence.

"Remarkable", he agreed and then added, cautiously, "It could help a few problems."

"Except ours, eh?" remarked Slick-Hair, keenly. It was a penetrating stare Elroy could not ignore.

"You mean -?" he asked, playing for time.

"I mean, our oil", declared Slick-Hair, quietly and firmly. "*Your* oil", he added, still looking directly into Elroy's eyes.

"My -?"

"*Your* oil, as well, Mr Fitzgibbon", emphasised Slick-Hair, "you've helped America ... uh ... *secure* it."

Huh, thought Elroy, helped America? Helped a corrupt, greedy cabal to pursue its avaricious ends. Oh, good Lord, how did he get into this?

"And now", continued Slick-Hair, icily, "we have shiploads of the goddammed stuff", and he glared even more intently at Elroy, through narrowed eyes, "floating around in the Gulf with nowhere to goddammed go." He breathed the last few words through half open lips so Elroy could see his gleaming white teeth, all bar the one with a glint of gold, bared at him.

"Well, I'm sure", began Elroy, helpfully, although not at all certain what he was going to suggest next, before Slick-Hair cut in again.

"I'm sure you know what to do." And Slick-Hair glanced at Bones as they both rose from their chairs, while he gestured to Elroy to do the same. Bones took a small bunch of keys from his trouser pocket and made towards the locked door. Elroy felt a pull in his stomach and had to catch his breath silently to retain an appearance of calm. His initial unease began to seem uncomfortably accurate. This was not going to be a cupboard, unless they were about to be transported into a popular fairytale world where suspended coats were transmuted into woodland trees. He grimly doubted it. Slick-Hair ushered Elroy from behind with a touch on his arm and the three minders sloped into the rear, screening off the exit door of the apartment. Bones swung the unlocked door inwards to the anonymous area, while Slick-Hair gave Elroy another polite touch on the elbow to follow.

He walked through with Slick-Hair just behind, the minders following, and blinked as he entered the starkly contrasting environment. No semblance of the domestic accommodation behind them. They passed along a short grey-walled corridor of a couple of metres, then through a second, heavy soundproofed door into a metallic-grey, featureless room. Elroy took it in as quickly as he could. The walls were all dull grey, the room almost square, about the size of an average living-room, roughly five metres across but more like a laboratory in appearance. It was lit by a couple of strip lights on the ceiling, the cause of his blink as they had flashed on. The centre of the square floor area, again grey - hard, cushioned linoleum - was almost empty. Along the side wall on the left and the one opposite the door was a continuous shelf or worktop, grey again, with four or five computer keyboards and screens ranged next to each other against the blank wall.

Elroy could not see straight across to the other side wall to the right as it was partially obscured by a large block of a chair, all in dark dull grey, masking the features behind. The chair was positioned sideways with its rear to that side wall; it had a high back and solid, square arms and seat, all padded in what looked like grey leather. In the instant he was able to cast his eyes around, Elroy noticed a range of electrical equipment on the shelf behind the chair, some knobs and switches visible, and a flexible cable snaking down to the floor and out of sight beneath the chair legs. There were grey office swivel chairs in front of the computer terminals and Slick-Hair motioned him to the nearest.

"Do sit down, Mr Fitzgibbon."

It jarred Elroy as the words recalled Bones' saccharine welcome in his own study, smirking slyly to 'Mr Jones', in what now seemed another lifetime, less than twenty-four hours earlier.

"We believe you may know what to do", repeated Slick-Hair, his unconvincing smile all but replaced by humourless determination. Bones logged into the computer with keyboard dexterity that surprised Elroy and gave the final lie to any connection with the gawping caretaker at NSA.

"I - " Elroy looked up enquiringly at Slick-Hair as he took to the seat. His mind was racing. The links: computer, NSA, Bones and what he might have seen, what they might know. Still, as his thoughts jostled together, he could not see how they might possibly have made a connection between himself and the seize-ups. Nothing that could be anything more than circumstantial.

"You - you are a brilliant man, Mr Fitzgibbon", broke in Slick-Hair. "If anyone, anyone at all, might understand what is behind this - this - madness", his teeth gritted again behind taught lips, "then it would be you. And that", he leaned closer so that his mouth was not far behind Elroy's ear, as they both stared at the screen, glimmering shiny silver behind an array of unfamiliar icons, "is what you have found out, eh?"

He drew back from Elroy and stood upright before continuing, "How do we know?"

He stared down at Elroy with a gleam of satisfaction.

Found out? What did he mean? Was he thinking along a different line?

"Mr Winston, please demonstrate to Mr Fitzgibbon. There are some things -", the thin smile ventured an uncertain return and Elroy felt he was being sneered at, "even the brilliant expert may not be aware of."

Elroy swivelled to look round at Bones, who was standing behind him in the centre of the room beside the large chair, the minders leaning on worktops near the door. The man Bones-Winston had reverted in some measure to the NSA caretaker; he was wearing those thick-lensed spectacles once more and smiled at Elroy from behind them. Elroy was momentarily disoriented, lifted back to the NSA computer room and the blue-clad gaping Charlie. But he was abruptly reminded of where he was now: the grin beneath the goggle eyes was the Winston crooked leer, not the Bones vacant grin.

As he stared at the opaque lenses, they shifted slightly to look past him, over his shoulder, as Bones raised a hand to touch a spectacles arm by his ear. It made Elroy turn to follow his line to see the screen display replaced by a couple of rows of characters which flashed into view. For a moment he was numbed by incomprehension, then he went cold as he realised what they were. It was the nightmare come true. The sequence of letters and numerals were the formula for the seize-ups: 'Piggyback'! How could it be! He swung round, trying to extinguish the dismay from his face as he looked at Bones again, glimpsing the smirking Slick-Hair at his side. Bones, still with the fixed grin, was removing the spectacles and holding them towards Elroy, revealing his sharp, piercing eyes once more.

"Memory glasses, Mr Jones ... Mr Fitzgibbon", he smiled with conceit.

"But you know about that, surely?" Slick-Hair interjected slyly at Elroy, "surely." He looked smug, at holding the advantage over an acknowledged expert in advanced technology.

Yes, Elroy knew about 'smart' glasses but big, bulky contraptions, reminiscent of night-vision goggles used by the military. 'Smart' technology was what he had warned Walt about: spy chips inserted into clothing. Likewise, it might be developed to legitimately incorporate miniature computers into clothing or hand luggage, providing access to internet sites for information downloads which could, indeed, be displayed on your glasses or an apparatus which looked exactly like ordinary spectacles. To the air force, it had been 'heads-up' display on aircraft windscreens for decades. Not yet, though, a personalised technology; not beyond the micro-spy chip Walt had anxiously patted his coat to find. All the rest was still in development for future application. Or so Elroy believed; but this was not his field, expert or not. He felt the shaky vulnerability of specialisation, where you know absolutely everything in your chosen field but it is a knowledge with blinkers, shutting you off even from closely-related disciplines. 'Memory glasses'!

His confusion must have registered, despite his attempt to conceal it. Bones was watching him.

"Visually connecting to the current screen display and tapping into the source code, and recording it", Bones relayed with more understanding than parrot-fashion repetition, as Elroy marvelled at exactly who this guy was. "Wireless, naturally", added the ex-caretaker.

Naturally, reflected Elroy. That was nothing new. Wireless information technology was even taking over from cords and cables in the domestic market, while it had been his own stock-in-trade for years. It explained the thick lenses for poor, dim-sighted Charlie, he thought sardonically: even miniaturisation has to be fitted in somewhere.

"So you see -" the ambiguity caused Slick-Hair to chuckle briefly before a hard edge returned to his voice, "we - Mr Winston", as he inclined his head to his co-conspirator, "have observed and recorded your commendable exercise."

Commendable? Causing widespread technical breakdowns leading to the same collapse in the oil market Slick-hair had just complained of, 'commendable'? Panic and confusion were battling inside him. They had the formula, it was there in front of his eyes, the very parade of equations which had been silently dissolving in his own memory. His panic was not knowing what they wanted from it, and him. The confusion was why they should describe it as 'commendable'. He wondered if his eyes were darting about wildly, in tune with his thoughts.

"I don't know who you are working for, Mr Fitzgibbon",
continued Slick-Hair, "your department, perhaps -", he must
have been referring to Elroy's legitimate federal surveillance
posting, if you could call it 'legitimate', "or even yourself.
Understandably so, it will be worth a fortune. But we rather
believe you should be maintaining your loyalty to us. You did
take the oath, after all."

He means LOTUS, Elroy understood, grimly. That oath, with
the unstated threats, before either he or Walt became aware of
the sub-federal subterfuge they had been dragged into. Even
now, he had no idea how much legitimate support was given to
the LOngTerm Unexploited energy Sources group or who really
did command the international strategy of the United States of
America. All he did know, he was in no position to argue about
it.

"We are prepared to overlook our disappointment in your - let
us not call it 'betrayal'", Slick-Hair proceeded tautly, "but if this
is the remedy, as I assume you to have calculated, it is fortunate
we have ... er ... met you in time."

Elroy's mind was racing to catch up but he still wasn't there.

"In time?" he asked, bleakly.

"Mr Fitzgibbon", Slick-Hair became matter-of-fact in tone, "to
reverse this - madness - will be laudable, to say the least, but the
ability to do so will be, shall I say, highly prized. I guess you
thought it would make you wealthy beyond your wildest dreams
but where should your true loyalties lie? Perhaps you had overlooked that and, as I say, we are prepared to exercise our
discretion, only - of course -", and he eyed Elroy grimly, "if you
in turn are prepared to co-operate now."

Elroy could not work it out. The panic was beginning to take
over from the confusion. Did they want him to use the formula
again? If so, where? How could he? Was he to become an agent
of corruption in some manner beyond his imagining? Besides, he
could not remember it all. Then he remembered the screen.
Before he could look at it again, Bones cut in.

"You've worked out how to stop it, haven't you?" sniped Bones.

"And maybe even planned to hold the country to ransom, eh?"
added Slick-Hair. "Shame on you, Mr Fitzgibbon. And you a man
of religion, an' all."

So that was it! They had somehow jumped to the conclusion this formula was the cure, not the cause!

"And there you were", Slick-Hair carried on, "all cosy in that room, working out your formula and, I guess, sending it up by NSA satellite - tut, tut, Mr Fitzgibbon - and testing if it worked, while helpful Mr Winston here - Charlie Bones -", another chuckle, "was only waiting to show you out through the door." At this they both gave a short laugh and Elroy was even aware of a snigger emanating from one of the minders.

"It didn't work", muttered Elroy, now realising he had caught up at last and might be able to extricate himself by feigning ignorance.

"No, evidently it did not", agreed Slick-Hair, "but you're a clever man, Fitzgibbon, I've no doubt it would not have been long before you got it right, which is why we have invited you here", he smiled smoothly, "and you can complete the task for us." He looked unblinkingly at Elroy and added, "which is what I am sure you would have suggested yourself, eventually, wouldn't you?"

He did not wait for an answer, probably knowing he would only be served with a reluctant untruth. But it was no help to Elroy, who now realised, distressfully, what was about to take place. He would be faced with desperate choices: to ratify the formula on the screen, whereupon they would very soon discover he had perpetrated the whole seize-up scenario - with the Lord knew what consequences for himself, and for Mariana and the children if it came to that; or he would have to tamper with the equations to nullify the formula. Either way, they would not get the result they had convinced themselves he could deliver. Before he could think further, Slick-Hair had grasped his chair-back and swung him to face the screen.

"So to business, Mr Fitzgibbon. It shouldn't take you long. I've heard you described as a genius in some quarters."

Elroy focused on the display of characters and then another horror struck him, although for an instant, as a relief. He was aware that part of the formula was missing. There should have been another row of characters at the top. Bones must have entered the computer room too late or not touched the 'record' sensor on the side of the spectacles quickly enough. Whatever the reason, the formula was incomplete. His surge of delight was mingled with dismay at the knowledge that he could no longer remember the whole formula himself. Staring at the screen did not bring it back. Even if it was what they wanted, he could not have helped.

"Come along, Mr Fitzgibbon", breathed Slick-Hair form behind his shoulder, "this is familiar territory to you. We shan't be impressed if you play dumb." The first hint of impatience was creeping into his tone.

"It's not all there", Elroy muttered bleakly at the screen.

"Well now, you might not be surprised to know we had worked that out already", remarked Slick-Hair acidly, and Elroy heard a sardonic grunt come from the direction of Bones behind him, "otherwise we might have been so overcome by our success that we would have forgotten all about you." Elroy noted the man was now becoming a master of sarcastic irony, replacing his erstwhile measured civility. "So - please - continue with your work. I can be patient."

Elroy hovered over the keyboard with absolutely no idea what to do. He could not supply what they wanted. Doubtless, if he just typed in anything for show, they would assume he was deliberately obstructing them. If he did nothing, they would come to the same conclusion. He was trapped. He felt suddenly, desperately alone. All the triumph of what they - he, Olivia, Walt, Bella - had achieved was becoming a bitter memory. An agony overtook him. Had the Power which had blessed him, had visited him, chosen him and bestowed the gift upon him, had it now abandoned him? He began to feel despair. You cannot despair, for God is with you. Is He? Was he, Elroy, just another pawn in the history of God's earth, cast aside once his job was done? Seek not your reward on earth, for you shall find it in Heaven. Is that so? Little comfort when you are left alone to your fate. Pull yourself together, man, this is not 'fate', this is not the Inquisition, nor even the fabled cells of Guatanemo Bay.

"I - " He looked up blankly at Slick-Hair. "I just can't remember right now."

"Well, that's fine", replied Slick-Hair almost sweetly, "we thought of that, too. We can help you on that." As he spoke, he turned towards the centre of the room and Elroy swivelled to follow him with his eyes. Bones - Winston - moved to one side, from where he had been standing in front of the chair. Elroy now saw it full-on for the first time. He noticed now that the flexible wire from the equipment on the shelf behind did not stop under the chair legs but was clipped to the frame so it wound up the rear and ended in two split lengths, partly concealed behind the back of the chair, and protruding over the top, each with a small dial or plate attached. Elroy stifled a gasp as he realised they were electrodes. In mounting fear, he noticed two other split connections with electrodes clipped close to the edge of the seat, where they would reach the lower part of a person's body.

"Wha -!" he exclaimed.

"Our *aide-de-memoir*", smiled Slick-Hair, clearly pleased with more of his linguistic agility. "I must ask you to sit down, if you would oblige." It was studied courtesy, loaded with menace behind the unwavering smile. "It has a high success rate, I assure you", he finished.

Elroy remained in his seat. Fear struck to his core. What was this? This was storybook stuff. This was allegations in Sunday newspapers, unfounded, unsubstantiated. Then he remembered Alan Cargill; and his own confiscated tie and shoelaces; and the soundproofed door; incident unheard, solutions denied.

Without thinking further, he leapt out of his swivel chair and lunged for the door, aiming to burst between the minders before they realised what he was doing. He was not quick enough. The bulky guards possessed sharper reflexes than their physiques suggested. The two either side of the door stepped decisively in his path, the third grabbed him from one side, while the two then grappled at his arms and torso. He fought. As big as each of them individually, he struggled like never before but his arms were pinned down before he could lash out, he was contesting with experts, experts who could disable without causing unnecessary damage or harm, and he was rapidly constricted like a fly in a spider's spun web, unhurt but immobilised. He was dragged and hauled to the big chair.

"Come now, Mr Fitzgibbon", reproved Slick-Hair, whose smile had faded but he had otherwise watched the one-minute drama dispassionately from beside the chair, "if all goes well, we are merely talking of, shall we say, jolting your memory. No other discomfort." Elroy had the clear impression that 'jolt' was not an accidental choice of word. He was pressed down onto the chair and only now became aware of the grey leather straps hanging from its two arms, as they were buckled over his wrists. A similar strap, which had been dangling out of sight behind the chair, was fastened across his chest. He was panting and sweating whilst he continued to struggle impotently and only indistinctly heard Slick-Hair saying, "Many of our guests find that a defective memory is swiftly repaired by this process." Elroy twisted his head this way and that but it did not prevent the two upper electrodes being attached to his temples by someone behind: it must have been Bones, now very much more of the Winston than the Charlie of distant memory.

"We'll leave it that, at first, shall we, Mr Winston?" Slick-Hair was standing facing Elroy while Bones withdrew his hands from the lower electrodes and went instead to the active keyboard.

"Now, Mr Fitzgibbon", said Slick-Hair, "how about if you dictate the missing parts of the formula as you recall them and Mr Winston will type them down. If your memory fails you at any point, we can just provide some small assistance at first", and he nodded to a point behind the chair where, unseen by Elroy, one of the minders had moved to the equipment on the shelf. The man made a very slight twist to a knob and Elroy twitched at the sharp stab at his temples.

"Just a tickle, eh, Mr Fitzgibbon?" smiled Slick-Hair, "quite often all the memory requires, we find. Anticipation of the *unknown* is a remarkable stimulant."

Elroy was panting from the struggle and heaving with trepidation.

"You can't do this", he ground through his teeth, "this is criminal. I'm not a terrorist, you can't just haul me in here. I'll tell as soon as I'm out."

"And your lovely wife - Mariana, is it? - and the children?" smiled Slick-Hair, as though inviting them all to tea. Elroy stiffened. Nothing had changed since his abduction. He and the whole family remained at risk unless he did all that was demanded. He quavered. But there was still nothing he could do. They would not believe that. They thought he was the ultimate expert - the 'genius'. How could he even begin to explain that the ultimate knowledge was beyond him, beyond anyone on earth.

"Now then, Mr Winston, are you ready?" Bones was sitting at the keyboard. Slick-Hair gave a slight nod to the minder at the controls. "Mr Fitzgibbon?"

Elroy could feel sweat trickling down his forehead, past the electrodes, and dripping from his face and jaw. He resolved to dictate some numbers, just anything, just anything to keep things going, to play for time in a game where eternity might not be long enough. He opened his mouth. As he did so, watching Slick-Hair's determined smile directed at him from the floor, Bones let out a shout of alarm. He was staring at the computer display. Slick-Hair jerked around to look and Elroy could see past them both to the screen. The characters of the incomplete formula were moving; not flickering or jumping as with a disturbed electrical contact, but dancing up and down and sideways and at irregular angles. Then they were cartwheeling over one another, leapfrogging - that's all you could describe it as - tumbling like alpha-numeral acrobats. Bones jabbed at the keyboard until Slick-Hair clutched his arm, crying "Don't!", in case the whole display should disappear.

"Get the glasses!" shouted Slick-Hair. "Play the formula back in!" Elroy could see the panic that this prize might be summarily snatched from Slick-Hair, LOTUS and the rest of them. Bones rushed behind the chair to grab the 'memory glasses' from the shelf. Slick-Hair turned to confront Elroy.

"What the hell's this, Fitzgibbon?" he snarled.

Elroy shook his head dumbly.

"Don' know", he replied, genuinely mystified.

Bones hurried back to face the screen, looping the spectacles over his ears. But he pulled up short. The screen was changing again. They all watched, stilled by it. The characters were slowing down and compacting into a linked bunch, each one touching another at different angles, some right way up, some upside down, some at varying slants. And then, as a whole joined-up unit, they began to glow and, with that glow, melt into a different colour. From screen-character black they glowed, shimmered and transformed into a soft, vibrant gold and - Elroy just gazed in astonishment; he could not see the other expressions from behind them - the individual shapes of the characters diffused and moulded together to form, slowly but distinctly, a pair of golden wings, spread to fill almost the entire screen. The shape was perfect, the individual characters completely vanished.

"What the fuck!" Slick-Hair took a step back. Then he broke forward to grab Bones by the arm. "Play!" He instructed loudly. "Play! Get the goddam formula back in. Play it back in, for Christ's sake! I don't know what the fuck that is but get rid of it. Play the fucking formula back."

The guy had at last lost his cool. Elroy was still only seeing the two of them from behind and observed Slick-Hair hopping from foot to foot in his anxiety, pushing and shoving at Bones to get him to switch the 'play' function. Elroy saw it must be tiny sensor pads on the spectacles' arms for 'record' and 'play' that delivered the equipment's functions. Bones reached to the left side of the spectacles beside his ear then staggered and cried out, clutching his hands to the sides of his head. As he staggered, he turned, trying to duck away from something and Elroy realised he was trying to pull the spectacles off but they would not budge. Bones was now facing him as he tore away at the glasses with anguished cries. The lenses were transformed. They were each filled with an image identical to the one on the screen: a pair of petite golden wings. Bones thrashed wildly about, trying to tear off the glasses.

"You've hit 'record'!" yelled Slick-Hair.

"I didn't!" cried out Bones, between savage moans as he tried to separate himself from the glasses.

Even in his own confusion, Elroy was certain Bones was right. He had correctly hit 'play'; then something else, whatever this was, had taken over. He watched in awed silence as Bones struggled, eyes each obscured by a pair of shining golden wings.

The minders rushed to Bones to steady him and help with the glasses. At last, with a yelp, he tugged them off and staggered into the arms of a minder. The glasses clattered to the floor. Slick-Hair dived for them and held them at arms' length in one hand. But the image was already fading. In a couple of seconds the golden wings had disappeared. Slick-Hair spun to look at the screen. The same effect. The last traces of the wings were fading into the silver background and were gone. He glared at the screen and then and at the glasses; and then at Elroy.

"Fitzgibbon! What the fuck was that?"

Elroy, still sweating, just gazed back.

"Don't know. Don' know", he mumbled, shaking his head with the electrodes still attached.

"Well, we might have to ask you some more about that", breathed Slick-Hair heavily, while Bones tottered to sit down on one of the other swivel chairs, rubbing his eyes and groaning quietly. Slick-Hair looked over at him.

"You okay, Winston?"

"Couldn't see", moaned Bones.

"You see now?" enquired Slick-Hair, giving the impression of being more concerned to lose an effective accomplice than his possible loss of sight.

Bones wiped his hands away from his eyes and gingerly opened them and blinked tightly, screwing them up and opening them again.

"Yuh ... yuh", he affirmed. "What *was* that?"

"We are about to ask the expert here about that." Slick-Hair looked savagely at Elroy, still held captive in the chair. "Get that formula back first." Bones smacked at 'play' on the spectacles and faced the computer screen. Nothing happened.

"It's gone!" Bones was frantically tapping at the glasses, took them off to repeat it, then replaced them, still trying.

"Is it in the computer?" barked Slick-Hair.

Bones leapt to the keyboard and his hands flashed across the keys. The screen remained silvery blank.

"Nope!" cried Bones, fretfully. "Gone. Can't get it back!"

Slick-Hair looked menacingly at Elroy. A phone rang. It was Slick-Hair's and he yanked it out of his pocket. His frown tightened and then he barked, "Okay."

"Release him!" he ordered a minder, gesturing to Elroy in the chair.

"What's up?" blurted Bones.

"Fuck knows!" swore Slick-Hair. "All going shit!"

Elroy was disconnected and unstrapped and allowed to step out of the chair. Slick-Hair headed for the door, followed by Bones, the minders ushering Elroy out between them back through to the apartment. There was an urgent rapping on the apartment entrance door. Bones opened it and a suited man plunged into the room.

"Jesus Christ! Sorry to call you. Goddam electrical storm or summat. Half the communications are off. We got signals going down all over the place. Need you up here!"

He was addressing Slick-Hair, who turned to Elroy.

"Seems you can enjoy the rest of your evening, Mr Fitzgibbon", he remarked stonily, some of his customary composure returning. "We'll see you tomorrow. Perhaps you could give these events some thought." He nodded towards the computer room door, which Bones was hurriedly locking behind them. He followed Slick-Hair out; the three minders took care to step through the doorway well ahead of any move Elroy might be tempted to make. The door shut behind them all and he heard it lock. He stood alone in the apartment living room, trembling and still sweating. He stumbled to the sofa and fell upon it, lying back, face staring at the ceiling. Then he rolled onto his side and could not prevent himself from sobbing into the cushion. The terror was taking its toll. He felt like a child. Then he realised it was not fear that brought the tears; it was not even relief. It was something close to gratitude and joy.

Perhaps, after all, he had not been abandoned.

PARADIGM : WELLBEING

She sat on the clean, dry rock, its sheen against her skin, her visceral garment of leaf and vine slipping from her shoulders, unneeded in the warmth of the day. Their child, steadied by her tender hands, was clasped gently as it sat naked between her knees. She smiled at his approach.

"He waits for you", she smiled. "He sees when you come. He knows you."

"I am his father, he is my son." He knelt before them, the hare and fowl swinging from his belt of knotted hemp, in rhythm with his own lithe motion. "He is well?" he asked, placing a strong brown finger under the infant dimpled chin.

"He is well", she smiled again, "always well. He moves a little, on his knees; he wants to be a man, like his father."

He laughed quietly and stroked the chin that flickered and chuckled at his touch.

Does he know I bring food for you to eat, so he can feed, too?"

His brow furrowed in light lines, caring to know the infant and his mother.

"He knows you hunt for us all and one day he shall hunt, too, your son. Life for more life."

And she took the son to her breast.

"I will prepare for us to eat, also", he spoke fondly to her, "life for more life." The sun shone in his smile and on her breast, and on the lips pursed there to feed.

"Life for life", she murmured, holding the child to her bosom and the man to her heart.

London

The phone rang. It was Paul, out late with friends at some club somewhere. One o'clock in the morning. Bella was already on her way to bed.

"Sorry, Bella." His voice sounded placatory, auguring a request or favour, especially considering the hour of the night.

"What is it?" Maybe she was a bit more mellow in her response tonight than she might customarily have been these days.

"Car won't start. Can you fetch me?"

"What!" Her tone was sharper now, fresh out of the bathroom and standing by the bed. "Get a cab."

"They're all busy, miles of queues and some have stopped."

"Stopped?" Her reason was telling her cab drivers don't just 'down tools' at the most lucrative time of a Friday night.

"Broken down", came Paul's voice, with the din of the London night around him. "It's impossible here", he cawed into the phone.

"Where are you", she wanted to know.

"Piccadilly."

"Aw, Gawd!" He was really expecting her to drive all the way into town to pick him up?

"Look, really sorry, Bel. Just never going to get home, else."

"Get a ride with someone, can't you?" She was feeling exasperated; he wasn't a teenage kid stranded.

"Can't. Jeff's car's broke, too. I dunno. Told him to get it serviced." There was a brief pause while he waited for her to respond. "Look, okay, Bella", he added, "it's late, I shouldn't have called. I'll see you later."

"Paul. Okay." What's the point in making things even worse, she thought; and it takes two. Play her part, maybe, this time. "I'll come. I'll phone you when I'm there, to find you."

"Oh, thanks, love. I'll pay the charge." He sounded genuinely grateful and offering to cough up the congestion charge. 'Love'. Really? She slipped on her jacket, picked up the keys and went downstairs.

Outside, a man climbed out of his hatchback and slammed the door shut in obvious frustration, as she was emerging from the garage. She drove off, amused at someone else in her husband's predicament just as she was setting off to retrieve him. Men! She was not concentrating on the road and had to swerve to avoid an abandoned car protruding at an angle from the kerb. She cursed softly and resolved to be more attentive. She noticed, as she drove into central London, that several people seemed to have had a night on the tiles, overdoing it or whatever, judging by the number of cars left by the roadside, often sticking out without being properly parked. Conscientious drivers, anyway, she reflected, avoiding the irresponsibility of drink-driving. She wondered whether Paul would have made the same decision if it had not been forced on him.

The hand gripped the phone more tightly, knuckles whitening. Two o'clock in the morning. End of the late shift, that hollow time halfway between fall of night and break of day, neither of which being distinguished in the artificial bloom of a strip-lit limbo like the inner office of the Heathrow Customs shed. Gordon Pierce was listening intently, his pursed lips grim, eyes staring out of focus at a point somewhere beyond the edge of his desk. His frown was deepening at what the voice at the other end was telling him, an explanation which was unfolding piece by piece. He spoke to interject, "What is it?"

The answer was crackling with more preamble and detail before it eventually reached its conclusion and Pierce spoke once more for verification before listening to the affirmative response and slowly lowering the phone to its cradle, staring rigidly at the unidentified spot ahead of him, stiffening with disbelief.

Intervention

God would like to have made a joke. The Almighty is not permitted jokes, of course, unless you count the bit of fun He had with Jonah, so he was constrained from this self-indulgence. Had he been free to do so, he might have joshed to his errant aide, "Been making a spectacle of yourself, have you?" and perhaps had a bit of a chortle. As it was, he more soberly observed, "Hmm, wings again?"

Gabriel shuffled, having only just clambered back over the edge of Heaven, and sat down.

"Boss?"

"Ahh ... Umm."

The Lord reflected it was no time for admonishments, which might, in the circumstances, have seemed a trifle pernickety, in the light of a mission successfully accomplished, irrespective of the style of its undertaking. Success, anyway, so far.

"Have we changed things?" grunted Gabriel.

The archangel was only half engaged in conversation, the other half of his attention already absorbed in making up for lost time between L3 and L4 (left foot, toes three and four, to decode Gabriel's private shorthand; or shortfoot, the witticism with which he had failed to amuse the Supreme Being on a number of occasions).

"Change? Yes. But we may only reverse the event; we cannot restore the previous circumstances. We would have to reverse everything back to a single prior occurrence. And even that itself", the Lord added, "might be the consequence of an earlier change." He knew Gabriel understood. In all their conversations about changing the future and revising the past, one factor was constant: as soon as a new chain of events began, as the result of a dislocation to the predetermined order of things, a myriad changes were set in motion. These - each a new link, or a link to a link, in the new chain - became the new order and could not be reversed. Humans had correctly defined it as the impossibility of travelling back in time to change the present, which then would have been the future. Murdering your own grandfather was the example most frequently cited. "This change", proceeded the Lord, unsure how much the excavating angel was taking in, "merely corrects a dislocation arising from a new chain which we were responsible for. We can intervene to prevent suffering if our actions have been the ultimate cause."

Which, roughly translated, sniffed Gabriel to himself while seriously focused on a point below his knees, means 'if we hadn't enlisted him to change things, and then someone hadn't turned up without being preordained - the 'biscuit' - and caused a delay, he would not have got into that pickle in the first place. So we got him out'.

Gabriel understood, even though he looked to be far more interested in other matters - or matter - right now. When they - he, the archangel of Divine instruction - intervened, the effect was not like the waking from a dream, in which nothing had been real. It was at times a rescue or at others, perhaps, an enlightenment but, whichever it was, it was reality altered; subsequent behaviour and attitudes would be different. Another new chain had begun. Events would not resume from the same point as before.

"So after we sorted that picnic", Gabriel meandered on, picking, flicking, picking, flicking, "people burned."

God was quite certain that the intervention to resolve the loaves, fishes and five thousand hungry mouths fiasco was not attended by victims in flames. He hoped His silence would say as much. A vain hope.

"I mean, that rescued Christianity, didn't it?"

"No, not precisely, no", contradicted the Good Lord, with a sigh. "Christianity owed its development to a great deal more than a single event, however necessary that particular intervention."

Gabriel sometimes amused himself with visions of what exactly might have happened to the carpenter had it not been for that smart piece of self-regenerating catering (introduced by yours truly, no less). Not a pretty sight, he generally concluded.

"No, okay, yes", he conceded, "all sorts of other things as well, okay", and his mind darted through the images of shepherds, amazingly solid sea water, the water-to-wine trick, disappearing diseases and a myriad others. "But just take that as the example, You know -" (God, although He was God, did not) "they burned all the witches as a direct result."

"Of what?" The Lord had listened to many of Gabriel's conjectures during their lengthy, indeed eternal, sojourn together but this was a new one.

"As a result of the loaves and fishes thing. And all the others, like You said. Stepping in and sorting it. No fishes ... no Christianity ... no burning."

Gabriel looked up at last and gestured the simple clarity of his argument with upturned palms resting on his knees, with a kind of get-out-of-that expression on his face.

Then he added, as a *coup de grace*, "So if *that* was because of us, because we changed things with the picnic, why didn't we step in to stop any of *that*, rescue any of *them*, I mean, You know", he shrugged, "like Joan of Ar-"

"Yes", the Lord interrupted him, firmly, "I do know."

He pondered in silence. He wanted to say it was because they could not trace every line back through history to separate the acts of self-determination from the acts of divine intervention, from the preordained chains of events, to determine which might have been caused by which, and which might not otherwise have occurred. The meddling would never cease. The fact was, on this occasion their own plan was both cause and effect and needed to be safeguarded, quite apart from their responsibility towards any individual entangled in an unforeseen predicament, triggered by a 'biscuit' in Gabriel parlance. The unplanned presence of someone who should not have been there, causing delay which led to entrapment. That was not the same as identifying His original influence on any selection of burnings, holocausts or other evils to justify reversing them. Was it?

Was it? He brooded, in a deific sort of way, fretfully. Cause and effect. Chains of events. 'Biscuits' and 'railway lines'. Was it not reasonable to suppose that all those hapless individuals, or others like them, would have been burned anyway, for some cause other than Christianity, as links in an alternative chain, regardless of any 'Divine Intervention'? Regardless of any 'miraculous picnic', for instance? Humans did not need religion to justify their perfidious behaviour so it surely was not His fault.

The angel was still watching as the Metaphorical Brow allegorically clouded over.

"Well, I was only asking." And he bent down to other matters, as one might say.

Salvation

"SALVATION."

The banner headline spread across the top of the New York Herald Tribune in bold capitals, a single word of declamation.

The east coast woke up to it this sunny May morning, fresh warmth blowing through opened windows, along verandas and down gleaming streets yet to acquire the dusty oppressiveness of high summer, blowing the word into minds waiting to be captivated at the dawn of a new day. The editorial team, with the rare presence of the editor himself, had toyed with a suffixed exclamation mark but eschewed its sensationalist flavour and settled upon their pronouncement as a simple statement of fact: SALVATION.

Others were less demure. As the sun traversed westwards, awaking middle America was greeted not only with the appended punctuation point but, further west and deeper south, the more dramatic, "SAVED!" and "SPARED!" Into bible belt - Dirk Donahoe country - and it became innumerable variations on an unashamed "THE WAY OF THE LORD!", until the sun spilled over breakfast table newsprint for its more, as they liked to suppose, sophisticated readerships, with "AMERICA FINDS SOLUTION" and "US WAY CAN LEAD THE WORLD."

One of the quieter ones, most appreciated in journalistic circles, was "TWIGG LEAVES LEGACY", despite its apparent attempt to foreclose any future achievements or further term of this presidency. It was about the only pun remaining unexplored in an exhausted lexicon of branches, roots, buds and seeds.

The President herself rolled over under the state bedroom duvet, floated a tanned arm against the patterned silk and revealed a proud smooth breast as she pushed the cover away, blinking at the sunlight streaming over her skin from between half-open curtains. She felt her legs part as she turned, ever aware of the animal between, and smiled the smile that oozed seduction even with no-one present to be consumed. She swung one naked leg after the other over the side of the bed, allowing a hand to gently caress her bare torso as she snaked to her feet and strode lithely to the en-suite bathroom. The hand followed habit and slid across the almost shaven triangle at the centre of her consciousness and she caught sight of herself in the full-length mirror. She stopped, taken aback. She suddenly understood that, for the first time, she was not influencing events or controlling policy with her most formidable power, her sexuality: her 'sex'. It was something else. She gazed at the magnificent bronzed reflection before her and was overcome not with pride but with humility. Something else had gripped her. Something had wrested control from those irresistible contours of gleaming peaks and beckoning hollows.

"My angel", she murmured.

There had been no physical contact but she had been swept up in a subsuming embrace and filled. Oh, Lord, she had been filled a thousand times before but not like this. It was still inside her. She looked at the body in the mirror as if she might behold the glow she felt within. "My angel." Only now, the morning after, did she fleetingly wonder how his nakedness might have appeared but then recognised she did not care. Somehow, inexplicably, he penetrated her whole being without touching her. Not for a moment did this woman of the earth admit a spirituality of experience. It was physical, invading her with its missive for the intellect. Its power was its logic. Yet - and her smile widened at the headlines displayed on the television which had sprung to life behind her - yet, she was prepared to adopt the rhetoric of religious fervour if that was the ocean upon which this new ship was to sail.

"See", grunted Gabriel, shaking a finger irritably, to disengage whatever was stubbornly adhered to it. "Sorted. Like I said."

There was a silver lining to every cloud, mused the Lord in one of the many little homilies he had gifted to various species. Even the ammonia clouds on Tryxx glinted at their edges if caught in synergy with one of its suns. And this particular glistening bonus, whatever else was manifested in Gabriel upon a return from Earth, was that he did not smell. Ironic that one of the most troublesome species in the mighty cosmos was one of its least malodorous. However, as so often with silver linings, this one was largely obliterated by its cloud: Gabriel's mood. Something about Earth rendered him obstreperous and argumentative after virtually every visit. God wondered if He was to blame, failing to imbue the angel with his own Love That Passeth All Understanding. A bit of Job's patience would have been better than nothing.

"I mean", declared the archangel, with an air of finality and a brush of his hands, in the manner of one who seeks to wrap up the discussion before it has even started, "that's it. Congestion - down. Pollution - down."

"Energy consumption, down", murmured Victoria Twigg, echoing the TV voices, as she stepped from the shower and reached for a towel. "Pressure eased on natural resources." She marvelled at how it was all falling into place. A phenomenon - freak or otherwise - to disable technology, a revelation in churches everywhere, and a nation apparently stirring from the nightmare which up to now had been termed 'progress'. The world must follow. Dependency upon the American economy determined that, with America using less and buying less, the other nations will sell less, make less, earn less, buy less. Less is more - where did that phrase come from - less is slowing down, discovering an inner contentment, co-operating to save the future. The world would smile and understand.

"See", announced Gabriel, "I told you."

God said nothing.

"It's like", grinned Abigail Jackson in the Wal-Mart aisle, on a shared shopping trip with her new friend Rita, "it's like when our fence blew down in the storm. The whole length down one side. Every day we could see Jerry and Jen next door; stepped out in the yard and there they were. Talked like we'd never before!"

"About what?" questioned Rita, undecided between chick peas and corn, a can in either hand.

"Anything. Nothing. Anything", beamed Abigail, "just passing the time. Nothing. Point is, we'd never done that. Just chatting. Never saw them, for the fence."

"*Your* fence", was Rita's mild rebuke, tossing the corn in the trolley, favouring the kids instead of Cal.

"Yeh, sure. I know. We put it up. Like, that's what you do, ain't it? Your yard, your fence. But - guess -" Abigail stood challenging Rita, a pack of fries poised above the trolley.

"What?" came Rita's expectant reply.

"We never put it back up!"

"Never?" Rita displayed her surprise. "No fence?"

"No. It would have been like building a barrier. We'd got so used to seeing them and talking an' all!"

Rita raised a pair of approving eyebrows at this expression of neighbourliness and decided she had completed her share of the trolley-load.

"This is the same", continued Abigail, happily.

"Yeh?" queried Rita.

"Yeh. Isn't it for you? All sharing things, seeing folks, co-operating, helping. Just making new friends. *And*", she rounded off with enthusiasm, "getting to know old ones a whole lot better!"

"Mm", Rita considered, thoughtfully. Yes, she had not really seen it that way but it was true for her, too.

"S'pose you're right." And she smiled in a comfortable sort of way. It was surely the case that relationships were more open and relaxed than they had ever been. And, why, she had scarcely spoken to her cute friend Abigail until her own seized-up Ford had thrown them together.

"You haven't put much in", noted Abigail, indicating the trolley.

"Aw, plenty", responded Rita.

"Sure?" smiled Abigail. "Here, have this on me; loadsa room in the car." She dropped a bag of fries onto the pile of provisions. In the old days, Rita might have flushed with embarrassment and protested at misplaced generosity. Now, she poked her friend in the arm with a grin of mock reproachment: she had done the same for her last week. And who's counting anyway?

The LOTUS chairman was on the phone to the 'observer' woman.

"What's the point!" he was complaining, fiercely. "Another Iraq is a non-starter if we can't shift the oil we've got. Oil's dead in the water!" He grimaced at the loud cackle at the other end of the phone. The 'observer' woman thought it had been a deliberate witticism and was laughing to humour him. Neither of them actually saw the joke.

"See", asserted Gabriel again, "no war, either."

"Well, I hardly think", began the Lord in response to this flight of imagination.

"No, that's what we said, didn't we?" argued the angel, "no avarice, no war. One leads to the other. If you get rid of one, you ge -"

He paused, looking up at the Almighty.

"Boss?"

Fully clothed, in a sleek twin-set and looking more the President than the predator this morning, Twigg pondered further.

Could she really be about to lead the country into reverse? Was Eldorado behind, not ahead of them? Extraordinary, but she believed it. It was within her. She was the medium, not the message. The television sages were still poring over the headlines. Salvation from calamity, they concurred. That was the message. Hitherto, responsibility to avoid the global apocalypse had been neatly deferred to a future generation. 'Action on climate change' studiously avoided any dramatic transformation of life today. Yet, suddenly, here it was. Action visited upon a startled populace, perhaps, but now clasped to the bosom of the community. The community of the Lord? Yup, that was the broadly expressed view. Apologists for secularism bit their tongues. This was no place for them now.

"My angel", whispered Victoria, dreamily, and rang for breakfast.

"I fear", spoke the Almighty, softly. Not that the Supreme Being feared anything in the whole universe, with the possible exception of Gabriel's return from Splong trips, but it was a turn of phrase that suited the occasion. "You may have overlooked something."

The look of resignation on the archangel's face was one he did not attempt to conceal.

"Biscuit?" he suggested, hesitantly.

"If you put it like that", agreed the Lord, Who wished he would not.

Oh, brilliant, thought Gabriel. No rest for th - but, as on many such occasions, he felt it inappropriate even to *think* to the end of that phrase.

Hoi Fong paced along the Shanghai sidewalk, shining shop windows dazzling to right and to left. The elegant throng skipped and scurried, chattering and smiling, fashionably clad from magazine pages and designer couture. They darted in and out of the bustling stores, emerging with smart bags containing the latest of everything: clothing, gadgets, music and video, stuff for kitchens, stuff for bedrooms, things for tonight, more for tomorrow. Everything that the young, and some older, Chinese had enviously watched the West enjoying and now they were participating, too. And catching up fast, even promising to pull ahead. Hoi was more energised by this brash modern metropolis than he admitted to Hwee Lo; yet it caused him to value the relative sobriety of Beijing, although the ancient capital city, too, was visibly succumbing to glitzy modernisation by the day. Forced to choose, he would select chickens and scrub in the setting sun any time. He was only here to visit a couple of dealers, taking his mind off the worry of delay at the English docks and fretting inquiries from Mr Teng. A group of twenty-somethings hurried lightly past him. He heard a snatch of their banter, laughing at the Americans 'sharing' things they had mocked the world with by hitherto acquiring in triplicate. A handsome lad pointed at the window they were passing and cried, "Imagine not having one each!" And they all laughed at the widescreen televisions on display, pulsing with the same commercials. "Crazeeee!" shouted one of them above the hubbub of street-life and traffic, before they merged with the crowd ahead.

Elroy had woken in his sealed tomb, deprived of the light of day. He had slept soundly, drained. Breakfast was delivered again and his hand shook as he raised the cup to his lips, until he steadied and took control of himself. His eyes kept being drawn to the locked door. Maybe a night's sleep had only delayed the inevitable. Rescued but not released; he shivered at the thought of when it might begin all over again. Miracles do not happen twice.

He started as the apartment door was abruptly opened and Slick-Hair stood there, a couple of minders behind him. A sardonic smile played on his captor's lips. Elroy's hands clutched at the sofa, where he had sat down in contemplation. The beads of sweat were gathering on his brow already.

"Good morning, Mr Fitzgibbon", was the smooth greeting, as though addressing a captive in a secret basement were a normal part of daily life, "it seems", he went on without further niceties, "your office is enquiring after your whereabouts. Unfortunate." He stroked his chin. "Questions might draw unwelcome attention. Perhaps it would be as well if you went back to work." That was all he said until they reached the top of the stairs and a minder was about to blindfold him. Then Slick-Hair looked at him without smiling. "We'll be in touch. You'll say you have been with Uncle Joe." Elroy knew what he meant. 'Uncle Joe' was the cover for any activity classified beyond anyone's right to know. It could only rarely be employed without arousing suspicion, through its catch-all quality, but was invaluable to preserve secrecy *in extremis*. Slick-Hair added a parting shot. "Don't delay. They seem anxious to see you."

Isabella had been roused from sleep by the blaring of car horns. Intermittent honking from what was normally a quiet suburban residential street. She got up to look out of the window to see the same halted car from last night, stationary where the driver had slammed the door and stomped away. There were a few others; she could glimpse one further up the road that she had swerved to avoid, only just in time. The sounds of horns came from irritable drivers having to skirt around these scattered obstacles. Her first reaction was at the laziness of drivers failing to retrieve their vehicles before traffic built up. Her next was translated into a broad grin, succeeded by a yelp of delight. Surely not!

She flung on some clothes and rushed down into the road, turned in the direction she drove last night and half-walked, half-jogged. Yes, there, that car she'd had to avoid; and that other one! She trotted on, passing others, making nearly a mile before pulling up, panting. Some drivers had been fruitlessly turning ignition keys, red in frustration, with no response. Others stood by, bewildered. Others may have come and gone already, seeking assistance. Those that noticed Isabella may have been affronted by the childish grin that could have been taunting them.

London! Now! Wow! Her mobile rang. It was Paul. He had risen much earlier to collect the car.

"Still won't start! Chinese rubbish!"

"You said they were good!" She could barely control herself.

"Well they're crap!" His voice was sharp and angry. "At least I'm not the only one!" She visualised him stranded in Piccadilly like a beached whale; okay, she mentally adjusted the vision, beached porpoise. "Looks like a scrap yard here!"

Paul could not for the life of him fathom the peals of laughter rippling down the phone as he cut it dead and jammed it furiously into his pocket.

Part Five

COMPLICATIONS

COMPLICATIONS

Uranium

"*Uranium?*"

Andy pushed the door closed behind him in dumbfounded silence, as he stared at Gordon looking up grimly from behind his desk. He whistled softly.

"Sit down." Gordon Pierce motioned to a chair. Andy dropped into it. He studied his boss as they viewed each other for long moments.

"But -" began Andy, puzzled.

"Yeh", nodded Gordon, acknowledging the perplexity.

"Reactor stuff?" suggested Andy, hopefully.

"No", responded Pierce, bluntly.

Andy shook his head, still staring uncomprehendingly across the desk.

"Enriched", Pierce confirmed.

"Jesus Christ", whispered Andy and gazed up at the ceiling, searching the bland cream paintwork for reason or denial.

"Weapons grade", Gordon added, as though any of his team needed to be informed of the sole purpose of enriching uranium isotope 238 to produce fissionable isotope 235.

"Fucking hell", breathed Andy, exhaling all the air from his chest in a single deep blow. "Here?"

"Don't know, Andy, don't know; that's just it."

"But -" Andy picked up his thread, "it's all accounted for, isn't it? It's not floating around like the powder." The 'powder' being the limitless quantities of heroin and cocaine they spent their daily lives hunting down. "It doesn't go missing", he asserted in the face of this fantastic notion.

"Doesn't it?" countered Pierce, glowering at him. "It's never all been fully docketed. Not since the Wall came down. All that chaos in the Soviets? Controlled disarmament? Joking!" He clenched a fist on the desk and then leaned back with an expression etched in worry.

"So?" queried Andy, in the position of one who depended upon senior officers for this kind of disclosure.

"Like the rumours say", shrugged Pierce, "always been estimated some chunks of it went missing. Never proved, never sussed."

"So why here?" asked Andy, following the logic of why Pierce was so concerned.

"Might not be", Gordon shrugged again. "They reckon some stuff that's been hidden in Russia for years had finally been traded into China."

"China?" quizzed Andy.

"Yup. Underworld, not official - not Government, you know."

Andy understood. The Chinese government went nuclear years ago and no doubt had enough enriched uranium not to have to delve into the black market for it.

"So why here?" repeated Andy.

"Might not be", with another noncommittal lift of the shoulders from Gordon. "But we trade with China. Stuff coming in all the time."

"So does everyone", objected Andy. "Second biggest traders after the States."

"I know, I know", sighed Pierce, heavily, "but we've had a tip-off. It could be here."

"Here? *Right* here?" Andy waved an arm in the general direction of the inspection shed.

"Maybe. Maybe. They don't know. Could be here, could be the docks, could be anywhere. Might be wrong altogether. Just ... I mean, look, Andy, you seen -?"

"Jeez, Gordon!" Andy cut in hotly. "How am I gonna miss bloody uranium! What's it like, eh?"

"Heavy", Gordon acknowledged, uncomfortably.

"Yeh! Right! So I'm gonna just *notice* if something like that comes through, aren't I?" He ran an aggrieved finger around his open shirt collar and shifted peevishly in his chair.

"Yeh, yeh, I know", nodded Gordon, conscious of offending his best investigative mechanic. Andy never missed a trick, as far as either of them knew. Well, if anything got past him, they would become aware of it sooner or later.

"How heavy, anyway?" grumbled Andy.

"Well, just, you know like I do, mate. Very heavy. For its size. Could be small but heavy. You know, I'm just telling you what I've been told so you can keep an eye open." He shrugged again. "Probably nothing, anyway." But he was worried, and it showed. You could miss a few smuggled jewels, and they knew sackfuls of powder evaded them every day. But uranium! Jesus Christ.

Andy grunted and got up to leave. He turned at the door, disturbed but mystified.

"Who'd be crazy enough to want to make a bomb?"

Gordon looked at him for a moment before replying.

"Who'd be crazy enough to fly planes into buildings? Your granny?"

Manchu

"What was so funny?"

Paul went straight to the kitchen for a drink and something for a very late lunch. He found Bella there, perched on a stool, munching an apple. She tried not to grin but had spent the whole morning unable to contain herself, breaking into periodic bouts of spontaneous laughter as she went about the house. She had excitedly phoned Ruth and - yes - cars were halted and randomly abandoned in that part of London, too. She had phoned other friends in as many quarters as she knew: it was the same everywhere. Some friends laughed with her, others were nonplussed at her squeals of delight, especially the occasional ones whose own vehicles had inexplicably died. "Well, not the biggest laugh I've had, Bella love", remarked one drily. She was just contemplating calling Elroy or Olivia when Paul stumped through the door.

"Oh, well, no -" she held her fingers to her lips, like a schoolgirl pretending not to laugh "just a picture of all those drunks trying to start their cars", she gasped, flippantly.

"I wasn't drunk", stated Paul, gruffly, as he reached into the fridge for a can. "Not funny at one o'clock in the morning, Square full of idiots and all you want to do is get home." He was even more fed up now, having spent the whole morning back in town, unable either to start the car, perched half on the pavement to one side of Piccadilly, or to get a breakdown truck. Too many people trying the same thing, apparently, and breakdown services spending ages with any vehicle they reached, without actually achieving anything. "Bloody Chinese cars."

"Well, you've just spent the last three months praising them off the planet!" She sang from her stool. She knew very well that almost anything she said was going to wind him up but she couldn't stop herself. This was magic. She was thrilled to the core with the realisation this could be all down to her - and those mad moments in the NSA computer room with Elroy.

"Huh", he grunted, "well maybe this was the test they needed; and they're crap."

"It's only the one you were driving last night", she observed lightly. "And anyway, you said other cars had stopped." She so wished she could spill out to him what she knew and the part she had played. This was wonderful. All that was happening in the States, back home, and now she had helped to bring it on here. She had been avidly devouring the news from the US, seen all the pronouncements and future projections, rejoiced in the implications for the planet. This was a million times more than she could have hoped to achieve by any number of marches. Oh, Paul. She wished she could tell him but he was just a car salesman right now, the worst animal to boast to about what she had done. Besides, considering the fragile condition of their relationship, crowing in triumph would only turn the screw. This was softening her.

"Yeh ...well", he had forgotten about the other drivers in the same predicament. There was Jeff and, yes, various others who seemed to have the same problem. He had been so frustrated, and so anxious to get himself home; and then this morning so preoccupied with sorting out the car one way or another and then having to leave it where it was. He had not really counted how many others there were. Yeh, rather too many for coincidence, now he thought about it. He looked at his American wife and the serious expression which she appeared to be straining to maintain. The States. Yes. The same phenomenon as they'd had there? God, no, he thought. Let's not get into science fiction. Maybe this was something, okay, maybe some common electrical fault but all it was doing was exposing cars with weaknesses. Sorting the wheat from the chaff. And this Chinese car was turning out to be chaff after all.

Back at the showroom on Monday, he was fuming. He took little or no interest in the reports of widespread car breakdowns - it was not overly dramatic, if you counted, anyway; maybe one in ten or less; media sensationalising as usual. That was what he thought about it generally but he was mad as hell the way it hit him personally. Customers kept phoning to complain their 'Mets' had broken down. He swore in the office, he swore around the showroom; he had to prevent himself swearing down the phone to customers and was aware of a tap on the arm from a colleague more than once as he was about to curse violently in the earshot of customers there in the showroom.

To Paul, it seemed the Manchu Mets, whatever other makes and models were seizing up all over London, were ten times worse. In fact, if he had stopped to count, which is what his staff were doing but could not get it through to him, there were only seven 'Met' breakdowns reported by customers by lunchtime. But that was a damned sight more than ten per cent of the thirty-five he had sold. When the eighth complaint came in at just before three o'clock, that settled it. Paul phoned the agent and stopped the order. The forty-five Manchu Mets still waiting for final import clearance at Folkestone docks could go back.

"Back?" came the alarmed response from the agent.

"Back!" barked Paul, firmly. "I've no contract to sell scrap metal!" And he slammed down the phone. The agent thought for a moment, sizing up all the legal and financial implications. There could certainly be a tricky argument about automobiles showing such susceptibility to faults only weeks after being sold. For starters, perhaps he should toss the ball back into Mr Choi's court. He and his backers were mighty keen to get this business. Maybe they would come up with an idea.

Discount

"Well, brother, you will have to offer replacements."

Hoi recoiled in shock. He had telephoned Teng as soon as the agent rang off after breaking the news. Suddenly, amusement at the US predicament had been wiped out by similar occurrences in London and they were affecting his own proud Manchu Mets, guaranteed reliable and fault-free! Teng had uttered sympathetic noises and insisted on coming straight round to the factory. Hoi had breathed a sigh of relief: some financial assistance, perhaps, in transporting the load back to Beijing, if that became necessary; or, better, exerting influence in certain quarters - who knew how wide and deep stretched the Society's tentacles. But instead the madman had sidled into his office to propose financial suicide! Hoi summoned all his reserves of composure.

"Brother Teng", he began, as deferentially as his domain would allow, "we really cannot -"

"Brother Hoi", Teng broke in sharply, a tone only tempered by the permanent smile which Hoi presumed had been fixed at birth, "you could challenge this legally and you might very probably win but", he feigned a sigh of resignation, "we cannot brook delay. Your payments", he added, meaningfully, "no doubt depend on those sales."

"But Brother Teng", urged Hoi, dismayed at this complete disregard for financial logic, "sales will be outweighed by losses from such compensation!"

"Why, no, brother, not at all", contradicted Teng, in the manner of one politely affirming his choice of tea, "you bring them back, repair the fault and sell them as new. You will lose nothing."

"Brother", Hoi explained patiently, whilst suppressing the turmoil seething inside him, "if this is the same as the United States, they have failed to repair a single car. They are still trying to ascertain the cause, which may be an alteration to molecular structure. If London -"

"Oh, poof!" exclaimed Teng, cheerfully, "we don't believe such science fiction do we? Modern vehicles full of electronics, affected by electrical storms, that is all! Even you could not expect the Manchu to be the only vehicle to be immune."

Hoi was about to point out there had been no storm in London but Teng peremptorily cut across before he could speak.

"Brother Hoi", and for once the smile had all but disappeared, "I know it is quite unnecessary to remind you", which is precisely what you are doing, Hoi thought, bitterly, "the Society has been most generous in its assistance with your international expansion and this will be nothing more than a passing difficulty -"

"Brother Teng", Hoi interrupted him, his thoughts a maelstrom of worries about costs, legalities, longterm product credibility, financial liabilities, not least those to the Society, "I do not have the resources to withstand unlimited refunds, even if the cars can be repaired here. I -"

But Teng listened only long enough to make his final point. He looked levelly at Hoi and almost seemed to have straightened and grown an inch taller from his affected poise of obsequious supplicant. "Brother. I am sure the Society will understand any difficulties and make arrangements to assist you. The Society has no interest in your business failing. We are all one together." And he beamed, clasping his hands in front of him. His eyes, though, were not smiling. "But those cars *must* reach the show-room."

He did not take his eyes off Hoi as he made his customary sidelong exit towards the door. As he was opening it to slip away, he paused as if with an afterthought, which Hoi considered later was probably as calculated as the rest of his peroration. "If necessary, you might offer discounts, too." He was gone.

Hoi slumped into his owner's chair. Discounts! Not just replacements! He dared not even ask his finance director to make the calculations; he would be aghast and goodness knows who might hear of it and what damage it might do to the firm's credibility. He would have to work at the figures himself, see if he could make them stand up. Perhaps he would be able to resell the 'dud' cars. Strange turn of phrase, he reflected, 'must get to the showroom'. Huh. Blow the showroom. Get them to the buyers, surely. He sighed and keyed in an accounts spreadsheet on the computer. Then he would have to phone the agent. Better phone Hwee Lo first; he would be late again.

Spaniard

The raised voices had been getting louder from above the shop.
Asif cocked an ear from behind the counter. Still ten minutes to
opening. This time he would get the boys downstairs before he
had to cope with all the customers on his own. There were a
group of lads up there again, he had heard footsteps on the
stairs an hour ago and the side door banging after them. He
thought there were more than usual; that Chinese man, maybe.
There was the sound of a thud, like a hand banging on a table
and a couple of muffled exclamations clearly audible. This would
not do. Not only did he need the boys serving with him, he could
not have the sounds of an argument for customers to hear. If
they were going to have their petty disputes with each other,
they could save them for times when the shop was closed or,
better still, take themselves somewhere else.

They were generally good boys, he sighed. Something about
the company they were keeping these days. They had visitors
who could be uncommonly surly, like that big Iranian lad - huh,
'lad': must be all of thirty - or just plain uncommunicative like
the Chinese man. He was entitled to be inscrutable if that was
their way but a civil greeting would not go amiss now and then.
Always scurrying furtively, that little man, like a mouse hiding a
piece of cheese but usually it was a big heavy bag he was either
struggling up the stairs with or folded under his arm on the way
down.

He glanced through the window and saw no-one was yet
hovering outside. The argument, whatever it was, was continuing
as he mounted the stairs. He recognised his own two boys'
voices but another was not Chinese but Spanish. Great Allah, he
thought, what acquaintances are they making now. He paused,
attentive. There was a mixture of tongues; some Asian and more
than one voice in Spanish; then they all broke into heated
English, perhaps the common language between them.

He had tried to learn Spanish once, not very successfully.
English had been difficult enough, when he had only begun
learning it at the age of five after the family arrived from Saudi.

Fortunately, he had been just young enough to learn phonetically, with grammatical assistance at school and at the mosque, so his English accent only bore traces of Middle- Eastern origin. But the singsong Latinate vocalisation was a tougher challenge, despite the Islamic heritage of the Iberian peninsular. He'd hoped to have found a closer affinity with the language but he had struggled. Nevertheless, his brush with evening classes had left him with a small vocabulary - and the ability to catch a bus or buy some bread, should he ever visit Spain!

He listened for a moment. The voices were indistinct now, reduced to mumbling but then the Spanish became more vociferous and he caught the word 'deal', perhaps it meant 'agreement', and then 'share' picked out from the rest he did not recognise. He continued up the stairs and knocked firmly, entering without waiting for a reply.

"Asif!" exclaimed one of his boys.

"Come now", said Asif, reproachfully, "it is time for work and the customers would hear all your noise. We cannot have loud arguments. It will be bad for business."

"Sorry, Asif", spoke up Abdul. They were all sitting about on the battered old armchairs with which he had furnished the room for off-duty comfort. He immediately noticed the stranger. A young man of over thirty, the oldest among them, with fine, dark olive features and shiny black hair. The Spaniard, obviously, and the man looked up at him furtively, with a greeting in a thick Spanish accent: "good evening, sir." The older 'lad' was there, too, the Iranian who seemed to dominate these little gatherings, and another lad whom Asif had seen there before, not one of his own.

Instantly, two of them made to grab or conceal, four or five Chinese dolls on the coffee table in the centre of the room. He recognised them immediately, even though he had only seen parts of similar ones protruding from a bag the last time he had been compelled to intrude upon one of their meetings. That time the additional visitor had been the Chinese man. The dolls must be the source of the pungent perfume which had afflicted his nostrils the moment he had entered.

The Spaniard jumped up hurriedly to leave, lifting a heavy leather bag at his feet and scooping two of the dolls into it. As he opened the bag for them, Asif saw it was full of others the same. The Spaniard appeared embarrassed and in haste to get away. One of the boys made a grab as if to prevent him taking the remaining dolls from the table and it caused him to lose his grip as he stood, drawing his hand away. The doll was propelled sideways and dropped several feet onto the hard, old-fashioned tiled fireplace. There was a sharp crack. Before the others could react, Asif stooped to pick it up, partly out of a hospitable response for their house guest but partly intrigued. He was surprised at its weight, which explained the noise of impact. The doll's colourful costume was parted at the back, as though the doll had been examined for some purpose. The back was split and the narrow crack exposed a silvery metal.

"What is this?" he asked, directing his question around the watching faces.

Without reply, the Spaniard clutched the doll roughly from Asif's grasp, dropped it into the bag with the others and made for the door. One of the boys started to follow in a gesture to prevent him, muttering, "that is not your share!", but the older 'leader' lad caught his arm and muttered in Punjabi, "Leave him. The Chinese man says the others will come presently. We'll have our share."

"Others?" queried Asif, wishing to be better informed of events in his own property.

"Nothing, Asif", assured Abdul. "Just these -"

"Eid presents?" Asif interrupted, sceptically.

"Yes, Asif," Mohammed joined in from his chair. "That's okay?"

"You have not ... stolen ... these, have you?" Asif asked, trying to suppress a very non-Islamic tone of suspicion.

"No, no! Of course not, Asif!" replied Mohammed. "Just a good bargain, you know?"

He knew Asif the businessman, even in his small-time way, would appreciate his boys striking a favourable deal.

"Yes, of course", nodded Asif, his unformulated doubts subsiding, "well done, boys." Then he added, "Most unusual dolls, very heavy for little girls to play with. Metal? Dangerous, don't you think?"

"They're more for ornaments, Asif", Mohammed assured him. "And not easy to break."

"That one broke", commented Asif.

"Well", laughed Mohammed, having talked his way into self-composure, "that's why they were cheap!"

"Ah", acknowledged Asif and decided to put it from his mind. Wheeling and dealing in dolls in London side-streets was no more unlikely than any other commodity. If his boys were engaged in shady transactions over goods of dubious origin, he knew he should take a closer interest but he preferred not to ask. He was running a kebab house. What he didn't know he couldn't be involved with. "Come now. We are late opening." He looked at his watch. It was two minutes past six. He detested even two minutes tardiness and he was always fearful it would lose him customers.

He cajoled them downstairs, bidding good evening to the three visitors, and hastened to open the door for the knot of clientele waiting outside. He greeted them warmly but his words were drowned by the sirens of two or three police cars speeding past, followed by the wail of an ambulance. What a noise, he thought. There were further sounds of sirens in the distance and he recalled having heard more from various quarters at other times earlier in the day.

Tut tut, he thought, are so many people being careless on one day? He and the two boys fell into the familiar pattern of serving. He smiled broadly at each customer he served. He wished his boys made more effort to do the same.

Tow

There was a loud crash in the dusk, just a few yards away: the unmistakable sound of a shattering plate glass window. Isabella jumped, heart in mouth, and looked around, fearfully. They were half a mile up the Edgeware Road in the fading light of Tuesday evening, waiting for Paul's car to be towed home. She had taken a taxi into town with him in the morning, in case the retrieval exercise required both of them but the rescue truck, which Paul had at last managed to arrange, itself abruptly broke down having only got them this far. Another had arrived to tow it away but had not returned. Most of the rest of the day on the phone, shuttling between car and nearby cafe, had finally secured an alternative so here they were again, waiting.

"Paul!" exclaimed Isabella. She clutched at his arm. They were sitting in the front seats of the Manchu Met, watching the street lights flicker on in the fading light.

"It'll be okay", he reassured her. The sense of danger was rife. It brought them closer in their anxiety, neutralising their differences. Lawlessness had begun just forty-eight hours after increasing numbers of cars and, as it turned out, random domestic appliances and electrical equipment had begun to fail.

The 'seize-ups' were quickly recognised as mirroring the American phenomenon of the past few months, from which the UK and elsewhere in the world had felt immune. Now, suddenly, it seemed to have struck London, to everyone's dismay except, secretly, Isabella's. She had rejoiced alone at home while Paul had been out. Now, it was just a matter of waiting for Londoners to respond in the same community spirit as Americans. Here, there was even a precedent: the fabled camaraderie of the war years and the Luftwaffe bombing blitz.

There was a second loud crash and muffled voices, a pause, then the sounds of running feet and cries of exhortation: "Quick"; "Take this one", were sharp retorts they could hear. Looters migh tavoid a couple in a parked car but their shouts and violent activity was a threat in itself.

All Paul's contacts in the trade had failed to yield a breakdown truck on Sunday, operators no doubt taking full advantage of double-time Sunday rates rather than provide free assistance to a fellow-trader. Monday had been occupied with all the Manchu Met complaints so this one remained where Paul had left it in Piccadilly on Friday night, immune from fines, clamps and tow-aways under the hastily-declared 'bug' amnesty (the term, 'bug', conveniently identifying a link with the Americans' experience and implying their blame for it, too).

There were more shouts and loud footsteps which clattered to a halt beside them. The car shook as a hand tugged at the driver's doorhandle, two or three men gathered hard up against the car. Paul had been careful to lock the doors from inside. They remained still, Isabella, petrified, gripping Paul's arm even tighter. She felt suddenly angry and lifted her head to shout at the potential car thieves but Paul saw her intention and clapped a hand on her arm and mouthed 'No!' at her. One of the men stopped to look inside and saw them. He sneered then turned to one of the others.

"People in it!" they heard.

The man's face peered at them again and the hand gave another pull at the door. A second voice called, "Leave it!", and the man straightened up out of view. There was a thump as he kicked the door panel belligerently. Then they ran off across the street. Paul and Bella watched tensely as the gang of three stooped at another car and tugged at the handle. Looking back and realising they would be seen, they disappeared round a corner and out of sight.

Bella was aware of a boiling anger growing inside. The British reaction was disgusting. This was not how it was to be! The first warning had been the unusual incidence of sirens and blaring fire engines. Then there were increasing news reports of thefts of cars abandoned and immobilised. The logic was impenetrable. If any attention had been paid to the American experience, cars in this condition were going to be so much junk metal. But the thieves were turning up with towbars and towropes, usually after dark, and with such frequency that police could catch only a handful. It was as though the States' experience had made it worse. People in London assumed within hours that none of their cars or appliances would be repairable. They did not take the trouble to find out.

America had gone months without a solution so people in London knew what to expect. 'Sharing' it might be, by some lights, if 'sharing' was taking from wherever you could find it: a car on the street, a TV or washing machine in a shop, any number of goods that could be carried from an unguarded house. There was an anger on the streets, a resentment at being placed in this predicament.

Quite who or what this anger was directed at was never specified. For those few who were apprehended it was expressed as persecution: 'something', 'someone', 'them' were responsible and snatching replacements for disabled property was nothing more than justifiable compensation. For two days, it had been getting worse by the hour. Police cars, fire appliances and ambulances on the streets; politicians' appeals for calm; tearful radio and TV phone-ins with the robbed. If one thought the British were incapable of such behaviour, it only needed the reminder of the riots in Liverpol's Toxteth, Bristol and Oldham in recent decades.

Bella's anger was turning to tears. She took her hand from Paul's arm and clenched her fists together. She felt a quaking apprehension, too, that this was because of her. 'Playing God'. No, surely. All she did was suggest it to Elroy. They both had been swept up in a mad, excited desire to spread the enlightenment among her fellow Americans to her adopted countrymen. Of all the nations in the world, surely the phlegmatic British ...

She blinked through watery eyes at the tow-truck drawing up ahead of them. Paul grunted with relief and got out, cautioning her to stay inside. Once the tow was attached, he opened the door for her to climb out for them to ride together with the driver. They glanced around apprehensively as they clambered up the step into the cab. The road was almost deserted. As they pulled off, Bella glanced down a side street and could see a flicker of flames from behind a building. A siren was approaching. They headed home.

Jilly

Another beautiful sunny morning and Jilly Hogan found herself walking along the high street with Pastor Donahoe. His brisk footsteps had caught her up and then he politely reduced his pace to hers. The church was a few hundred metres ahead at the end of the uneven line of shops, bars and parlours. He was obviously on his way there.

"A wonderful morning to you, Mrs Hogan", breezed Pastor Dirk. "And how's your Jim, may I ask?" He held a fondness for any couple such as these, particularly when the memory of their marriage in his church was so fresh.

"Aw, he's just fine, Reverend, busy at work as always." Jilly gave him a huge smile that radiated all the warmth of the sun on both their faces. Sometimes she felt a slight spasm of embarrassment at the attitude of herself and other teenagers in the town when the new Pastor had arrived to 'take up his mission', as he often phrased it in the church newsletter. They had sniggered with lowered heads in their pews, tickled by his fervour and at times anguished supplication to the Lord Jesus. They viewed it as OTT - over the top - and on occasions passed each other scribbled notes predicting how many times he would utter 'praise' during the course of a service. Shamefully, a few boys had been known to bet a handful of dimes on the wager.

Now, and most especially since her wedding and the unambiguous joy he had bestowed upon the religious ceremony, she saw him for what he was: a passionate, devout servant of the church, unafraid to expose his naked emotions in pursuit of his evangelism. It seemed almost natural now - if any such Divine event could be described 'natural'! - that he should have been blessed with the 'smiling Jesus' revelations. Now, she and others could only hold Pastor Donahoe in awe.

"Was that you and your Jim with some friends I saw picnicking in the fields on Sunday after service?" he asked her.

"Aw, gee, yes, and the weather so beautiful an' all", she beamed.

"Sure, I never seen so many folks out and about, picnics or jest walking", chuckled Donahoe. Indeed, there were many more people out and about on foot than there had ever been since not everyone had a car to drive.

"I know, Pastor. We cain't get around in cars like we did", smiled Jilly, "an' anyways, we never did these things since we were kids. 'Most like we'd forgot them."

"Sure thing, dear", he agreed, "folks tell me they never seen each other so much as just now. Them things", and he indicated one of very few cars to be seen, parked at the roadside, "sealed 'em up and carried 'em away, like corn in a can." There was an Italian-looking guy running a finger down a scratch the length of the vehicle and muttering furiously under his breath. Donahoe thought he recognised him as an occasional visitor to the town, a salesman of some kind; rumoured not to be popular in these times, as he habitually drove by without offering a ride in the way which had become customary now. He did not know him by name and did not pause to notice how Tony Delgardo was enraged and swearing vengeance on whoever had violated his precious automobile.

"And you, Reverend", laughed Jilly, giving him a little playful dig in the elbow, "I only ever seen in you in your Chevvy till now."

"Shucks, I know", grinned Dirk, knowing full well he had been the first to jump in the auto just to travel a few paces down the street, "meeting beautiful gals like you now. Didn't know what I was missing." He was grinning broadly, the sun spilling off his cheekbones in a tanned glow.

"Aw, Reverend." Jilly smiled and blushed. "But anyways, you going to chapel today?"

"Ah, my dear", he smiled, "a pastor's work is not jest for Sundays. I'm going to give thanks and to pray."

"Give thanks?", she asked, interested.

"Yes, my dear", "thanks for all you generous folk giving money for the poor. I did not know America had so many kind hearts."

"Aw, me and Jim cain't give much, even now." Jilly felt sheepish, although it was true that spending so much less on gas for the erratic cars and not bothering to rush out and replace things that did not work with others liable to break as soon as you got them home, was leaving more spare cash than they had expected. It was something the President had said as well, about how people less well off did not have to wait for raising taxes to help them. There was such a spirit around these days! She knew some folks were being more than generous, though they did not make a big noise about it.

"It all makes a difference, Jilly." She liked it when he used her Christian name, like when she was fifteen. 'Mrs Hogan' made her feel proper married and special but 'Jilly' was for friends and, for all his intimidating authority in the pulpit, she liked to think the religious father at her side was really her friend.

"Well, here I am." The pastor stopped. They were outside the broad open space before the steps to his church.

"Oh, lawdy!" And then she paused, embarrassed at her petty profanity.

"Hah, my dear", he laughed, "our Father minds not how you take his name if it shows you remember him!"

"Well, gee," blushed Jilly, "I jest hadn't realised I'd walked so far, right past the stores." She had been engrossed with his company and missed them all.

"Ah, well, regrettably I must leave you", he smiled again and began to turn to the church.

"You goin' to pray, you said?" Jilly could not help herself asking.

"Yes, my dear." He paused a moment. "Praying for our brothers and sisters in England."

"England?" She was puzzled.

"Ah, yes", he sighed, with a look of concern. "They have troubled times. They don't seem to see the same as all you folks here. Everywhere here", he added with a broad sweep of his arm intended to encompass all America.

"In London? What they doin? That stealin'?" she asked. She vaguely recalled some news reports over the last two or three days. The same kind of breakdowns suddenly occurring in cars and other things in London. The Brits reacting aggressively, causing trouble there. 'Riots' she interpreted it. Shops smashed up for folk to steal washing machines and things. Pictures of broken windows. Even police camera video showing men trying to steal abandoned cars. It had not been like that here. Not small town America, anyways, although there were some reports of violence further north in the cities. Nothing like London seemed to be.

"I don't know." Dirk Donahoe shook his head, sadly. "But I must pray for them to stop. Maybe to take it more like the folk do here."

"Why's it so different there, do you think, reverend?" Jilly had little knowledge of any other country beyond America. Jim's family was originally from Ireland but neither of them had been there.

"I don't know, my dear." He looked into her wide, enquiring eyes. "Maybe ... maybe .. they have not found the Lord." He was aware, much more than she would be, that the two nations, famously 'divided by a common language' were also separated by completely contrasting measures of religious faith. There was nothing a poor American pastor could do about that but pray for them.

"Poor souls", whispered Jilly to herself as Dirk Donahoe smiled, sadly again, and turned towards the church steps.

Park

"I gotta get away, Walt."

They were in Central Park in the brilliant early evening sunshine, at Elroy's insistence, and deliberately sprawled on grass close to a loudly chattering group of young people, students probably, who also had a portable hi-fi blaring pop music beside them. Walt had suggested that summer clothing they both wore, T-shirts and casual trousers, did not lend itself to stitched-in 'bugs' like a winter overcoat might but his friend's tone had been firm and urgent, as it was now, in his declaration of intent. Walt wondered if paranoia was creeping into El's psyche, requiring such an intrusive noise blanket in wholly improbable eavesdropping conditions.

"Get away? Where? Whaddya mean?" Walt was conscious of adopting a conspiratorial tone whenever he spoke with Elroy now, such was the labyrinth of subterfuge the big man had introduced into his life.

Elroy looked at his friend. He had not told him about his capture and the events during it. He had waited until he could choose these surroundings, safe in the knowledge they would not be overheard. Now he relayed the whole sequence, beginning with the ambush in his house and the disconcerting transformation of 'Charlie Bones'. He told Walt of the apartment, Slick-Hair, the equipment room and the chair. He finished, falteringly, with a description of the 'memory glasses', the erasing of the formula and the 'wings'. His friend listened in subdued silence. When Elroy had done, Walt crossed his legs and sat with his head down, thoughtfully picking at blades of grass and twisting and crushing them between his fingers.

"Jesus, El", he muttered, at length, ignoring once again his friend's religious sensibilities.

"So, see", pressed Elroy, "I gotta."

"Where to?" Walt asked, squeezing yellow-green sap between finger and thumb.

"Dunno", Elroy replied, leaning forward, elbows resting broodily on knees, "but they're not gonna let it go, see?"

Walt nodded. He had never liked the look of Slick-Hair, who seemed to view both of them as intruders at LOTUS meetings, instead of experts seconded for their specialist abilities. This explained it, if the inner conclave was prepared to use any means to promote its interests. He remembered Elroy's previous warnings, the Alan Cargill death and other misgivings. He had been naive to pretend they did not apply to themselves.

"They'll soon know if you just disappear", said Walt, "and what about Mariana and the kids. You said that guy -"

"Yeh", cut in Elroy, sombrely. That was his worst fear. The fact they had already alluded to Mariana. The guy had not needed to spell it out, it was quite clear. Elroy could not risk anything that might turn their attention to the family in retribution.

"Olivia -", began Walt, slowly.

"Yeh?" Elroy looked up as his companion paused, contemplating.

"She said - you know, this London thing -" For a moment they both smiled ruefully. It would have been a shared triumph but for the English reaction and now Elroy's deeper predicament.

"Yeh?" queried Elroy again.

"Well", continued Walt, frowning, "she said there's a call out for anyone who could help over there."

"Well, no-one's succeeded here", countered Elroy, which they both knew anyway, "so what's the point?"

"I don't know", replied Walt, "The Brits seem to think anything's worth a try but they're asking for someone here who's been working on it already. Olivia says they're following the same line, as though it's something molecular in the atmosphere."

They smiled ironically at each other. It was odd being the only people to be aware of what had actually happened, along with Olivia, and of course Isabella. Talking about it from an alternative viewpoint was rather like being told a news story which you already knew was completely fabricated but could not admit your superior knowledge.

"I guess", continued Walt, turning it over in his mind, "you'd be as well qualified as anyone."

"I don't work with the NSA", objected Elroy.

"No", agreed Walt, "but you're the expert in signals and all. Maybe if Olivia could persuade them. Well", he looked up optimistically, "it would get you out of the country for a while and it would be legitimate."

"Yeh but I couldn't do a damn thing, could I?" protested Elroy. "I *started* it, remember? I aint got a clue how to stop it!"

"Yeh, but they won't know that, will they? Buy some time", suggested his friend.

"Well, maybe", considered Elroy.

"I'll ask Olivia", said Walt.

Elroy's frown lifted as he viewed the possibility. The young crowd beside them suddenly jumped to their feet and scattered away down the path, leaving the two men to some peace in the evening sun.

Heavy

Gordon Pierce was under the strictest instructions, on pain of all manner of horrible fates; amongst them, kippers for tea and the permanent withdrawal of all Laura's love and affection "for ever and ever, Daddy!" Forgetting the doll again, which he had been so impetuous to mention without having it to hand, would render his immediate future one of indescribable woe. Had he never uttered the words, "Guess what I've got for you", at least until he had actually remembered to bring it with him, life as he knew it would not be hanging by such a delicate thread.

His desk now boasted two sheets of paper, at opposite corners, with the single word 'doll!' scrawled in large black letters. There was a note in his diary, a knot in the short tail of his tie, another 'doll!' sheet punctured over the door handle and another one placed on the floor between desk and door. If all this failed, and with some due care, attention and devotion to paternal games-playing, he did not doubt he could ultimately win back his daughter's favour, but kippers - ugh!

Quite why he had persistently overlooked the wretched object was a mystery. There it was, bright and colourful, nestling at the top of the stationery box. How could he keep missing it! Anyway, today, no. He stooped to pick it up and it lifted easily from the box. He still had the impression it should be heavier. This was the one from Andy's mate, that he got with the car. Gordon recalled their joke about inconsistent workmanship, 'cheap Chinese', all likely to be of different quality. Funny how both Andy, and Derek down in Folkestone, had used the same phrase, 'heavy buggers'.

He turned the doll in his hand. Not as though he, Gordon, was a 'strongman'. Certainly less so than Andy the mechanic, who wielded tools and manhandled bulky import goods all day long. If anything, he should be more aware of its weight than Andy, but he would not go out of his way to describe this one as 'heavy'.

"Heavy bugger", he mused. Heavy? He turned it over again, its full length from head to feet extending nearly to his elbow. Heavy. Where had that word cropped up recently? His thoughts abruptly halted. He had used it himself in response to Andy's question: 'heavy' uranium. A sudden flush of guilt ran through him, the consciousness of a responsibility which may not have been fully discharged. An unprofessional oversight.

He clenched a fist; the palm was sweaty. He turned to the desk with quickening concern, frowning with worry, and snatched at the phone, dialling the internal code for Folkestone, then Derek's direct extension. 'Heavy'. Some heavier than others? Or just an illusion. How would he know, without another to compare? He drummed fingers on the desk to calm himself. Come now, he could make no associations. Many a time had 'professional instinct' led him up a blind alley of suspicion. Then again, there were all the other times .... a female voice answered. Derek was on a day off. In tomorrow.

Gordon replaced the receiver. Damn. It would have to wait. So would the doll. Sorry Laura. I'll play doctors and nurses or whatever you demand, he vowed to himself wryly. He must first know what he was carrying home. There were no traces; the dogs would have detected that. Even that ghastly perfume was fading; and the doll was definitely solid wood. He breathed a sigh. The trouble was, it was drilled into him to suspect everything. Think of all those innocent, enraged holidaymakers emptying their suitcases on Passenger Arrivals! Nevertheless, he frowned,

there was something he could not explain. He had an idea how
he could check it with Derek. He placed the doll back in the box
and covered it with some loose pads of paper - as if that would
make a difference! He opened the door to leave, ready to brace
himself for brimstone; and kippers.

Attention

Had God not been God - and that bizarre thought had actually
occurred to Him - He could have sighed and said 'Oh My Dear
Lord'. As it was, He bit His metaphorical tongue and just sighed.
(Hey ho, a few more constellations unexpectedly on the wobble).
Splong. He could tell that odour anywhere. He glanced disapprovingly in the direction of the errant archangel, crouching
fresh - though that was not the most appropriate word for the
moment - back from his interplanetary excursion, and wondered
if it had been altogether wise to share another gift with various
among His species, the sense of smell, and should have simply
let them keep it to themselves.

"Guv?"

Gabriel had not been around for most of Eternity without being
aware when he was the object of less than tasteful attention. He
looked up and tried to surreptitiously wipe a finger.

"Was it really necessary?" the Lord observed, with studied
calm.

Gabriel feigned an expression of blank incomprehension,
which would have deceived few mortals or other beings so it was
pretty much a waste of effort trying it on the Lord.

"Taking leave, in the circumstances", added the Almighty,
overlooking the silent 'Who? Me?' charade.

The angel shrugged, defensively, "Well ..." he began.

"Well?" prompted God.

"Well, You know -" Gabriel shuffled uncomfortably again.

"Actually, no I don't", murmured the Lord, in that fashion
which might be dry and ironic if expressed by any among the
cosmic multitudes but, uttered by the Supreme Being Himself,
was swathed in beneficence and disarming solicitude.

Gabriel had also been around long enough to recognise when he was not being disarmingly solicited.

"Well, You know, they might have been wondering where I was."

The Almighty was infinitely mindful that the Splongies, for all the affection with which they might regard the itinerant archangel, could manage without his presence for a good deal longer than Gabriel might like to pretend.

"Really? Well, I trust you set their souls at rest."

"Well, yes, maybe", conceded Gabriel, doubtfully, conscious there was only one official Rester Of Souls amongst them.

"Good. Because I think we may need to pay a little more attention to immediate ... complications."

Gabriel was in no doubt what 'we' meant. He had assumed, though, that this Earth business was more or less done and dusted, hence his covert flit to Splong, while No-One was watching (ha).

"Complications?"

The Lord was almost moved to sympathy at the look of gloomy resignation before Him but He really could not do with Gabriel just disappearing at will, right now. Humans being humans, it was not, well, it was not absolutely, completely, altogether proceeding as He would have hoped. Call it self-determination, call it free will, call it plain, uncomplicated accident, call it whatever You liked, there was only so much He could preordain, as he had already tirelessly elucidated to his loyal aide.

That same loyal aide knew what to call it.

"Cretins", he muttered under his breath (as if No-One would hear).

PARADIGM : CHANGE

He held her in his arms, they standing upon the rock, the sun only beginning its ascent into the day. Their infant slept in the sheltered hollow behind. Her eyes were on the shimmer before them, glinting and gleaming in splashes of silver amid the dark hues of blue and green.

"Is it changed?" There was fret in her troubled mien.

He followed her gaze and looked with her, then shook his head, untamed locks flicking across his uncertain brow.

"Is it changed?" She frowned now, also, eyes intent upon their sea.

"Changed, dear one?" And he turned to watch with her again.

"The colours." She spoke unsurely and he heard the firmness melting in her voice, as the sun so melted on her golden skin. He held her more closely, in love and desire, his loins beating at her subtle lure.

"The colours?" He frowned to the sea. "Are they not the same? Is it not the sun bringing new colours for the day?"

"I thought I saw other colours", she passed a light sigh, "not of the sun; not of the day."

"It is your joy, our joy." He pulled her closer to him, so her thighs were pressed against his, and they each felt the strength and warmth of the other. He cast their eyes to the sleeping child. "Our joy, as you are mine."

"And you are mine", she breathed, feeling the hardness of him rise against her and the hunger in his hands bringing her to the lust of his loins.

"Let the sea be the sea", he urged, "it is but our joy making it seem dulled today."

"Yes", she breathed again, allowing him to draw her down, down to the rock, to lie against him and to hold him, hard and long, before he took her and her soul swam, as the silver twinkled on the darkening of the blues and greens beyond.

Weight

"Weight? Blimey, Gordon."

The thing about Customs was, once you had seen a job through, checked it and either it was clean or you had captured some contraband, that was it: finished. You liked to think it was sorted, a tick in a box, assigned to the next stage in the process or else cleared for import. Job's a good 'un. You did not want to have to revisit it once you had closed the book on it: there were plenty more potentially suspect consignments, queuing nose to tail for your attention. Anyway, Derek in Folkestone had not given much thought to the Chinese carload since Gordon Pierce at Heathrow had told him they were all likely to be clean. It was not a cop out; it was just an efficient way of dealing with goods when colleagues communicated with each other between ports and air terminals. But now here he was again, on about those bleeding dolls!

"Sorry, mate, I just need to check, if you've got the data."

"What about you?" asked Derek down the phone, "haven't you got it?"

"We didn't go by weight", explained Gordon, "we'd a tip-off about powder so we stripped a few of the cars out. My Andy went through the chassis frames, running boards and all that; didn't just go by weight."

He was choosing his words carefully, embellished with some tactful, if inaccurate detail. He did not want to rile his colleague but he knew the port would often check by comparing the vehicle's manufacture weight, in its documentation, with the deadweight at the port. It was the only way they could cope at times with all the vehicles coming off the ships. If there was a discrepancy it might indicate the weight of concealed contraband. Then they would do a search. He heard Derek's quiet sigh coming down the line.

"Have you got deadweight against document weight?" Gordon added. "That would give the dolls' weight, eh? There was nothing else in the cars."

"All those flags", rejoined Derek. He was referring to the decorative bunting adorning the Manchu Mets.

"Oh, yeh", replied Gordon, dismissively, "but they were nothing. Bits of paper. A few grams. Those dolls were a kilo or more."

"What's the problem?" came Derek's voice, indicating signs of trying to avoid this turning into a full-scale investigation for his pal.

"Dunno, really", admitted Gordon, "just got an idea. I got one of them with me."

"A doll?"

"Yep."

"Well, you're okay, then," chirped Derek.

"No, but," responded Gordon, "it don't feel right. Too light."

"Aw, come on, Gordon, how would you know? You know what it's like, remembering."

They all respected one another's judgement and they all sported a history of memorable 'strikes', built upon a mixture of hunch, experience and sheer, solid professionalism. But they were all human, too, and Derek knew there had been times when his own suspicious imagination had deceived him, over weights, packages, shifty looks, and the like, and he was sure Gordon had been similarly misled on occasion.

"Yeh, I know", acknowledged Gordon, "but I just reckon I should check it out. You got the weights?"

"Yeh, probably", Derek conceded in a resigned tone. "You in a hurry?"

"Well, when?" Gordon was aware there was a limit to how he could press a colleague who would be similarly swamped with work.

"Maybe tomorrow if I can put someone onto the archive." For all the efficiency of computer files, Derek knew his secretarial staff could not immediately disrupt their routine duties for a check on goods already cleared, unless there was urgent evidence of high-level smuggling.

"I guess one more day", agreed Gordon, reluctantly, in circumstances where it had taken him weeks even to consider something might be amiss.

"It'll be tomorrow, unless something else goes 'bang'", Derek assured him, conscious of the anxious edge to Gordon's voice. They stuck by each other as much as they could, all the Customs teams. Theirs was a routine occupation which could nonetheless unpredictably propel them into high-profile public controversy, and become uncomfortably political, if a serious systemic flaw was exposed. The day-to-day hazard was to unwittingly allow the volume of Class A drugs evading their net to develop into an escalating crisis, with condemnation heaped upon them from all sides. However, there were other dangers, from weapons to fatally toxic substances. The fact they were sporadically uncovered did not mean none were getting through. The teams at any of the entry ports and terminals could never entirely dismiss an under-current of nervousness from their minds.

"Thanks, mate. I'm on 'days' again tomorrow." Gordon looked at the clock on the wall. Still only half-past-nine in the morning. He glanced at the partially-concealed doll in the stationery box. It would just have to 'wait'. He grunted and grimaced at his unintended irony.

DNA

"This is Elroy Fitzgibbon."

"Hi. How d'ya do." Elroy smiled his greeting to the senior section manager in the impressive GCHQ building - the smart, modern and aptly named 'doughnut', circular complex - nestling in the leafy Gloucestershire countryside of western England

Elroy had never been to Cheltenham. In fact, he had only been to Britain twice before. That was more than most of his fellow-countrymen, being one of less than twenty per cent of Americans who possessed a valid passport. Just because Hawaii was across a slice of the Pacific, he jokingly reminded some of his friends, did not make it 'foreign'. His own first trip across this other 'pond' had been for a week as part of his early training, based at the Goonhilly surveillance establishment near the Lizard.

He had been unimpressed by Cornwall, not aided by chilly, drizzly weather that week in August. Not helped further, just as the weather brightened up for the sun to shine through a cool sea breeze, to be informed that a thirty-minute drive across to the north Cornish coast would have presented him with sand and surf to match even some on the eastern seaboard back home. Too late, it was a chance, 'haven't you been to?', remark in a pub the night before the drive back to Heathrow.

His second visit had been a similar length of time with a group from the golf club to watch the Open at St Andrews in Scotland. Again, it had been something of a shock to the system to leave the hot July humidity of New York for the 'fresh' - as the locals euphemistically termed it - breeze of the Scottish links facing the North Sea and that masochistically exposed famous old course. The destroyer of many a golfing reputation, he marvelled that it had not put paid to many of the golfers themselves: hypothermia, or even terminal frostbite.

He marvelled, too, at the ease with which Olivia had arranged his instant secondment to Government Communications Head-quarters here in Cheltenham. They had jumped at the opportunity, she explained to him, to acquire the services, albeit temporarily, of an expert who might be more closely acquainted with the 'seize-up' phenomenon. He protested when she described how she had listed his surveillance achievements to her NSA bosses, which they seemed to be aware of anyway (although she and they would only know about the 'official' ones) and the close interest he had taken in the sudden immobilisation of cars and powered equipment in the US.

"Honestly, Livvy!" he had exclaimed, "you know very well how I'm involved with it and it's *not* to find the cure! Anyway", he grumbled, "it's all gone. I can't remember the formula, even if that would provide a way to reverse it all."

She had gazed at him in mild reproachment.

"El, hun, I got you here, away from home. Walt said that was vital. He told me about your experience. Yeh?"

"Yeh", he had grinned, ruefully and appreciatively, "you got it sorted. Now I'll just have to sit in front of a screen and pretend I'm figuring it out. Right?"

"Right", she had smiled on the flight over. Walt, in the seat on the other side of her, had grinned, too. Somehow, this tortuous deception was almost a game compared with Elroy's recent trauma.

He reflected that he should not be surprised at Olivia's influence and the respect she clearly commanded here. The links between the surveillance teams of their two countries were closer than their fellow citizens might have guessed. As for women in positions of authority, it was one of the conceits of America to believe it was always first in everything forgetting, perhaps, that little old Britain had beaten it to the line with its first female head of Government, the redoubtable Margaret Thatcher, not to mention placing women at the top of its own home security service, MI5. By those standards, Olivia Brown, a section head at the NSA, still had a long way to go. Even so, it made him reflect that it was soft, unassuming, peach-and-pretty Livvy who was the career woman, not feisty, uncompromising, excitable Isabella, whom one might have predicted to be the natural leader. Such are the ways of men; and women.

"They always turn to us", the manager was saying, "when they think it's 'something in the ether' but don't have the foggiest what it is." He shrugged with a smile. "But it's great to have you here while we've got this problem in London. You've been studying it in the States? Any progress?"

Elroy demurred with a smile, saying they came to him, too, when they were stuck for an explanation but suspected waves, rays or rogue signals. "Anyways", he offered, "I guess we're right on the spot here and thanks for giving me access."

"Not at all, my friend", smiled the manager again, " a problem shared, and all that." There was something of the military bearing about his fifty-ish air of authority and Elroy and Olivia both guessed he was much more the armed services appointee than the signals and surveillance man.

The section was obviously well briefed on Elroy's arrival. He had only been typing away, creating meaningful-looking formulae at his keyboard, for a couple of hours before one of his new colleagues addressed Olivia, who remained present as a matter of protocol, doing little but appearing to share opinions with Elroy as he worked.

"Excuse me - Mrs Brown, is it? - I wonder if Mr Fitzgibbon can make anything of this?"

It was signals 'traffic' picked up by one of the many listening posts.

"Sorry, sir", the surveillance team member turned to Elroy, "I know you're not here for this but, with your experience, maybe you'd know something."

The stream of code was apparently linked to a triangle of sources.

"One is China, sir", the operative was explaining, "the others are Spain - could be Madrid - and almost certainly London. Early days. We've been tracking them for a few weeks but only just made the links. Codes vary with each message. Probably not a problem to break but they're not from amber or red sources so we've just been monitoring the patterns for now."

Elroy knew that 'amber' or 'red' would necessitate degrees of priority decoding, as demanded by their designation, linked to known or suspected terrorist or other 'enemy' sources. He took a quick look at the code. It's superficial simplicity belied a deeper subtlety, probably implying that an initial 'break' would reveal a string of gobbledegook: a kind of code-maker's double-bluff or decoy. He had been caught out several times by this technique early in his career, more than once being embarrassed into silence after shouting 'eureka!' across the office before humbly submitting a kindergarten nursery rhyme or jumbled alphabetical chain to the ironic scrutiny of his immediate superior. However, now, his genius was legendary, even here where you were still liable to bump into the original arrogance of empire, stalking any corridor. He had long left codebreaking and signals intervention behind, now that he held the dubious honour of foremost perpetrator of communications manipulation. Nonetheless, interception and interpretation still held its peculiar fascination: there was nothing quite like the satisfaction of unravelling someone else's fiendish labyrinth of conundrum; it was the exalted pinnacle of the crossword puzzle-solver. Cracking the code. It was like turning the surface of the world inside out and exposing all that covertly crawled within.

"There's a repeated word here", muttered Elroy.

"Sir?" inquired the young operative, willing, not jealous, to be awed by a superior skill, a higher intellect. "A word?"

"Yes", muttered Elroy, examining the meaningless array of letters and numerals covering the half-dozen pages before him.

"What word, sir?" The young man was leaning eagerly over Elroy's desk, trying to peer upside down at the pages.

"Hm," said Elroy, thoughtfully, "could be something like, 'toy', or maybe 'model'. Hm", he pondered again, "or artifice."

"But they're nothing like each other!" The young man was no idiot, or he would not belong to this high-calibre team, but he still had plenty to learn, and he accepted that.

"No, that's right", murmured Elroy, passing a finger along the lines of characters. "It's the DNA principle. You know that?" He looked up at his earnest disciple.

"Mr Fitzgibbon?" There was puzzlement on the youthful brow.

"You know DNA, the human genome, is largely comprised of a random jumble of meaningless characters, all masquerading as part of our genetic code?"

"Sir?"

"The key to solving the riddle of DNA was to establish which repetitions of character sequences were real code, representing genes which actually existed and performed active functions, and which were just chaff, representing nothing at all. Since the real code, the functioning sequences, were embedded within the vast strings of chaff, it was like looking for straw in a haystack. Yes, of course, it's all straw; but if you look hard enough you find that a small percentage of it is more orangey than the rest. Actually, more than just one shade of orange, but once you have learned to recognise it, you can find it all. But it still takes time."

The young man stood waiting for something more by way of enlightenment, like a dog with half the bone.

"Every gene is coded with the same four characters but in a different order, in different lengths and repeated a different number of times, interspersed at different and often irregular intervals with the 'chaff' character sequences. This code is following the same principle."

"But those words - 'toy', 'model', 'artifice' ", protested the ingenue, "they don't use the same characters."

"Sure", breathed Elroy, still intently studying the character configurations, "that's because this sequence is using an alphabet of twenty-six letters and a numeric of ten single figures, including the 'zero'. DNA code only has an alphabet of four characters. The principle is the same: which is the active sequence and which is the chaff. If you have a total of thirty-six characters in your 'alphabet', a lot of chaff can look like the real thing, and vice versa. So we have to find which is which."

"And you think it's 'toy' or one of the others?" interjected Olivia, who was listening with as much attention as the budding young surveillance expert.

"One of them, or something similar, would be consistent with part of the pattern", concurred Elroy, "but then again it might not." And he beamed at them both, as he stood and stretched his big brown hands above his head. "That's the problem. And that's only one word. But if I'm right, it's a keyword and probably alerts the decoder to how to find the rest of the message. But, like you say", he lowered his arms from their great stretch, "it might be nothing more than someone fooling around. Ordering toast and tea."

"Or toys", said Olivia, keenly.

"Maybe", and Elroy grinned. "But, hey, hadn't I better get back to cars that won't start?" He gave a subtle glance at Olivia.

"Of course, Mr Fitzgibbon", nodded the young man, "thanks for the tip. I'll keep an eye on this." He scooped up the sheaf of papers and returned to his workstation. Olivia and Elroy exchanged the slightest of smiles as they resumed their positions.

Traffic

"So much traffic!"

Their roles had been reversed for a change. At any rate, Hoi Fong was the one who had arrived home first, thankful for a shorter day, when he could leave the factory running smoothly without need for his watchful eye. Hwee Lo had put Soo Wong in the baby seat, fold-up pram in the car boot, and driven to the city for some fashion shopping. It was time to treat herself after months of maternity clothes and further weeks at home in constant devotion to baby care.

But the traffic! Was Beijing even worse than she remembered it? Surely it did not alter so much in the few short months she had confined herself to rest at home and devoting attention to Hoi Fong during this worrying time with the London cars and the Society. Absence must have dimmed the memory: the memory of the stop-start crawl into the shopping centre amid blaring car horns, traffic lights always ambushing on red and the angry impatience of fellow drivers. Then the parking! She had considered parking at the factory but she preferred not to mix her own life with her husband's business. She would be fussed over, offered tea, eventually driven into town through the same traffic jams only to arrive even later than if she had stayed on her own. No, she put up with the hunt for the elusive multi-storey parking space in order to preserve her independent schedule.

Soo Wong, strapped into her seat in the back, took it all in her stride by sleeping soundly until gently unfastened and lifted into her pram. Her dear baby child. A pity she felt obliged to cover half her sweet face, and her own, with the anti-pollution masks so commonplace now in Chinese cities. Deemed to be a necessary filter against the torrid exhaust fumes and goodness knew what other cocktail of vapours suspended in the hazy street atmosphere. She and other citizens regarded the shops as welcome refuges, sanctuaries in which making a purchase sometimes became a secondary objective.

"Traffic?" Hoi beamed fondly at both of them, embracing Hwee Lo and kissing her lightly on the brow, before taking Soo Wong to cradle her in his arms.

"Oh, so much traffic, my dear", sighed Hwee Lo, sinking into the sofa.

"Ah, but it is our living, my dear", Hoi smiled with his chin nestling on the baby's dimpled cheek, "it is what provides us with all this", and he swept his eyes around the comfortably-furnished room.

"I know, my love", she smiled at them, he standing above her with their child cuddled to his chest. It was a difficult case to argue, when their own prosperity owed itself to the very discomfort she and millions of others experienced in their increasingly congested cities. "You are home early", she observed with approval. So often of late she had waited long into the evening for him to return home. He smiled in response and looked more relaxed, less fretful than recently.

"The London order is being delivered."

"Ah, good", she allowed her relief to show on her face, too. "Many cars to replace?" He had told her of the Society's pressure to exchange Manchu Mets disabled in London, for identical models, at no charge; and even offer an additional discount to the dealer if it was necessary to save the order.

"Yes, perhaps eight", he acknowledged, "but at least the order goes through so I felt I could leave earlier today. So here I am to greet you." He grinned more broadly, as he gently rocked Soo Wong in his arms and added, "would you like some tea?"

She smiled with simple delight as she received Soo Wong from his arms so he could set about the domestic task. It was a pleasure shared between them when they were able to indulge in the normalities of home life, when the husband made a pot of tea and they played together with their baby child. Hwee Lo laid the babe in her luxurious bamboo framed cot.

"Give her a toy to play with and come to make the tea with me", Hoi called as he made for the kitchen.

"Oh, my dear, she is scarcely old enough to play", chided Hwee Lo, with a smile. "But perhaps you might have one of those dolls to keep for when she is older."

"The car dolls?" He peered out from the kitchen doorway.

"Yes, you described them as so colourful", she replied.

"Goodness gracious", he scoffed fondly, "they're much too large and heavy. I really don't know why they insist on providing one with every car. I cannot imagine even those big English children playing with them. They're more like weapons than toys." And he laughed, while she chuckled with him.

"Cousin Wu visited this morning", remarked Hwee Lo, as if one amusing thought led to another.

"Ohh", Hoi gave a mock groan. "More pots?"

"How did you guess?" she giggled. "But he returned a pot we never had. See: on the drainer."

He glanced and saw the 'stranger' utensil, drying from its returning rinse.

"Not ours?" he queried with an amused raised eyebrow.

"Never. Would I buy one like that?" It was a florid pattern of red, blue and green flower petals, shaped like a bloated urn.

"Do you know, I think he must be digging them up from the garden so he has an excuse to visit." Hoi smiled broadly at his idea.

"Well", she added, "he was at pains to say that if ever we should need *his* help ..."

Their eyes met and they broke into more giggles, facing each other from lounge to kitchen doorway. Poor Wu. As if there might ever be anything he could do for *them*.

Brick

"You must be pleased." Olivia smiled at Elroy beside her in the front passenger seat of the private hire car.

"Sure", he smiled back at her. "But", he added, "it wasn't down to me. Ya know that."

"Well", she countered, "who else could have done it?"

"Okay, sure", he agreed, "I had to know what the formula meant, ya know, to put it together but Livvy, hun, there were things in that I could never have invented. That was genius." He gazed out of the window at the Berkshire countryside rolling past the M4 motorway. "More than genius."

"Like you?" She grinned at him.

"No, hun, I just wish. You know", he turned to look at her, "maybe it was like Beethoven, or Michaelangelo, maybe it wasn't their genius, maybe it was something got inside them and ... changed them. You know, beyond themselves."

"You felt like that?" She was conscious of his awe.

"Yup. Yup, I did." He turned again to the window to watch middle England spinning by. They were heading back to Paul and Bella's in London. It was one of those minor subterfuges they had all concocted between them. Elroy and Olivia were checked into separate rooms in a Gloucester hotel. They had duly collected their keys and gone to their rooms after the day's work at Cheltenham. Then they had left fifteen minutes apart and rendezvoused at the hire car depot a few streets away. Even if it was noticed they did not return to their rooms for the night, it was no business of hotel staff to comment and, as Walt had said as he took a cab to meet Bella while they headed for GCHQ, no-one would guess where they had gone, and only themselves in the car to know.

"Anyway, you must be pleased", repeated Olivia, accustomed to talking while driving on English roads from her regular trips to the old country. "Whole States calming down", she added, "whole different attitude to possessions and money, an' all. Almost like everyone had been waiting for it but needed to be shown."

"Or given no choice", chuckled Elroy.

"'Spose so", she smiled, "but no-one would have imagined." She shook her head, mystified by the momentous turn of events.

"Sure. No-one." Elroy turned to watch the urban advance begin to submerge the countryside. He was equally bemused by all that had sprung from that traumatic but joyous encounter in his study. Then he remembered they were in England now and the very bricks and roofs of the houses, clustered in their tight residential bunches, seemed to bear a veil of foreboding. "Pity about here", he muttered.

They became silent as the traffic intensified and Olivia had to negotiate a stretch of the notoriously congested M25 motorway - worse on every visit - before turning again towards North London. She spoke once while stopped at traffic lights.

"You were very patient with that young guy." She was smiling to herself as she recalled Elroy's explanation of the 'DNA' code at GCHQ.

"Aw, I guess he knew most of it already", scoffed Elroy, "probably just being polite."

"Toys?"

"Yeh, likely", he grinned. "Sounds like someone in Spain trying to avoid import duties. Get toys, or something, shipped to England, then smuggled out again."

"A bit complicated", observed Olivia.

"Yeh, well, they do these things to throw security off the scent." He grunted in mild amusement. "At least it ain't drugs or weapons."

Their only other exchanges concerned signposts and directions and the frustrations of the stop-start shuffle through the edge of the city.

"What's that?" remarked Elroy, suddenly. They had wound their way in a diversion through some side streets, apparently to avoid a fire-damaged property. They were almost stationary in the narrow street. Olivia looked past Elroy to where he had indicated. There was a huddle of twenty or thirty Afro-Carribean adults crowded over the steps to a small church, craning to see and hear what was inside.

"Can we pull in?" asked Elroy. He felt a kinship and was intrigued by what appeared to be an overflowing church service on a Thursday evening.

"Well ..." Olivia peered ahead, dubiously. "No, okay." She swung left into a side road and perched the car half on the pavement. They got out and locked up. Elroy was greeted at the back of the crowd with warm smiles of welcome; Olivia a little more indifferently.

"Brothers and sisters!" They could hear the preacher's voice through the open church doors. The crowd edged up the steps and Elroy's height allowed him to see over heads, into the church and to the backs of brown necks, coloured hats and scarves and the full range of hairstyles. All were on their feet and crying out responses to the preacher.

"Pray for our brothers! Pray for our sisters!" called the preacher from his elevated pulpit. "We pray to you, oh Jesus!" he declared and the congregation chanted the refrain: "We pray to you, oh Jesus!" All eyes swung around to stare up at the window behind them, in bland patterned stained glass with no figure etched into it. Elroy's eyes widened and Olivia clutched at his shoulder, raising herself on tiptoe for a better view. There was disappointment in the eyes they could see.

The preacher was bemoaning the lack of faith among the wider population - "our brothers and sisters in the Lord" - inclusive of all races and colours but with less-than-subtle references to "God's children who have gone astray." The fervently chanted responses were an admonishment of a mainstream culture well-advertised in its secularisation, its acknowledged lack of belief and minimal church attendance. Without speaking to each other, the two American onlookers each wondered why their similar nations were, in this issue, so unlike. Except for these people, my people, thought Elroy as the black passion and zeal washed over them from within and onto the steps of the church.

Just then there was a crash and a gasp from the congregation as a side window shattered and a brick or large stone hurtled through and among the people. There was an enraged shout as it became immediately apparent that someone had been hit. The whole crowd turned and began to surge towards the doors, seething in its determination to seek out the perpetrator. The massed eyes in black faces seemed to be glaring directly at them.

"Quick!" Elroy grabbed Olivia's arm and tugged her around the corner to the car.

"Quick! Get going!" he commanded as they clambered in. Olivia started up and drove straight down the narrow road ahead to get clear.

"Okay", breathed Elroy, after they had rounded the block and rejoined the diversion.

"Were they going for us?" stuttered Olivia, still shaken.

"No, no, I guess not. But they'd soon know we were strangers. No place to hang around."

They found themselves back on their main route. They were silent again, subdued by the febrile clash of religious ardour and threatening violence. They remained unspeaking as they passed occasional motley groups tugging at the doors of parked cars; and when they skirted a building ablaze, siren-blaring fire appliances racing past them to the scene. Elroy found his troubled thoughts darting back to the NSA computer room and he could not dispel a feeling of shamed responsibility. The shame deepened when he realised he was subconsciously blaming Isabella. It had come from both of them, he had to acknowledge that.

He saw too, in his mind's eye, that sea of black faces turned in supplication towards the church stained glass window, eager for the fabled vision to appear. He wondered if, despite their brimming faith, they were being ignored or abandoned, consigned to an association with the wider society of which they and their preacher had declared such righteous disapproval. He could not presume to know the answer.

Weighed

"Nine-eight-one-point-five grams. How will that do you?"

"Two pounds."

"Give or take."

"A bag of sugar, more or less. I thought they were heavy buggers", observed Gordon. "All the same? Sure?"

"Yeh, yeh." Derek's voice was already edged with the beginnings of impatience. "We ran each one for you: all computer checked, anyway. Document weight against dead-weight on the weighbridge. Every one. Nine-eight-one-point-five difference."

"Exactly?"

"Gordon!"

"Yeh, okay, okay, sorry, mate. Thanks for doing it." Gordon's mind was racing. Naturally, he had already weighed the doll in his office and it was barely two-thirds of that weight, the weight of each doll in Derek's result. So some weighed more than others. Why? And how many? And which ones? He was still troubled by the awful thought but it still did not add up logically. "Look, Derek, mate..."

"Yeh?" The response down the line from Folkestone was cagey.

"You don't have the *volume* of each doll, do you?"

"*Gordon!*"

"Yeh, yeh, all right." Gordon replied hurriedly. "I just thought -"

"Gordon, mate", Derek's tone changed to comradely patience for his increasingly tiresome colleague and friend, "why should we even *dream* of measuring their volume? It's a solid, irregular shape, not a bleeding block of dope."

"Yeh, okay, I know", Gordon sounded deflated. And a bit tired. Derek was not to know this had been occupying his daily thoughts and keeping him from sleep at night.

"Look," Derek continued with genuine understanding in his voice, for a colleague who, for whatever reason, needed support, "you want the volume? Remember your old physics class?"

"Uh?" Strange how Gordon had plodded doggedly through weights and measures, expansion and contraction, solids and liquids, to get his exam passes, never supposing at the time that it would be a necessary qualification for his chosen career. Even then, only portions of it had retained relevance to the practical job in hand. However, he was listening.

"Oh, Gordon", Derek groaned in mock disappointment. "Remember? You can't measure the cubic volume of an irregular solid object with a ruler, so?" He was teasing.

"So?" Gordon mumbled, his mind on the weights of dolls, not classroom physics.

"So you stick it in a measured container of water and get the cubic measurement of the displaced volume - how much more it fills the container. Yeh?" Apart from the lightly taunting 'yeh', Derek, at that moment, could just have been Gordon's old moustachioed, bespectacled, nicotine-stained, frowningly displeased physics teacher. "And that's the volume of your ... doll."

Gordon could almost see the lips smack with disdainful satisfaction and the orange forefinger make a delicate pass to catch the nose-drip before it entered the jungle of moustache below.

"Hey, mate." Gordon's recollections were displaced by a smile of gratitude. "And you haven't got the weight by volume of -?" Then he broke off. This was beginning to sound too crazy. He had better find out for himself. Even Derek would not be able to keep this story to himself if it turned out to be the howler of the year.

"Of what?" Derek had no wish at all to jump through any more hoops but his interest was aroused.

"No. Nothing. Just need to check the volume of the wood in these dolls", he covered for himself, "in case it's restricted."

"Oh. Banned hardwood?"

"Yeh, yeh", Gordon wanted to be quick to agree, to avoid more questions.

"Christ, Gordon! You had me doing all this for hardwood?"

"No .. Yeh, no. We've had a warning about toxic resin. You not had it?" Gordon was thinking quickly and lying through his teeth; not much thanks for a friend's diligence on his behalf.

"No, no. Guess I'd better check. Resin? Powerful stuff?" Derek sounded concerned he might have missed an official directive.

"Maybe. Anyway, don't worry for now", Gordon rounded off quickly to disguise his embarrassment. "I'll do the work on it and let you know. Thanks for the help. And for the physics", he added, with the smile returning to his voice. Derek noticed. His was a smiling reply.

"No problem, any time." He added the last words without any intention of being taken seriously; and he was fairly confident Gordon would not dare, for a while anyway.

"Look, I'll make sure you know the results straightaway", Gordon emphasised.

"Yeh, sure, thanks, see you." Derek put down his phone, still wondering if there needed to be so much fuss about some hardwood resin. However toxic, it wasn't going to blow up the planet.

Gordon sat for a moment, picked the doll up and thought. Then he moved to his office door. Time for action. Still not yet ten in the morning. He had to do a bit of schoolboy physics, find a measuring tank somewhere - the lab would have one - and then find that other volume-by-weight. That would be easier. It would be on a chart in a manual. He knew the results he did not want to see.

Problem

"I mean ... what I mean is..."

For once Gabriel was not engaged in any unsavoury organic investigations. He was lying on his back gazing into Heaven. This was not the same as gazing into 'the heavens', which he could have done almost anywhere in the Universe except, for example, on Cryxx during an ammonia storm, or in Scotland on a typical summer's day. Once actually inside Heaven, you could gaze into, up, along or down it into infinity but you could not gaze at 'the heavens' for, in Heaven, such a view did not exist.

Actually, that only technically applied to mortal souls, had there been any there. Gabriel, and of course the Good Lord Himself, could shift dimensions at will and thus create a bifocal view of Heaven and 'the heavens' - that is, the Universe - whenever they wished. Gabriel was sometimes struck by the emptiness of Heaven and felt almost sad for all those species - which was not *every* intelligent cosmic species, you understand - who thought they would end up there. He considered they were better off out of it, anyway, because there was absolutely nothing to do. Peaceful, yes, but you could only stand so much peacefulness before it started to drive you mad; and then there was the rest of Eternity to get through.

At least he was often busy, which would not have applied to all the souls drifting aimlessly around for ever, bored out of their skulls (which, he conceded to himself, was only in a manner of speaking since, by and large, they would have left their skulls, and other physical manifestations, behind).

Huh. A sight *too* busy, he grumped to himself.

"I mean", he objected, "we just leave them to it, don't we?" He lowered his eyes, taking a chance, "You said we can't just go on meddling. We've done avarice: more sharing, less pollution, less congestion, cleaner future, less crime -"

"Crime?" The Lord cut in, sharply.

Gabriel looked ruffled. "You said ..."

God agreed He had calculated that less emphasis on materialism would, ultimately, lead to a fall in many types of crime, partly because goods would lose their black market value, partly because the acquisitive culture would be supplanted by one in which possessions, acquired by whatever means, would assume a subsidiary rather than a primary role. The full effect, however, would take some time and would have to spread far beyond its origins. The current fall in crime, coinciding with the first manifestations of change, was entirely predictable, driven by the unreliability of the very articles which might otherwise attract criminal attention, thus drastically reducing their value. The violence which might have been deployed in pursuit of such crime consequently diminishing, too.

"However", the Lord reminded his disgruntled, if angelic, adjutant, "the matter is not proceeding in the same manner everywhere. There are problems."

"Aw, but we didn't plan that", protested Gabriel, aggrieved that an unpreordained dislocation - a 'biscuit' incident - was threatening to make yet more demands on him, as if he had not put himself out enough already. Peace! He should be so lucky.

"No, but we still have to pay attention", countered the Lord, sensing the onset of one of those endless circular discussions in which He, the Lord God Almighty, had to justify and explain Himself to him, the supposedly obeisant archangel.

"Well", the aforementioned archangel shuffled, averting his eyes once more, in order not to be seen to acknowledge who 'we' and 'paying attention' might be referring to, "I was."

"Was?" queried the selfsame Lord.

"Paying attention."

"Oh? And the church?"

"Boss?" Gabriel had the uncomfortable feeling he had been caught.

"The church where they all looked around, expecting." God considered that, if He had wished to be a teacher, or indeed a father (following the tenets of certain mythologies), whose roles embraced the goading and cajoling of others, He could easily have been so. The virtue of, alternatively, being God was that He should be spared such petty aggravation. Unless He happened to be the God with a particular archangel at His side.

"Well, I ..." hesitated the same angel-at-the-side-of-the-Lord, as he recalled the expectant sea of black faces for whom he had arrived just too late, as a brick abruptly curtailed any further thoughts of retrieving the situation.

"Yes?" The Lord was waiting.

"I ... forgot." There are times when it is fruitless to pretend you have not been dallying in a more favoured neck of the universe and just admit it.

"Fancy", murmured the Almighty.

"But anyway", blurted the angel, leaping to his own defence, "what could I have done with coloured patterns, anyway, no face there?" He had been singularly proud of all those smiling features but even he required the raw materials - a face - to work on.

"Hm." The Almighty was mindful of that and also of the issue of forgetfulness, a subject which had the uncomfortable habit of returning attached to an unfortunate French saint, to mention but one. He was disinclined to pursue it further just now. "It may have been just as well", He mused in reflection, aware of the wider scepticism with which such a phenomenon might be greeted in that community, which for long had been less spiritu-ally receptive than their cousins overseas. It was part of the problem.

"Anyway!" The Lord's meditation was interrupted by a sud-denly cheerful archangel, additionally relieved he was not to be taxed further on his memory lapse. "It'll all be over there any time now", he chimed, perceiving the resumption of unchallenged visits to wherever he wanted, "then it will all just spread naturally. No ... 'dislocations'."

He was content with his analysis. Like a storybook, it would all turn out right in the end.

"See?" he added, for good measure.

The Lord pondered. Optimism was a two-edged sword. On the one hand, it could propel successful outcomes simply through its own unstoppable momentum. On the other hand ...

On the other hand, He was unwilling to quell such spirit and hope. It was not what God, after all, was about.

"Of course", agreed the Good Lord, with as much confidence as he could muster.

It seemed to satisfy the angel.

Code

"Mr Fitzgibbon."

The young operative - Martin Timmis, it turned out his name was - was hovering at Elroy's side. El was relieved at any interruption. He was beginning to weary of creating and manipulating contrived formulae, in a show of attempting to analyse the 'bug'. Every now and then he would run a 'test' with one of the senior analysts only to find that - surprise, surprise - it threw up a complete blank in terms of penetrating possible causes and remedies. Nothing worked. Elroy feigned due frustration and puzzlement before returning to his workstation to 'try something else'.

"I think you were right, sir."

Elroy looked up at him. The man was every inch how a big, broad, laid-back American might imagine a British civil servant to be. Neat, short brown hair, pale and earnest-looking, jacket removed for the warm summer day - typical inefficient English air-conditioning - but tie still knotted at strangulation position against a buttoned collar. Striped shirtsleeves and cufflinks completed the perfect portrait. Elroy grinned.

"Yeh?"

"I can't fathom all your DNA theory, sir, but I've found the repeated word. It's definitely 'doll'.

"Not 'toy'?" queried Elroy.

"No. There's a spare repeating letter, not always the same one, obviously there to confuse and create an alternative four-letter code word; but 'doll' is the word which repeats in the thirty-six characters. Maybe you could help with the rest?" He looked suitably deferential, yet unable to prevent the excitement of his discovery from forcing an intrusion upon the great American's infinitely more important assignment. He added: "I think it's more or less talking about delivery and receipt, like you said."

He handed across the sheaf of paper and Elroy gestured to him to pull up a chair at his side.

"No 'artifice'?" grunted Elroy, peering at the rows of jumbled letters and numerals.

"I think that's 'delivery', sir. Eight characters, but different ones, repeating but not always in a continuous sequence. When it's split into two 'fours' one could be 'doll'."

Elroy examined the rows more closely, paying attention to the sets of four and eight characters which Timmis had high-lighted. It was clever. Utilising the full 'alphabet' of twenty-six letters and ten numerals, the code used some repeated sets of the same characters, but not always in the same order, but also selected different characters to represent the same word, which was only evident by the spatial relationships between characters.

Thus 'doll' was represented both by '1,G,X,B' - but not always in that order - and also by sequences such as 3,O,M,E. In the latter, each character in the '1,G,X,B' sequence had been replaced by the sum of itself and the next one in the set of thirty-six. Thus, '1' became $1 + 2 = '3'$; and 'G' (the seventh character) became G + H (the eighth character) = 'O' (the fifteenth character), and so on. Then the code-cracker had to spot where the sets of four were not only different characters but not in the recognised 'd', 'o', 'l', 'l' order.

"But that's as far as I've got, sir."

"Took some time, eh?" Elroy looked at him, with a wry smile.

"It's quiet here at night, sir."

Elroy noticed the bleary-eyed appearance was probably the result of overnight devotion to duty, rather than that of the congenital public servant fashioned in the womb. He respected the dedication of a fellow-professional.

"Well done", he beamed. Then turned back to the sheets of code. This was what separated him from most. Young Timmis would have slaved for hours with computer programs but this kind of code was used between just a few communicators, who would separately share the basic principles between them, making it too randomised for most computer analysis.

Elroy, however, once he had made a start - and in this instance, Martin Timmis had done the legwork for him - could see through the tangle of disguise in a manner which defied the logic of the computer. A computer would analyse at lighting speed but it would have to recognise what it was analysing. Elroy's genius was to be able to visually and mentally penetrate the contrivance of chaotic undergrowth which masked the message concealed within. A computer had to, somewhere, recognise logic. Elroy's unique skill was to analyse chaos. It was back to his analogy of finding straw in a haystack or, as a colleague had once labelled him, being 'X-ray El'.

Young Timmis sat quietly to one side. After about ten minutes, Elroy leaned back, smiled and announced, "Yup, dolls from China. Getting into London somehow - maybe concealed inside something else - then sold on to Madrid. And there seems to a complaint about payment. All a bit heavy duty for a load of party toys. Still", he clapped Timmis on the shoulder and gripped him warmly, "you could tell your Customs guys. Still avoiding duty, ain't they? Mebbe they're high value and they're saving themselves some big dough."

Timmis smiled with some pride. He suddenly felt he might have a real future.

"Next time", chuckled Elroy, "it might be guns, or gold, or dope, then - whaddya say here? - bullseye!"

The young civil servant allowed himself a restrained grin in response and gathered up his papers. He would phone a Customs contact. Then he would email and make sure he copied in a few top suits in Cheltenham. Dolls or no dolls, he'd cracked a code.

Check

"What! Jesus Christ All Mighty, Gordon!"

"Yeh. Look, I know. I'm sorry, mate. I - you know - I had to check it first." Gordon had braced himself for this moment but it was not easy, nevertheless. Failing to share a confidence with a good mate and colleague was one thing. Getting him to run around like a headless chicken doing spadework on a completely fake pretext was something else altogether. He felt as genuinely humble as he sounded.

"Jesus Christ", he heard Derek breathe again down the phone, before adding, "enriched?"

"That's how it works out. If it was in a volume the same as one of them dolls, the body section would weigh spot on nine-eight-one-point-five grams."

"Shit. Spot on?"

"Well", Gordon qualified his tone, "allow forty-eight grams for other doll parts, clothes and casing - I weighed them separately. Yeh, spot on."

"Shit." Both men were thinking hard and quickly. Gordon could hear the heavy silence all the way from Folkestone. He had rigged up the water displacement test - funny how it all came back to him once he had started. Sinking a doll into the small tank caused no more amusement in the lab than many another experiment undertaken to analyse metal cloaks of concealment, corrupted chemicals and other devices of illusion in the world of contraband.

"Yeh", Derek's voice continued, "but yours is wood. They could all be wood - some heavier."

"Yeh, they could, hell of a lot heavier", agreed Gordon, sceptically, "but do you like the coincidence?"

No. Not a soul who worked in Customs liked coincidence. Coincidence meant suspicion. Coincidence was not part of the natural order of things. 'Coincidence', in their experience, usually meant something was afoot.

"Right. No." Derek could do nothing but concur.

"So we'd better bloody check, eh?" continued Gordon, urgency returning to his voice. "Mine have all gone from here, bloody weeks ago. Where's that shipload of yours? Still there?" He was referring to the Chinese cars held up at the docks holding yard.

"Right. I'll stop 'em leaving." Derek, equally firm and urgent, prepared to put down the phone. "Well done, anyway, mate. Shit!"

Gordon put down his own handset. He looked at the clock. Five-fifteen. He could hardly be faulted for all he had achieved in the three hours since coming on duty. Maybe this was all something or nothing. It seemed just too extraordinary, even in their endless game of chance and fantasy. But - just in case there was more to it - at least they had sussed it out in time. Nipped it in the bud.

"Thank Christ for that", he muttered and leaned back in his office chair.

News

It was Walt who opened the door from inside Paul and Bella's town house and gave Olivia a huge hug as she entered, while Elroy hovered behind her. He had to pause as the pair of them enacted a kind of Hollywood reunion on the threshold in front of him, complete with lingering kisses and arms straying across waists and buttocks. They looked for all the world as though they would sink to the floor in sexual entwinement and he thought they probably did behind the privacy of their own front door. Walt moved his head from his wife's close encounter to greet his friend, quite unabashed at the semi-erotic show he had just displayed.

"Hi, El. Good day?" Walt grinned.

"Yeh, thanks", Elroy grinned in return, delighted at his friend's complete lack of embarrassment. Dear Lord, he truly loved his glorious Mariana but neither of them could abandon themselves so unselfconsciously in front of even their closest friends. They were walking through the entrance hall into the lounge, where Bella was just entering with cold drinks from the kitchen.

"No Paul?" asked Olivia.

"Still at work", said Bella. She was about to add something but Olivia was breaking in to question Walt, as they all took drinks and sank into chairs and sofa.

"Been into the city, hun?" She asked.

"No. Jeez. Another day here", smiled Walt with a shrug. "Too much hassle." He had stayed in the house all the previous day, as well, stranded by a combination of scarce taxis, impossible to rely on when so many had the 'bug', jam-packed public transport and the unpredictability of the kind of incident you might unexpectedly encounter, even in the heart of the West End. It was not exactly 'gangs roaming streets' like some futuristic movie but it was not guaranteed safe, either. Isabella had offered him a lift on both days but she had to make calls the other side of town and could not be precise about when and where to pick him up on the way back.

"So another day with CNN?" checked Olivia.

"Yup", said Walt, "hey, and I tell you, it just keeps rollin' along!"

"Yeh?" Elroy's eyebrows rose in interest.

"Yeh", continued Walt, enthusiastically. "Yesterday, that stuff about everything just simmering down, statistics on lower energy, less oil, less cars and all that. Now they're doing measurements: air's cleaner already - new figures today - even crime, you know, ain't nothing worth stealing -" They all laughed. "And", he continued, "seems there's so many more folk either at home or out and about on foot, there's just more protection and the bad guys can't move without being seen!" They laughed again. It was unreal. It had all moved so dramatically since that first day they sat around the television with Mariana, gaping in amazement at what they had begun. They? The others all knew it was Elroy really, and how he said he'd been 'chosen'. They also had Mariana in their thoughts.

"Got you another coupla phones, El", said Bella, as she handed him two new mobile handsets.

"Aw, thanks, hun", Elroy beamed gratefully.

It was another of their precautions: frequently changing phones and sim cards for Elroy to call his wife so nothing would be traced to him or his whereabouts. However much they delighted in the way everything was turning out, there was no forgetting Elroy's 'capture' and the fact he was now effectively on the run.

Elroy put his daily call in to Mariana while the others chatted, overhearing his affectionate concern and assurances as they did so.

"And", Walt eagerly proceeded with more of the day's news, "Now - guess -"

They waited, knowing it was becoming impossible to guess.

"Troops out!" Walt proclaimed.

"What?" exclaimed Elroy, disbelievingly.

"Well, not *now*", explained Walt, "but Twigg's announced troops'll be drawing back in various parts, mainly Asia, Middle East."

"Wow", breathed Elroy.

"She says it's for world peace", he added, cheerfully, "and anyways the States don't want to be seen aggressive any more."

"Don't need to poach anyone's oil anymore, you mean", chimed in Bella, in sardonic amusement.

"Whatever", acknowledged Walt.

"Yeh, whatever", nodded Elroy, sagely, "less war, maybe."

"You reckon?" joined in Olivia.

"Well, why the Yanks ever gone to war these last few years?" challenged Elroy, "only to get something that ain't ours: either a country's oil or the whole goddamned country itself."

"Well, maybe", murmured Olivia, quietly, "just maybe ..."

They all nodded and sipped their drinks.

"Not all sweetness and light though", remarked Walt. They looked up at him. "Some trouble brewing over jobs. Companies saying they can't hold out much longer."

"Job cuts?" asked Bella.

"They sayin'", shrugged Walt.

"Well, won't matter", said Elroy, "whole thing is, folks spending less money now."

"Yes", agreed Olivia, "but the extra's going on welfare. If jobs go, that whole aspect will be lost, won't it?"

"True", nodded Walt. "Anyways", he added, "Twigg's facing Senate. Big showdown coming up. Companies still complaining. Still can't fix the 'bug'" - they all chuckled - "sayin' it's like a bad dream."

"Tell that to the folks with their new quality of life", remarked Bella.

"Yes, but it's a point, isn't it?" interjected Olivia. "The economy can't just collapse completely."

"Talkin' trade wars, as well", Walt offered by way of more news talk.

"Yeh?" asked Elroy.

"Yeh, you know, we've announced import restrictions to protect our own industry when no-one's buying as much. That hits China worst. So the Chinese are slappin' up barriers, too."

"Will that matter?" asked Bella, "if we don't need their stuff and aren't producing as much as we did, anyway." She barely realised she had adopted 'we' and 'us' in a subconscious identification with her homeland. Drama, crisis and uncertainty takes a heart back home.

"Well, we cain't sell nothin' at all", commented Elroy, "and if our own folks ain't buyin', we gotta sell it somewhere."

They brooded a little on this. Utopia always seemed to move a step away as you approached. Just like you could never find the end of a rainbow.

"Anyway", Bella spoke up, brightly, "we're off to the show soon."

"Show?" Olivia turned to her.

"Oh, yeh", grinned Walt. "Forgot to tell you. That's where Paul is. Getting it ready."

"What?" asked a puzzled Elroy.

"The Dragon Show", grinned Walt again, relishing the suspense.

"Paul's Chinese cars", explained Bella, "his next delivery came today. They always put on this show for the arrival."

"Who do?" asked Olivia.

"The Chinese", explained Bella. "It's amazing. I missed the first one and heard so much about I had to go to the next one. Wonderful Chinese dragon and dancers."

"You're kidding", scoffed Elroy.

"No. Straight", assured Bella. "Paul's really keen you see it. He pretends it's a whole loada fuss but, really, he's chuffed it's the only one in town."

"When?" asked Olivia.

"Now", said Bella, looking at her watch.

"I'm starving", grimaced Olivia.

"Oh well, I got some sausages and egg, that okay for now?" smiled Bella. I mean 'now' - we'll go straight after that. Yeh?"

"Yeh, okay", grinned Elroy.

"They're very pretty", remarked Walt.

"The sausages?" queried Elroy.

"The dancers, hun", Bella smiled.

"But we won't tell Mariana." Olivia smiled, too, and stepped over to give him a little hug. He grinned. He felt more relaxed than he had for weeks. They all felt like a bonded team. They did not dare speak, even think, of changing the world; but the bond carried them all into the kitchen to share preparing the eggs and sausages together.

Gone

"Gordon, they've gone!"

Gordon Pierce's hand trembled as the phone nearly fell from his grasp.

"Gone?" he echoed in dismay.

"Yeh, left the yard. This afternoon. Six transporters."

"I thought -" stuttered a bewildered Pierce.

"Yeh, I know, I thought they were stuck there: import dispute or something", replied Derek, tensely. "But the documents were suddenly cleared, the drivers turned up and they left."

"When?" demanded Gordon, collecting his thoughts.

"About three o'clock."

Gordon studied his watch. Six-thirty.

"Where were they going?" he asked Derek.

"Dunno. London somewhere." Derek was shaking his head and Gordon could almost see it down the phone line.

"Well, Christ, Derek, where?"

"Look, I got someone on it. Tracing some dealer in North London. I've got one of the women on 'lates' to find the address. Just thought I'd better ring you straightaway. Oh, and did your Heathrow guys get the GCHQ message?"

"What? No. What was that?" This was an extra complication Gordon would rather not hear about.

"Could be something or nothing", said Derek. "They reckon they've cracked a code with messages between China, London and Madrid -"

"Madrid?"

"Yeh. Consignment of Chinese dolls, they reckon, using London as a mask for passing into Spain duty-free. Could be our little fellers, eh?"

Gordon groaned. This might confirm his worst fears, creating a load of fuss for nothing more than some toy dealer trying to evade import duty for the Christmas market; or get them undercover into Spain because they weren't up to EU safety standards and would be impounded. Either way, no-one would thank him for stirring up his corner of Customs and Excise like a nest of hornets to capture some crap oriental dolls.

"Right. Thanks. Derek, I wish I knew what the hell all this is about", was all he could find to say.

"Gordon, you know it's probably nothing."

"Yeh, I know", agreed Gordon, reluctantly, from Heathrow, "but we have to follow this through, mate. It can go in the bloody Christmas storybook afterwards. I won't care who laughs once I know it's all clear. Christ, man", his tone was suddenly urgent and anxious again, "we've got to find them!"

"I'll get back to you. Half-an-hour, tops."

Gordon heard Derek's phone click off. He sat staring at the wooden doll, smiling at him over its colourful costume. What did it know, eh, what did it know?

But

"But -"

"But -" The Lord summoned all ... well, no, actually, He did not summon anything like *all* His patience. Not remotely all of it. He never, ever, ever had to summon all His patience because not only was His patience deep, profound and passing all understanding, it was also infinite. Even when sorely taxed by the foibles of the Glonxpkites (tricky, but have a go at it), the vagaries of the Blabbbbbbs (easy, once you get round all the 'b's) and the contrariness of the Humans, not to mention the persistence of the archangel Gabriel, God never had to summon more than a smidgin of His boundless patience. Where a Tryxian, a Cryxite, a Splongie or a Human might have to scrape the barrel for the last iota of available patience, utterly exhausting the immediate supply, to God it was just a scoop, or a dollop, spooned up from His infinite store. So. God scooped up a dollop of patience, which would be a veritable mountain to any of His beloved species but made scarcely a dent in His own limitless supply, and continued.

"But", repeated the Supremely Patient One, countering the muttered objections of faithful angel, "there will never be a perfect time."

He could see that Gabriel was still thinking 'but' and was on the verge of saying 'but' again so He carried on before the angel could actually utter the word itself.

"If such a perfect time were to exist", persuaded the Almighty, "our intervention would not, by definition, be required in the first place."

Gabriel was about to have another go at repeating 'but'; however, he sensed perhaps it was an occasion either to extend his vocabulary or say nothing. He said nothing.

"We chose *now*", the Lord reminded him, "because, in their terms, it might not be too late and because ...." His voice drifted away. Gabriel looked at Him.

"Because", the Lord resumed with a low sigh, "there may never be a better time, let alone a perfect one, however long we wait. If", He continued before a further interjection could be discharged from the angelic lips beside Him, "at the same time, if there are occurrences which might undermine our purpose, we may have to ...adjust ... their consequences."

"Nudge", translated the archangel.

"I suppose so", sighed the Good Lord.

"Preordained 'occurrences'?" muttered the angel.

"I beg your pardon?"

"These occurrences", pursued Gabriel. "You must have preordained them?"

God was not accustomed to being challenged on the logic front.

"Perhaps", He replied, guardedly.

"So if You knew they were coming", urged chief Patience-Tester, "why couldn't we have avoided them? Picked another time", he added, truculently.

When You are Lord of the Whole Universe, whose entire unfolding You had a brave shot at completely preordaining from the Very Beginning, You do not particularly keep on top of every nuance of every detail on every planet in every galaxy for all time (all their times) thereafter, however legend may have it otherwise. Perhaps events sideslip into new preordained paths - 'biscuits' and 'railway lines' - when You may not necessarily be looking. Whichever path is taken, all events are ultimately accounted-for, one way or another, but they are not always in the place or the time You originally ordained. It's not as straightforward as people - and other species - might think, being God, He sometimes reflected, which means ... He continued His thoughts aloud: "Inconvenient events might occur, whatever time we chose."

Gabriel wanted to argue that events could hardly be 'inconvenient' if they were all preordained but he realised they had been over that one: there could be 'dislocations' from acts of self-determination; or merely brief dislocations in preordained time. And now here they were, avowedly influencing only *attitudes,* not *events*, only to find that other events, already passing along their own preordained paths, were getting in the way. And needed to be dealt with.

"Is that what You meant by 'quite a lot of nudging'?" he grumbled.

"Those were your words", reproved the Lord, "however, yes, if you put it that way. What -"

" we have started..." The angel completed, with a resigned grunt.

"Precisely", confirmed the Almighty.

They were both silent.

"But -" At last Gabriel was no longer able to hold back: "At this rate -" and there was definitely a grumpy tone to his voice - "I'm likely to have to be in two places at once. I mean -" He looked up, with a wounded expression.

God regarded him in His infinite wisdom, trusting that would be sufficient without actually having to remind him that such a feat had not been so onerous an imposition at other times.

Gabriel was well-acquainted with the infinite-wisdom look. It generally meant checkmate so there is no point in making a move. It did not prevent him from trying, though.

"Can't we just leave them to sort -"

"No", interrupted God, firmly; although He suspected He might be wishing they could sort it out for themselves, before very long.

Dollars

"Whatever -!" Asif looked up from the fish portions he was stirring in the fat.

The roar and whine of a car engine, and a frantic screech of brakes outside, drowned the bubbling of fat in the fryers. There was a sudden clattering of footfalls down the stairs and the thump of bodies hurling themselves as a barricade against the side door, as there came a frenzied banging at it from the other side.

Asif turned to the rear of the shop, dropping the spatula on the counter and hurrying through the plastic strips in the opening. His two assistants, Mohammed and Abdul, were leaning their whole weight against the door, which was shuddering from the battering outside. The hammering of fists was accompanied by muffled shouts of anger. The boys looked up at Asif in consternation, then turned again to push against the juddering door, as though its spring-latch would not be sufficient defence on its own.

"Asif!" Abdul gasped, head down between shoulders as he pressed against the door. The shouts outside became more distinct and were transposed into words of Spanish mixed with broken English.

"Let us in! Hey! Where are the goods!" There was threat mingled with anger.

The two inside stood up, relenting before the door cracked under the assault.

"Okay, okay! Here!" called Abdul, releasing the latch.

The Spaniard of the other evening sprang through the doorway, followed by two more like him They started to make for the two Asians then they caught sight of Asif and halted, fuming. Abdul turned to Asif hotly and began to blurt out an explanation:

"We thought it was the Chinese!" Then he paused, glowering as he suspected he may already have revealed to much, while Asif's imagination groped with the unlikely threat posed by the little Chinese visitor of recent weeks.

"Ab!" Mohammed glared at his friend and continued in Punjabi, "*Say nothing! Nothing!*"

By now the Spaniards were issuing a volley of protests and demands in their own language, too rapid for Asif to follow, although he thought he might have heard 'goods', accompanied by a negative shake of a forefinger. The verbal torrent was lost on Mohammed and Abdul, too, who held up hands, crying, "English! English!"

All of them abruptly turned to scramble up the stairs, with Asif following behind, taking an anxious look at his watch which informed him it was only ten minutes to opening time. Once in the upstairs room, the argument broke out fiercely again, with Asif watching bemusedly from just inside the door. His boys were demanding money, the Spaniards were demanding the rest of the 'goods'. The Asians shouted and gesticulated that they could not hand over more of the goods without the cash to pay their suppliers - or at least this was the gist of what Asif understood from the spate of half-articulated exchanges. The two sets of protagonists paused for a moment, scowling at each other in a mutual impasse. Asif took the opportunity to insert himself into the dispute, taking a step towards them from the doorway.

"What is this?" he demanded, gently but firmly, "more of these Eid dolls?"

"Oh, Asif", groaned Mohammed, despairingly.

"Well, what then?" demanded Asif again.

"Yes, yes, the dolls", cut in Abdul, hastily, anxiety etched all over his youthful features.

"Well, then", proceeded Asif, levelly, "if it is simply a problem of cashflow, and you must pay before you can deliver, I shall take some money from the till. These dolls, are more coming soon?" He smiled benignly at the three Spaniards, who regarded him stonily.

"Asif", began Mohammed and spread his arms helplessly at his sides. "We can't -"

"Not at all, my dear boy", reproached Asif, whose troubled countenance had been relaxing into a paternal smile as he resolved their difficulty, "tell me how much you need." He thought he discerned a sneer from the leading Spaniard out of the corner of his eye.

"Come now", smiled Asif.

"Asif", began Mohammed despairingly again, "there's no way -"

His attempt to deflect the gracious offer was checked by his shorter companion, who looked up fiercely at Asif, hot and red-eyed, and half-panted, half-shouted:

"Ten million dollars!"

He paused in the shocked silence before repeating, for emphasis: "*Ten million*!"

Asif rocked, stunned. There was no sound, the Spaniards glaring at Mohammed and Abdul, who in turn were staring in guilt and confusion at Asif. Asif found he could not speak, as his eyes flicked between all five before him. At first he wanted to laugh at the joke but the expressions on the other faces drained all comedy away. Dollar bills twisted and turned in thick wads in front of his eyes but he could not visualise enough of them; he had no idea what ten million dollars looked like. Ten million! He continued to turn his numbed gaze from one to another. At length he spoke, weakly and very quietly.

"Boys." He shook his head uncomprehendingly and moved slowly to one of the old armchairs, two of the Spaniards parting to let him through. He was no fool. Ingenuous and trusting to the point he desired to believe ill of no-one, but by no means unaware of the world around him. The sullenness of youth, serving at his side in the shop, the unwillingness to communicate with any but others of the same ethnic origin, the broody looks and those upstairs meetings which now adopted a furtive dimension he had dismissed hitherto. He stared up at Mohammed.

"What is in these dolls", he asked, softly.

No-one spoke but he waited silently for an answer.

"We can't tell you, Asif", Mohammed muttered at last, his evasive look betraying both embarrassment and fear. Asif regarded him steadily, before turning his gaze to the other.

"Abdul?"

All the while, the three Spaniards hovered in the room, eyes darting between the three from the kebab house, boss and assistants, alert to how much information would be surrendered. Abdul shook his head miserably in response to Asif and studied the floor.

"This ...money", Asif was enunciating his words heavily and carefully, as he gradually came to terms with the wildly improbable, "you were to bring it?" He addressed the leading Spaniard, unable to suppress the image in his mind of an enormous soft leather bag bulging with banded wads of currency poking out of the top.

The Spaniard nodded, sullenly.

"Only after we have all the goods", he muttered.

Asif was beginning to link the pieces together although it still made little sense. Their sullen appearance could be interpreted as unease now; he wondered if they were being inexorably dragged out of their depth. Abdul looked as though he wished it were all a bad dream; Mohammed seemed temporarily marooned in uncertainty.

"Who uses these dolls?" Asif asked him.

"Mohammed shrugged. "They have some, our Iranian friend keeps some", he replied.

"And you have not made a payment yet?"

Mohammed shook his head.

"And who do you pay", asked Asif, "who brings these dolls?" It was incongruous to be referring to children's toys when he could only fear and imagine what they really were. "Is it drugs they contain?"

Just then there was a another hammering of fists at the door below. Abdul and Mohammed looked at each other in trepidation, then relaxed as they heard the voice shouting from outside. Abdul leapt to the door and down the stairs, to return moments later accompanied by the Iranian, who stammered out, "A message! They're coming tonight!"

"The goods?" barked Mohammed.

"Yes, yes", replied the Iranian, still catching his breath, "and *them*!"

"They want their money!" Abdul exclaimed.

Their two faces were struck with fear, Mohammed imploring the Spaniard, "And you will have their money?"

The sullen Spaniard gave a brief assertive nod.

"Yes, yes, of course."

"You have ten million dollars?" Asif asked him, incredulously.

"It is ready", the man muttered.

Abdul broke in, "They won't believe us if we haven't got it! They -" And he choked fearfully. Mohammed gripped him by the arm. It was dawning on Asif that his two boys were nothing but pawns in the game. They - and he, his own shop - merely a cover for these others, and whoever they so feared who conveyed the goods and demanded payment, to transact their business. There was a distant rattle of the shop door. Asif looked at his watch in dismay. Five minutes late! He turned to the Spaniards.

"You had better go", he said to them. "Come back later, please." He addressed the Iranian. "What time?"

"Ten o'clock", was the response.

"The dolls?" checked Asif.

The Iranian nodded.

"And these other people, whoever they are?" demanded Asif, firmly.

The man shrugged.

Asif spoke to the Spaniards again. "Go, please. Come back at ten. You will have your dolls." Whatever they are, he thought grimly to himself. The Spaniards set off down the stairs, followed by the Iranian.

"Come", Asif beckoned Mohammed and Abdul to follow him into the shop. "We shall speak later."

He strode to the door to let in the customers. This time, their patience had been exhausted. There was no-one waiting.

Doves

"What do you reckon to the troop withdrawals?" commented Walt to Elroy, as they sat in the back seat on the way to Best Cars, Olivia sitting in the front, beside Bella at the wheel.

"Wow", responded Elroy, "she's sure got the message. I'd never have guessed the President would come on board so quick - if at all."

"Yeh", grinned Walt, "she must have seen one of those church visions."

"Mm", Elroy smiled thoughtfully. He recalled the glow that seemed to shine from within Victoria Twigg as she stood making her announcement on the White House steps. There had been something unnervingly familiar about that glow. "Well", he picked up Walt's original question, "it's sure gonna change things around. No more Mister Policeman America."

"Yeh. Not going to be tomorrow, though", suggested Walt, "a 'phased withdrawal'."

"Huh", snorted Elroy, "we supposed to be doing that for years."

"Yeh, I know", agreed Walt, "but this time it looks real. The military are arguing but looks like Twigg's got both Houses on side. They've been canvassing Senate and The Representatives and getting majorities for her."

"You know a lot about this", remarked Elroy.

"Hey, man", chuckled Walt, "all I've done for two days is watch CNN while you've being sorting the bug." He grinned and dug his elbow into his friend's side.

Elroy laughed as he recoiled.

"They've been talking about terrorism", added Walt, looking out of the car window at the gathering sunset over London's troubled streets.

"What? More of it?" queried Elroy.

"No. Less. Well, you know, it's hawks against doves again but it's the doves winning this time. Saying if the US pulls back everywhere a lot of terrorism won't have targets any more."

"It's not always our own guys getting hit", objected Elroy.

"No. But it's often because we're there, isn't it - you know that from your eavesdropping, yeh? Either they can see us more or less running their country or propping up their government or just plain interfering. We just never thought we could leave them before."

"Or their oil." Elroy sniffed. "So we pull out and leave them to it?"

"Yeh. Doves calling the shots right now. All part of that 'leading the world' she said that day, remember?"

Elroy nodded. He remembered where he saw that inspiring speech, too, in his prisoner's 'cell'.

"'Course", Walt went on, "as one of the experts said, it'll only take one or two 'nine-elevens' - anywhere in the West - and Uncle Sam'll be back in there, kicking ass like never before."

"Hm", pondered Elroy, "a gamble. Wait and see."

"Guess so."

The car swung through a tight curve as Bella pulled into the Best Cars forecourt.

"Here we are, guys", she called brightly, switching off the engine.

Address

"Best Cars."

"Never heard of them", Gordon replied.

"I thought you said your mechanic -" came Derek's voice from Folkestone.

"Yeh", said Gordon, "but he only said his mate bought a Chinese car, didn't say where. Anyway, what kept you." He looked anxiously at his watch. Eight-thirty. Two hours since their last call."

"Come on, mate", Derek sounded worn, "there's all hell down here, high tide: we've got all the big ones coming in."

Okay, Gordon knew the problem. The big container ships had to wait for the tide then all started unloading in quick succession, creating a sudden influx of cargo for Customs inspection.

"Yeh, okay, thanks for getting it", acknowledged Gordon. "What's the address?"

Derek carefully dictated the Best Cars North London address down the phone, adding that he'd send it on a fax immediately, for confirmation.

"Do you want the phone number", asked Derek.

"Yeh, okay", Gordon sounded unconcerned, "just in case."

"You not going to phone them?" queried Derek.

"No, don't think so", responded Gordon.

"Think they might be in on it?" Derek quizzed with interest.

"Well ... no, I doubt it but no point in warning them, if they are."

"If it's anything, anyway", remarked Derek. "You sending a squad?"

"Yeh, soon as ..." Gordon confirmed. He had already ordered a raiding team to get ready.

"From your depot?" asked Derek. Raids, especially when they took place away from Customs sheds or entry ports, were hedged with intrigue and excitement, not to mention potential danger. "Tooled up?"

"No. Hell, no. I don't want to waste time getting the Met, and firearms authority", Gordon declared.

"You think it's safe?" queried Derek, uncertainly, hesitating to remind his colleague of precautionary procedures. "If it's what you're suggesting, they're not kids you're dealing with."

"No. Sure", agreed Gordon. "You think I should get the Met?"

"Get them on back-up", suggested Derek, "they can carry a couple of guns for routine. Only take half an hour."

Gordon looked at his watch again. Another half-hour would be lost. It seemed like the pattern was for the dolls to be sold with the cars, or at least some of them. The most he could do was intercept them at Best Cars and seize them all before they disappeared with the showroom's customers. They weren't all going to be sold and driven away in the next couple of hours. He was puzzled. Andy's mate's doll was wood and it was lighter than the weight discrepancy from the weighbridge and the uranium volume-by-weight check. Anyone smuggling something dangerous wasn't going to let it slip into the hands of random car customers, anyway. Maybe certain cars were bought by 'middle-men', with specified dolls included in the sale. It did not add up.

He felt some beads of sweat tingling under his collar. He could be making a big fool of himself - a whole page in the Christmas magazine! It was all too complicated, with too much left to chance on the part of whoever might be behind this. So, it was all too possible that no-one was behind it. Nothing to be pursued. Just some shoddy Chinese toys after all, so badly manufactured that they were made with different materials and of at least two different weights. The best he might hope for would be to haul Trading Standards in to confiscate the whole lot for toxic coatings, loose nails and all the usual foreign toy hazards. He quailed at the thought - and the headlines: 'Customs Blunder. Team Raids Dolls House'.

"Yeh, yeh", Gordon nodded at the phone. "I'll tell the Met. Probably false alarm but play safe."

"Okay, good luck and", Derek added with a chuckle, "the wife wants one with pigtails and a gold ribbon."

"Sounds more like your type, that", retorted Gordon in amusement. He heard Derek's cackle and the phone click off.

Okay, so he would put in the routine precautionary call to the police, give them the address and then - oh to hell with it - he would set off with his team, anyway. If this was all going bad on him, he'd rather sort it out before the force even arrived than be caught with egg on his face as they came leaping out of the back of their van. If the worst came to the worst, he would just sit tight with his men and wait for the back-up to arrive.

He went to the office door. There was that doll, still smiling at him. He could not help smiling back, despite his anxiety. It was the first time he'd noticed it had pigtails tied with gold ribbon.

Vigilante

Paul himself let them in through a staff-only door and slipped them to the side of the crowd, where they could see the showroom was packed. Word had got around. The fact that the entertainment was free, together with the vividly reported delicate beauty of the Chinese dancers, had ensured an overflowing attendance. Paul had grunted disparagingly to one of his senior sales staff that they might all be time-wasters. He had even toyed with the unrealistic notion of only allowing entry to those who paid a holding deposit on a Manchu Met. He was swiftly dissuaded by one of his more pragmatic sales team, who reminded him this was a promotional exercise, not a hard sell, and Paul could scarcely complain at all the free publicity. Television and radio had lost interest, now that it had become a recurring event, but sheer word of mouth and a variety of 'what's on' announcements maintained an extraordinarily high profile for the 'dragon dance'.

Olivia marvelled at the eager anticipation of the audience.

"Well, I guess it's a change from ugly scenes", she enthused in reference to London's week of troubles. "More like home tonight."

"Yeh", agreed Bella, "except I heard some stories of violence today."

"Back home?" asked Walt beside her.

"Yeh. Not the first but more than before."

"Nothing like here", commented Paul, who by now had been brought up to date on the basic details of the 'bug', with the close involvement of Elroy, Olivia and Bella carefully omitted. Walt had filled in details without giving the game away. The two men found they got on well, thrust together unexpectedly in the same house, and now able to build on their previous brief acquaintance in New York and London.

"Well, no, not like here, maybe", Bella chipped in, "but I heard on the car radio: some vigilante groups."

"Eh?" interjected Elroy, on the edge of their little group,

"Religious groups", explained Bella.

"The Klan?" Olivia exclaimed.

"No", replied Bella, "not the same, not them, but it seems there's religious groups patrolling towns, talking about the 'vision' and 'acting for God'."

Elroy groaned softly.

"How?" asked Walt.

"They say it's only isolated cases", continued Bella, "but some people have been threatened, and some beatings, if they're not sharing - car rides, mainly, ya know."

The deep clang of a gong, followed by a rattle of drumbeats, lulled their conversation and hushed the expectant throng. All eyes swung in front to the showroom floor, drawn by the entrance parade of dancing girls in their black-and-bobinned mannequin hairstyles and silken gold, silver and red traditional dresses flowing to their ankles. The dainty, smiling dancers swirled into an arc and gestured to the rear of the showroom as, with a clash of cymbals and blare of classical Chinese music, eyes and mouths in the audience gaped wide at the entrance of the dragon! The swaying, giant, skirted beast, in green and gold, pranced and tossed from its red-rimmed mouth to its many-spiked tail, until it took centre stage. Then the show began.

Belief

"Who's side are we on?" Gabriel grunted, picking messily at the toenail next to the big one on his left foot.

"Side?" God looked down and then quickly away, to avoid the mild wave of nausea that accompanied any accidental observation of Gabriel's assault on his feet.

"Well, they've all got You on their side, as usual", Gabriel responded, without looking up from his sculpturing. "You know: 'God be with us', from one lot; 'the Lord will bless the true believers', from the other lot."

God sighed. One of those deep, soft, long sighs, which sent a tidal breath across a swathe of universe, shunting a couple of comets off their courses and thereby changing the future of a planet or two, a couple of million years (their time) ahead.

"Well?" insisted Gabriel, flicking away an obstinate particle of indeterminate colour sticking to his finger.

"I don't take sides", sighed God again, wearily (another comet, another planet. Hey ho.)

"According to them you do", retorted Gabriel, continuing to forage. "According to them You're on all their sides. Until one of them loses; then all of a sudden they go all quiet about You. Have You noticed how the losers always stop claiming You were on their side, once they've lost? According to them, You're not a losers' God, only a winners' Go-"

"All right, all right", The Lord cut in.

There was a pause in the Cosmos.

"...They've got a point, though -" Gabriel turned his attention to the gap between the fourth and fifth toes on the other foot "from the believers' point of view. I mean, how could there be a God for *unbelievers* if they don't believe in You in the first place? The unbelievers can't have it both ways - from the believers' viewpoint, that is. The unbelievers are not believing in You, but a different version of You, and still expecting to have You on their side. Until they lose, that is; which is why the winners are always the believers, whichever side they are on."

He flicked a bit of something not very nice in the general direction of God. "Oops, sorry", he glanced up momentarily, before focusing on the offending crevice again. "Of course, some of them say it's possible to have a God - sort of just knocking around somewhere - without everyone having to believe in Him - You - and they're absolutely right there, aren't they, Guv? But then again, that's easy 'cos it doesn't make any difference to them if there's a God they don't believe in, if they don't believe in ... You ... In the first place, if You take my meaning. I mean, if I didn't *believe* there was stuff to be got out of here -"

Gabriel was prizing the next two toes apart to examine the secret contents of the space between,"I wouldn't have to do anything about it. But I *do* believe it, so -"

"Yes, yes, all right! All right! All right!"

God felt slightly sick as he glanced at the excavations of his loyal aide and moved away a little.

Belief! That was the most absurd thing of all, that His very existence, as far as humans were concerned, rested on whether each of the billions of them *believed* in Him or not. Not *fact* but *belief.* The earth was round: fact. The sun was a ball of fiery gas: fact. Father Christmas - 'Saint' Nick! Ha! - was a large number of otherwise normal men dressing up in red suits and white beards and consuming immoderate quantities of whisky and mince pies in the fireplace: fact. But God. Oh no, God - He - was entirely dependent on *belief.* If someone *believed* in Him, He existed. If there was no belief, then - *pooff!* - He was gone. Or rather, had never existed in the first place. How utterly, utterly ridiculous. It was not a question of whether Gabriel *believed* in the gunge between his toes, it was there anyway. It existed regardless of whether he believed it did. But not God, apparently; He had to be believed in, otherwise He just did not exist.

Hadn't He done enough? Hadn't He gone to great lengths to ensure that all those 'miracles' of Jesus actually worked so people really would accept him as God's messenger ?(Okay, okay, 'son'; He had let that go as part of the deal, at the time). And Mohammed. Look at that one. An unremarkable man - all right, sincere, dedicated, *driven* by a passion for a moral code but no more likely than any number of visionaries to carry God's torch - *transformed* by one spellbinding encounter in a cave into God's prophet for centuries to come. (One of Gabriel's finer achievements, that cave episode, God had to admit).

And yet ... and yet ...it was not a single belief in a single God that had arisen as a result. What Gabriel said was true: not only was He, God, claimed by each set of beliefs, He was moulded by each into an image of *their* choosing, not His own. And when their behaviour reached extremes, when they in-flicted suffering in His name, when they took His name - as they accused each other - in vain; or would it be better to say 'in vanity'; what was He then? A plasticine God. A God of many shapes. A God for all, but different for each. The God in the Hall of Mirrors.

"So...?" Gabriel had decided the God Of Many Silences had been left long enough in Divine contemplation.

"Mm...yes?" The Lord was torn from his thoughts back to the world of reality, if one small planet in a distant corner of the Universe could be so assigned.

"Whose side are we on?"

Dropped

"Wooooooh!"

The audience whooped in time with the dolls as they were flung into the air by the dancing girls emerging from beneath the dragon's skirt, almost reaching the high ceiling of the showroom. There were wide smiles of delight on every face, upturned to watch the silken-clad figures twist and turn in their trajectory, to plummet back into the waiting hands of the dancers. Everyone gasped in admiration at the pinpoint accuracy as the dolls all reached their summit at almost precisely the same height and were caught simultaneously by the smiling mannequins, who continued the downward sweep of the dolls in a synchronised bow.

"See!" Bella turned to the others, clapping her hands in glee. "Aren't they spectacular!"

"Sure thing!" and "Wow, yeh!" Walt and Olivia cheered and clapped together.

Elroy turned to Paul, a sudden recollection coming to him.

"These dolls come with the cars?"

"Yes, that's the whole idea", beamed Paul, proudly.

"From China?" asked Elroy.

"Well, yes", affirmed Paul, "*with* the cars", as though it would be unlikely for cars and dolls to arrive from different countries.

"Gee", murmured Elroy, thinking of the GCHQ code and Martin Timmis.

"Not smuggled, then?" he half-joked to his host.

"Smuggled?" Paul looked at him in surprise. "These don't look smuggled, do they? This is about as public as you can get!"

"Yeh, sure", Elroy agreed, puzzled. A peculiar coincidence. Chinese dolls the subject of secret coded messages; and Chinese dolls here on public display, to be given away with every Chinese car: no secret at all. A jigsaw where the pieces refused to fit together. He shook his head and gave up to watch the show.

Now that there were forty-five cars and dolls newly arrived, all to be freed from the dragon's curse, the ceremony had to be performed three times in succession but nobody watching minded. It was such a mesmerising show, it was like being offered two encores and no-one wished it to stop. Between each repeat, the dragon swayed out of the rear door of the showroom, while the girls returned the dolls to tables covered in silk cloth, with the cars displayed behind.

"I don't know why the dragon has to go out and come back each time", muttered Walt, as the ungainly beast, with its array of human legs, staggered through the door to vanish for a few minutes before returning.

"Well I guess they need a breather after that", smiled Olivia, as they waited for the third and last performance. The fixed smiles of the pretty girl dancers looked slightly glazed by now and there were some chests lifting and falling more heavily than when they first made their entrance, with even a few wisps of jet black hair out of place. The onlookers clapped the more enthusiastically, though, perhaps because it was the last repeat, perhaps to encourage the performers, whose movements, both dancers and dragon, were not quite as perfectly co-ordinated as before.

"Whoa!" Elroy exclaimed as the dragon swayed clumsily close to them, its tail swailing in a loop across the floor within inches of their feet. As the dancers completed their routine with the dolls for a final time, there were a few trips and stumbles as they ducked under the dragon with the dolls, and when their hands reappeared to toss them sky-high, the smiling dancers emerging to catch them were a decidedly more straggling bunch than in the first performance. It was just one last effort of skill and timing but the dolls had not flown upwards in perfect unison, the girls beneath had to dart in different directions. There were a few grasping hands, fixed smiles momentarily slipping, and then one wild-eyed girl lunging vainly too late, and a loud crack as a doll hit the hard showroom floor.

There was a gasp and groan in sympathy from the portion of the crowd nearest, over where the four friends and Paul stood. The front row had started backwards a half-pace, at the crack and flailing hands of the dancer who had missed her catch. The doll had split in two, the head separated from the body and rolling towards the feet of the onlookers. Elroy instinctively bent to pick it up, as did a woman next to him. He saw the raw metal sheered off at the neck and barked at her, "Don't touch it!"

The dancing girl had slipped to her knees with a terrified look and was groping at the doll's body to retrieve it. With the head in his hand, Elroy snatched up the body before the girl could reach it, shouting at her, too, "Don't touch it!" He did not know where he had seen that metal before but something was ringing alarm bells. Paul came over to him to relieve him of the doll and restore order. It distracted Elroy's attention and allowed the girl to gather her wits and grab both pieces from him, making as though to fix them back together in her hands, covering her confusion with a gesture and a smile.

The music was still playing through the loudspeakers and the girls swiftly composed themselves into an orderly row to take a bow, the audience began to clap and cheer, the dragon swayed and bowed and, as the audience regained its confidence it broke into wild applause, forgiving the minor mishap. The dancers and dragon together took their applause and the dancer with the broken doll twirled under the dragon's skirt to re-emerge with it miraculously complete once more, held aloft for all to see, her look of terror replaced by her shop-dummy smile. The crowd applauded further at this display of 'magic', as the show ended, the dolls were placed on their table and the dancers and dragon made their exit to the rear.

As the applause died away, Walt remarked to Elroy, "They must have one or two spares in that dragon, for breakages. She looked like death when it broke."

Elroy grunted unsmilingly in response. He wanted to recall where he had seen that queer, silvery metal before and why it had suddenly unnerved him.

"Let's go see those dolls", he suggested. Just as they moved, there was a disturbance as a number of uniformed men burst through the ranks of onlookers and strode onto the performance area. One among them addressed the audience.

"Ladies and gentlemen. Sorry to interrupt your evening. We are from Customs and Excise. We have to conduct an inspection!"

There were murmurs of surprise in the gathering.

"Who's in charge?" the uniformed officer continued.

Paul stepped to him.

"I'm the owner. Paul Best", he began indignantly. "What's all this about? You'll ruin my trade!"

"I'm sorry, sir", Gordon Pierce confided to him, "We have to arrive without notice. We don't know who might be involved."

"Involved in what?" Paul was close to exploding, as the hushed audience stared at the two of them.

"Can't say immediately, sir, but let me explain to your guests, if I may."

"Okay, go ahead", scowled Paul, seeing this might excuse him from the responsibility of spoiling the evening.

"Ladies and gentlemen", Pierce addressed the onlookers, "please accept my apologies. There is no suggestion the establishment here -" he indicated Paul Best beside him "is involved in anything untoward but we have to conduct an inspection if we believe there may be compromised articles inadvertently brought onto the premises. Do continue with your evening. We can carry on quietly in the background." He nodded to Paul, who took up the message.

"Yes, everyone", Paul called out, "at least they waited till the show was over!" There was a ripple of laughter. "There's more drink and buffet and the cars are here for you to see .. and the dolls!"

"In a moment, sir", Gordon Pierce advised him in a low voice.

"Eh?" responded Paul.

"It's the dolls we need to see, sir. If they're clear, you can have them."

Paul look bemused, then realised the other half-dozen Customs officers had already surrounded the table of dolls, preventing anyone from getting to them. He followed Pierce to the table. An officer turned round. "Checked the first two, sir. Wood."

"Wood?" Pierce frowned.

"Yes, sir, look." His colleague showed where he had parted the costume at the rear and struck the doll's back with a sharp knife to split it open. It was solid hardwood. Gordon frowned again.

"Check them all", he ordered.

"Here, sir", asked another officer. "Aren't we taking them?"

"I need to know, now", said Pierce, gruffly, the Christmas magazine cover-story growing bigger and brighter in his mind's eye. He knew they could not possibly *all* be wood. Derek had the weights. Okay, supposing he had not actually weighed and checked every one; suppose he'd told Gordon he had but actually stopped after the first dozen and assumed they all weighed the same. That would explain some being heavier than others without Derek being aware of it. He would have it out with his colleague later; first, find the heavy ones.

It only took half an hour. Every one, all forty-five, were made of the same wood and, as Gordon had instructed one of his team to bring a digital balance, each checked at the same weight, just overthree hundredgrams, barely one-third the weight Derek had confirmed. It was not possible. This was the same consignment. The same forty-five cars containing the same forty-five dolls. Each doll should weigh, according to Derek, nine hundredn and eighty three grams. You can allow a bit of leeway for inaccurate measurements but not two thirds of a kilo! They all weighed the same as Andy's doll, from a different consignment. Gordon felt he was going mad.

"I hope they're being careful", commented Elroy to Paul, watching from the buffet table.

"Why?"

"I don't like the look of that metal. Can't think what it reminds me of."

"I heard them say something about wood", Paul commented. "Where do you get metal from?"

"That one that broke", said Elroy. "Told the girl not to touch it. Can't be sure."

Paul shrugged. He called over to the uniformed group clustered at the table. "You found any metal ones?"

Gordon Pierce heard and looked around, surprised.

"What do you mean, sir?" He felt little hairs prickling at the back of his neck.

"My friend says they're metal."

"Sir?" Pierce came across the few yards to Elroy.

"Aw, nothing, I guess", explained Elroy. "One broke in the show. I picked it up. It was metal. Didn't like the look of it. Can't think where I seen it before. But they replaced it - I guess with one of those." He nodded across at the table. "The dancer looked terrified, like she'd really screwed up."

Gordon's mind was a ferment.

"Where is it now, sir?"

"The metal one?" replied Elroy, "I guess they took it with them, instead of the spare."

"This show, sir", Gordon turned to Paul again, "what do they do?"

Paul described the dragon dance with some relish, having witnessed it often enough for every detail to be imprinted on his memory.

"So the girls dive, as it were, under the dragon and then toss the dolls out again, and catch them?" Gordon went over the sequence.

"Yes, that's right", confirmed Paul, "pity you missed it."

"Yes", Gordon shook his head in rueful agreement. A pity he missed it, indeed. "The same dolls?" he queried.

"Same?" Paul looked puzzled.

"They threw out the same dolls they took under the dragon?"

"Well", Paul shrugged helplessly, "not much point in having two lots of them, except for those spares." Elroy nodded in agreement.

Gordon was wondering if some pieces might fall into place.

"And the dragon leaves for a few minutes between shows?" Paul nodded. Gordon thought for a moment. "Did you seethe Chinese leave, sir?"

"What, tonight?" asked Paul, about to add he'd been stuck inside waiting for Customs to stop disrupting his promotional evening.

"Any night of these shows, sir. There have been others, haven't there?"

"Yes, two others", affirmed Paul. "No they just slip out and away. I suppose. I'm still with my punt - guests. I saw that Mr Sing, their compere guy, leave once with a suitcase -"

Paul stopped speaking. He was visualising that first evening when he had sought out Mr Sing to congratulate him on the entertainment and found him packing some dolls into a bulging suitcase. He had not taken much notice, assuming them to be spares for breakages, like Elroy this evening.

"Suitcase, sir?" Gordon was staring attentively at Paul.

"Yes, with dolls - spares, like tonight, I suppose."

"A full suitcase?" Gordon asked, disbelievingly.

"Well, yes, looked like it."

"Like a full set of spares?" Gordon asked, sharply. "The dancer looked frightened?" He addressed Elroy, who nodded. "As if she'd blundered?" Elroy nodded to agree with this possibility. Gordon pursed his lips then added, grimly, half to himself, "They've been switched, haven't they?"

"Eh?" Paul was not following this. Elroy was seeing the jigsaw pieces find their positions.

"Sir, that charade with the dolls - yes, I wish I'd seen it - disappearing under the dragon then coming out again, they were probably changing one complete set of dolls for another. Leaving the substitutes in the room, taking the car dolls round the back in the dragon, then bringing another set of substitutes inside the dragon, ready to swap with the next batch of dolls from the cars. Every set of dolls from the cars ending up round the back, with substitutes left here in the room!" There was rising urgency in his voice as he worked it out. "Where does the Chinese man go next?" Now there was an element of panic. Vital minutes were being lost.

"Just out the back", said Paul, indicating the exit door to the rear.

"Quick! Ron! Dave! Round the back! Stop the Chinese!" barked Pierce, leading his men in a charge, past backroom offices and stores. The Customs team erupted in a bunch outside in the rear yard.

"There!" cried Pierce, pointing at the Chinese man, Sing, and a swarthier companion, heaving a sturdy leather bag into the back of a small blue van fifty yards away. The two Chinese looked up in dismay. Sing scrambled to the front passenger door and leapt in, his accomplice jumping into the back of the van, hauling the bag in behind him. Pierce's men were almost upon the van when it lurched away - a driver must have been ready to make a dash for it - and sped down the incline to the road, the Chinese heavy pulling the van doors shut behind him. Two of Pierce's men made a grab for the rear van doors but missed their grip and footing, tumbling to the ground as the van accelerated down the street. Pierce looked around wildly for a vehicle to give chase but realised none could be started quickly enough. Their own cars were parked on the front forecourt and there were only locked cars and service vehicles in view.

"Shit!" He panted, as the last glimpse of the blue van disappeared from sight in the gloom of dusk.

Trap

Tony Delgardo felt real swell. The soft top was open, the sun was shining down, he was looking good (he knew that) and so was the car, newly-valetted. He wanted it to sparkle inside and out, although the guy sprucing the interior had commented, "Sure is neat and tidy, Mr Delgardo, hardly needs a wipe around. Not many folks get in these back seats, eh, with their dusty feet on the floor?"

Had Tony not been feeling so pleased with the world at large, and himself in particular, he might have thought there to be a mite meanness to the guy's tone and the look in his eye. But Tony had no mind for such reflections right now. So what if he gave the finger to suckers trying to hitch a ride. He was a busy guy. So he was not one of those losers on short time in a car plant or a vacuum cleaner factory. So he was in soft goods, not electrics. Any fool knew a toilet roll would never break down on you (he laughed to himself) and would folks stop using them? (He laughed again). Same with towels. And soap. And washing powder. So people still washed their clothes, (except in each other's washers, for fuck's sake!). He was shifting as much 'smooth and gentle' as ever.

He looked at Suzy Rose's delicate, soft-gold hands on her lap in the passenger seat beside him. They would never go red raw with washing and cleaning, not while he was with her, anyways. Soon as she showed signs of beef steaks for hands, that would be her, straight outa the window. She smiled sweetly and seductively at him. He smiled back and was aware of the faint stirring in the familiar way.

He'd had the scratch removed and polished. If he found the shit who did it, he would sort him out so he'd know never to go near Tony Delgardo's wheels again. Like his father's friends used to teach lessons in the Bronx. His old man never let him see a 'visit' take place, though once when he was a kid he heard some screams of pain from around a street corner before he was hurried away. Sometimes he saw men with bruises showing around the sides of dark glasses, or with an arm in a sling, or on crutches; men who had looked fit and well a day or two before. "Never do wrong, son, never do wrong", his father would say, "except if they done wrong to you."

They were on their way to a 'dead cert' client, who always bought. Tony made doubly sure of a deal every time by taking Suzy with him into the man's office. Some clients did not welcome female intrusion into business, in some traditional old-style places, but this jerk was quite the opposite. In fact, Suzy Rose amply justified her 'secretary' billing on these occasions, cutely aware of just the right moment to cross and uncross her legs, in a skirt just short enough to tantalise yet deny proof of whether she wore anything underneath. It was at moments of decision-making that her secretarial support became most valuable when, hovering over Tony's invitation to sign for a formidable quantity at a considerable price and with a flustered eye upon Suzy's endless thighs, the man duly did so, much beyond the limit he had privately set himself.

The town had become a degree troublesome lately. Even Tony could not entirely ignore the angry glares from townsfolk on foot or watching him speed by an elderly resident waving her free arm for a ride, with a heavy shopping bag weighing down the other. He had seen some fists shaken in his mirror and scowls when he entered a store for some cans and cigarettes. So what. Losers. The client had been particularly intent on establishing the time of their appointment on this occasion. Usually, he just said, "I'll see you when I see you", but today's visit had been pinned down to an exact time. "A busy schedule", the client had explained on the phone, evading any further explanation. Tony had dismissed it as a quirk. The guy must be making certain there would only be the three of them, not having his own matronly secretary siphon Suzy away for coffee and cake. Suzy's nether regions could receive uninterrupted attention, the offending matron doubtless already despatched on some errand the other side of town.

Tony grinned to himself again and squeezed Suzy's exposed thigh as he turned into the quiet side-street off the main road through town. He anticipated a big juicy order with top commission. Strangely, the client was already at the door of his premises to greet the pair of them, stepping out with a raised gesture of his arm as the car pulled up. Tony's grin widened, with a knowing look directed at the man and then at Suzy. The client did not respond as Tony might have expected. His mouth twitched into a nervous smile, not the familiar suppressed leer.

As Tony made to fling open the car door, his eye caught a movement in the wing mirror. A group of men had appeared behind the car, five or six of them. Something made him look up ahead and another group, about the same number, were approaching the front of the car; both ten metres or more away. Delgardo's immediate reaction was confusion, that they should have materialised unseen out of doorways or hidden passages without warning. There was no reason for them to be not there one minute, and there the next.

His next reaction was driven by the looks in their eyes, fixed on his. Instinctively, he snatched for the key, still in the ignition, but before he could turn it the client wrenched open the car door and pulled Delgardo's arm away from the dashboard. The violence of the motion caused Suzy to let out a sharp cry of alarm. Tony cursed and struggled to free his arm and could see out of the corner of his eye that both groups of men had moved to encircle the car; some were holding sticks or rods. Distractedly, Tony allowed his arm to be wrenched further from the ignition, jagging the key against the wheel, knocking it from his fingers onto the car floor.

He was suddenly conscious of how punctually he and Suzy had arrived, to take maximum advantage of their sleazy dupe. He had been only too eager to fall in with the client's request. This was the appointed time. A rough hand was pulling him from the car. Suzy Rose was beginning to tremble and emit little yelps beside him. The welcome party had been waiting.

Jihad

Asif stood facing them in the upstairs room.

It had torn at his gut to fabricate the pretence, written out in black marker pen on a sheet of paper and taped to the shop-door window: 'Sincere Apologies. We Have Closed early This Evening Due To Staff Illness. Very Sorry For The Inconvenience. Open As Usual Tomorrow'. In truth, it could be said there was ill health among them, for it made him sick to his stomach, the churning apprehension of an evil being unveiled before him: here, in his own humble kebab house.

"Sit down", he commanded, quietly. Mohammed and Abdul each sat in a manner both anxious and sullen, reluctant to meet his eyes.

"What is in those dolls?" he asked, gravely.

They continued to half look at him, then away.

"Is it contaminated?" he persisted. "Is it a poison?"

He knew little of chemistry. He understood only that any solid, heated to a sufficiently high temperature, would turn to liquid, then eventually to gas. Perhaps a noxious, fatal gas. The two confederates, mere youths to Asif, shook their heads, dumbly, expressions mutating between the wretched and the resentful.

"Is it evil you have been persuaded to do?" Asif provoked them to respond.

Abdul's head lifted to face him, a ferocity lighting his eyes.

"It is for Allah!" he declared, vehemently. "It is for Islam!"

"Islam?" repeated, Asif, deeply troubled at this confusion of aggression with their faith.

"It is for the jihad!" Mohammed burst out, joining his companion to glare up at Asif.

"The jihad", Asif denounced in steady tones, "is nothing but savagery."

"It is for Allah", repeated Abdul, hotly, a flush glowing even beneath his dark olive skin. "It is for the people of Islam. It is against the unbeliever. Down with the aggressor against Islam!" He thumped his knees with his fists. Mohammed pressed his lips tightly together, still glaring at Asif, then spoke grimly, becoming for a moment old beyond his years.

"It is a war against evil, Asif", he asserted.

"Evil?" Asif looked at him. This young man, at turns moody, honest, passionate, yet at times relaxed and good-humoured. What had infected him? It seemed the corruption of their faith, at once proclaimed and denounced in disparate quarters of the world, a distorted image he so despised, had at last insinuated itself under the very portals of his own life. "Evil?" he repeated, solemnly. "Is what you prepare not evil? What would you do with these dolls?" He paused. "Do you mean to kill people?"

Their two heads bowed to the floor, quavering from side to side, not meeting his gaze. It occurred to Asif that perhaps, whatever plan they had been formulating, whatever terrible deed might be perpetrated in the name of Islam, it may not have directly entered their consciousness until this moment that what they conspired to accomplish could actually bring the lives of ordinary people to an horrific end. Real, brutal death arising from misguided intentions and devout aspirations. "Do you intend to make people die?"

Chase

"Why didn't you like that metal doll, sir?" Gordon Pierce eyed Elroy suspiciously, as they stood, still breathing heavily in the Best Cars rear yard.

"Don' know", replied Elroy, guardedly, "there was something not right about it."

"Yes", agreed Pierce, doubtfully. "You some sort of expert?" He had recognised the American accent and began to wonder what it was doing here at a London car showroom, with more than a layman's awareness of the situation.

"He's a signals specialist", Olivia stepped forward to put it simply. "He works with the US government - and over here with the British."

Pierce was puzzled at the second American voice, and an American woman of some authority, not to mention a US 'signals specialist'.

"You've got an idea what this is, haven't you, sir? If it's what I think it is, that makes two of us."

Elroy looked worried. Sure, he'd formed an impression immediately he saw the broken doll and felt its weight but the notion was too absurd.

"I guess I thought", he hesitated, "it looked like -"

"Yes?" Pierce prompted him , anxiously.

"Uranium."

"*Uranium!*" Olivia burst out in horrified amazement.

Elroy wanted to backtrack from naming the apocalypse. "it looked like uranium but, man, it can't be so I guess I just wanted to warn people in case -" he shrugged. In case 'what', he did not know. He inhabited a world where innocent objects turned out to be dangerous, and vice versa; it invaded his mind with suspicion and doubt.

"It is uranium, sir," said Gordon, sensing he could take this man into his confidence if it shed some more light, "Enriched. Weapons grade."

"Lord!" Elroy gasped.

"I've been checking weights and volumes. Yes, it's not possible, is it? But you know what you saw. That's all I needed to hear."

Pierce looked drained. All the strain, the agonising in his mind, the pursuit of evidence, and now the terrible quarry slipping from his grasp; it was all suddenly taking its toll. He turned back to Paul.

"You any idea where that Chinaman comes from? An office?" His question was tense but weary.

Paul looked blank. Come to think of it, all the contracts had been brought to him by Sing for signing. The only addresses were Best Cars and Mr Choi's factory in Beijing.

"Well", Paul spread his arms impotently, "how should I know, I mean ... wait a minute ...no, look there's probably no connection but", he was fishing through his memory for that bizarre image of the little Chinese man emerging from the back of the kebab house with a large empty bag under his arm, "but I saw him soon after the first delivery." And he described the circumstances, rounding off with, "But, you know, the guy just likes kebabs, eh?"

The next few minutes passed in a flash. Gordon Pierce had come this far; now any flimsy lead was worth following. He had Paul get the nearest available car on the forecourt, with just seconds to delegate the rest of the evening to his showroom manager; then the Customs team piled into their cars, all instructed to follow Paul to the kebab house, as fast as safety, if not the law, would allow. Elroy had got himself in the back behind Gordon and his driver. Bella, with Walt and Olivia, climbed in with Paul, determined not to miss out, as he raced a car into the rear yard, around the building from the front forecourt. Gordon groaned inwardly. Chasing off to a kebab house because a Chinaman liked kebabs was uncomfortably close to some of the more embarrassing news headlines they had generated in the past. Too late now.

Paul shouted to the other drivers to follow.

Gordon's fists were clutching at his thighs, his face darkening with dread.

"Move!" he barked to the driver, fingernails gripping through trousers to dig into his skin.

"Move! Move! Move!"

Two

"Do you intend to make people die", Asif repeated, firmly and quietly, not allowing their silence to evade his question.

The young men shifted where they sat and appeared about to respond, whether to dispute or justify, but there was a thundering at the door downstairs. Mohammed and Abdul looked at each other in trepidation. The hammering of fists at the door became mingled with muffled shouts in a language Asif could not immediately identify. The two young men trembled visibly, interpreting the foreign tongue with fear in their eyes. Abdul blurted an exclamation.

"The Triads!"

"No!" Mohammed cried as if attempting to deny an irrefutable reality.

"Chinese?" queried Asif, unnerved at their alarm. Their eyes darted to him and back in fright towards where the tempest of banging and voices was drumming up the stairway. There were a couple of heavy thuds. Fists had given way to shoulders battering the door.

"Let them in, Mohammed", Asif instructed.

The boys looked fearfully at each other.

"Asif -" Mohammed began.

"They will break the door down if you leave them", Asif said, still calm. He was issuing orders not over the seasoning of meat or the washing of salad but concerning conflict, fear and strife. Yet the light of a spirit which had been growing in him in recent months was shining on an inner strength. If it meant power, he would not have wished it so. He was a humble man. But if strength was borne on humility, he would accept it. If so, it was strength which fought with doubt, for he could not tell if his action would prove wise or foolhardy.

"Go", he commanded.

Mohammed rose obediently to the door, muted by his master's strange spell. He trod uncertainly down the stairs. A moment later there was a clatter as the door was flung open amidst sharp exchanges in Chinese and accented English and then pounding footfalls on the stairs. Sing and three stocky Chinese accomplices with pigtailed hair plunged into the room.

The three each carrying a large, heavy, bulging leather bag, which they dropped to the floor, a doll's arm or leg poking out of a couple of them. All four glared at Mohammed, who had stumbled into the room just ahead of them, and at Abdul.

"We have the remainder!" declared Sing, indicating the bags, "Now you pay!"

"We wait for the Spanish!" Mohammed replied, fiercely, with a wide-armed gesture.

"You say this before!" charged Sing, angrily. "We bring these a long way! Now you pay!"

His thin little face narrowed venomously and a pair of his fingers twitched at his henchmen. The three stepped towards Mohammed and Abdul, who noticed that two of the men were slipping brass knuckle-dusters onto the fists. They both started back, fearfully.

"So you will pay?" Sing smiled now, a thin crack in the weasel mask.

"We have no money -" Mohammed protested, his eyes faltering between the three Chinese cornering them.

" - until the Spanish -" Abdul finished.

"No Spanish!" snapped Sing. "The Spanish pay you. They have many dolls already. Where is our money?"

The three Triads had squared up to Mohammed and Abdul, less than an arms length from each, blocking Asif behind them.

"The Spanish will not pay until they have all", stammered Abdul.

"But you keep some", contradicted Sing. "These are yours."

"No", gasped Mohammed, feeling rank breath on his face from sneering lips in front of him, "they still take more."

"So they will see what happens if you do not pay - and if they do not pay", Sing snarled. His gang moved on cue, raising fists with glinting knuckles. Mohammed and Abdul both cowered, arms lifted in defiance.

"Wait!"

Asif had been gradually excluded from the proceedings, the Chinese having almost forgotten he was there. They were halted by the commanding tone behind them and turned.

"Let me speak to these boys", he continued. He addressed Mohammed and Abdul together, solemnly.

"You were to keep these dolls?" He looked for confirmation of what they had already hinted earlier.

"Some", muttered Mohammed, bowing his head.

"It is for Islam", blurted Abdul, ignoring the threat for a moment.

"And you would do harm?" Asif insisted.

"The jihad", Mohammed mumbled, stubbornly.

"Haw!" cried Sing in scorn. "See! You have your dolls for your little war! We take our money!" The three heavies began to lurch towards the two young men but suddenly stopped. Sing paused, too. Mohammed and Abdul frowned and peered. There was a glow in the room, a glow of unnatural light. They all looked and saw it was coming from Asif Hassan. He stood and now appeared to tower before them, although they could see he had not physically altered. Except for the light. The light was coming from him, as though from inside him. His skin shone. The glow came from his body, too, through his clothes, in the manner of an ornamental figure lit from inside. He turned slowly to the two boys.

"Prophet!" gasped Abdul, wide-eyed. Mohammed's mouth dropped open. The four Chinese gazed in bewilderment at the bearded, towering, illuminated man.

"No, I am not he. But I bear his message. Would you do evil in the name of Islam?" boomed the voice from within Asif Hassan.

The two shook their heads in stunned disbelief.

"Would you kill, in the false name of the Qur'an?" The voice vibrated about the room and the lamp hanging from the ceiling dulled, outshone by the light from this man.

Abdul began to cry. There was a small sob then his eyes watered. Mohammed choked and seemed about to protest but was overcome by the vision shining before him. It was not possible the Prophet should return amongst them. The Koran forbade the notion. But he was overwhelmed by the purity of spirit pouring out to them and the light which filled them.

Just then Sing shook off the spell.

"Hah!" he cried. "Tricks! We know your tricks!" and his three men blinked as though from a trance and began to move menacingly again. This time, though, Asif turned purposefully to face them instead. All four Chinese men wilted and froze. The man in front of them, glowing with light, was not the kebab shopkeeper Asif Hassan. What they each saw, they could not explain. It was a small Chinese man with goatee beard, bowed slightly towards them. The voice changed. It did not boom at them, it spoke softly and in friendship, with the admonishing tone of a teacher to recalcitrant pupils.

"Do I not teach of honour? Do I not teach of a noble life? Do I not teach respect for life? Do you betray our ancestors?" The figure inclined his head in rebuke and stood mildly looking at them.

"Confucious!" Sing staggered where he stood, hand clutching heart. "You - you - come!" The three henchmen blinked, confused. One trembled slightly, another just stared in bemusement. The figure, Asif Hassan, turned again to his boys and glowing with light they saw the tall, bearded prophet; he turned again to the Chinese and they perceived the slight figure of the ancient philosopher. He turned and turned again, slowly, measurably, being only what each separately, the Asians and the Chinese, saw. There was not another sound in the room; except for one, which none of them heard.

"Gabriel."

"Guv?"

The six other heads in the room quivered in surprise at this query addressed to no-one in particular by the awesome figure before them.

"Are you forgetting?" came the unheard voice.

The prophet-philosopher figure blinked imperceptibly, unnoticed by those in the room. It did, however, groan and spoke nonsense again.

"Yeh, okay, Boss."

There was another imperceptible motion within the figure, again unseen, a minor tremor or judder, but the dual-image continued unchanged and resumed its former bearing.

Suzy Rose was sobbing and shrieking, crying and screaming for help but the narrow side-street was deserted, except for themselves. She was held, struggling and kicking, by the client, who did not look as though he was enjoying it half as much as he might have hoped. He held her from behind, with her arms pinned to her sides, but his shirt was torn and there were scratches on his face. Tony Delgardo had his back to the wall, surrounded by a semicircle of twelve men. Most held a stick or a rod.

"What the fuck!" He shouted defiantly. There was already a bruise on his forehead and around one eye. His shirttails were hanging loose and the knuckles of his right hand were red and bloodied. "Is there some new fucking law about giving rides, eh? You gonna fucking tell me that, eh? Well you cain't come doin' the law's fucking business! I got my rights! You wanna take me to court, okay?" He stood, breathing heavily with his body pressed back against the wall. The man in the centre of the arc, slightly rotund and with a more respectable air than some of the others, rough and ill-kempt in jeans and checkered shirts, spoke evenly to Delgardo.

"This *is* the court."

"Eh?" The salesman looked at him, belligerently.

"This is the court of our Lord." The man eyed him directly, metal rod held loosely in one hand. "Our Lord has spoken, mister, and you aint listened. You aint been behavin' like the Lord says you should." Perhaps he was less respectable than he made out, maybe he was intent to speak the language of his comrades. There were various "yehs" and "rights" of agreement and hands re-gripping weapons.

"So you're doing your fucking Lord's fucking dirty work for him!" blared Delgardo, ferociously.

This was too much for them. The men reacted like a single body and weighed towards Tony, rods and sticks raised in fury. He made to fight then was aware he could do no more than defend himself with arms around his head and crouching for protection. A stick landed with a crack on his forearm and he cried out in pain. Suzy Rose screamed in response when she heard him. She was going to watch him be killed. Murdered. Another blow struck with a thud. The men were shouting savagely. But there was another sound. It was like a low howl but it was also a melody. Afterwards, those men who could recall it without shaking to their boots said it was as though there was a choir singing in the wind. A hollow, howling song.

It must have been the wind, they said, because they felt it. It suddenly swept around them, lifting shirts, blowing hair, even throwing them off-balance. They all turned, distracted, to see what it was. At first there was nothing and they might have returned to their malevolent exercise but there was a dust-cloud.

A swirling of dust from the street in the wind. As they watched, its swirling motion slowed and the millions of dust particles danced and eddied into a form. The men were transfixed. Even Tony Delgardo, crouching by the wall, and Suzy Rose, simpering and sobbing in the client's grip, stared.

Two parts of the shape, one on either side, began to spread outwards. At the same time the sun shone. Leastways, they marvelled later, it seemed like the sun, except there weren't no sun shining directly down the street, at the angle of a sunset but bright as noon. It was behind the dust cloud, it shone through it. The dust became a golden glow, it took a firmer shape; it was dust, it was like a blurred image but there was the outline of a head, a body flowing like a garment to the ground and - lawd, they never could believe it theirselves so it weren't no surprise they could persuade no others - those two shapes at the sides, they spread, and spread, until they were two perfect wings, two perfect angel wings, shining like dust with the sun behind. The low howl of the wind-choir sang on. The men, the client, Tony, Suzy, all just stared. Then the almost respectable man shouted, angrily and fiercely.

"You taking our Lord in vain! You will be damned, whoever you are! Get outa here! What is this! Blasphemy!" He was becoming incensed and it aroused his companions likewise. They lurched towards the dust shape, sticks and rods raised in mounting fury. They were shouting, "blasphemy!" "The Devil!" "Mock the Lord!" They had become a mob in a rage, moved beyond their mortal wrath against the sinner salesman. "In the name of the Lord!" yelled the respectable leader and led a charge at the dust cloud.

"Quick!" called Delgardo to Suzy Rose, who had been released by the client as he ran with the mob to arraign the giant dust-angel in the street. The car still stood where it was. They tripped and stumbled to it and clambered in. Tony peered with hazy vision and groped at the floor for the keys, still there. His hands shook as he started up and Suzy clutched his arm, shivering, shaking and sobbing as they roared down the street.

The gang of men did not appear to hear them leave. They were flailing with sticks, rods and fists at the glowing dust-shape, hacking at the huge wings, trying to reach the head above them to decapitate it, though it swayed well above a man's height. As they laid into it, shouting and calling on the Lord, the shape disintegrated and dissolved, the dust filtered into the air, the light faded from it, the wings dispersed like seed cast to the wind and the group of men were left alone in the street, shaking they thought with outrage and self-righteousness but later, alone in their beds or with lonely wives, more than one trembled again without knowing why.

"Go, boys", commanded the glowing prophet-figure. "Retract while you can. Go to your cousins. You will be safe."

Mohammed and Abdul blinked. Their awe was undiminished but the incongruous utterance of "Guv", and "Boss", in the midst of this mystical experience made no sense either from the lips of their Asif or from whoever he had become.

"Go boys", he repeated in that booming, ethereal voice.

The Chinese, too, were still taken aback by the Confucious figure which had just inexplicably spoken in an idiom they only knew from London's local life.

They were all shaken out of their trance by a rush of footsteps on the stairs. The door had remained ajar below. The three Spaniards bounded into the room and pulled up short at the scene and the glowing figure. Instantly they spotted the bags, exchanged looks with each other, saw they had broken into a situation where no-one seemed fully alert, each grabbed a bag and made for the door, lugging the heavy weights with them. The Chinese were the first to react, Sing leaping to block their exit and shouting, "Money!" His henchmen, slower to rally from their stupor, began to turn but then the diminutive Confucious figure called to them.

"Do I not say", he began, through his aura of light, but Sing turned on him, angrily.

"You say nothing, impostor! You say who you mock! You mock our tradition!" And with that he jumped from the doorway to lunge at Asif Hassan, whipping a knife from under his jacket.

The Asif-prophet turned to Mohammed and Abdul.

"Go now, go now." The voice remained calm and deep but now with a suggestion of urgency. They saw their opportunity. The Chinese were confronting Asif, the Spaniards had for the moment halted in their tracks, amazed at what they were seeing which, to them, was a glowing figure of light looking much like the kebab shop owner, and the doorway was clear. The two Asian youths slipped past the little crowd but were dismayed as they looked around to see all four Chinese about to attack Asif with fists and knives.

They hesitated, compelled to assist him but they were overcome by what they saw next. The figure, Asif, separated silently into two, a small, wizened Chinese man with a goatee beard appearing to one side and moving slightly away. The Chinese party all lunged at this figure, ignoring Asif, standing tall above them. Asif-the-prophet, still glowing in light, turned to Mohammed and Abdul and they could see a slight smile.

"Go", he commanded.

They turned and hurtled downstairs, into the street, and ran for their lives.

As the Chinese quartet were about to lay into the Confucious figure with demented fury, the Spaniards, gaping in amazement, saw no-one was paying them any attention, nudged each other and hurried quietly down the stairs with the bags. All they heard behind them were cries of fear and alarm. The Chinese were delivering a hail of blows with fists and knives, then recoiling in shock. The little goatee-bearded man was not collapsing under their barrage but proceeded to shake and vibrate where he stood, before slowly dissolving into the air. The Chinese pulled back in horror, gawping and stuttering at the empty space in front of them. Then they realised there was still a culprit in the room. Asif stood staring at them. The light had faded but he was still imbued with a strange glow. They glared at him and began to advance, arms raised. But they were halted by a loud rapping at the shop door beneath and a shaking of the handle.

"Open up! Customs and Excise! Open up!" came a voice from outside the shop. The four Chinese looked in panic at each other, pitched around and hurtled down the stairs, out through the side door, and disappeared up the street only moments before one of Gordon's men turned the corner of the shop to check for other exits. He saw the open door and called over his shoulder.

"Gordon! Here! Door!"

Pierce and the rest of the team hurried around, followed a few yards back by Paul, Elroy and the others.

"Who's there?" Pierce shouted up the stairs. There was no response.

"Come on", he instructed his men. "Careful." He had decided against involving armed police and was fearful now of the possible consequences. They crept slowly up the stairs, pausing each time one creaked. When they reached the room they were met by a bearded, benign Asian gentleman, who just smiled at them at first and then greeted them.

"Good evening, gentlemen, is there anything I can do?"

It did not take the Customs team long to establish the building contained no dolls, bags or Chinamen even though the Asian gentleman could not have been more helpful, indicating all the nooks and crannies they might otherwise have omitted to inspect. Gordon noted that the gentleman - Asif - and Paul greeted each other and exchanged a few words. "Good kebabs", explained Paul.

As they left, Gordon could only shrug in frustration. He still had no proof there even was another set of dolls. Just bits and bobs of hearsay, and 'spares'. He thanked Mr Asif Hassan for his assistance. He only really worked out afterwards what was odd about the man. The strange glow about him, which faded even while they were there.

Madrid

Olivia drove Elroy early back to Cheltenham on Friday morning. They wanted to call in at the hotel on the way, check into their rooms and appear for breakfast. Eyebrows would be discreetly raised at the reception desk but their visible arrival at the breakfast table should quell gossip among waiters and any fellow guests who might be taking more than a passing interest in their movements. The news on the car radio shook them out of their preoccupation with the previous evening.

'Numbers of cars and other vehicles which have been immobilised by the mystery 'bug' over the past few days are now reported to be functioning normally. Drivers and service garages are advised to check whether their vehicles may now be clear of the undiagnosed fault'.

Elroy did a quick mental count and gave a wry smile.

"Six days. 'Repaired theirselves'."

"What?" Olivia had been attentive to the road ahead.

"Six days", repeated Elroy. "You remember: the trial 'seize-up'? Six days. I don't really know what I did in that computer room after the main formula. Hitting the wrong keys, I don't know. Or something - someone -" he rolled his eyes uncomprehendingly - "fixed it so I hit the six-day trial for London. Yesterday was the sixth day. I don't know." He shook his head at the approaching Gloucestershire countryside.

Olivia glanced at her companion, absorbed in his mysteries. He caught her eye.

"Clever, eh?" he smiled.

Inside GCHQ, Martin Timmis was on to them almost the moment they had arrived. The message triangle between China, London and Spain had changed its code. Timmis was stuck. Elroy examined the array of characters on the print-off and grunted.

"Different character sets, same alphabet, that's all. Find what they're now using for 'DOLL' and we've got it."

They pored over the code for an hour or more, Timmis mainly watching at Elroy's elbow as he tapped different trial combinations into the computer. Then Elroy leaned back.

"My Good Lord", he muttered.

"What is it?" asked Timmis, eagerly. Elroy continued quietly for a while, his brows furrowing deeper, with some intermittent gasps of concern.

"Oh Lord", he said at last, Timmis and Olivia both hanging on his words.

"I think this is what we were mixed up in last night." He looked at Olivia, images of Chinese dancers and a chase through London streets, subconsciously shared between them.

"These dolls", he measured out his words, "they seem to get from China to London. Livvy, they must be the same ones we saw, otherwise, some coincidence!" She nodded. Martin Timmis looked perplexed.

"And Spain", he continued, "it's probably a subversive group -"

"Madrid?" asked Timmis.

"No, not where they're based, necessarily", Elroy frowned at the pages of code, "but they keep referring to it. Spanish rebels?" He looked queryingly at the British Intelligence man.

"Could be!" exclaimed Timmis, "Spanish Islamists! They did Madrid before - the train bombs!"

They all recalled the bombs planted on peak-hour trains in Madrid in 2004 and the death toll among innocent commuters. The masterminds behind the outrage were never identified but eventually, three years later, over twenty people were convicted, mainly muslims from Morocco - and from Spain. The hand of Al Qaeda was suspected in the background but, as always, unproven.

"So they could be at it again", breathed Elroy, heavily. "And this would be something else. A word, or a series of characters, but I think I can pick the word, keeps cropping up."

"Which one?" Olivia bent forward to peer at the unintelligible scramble of letters and numerals.

"Uranium." Elroy was slowly clenching and unclenching a fist as he uttered the word. "I think that's what I saw in the doll and the Customs man said the same."

"The one that broke?" asked Olivia.

"Yes", replied Elroy, thoughtfully, "the girl was terrified. No wonder, if she knew what it was."

"But - but -" Olivia looked puzzled, " we followed the Chinese to that kebab house -"

"We *think* we followed them, "Elroy reminded her, "but we never saw them, did we? No Chinese. No dolls. No Islamic extremists. No Spaniards, come to that. Just an empty house except for that weird kebab man."

"Yes, but suppose", Timmis had been engrossed in their conversation, with no heed as to whether they had been in London overnight, not Gloucestershire as expected, and had been gradually catching up with them, "suppose it all happened before you got there. The dolls were handed over to whoever wanted them -"

"Spanish?" Suggested Olivia.

Elroy shrugged to acknowledge the possibility.

" -and they'd all gone before you arrived", Timmis finished.

"Where do Islamists come into it?" asked Olivia.

"We don't know if they do", observed Elroy, "the connection is London. Could be anyone."

"Qaeda or one of those groups might be funding them", mused Timmis. "You're saying it could be uranium. My God -" as the full realisation struck him " - I can't think of any other group with the money ... or the brutality", he added.

"I don't get the Spain connection." Elroy shook his head.

"We have had some stuff going through lately", Timmis pondered aloud, "from what we call the 'nutters'. Easy code. Don't know why they bother . Talking about reclaiming Spain for Islam."

"Islam?" Elroy expressed surprise.

"Yes, sir. Spain was a Muslim state until about five hundred years ago. There are a handful of Islamic radicals who still want it back. 'The Islamic Iberian Peninsular'", he quoted the mantra. "Destabilising the government is always the first target of revolutionaries, whatever you think of their brutality. Remember, in 2004, it effectively changed the political landscape: the Spanish governing party were ahead in the polls till the bombs, then lost the election."

They all reflected in silence for some moments. Elroy spoke first.

"So. Madrid. And now something bigger."

"Fits their agenda, sir. Those particular Islamists would have an interest in destabilisation."

"But", complained Olivia, "it just turns the people against them. It doesn't promote their cause."

"Yes, madam", said the ever-courteous young Timmis, "they're clever, they're callous, but they're not very bright when it comes to politics and psychology. That's probably why they never achieve their ultimate goals. They just cause death and mayhem, time after time."

"Only this time", Elroy spoke grimly, "they've got the ingredients."

"Ingredients, sir?"

"Uranium", explained Elroy. "For the bomb."

PARADIGM : SIGNS

He strode from the edge of the forest across the dry, dusty clearing, to their rock, in the day's late sun. Her smile seemed grave as she rose to greet him, yet she brushed his cheek with hers, in love, as always, and caressed his lips with hers, the same.

"I have found a fish", she said.

"Ah!" His voice was light with relief and pleasure. "That is good, for I have not brought as much for us as I should." He felt a tug of shame that he had not, this first time, caught enough for their needs. "It has been a difficult day." He felt at his side, where the one small rabbit swung. He spoke low at his want of reward for the day. "There have been but few to hunt. I know not why. But with your fish -!" His voice brightened.

"No." She lay a finger on his cheek and took his hand. "It is not one to eat."

She led him to where the fish lay; where she had lain it, on the rock's edge by the sea. A good fish, the length of her arm. It would provide more than a few full meals for them both and to make her milk for the child.

"But you have been so clever to catch it!" There was pride in his words, and delight, even though it was not the fruit of his own endeavour.

"No", she said. And then he saw its bloated side, the lumps, a few, that were like boils under its scales, and their bad colour of black and dark green; and its open gill, sore red and swollen and a deep yellow puss that had seeped from it. She stooped to turn it over and he saw that one boil had burst and torn a gash in its side, with black parts amongst the exposed flesh. And the other gill the same as the first.

"It had almost died", she said. "I took it from the sea so that it might not pass its disease to others." Though she knew, and so did he, that it might have taken the disease from others, also.

He placed a hand upon her shoulder to console her for the fish, and for the lack of food.

"Why is the sky so?" she asked. "Is it because of the fish?" They look up at the sky together. It seemed in sorrow, or in some anger. Heavy curls of black and grey and sombre red against the deeper blue, and rims of darkest gold tinged the fading sun.

"It is but a storm", he said, "and the sea may make both life and death and still provide for us. The fish was old and met its time to die, as all things do. The sky knows this, as do we."

He put his arm around her to walk away, and to their child, but the sea held an anger, too, and cut at their rock and with a stain at its edge, in a manner they had not seen before.

Stuck

They were saddened they were parting in ill humour. It was as though the shared experience and intrigue which had bound them so closely had become fractured: thin scar lines on the smooth glaze of their camaraderie. Bella had been the most vociferous and perhaps the other three privately blamed her for starting the fission.

"It makes me puke!" she exclaimed, as they watched the television news that Sunday lunchtime. "I never thought the English would disgust me!"

The 'remarkable' and undiagnosed recovery, not just of motor vehicles but, as it turned out, domestic appliances, too, had so far had no effect on public disorder. It seemed the preoccupation with immobile cars and defunct washing machines and the like had diverted attention from the deeper malaise which had already been brewing: the general decline in economic activity. Several large companies had taken advantage of the buoyant public response to the return of technological normality - and the expectation nationally that the 'bug' would not now spread beyond London - to announce impending cutbacks in production, with the warning of expected redundancies.

The weekend press and media had been dominated by growing public disaffection. Generally, the United States was blamed. Its 'bug' had been a blip, a distraction from the real issue of what was proclaimed by their President as a deliberately deflated economy, dragging the rest of the Western economies with it. Scant credit, if any, was accorded their declared aim of 'saving the world'. 'Arrogant Yanks', was the majority verdict. Not only had the London populace not responded to technological chaos with the goodwill of their American cousins but, now it was over, resentment at declining economic circumstances was released once more. Now, too, following London's example, there was a lawless consensus among a significant minority across the nation of how to express such discontent. Already on Saturday, and especially Saturday night, there had been sporadic instances of looting in a number of provincial cities across the UK. Now that the 'credit economy' of the past few decades was running dry, the ingrained habit of acquiring and possessing would not be denied: the answer was to take, steal, loot. Possession had become an inalienable right.

"They're pigs!" snorted Bella again and there were hot tears of distress in her eyes. She had directed that remark at Paul, the only English person amongst them, as if to apportion him all the blame. The softer surface of their relationship, which had been drawing them imperceptibly closer, was once again punctured with barbs of hostility.

"Oh come on, love", protested her husband, "it's not everyone."

"Soon will be, by the looks of it", retorted Bella before turning on her friend, Olivia. "And the Yanks are the same." She berated the air in their lounge. "Look what they're doing!"

British and American news channels had all been reporting acts of violence, said to be by vigilante gangs with religious associations against people identified as challenging the 'sharing' culture. Such attacks were being justified 'in the name of the Lord'.

"Only a few, only a few Americans", countered Olivia, mildly, "we couldn't expect that *everyone* would behave right."

"But it's disgusting", cried Bella, shaking her head, her brown curls dancing around her ears, "they say they're doing it for the 'Lord'! What kind of religion is that!" She shot a glance at Elroy. "It's the Klan all over again!"

"Hey, Bella. No, no", protested Elroy. But he was uneasy. At that moment television news pictures focused on the battered face of a man in Seattle, claiming to be the victim of a 'Lord's Justice' group. He admitted he had kept himself to himself and had always been nervous about mingling freely with the rest of humanity. He did not share but nor did he borrow; neither did he have much cause to communicate with his fellow citizens. The doctor said he would be in hospital for a week or so for brain scans. There were other reports, too, including one of a narrow escape by a salesman in Louisiana when his assailants were trapped in a local dust tornado. Details of this were vague and somewhat colourful but the gang escaped unharmed, which was more than could be said for the bruised but lucky salesman.

"And the Chinese!" declared Bella, fiercely.

It was true. There was limited coverage of disturbances in parts of China, mainly the cities, where they, too, had been experiencing the effects of diminished trading options with the United States, hitherto the 'engine of the world's economy'. So far, it was just the inevitable reduction in sales across a whole range of products but now there were hints of possible import quotas, even complete prohibition, and retaliatory restrictions imposed by the Beijing government.

"Well, maybe just give it time", observed Walt, moderately, "Twigg's plan, eh? Lead by example, show the rest of the world a new way that isn't just make, trade, buy, pollute, grab, grab, grab. Maybe they need time to see it."

"Maybe they won't see it all", remarked Paul, drily, privately resentful that this bizarre episode had offered nothing but disruption to business - not least his own - with no compensatory merit as far as he could determine. The four Americans brooded. It was not that they had fallen out but each, individually, was harbouring some guilt that this marvellous, wonderful, Utopian adventure was beginning to curl at the edges. Or perhaps it was not. Perhaps these were just temporary disturbances along the way, inevitable stumbles by a world blindly groping to comprehend.

They would have wished to hug and laugh and congratulate each other as Bella and Paul and Elroy accompanied Walt and Olivia through to the Heathrow check-in that evening. Elroy had been quite glad to accept the invitation to stay on at GCHQ to try analyse the sudden ending of the London 'bug'; it kept him safe in the UK, although he would miss Mariana and the children even more. They did all hug. And they smiled. But there was a troubled, uncertain look in the eyes of the four Americans as they parted.

Earlier, while it was still dark in London and they were wrapped in sleep, Hoi Fong, in the light of a new day in his Beijing office, took a phone call. It was from Mr Teng.

"Brother." Hoi winced at the unbrotherly tones in his ear. "I trust you are preparing the next delivery to London."

"Brother?" Hoi Fong did not have the next delivery prepared, no. He was certainly anxious to continue with the deal, preferably on improved terms, but he was aware the previous order had only just been delivered and to press so soon would be to invite expectation of further discounts. He did not want to promote the perception of a 'buyer's market'.

"The next delivery. As soon as you may", urged Teng in his obsequious purr.

"Brother Teng", replied Hoi, as evenly as he could contrive, "I doubt whether the dealer is quite ready to re-order and I would not wish him to think-"

"Brother Hoi Fong", broke in Teng, the emphasis on the formality of using both forenames, "I repeat, as soon as you may. If necessary, a discount-" The thin voice allowed silence to convey the message.

"Discount?" repeated Hoi, bleakly. There was no response, except for a polite, "Good-day, Brother Hoi" and the click of the phone as he hung up. He wondered what the Society expected from an arrangement in which their own return was compromised by the very pressure they exerted to accomplish it. Business does not function the same as extortion, he reflected sardonically.

A few hours later, he was still fretting when he took another phone call. It was Hwee Lo.

"My darling." Her voice was tempered with anxiety and frustration. "Can you collect me?"

Her car had halted in the middle of city traffic, while on a shopping trip with Soo Wong in the child seat. They were stranded. Taxis were all booked - and some appeared broken down anyway. Some other drivers were experiencing difficulty, too, heads bent over engines, searching for the fault. Some breakdown trucks had arrived but all to order and none to spare. He was her only help.

He sighed.

"Of course, my love."

The traffic was a nightmare, she said, and she was so sorry and if it was only for herself she could perhaps make her way home eventually but Soo Wong -

"Of course, my love." He did manage a rueful smile, for he loved them both.

Elroy, Walt and Olivia were still somewhere high over the Atlantic Ocean and did not hear about Beijing until later.

Girl

"Or maybe if I was a girl, then ..."

God, being God, had no difficulty concentrating on several things at once. It was a piece of cake, in fact, to monitor the births of a couple of new stars, do a running check on the different evolutionary phases of a dozen planets and their multitudes of species - or not, as the case might be - note how much substance, alive or inert, was being swallowed up by any active black hole, and even keep a weary eye on the fractious Humans. All at the same time. Until, that is, Gabriel started on one of his discourses then, all of a sudden, the kaleidoscope of sharply focused incident upon which the Lord was effortlessly dividing his attention dissolved into an indistinguishable blur, supplanted by the cerebral perambulations of one solitary angel. Worlds tremble, ye whose fate hangs in the balance while Gabriel cogitates before the Lord.

"Girl?"

"Yes, you know -"

"Yes, I do know what a girl is." Only God could have said this free of sarcasm and even He had to try quite hard.

"Yes, well", Gabriel conceded, not really intending to suggest the Good Lord was not *au fait* with all of His species, "I mean, they *like* girls."

"They?"

When called upon, in circumstances which required it, God could, if driven to necessity, identify all the myriad creatures in His mighty cosmos. However, He was inclined to regard it as rather a waste of time, despite that commodity being in limitless supply. The notion of watching over each and every one of them, on a second by second basis, was endearing, undoubtedly, but fanciful to say the least. Even the Ultimate Deity had better things to do than be a kind of supernatural CCTV system. All those ants, flies, elephants, little squiggly amoeba, well, they were all His creatures, sure, but they were all preordained at the dawn of creation and after that it was up to them to get on with it. And that was just Earth. What about all those minute,

pulsating Zigliotnns, which crawled tirelessly over the Bllutquip-
pzzts (sorry), keeping them clean (well, more or less clean, in the
grand scheme of things)? The idea that he was ever-present
among them all the time (there's that word again), too. Well,
Dear Lord! Enough said.

So, when Gabriel came up with an 'it' or a 'that' or a 'they',
the Lord had to concentrate a bit to work out which of the 'its',
'thats' or 'theys' His loyal but incorrigible angel might be allud-
ing to.

"They. Them." Gabriel was muttering, chin on knees, having
a good old poke around, too absorbed in the task to exhibit,
unwisely as it would have been, the impatience of one who might
be repeating himself in order to state the blindingly obvious.
"Down there."

"Ah. Um. Yes." The Lord's contemplative musings were
brought back to Earth, as it were.

"Yeh, well, I mean", muttered the foraging angel, "if I was a
girl -"

"Gabriel." A warning shot.

" - If I was a girl, they'd -"

"Gabriel." Cannonball water plume just across the angelic bow.

Gabriel looked up at his Supreme Commander and adopted a
slightly more conciliatory tone, as of the child who argues that
ice cream must be good for you, even before dinner, because it
tastes so nice. He was aggrieved. Being attacked was surely not
part of the plan, even though, when it came to prophets, preachers, messengers and saints, being attacked in the name of
religion was pretty much par for the course on Earth. All the
same, it was not something an *angel* expected.

"The point is, they're not *suspicious* of girls. Girls can, well,
You know, get away with more. Well", he added, realising this
was not necessarily, in terrestrial terms, a universal truth, "in
some parts anyway."

"You are not a girl."

"No, but -"

"You are an angel." God wondered sometimes if that guileless
phrase might be subjected to closer analysis if people were
aware of quite where the comparison came from. Gabriel
glanced up at the all-too-familiar darkening of deific clouds.

"Well", he mumbled truculently, "tell *them* the difference."

"I beg your pardon?"

0"All that stupid long hair and robes and pretty smile. You know - girlish."

"Gabriel." It was one of those long sighs of resignation which swept through the black emptiness around them in a manner which would end worlds by new trajectories and even create new life by the kindling of new stars.

"All those pictures", the pained archangel was complaining into his shins, "they make me *look* like a girl, don't they?" He paused, hunched with his arms around his legs, staring ahead now. "So why not?"

"I don't think ..." But the Lord gave up at this one. Sometimes there was just no answer.

Gabriella

President Twigg sat in the back of her chauffeur-driven limousine with the rising tide of complaint and criticism on media airwaves buzzing in her ears. Fortunately perhaps, she had not been privy to some of the unbroadcast - and unbroadcastable - tirades resounding in selected boardrooms and executive offices across the land. One such might have been heard - and indeed probably was - from outside a typical hallowed enclave on the twenty-third floor of a high-rise office block adjoining a car manufacturing plant in Detroit.

"Fucking crazy, fucking brawd!"

There was no longer any care to connect with a buffer of papers nor restraint in the physical gesture accompanying the outburst and the big hand smarted and stung from its dramatic collision with the polished tabletop. Each of the anxious, muted subordinates twitched involuntarily in their seats as if the pain were their own.

"Didn't I say?" thundered Max Drummond at the array of half-averted timorous eyes. "Now not only is no-one buying a goddamned thing here, the goddamned fucking Chinks aren't buying from us either! Jeeesuz Chri-i-ist!"

He slammed into his chair at the head of the table, discreetly resting his smarting palm on the soothing cloth of a trouser leg out of sight.

"Well, Max", began the sagacious Abe, "we did slap on our own import controls first."

"Hmmph", Drummond grunted, unable to deny that observation. It had all happened in the space of two or three days. The United States had no choice but to impose import controls, the President had explained, because the American economy, in controlled deceleration (she was careful not to say 'recession') needed to focus on self-sufficiency for the protection of home manufacturing and produce. She had made no mention of exports but it was clear to all the pundits, as it must have been to her, what would happen next. It was part of the 'plan', she reassured her advisors and supporters. It was the logical consequence of winding down an economy to a lower gear, where all Americans would share the new spirit of community in which they were already participating, and into which other nations would be involuntarily drawn, deprived of the global driving force of America's trade.

It was, she declared, her 'vision' and her 'legacy'. Nevertheless, she conceded the inevitability of short-term retaliation. Within twenty-four hours China had banned all imports from the United States. It was, agreed most commentators, a case of 'cutting the nose to spite the face' and China's economy would only the more rapidly fall into slower step with the States as a result. And that was without this other thing.

"Anyway", Drummond brightened, while slouched in his chair, inasmuch as his big, square frame could ever slouch, "serves them fucking right!"

The mice, and Abe, looked at each other.

"Serves who, sir", asked the ever-more-emboldened Tom.

"The Chinks, you fucking idiot!" snapped Drummond, as young Tom slithered down a few crucial rungs on the ladder of confidence.

"Max?" The sage Abe had long since learned the accepted mode of response, seeking enlightenment without challenging the great man's sanity.

"The 'bug', man, the 'bug'!" Max Drummond broke into a salvo of uncharacteristic guffaws, customarily familiar only to top dog golfing partners over a lewd joke at the bar.

Of course, ah, the 'bug'. The others nodded to each other and considered it prudent to smile.

"That'll teach 'em, eh?" Drummond grinned fulsomely at the gallery of artificial smirks humouring him.

Victoria Twigg was astonished at that turn of events in Beijing. Only the capital and nowhere else in China as far as could be discerned. It was almost like a domino effect, following so soon after the London phenomenon, itself a replication of the original Virginia 'six-day standstill'. She was much more disturbed - and not at all amused - than the likes of Max Drummond.

Public reaction in Beijing was similar to London, without the rampant public disorder and looting. Chinese citizens had experience of their government's uncompromising response to popular revolt. However, the rising level of public discontent was clear from reports of crowds gathering in public squares. It was equally apparent that international misgivings about Beijing authorities' potential reaction were not fulfilled. The government 'advised' its citizens not to gather in groups of protest but also issued edicts condemning the West for allowing a 'technological virus' to infect the capital city of the People's Republic. It was only a step away from accusing America, with lapdog Britain in support, of deliberately sabotaging Chinese technology. It also allowed the Beijing population to gather in a number of public protests in defiance of government orders, while that same government, with the world's media in attendance, increasingly turned a blind eye.

International goodwill and kudos, so recently garnered, was not going to be lightly squandered. While the citizens of Beijing, with the reliability of prized and desired cars and modern equipment faltering all around them, were of no mind to pause and take stock of a burgeoning economy they were only just beginning to enjoy. They did not dare loot but they railed and complained, ever the more vociferously as each day went by. And no-one shared. No-one shared a blind thing between them. They were too angry.

Twigg gazed at the back of her driver's head. There was something unsettling about the Beijing development. Quite what this mystifying 'bug' was, still no-one knew, but it was already exacerbating China's negative response to economic restraint.

She had been offered a message, a 'vision', which foresaw the possibility of a new world order led, paradoxically, by America, the great polluter and insatiable invader, throwing itself into reverse and offering the prospect that other nations might eventually follow suit. There was no suggestion the process should be accelerated with shock tactics elsewhere in the world, antagonising whole populations in consequence.

The head was unfamiliar. It was not her regular driver. Twigg was looking at a short bob of shiny, almost black hair, African curls which had been teased, straightened and conditioned into luxuriant locks falling to just above the uniform's collar. She could not recall having a female chauffeur before. It rather pleased her. If the President could be a woman, why should the trade of professional drivers be an exclusively male preserve? Women were better drivers, anyway, it was a documented fact: more careful, more reliable. Twigg leaned forward.

"Is my regular driver not available?" She did not wish to sound churlish and, really, she delighted in the change, but she felt she should have been informed.

"No, maam; sorry, maam", came the polite reply, without a turn of the head away from the road. It was a rich Afro-American contralto voice, matching, Twigg considered, the hair. "He felt not quite well."

In truth, he had felt most peculiar, for no definable reason. Not sick, nor faint, nor with a sweat or headache; but indescribably *peculiar* and he had to admit to his new female colleague that it might be best if he did not attempt to drive the President today. Fortunately, his new colleague, whom he had not previously encountered, was right there in the chauffeurs' lodge just completing her induction. It was an additionally happy coincidence because he had only begun to feel 'not quite right' when she had stepped through the door and there was no-one else on shift to relieve him.

She had looked at him with those deep, brown eyes, most concerned that he might not be well enough to discharge such a vital responsibility of state. There was a wisdom in those eyes - call it feminine intuition - and her gaze seemed to profoundly understand as his knees buckled and he slumped to a chair. "Gawd, yes", he acknowledged in gratitude, "I might have a crash with the President. You've saved my skin. I owe you." She had smiled and said no trouble, you're welcome. He could not remember much after that. Perhaps he had fallen asleep for a while.

"Well, I guess I can thank you for being around", smiled Victoria Twigg, there's always a back-up but it's the first time I've had the pleasure of being driven by a woman."

"Yes, maam, it's an honour."

Twigg smiled again and saw two deep, brown eyes twinkling back at her in the driver's mirror.

"What's your name?" she enquired.

"Gabriella, maam."

"Ah, nice name", commended the President.

-302"Thank you, maam."

Twigg looked out of the car window and was surprised to see unfamiliar surroundings. The route taken would not be questioned by her security team in the car behind because she had given specific orders against interference so she could be driven around the city undisturbed, ruminating over this most improbable period of her Presidency. An economy faltering below the safe level for equilibrium amid swelling murmurs of rebellion. Her mighty stature of charisma and sexuality might not be sufficient for much longer. What should she do next? She was alone with her dilemma.

They seemed to have arrived at the city outskirts. Gleaming streets and towering skyscrapers had been supplanted by untidy three-storey tenements, amongst older clapboard houses and gaudily-painted shanty homes of cheap panels and corrugated tin. There was no reason to take her on a social education tour, she fretted.

"Where are we, Gabriella?" She adopted her lofty I-Am-Your-President tone.

"We are here, maam." The driver was drawing to a halt and a moment later stepped out to hold the door open for her President.

Twigg looked up at the chauffeur without getting out.

"I did not ask to stop here", she stated, coolly, despite her liking for this Gabriella.

"No, maam." The chauffeur eyed her, unabashed. There was something about those eyes. They drew her. Twigg found herself alighting from the car, as if the eyes were magnets pulling her. Those deep, deep eyes. Somewhere ...somewhere ... had she seen them before? How could she? She wondered if she was losing control of her reason, half-mesmerised by those eyes, set in the dark brown face, with the pretty, stubby African nose and the big lips with their slight, solemn smile.

"Gabriella." Twigg tried to reproach the chauffeur, a mild reprimand for acting beyond her remit, but the words would not follow across her tongue. She knew she was staring at those deep, brown eyes but could not pull away. Then, as she looked, she was aware of a charge thrilling through her, something she only associated with the hot allure of a man. But this was not sexual. It was warm and devouring but embraced her soul, not her loins. The chauffeur spoke from within the spell.

"Maam. We are here. It is where you must be."

"Must?" Victoria echoed distantly, She turned and saw they had halted outside a small church. White-painted walls gleamed in the afternoon sun. The last few worshippers - all black - were making their way up the slab steps to the arched wooden doorway. Singing could be heard from inside. She turned her head back and Gabriella the chauffeur was still smiling at her.

"Yes, maam, 'must'. It is where you wish to be." The voice was firm but in friendship. The lips and eyes were smiling together.

Victoria Twigg understood. In her isolation in this moment of crisis, she was not alone. She smiled in return. Those eyes, those eyes. She turned again and walked to the steps of the church.

Doubts

"I mean", grumbled the grumbling one,"leaning back with an irritable flick of the finger and shake of the hand, "do we really have to?"

"Have to?" murmured the Lord, not yet having found a way of nipping such dialogues in the bud, in all the Eternity they had occupied prior to the bit they occupied now and did not hold out much hope of things changing for the rest of it.

"Have to keep saving them and rescuing them."

"Under normal circumstances", the Lord acknowledged, guardedly, "we would not intervene, but ..."

"But?"

" ...but if there is a threat to the Plan..."

"I mean", declared Elroy, the two of them perched on stools over their bourbons in a New York bar, "suppose there *is* uranium in rogue hands."

"But we never saw it", insisted Walt.

"No, well, y'know, I think I *did*, that's the point. That doll, that silvery metal. And the weight. And that service guy - Customs - he sure heated up when I told him what I thought. And he was in a helluva state when the Chinese got away in their van."

"Well..." Walt shook his head, doubtfully.

"Point is", Elroy was marshalling his thoughts as he spoke, "if terrorists make a bomb -"

"Phew." Walt shook his head again, this time in consternation.

"Well, not only would it be a catastrophe, it would change all this." He jerked his head to generally indicate the world around them, "No more America drawing in its horns, leading the way in world harmony." He gave a short, sardonic grin. "We'd be tooling up, marching back in everywhere, big boots and big guns, kicking any ass that even so much as winked. And all this 'new order' would be forgotten as fast as you can say Uncle Sam is Number One. And Hell is you forgetting it."

Gabriel pondered, morosely.

"Cretins", he muttered.

"I know, I know!" Gordon Pierce was scratching his head and flinging his arm out in a despairing gesticulation, while the other hand clutched the phone.

"Well, if you haven't seen it and didn't find it, all you've got for evidence is those weights."

Derek was attempting to persuade Gordon of the illogic of his continued pursuit of vanishing or nonexistent uranium.

"But that doll", Gordon reminded him.

"Yeh?"

"The one the American guy saw, broke. He thought it was uranium."

"Thought?" queried Derek, sceptically.

"Well, he's a kinda expert", Gordon responded, defensively. "And the weights match up, Derek, the *weights*."

"So where's it gone?" challenged Derek in his Folkestone office, hovering between images of wild geese and haystacks.

Martin Timmis, working late, identified two more messages in the triangle. The first, from the Spain apex, indicated that something - dolls? - had been received. The second seemed to contradict the first and could have been an urgent demand for something else. However, the code structure had been changed again and Timmis could not be certain he had deciphered it correctly. Nor could he identify the expected item. He emailed both messages to Elroy.

"But it's not sorted, is it?" grunted Gabriel.

"No, it is not." The Lord could scarcely disagree. The facts spoke for themselves. A threat muffled but not extinguished.

"So..." Gabriel paused, reflectively.

"So..." began the Lord.

"So", Walt speculated, "even if there *is* uranium in the wrong hands, if we *did* see it and it was in all the dolls, and they got away with them, is that all they need?"

"Well", replied Elroy, "most of the stuff is not difficult to get hold of: shell casing, igniter, foam padding, that kind of thing, but they can't detonate it without plutonium. Not the do-it-yourself kind of bomb."

"So, d'ya reckon they'd have that already?" asked Walt.

Elroy shook his head.

"Who knows? But, hell, Walt, they'd be crazy. This is not semtex. You don't play around with this stuff."

"So..." continued the Lord, "we have to protect what we have-"

" -started, we must finish." Gabriel completed the phrase with a shrug.

"Precisely."

"Avarice", brooded Gabriel, mulling it over, "pollution, consumption, climate..."

"No more than a beginning", the Lord reminded him.

"Is it worth it?" asked Gabriel, with a concern this was not all a wasted denial of more pleasurable excursions.

"So far, yes", murmured the Lord, aware of the flaws.

"And now ...?" said Gabriel, looking up.

"Disease, famine ...", the Lord recited from the list with which they had begun.

Gabriel suddenly found he could not suppress a grin. Tiresome though these duties could sometimes be, he harboured a secret pride in his accomplishments. He fancied himself awarded all the accolades at an Oscars night for angels at which, being the only one, he would confidently sweep the board. Recognition, that was all, just some recognition.

Senate

Senate was an expectant babble of voices. The President was, it was deemed, exercising her female prerogative and was, as usual, late. Will Jerome, fielding press speculation in the manner of a demonic catcher, was driven to even greater distraction than usual as to the whereabouts of the Chief.

"She called from the car just now", Renee Fleck assured him on his cellphone, "been to a church."

"What!" Jerome exploded. The number of times he'd had to cover for delayed appearances due to extended attention accorded a variety of handsome young 'diplomats'! But church! What's she doing in a church, for God's sake!

"Come now, J", cooed Renee in ironic reproach, "you know she's gone all spiritual lately. That's this whole thing now, isn't it?" Sure, Jerome reflected, grudgingly. He had lost track of which came first, the nation's reborn faith or the Leader's enlightened direction to adopt a new vision, but he could not deny the altruistic fervour which was still rippling through America, like an irresistibly advancing wave, albeit its advance already breaking over sporadic but multiplying rocks of dissent.

Returning in the car, driven by the enigmatic Gabriella, Victoria Twigg sat back, her mind a blur. It was true, so true, why had she not seen it for herself? This was the next, inevitable step. It had taken a black gospel preacher to show her. And some preacher. Those eyes. Those penetrating brown eyes. She had been invited to the front, respectful looks upon her, as though she had been expected there. A few hands reached to touch her arm or briefly clasp her hand. A vacant seat awaited her and the preacher smiled a welcome; wide warm lips beneath the deep brown eyes.

The eyes seemed never to leave the President during the sermon; but you could not call it a sermon, it was a cry, a clarion call for the dispossessed, the shunned, the lost brethren. Twigg felt it surge through her and ... and ...there was that thrill of energy pulsing in her core which she could liken to no other experience except ... except ... that singular, phenomenal encounter in the Oval office, with that extraordinary young man whose name for some reason she just could not recall. When she left the church, the singing and exhortation bearing her down the aisle, she was floating on air.

"Thank you, Gabriella." Victoria spoke dreamily and touched the chauffeur lightly on her shoulder to communicate her gratitude. "That was a wonderful service, a divine preacher."

"Yes, it was, maam; thank you."

Victoria Twigg trembled an instant and saw the chauffeur's eyes reflected in the mirror. Those deep, brown eyes appeared to shine with pleasure at the compliment. It was as though the girl had been in the church, too, while waiting in the car outside. Ridiculous notion. Perhaps it was her church, her preacher and she had been instrumental in organising the President's visit. How she had achieved that without being the scheduled driver, Twigg could not imagine, but she had inexcusably abused her position and Victoria could never thank her enough. The car swept beneath the Capitol ballustrades, Twigg exchanging a last look with those eyes as she alighted and stepped away.

The babble was stilled as the President entered. There had been plenty of time for the virus of disgruntlement and malice to pass from senator to senator, an infection to which even her own supporters were proving less than immune. The more the talk, the darker the crisis. Declining economy, slumping sales, threats of mass redundancies, trade war with China and now that huge global rival joining with India and most of the rest of Asia to initiate trading cartels between themselves, to the exclusion of renegade United States.

Fuelled by resentment and rebellion amongst populations not willing to be denied participation in a lifestyle they had hitherto only envied from afar, they mocked and derided America's vain attempt to promulgate a halt to progress. If the arrogant Americans wished to wither upon their own stem, that was their business; now it was the turn of another part of the world to reap the rewards of economic opportunity. And they were strong enough to do it without the West. The consequences for the United States, rumbled the senators, were dire. Instead of leading the world they were being barred from it. They were going to slide backwards into a primitive market economy!

The President spoke.

"Senators, representatives of the people of the United States. We have reached the point of a new direction. It is time to turn."

Some groaned. Others brightened. Was this an admission of folly, a time to reverse? The President continued.

"Members of this House. Together we have an awesome duty to discharge." And she looked awesome herself, as the assembly was reminded once more of the aura of this acknowledged leader of the western world, standing in bronzed grandeur before them. Male hearts fluttered in desire, female in grudging envy. "We have to maintain our great nation on a steady course, even in the new waters we have only recently charted, and still ensure that ours is the land where opportunity remains open to all. There is concern that our new-found celebration of community may be to our disadvantage; that our adoption of a new responsibility to the future of this planet - the only one we have - may result in our own destitution!"

She rang the word 'destitution' around the chamber and some felt it was being used as an accusation of their own exaggerations.

"But I have been shown that we can achieve both ends." Twigg appeared to draw herself even higher than her natural six-feet-one-and-a-quarter inches and exuded even greater pride. "We may repay one of our most burning debts and, in doing so, contribute both to the world beyond our shores and to our own future. We shall no longer be the great polluter - we are learning new ways even now - nor the unrepentant thief."

Thief? What was she talking about? Was this another Victoria Twigg tightrope act, precariously balanced between vision and insanity?

"It is time to make amends, to return to where we once only seized by force; to where we still only take on our own terms. It is ironic, senators, that it is a land to whom millions of us owe our ancestry yet we treat it like we would never abuse our own grandparents. It is a land to which we can return in a spirit of honour and mutual advantage and at the same time support our own new way of life. America shall be neither spiritually nor economically impoverished!"

This was a declaration in triumph, words which might otherwise have suggested humility born of desperation. But no, this was an exultation in a cause. The light from within President Victoria Twigg's eyes shone with the message she herself had received but an hour ago in an ordinary church amongst their own black brethren, a reminder to them all of mixed descent with a common goal: their own future.

"Members of the Senate", she declared, "it is time for America ..."

They were quite silent. No shuffle of foot. No cough. No whisper.

"...it is time for America to turn ..." And she held them in her own spell now.

" ...to Africa!"

Part Six

GAINSBOROUGH

GAINSBOROUGH

Africa

"Africa? ...Well, lawdy sakes, I jest don' know, Mary Jo, honey. We'all jest gonna have to listen up to the President, I guess. Have a nice day!"

Jerry Corrie jabbed a big flat thumb at one of the modest row of knobs set uncertainly in the fretsawn facia mounted on the rickety table in front of him and leaned back to take a swig of beer, while one of half-a-dozen 'Sally's Soft Cream Soda' jingles fired across the airwaves.

"Lawdy, Al!" declared the South's lankiest and most popular morning 'jock', with a roll of the eyes aimed through the glass panel dividing egg-carton soundproofed studio from dexian-frame, tangled-wire control room. "Africa, Africa, Africa! Whadd'I say? It's big and black, and fulla big blacks!"

He was treated to a few short stabs of guttural laughter from Al the engineer in his headphones before the jingle's end launched him back at the microphone hung above the table.

"This is WPPJ One-Zero-Three-Point-Five Chattanooga Tennessee, this fine an' dandy mornin'!" hailed Jerry to his listeners far and wide. "Get yer fingers on them dials fer four-two-three, six-four-two, two-two-two, on the Chattanooga Two-Two Show! An' a big 'hi' an' mornin' to y'all. Who's next out there?"

There was another despairing roll of the eyes as your tall and friendly Chattanooga chat host listened to yet another of the morning's shocked and confused, bewildered and outraged. They played to a sympathetic ear.

"Yeh, sure thang, Earl, my friend. Debt? Nobody ever cancelled your debt, did they, Earl?"

"Sure, no, Jerry!"

"No, me, neither", chorused radio's man of the people, "I'd havta shoot my bank manager first!" (Brief pause for effect). "Hey, now that's an idea, eh, Earl?"

And a few thousand smiles and nodding heads warmed some more to the familiar voice that said all the right things to them.

"You gotta loan, you gotta pay it back cos it sure don't belong to you. That's how I was brung up, how about you?"

More nods in kitchens, cars and parlours; grimmer, with fewer smiles this time.

"Aid?" In response to another from the simmering brew. "I could do with some aid myself, eh? It's *my* taxes, yeh?"

When astutely expressed in terms of personal taxation, and the destination of so many reluctantly-tendered greenbacks, the new Federal policy of cancelling all remaining African debt, and tripling even the current aid budget, raised some purdy disparaging frowns across America.

'Has Twigg betrayed her roots?' served as a favourite headline in various quarters, conveniently forgetting the President was herself from impoverished stock, south of the border, if not actually coal-black from over the ocean. Also conveniently overlooked by many popular organs of the media, in the first twenty-four hours, was the 'trade 'n' gain' aspect of the announcement. This was in part because the White House chose not to elaborate further until the significance of 'No Debt, More Aid' had sunk in.

The delay was also because it took Victoria Twigg a full twenty-four hours to persuade the Treasury, with her complete repertoire of smouldering eyes, towering breasts and beckoning legs and - on this especially demanding occasion - piercing intellect, that the plan would work. Without admitting it, she was having to simultaneously persuade herself since, up to that point, she only had the inspiration of a bestowed vision in a humble chapel to guide her.

But yes, it could work, the suits were compelled to concede, brains and groins pounding in turmoil, it could work.

"It *will* work", the President asserted, imperiously. They wondered if this, like the revelation on the White House steps, was another vision.

Aladdin

"New for *old?* Is she fucking mad! This isn't goddamned Ali Baba!"

Big hand - crash! Entire group - wince - both he who owned the hand and those who were glad they did not. You had to be either courageous or foolhardy to speak next.

"Aladdin", suggested Tom, nervously.

Abe tried to dig him in the elbow but missed.

"Eh?" growled Drummond.

"Aladdin", continued Tom, gaining some confidence, "new lamps for old."

There was an uncomfortable silence around the boardroom table.

"Eh?" Max Drummond glowered at callow, brave, reckless Tom. "Lamps? Who's talking about lamps, you fucking idiot. Cars! I wouldn't care a goddamned fuck if it was lamps, would I?"

He glared at Tom, waiting for a response.

"Would I, eh?"

"Er ... no, Max ... Sir." Tom was colouring in his cheeks, beads of sweat glistening on his upper lip. The other five sitting around the table with Max Drummond were ever so glad they were not Tom.

"Maybe you'd like to go work in a lamp factory, eh?" demanded Drummond of his hapless subordinate. Nobody else felt much inclined to break the silence after that and the meeting was soon over but only after Abe had managed to say, "Battery cars, Max. Cheaper to make. We only didn't go for them while we had a solid production line of regular cars. But look where we are with them, now. I think we'll get our money on this deal. Batteries into new and old cars and sell them on this tax break - and on the cash the Government's giving the Africans. She wants it to work. It *has* to work. I don't think we'll get hung."

"Hmmph", grunted Drummond but he knew Abe was wise and he invited him to his Chairman's suite to talk it through. Abe made a mental note to give young Tom some friendly advice on how to handle the Max Drummonds of this world.

Hill

"Who's that?"

Elroy tilted his head to ask Bella above the hubbub of the party. He was indicating a lean man near the door, in close conversation with a young Chinese woman, pretty and elegant in short Chinese silk cocktail dress, delicately balancing a glass of white wine in her slender pale fingers. She was smiling at him. He was gazing adoringly at her from his ascetic features, in his considerably less fashionable attire of loose-fitting trousers, dowdy brown jacket and almost matching brown shirt and tie.

"I don't know", replied Bella. "I'll ask Doug." She called over to their host.

"Hey, Isabella!" Doug moved across from a bunch of partygoers, glass in hand, and gave her a friendly one-armed squeeze around the waist. "Almost an anniversary, eh!" Good old Doug, she thought, never the most observant character, unless he was eyeing up his next conquest. She flicked her head from side to side in a noncommital way.

"Oh", he grimaced apologetically, "you two still ...er..." He held up his free hand, palm down, and wobbled it in a *comme ci, comme ca* gesture. She nodded slightly. "Oh, well, okay my love. Just thought maybe same place, same people - more or less", he chuckled, looking round at his guests, noting Paul with a group on the other side of the large lounge. "I mean, it was me brought you two together here, eh?" She smiled at him. Yes, Doug's party all those years ago. She and Paul, a match made for ... oh dear, she thought. "Anyway", Doug breezed on, smiling at Elroy, "you met any interesting people?"

"Elroy was just asking", said Bella, "who's that over there? ... You mean the Chinese girl, El?"

"No, no", Elroy chuckled sheepishly, genuinely wishing he had Mariana at his side. "No, I mean the guy; I almost think I've seen him before."

"Oh, that's Gainsborough Hill. Some kind of scientist, I think", replied Doug. He's come with some friends of mine. I wouldn't even have remembered his name, except it's not the sort you quickly forget."

"Who's the girl?" asked Bella.

"Ah", Doug leered, knowingly. "He's married, I gather, but that's his bit of ... you know", and he tapped the side of his nose, winked and leered some more. "Anyway", he breezed at them both again," Can I get you both a drink? No? Okay. Food's in the other room." He waved his glass vaguely at a doorway and stepped away, moving to join a couple of rather glamorous women with their partners. Not that it would deter Doug, thought Bella. He would insist they each ought to have one of his business cards - "just in case" - slip one into each handbag while partners were away collecting drinks, with a cheery aside about the days he had to sadly drive to lunch, solo in his Aston Martin - "such is life!" - then wait until the first one took the bait and phoned him.

There was plenty to fill the party conversations. People were aghast at the behaviour of their fellow-countrymen, not that this privileged quarter of London society felt much affinity with the general hoi poloi. "Shocking!" "Disgraceful!" "Nothing's safe any more!" at the continued spates of thefts and break-ins characterising daily life, in which the perpetrators were refusing to accept that redundancies, short-time working and less money meant that you could not continue acquiring possessions like before. And as for China! All those reports of demonstrations on the streets, some shop looting as the protests grew bolder and even a sit-down demonstration in Tianamen Square - tempting a repeat of the disaster of all those years ago - with Beijing apparently hit by the same 'bug' as America and London. This time, however, the Beijing government was content to leave it alone and allow maximum international media coverage. The implication was clear: this is America's doing and now we, the Chinese, are going to do without America.

Once it became clear there were two Americans at the party, Elroy and Isabella were the focus of much attention. It was a mixture of veiled accusation at the perceived US policy of attempting to force economic contraction on the rest of the world and fascination at the new behaviour of ordinary Americans themselves. "Are people *really* sharing cars, televisions, and all that?" "What's this about the new American way of life?" "Isn't this just another way of the States trying to dictate to the rest of the world? First it was war, now this!" "And what's this about giving cars and things to Africa?"

Elroy and Bella fielded the questions between them. Elroy himself had phoned Walt the day before just to check he was hearing this latest news right and that it had not become ludicrously distorted in its media translation across the Atlantic. But no, it was true, the plan was to more or less force - incentives first but laws were threatened if necessary - all car manufacturers to take back all the 'bugged' cars and replace them with battery-driven versions at half-price. 'New for old' it was popularly termed. The manufacturers would then convert the 'dud' cars to battery power for export to Africa at a fraction of market price, but with huge export discounts and tax reductions making it financially viable provided it was a large mass production exercise.

Any American who, now accustomed to managing without two or three cars, and sometimes without even one, wanted cash instead would be paid cash, heavily subsidised by the government (as Abe had patiently explained to a gradually-subsiding Max Drummond). And all this Federal Government money? Financed by massive reductions in the purchase of military hardware. It was pointed out that one military jet was worth about a thousand motor cars. And then Africa would need new roads throughout the continent; and new factories. The government would subsidise companies to export the technology, set up home production in as many African countries as possible and finally, perhaps, drag them into the twenty-first century.

"Hm", mused an economics analyst among the guests, "it's far too radical for anyone to have even remotely suggested it before. But the States has been going down a very radical road. And the strange thing is, they *need* Africa. They need a whole new consumer continent to replace their own, with its economic downsizing. It's not just altruism; but if at the same time it modernises the whole of Africa in twenty years instead of a hundred. Well, that's probably what all the pop stars and activists have been demanding. Although, they would be the last to have this kind of vision. She's a remarkable woman, that President."

By the time the economist had finished this exposition, quite a group had fallen silent around him to listen, even though most were not quite sure what he was envisaging. Elroy took advantage of their attention being diverted from him.

"I'm sure I know that guy, Bella. Like our host, Doug, said, it's the kind of name that sticks: Gainsborough Hill", thinking, 'some people have weird parents'. "Do ya mind if I go see him?"

"No, sure, hun", Bella smiled. There were a few familiar faces she had not got around to. She wandered off to greet one of them.

"Hey man .. Gainsborough?"

The brown-jacket man looked enquiringly at the big, black American who had appeared at his side.

"Er -" he began; then a smile played at his mouth. "El? Elroy Fitzgibbon? Wow! How could I possibly not recognise you? Have you changed, shrunk or something?"

They both suddenly guffawed and clasped each other in a huge hug, Elroy delighted at the long-forgotten quirky sense of humour.

"Elroy Fitzgibbon!" declared Gainsborough Hill, taking a step back to look at him. "Must be fifteen-"

"More", grinned Elroy.

" - seventeen years?" Hill was beaming.

"Yeh, guess so", grinned Elroy again.

"What on earth are you doing here?" exclaimed Hill in amazement.

"Isabella Best", Elroy raised a hand to where Bella was chatting, "and Paul, her husband", with a similar gesture towards Paul, "new friends of mine; I'm staying with them. Are you still in Signals?" It seemed like yesterday when they met during that week at Goonhilly.

"No", replied Gainsborough Hill, "that was just some basic training. I went back to pure physics. Research. Oh, by the way, this is Vicki." He smiled at his Chinese companion and reached for her hand. "She has an unpronounceable Chinese name so she's Vicki. And she's from the Embassy", he added, quickly, as if to provide her with a legitimacy that distanced her from any other assumptions which might be made.

"Hi", Elroy smiled and shook her hand. She smiled too. "Research?" he continued to Gainsborough, interested, "anything exciting?"

"Well, transport, really." Gainsborough appeared a little bashful.

"Buses?" joked Elroy.

"Huh", Gainsborough smiled, "No. I thought I might have changed the future, except I can never crack the fundamental problem. You know what it's like."

"Sure", replied Elroy, intrigued. "What is it? Hydrogen cars?"

"No", chuckled Gainsborough, "bomb up the buttocks? - sorry Vicki - no, can't talk about it. They all think I'm crazy anyway. But come and see the lab."

"Okay, sure." Elroy did not recall Gainsborough as crazy. Level-headed English mathematician, from what he could remember. They exchanged phone numbers. Elroy felt he was being shown a new future almost every day. Put visions and mathematics together and ... well.. he had seen for himself where it could lead. He would call Gainsborough tomorrow and fix a visit.

PARADIGM : DOUBT

The sun burned the sky. Sharp jags of dull red and livid yellow struck out from the lowering sun, scything through lakes of black and grey blotting the deepening blue. His steps were of pride tinted with shame, as the sky's tints warned of a new time. Their rock, as he approached, glinted with the hues of the sky and the sea spat as in spite from dark waves below. His shoulders were hunched and his step more slowed than of custom but not, in this, of shame. His shoulders bore the weight of a lamb. Yet his eyes were dark.

"You come in time", she smiled in warmth. "I hoped you would not be late. The sky -"She looked above "a storm?"

"A kind of storm I have not known", he spoke sombrely as he drooped a shoulder for the lamb to slip to the ground.

"A lamb?" She looked in surprise at the dead beast at her feet.

"The hunt was poor", he confessed, taking her hand to be forgiven, not being the hunter to provide for her, and for their child. "So many beasts diseased, and birds already fallen from the sky, we could not eat. So many", he let out a sigh, a sigh for unknown times, "I could have killed but they would not run, nor fly from me, but would look and wait for the blade and would have me bring them back for us to feed, diseased or already dying."

"The lamb?" She asked.

"Left by its ewe", he owned, averting his eye.

She reached to touch his hand, knowing his shame.

"We said we must not take the deserted lamb or abandoned calf, my dearest, for it may have been left sick and unsound."

"This one is not so", he replied, tightening her hand in his, "perhaps lost, I found it lying. It was too young to fear. It was too easy for me -"

He looked away again, away at the fitful sea, mocking the hunter with his lamb.

"Let us prepare to eat", she said, letting her hand caress the noble thigh at her side, "the beast and fowl will return in health. Perhaps when the sky -"

But the sky churned as they looked and the sea mauled at their rock, as they turned again to feed on the lamb and for her to feed their child.

Terror

"Brother Hoi."

Hoi wished the man would not sidle into his office without even asking his secretary to buzz to let Hoi know he was coming through. He could not be expected to wait to be invited in but at least he might allow his arrival to be heralded. Instead, it was always like being surprised from behind a pillar, or from a concealed alleyway; and Hoi could never suppress a start of displeasure, which he hoped would pass unnoticed by his 'brother'.

"Brother Teng", Hoi greeted him civilly, as he settled his nerves.

"Brother Hoi", proceeded Teng, inclining his head as though subserviently requesting a favour, "we are reducing our exports for a little while."

"We?" asked Hoi, involuntarily emboldened by the effrontery of the man, suggesting that the commercial business of the Manchu Motor Corporation were somehow a collaborative enterprise between the two of them.

"Hm, yes", Teng smiled at what he perceived to be mild banter, "that is, we do not need to make -er - deliveries during the next few months."

"But, brother Teng", protested Hoi with dignity, "we must continue with our trade. "Besides", he continued, meaning to play the card to his advantage for a change, "my debt to the Society must be repaid."

"Yes, yes", Teng responded, with a degree of impatience, "I am sure we can accommodate that. However", and he clutched nervously with his fingers at his jacket cuff, "we must be sure not to overplay the market before our deliveries continue."

Our deliveries? thought Hoi. Who is manufacturing and selling these cars? And whose livelihood depends on it?

A phone rang in Teng's pocket. He took it out and answered.

"Indeed, yes", he confirmed anxiously to the caller. "Precisely. Yes, I am making it clear ... when our deliveries resume - the main one, yes, brother, there will be exports as usual." There was a short pause as he listened anxiously. "Yes, our operative is in place. She is reporting - but there may be nothing to learn." He emphasised this as though to lower expectations, then put the phone away, slightly abashed, and addressed Hoi. "It is important to make a delivery in six months from now, brother Hoi, that is all I am saying. To maintain demand until then. Therefore, it might be wise to reduce the volume in the meantime." He was determined to make his point, in the manner of one, it was evident to Hoi, who was under pressure to do so.

"And the dolls?" enquired Hoi, mindful of their sales value in England.

"Dolls?" asked Teng. "Oh, I don't know -"

"Brother", Hoi interjected, "our London people say they are very important - a valuable 'gimmick' is their word."

"Oh, yes, yes", agreed Teng with some impatience, "I'm sure we can find some."

"And dancers?" added Hoi, wary that the elaborate promotion of Manchu Mets, of which he himself had been dubious initially, might be undermined by the Society's sudden withdrawal of interest in these sales frills.

"Oh, yes, yes, of course", acknowledged Teng, as if none of this held any interest any longer. "But just be sure there is an order to be delivered in six months. We shall be in touch."

He was on the point of leaving when there was a crash from outside, muffled by the window partition and the hum of manufacture below. Hoi shot in alarm to the window and could see men leaving their workstations to hurry down the production line to a point just out of sight. He looked anxiously at Teng, who nodded, "I'll be going now, brother", but Hoi dashed past to leave him to depart on his own. Down on the factory floor there was a commotion of workers and office staff running together towards the shattered plate glass window by the entrance door, sheets of fractured glass covering the concrete floor. There was a large brick lying amongst the shards and splinters, with a loop of string around it and a large white label attached. No-one had dared touch it until the boss appeared. They stood in a horseshoe around it. Hoi rushed to them, then saw the brick. He darted to pick it up and the label fluttered in his face. There was one word - the same - written on both sides: 'American!'

Hoi's heart missed a beat. American? He fumbled his way back upstairs, leaving the staff to sweep up, all muttering excitedly amongst themselves. Who? Why? American? Hoi's mind was filled with trouble. He sank into his plush leather office chair, head bowed forward to rest on two forefingers. American? He had no association with America. But he dimly saw an explanation swimming into shape. America, UK, London: he was trading with London. It was well known. Much trumpeted, in fact, in Beijing, as a coup for the private manufacturer. Was someone associating him with the new American isolationism, blamed for China's present economic hiccup? He was trading with one half of the 'special relationship'; was that enough to indict him? He shook his head, sadly. Did he invent the 'bug'? Was he President Twigg?

He was suddenly jolted out of his brooding by his mobile phone. Phones! Doors! People invading silences! Was there never to be peace! He answered it. At first he heard only sobs; sobs and stifled gasps. Then more sobs. His heart began to heave and race wildly.

"Hoi Fong! Hoi! Darling! Please come! Come! Oh, my Hoi Fong!" It was Hwee Lo! He was gripped with fear. He had never heard her like this! So distressed! In danger!

"What! Where are you?" He cried down the phone.

"At home! Home! Please come quick! Quick! Oh .. Oh ...!" She was sobbing frantically. He could not bear it. He was not with her. He could not see her. Where was Soo Wong? His mind was scrambled into a fit of wild imaginings.

"Home? What is wrong, my love? Tell me!" He shouted at her unseen, beautiful face, tears he could see streaming down it.

"Men!" She wailed at him. "Men! Here!" She sobbed and sobbed. His heart was wrenched. "Oh, please come, please come!"

"I'm coming!" His finger shook as he stabbed the phone off. Then he lunged at the desk phone and called up the man he knew he had to have with him. Cousin Fo of the police. He drove like a madman out of the city lights and into the dark, along the scrub-lined country road, black twisted shadows of skeleton trees springing into the headlights on either side. He roared over the rough, unmade track to their house and saw car lights bathing the walls in their gleam. There were dark figures flitting about in the beams until he saw they were hurling objects at the walls. He heard a window smash and saw that two or more were already broken.

He screeched to a halt behind the nearest of three cars pointing their lamps at the house and leaped out, shouting in fury. Figures turned to see him and they were men holding stones to throw and waving sticks in anger. When they saw him they began to advance upon him and he did not know what he would do next. He only wanted to get to the house to protect his Hwee Lo and Soo Wong but his way was barred and menaced. He stopped, irresolute. Then there was a siren, a wailing upon the road behind, from where he had just driven.

In a moment, headlights appeared and swung and bumped over the scrub track, and a police light flashed on the car roof. Four officers jumped out, shouting, and the figures around the house could be seen scrambling to their cars and, before they sped off, shouting and swearing, "American! English! You are cursed with them!" The police let them slam away into the dark.

"Cousin Fo!" breathed Hoi, gratefully, and clasped him about the arms. He and the officers rushed to the house. Inside, Hwee Lo was sobbing and trembling and hurled herself into Hoi Fong's embrace, her wet cheek pressed against his chest. He was suddenly angry, furious that his dear wife should be threatened, a scapegoat on his behalf. They sank into a chair as Fo and his officers examined the broken windows and furniture damaged by incoming missiles. There was rubble and glass here and there on the floor. Fo began to instruct the men to clear up.

"It's all right. It's all right", Hoi said to Fo. "We shall manage." Fo understood. They needed to be left alone. They would ask questions and try to establish identities in the morning, though he knew it would be of little use. This was anonymous, parochial terrorism. He was aware of its source. He even held some private sympathy, though he would not let it interfere with duty, even less to help a cousin. But there was an anger. An anger at being dictated to by America and, as far as the Chinese were concerned, all the West was America, or its cohorts were. Just when the world had been growing smaller and closer, there was a new wedge driven through it. The madness of trying to halt progress; the arrogance of doing so just when half the world was learning to savour it. Then you sold cars to the West which caught the 'bug'; then the bug came to Beijing.

Then people simply did what they had always done, in any language: they added two and two together. He looked at his cousin, hugging his sweet wife in his arms and shook his head sadly. "We shall go", he whispered. Hoi looked up and smiled: "Thank you for coming." Fo smiled, too and left with his men.

Hoi Fong held Hwee Lo as her sobs gradually subsided and her breathing calmed. Soon, he led her to bed and helped her undress and then lay, still holding her, until he knew she was asleep. What had he done wrong? He sighed and there were tears in his eyes, too. He heard some little snorts and snuffles from the next bedroom, through their open door. Soo Wong must have been asleep the whole time and had not heard a thing.

Decision

"We can't do that!"

It was not really up to an angel to offer strident opinions upon what should or should not be done, observed the Lord to Himself. Even if He had only one angel - an archangel, no less - and one who did, He had to concede, prove an invaluable confidante on many a ticklish occasion. Nonetheless, His one and only angel was not, as far as He could recall, put in Heaven to be judge and jury on the Almighty's chosen strategy. God's purpose was precisely that: a carefully charted course through the infinity of space and time. All creatures, every beast that walked, every bird that flew, every zangt that dissolved, every grivloco that banged, every ... and so on ... and so on ...He mused. Except, He frowned (dark matter coalescing all over the universe), this was perhaps a bit less of a calculated stratagem than an act of desperation.

"*Can* we?"

Insistent, demanding, relentless; why did He seem unable to exercise more choice as to when and how His loyal adjutant made his contributions to the matter in hand (Hah! Apt choice of phrase, not lost on the Good Lord, even at a time of trouble).

"We *can't!* I mean, You said ..." Gabriel broke off in the nearest thing to exasperation he dared and stared up at the Lord and Master.

"I said?" The Lord responded at last.

"Yes", the angel said with an emphatic nod, "You said we can't change *events*. Only attitudes." He bent down to examine a neglected crevice but it was a half-hearted diversion. He knew it was not his prerogative. It was not he who was Lord over Time and Space. His was not the grip in which lives were held in thrall, from which suspended galaxies wheeled and revolved, by whose ordinance the teeming trillions of His creations danced and turned their patterns through infinity. He was only an angel Even so, he knew a gamble when he saw one. "We can't change the future. You said that."

"I ...." began the Lord with a sigh. He paused. Yes, He had said that. He had pontificated about cause and effect and the myriad consequences of interpolating just one small adjustment into the course of history. But this was not one small alteration. This was going to be a momentous intervention to salvage the whole project before it was too late. All or nothing. Somehow, somewhere, the dislocation had crept in; plunging nations into sudden upheaval, instead of gradually assimilating the new order, the new way of life. Now: division and discord, disagreement and distrust, schism and conflict. It was not how it was ordained to be. Ah, ordained! But for that unpredicted dislocation, the interloper in the computer room... If only. Hah. Here He was. God. The Great Ordainer. He, speculating 'if only...'

"If only..." He murmured aloud.

"Eh?" Whimsy was not going to satisfy a certain angel in this mood. "If only what?"

"If behaviour is the priority - *influencing* behaviour -" God took up a more determined tone "extreme measures may be employed to achieve that end. After all, our aim is to help ..." He paused again. Even He, the Good Lord Almighty, pausing almost as if to summon the argument to convince Himself. "By eliminating -"

"Avarice?" The archangel looked up at Him.

"And the means by which it is expressed", the Lord affirmed.

"Competing, acquiring, possessing", interjected the angel.

"Indeed, yes", God agreed, "But if, through this single step, they were all to perceive one vision so distanced from any present reality, so fundamentally redirecting their future, perhaps ... perhaps... they would forsake their differences and develop that vision together. One which solved so many problems at one stroke."

In all his journeys through the mighty cosmos, Gabriel had never seen a flying pig but wondered if he had just missed a couple now.

"'Perhaps'?" queried the angel, "'Perhaps'? I thought You preordained everything." He knew he was being rather bolder than custom would normally allow but he also knew who would be politely invited to go and make it happen. "Can't You see the future?"

The Lord bestowed his angel with a studied gaze. Yes, He could. He could see two or three futures, or more. Even He, for reasons much debated between them, could not predict which of these futures would actually occur.

"Which future indeed?" He murmured, and then, "Mm. So hadn't you better be going?"

"Me?" Gabriel wanted to look around as though there were a whole host of angels to choose from. However, he had tried that one before, notably when there had been a cave, a stone and a temporary impersonation to be undertaken, and it had not gone down very well at all.

"Yes, Boss." He heaved himself up and drew towards the edge, cheering himself up with thoughts of wings.

Card

The pair of little black, curved pigtails bobbed past the shop window and behind the strip of advertising and credit card posters beside the door frame, to reappear in the door window, a few inches above the small hand pushing down on the old brass handle. It was a modernised 'corner shop' in north London, where some care had been applied to retaining a few of the original fittings under the onslaught of glass and chrome.

The door handle was one of them. The jangling bell announcing a customer's entry was another. The diminutive Chinese girl, all of nine years old and barely halfway between three and four feet tall, knew exactly what she wanted and headed for the display racks of birthday cards. She arrived at the till, moments later, clutching a bulky card that played a tune, in one petite hand, and a couple of two-pound coins in the other. She looked up with a wide-eyed smile. Sarah Potts smiled down at her and took the card and money.

"Thank you, dear, that one? Three pounds ninety-five, please. I know", she gave a sympathetic grimace, "they *are* expensive. Are you sure you want this one?"

The girl's smile faded and she nodded seriously.

"Of course, dear", agreed Sarah, knowing how important a fancy card with a tune could be to little girls, "you like this tune?"

The girl nodded again, her pigtails dancing by her ears, as she watched her four pounds being placed in the till and a five-pence piece returned to her waiting palm, followed by card placed in its paper bag. Sarah shook her head disapprovingly.

"I know, dear, they cost far too much but", she added brightly, "I'm sure it will be appreciated. Is it for someone special?"

"My sister", nodded the little mite, still with her serious expression.

"Big sister?" enquired Sarah Potts.

The girl nodded again with a shy smile. Then, instead of turning to leave, she asked, "Can I have some scissors, please?"

"Scissors?" Sarah frowned. "Whatever for -" But she was halted by the girl's serious air and the solemn gaze of her deep, brown eyes. "Well, of course, my dear." Sarah reached under the counter for the scissors she kept for cutting sticky tape and opening packs of labels. The girl clasped the scissors in one hand, while her fingers fumbled to withdraw the card from its bag, leaving the envelope inside. She opened the card, which immediately began playing 'Happy Birthday' in clinking, metallic notes. Then, as the kindly shopkeeper observed in some dismay, the girl deftly sliced open the bulky centre of the card, with the scissors, revealing the miniature assembly of speaker, battery cell and microchip.

"Goodness gracious", declared the disconcerted Mrs Potts and would have reached to retrieve the card but the girl looked up with her solemn eyes, handing back the scissors and asked again, "Can I have a pin please. A big pin."

"A pin?" asked Sarah, a little faintly, "*Well* ..." but found herself involuntarily seeking out the old hatpin she kept beside the till as an utterly futile weapon to ward off thieves. A service into which, fortunately, it had never been pressed.

"Here you are, dear", she said weakly, as she offered it headfirst to the strange child, who accepted it with the same solemnity and, with the opened card still playing its 'Happy Birthday' in the other hand, poked and stabbed at the exposed musical device, with some precision. The tune coughed and began to miss some notes.

"Goodness me, young lady!" exclaimed Sarah Potts in dismay, "whatever are you doing!" And she did reach down this time to take the card out of the little vandal's hands but she was met by a penetrating gaze and then a disarming smile as the pin was placed carefully in her outstretched hand. Sarah could only draw herself upright and smile in return, when she heard the girl ask, "Can I have some sticky tape, please?"

Sarah Potts felt as though she was taking part in a nonsensical dream as she handed over a short length of tape, which the girl proceeded to apply to the card and music box, sealing the two together again and returning it all to the paper bag. "Thank you", she vaguely heard the girl chirrup, as she watched the departing pair of heels, in neat black schoolgirl shoes, as the dainty hand depressed the old door handle, the bell jangled, hand clutching paper bag and pigtailed owner departing into the street outside.

"Well, I never", breathed Sarah Potts, in a daze. "Well, I never."

Not long afterwards, Paul Best glanced up to see a pair of black curved pigtails bob just above the window frame of his office and then disappear in the direction of the showroom. While he was still puzzling it out and deciding whether he should leave the sales chart to investigate, he was summoned anyway by a call from a salesman.

"Hey, Paul! Check this out."

Paul Best grunted and took himself into the showroom. The salesman was standing with a small Chinese girl in pigtails beside a Manchu Met bearing a 'Sold' sign on its windscreen.

"Paul", said the salesman, cheerfully, "this little girl wants to put a birthday card in this car for her sister."

"Uh?" came the puzzled response from Paul.

"She says one of the 'Mets' is being delivered to her sister on her birthday - tomorrow?" He turned to ask the girl, who nodded and smiled demurely. "And she has this card to put in the car." The girl held up her white envelope.

"It's not a bomb, is it?" Paul addressed the child with mock concern. She gave a little shudder and shook her head solemnly.

"Only joking", Paul chuckled. "What's your sister's name?"

"Vicki", she replied.

"Okay", responded Paul, "and has she ordered this car?"

"It's a present, apparently", grinned Mark the salesman, "from a Mr Gainsborough Hill, she says." The girl nodded with her serious smile.

"Okay, check it out, Mark. This 'Vicki' and the buyer", instructed Paul. Mark disappeared to the office. Paul stood, casting his eyes around the showroom, while the Chinese girl remained motionless, looking up at him, saying nothing and clutching the large envelope in her two small hands. The salesman returned.

"Yup", he smiled, "that's it. Ordered and paid for by Mr Gainsborough Hill, to be delivered to Miss Vicki Tong."

"Okay then." Paul smiled slightly at the diminutive Chinese waif. "A surprise card for your sister, eh?"

The girl nodded again with that serious smile.

"Okay, Mark", said Paul, "open the door for our friend and she can put the card in herself."

The salesman opened the driver's door. "There you are, miss."

The girl took a couple of little steps and leaned in to place the envelope on the driver's seat, face up with the neatly-written words, 'Happy Birthday Vicki' and a tidy 'x' after them. She suddenly broke into a broad, happy grin and hugged the salesman, stretching her arms up around his waist. He grinned back.

"Hey. Nice surprise for sister, eh? Here, I'll show you out. Do you need a lift home?"

The girl shook her head happily, pulled away and skipped off down the corridor. The two men followed to see her dancing down the street, pigtails bouncing in their tight curves about her ears.

"Those pigtails", chortled the salesman to Paul, "they look like a pair of little wings. She might take off any minute!"

Paul gave a snort of amusement and they each returned to their work.

Car

Gainsborough rolled over in the large bed, crumpled satin sheets more under than over his body, orange glow of street lamp filtering through the thin curtains of the central London apartment. He peered down at his spare frame. Not bad for forty-five but not exactly an athlete. 'Wiry' might be an approving description, overlooking the tendency for skin to crinkle here and there on his torso, rather than remain taught over muscle. Muscle? Not too much sign of that but at least there was not the telltale pout of a spare tyre. Still, what did she see in him when she could have any young geronimo half his age?

His eyes passed adoringly over the pale form at his side, likewise part-uncovered and shining softly in the milky-amber light. She was naked with her back to him, spread with her bottom upwards and the smooth creamy, unbroken curve of her shape rolled from neck to buttocks in a soft, undulating flow. He reached to gently caress the small of her back and the neat red triangle tattoo just above where her cheeks parted. 'A family emblem' she had told him, a sign of fidelity and love. Love. Ah. He was besotted with her, if that was love. She stirred and curled over to smile lazily at him, black eyelashes fluttering into wakefulness.

"Mm?" she hummed dreamily and leaned to kiss his shoulder, laying at her side.

"I'll have to go", he murmured, regretfully.

"Oh, so soon?" she purred in disappointment.

"1 o'clock. Working *very* late", he grinned wryly at her. Emily could only be fed the 'difficult problem' excuse up to a certain hour. Even research physicists can't pretend to work all night. It had been a wonderful evening. The car had been a triumph, even though he was walking a tightrope of deceit, telling both women he needed to use the car himself - just a favour to him - and she and he would share it equally. There was no question he could actually have bought his girlfriend a car! But he was infatuated, he admitted it to himself, and she had so loved the car in the showroom. Dividing the same vehicle between three was going to present some challenges in the future but never mind that tonight. They had wined and dined in Vicki's apartment, then made love for hours, first on the afghan rug, just a passionate tumble from the dining table, and then in bed. He wished they were not always under pressure to complete their whole experience together in time for him to return home to the marital bosom. Only occasionally had he been able to stay here the night.

"One day", she reached to whisper in his ear, "one day we shall stay for ever."

Bliss. She had been hinting lately that he should leave home and remain with her permanently. Despite the disintegration of his marriage, he felt an irrational loyalty to Emily, as though it was all his fault and he should be trying to achieve a repair. Friends said, 'it takes two' and 'you can't just blame yourself'. Some periods at home were an unbearable succession of spites and rages, each of them rising to the other's bait, and he wanted to believe it was never he who started it but he could not be sure it was so.

"Yes, my love, we shall", he breathed to Vicki's lips, before kissing them softly and then again fully, reaching deep into the luscious embrace of her mouth. They clung, their warm bodies moulded together, until he forced himself to swing decisively onto the edge of the bed. He switched on the bedside light. The birthday card was lying on the little table. He chuckled and opened it. It began its feeble attempt to play its tune, jumping and repeating notes and beats.

"My lovely card", she smiled as she heard it.

"Huh", he laughed quietly, "sorry it doesn't play the tune properly." He had anticipated her squeals of delight at seeing the Manchu Met and was duly rewarded by making sure he was present at its delivery; but he'd been taken unawares by the unexpected card, her pleasure and her praise for his 'thoughtfulness'. He had quickly gathered his wits and assumed appropriate bashfulness. He would have to thank and congratulate the car showroom: 'Get Extra Best - The Best Of Extras'. The single capital letter 'G' and an 'x' inside the card was just the right touch - although perhaps they had simply been nervous of spelling his name, he had smiled to himself. And surely not their fault that its attempts to play 'Happy Birthday' sounded like Kermit the Frog with hiccups.

"Oh", she scorned playfully, "it nearly gets it right."

"Nearly!" he laughed. "It's got no 'Ps', half a 'b' nearly lost under the 'ir', nearly misses the 'd' and adds a couple of 'ays' at the end!"

"Well, didn't you try it first?", she laughingly chided him and reached over to fondly poke his back.

"Well, no, I trusted the shop!" he protested, inventing rapidly, nearly caught out. "Anyway..." he turned to her, "I have to go. You can play the tune till the battery runs out!" She poked at him again but missed and lay back on the sheets. He dressed, kissed her and left. "See you soon, my darling."

Birthday

"Welcome to the humble scientist's den", greeted Gainsborough, with a dry smile, as he led the way into his research room. Yes, you wouldn't describe it as a 'lab', thought Elroy, as he took a quick look around. Nor an 'office'. It was more like an old-fashioned open-plan schoolroom, half-a-dozen work areas, separated by half-partitions across a long narrow room. A plain, indeterminate wood provided the surface for all desks, tables and work shelves. Gainsborough's semi-private section was at one end of the long room, occupying a large corner space. A plain wooden worktop ran along the whole windowed, long side of the room, bisected at intervals by the partitions, and offering a view from the second floor over a nondescript part of the city of London. Two plain wooden tables covered in piles of papers in the centre of the room served as the office filing system.

An anomaly of a building. A Nineteen-Fifties three-storey research institute; this one focusing on atmospheric measurements, chemical constituents in the air at innumerable locations and elevations, ratios of population densities to pollutants, and goodness knows what else. Through changing circumstances, it had assumed a greater importance now, in analysis of the effects of climate change, than when it first opened, when coal-smog, and sulphurus fog were the principal concerns. The whole room was quiet, occupied only by men, bent silently over desks or computer terminals between the partitions, about five or six of them in all. There were subdued murmurs of greeting from a couple nearest.

"However", confided Gainsborough, when they had sat down at a computer near the corner, on the window worktop, "it's a bit like academia: we're encouraged to develop our own lines of research - just in case we ever make an historic breakthrough. Him - over there", he indicated a man of sixty-something in a short-sleeved pullover and checked shirt, scribbling into a notepad, "he's devoted years to finding a mathematical formulation of ageing, trying to find an answer that biology has so far missed."

"Looks like time's running out for him", grunted Elroy. "And what about you? You said they think you're mad, here."

"Oh, yeh", Gainsborough shrugged, sheepishly, "just beavering away at some transport projections."

"Eh?" queried Elroy.

"Well, honestly, I can't say, it's too vague and half-baked so far." He was tapping at his keyboard and the screen suddenly displayed several rows of characters, some separated by 'equals' or other algebraic signs, others one on top of the other in the familiar 'divide' equation. "There."

"Got a lot of 'Ps'", commented Elroy, although he could not fathom what it was all about; it bore no relation to code or signals.

"Yeh", agreed Gainsborough, forlornly, "it's my wild card. I keep adding more 'Ps' to try to make it all work."

Elroy was intrigued but knew he could not interrogate a fellow-scientist about his private work. There was many an embarrassment spared by quietly screwing up and throwing in the bin years of work in search of Eldorado, best never revealed and never mocked. Nonetheless, he loved to search for patterns, even in formulae whose purpose was entirely concealed from him.

"Is that 1-r or I-r - numeral or letter?", he asked about a two-character sequence which repeated a number of times.

"I-r - the letter", explained Gainsborough.

Elroy chuckled softly.

"Ah, well", he remarked, "you been writing songs?"

"Uh?" Gainsborough peered at his rows of characters.

"There", pointed Elroy, "you've almost got 'birthday', if you ignore the numerals inbetween. Except there's no 'th' in the middle. Sorry", he added with a chuckle, "just my flippant attitude to someone else's years of labour. Just spotting irrelevant patterns. Like seeing a face in the clouds. You know how it is. I'm just glad to see someone else going mad over figures that don't add up."

But Gainsborough had gone quiet. He was staring at the screen. He was starting to hum to himself, then softly singing out the words; and feverishly trying to remember the ones he had listened to most recently. "Ha - y brth - ay - ay - ay ... to ...you; Ha - y brth - ay -ay -ay ...to you; Ha - y brth -ay -ay -ay ...." and so on. Elroy looked quizzically at him, wondering how his fatuous remark could have set a fellow-professional off singing to himself. Then Gainsborough stopped singing and sat staring at the screen. If there are no 'Ps', he muttered to himself ...and, yes ... if the 'b' was under the i-r ... i-r divided by b ...and lose those 'ds'....no, not all of them ...'*nearly* misses the 'd'. He was erasing all the 'Ps', some of the 'ds' and placing a horizontal divide between 'ir' and 'b', one over the other.

"This is mad," he suddenly declared out loud, leaning back and staring in growing astonishment at the equations in front of him.

"Oh my God." Gainsborough's hands were trembling as he reached again to the keyboard.

"You all right?" asked Elroy, a little anxious for him. But Gainsborough was ignoring him and muttering again.

"If 't' equals -" and Elroy could see he was inserting the letter 't' at specific points in the equations, then, similarly, the letter 'h'. (The missing 'th'? Elroy wondered). "Oh my God", muttered Gainsborough again, and his words were stuttering as he spoke.

"And add 'a-y' and 'a-y'." Elroy watched in puzzled fascination as the physicist's fingers flashed around the keyboard, manipulating and rearranging the characters of the equations. The fingers were shaking and Gainsborough's breath was emitted in short gasps. He suddenly leaned right back in his chair and Elroy could see he had gone deathly pale, his sallow features drained of all their sparse colour.

"Oh ... my ... God", breathed Gainsborough, very slowly. "Oh ...my ... God." He was silent for a moment in his fixed stare at the screen and then suddenly, violently leapt to his feet, arms outstretched above his head, fists tightly clenched and yelled at the top of his voice, "Y - E- E-SS!!"

All the faces down the room looked up in surprise and two or three colleagues began to make for the corner area to see the cause of this eruption. Gainsborough, still on his feet with arms outstretched, pumped the air with his fists a second time, with a second, rasping "Y-E-S!" and turned to Elroy, flinging his hands down to grasp the big American tightly on each upper arm and stared wildly into his eyes, mouth wide in a joyous grin. "*Yes!*" he hissed one more time, a look of triumph all over his face. And then again, and Elroy could feel the steel of the man's grip through the firmness of his jacket sleeve, "*Yes!*"

Two colleagues had reached him and looked on in amazement but another, a senior figure also joined them.

"Come on, Hill, save it for home, if you don't mind. When your fanciful meanderings finally get somewhere we'll all be very glad." The man spoke with irritable irony and Elroy recalled again Gainsborough's comment on how he was thought to be 'mad' here. Clearly, there was little sympathy for *his* time spent on individual project research.

"Oh, fuck off, Barnes!" exclaimed Gainsborough with unexpected venom. "Go and finish your crossword."

Barnes stood stunned for a moment and then responded in chilled tones, "I'd be grateful if you would leave us for the rest of the day, Mr Hill. We shall talk tomorrow, if you don't mind."

He turned abruptly and walked off.

Gainsborough was trembling but Elroy doubted it was fear of his superior colleague. Something more momentous than that. Archimedes must have leapt out of his bath shouting "Eureka!"

in similar fashion. Gainsborough was keying a 'save' into the computer and watched it boot off.

"Come on." He grabbed Elroy by the arm and virtually towed him to the door, with brief nods to gawping colleagues. Outside, he was panting and trembling. Elroy was afraid he might collapse on the pavement.

"Here", said the American and took his turn to guide by the elbow, steering them both across the street to sit on a bench set back under railings.

"What is it?" Elroy asked after they had sat for a few minutes in the rumble of traffic noise.

"Look, Elroy, I'm sorry, I can't say." Gainsborough was still shaking slightly but more in command of himself than a few moments before. "You know how it is. It could be nonsense. I'll have to test it. It's too ...too ...outrageous. They were right to think me mad. I don't even know why I was working on it. I thought maybe it would help pave the way for developments over the next few hundred years - literally." He gazed dumbly ahead of him. "But not now."

Before Elroy could say anything else, his companion continued, "It came from that card, you know."

"Card?" Elroy was confused.

"A birthday card to Vicki. She thought it was from me - I had to pretend - but it wasn't. The showroom put it in the car. But it didn't play the notes properly."

Elroy was catching up with him.

"'Happy Birthday'?" he asked.

"Yes....but it was a dud card, it missed out some notes and almost ran others together. Elroy, this is weird, ridiculous ... impossible. When you spotted those letters in my equations ..."

"Like 'birthday'?" checked Elroy.

"Yes", nodded Gainsborough, seeing it again in his mind's eye, "I realised - bizarrely - I mean I just can't explain it - the missing notes and letters in the card tune, they nearly matched my equation but not quite."

"And when you matched your formula to the card ..." added Elroy.

"Yes! It was the clue. It was where I'd gone wrong and I might never have spotted it myself! Would have gone to my grave -" He broke off and gazed ahead again. "Because that equation now, it bears no relation to any of our logical rules of physics. It breaks open a completely new concept. Based on what we know so far but beyond what I - or any of us - would have conceived on our own. Elroy, it's not possible. But looking at those equations just now, I think it actually might be."

Elroy felt a shiver within.

"The showroom sent the card?" He asked.

"Put it in the car", affirmed Gainsborough.

"You saw them?" asked Elroy.

"No, I wasn't there", replied Gainsborough, "but it wasn't anyone else. Just made it look like it was me - very subtle, very thoughtful of them - wrote a big capital 'G' inside and a 'kiss'. Vicki was knocked out." He smiled at last.

Elroy did not know why he suddenly felt cold. The sun was shining. It was a warm summer's day in central London but he felt shivery and wrapped his arms about himself. He looked around, eyes darting this way and that. Were they not alone? Were they being watched? All the time?

"I had a formula", he said slowly.

"Yes?" His companion looked up from his own thoughts.

"Yes ... but ...never mind." He felt he should explain that he, too, discovered the impossible in inexplicable circumstances and the impossible turned out to be reality. Yet it would be like men swapping stories of improbable holes-in-one or of fish whose size expanded even as the catch was retold. What they had each experienced might not quite fit into the catechism of the competitive raconteur. So he said no more.

Petal

Is it a petal blown on the lightest breeze, that catches her eye? Seen in a glimpse, then gone? Would the petal have been there, in that instant, if the seed had been sown one hour earlier? Did a phone ring? Was there a caller at the door? Was the seed, at that moment, just one finger-pinch from the earth? Delayed. A difference of one second. When was that second lost? Or was it a woman ahead, crossing the road, whose hair, caught in the same breeze, flicked across an eye? Causing her to pause, just a moment to brush it away. A distraction to the observer. Would the hair have been already too short to cause the pause, had the hairdresser's schedule not been disrupted the previous day by the traffic pile-up when a dog darted across the road? Chasing another petal? Or the same one, from the seed sown not later but earlier, for a different reason? One event hastened. Another delayed.

And had not either of these, or any other, occurred at just that moment, to catch the eye, distract the attention, just for that instant, would her pale, delicate finger not have allowed the lipstick tube to fall and slip under the seat, to nestle half-concealed beneath her feet, as she drove whilst adding that brighter touch to her oriental smile? Distracted, attention waylaid, only for an instant, then hurriedly closing handbag cradled on knee, and then forgetting, attention restored to the road, for a discovery to be made later, which would otherwise not have been made.

Which of these occupied a place in the preordained order of things? Or which, in another order, destined for another time, another past, another present, another future? Which was this, our present order; which another, where the change? How can we know? Do we ever know? Does He know? Which of these?

Which future indeed?

Something

"They need something - *something* - to bust them outa this ...crap!" Bella declared, fiercely. Elroy could see the bones of her knuckles tightening over the steering wheel as she drove, her eyes jerking from side to side at the evidence of crime and disorder. Every now and then a shopfront boarded up or sheets of plywood covering shattered display windows, the premises still gamely open for business. "Why are they like this, Elroy?" She cast a sideways look at him then back to the road, on their route home from collecting him at the research labs.

Elroy said nothing, lost for an explanation. It really did appear that America's lead, driven by the remarkable flocking to faith -

a flocking, it had to be said, borne on a bubbling ferment of willing belief - was derided and rejected here. Parts of London, and some quarters of other towns and cities, had taken on the appearance of peacetime violent disorder, reminiscent of Belfast at the height of the 'troubles': blackened buildings, those damaged shopfronts, armoured police vehicles - and army - on prominent patrol. It was infectious, too. It was spreading. There were intermittent reports of similar scenes across continental Europe, particularly in countries most vulnerable to dramatic economic change. Small groups of rioters and looters left their mark in Germany, Poland, the Czech Republic, Slovakia, Italy. Nothing widespread but all indicative, and disturbing.

"Don't you think?" challenged Bella, eyes still darting this way and that. "Something to change the focus?"

"Visions?" remarked Elroy, sceptically.

"I don't think they'd accept that here", muttered Bella, disparagingly. "I don't know why. Something - if they won't change life like in the States back home - something just to change their ... direction. Make them see a different future. Inspire them to behave ... differently."

Elroy did not know why but he suddenly visualised Gainsborough's eyes triumphantly staring into his and that exultant, "Yes!" What had he seen? What was *his* revelation?

"Precisely", remarked the Lord, "a breakthrough that won't be abused."

"Where they won't flaunt it", grunted Gabriel, sitting bent over knees, assessing exactly where his attention might most keenly be required next.

"That is the hope", answered the Lord.

"Hope? Can't we do better than that?" Gabriel was loth to think all his artistry might be to no avail.

"It is clear", replied the Lord, "that such a discovery where it is currently originated will more probably be extended to all in a spirit of co-operation and unity, than if it were a phenomenon to emerge elsewhere as an instrument of competition and unique advancement. That is our design."

"Well, that's it then, that's what I said", declared the angel, conclusively. "Here they won't flaunt it, others would. I mean, boss -" he paused to look up at the Almighty with a frown.

"A discovery of this magnitude has to be shared - by all - not wielded as a trump card", murmured the Lord in agreement, though his words were clouded in a frown of doubt.

"I mean -" Gabriel's tone, too, was fretful, although his concern might have been the unimaginable inconvenience placed upon his good self if things went awry. "This is bigtime. I mean this is not just a little nudge, I mean -"

"Yes, yes, I know", sighed the Lord God Almighty, only too aware and not needing to be reminded by an angel, arch or otherwise, thank you very much.

"Well, You know what I mean", Gabriel subsided into a little sulk and muttered into his knees, "more like a shoulder charge than a nudge."

The Lord held His silence.

"So what's this about 'hope'", the angel pursued the point again. "It's all fixed, isn't it, once You've sorted it, preordained it?"

The Lord assented without speaking, seeking to convince, where His own conviction might be lacking. Being One Who sees most and misses little, perhaps the falling petal, the wisp of hair, or some other such, had not escaped his attention. Dislocations to the preordained order. Which future, indeed?

"Anyway", chortled Gabriel, suddenly, "what did You think of the pigtails? Different, eh?" And he chuntered and chuckled as he prised apart the two smallest toes on his right foot. "I mean, You keep saying 'no wings'" And he giggled irritatingly at his feet.

The Lord refrained from comment but moved off a little and, despite seeing everything all the time, contrived to look the other way.

Lipstick

Emily's cream-and-rose complexion was flushed to a hot pink, with blotchy white spots of anger on her cheeks, framed by her short, straight, dark brown hair.

"What is *this*?" she demanded as Gainsborough entered the kitchen. She was standing at the other end of the rectangular wooden table which, he noted, was not laid for an evening meal as usual. Instead, it was bare but for the cruet and slender glass vase of flowers, and she was holding up a small, shiny object between thumb and forefinger.

"What's what?" he stared blankly, sensing with dread that he was about to be embroiled in yet another barrage of raging hostilities.

"*This*!" she stretched her arm towards him.

"I don't know", he stated honestly, not recognising anything familiar about the short, tubular, gold-coloured object she held out. He saw it was open at the end pointing at him, that was all.

"Oh, well it's the sort of thing you *wouldn't* notice!" Her eyes were gleaming and looked hot and watery. "Since you've spent years not noticing *anything* that's not to do with figures and numbers and computers and you saying one day you're going to save the world or whatever other stupid idea you're wasting your life on! *And* mine!" She turned the thing in her fingers so the open end pointed at her and she stared at it. "You don't see anything else", she spat, bitterly, then glaring at him with venom, "unless its got two legs and a pair of tits."

His heart was sinking fast. He still did not know what the object was but he had a desperate sense of what the connection was going to be.

"You don't know what this is?" she shook it at him, still grasped tightly. "Lipstick."

"Lipstick?" he repeated feebly, reaching down with a hand to steady himself on the table.

"Lipstick", she assured him, forcibly. "Yes, lipstick", her voice rising again, "only you wouldn't know because you never buy me any, you wouldn't have the first idea where to look or what to buy or, probably", she sniped, "even how to take the top off. Unlike some other tops you're probably an expert at!"

"Well, what's it got to do with me?" he asked, stoically, his mind racing with wild images of Emily invading Vicki's apartment, despite not knowing where it was, or his pockets searched and improbably yielding lipstick, or ... or ... where could lipstick, he and Vicki all be connected together?

"What's it got to do with you?" she breathed heavily. "it was in your car. *My* car!"

He felt himself buckle inside."Well", he suggested bravely, while his nerves tingled, "it's yours then."

"*Mine?*" she shouted across the table. "That *shows* how much you notice! Do you think I'd wear this trashy colour! I'm not some tart!"

He felt his own blood rising, as he visualised Vicki's beautiful red lips set in her pale, flawless complexion. His anger was being provoked to defend what he adored. She was pointing the open top at him again and now he saw the bright colour inside. He flushed palely through his sallow features.

"We-e-ll", he stammered, controlling himself, "how can you tell just from that?" He was helpless, trapped, but flailing to find a way out.

"Because ... see this?" She leaned forward and stroked a finger across her lips, which were her natural soft light pinkish-beige. "Because I hardly ever wear lipstick, do I?" She pulled back upright again and hissed, "Not that you would know." And then added, icily, "It's that bloody Chinese bitch, isn't it!"

"Chinese?" he continued to parry ineffectually.

"Yes! The one you've been seen with at parties - oh, don't think I don't know! - and even with your arms round her in the street!"

"Oh, her", Gainsborough rallied, defensively, "the one from the Embassy..."

"Don't you 'Embassy' me! She's a foreign tart who's picked you up I don't know what for - God! You're lucky you've got *me*, let alone some young model who must think you're worth something! Well, I'd soon tell her!"   Emily's cheeks were heating to a burning red and Gainsborough could see that tears were welling into her eyes. "And in *my* car!" she berated him furiously. "And under the *driver's* seat. You actually let her drive my car! How could you! How could you!" Her words were becoming punctuated with sobs and she sank into the chair at the end of the table, her head bowed. He was feeling helpless, hopeless, desolate but something in him was chal-lenged, too.

"I can't help it!" he blurted out. "I can't help it if someone just turns up when I don't feel close to anyone -"

"*Close?*" She looked up, eyes flaring at him.

"Yes!" He was heating now, too. "When have you even touched me?" He knew it was a weak argument. He knew the withering of affection had to be a two-sided thing but now he was aware of the contrast, a comparison he had avoided by the simple expedient of going to work, staying out late, spending all the available moments with Vicki, as few as possible with Emily. Now, he confronted it. Across the table was the empty tunnel of a drained relationship; outside this house was the brilliant light of reciprocal love. "You should hardly be surprised!" He barked it across the table and knew it was an admission as well as an accusation. The confrontation he had shied away from was all at once a raw lesion.

"Well, no I'm not surprised!" She rose from the chair but she was supporting herself on the table as she faced him, tears now staining her hot cheeks, eyes pink-rimmed and watery. "I've known for months! Your petty excuses - 'working late'! - perfume on your shirts! You think I'm *stupid*? But now..." she broke into sobs again. "but now - *this* Now you mock me with it. And even - *even*! - let her drive my car! Well, you can go. GO!" She suddenly, violently, hurled the lipstick at him, striking him on the cheek. "GO! ...and don't come back ...until ..." She broke down into sobs again.

"Until?" He felt hot but he spoke calmly, a kind of fateful calm.

"Until!..." She stared directly at him again through tears and red heat. "*Ever!*" She shouted and reached to the centre of the table, grabbing and hurling the vase of flowers at him. He jerked violently to one side to avoid it, as it crashed to smithereens against the wall behind, stalks, water and delicate petals showering to the floor. "EVER!" she repeated. *"Ever... Ever ..."* She had collapsed, sobbing, onto the chair, head buried in her arms on the table and continued to sob and groan into them without looking up: "Go! .. Go! ...Go! ...Go!... Never come back ...Go! ...Go! ...."

He felt emptied. Something had slipped away, something he could not retrieve. It was something he had tried to cling on to, for both their sakes, perhaps hypocritically, but now it had gone. He turned and walked firmly, but shaken, out of the house.

Leaving

"Uh-oh."

Gabriel sat with his chin resting on hands, elbows on knees, gazing ahead.

"Did You see what I see?"

Now *that,* in the Company he kept, was a very silly question.

"Yes", He replied, sounding a trifle weary, "I did see." And He fixed the angel with a look that said, 'What did you think, that I'd missed it? And no allusions to French martyrs, please'.

"Yeh, well", Gabriel saw that look and shuffled uncomfortably. "Just thought I'd mention it."

Gainsborough flung himself into Vicki's arms, the moment she opened the door. He had not intended or expected they would make love. He had only sought her companionship, a solace, stability of fondness in the tempest. But they did. Somehow, she understood the turmoil inside him, that it demanded to be released and they fell to the bed, tearing off each other's clothes, becoming engulfed in passion until she felt his outpouring inside her, and it blending with hers, and they subsided to lie still but gently caressing and holding and softly kissing and murmuring as daylight slowly faded and they were gradually enveloped in the cosseting gloom of the dusk.

Then he quietly told her. But there was a tremble in his voice as he described it, whispering with his face to her cheek, his lips close to her ear. He told her of the card, as they giggled at their recollection of the tune, but he told her of the coincidence, of the missing notes, the letters they represented, of his equations and what they now implied. His words stumbled, his breath panted, she was the first and only person he had told, told the whole extraordinary truth.

She tried to control her reactions and hoped he did not feel her stiffen with her own excitement. She caught her breath, thinking, if this was true, it was beyond the wildest dreams of her mission. Her task only to befriend, entangle, listen, enquire, absorb, so often with nothing of note to report. 'Just having a good time?' she would be chided back home. Bright and educated as she was, she was not sure she could quite take in what he told her. She clung to him, drawing him closer, and he felt the warmth of her love. She was trying to devise an outcome; and then suddenly he was saving her the trouble.

"But how can I do it, Vicki?" he rolled over on his back with a sigh. "How can I work here? They're more or less kicking me out at the labs. I *am* kicked out at home. Even if I just stay here with you -" And he reached out to stroke her torso "how can I find the space, and the time, amid all this - anger!"

"She told you to leave?" Vicki touched his hand as it lay on her stomach.

"Yes, but ..." His voice trailed off. It was not a situation he had seriously foreseen.

"You could come with me." She had turned so her lips, now, were brushing his cheek as she spoke, her moist, warm breath spilling from her. Her delicate fingers traced a path across his stomach. He could feel the beginning of arousal again already.

"Come? Where?" He was mumbling to the ceiling, swimming in her caress.

"You know I have to leave soon?" she whispered.

He started and turned to her.

"Leave? No! When?" He was drawing her to him as though to prevent her going.

"Sshh." She put her lips to his. "I was afraid to mention it because ..because I want us to stay together. But - my work - I have to go back sometime." She could feel his tension, his grip tightening on her waist. She was thinking fast. This was why they employed her: to improvise in altered circumstances. "But now you can come too."

He relaxed slowly and lay back again, staring at the ceiling, now amber-tinted from the street lights. He began to smile.

"Oh, brilliant!" snorted Gabriel. "Don't tell me this is part of the plan!" Knowing very well that it was not.

God remained silent, in deep contemplation. At least, that is what it looked like. He could have been thinking about a completely different planet, for all Gabriel knew. Since God moves in mysterious ways, He can look pretty mysterious, too, without a companion angel having much idea of what He is actually thinking. However, this angel, on this occasion, was fairly sure the Good Lord was not very pleased.

Gainsborough's thoughts were opening on a whole new world. He dared not imagine it could happen.

"With you?" He frowned and smiled at the same time, turning back to hold her. "Where ..." He could not formulate the idea. "How...?"

"You have your passport?"

He murmured, "Of course", and kissed her, lightly.

"How long will the work take?" she asked, wishing to sound concerned, not pragmatic.

"If it succeeds?" he replied. "To actually build it - probably a year or more; maybe six months if I worked like a slave. But I'd need the materials and support. That's the trouble. I'd have got all that here."

"I can arrange that", she said.

"Over there?" He queried.

"Of course", she hugged him. "I am with the Embassy, you know."

"Perfect", remarked an archangel, sardonically, "just perfect."

They hugged and cuddled and giggled and laughed. Deep inside he felt a guilt for Emily but it was too late. Perhaps it had been too late for some time. He salved his conscience with the thought he had hung on, he had tried, he had given their relationship a chance to rekindle. Then he felt Vicki's soft hand slide over his thigh and her lips press to his neck and he realised it had been no contest. She was his, he was hers. It was done. He would go with her. They made love again. And again. Between times, as the night grew late, and as the sun rose in Beijing, she slipped to the other room while he slumbered, and made a long-distance call on her mobile phone. She tried to maintain a professional calm but her voice trembled in an excited whisper. So excited, she almost choked, clasping her fingers to her lips, afraid he might waken and hear.

"You know how there's never a perfect time", grunted the archangel again, "You said."

There was only troubled silence from the Almighty.

"Well, this is definitely it, isn't it? *Never* the perfect time."

"Gabriel", sighed the Good Lord.

"I mean ... weren't we just saying -" as a finger jabbed into a crevice " - how here, *this country,* is where it should be 'discovered', where it might be shared, not flouted?"

The Lord could only assent in grave silence.

"But *now* look where it's going to end up", ended the angel, with a sullen flick into the void ahead.

The Almighty said nothing, knowing only that, whilst a chance act of self-determination, might ultimately - perhaps by a petal cast into the wind at an unpreordained point - migrate a whole world's destiny from one preordained path to another, it could still be influenced for the good. They - He and his archangel - continued to have a part to play.

"Is it really worth continuing?" grumbled the angel who, frankly, could easily discover many better things to do with his time.

"We must", sighed the Lord. "For now, we must."

PARADIGM : WARNINGS

The sky was split by skeins of silk, like mourning veils, splicing the haze of a rabid sun. Above, the orb lurked sourly behind its uncomely shroud, yet beat with the heat of fire upon their rock. She stood, her feet glowing ruddy brown in the eerie light, which spilled a lurid sheen upon the ground. Her infant lay cradled to her breast, held soft and tight, sleeping and fed, while he looked upon them both in pride.

"The lamb we ate", she said, "tasted ... funny."

"Funny?" he asked, with an uncertain frown.

"Not ... funny", she confessed, "but not ... right."

The sea heaved as though it were not well, not right, too, she mulled, as she reached for his hand and the waves of dark grey, streaked with red from the sky, chopped and lapped at their shore.

"It seemed to me to taste .. good", he said, knowing how he took the failing lamb, abandoned in the clearing by the forest, by a ewe which would otherwise have clung as a mother will. "The herbs you cooked it in were fine, a fine meal for us." And he grasped her hand in love and knowing how well she cared for him and their child.

"I picked more", she said, "to make it taste ... right."

He turned to kiss her so she laid their child on its bed of leaves before he gently pulled her with him to the ground, the while kissing her slowly and yet more low so his kisses reached her soft belly with its new lines and further beyond. His words came as a purr to her.

"It tastes ... right ... to me here", and she heard the desire in his voice and felt his hot lips and tongue where she had, in her manner, used the lamb's grease for their greater pleasure. Her thighs quivered as she felt his tongue lick smoothly at the grease and felt his love for her.

"Then so it is good?" There was a doubt in her voice, though it quivered, too, with his passion, and with her own.

"So, yes, it is good my love", he breathed into her loins, for he wished to forget the lamb and he, the hunter, had taken it for their food and for her milk. And he drew her body to his, stroking her back with his strong lover's hands. His fingers passed over her silky smooth skin and felt the cluster of small pimples which he was certain he had not felt before but did not remark much now, as his passion took them both and the dark waves lapped at the edge of their rock, leaving their new trail of simmering foam to linger above the tide.

Part Seven

TIME

TIME

July

July. Hot and sultry in New York, Chicago, Dallas, Vegas, LA, Shanghai and Beijing. In London, it was the usual bit of this, bit of that. Wimbledon, earlier in the month, had been alternately plagued and blessed, by wet days and strawberry scorchers. Isabella had secured tickets months before on the internet and made a couple of visits with Ruth in the second week, one damp and miserable, one a blazing hot day. As ever, she did not even attempt to persuade Paul to accompany her. He held no interest in any sport these days and spent more time than ever at the showroom, dreaming up gimmicks and slogans. Sales were slow. The unexplained restoration of cars to normal working order, after a week of chaos in the capital (six days, as some pedants insisted), had not altered the fact that the UK economy was still struggling to fend off recession, along with all the world economies sinking into the mire caused by America's perverse change of pace. 'Swamp', 'disastrous' and other labels were routinely employed by media, politicians and public alike, to Bella's frustration and increasing despair. This was the new American dream - their own fantastic dream - which no-one else seemed prepared to accept or follow.

She would have liked Elroy's company at Wimbledon. A golfer, maybe, but he would have revelled in the days of tennis. However, he had flown back to Mariana as soon as GCHQ accepted his assurance there was nothing more he could do. Bella was struck by his account of that physics guy in the lab, his shout of - triumph, it appeared to Elroy - and the wild look in his eyes. But in a year of extraordinary experiences perhaps a slightly eccentric British scientist having a 'Eureka' moment was not going to occupy a place very high up the scale of significance.

"It was the birthday card that was weird", recounted Elroy, "according to how he described it."

Anyway, the guy had gone, too, apparently. Just disappeared. No-one knew where; except that his Chinese girlfriend - 'allegedly'had vacated her apartment. This was all a mixture of hearsay, gossip and newspaper tittle tattle. Nobody really seemed much interested. One bitchy remark from a colleague, quoted in the Daily Telegraph, suggested he may have just given up and gone because 'he couldn't face his best years were behind him." If it had not been for the minor scandal of the Chinese Embassy girlfriend, itself diluted by blank refusal to comment on the part of her employers, the story might not even have made the depths of the inside pages where it was easily missed, anyway.

Paul sagged into the sofa one evening, grunting thank God he had no more Chinese cars for a while. He had stopped further orders until well after Christmas because of the sluggish market.

"Did they complain?" Bella asked, meaning the Chinese and feeling she should contribute with a response to prevent the hesitant warmth in their relationship from sliding back down the thermometer to 'chill'.

"No." Paul admitted he was surprised; the agent had taken it very politely, almost as though he was about to suggest the same thing himself. Paul had been intrigued to see a police car outside the kebab shop one day, explained later in the local newspaper, in an excited headline, 'Kebab Drugs Raid!' However, nothing had been found, to the disappointment of some bohemian locals who had briefly entertained the notion they had maybe indulged in something more stimulating than doner meat or griddled lamb.

Asif, serenely innocent to the officers of the law and the outside world in general, had sent word to the boys to stay away and not return for many months. He recruited some more assistants, from within the family circle, and continued to feel a strange awakening inside himself. Try though he might, he could not recall in detail the events of that dangerous night. He remembered the violent Chinese intruders, he recollected the presence of the Spaniards, along with Mohammed and Abdul. He knew he had spoken to all of them, in turn perhaps, he was not sure, and they had all departed, whether because of what he had said, or of their own volition, he did not know. He thought he recalled urging the boys to leave for their own safety but the words he used did not spring to mind, as if they had not been his own.

And now he felt unsettled within himself. Moreover he had involuntarily stepped into a travel agents along the short parade of nondescript shopfronts further down the street and come away with a couple of brochures for Spain. He thrilled with a whiff of anticipation as he thumbed absentmindedly through them at home. He had no idea why. He had no intention of taking a holiday in Spain, or indeed anywhere.

"You did leave something behind?" remarked God, feigning the air of a merely passing interest, not wishing to imply the remotest possibility that a not altogether predictable angel might overlook anything.

"Mm", mumbled Gabriel in a manner which might mean 'Yes' or might mean he had just extracted an object or particle from a place in which it had hitherto been inextricably lodged. As Gabriel had not actually completely occupied a living being before, not in all the visitations to all those multifarious worlds, this having been a uniquely urgent, even imperative act to preserve one who might be another vital instrument of the plan, he could not draw upon previous experience. He did not feel as though any part of him was missing. On the other hand, with the capability of one who could be in more than one place at once, he sensed that a small, inspirational element of himself was successfully, and simultaneously, in *locus operandis*, elsewhere.

"Mm", murmured God, "Let's hope so."

Gabriel looked up, seeing an expression of concern rather than doubt, then shrugged and got back to the matter in hand.

Interval

And in the six months that followed, these things came to pass (which is a suitably biblical way of putting it, isn't it?).

The signals and the whole 'uranium' issue went cold. Until his attention was diverted by the episode with Gainsborough in his lab, Elroy had reacted with genuine alarm to Martin Timmis's signals report. He knew immediately. He had told himself the missing ingredient would probably be plutonium. He alerted Timmis. Timmis got straight onto Customs. Customs - Gordon, Derek and all the other teams - went to 'Red'. Then there was a third signal Timmis intercepted. With Elroy's help and a couple of encrypted email exchanges, he translated it as a 'halt'. They both wondered if their own intercepts had been detected. Anyway, it all went quiet. The 'triangle' was dead.

"Autos For Africa!" ranted Max Drummond. "What is the fucking woman *on!*" But he could not ignore the figures. Sales were moving back up - not to their previous levels but no longer on the floor - as soon as people understood that, for whatever undiagnosed reason, battery-and-petrol-driven, dual-power cars had so far been unknown to 'fail'. And President Twigg's 'Autos For Africa' slogan tapped into the American conscience: their new role as leaders along the pathway to Save The World. It was all fitting together in a perfect circle: people got their 'wheels' back - insofar as they wanted them - and at the same time were contributing to the revival and modernising of a whole continent.

Funny thing was - and this was the triumph for Elroy, Olivia, Walt, and Bella in touch with them from across the pond - folks did not revert to using cars like they used to. They still shared. They still walked when they could. They stuck with the new life instead of going back to the old. There were more cars parked in garages and driveways than ever there were before. It helped with the unusually harsh winter: the habit, now, of spending more time in each other's homes, each other's cars, each other's lives, kept down energy consumption across the board. They watched news programmes together, which told them of the troop withdrawals around the globe - our boys coming home! - and of a recorded decline in international terrorism. They didn't even complain much about the swingeing aircraft fuel tax which President Twigg had slipped through Congress; scarcely the most adventurous travellers, Americans simply flew less and cyber-communicated more.

And Africa. This was big. All that stalling on which countries had their debt cancelled, what conditions were imposed, all that was swept out of the window. "Someone has to make the first move", declared Twigg from the White House steps again, ingeniously suggesting to dumbfounded news crews that nowhere else had even contemplated this before the United States did. With their jaundiced attitude to politicians, the hacks accepted her pronouncements more reluctantly than the public to whom they were disseminating this fairytale. The American people embraced the whole notion with delight and pride, as testified by countless street interviews and media phone-ins.

"Am I on the wrong planet?" growled Joe Kirk, scratching his grey-stubbled chin and watching his fingers type sentences he would have shot himself for a mere year ago.

It was only a beginning but the idea of cancelling all debt and quadrupling aid at last provided all fifty-four African nations with some real and independent 'start-up' spending power, just as significantly for those who were already making limited progress as those who began from a baseline of abject desperation. The only 'hedging' was to make pretty damn sure the money did not simply line the pockets of African politicians as it had before. It took a bit of arm-twisting to get the right guarantees and the necessary monitoring but the carrot of international prestige (plus a legitimate share of the spoils) and the stick of punitive sanctions was beginning to do the trick.

The other ingredient was American manufacturing industry. Deprived of the bottomless pit of home consumption, which it had previously enjoyed, the Twigg plan of incentives, subsidies and tax breaks encouraged factory-constructors, equipment manufacturers, road-builders - you name it, they were there - to literally take their trade into that vast, impoverished, underdeveloped continent instead. A continent which had hitherto been no more than a camping ground for a few multinationals out for a fast buck was now becoming America's new marketplace. And of course, thanks to the campaigns of a motley mix of politicians and pop stars in recent years and decades, Africa was already 'on the agenda'. It just needed something, someone to plunge right in. That something was the United States. That someone was President Victoria Twigg. Streetchild of poverty, wanton lover, twenty-something orphan, now only just forty-something loner in a crazy, mixed-up world, President Victoria Twigg.

Suddenly Africa was acquiring roads. Why? You sell eco-friendly battery-driven cars to Africa at knockdown prices, it has to have roads, doesn't it? Who builds the roads? Why, sure, American construction firms who have just suffered best part of a year of recession. (Although nobody ever dared use that word! Not when the President was looking, anyway; she might conquer with her thighs but she could kill with a look). Who buys the cars to drive on the roads? Why, sure, Africans: Goans, Congolese, Angolans, and the rest, who now have real jobs. Doing what? Why, sure, building roads, of course!

And so it went on: schools, hospitals, houses, more factories. One whole continent - well, half of it: the United States - was starting to earn its keep by dragging another whole continent - Africa - into the modern industrial world. The folks back in the United States, it preserved their jobs, too, just when things had been getting a bit tight. Now they were making factory machines for Africa, cars for Africa, cranes for Africa and then, of course, washing machines, vacuum cleaners, computers, clothes, hair-dryers - oh, how long is the list of contemporary needs! - for the people of Africa. The final triumph was to match this surge in industrial activity with the new order of America's dramatic transfer to eco-friendly, self-sustaining power-generation. A transfer which would take decades to complete but was now demonstrably under way.

Not only that: in the new factories, the people of African nations were beginning to make some of those things for themselves, too; and driving to work on new roads in new cars. It was a partnership. On an intercontinental scale. It was only a beginning. In six months, this was the vision for the future rather than the reality of now but progress was rapid, achievement was astounding. Everyone was a winner so everyone - in both continents - strove hard to win. The vision still perceived a beautiful land, from ocean to ocean, with jungle and mountain, shimmering prairie and menacing desert, but linked by ribbons of modernity to the twenty-first century. The vision saw disease being reduced, life expectancy increased, famine eliminated, poverty ameliorated, warfare and strife replaced by comforts and a slow but steady crawl towards relative prosperity.

"I can see an Africa which will take its place beside Europe, Asia and America", was the proud declaration of the Prime

Minister of Mozambique. And "the poor shall at last inherit their own earth", echoed the Anglican Archbishop of South Africa.

Gabriel smiled and admired himself for having selected the 'avarice' card to flip the whole deck. God pretended He had not read the angel's thoughts and said nothing.

The Mozambique Prime Minister, as it happened, chose a bad analogy. Resentment at America's unilateral decision to slow down the ocean-going tanker of world trade was driving the nations of Europe and Asia closer together, determined to discard their dependence on the vagaries of an American economy incited by the wild ramblings of its maverick leader. India began to throw off a generation of suspicion and enmity to hold hands with China on one side and Pakistan on the other. All three established comprehensive trading deals with Russia, Japan, Korea, Thailand, Malaysia, Singapore and the oil states of the Middle East. Australia and New Zealand, already aligned through geographical proximity to the southern Asian countries, were drawn in. The steady rise in industrial, transport and domestic pollution was monitored but nobody took much notice in these competitive conditions. There was but one unifying thought: just because America got there first and has it all, does not mean it can decide when everyone else has to sacrifice the opportunity of catching up. It's our turn. It's our turn, President Victoria - supercilious- Twigg, it's our turn.

Initially, the UK and the rest of Europe had no choice but to struggle to accommodate shrinking economic activity, dragged below the waves of recession by the great American slow-down. But their inclination was to fight back. No more 'seize-up' phenomena occurred to provoke their ire but neither was there any popular 'sharing'. No new life culture was emerging. Among the nations of the West - and the old east of Europe - separated by the Atlantic from the United States, there remained resentment, with incipient and not infrequent overt violence. Governments had to invoke authoritarian powers to exert control. Whether it was they had no 'Twigg', or insufficient goodwill, or no true God - or no abiding belief in One - the Europeans sought not to embrace but to resist the 'new order' from the New World.

Their answer was Asia. Links already forged in recent decades, through a mix of trade and politics, assisted by the

mingling of cultures from a century of migrations, were doubled
and strengthened. The bonds with America, fashioned by treaties through wars hot and cold, and by decaying ties of ancestry
and affection, were being loosened. The urge was to protect a
lifestyle, not be taught how to live.

While in Another Dimension, there was troubled concern. An
extraordinary 'invention', which would launch science forward
by hundreds of years, had - by an unpreordained dislocation -
been transposed from a declining old democracy, where it
might possibly have been developed for global interests, to one
of the contemporary seats of international rivalry, jealousy and
competition. And it would be anyone's guess - including God's -
about the outcome. But it was, as Heaven's two occupants
might have been observing, too late now.

"That's what comes of nudging, eh?" Gabriel felt emboldened
to remark, sensing more unwelcome visitational excursions
lying in wait.

"Mm..." The Lord acquiesced in a tired sort of way, not that
the Lord God Almighty is susceptible to fatigue in the manner
experienced by any of His myriad flocks. A trifle worn He
nevertheless felt.

"Well don't say I didn't say", groused the angel into his knees
and winced at the sudden ferocity of his own scouring. "Ouch."

Outwardly, the Lord remained serene and impassive, although inside he did squirm just a little; but that may have been
prompted less by the company He kept than His ability to see the
future.

Part Eight

CAR

CAR

Work

"Is it not yet finished?!"

The words were hissed angrily in Cantonese at the little dour man Gainsborough had come to recognise as 'Mr Teng'. The speaker was another dapper Chinese of similar appearance and age, if slightly heavier, also in smart dark suit, white shirt and dark tie, but with a thin scar running partway down one cheek. The two men were passing close by, catching a glance across to where Gainsborough worked.

"You said six months!" Teng's companion hissed again, though this time it was mere Chinese garble to Gainsborough.

He had managed to pick up barely more than a few words and phrases in this difficult tongue but, 'finish', and derivations of the word, had become familiar, particularly lately, in guarded conversations around him. He had asked Vicki to translate it.

Okay he had estimated six months and now it was creeping over seven. But what was the problem? This was science, not painting by numbers.

"Good-day, Mr Hill." The man Teng paused and looked towards him with a little deferential nod. Obsequious, thought Gainsborough. "The work is almost complete?"

"Shouldn't be long now", returned Gainsborough with a polite, if brief, smile, raising his head from his polished test bench of microchips and circuitry beside the Manchu Met.

The larger man gave a peremptory nod and turned so that he and Teng proceeded on their way along the factory floor.

Things had not turned out entirely as Gainsborough might have hoped. Initially he was treated like a visiting head of state. The moment the plane touched down he and Vicki were greeted by Government officials, warm smiles, enthusiastic handshakes. They were whisked off to a VIP reception, complete with ministers of the Interior and Industrial Technology. There was traditional Chinese entertainment of music and dance - entrancing mannequins with fans and the daintiest of feet - and the most exotic Chinese banquet he could ever have imagined. He was treated to so many deferential bobs and bows he thought his head would fall off nodding in response. In several days that followed there were tours of historic Beijing, a trip to the Shanghai metropolis and an excursion to the marvel of the Chinese Wall. All this in the company of Party officials, Government people, tidy men and women of considerable authority, who accorded him knowing smiles with their discreet remarks.

"Your work ... We are most privileged."

"You are helping China to change the world."

"To regain its rightful place", added another as they surveyed the breathtaking vista of the ancient country from atop the astonishing Wall.

Gainsborough did not believe they had all been told the details, not in the light of the utmost secrecy to which he himself had been sworn. But it was clear they had been informed he had brought with him a scientific breakthrough which would set their country apart.

"For the greater good", he was assured by more than one over-deferential official, as if anxious he might doubt their motives.

They need not have worried. He was fresh from the turmoil of his immediate past and was of a mind to agree with them.

"Look how the United States is trying to drag down the world economies for some foolhardy and selfish cause!" he heard his Chinese hosts declaring.

"See how the nations of Europe have fallen into disorder and disarray as they struggle with American-imposed recession!"

He heard himself agreeing, with increasing enthusiasm, that the mish-mash of disparate societies of the West rendered both the Old World of Europe and the New World of America unreliable repositories for the future safekeeping of mankind.

"Your people are protesting, too", he did observe once.

"Yes! Precisely, Mr Hill!" came the reply. "How can we expect them to bow down uncomplainingly to the American will? We who are only now beginning to enjoy the fruits of modern economic development? Why should we slow down?"

"Share our cars?" someone laughed at his side.

"Walk to work?" another would chortle in scorn, "then stay home at night to watch our neighbour's TV?"

"But we do accept", a clearly senior Party man acknowledged, "that if we can develop without further damaging our own planet - our only home - it will be to the advantage of us all."

"The whole world", added a professorial figure listening-in.

"See. Maybe it'll be okay", Gabriel grunted, only part of his attention focused on the scene below, the rest absorbed in matter closer to hand. "Even if You didn't exactly plan it that way."

The Good Lord maintained a noncommittal silence.

"Quite, quite", conceded the Party man, a little brusquely, Gainsborough considered, "and it will give us the power -" the man's voice appeared to swell with a tremor - "to do so."

"Power?" queried Gainsborough.

"Hhm", the Party man emitted a small cough, "the *ability*" - he was selecting his word carefully - "to lead the way."

"Of course", Gainsborough smiled hesitantly.

"So that is why we so welcome your decision to work with us instead of with the West, sharing your genius with us."

He had occasionally wondered how much of it was truly his own decision.

He was delighted with the technical facility they provided. Grateful for their wholehearted support. No curmudgeonly scepticism, no mockery, no snide remarks. He was given full rein and all he needed. It was his dream come true, while he ceaselessly marvelled at the formula which he, incredibly, had created. No other scientist in the world could have envisaged it; nor, indeed, it troubled him to admit to himself, could he.

He had expected it all to be fitted into a smart, ultramodern lab. On reflection, the car factory was probably a sensible decision. They wanted him to develop the prototype in a contemporary passenger vehicle; custom-designed carriers could follow later. He had no practical objection: his only real aim was to complete the invention. It was just an odd working environment. The hum of the factory around him was only partially shielded by the open partition separating it from his improvised lab. Still, as they said, it avoided having to transport a car to him and perhaps knock down half a lab wall somewhere else in the city to get it inside.

He could not fault the construction of the test bench, nor the provision of electronics equipment; and if he needed anything that was missing, he only had to mention it and he received it within the hour, of the highest technical quality he had ever seen. This was China, he mused to himself. Eat your heart out, England.

They left him pretty much to himself, except for these increasingly anxious visits by either Teng alone or with a humourless cohort. On its own, this would not have been loneliness. God knew! He had craved this degree of research solitude for years. But he was seeing less and less of Vicki, too. If he thought about it, which he did not like to much, she really had not spent a great deal of time with him since they arrived. Not since that whirlwind week of official welcome. Then it had been as much a series of smiles across crowded rooms as anything more intimate.

He had imagined them sharing a plush apartment after the luxury of those five-star hotel rooms that first week. The apartment they were taken to was clean enough, well-equipped, modern, but scarcely upmarket. More like a holiday flat on the Med, really. Plastic, chrome, cheap polished wood and not particularly comfortable chairs and bed. Vicki explained it wasn't actually hers.

"I would have made it a home for us, my darling", she smiled sympathetically.

It was just a bit grey and forlorn, he considered. Which was precisely how he had come to feel at times, and more frequently as the months drew on.

Quite soon after the first week, she began to disappear for days at a time.

"I'm so sorry, my darling", she breathed into his ear, as she stroked his cheek with a delicate finger, "I wish I could just stay with you but they know you are looked after at your work and they expect me to do mine." He felt a part of him shrink away as she slipped through the door. Just for a normal working day, initially; then two or three, then a week, then a week and a few days more.

"They send me around the country, my darling", she whispered as they lay in bed one night in the second month. "The Government is a tough employer, you know."

They made love. Oh God, they made love. Each time she returned, he kept her in bed and wrapped in his body as long as he could. Then she was just as she had been in London. She joined his excitement at the work. She asked him to explain the separate stages of development, the landmarks and milestones week by week. He was struck how concerned she was that he should reach his earliest target of six months - by 'working like a slave', he recalled his own phrase - rather than take a year. "The sooner you finish, the sooner we can truly be together, my darling", she soothed him. Then she teased him a little, saying she would schedule her returns for the completion of each stage to finish in six months.

In her absence, and his own solitude, it was a goad to drive him on. He was working all the extra hours necessary so that he could phone her and say he was ready, he had completed the next phase. Miraculously, she would reappear that same evening. Sometimes she phoned unexpectedly first, anxious to see him, anxious that he should have reached the next goal. More than once he had to reluctantly explain he still had another day to go. But she could return anyway! No, she declared she must not distract him. Regrettably she would wait another day. Regrettably! Desperately! He drove himself on.

Six months! Where had he plucked that wild estimate from! It should have been a year. Or even two. Yet she had seized upon his rash optimism, despite a dogged reappraisal of the task once they had arrived. She had frowned, then smiled, scolded then encouraged. She had listened to the impossible schedule he described and she had taken its targets for the times when she would return. She was helping him, she said, complete his task so they could once again lead their lives together. He had protested in love that he could work while she was present but she would reach a hand down to hold him while she dissolved her lips into his and he would sink in a daze as she smiled and told him he could not. He could not work while she was there. She wanted him to herself, their lives together completely.

In the meantime she would return just at these intervals. His reward was her return. She did not say as much but it was the truth. He could have lied. He could have told her he had completed the next stage just to see her and feel her but he could not. He had to be loyal to her honour. So, working all hours to be with her, by stages and so briefly, by endeavour and lust, it was now almost complete.

Convoy

"Jesus Christ!"

"What the fuck!"

"*Down*!"

The shouts were drowned to soundless mime as the MiG jets roared and screamed so low the officers on the bridge felt like they were taking a direct hit in the instant before the four aircraft soared high into the sky above the deep blue ocean, wheeling on wing tips against the sun for a second dive.

"What the flying fuck ..!"

The first officer scrambled upright, grabbing his cap where it had fallen on the bridge deck. All six uniformed men had ducked involuntarily at the deafening violence of the threatened assault, a couple of them tripping and sprawling at the shock. The warplanes had come from nowhere, approaching the huge oil tanker at lightening speed, five seconds from eye contact, two from identifiable shape and direction, to impact. Or so close to impact it felt like a 'hairbreadth' away.

"What the goddam fools playing at!"

The third officer grasped the wheel, glancing at an instrument panel to check their computerised course was still true.

"Chinese!" cursed the captain, straightening his jacket with a grimace and peering out to the rest of the convoy. "Going for *Hoover* now", he muttered, grimly, as the flashing silver formation swooped a mile high and a mile distant, plunging to 'buzz' their sister ship, *Hoover*, to starboard.. He turned to look past the gleaming white, wood and chrome bridge fittings and instruments to see *Ford* slung low just inside the port horizon.

Grant, Canyon and *Coyote* were aft, in a parallel line, half a mile of safety between each. The officers on the *MV Bush* watched as the close formation of four jets swooped away from *Hoover*, overhead to *Ford*, then out of sight, presumably to give a fright to the rest of the flotilla behind.

"Chinese?" queried the first officer.

"Yup", affirmed the captain, still peering at the sky for a further sight of the intruders. The aircraft underbellies had been so close, their insignia and markings had been clearly visible, even in that instantaneous pass. "Slitty little yips."

The communications bell rang on the bridge, answered by the second officer, who was one who had ended up all legs and arms on the deck and was still dusting himself down. There was an urgent request from below to know what the muffled, if loud, noise had been. The second officer explained, taking pains not to paint an alarmist picture to be conveyed to the skeleton crew at their dispersed stations about the vessel. The tanker more or less ran itself but they still did not want crew rushing up on deck in unwarranted panic.

The captain had already received coded word from base that Beijing was threatening to intervene on the deal. Earlier today, as they passed out of the Indian Ocean through the Indonesian Straits, a Chinese Navy patrol corvette had intercepted within a couple of hundred metres, flashing a demand that he respond to a Beijing Government message he had ignored that morning. The message had warned him to change course. His contract, with a fat bonus for keeping to schedule, was to get to the world's largest harbour, Singapore. A former Navy man himself, he wasn't about to turn tail all the way back to the Gulf. No way was he going to be intimidated.

"Anyways, what can they do?" He had barked the question to the contact at base, after the patrol boat encounter.

"Nothing", came the firm reply. "All show. Ignore them. Carry on."

Goddamn, he thought to himself now, bearing north towards Singapore harbour, he had not expected warplanes.

Six supertankers. All brimful of oil from that new Kuwait terminal. This was a private deal, so he had been informed. Now it was looking as though the Chinese Government might show scant regard for privacy.

Deep inside 'Apex Insurance, NY', Slick Hair and the LOTUS chairman were fuming. The deal was neat. Millions of barrels of oil they couldn't trade in the States. Get the tankers to Singapore, change flags, get accredited Chinese import certification (money talks), acquire Asian crews and sail on to Shanghai, where they were clamouring for the black gold. The world's fastest growing economy, soon to be the largest, and no oil of its own. What a convenient irony!

"Fucking mad Chinks!" snarled Slick Hair.

They both knew that the new Asian trading agreements meant vast Russian oil resources were now being redirected to China; so were much of Iran's, Iraq's - despite the continuing US presence - and Saudi's. Even Libya, for God's sake, supposedly cosying up to the West in return for diplomatic favour, was rumoured to be turning its attention to the solidifying Asian block. Nevertheless, the LOTUS calculation was that any oil, from anywhere, especially arriving under a neutral flag of convenience, would be welcomed with a blind eye by China, ignoring its blacklisting of USA trade. The two men conferring in the boardroom at the end of a steel corridor in the bowels of 'Apex' ordered a 'continue' message to the convoy.

Three hours later, the ships were entering Singapore waters. The *Bush* received a radio message with coded authorisation from the Singapore Government Defence Department. Words to the effect: 'Turn back. Do not enter Singapore waters, do not approach the harbour'.

Communications sped between the ship and base. LOTUS response was to proceed as ordered: "They can't stop you, it's a private contract." The captain looked up at his mast: the Stars and Stripes had already been replaced by the neutral flag. All according to plan.

Half an hour later, a Singapore Navy patrol boat skimmed a hundred metres to fore. A voice barked through a loudhailer, demanding to board the *Bush*. There was a nervous query to base from the captain. "Proceed", came the response. 'Permission to board declined' was flashed to the patrol boat.

The request and reply were repeated, while the Singapore vessel surged and turned ahead, then sped back towards the distant outline of the huge harbour.

Twenty minutes later, there was a deafening scream of jet engines and dark shapes appeared overhead. The MiGs were back. This time there followed radioed warnings to halt and reverse course. The jets continued to wheel and buzz all around the six tankers, angry gnats circling their quarry. Tense officers stood stiffly on all six bridge decks, wincing each time the planes screeched down upon them. "Continue", came the terse instruction from New York, "this is not war, This is private."

Suddenly, there was a sharp rap and crackle along the flat cargo deck of the *Bush*, a series of bright sparks tracing a line towards the bow.

"Jesus Christ!" exclaimed the third officer, "they're shooting!"

The MiG was wheeling away into the sky ahead, following the same line as the sparks from machine gun bullets. The captain ignored radio and was on the phone to LOTUS in an instant.

"Jesus fuck!" breathed Slick Hair. "They can't do this!"

"They just did!" barked the captain, white knuckles clenching his phone.

It was clear. Beijing was prepared to risk a response from Washington, gambling on their right to refuse entry to their allies' waters to avoid anything other than a war of words.

"They're not going to shoot you out of the water, for God's sake!" declared Slick Hair down the phone.

"Maybe not, maybe not!", shouted the captain, "but they can mess up our decks, our radar, even our propellors ... anything ... make our lives goddamned hell! And we'll still not get entry."

He ordered all six tankers to stop full ahead, which would take them each through another three miles of water anyway, while he waited.

The LOTUS chairman frowned, grimaced, cursed under his breath.

"We can't let the White House get involved", he stated bluntly.

Slick Hair matched his frowns, in silence.

"Any confrontation, they might ask questions." The chairman was thinking aloud.

"Where the oil come from?" Slick Hair posed the likely question.

The chairman nodded, grunting.

"Safe, isn't it?" asked Slick Hair. "Can't trace it ... Fitzgibbon-"

"You think he knows everything?" The chairman looked up, sharply.

"He done a good job..." began his colleague, doubtfully.

"Yeh? The formula? No help there."

Elroy Fitzgibbon had brilliantly set up a complete decoy communications network to disguise the diverted oil from Iraq via Kuwait but, Slick Hair conceded to himself, appeared to have genuinely no idea about the formula in the interrogation room, whatever 'persuasion' he might have been subjected to, had circumstances allowed. He was not infallible.

"Sure", he admitted.

"So he could guarantee no-one - but *no-one* - will suss the oil?" The chairman fixed Slick Hair with a penetrating stare.

Slick Hair lowered his eyes. The consequences of such a discovery could not be contemplated. Too many people had been kept out of the loop - right up to the President - for any wriggling to get them off a very big, sharp hook. Enron would seem like a tiddler caught in a kid's net.

"Singapore's letting the Chinks in", muttered the chairman. It was becoming transparent. The newly-tightened links between all the Asian states included treaties of co-operation that submerged the guarded formalities of recent decades. More than half Singapore's population was of Chinese heritage anyway, notwithstanding the country's image as the 'western jewel of the east'. Now, today, Singapore was confirming that bond by allowing Chinese warplanes to buzz US merchant tankers and dictate - or, rather, refuse - their passage any further into Eastern waters, including its own commercial harbour.

"They're not going to sink them!" protested Slick Hair,

"Like the captain said", grunted the chairman, "they don't have to. Mess the ships about a bit. Create an international incident. And they don't even know about *us*. *Yet!* " He spat the last word into the empty air of the room.

"Or do they?" Slick Hair followed the chairman's line. Suppose Fitzgibbon's system's weren't foolproof. Suppose someone, whether US, Iraqi or even Chinese, was already having suspicions, making calculations about the origins off all this oil. This was an incident to steer well clear of. "So?" he added.

"The alternative", brooded the chairman into clasped hands, elbows on the polished table. It was more complicated than a quick offload at Shanghai but, hell, longterm it could be an infinite cash mountain.

"Africa", affirmed Slick Hair, a glint now in his eye.

"Africa", nodded the chairman, a knowing smile dispelling his grim expression. "Turn the goddamned ships around." He rose from the table. "Where is Fitzgibbon, anyway?"

"Here. New York. Doing his regular job", responded Slick Hair.

"We need him", stated the chairman, bluntly. "in Africa." He stooped to pick up his black attaché case from the floor and straightened to look at his colleague. "Get him."

Stats

"Walt. Have you seen this?" Olivia was calling from the study, where she was scrolling through a page of news online. Walt was busy in the kitchen pouring a couple of Sunday morning coffees.

"It's amazing", she called again.

"What?" He emerged through the door, bearing the mugs.

"These figures." She looked up from the screen and smilingly accepted her coffee. "Do you think El knows about them?" She took a hot sip. "Ooh, thanks."

"Dunno", replied Walt, looking over her shoulder, "been trying him on the phone. Cell's on voicemail."

"The house?" she asked.

"No reply there, either."

"Probably at Mariana's ma", suggested Olivia, looking back to the screen.

"Yeh, guess", agreed Walt, mug to lips and looking at the computer screen. "What is it?"

"See - the latest statistics. Amazing." She clicked back to the top and scrolled down again, reading them out as he watched.

Oil Consumption	*Down*	*42%*
Electricity Consumption	*Down*	*31%*
Coal Extraction	*Down*	*34%*
Air Pollution (carbon dioxide)	*Down*	*23%*
Average Ozone Depletion	*Reduced*	*16%*
Aircraft Passengers	*Down*	*31%*
People Below Poverty Line	*Reduced*	*2 million*
Poverty Reduction in 5 Years	*Projected*	*10 million*
Major City Traffic Jams	*Reduced*	*90%*
SUV sales	*Reduced*	*88%*
Dual Power Battery Car Sales	*Increased*	*343%*
Military Demob Projection Combined Forces		*87,000*
USAF Fleet Reduction	*Projected*	*36%*
US Navy Fleet Reduction	*Projected*	*31%*
Anti-US Terrorist Activity	*Reduced*	*24%*
US National Recorded Crime	*Reduced*	*17.5%*

"How about that*!*" she declared with a grin, leaning back, hands clasped behind her head.

"Wow!" was all Walt could exclaim and reached to the keyboard, scrolling up to take a second look.

Elsewhere, locally, Jim and Jilly Hogan were seen *walking* to church, meeting all six Brents also on foot and *even* the aged Williams spinsters, complete with almost equally aged walking sticks. All cheerfully greeting each other in the warm Spring sunshine. They all hailed Pastor Donahoe, also devoid of gas-guzzling automobile.

"Thought you'da had one o' them newfangled battery cars bi now, Pastor", called out big Bill Brent.

"Jest kinda got used to mi legs agin, Bill", laughed Dirk Donahoe, as they all mounted the church steps together, Jilly putting a hand under a Williams elbow for support.

Someone else remarked how they'd seen that salesman guy giving someone a ride. True, it was Tony Delgardo, even with pretty Suzy Rose in the front seat at his side.

And Los Angeles, to take just one example, had announced a plan to build eighty miles of new sidewalks along its half-empty roadways.

"And not even a pig in sight", muttered Gabriel to himself with a grudging grin, taking an upward glance, just to check.

"The world will see it can be done!" announced President Twigg proudly, from the White House steps. "It is enough to know we all have to share this one small planet. America had been the worst offender. Now we have begun to turn the tide of our own transgressions, others will see they, too, can enjoy a modern society without destroying the very world which sustains it."

"Uh-oh." Gabriel cast an eye upwards, before bending to dig at something deeply embedded somewhere, "just seen one."

God said nothing.

Battery

Hoi Fong was brooding in his - and Cousin Wu's - favourite bamboo chair as he watched the CNN news from America. But it was not capturing his attention. He knew the story off by heart, anyway; as did any reasonably aware and television-viewing Chinese. America was 'saving the planet'. Saving on aircraft fuel, saving on auto gas, saving on domestic and industrial energy, saving on factory emissions, cleaning their air, restoring their ozone (as if you could partition off your own section of ozone layer from everyone else's!), beginning to stabilise the climate. Why wasn't the rest of the world doing the same? Not only that, the United States was developing a new, modern future for the whole continent of Africa, too!

But Hoi and the rest of China knew all that. They also knew that the US had a hundred years' start on them in economic development so it was easy for America to look down from its summit of materialism and decide it was time to descend to a more temperate zone. Did it consider those who were still clambering out of the foothills, yet to savour the full rewards of their endeavours? No, it appeared America did not. Anyhow, China was contributing with its 'green cities' project wasn't it? Eco-friendly urban development?

So, that was largely neutralised by continual commissioning of new coal-fired power stations, pumping (partially-treated) sulphur into the atmosphere. Progress demanded compromise;

but a compromise they could justifiably ignore, it was tetchily remarked in Beijing, when it came to China's own expanding interests in Africa. But Hoi was not going over old ground in his mind, while his eyes stared blankly at the television.

No, he was thinking of the Englishman. And the girl. He understood she worked for both the Government and the Society. He doubted the Englishman was aware of that. On one of her occasional visits to see him, when they behaved like young lovers - ridiculous at his age! - he noticed Teng sidle up to her afterwards and appear to congratulate her, briefly grasping her by the hand, nodding and chuckling in his humourless manner. That was after her *formal* welcome to the factory by the government officer assigned to the Englishman.

And that was another thing: being 'bestowed' with the 'honour' of accommodating a Government research project, including donating one of his own Manchu Mets to the work, much against his inclination but without any choice in the matter. And *then* finding that 'brother' Teng was involved as well, slinking in and out not to see him, Hoi, any longer, but to creep along to the new 'research lab'.

The Society! One end of his factory had become the exclusive preserve of a foreigner who was doing what he liked with a valuable Manchu Met, in cohorts with a Government lackey, Teng of the Society and a girl who seemed to have some attachment to all three. At length, his irritation emboldened him sufficiently to confront Teng on one of the latter's unannounced visits.

"Brother Teng."

"Yes, Brother Hoi?"

"I feel I should be better informed about activities within my own factory."

"Brother Hoi?" The ingratiating smile could have been painted onto his features.

"The Englishman's project. I should know more of what is taking place in my premises. You and your companions, you come and you go -"

"For the esteemed Government of the People, Brother Hoi", Teng interrupted, as to remind Hoi where his loyalties should lie.

"Such secrecy", Hoi mildly protested, though he felt far more insulted than he showed.

"Secrecy, Brother Hoi?"

"For a *navigational device*, Brother Teng? Am I not enough a figure in this industry to be better informed of a new devel-"

Teng cut him off. He was still smiling but his eyes were hard.

"Brother Hoi." Somehow the man's tone managed to be smooth and sharp at the same time. Like a rapier. "If it is our Government's wish to withhold to itself until it is ready to make its own announcement ..." He did not complete his sentence. He did not need to. Hoi knew. Every Chinese citizen knew. Their Government would keep a secret about the colour of the sea, or the shape of a cow, if it chose, and if it could keep the information to itself.

"And the Society?" Hoi queried.

"Ah", Teng blinked, as though his own presence and continued interest in the car project had been completely invisible these last few months. He smiled lightly at Hoi. "It is family, you know. The Society and the Government."

Hoi could have guessed it. Indeed had half done so. Family, Society, Government, the three were inextricably intertwined. Had been for centuries. China would never term it 'corruption'; always 'co-operation'. Through a family link, he did not doubt, both the Government and the Society exercised an interest in this project. Teng's own conceit allowed him to slip his guard and smugly boast that the Society had arranged to take advantage of it first.

This was what was troubling Hoi Fong now. Nobody was telling him anything. The next delivery of Mets to London should be almost ready. Teng kept stalling him, saying they were waiting for the dolls. Hoi knew he could not argue with that, since he was the one pressing to include dolls and dancing girls as before. It was the next thing that bothered him enough to tell Hwee Lo the same evening, a good seven months after the Englishman had arrived and London constantly on the phone enquiring about shipment of the Mets.

He rose to give her a long warm hug as she set the tea down in their lounge. She was secure in his love but knew when its demonstration also reflected a troubled mind. She looked into his eyes, waiting.

"My love", he said, "I do not know what they are up to."

She was aware of his disquiet about the imposition of the research project. She let him continue as they sat side by side on the sofa.

"This evening as I was leaving late - I don't think they realised I was still there - I saw their men carry a large battery, or so it seemed, and place it in the research car."

"So unusual?" she queried, mildly.

"Very large, my love, and in the boot, not the engine space."

"You asked them?"

-302"I questioned Brother Teng." He grimaced as he spoke the name. "He said had he not told me it was to be a battery car."

"Battery car?" she asked, puzzled.

"Dual power, they're called. Petrol and battery-driven. America is making many."

"Ah", she acknowledged.

"But it was clearly very heavy, And the Englishman had already gone home. And they should have asked me!" he suddenly blurted out in anger. "These are *my* cars. I did not request a battery car. My customers do not wish it. I allow them to install their new navigation device - and it is hardly a new idea, my love - but now they meddle with the car itself. Who is making these cars! Is it not *my* factory?"

She wrapped an arm around his neck and pulled herself to him.

"Come and see our Soo Wong, my love. I think she will walk for you soon."

Their child was in her playroom, sitting inside the bamboo playpen, testing the durability of a furry toy, whose life expectancy looked ominously short. Hoi's face spread into a broad smile as he bent to pick her up.

"You going to walk for me, my little Soo?" he grinned, giving her a peck on the cheek and placing her on the rug, kneeling down beside her. The tot lurched onto all fours and made a grab at his jacket lapel. He remained still while she attempted to haul herself upright but her dimply knees were giving way as he caught her under her shoulders and lifted her above his head. Soo Wong chuckled down at her father from under her shock of straight black hair, suspended above his smiling face. Hwee Lo smiled and giggled at them both.

All thoughts of cars, dolls and batteries had been duly banished.

Triangle

Plutonium. It had to be. It could only be that. The wing dipped over Nova Scotia for the plane to turn eastwards across the North Atlantic, allowing Elroy to see the snow-flecked island thirty-seven thousand feet below. Perhaps he was over-reacting but he could not risk emails, texts, file transfer, phone calls, any electronic communication, however encoded or encrypted. He had to work with Timmis in complete confidentiality at GCHQ, just the two of them face to face, on these new signals.

He felt guilty he had not even told Olivia. And Walt. But he no longer knew who was watching, or listening. Any one of them absent from their regular jobs might draw attention from an unwelcome source. Even his own departure might not have passed unnoted. Hence, the precaution of getting Mariana and the children away to relatives in Minneapolis. As far as 'Research Electronics Inc' was concerned, he was taking a couple of days off by himself in the mountains. If Olivia - and Walt, who would surely insist on accompanying her again - made similar excuses for absence to support him, the coincidence would be unlikely to evade anyone with an interest in their whereabouts.

"Martin, I've been thinking this whole thing through."

"Mr Fitzgibbon?" The intense young GCHQ man looked earnestly at Elroy in the private office allocated to them.

"You can call me Elroy, man", grinned the big American, slapping a broad hand on the Englishman's shoulder.

Timmis smiled nervously at his new-found mentor, who was poring over the sheaf of gobbledegook in front of them. This time it had all been emails. Tortuously encrypted. It had been equally tortuous to unravel the encryption but Timmis had done it, only to reveal a parade of jumbled characters which refused to submit to the pattern they had analysed the previous summer. Or, rather, the awed Timmis conceded to himself, which the genius American had cracked more or less single-handedly; the crucial part, anyway.

"It follows a pattern again sir - er, Elroy." He looked expectantly at the American, as though seeking approval. Elroy looked up and smiled in acknowledgement. "But", continued Timmis, "the repetitions still don't make sense."

"Hm", brooded Elroy, "been thinking it through, like I said. Anyways, first off, it's the spaces, not the words here."

"Sir - Elroy?" Timmis could not stop the bashfulness clouding his expression.

Elroy did not glance up this time, except to hand Timmis the top couple of sheets.

"The spaces between the characters which make up the words are what are encoded," he began to explain. "Only those characters have been given the 'add itself to the next in the thirty-six character code' treatment. When you decode each character, the sets between the meaningful words all show up as nonsense, revealing the uncoded characters of the message words as the only ones that connect to make sense." He reached up to point at the pages Timmis was examining. "It's clever because the meaningful characters aren't joined together but hold it away from you a bit and you can see them."

Sure enough, Timmis stretched his arm out, squinted and exclaimed:

"Oh, yes! A 'one', then a row of 'xs', 'ys' and 'qs', then a '0'!"

"Yup", agreed Elroy, "if you read along you'll see 'million': 'ten million'."

"Good Lord", exclaimed Timmis, completely unaware of his companion's religious sensitivities, "it would take them ages to decode this."

"Humph", grunted Elroy, "they'll have a computer program, or even a sliding grid, like an old-fashioned slide rule. It'll take them seconds. It's just plain aggravating doing it this way, that's all." Timmis was marvelling the man could do it all; he must have a brain like a room-sized computer, never mind a slide rule.

The explanation suddenly occurred to Hoi Fong as he awoke the next morning after a fitful night's sleep. He had deliberately stayed until last in the factory the previous evening so he could pad softly over to the 'research' Manchu Met in its semi-partitioned bay. He unlatched the boot with his master key and found himself frowning in puzzlement at the open car boot. It was empty. There was no large battery inside. No battery at all, despite having seen it placed there with his own eyes. Now, wide awake and trembling at being the victim of subterfuge in his own factory, it hit him. They must have switched the cars! The one with the battery would now be waiting in the export line for London. They did not want him to interfere. Hah! He could still protest and halt the order until everything was explained!

He paused only for a brief bite of breakfast, leaving Hwee Lo holding a nearly full wok, before he sped to the city. He rushed into the factory, with a hasty 'good morning' at the security gate, and pulled up abruptly at the long space where the line of brand new 'Mets' had been. Of course! He had forgotten. The shipment to London had been loaded onto transporters overnight for an early flight. They would already be at the airport! There was no way he could justify halting the departure at this stage.

It was not as though he could think of any vital reason why the 'battery car' should not have been exported with the others. It was just the principle! They - the Society - were going behind his back, swapping the cars for no apparent reason and meddling with the terms of the contract! Would the English dealer want one battery car substituted in the order? He had not asked for it. He could be a prickly customer and had once threatened to return a whole batch. Hoi fumed. He would speak to Teng as soon as he saw him. He walked over to the 'research bay', where Mr Hill seemed unconcerned that his prototype had been removed and replaced with an ordinary 'Met' which would be no use to him.

"Yes, Mr Choi", Gainsborough assured him, though with an awkward look, "the project is ready to test." He had felt compromised by being party to the deception.

"Test?" queried Hoi, with a little belligerence, implying he did not want his customers involved with an untried commodity.

"Er .. on the market", added Gainsborough, hastily, "see how they like it."

Hoi bristled inside. Sending a dual-power battery car with a prototype navigation system to a valued customer without even consulting him! He could only think the car had been replaced by another in the bay to prevent him suspecting the exchange before it was too late. He shot an accusing glance at

Gainsborough, who now, presumably, having been part of the plot, had nothing left to do but collude in hollow pretence.

"Ten million ... dollars?" Timmis was adding it up in his mind.

"Seems like the Triads thought they should have received it already", Elroy suggested. They had the sheets of deciphered code on the desk in front of them in their private office.

"And the plutonium," added Martin.

"One lot wants it, the other lot's still got it," affirmed Elroy adding grimly, "and the first lot can't finish the job without it."

"And vice versa with the money", concluded Timmis. "Good heavens, Elroy -" He was at ease with the name now "that's dangerous stuff. They can't just ship it in a cardboard box."

"Nope", agreed Elroy, "have to pack it inside lead or something like that. Heavy, solid."

"But what transport?" argued Timmis. "They can't just get a lead box through Customs - China to London?"

Elroy paused in deep thought. Then suddenly shot bolt upright. "The cars!"

"Sir - Elroy?" Timmis lost his composure at the outburst and almost reverted to familiar formality.

"What's the bet there's a delivery of those Chinese cars on the way?" declared Elroy, fiercely.

"The dolls?" Timmis was looking doubtful again.

"Well, maybe ... no." Elroy brooded for a moment. "No, they won't try that again."

"They won't try the cars at all, will they?" objected Martin. "They know we know."

"Could be whole double-bluff, couldn't it?" Elroy's eyes gleamed. "Hell, your Customs guys need to know anyway, don't they? Can't risk leaving them outa the loop!"

Timmis had to agree, though he wondered what fool Chinese criminals would use the same method of transportation after their close shave last time. And with a rod of plutonium for goodness sake!

"See", Elroy contemplated aloud, "if that was uranium ..."

"In the dolls?" prompted Timmis.

"Yuh."

"But you didn't know", Timmis said, doubtfully.

"No", agreed Elroy, "but I was pretty damn sure. And it tied in with what the Customs guy said he'd worked out."

"But you didn't find the dolls."

"Nope. They just disappeared. But if they connect with our 'triangle' ..."

"Toys - dolls." Martin completed Elroy's train of thought.

"Yep. And if the triangle starts with where they come from-"

"China."

"Yup, And then they go to -"

"London?" queried Timmis, unsure he was following the trail.

"Yep, I know", acknowledged Elroy, knowing it sounded a somewhat contrived stitching-together of threads, "but if that only happens to be the midpoint before they end up in -"

"Spain!"

"You got it. So, like we said already -" Elroy was referring to their conversation of some months earlier. "who's got the dollars to buy all that uranium -?"

Timmis nodded in growing comprehension.

"and who's already backed terrorism in Spain -" Elroy continued, as Timmis nodded again, more thoughtfully.

"and who have a strong base in England, especially London -?" Elroy finished, looking up at his junior partner.

"Islamists", breathed Martin Timmis, his eyes widening, seeing the sequence of signals over the last several months all click neatly into place.

"Yep", affirmed Elroy, "and what bunch of criminals can you see getting hold of Soviet uranium, with tentacles stretching between China and London and probably the means to convey it from one to the other?"

He leaned back, hands clasped behind his head, watching the realisation dawn on his English companion's features before he spoke.

"Triads!"

Heaven

"You know this Heaven business", hummed Gabriel, who was squatting, gazing out at the emptiness.

"Mm." The Lord's response was noncommittal, hoping, as ever, to suppress further angelic utterances by His own silence. Besides, he had never really regarded Heaven as a 'business'; rather, it just *was*. Like the angel's vocal chords.

"I mean, some of them still think they're coming here."

If God could feel uncomfortable, which of course He could not, He would just now. He did, however, wish His loyal servant would not raise such subjects. It was not as though he had ever directly informed them they would come here, had He? Just another of those misconceptions creeping into the transcripts somehow.

"It's not as though You ever told them they would come", muttered the angel, disconcertingly as though *he* were reading *God's* thoughts.

"I mean, what would they *do*?" The archangel gazed at the bleak emptiness all around them. Featureless, he thought to himself, to say the least. Not even any paint drying.

"Probably start killing each other", he grunted, bending to a more pressing concern, apparently ignoring the contradiction of already-deceased souls becoming engaged in mortal combat.

"Lets You off the hook with the Day of Judgement, though."

The Good Lord Almighty did not often wish to be alone, fairly difficult anyway for One who is everywhere all the time. You are usually going to be rubbing (metaphorical) shoulders with some living organism somewhere or other. However, this was a moment (if you put it like that) when He could quite cheerfully manage without the company of the other of Heaven's inhabitants.

"I mean, You can't judge nobody."

God felt almost relieved to be able to divert this dialogue along the path of corrective grammar.

"You can't judge *anybody*", He reproved.

"No, no: You can't judge *nobody*", declared Gabriel from his squatting position, with a vague gesture at the barren vista. "If there's nobody here", he added by way of helpful explanation, "to judge."

"Anyway", the angel looked up again at the Benign Presence nearby, "where would You have started? If they'd all come up here?"

He looked around. The Lord supposed Gabriel must be in the process of visualising a Heaven teeming with souls.

"Nightmare", pronounced the archangel, levering a foot into his lap. "And what would You have said? 'Never mind if you've been horrible down there, or thought praying was all you had to do. You're here now. Forgiven - "

"Gabriel." One of those warning shots again, unheeded as usual.

" - 'So have a nice day, My flock. Serves you right if you're bored to death'."

Numbers

Andy looked quizzically at the printed 'electronic declarations' in his right hand.

"Twenty-six", he called, without conviction.

Gordon Pierce, at the other end of the line of Chinese cars in the hangar, jotted the figure onto his clipboard, then called back.

"I thought you said twenty-five."

"Well..." Andy looked at the docket in his left hand. "I did ...but..."

"Come off it, Andy", called Pierce, "let's get it right."

"Well..." Andy shook his head. "I got twenty-five on the Beijing exportation docket. But I got twenty-six on transportation."

"Well, those Chinese never could count", called back Gordon. "You tried getting the right change for your chop suey?" He laughed. "How many cars we actually got?"

Andy still looked puzzled.

"Twenty-six."

"Sure?"

"Yeh. Counted 'em."

"You and the Chinese?" Gordon laughed again, then added, "Well, your twenty-five docket's obviously wrong. Tell our friend we'll do 'em now."

Pierce indicated the Chinese sales agent standing by the hangar doors, with a mobile phone clutched to his ear. A swarthy fellow in dark glasses and black leather jacket, not looking much like sales agents Gordon had seen in the past but it takes all sorts, he told himself. His clearance was okay. The Chinese man watched as Andy walked away from him down the line of cars towards Gordon, then he spoke furtively and urgently into his phone.

Gainsborough's heart had been wrenched. They told him if this went wrong he would not see Vicki again. Teng and one of the familiar cohorts had moved up on him, beginning with pleasant congratulations on completion of the work but standing oppressively close, in their dark jackets, their inscrutable features, their narrow eyes. They told him what they were going to do. He responded that the system could not be guaranteed to be accurate over great distances until tested. He did agree that if a short-distance experiment turned out to be a hundred per cent reliable, as anticipated, that would be a good indicator for more ambitious trials.

They also told him Vicki would be delayed - until success had been confirmed. He knew what they meant. He could feel his heart at the point of breaking. They stood with him now, Teng with mobile phone to his ear. The little man was waiting for something: information, or an instruction. Suddenly his expression changed. It was both tense and excited. His eyes turned to Gainsborough and they almost flashed as his voice cracked into a sharp: "Now!" Gainsborough hovered taught over the console and jabbed his finger on a button. A green light flashed. Teng's features broke into a sly grin.

Twenty-Six

"We going through all these ruddy dolls again?" asked Andy, holding the one from the first car out in front of him.

"Course!" declared Pierce, emphatically.

"Well, they're not going to try that again", objected Andy, who regarded any obvious wasted effort as a hugely unnecessary misuse of his hard-pressed time. "They're bound to have heard about that showroom and us and the dolls."

"And won't they think that's what we'll reckon - don't bother 'cos they won't try the same thing again? You not heard of double bluff?" Gordon was looking determinedly at his subordinate. No way was he going to be taken for a mug; it was too close a call last time.

Andy sighed and took his chisel to chip away at the doll's back - just to expose the metal, as Gordon had described it.

"See?" Andy placed the last doll on the inspection bench, it's gaudy Chinese costume open at the back and a small exposed cut in the body revealing solid hardwood.

"Twenty-five slightly damaged wooden dolls."

"Twenty-five"? asked Gordon, sharply.

"Yeh -" Andy glared at this further interrogation of his mental reliability.

"I thought you said twenty-six." Pierce was frowning as he began to wonder if Andy was quite on top of his work.

"No", Andy began, "twenty-five, like I said..." His words faded to a halt as he reached to the end of the bench for the print-offs. He found the two from China. "See - twenty-five", Then he looked at the second sheet. "Twenty-six..."

Pierce tried to suppress his exasperation.

"Andy, you did all that before. Two dockets, two different numbers. You said we've got twenty-six cars so twenty-six is right. Okay?"

"No .. Look -"

"I compliment you", remarked Teng, still with the trace of a grin and listening to his phone. Gainsborough shrugged, concealing his pride. He did not know what game they were playing but his formula seemed to be working, according to whatever Teng was being told.

Andy walked briskly down the line of inspected cars, each of which he had more or less taken apart and put back together again over the past three days, not to mention the ruddy dolls. He called out from the back of the line.

"Twenty-five! See!"

"Andy..." Gordon's tone was becoming heated. "When we started this you told me twenty-six. You counted ... so you said." There was more than a trace of heavy irony in his voice now.

0"No, I didn't..." Andy's voice tailed off again as he tried to remember. Had he counted twenty-five or twenty-six? Which docket had been correct? He felt confused. And embarrassed. He might only be a mechanic but sure he could count to more than ten. He counted them again, walking slowly down the line this time. He reached Gordon, who was watching and waiting, resigned exasperation written into his face, like a father watching his naughty child pick up the toys he'd strewn around the floor.

"Twenty-five", declared Andy, emphatically, "like I said." And looked as meaningfully as he could at his boss.

Gordon snatched the two dockets from him, briefly examined both, then deliberately tore up the one with 'twenty-six' in the 'goods quantity' box and handed the pieces to his mechanic. "Maybe you'd better have tomorrow off, mate. Get these bloody Chinese cars out to the yard. And tell him" - tilting his head towards the impassive Chinese sales agent who had been in attendance, mobile to hand, the whole three days "we're done." Andy signalled to the man and they saw him speak animatedly into is phone once more.

Gainsborough had not been allowed home. They had brought a mattress for him in the corner of his lab area and escorted him to and from the washroom, bringing meals and drinks to where he worked. Three days. Vicki haunted his mind. He was sure she would not have been at home, even had he been able to go there. This was not finished until they let him go. Now Teng was on his phone again, listening intently, hand raised. "Now!", came his retort, as his hand fell. Gainsborough jabbed the button. Teng listened into his phone and then broke into a broad smile - as broad as his thin sallow features had ever allowed, as far as Gainsborough could imagine. Nor could he imagine why it was so important to disguise the existence of the car as it entered England.

"Congratulations, Mr Hill!" The man was positively beaming, as he turned towards the factory door.

"Here, mate." The driver of the leading car transporter slapped his docket copy onto the customs office desk, picked up a ballpoint and crossed out '25', replacing it with '26'. "Someone's cocked this up somewhere. I'm expectin' twenty-five of these cars an' I got twenty-six. Good job we got room", he grumbled, thumbing towards the three vehicles in the yard. "Can't someone count?"

The customs official examined the docket and shook his head, puzzled.

"I'm sorry, sir. Must be a clerical error. Our inspection teams never get it wrong. They're all checked or they wouldn't get to the yard. You have twenty-six cars?"

"That's right, mate. We're off now." The men smiled at each other, no harm done. Not their mistake, some jerk of a clerk somewhere between here and China. When the discrepancy was pointed out to Gordon Pierce he had to wait for Andy to return from his day off, whereupon they had the most enormous row and it was some time before either fully trusted the other's judgement again.

PARADIGM : DISORDER

Her hand stroked the firm, delicate back, already strong
like his father's, yet not able to withstand any but the
softest blow but would one day grow to be a man's. Her
fingers trembled as they touched and a tear welled in her
eye as she watched his approach from the hunt. His stride
was slow, not with the eagerness to greet her that was
their custom. She looked for what might be hung from his
belt that would feed them and defy the glowering sky that
leered above the sea. From the distance, it appeared he
bore a vine and she caressed their child in apprehension
of what sustenance might be brought.

"What is it?" she spoke out as he came near but she
could already see.

"It is a snake." His voice was low and humble, as he slung
it from his side and it lay, limp and twisted at their feet.

"It is not good to eat", she whispered, her hands
trembling on her infant's skin, "my milk is already
poor, he will not feed."

He saw her lips falter as they moved and felt the despair
rising in his own soul. He reached to clasp her arm, and
lay his other hand upon their child, torn as a father who
could not provide for his only son.

"Does he not take your milk", he faltered, his taught
frame lessened by the hurt of her words, "the snake is
good, it will be good, if it is well prepared, I caught it
unawares; the hunt is .. spare ... too many animals are sick
or already dead. The air ..."

He held them both to him, his arms wrapped around her
and their child. He felt its ribs and then the pimples, some

of them small lumps, upon its back, and he started back, his face screwed in alarm.

"He has them, too?"

She lowered her eyes.

"He does not feed so well, my milk is turning sour. The lamb .. and now .. a snake .. And the air .. it is not good to breathe .. he coughs ..."

"I shall prepare the snake, it will be good, you must eat, he must feed, your milk will be good again." He spoke with tears in his eyes, he, the hunter, with unbidden tears, while the skulking sky tainted the air and the sea writhed and scowled beneath.

Gender

"Or maybe if they thought of You as a woman", Gabriel grunted, scooping something surplus to requirements from between a little toe and its nearest neighbour. He was conscious of the silent response and glanced up at the Lord's less than benign expression.

"I mean", he continued, by way of conciliatory explanation, "I mean, you know, a wom..." His words tailed off as The Almighty's metaphorical brow continued to darken. "... as opposed to a ..." the angel shrugged defensively, as though considering his remark a not particularly provocative one. " ...a man."

The subject of attaching a physical entity to the Supernatural Deity was always an awkward one and one of the few things in the universe the Lord remained sensitive about. That, and Gabriel's personal hygiene. On Ggrrukunge (extremely difficult to translate, as the planet's name is derived from the noise of an annual ion storm which sweeps by, causing total havoc in about ninety seconds).

Anyway, on Ggrrukunge, the Ggrrukungites (for want of a more imaginative name) acknowledge the Supernatural Being quite differently: not as a physical entity, or a kind of super-personage, but as a pervasive presence, somewhere in the 'ether'. They call It 'Suphhooooooooe', like a long drawn-out breath, indeed almost as the antidote to the 'Ggrrukunge' storm, identifying it with a corrective, stabilising, purifying force in nature. Its flipside - its punishment facet, if you like - is reflected in Its failure, or refusal, to make good, rectify or negate bad deeds or evil events. Much like Earth's God, or Muhammed, or the Buddha, even, but without being cast in the image of the species itself.

On Splong, the Deity is different again and is represented, simply, by a gigantic mutant Splongie, a sort of Big Monster Splongie, with various unsightly additional appendages and eyes and ears protruding from every quarter. Grotesque, God deemed it, while admitting it was an effective image for keeping the Splongies in order, as a remarkably genial and docile species they proved to be.

Unlike these humans, who were in a minority in conceptualising the Almighty more or less like one of themselves: usually elderly, with a flowing white beard and a flowing white robe; indeed, much like a grandfather version of how Jesus was familiarly portrayed. (Or Muhammed, if such a portrayal had been permitted). A male representation, anyway: definitely not a woman. God was not too keen on any of these manifestations but accepted that, if He was to 'exist', or be believed in, He would inevitably be endowed with an image of one sort or another by every intelligent species, including the humans.

"I mean -" (spoke he who never gave up). "I mean -"

"Gabriel -" It was a warning shot; a shot, typically, ignored by one bent on a pressing train of thought.

"I mean, they refer to *ships* as women."

"I beg your pardon?" The Lord's incredulity was acquiring stretchmarks.

"Ships", uttered Gabriel, matter-of-factly, "You know, things that float on wat -"

"Yes, I do know what ships are." If this were not the All-Caring Fountain Of Love, the tone might be misinterpreted as 'curt'.

"Yes, well," continued Gabriel, undeterred as usual, "all I mean is they don't have to refer to *everything* as guys?"

"Guys?"

"Men, male, masculine", huffed the angel, and hunched over his feet in silence.

"If you are suggesting", the Lord remarked after a brief pause, "that they should invest the ... uh ... Deity with the feminine gender, instead of -"

"Well, yes", Gabriel perked up animatedly, "Exactly. Might they not be so..." And then broke off, as his mood suddenly became more contemplative, almost wistful, "...so...violent ...aggressive ... dark!" He blurted the last word out staccato fashion, ejecting it from the back of his throat as if it had been a foreign object, stuck there, impregnated with all that was wrong down 'below'. Of course, this presupposed a universal acknowledgement of the existence of his Lord and Master; a patchy belief, to say the least. And of course, there might be many a human male who would take issue with the notion of a world governed in harmony by the soft feminine touch. Quite apart from experiences concerning rolling pins or projectile domestic objects (teacups, for example), broader history held its own reminders. Boadicea and Catherine were two which came immediately to mind, not to mention the present incumbent of the Oval Office.

The Lord shuddered inwardly at that utterance, 'dark!' He had never really considered Himself (from an Earthbound perspective it is somehow impossible to say 'It' and 'Itself' so we won't get into that) as being of one or other gender, from a human standpoint. If pressed, however, He would probably have to say 'masculine' or 'male'. It did not strike a harmonious chord. It was more comfortable to identify with the concept of 'Suphhooooooooe' or even 'The Mighty Splongie'; but as for 'woman' or 'feminine'? Why did that not seem right? Why, if He could be a male 'God', could He not be Godde, or Goddey, or even Goddelle?

If He could not influence mankind's (there's 'man' again) perception of 'Him', what *could* He influence? Somewhere deep in the darkness of Creation, He had invented the question but not the answer. But he suspected that, if the masculinity of 'God' was part of the problem - part of centuries of excuses, justifications and sublimations - it was a symptom not the cause.

"Guv?"

The Almighty was about to confirm that there was never going to be a perfect time and the time was, indeed, now. That, male or female, God or Godelle, They could either surrender to the 'dark' twists and turns of human behaviour and let them determine their own fate, or They - he and the archangel - could continue in their efforts to influence the eventual outcome. He was about to say all this but when he turned to look, Gabriel was already waiting.

"Guv? What now?"

Real

"Is it real?" asked Olivia.

"Or unreal?" Walt responded with a wry smile. "I sure wouldna bet on it a year ago."

They were sitting together watching television again. A CNN documentary about their changed way of life. The neighbourhood sharing, which had not diminished even after the restoration of most domestic equipment to full working order; the half-empty, previously bottlenecked freeways; the downsizing of car showrooms and electrical stores contrasting with the vibrant economy in manufacturing automobiles - dual-powered - and consumer electronics, now driven by export to Africa instead of domestic sales. The documentary was entitled, 'Smiling America', an oblique but resonant reference to the 'smiling Jesus' images which were credited with starting it all. These abided only in the memory now, although some expectant eyes still turned towards stained glass windows on Sundays, just in case. (Not a hope in Heaven, as far as a certain angel was concerned but they could not be expected to know that).

The TV programme focused on smiling faces, too: the grim, determined expressions which had characterised so many American visages, now replaced by relaxed good humour, apparently the prominent feature of workplace, home and street. Streets, it was shown, bustling with people on foot; 'feet' the new 'wheels' as someone had coined the phrase. Thanks to the 'Autos For Africa' policy, now accompanied by just about everything else required in modern life for Africa, wealth was still being generated as before.

Now, however, it was being spent differently. Less on home energy consumption; much, much less on auto gasoline; more on leisure pursuits; more on charity and community work; more, too, on tax but not so much that it hurt; enough, though, to finance the anti-poverty programme. 'The poor will be history' had become a favourite Twigg phrase, if not an entirely original one. The big federal expenditure was being switched from defence and armaments to subsidising alternative energy for industry. The new Clean Air Act was supported by solar, wind, water and biomass energy generation for power plants which had hitherto gobbled up oil and coal. The automobile manufacturers were even beginning to look more seriously at hydrogen, for all its problems of bulk and storage.

Okay, all this was in its infancy, everyone knew it and the TV commentator acknowledged that, but it was change at the speed of light compared to the inertia which had suffocated such proposals before. If it had not been for these reminders in the media, many people might already have forgotten how such an about-turn in contemporary American life had ever occurred.

The seize-ups had come and gone, leaving only the sharing habit in their wake. Scientists and engineers were still frustrated by the cause but no longer had 'dud' machines to examine, since they had all 'repaired theirselves'. Folks quivered at the memory of 'smiling Jesus', those who had witnessed the miracle, but were not blessed with its return and it was already fading into folklore.

There was just a sense of wellbeing and perhaps a bit of a holier-than-thou glance at the rest of the world, too. And some puzzlement, resentment, that the American example appeared not to be admired and copied. It was not Utopia, the TV programme was at pains to declare; crime had not vanished, but reduced; poverty was not eradicated, but shrinking; dissent was alive but, hey, this was the greatest democracy in the world, where would it be without argument? You can't have three hundred million Americans all agreeing on the same thing, the same outcome, the same revolution. For that was what it seemed to be: a social, economic, spiritual revolution. If this wasn't a documentary it would have looked like a fantasy.

"I just wonder", frowned Olivia, "is it fragile? What would it take to break it?"

"Break?" Walt raised an eyebrow with a shrug. "Anyway", he grinned mischievously, as the credits rolled at the end of the programme, "How fragile are you feeling tonight, baby?"

He lunged at her, still grinning, and she skipped out of his reach to switch off the television, then shrieked and giggled as he caught her, hugged her, planted his lips on hers, then pulled her towards the stairs.

"Ooh! Careful!" she laughed, as he wrestled her into his arms.

"Don't worry, Miss America", he snuffled into her cheek, "I aint gonna break yer, just make yer!"

It took remarkably little effort to grapple her up to bed.

Spain

It all happened in a rush, or at least appeared to, and if you were privileged to have an overview, which was only accorded to Gabriel, anyway, and he was only half paying attention. And God, of course, Who is everywhere all the ti - well, you know the rest.

"See your people want Spain as well now!"

Something stirred inside Asif, something he could not identify.

"No, no, not my people", he sighed with a sad smile, handing over the bulging paper wrapper of pitta bread, kebab and salad. Paul noted the belligerent expression on the face of the customer next to him as the man received his steaming meal. Seemed a trifle ungrateful in the circumstances but Paul was uncomfortably aware, too, that he was once again outside the news loop. It did not used to bother him but maybe it was taking him by surprise once too often. He did not notice the troubled expression in the kebab man's eyes as he received his own takeaway, nor could he have known how strange the man felt. He just got himself home with his question.

"What's this about Spain?"

"Er?" Bella stuck her head around the kitchen doorway, as Paul unwrapped his cheeseburger and salad.

"Something about Spain, I heard at the kebab place?"

"Oh, yeh."

Paul felt a warm wave of quiet relief that he was not being confronted with aggressive accusations of ignorance. He could not lay his finger on it but they both seemed more at ease with each other lately. Maybe the temporary separation across the Atlantic, maybe the turbulence of life in London, which they both abhorred, maybe the uncertainties of life in general these days. Who to turn to for companionship but your own partner?

"Yeh", Isabella continued, following him into the lounge, "Islamists. Fundamentalists. One group of them. Saying they want Spain to be Muslim again."

"Again?" he asked as she sat beside him at the other end of the sofa.

"Yeh, you know -" she might have spoken it as a sardonic rebuke a few months ago but now she was just offering it as information "southern Spain was Muslim until about five hundred years ago. A group on the news today - saying the States is betraying the Middle East by not buying its oil -"

"Well!" Paul exploded over a mouthful, "That's the whole point isn't it! Not using so much oil!" It was partly an expression of protest, Bella knew, since his business - their prosperity - was directly linked to oil.

"Yea", she drawled in that Brooklyn burr, "there were already some voices raised over there - American economic warfare and all that -"

"Rubbish!" declared Paul.

"Yeh, well, you can see how they take it. They thought they were sitting on at least thirty years of oil cash, now they can't sell it - not to the States, anyways. Anyways", she went on, "this group said today the West is betraying them - they mean America but it sounds like a good excuse."

"Excuse?"

-300"Yeh, for saying they want Spain back."

"A bit of a weak link", mumbled Paul with his mouth full.

"Well, you know what they're like."

"Nutters", agreed Paul. And he was pleased she drew herself slightly closer, making as though to sit more comfortably but he felt comforted, too.

"But they're not", muttered Elroy, grimly.

"Not what?" Timmis asked, though it was he who had suggested it.

"Mad", elaborated the American. "And My God -" Martin Timmis was still unaware this mild expletive was one that rarely passed his colleague's lips "if this is the same group", continued Elroy, another sheaf of coded emails in his hand, "and they're getting ready to receive -". He stopped, unable to articulate the abyss.

"Plutonium", Timmis slowly spelled out the word that completed the American's sentence.

"To go with their -". Again Elroy found himself unable to contemplate the menace in word.

"Uranium", Timmis finished it for him again.

They looked at each other, then both involuntarily cast their eyes to the streams of characters on the pages in Elroy's hands.

"But", Elroy looked up again in despairing bemusement, "if it wasn't in the cars, where is it?" Customs had reported drawing a blank, with more than a hint of being put to an unnecessary waste of time on his, and GCHQ's, whim.

"Oh My Lord", Elroy breathed, after a pause in which the implications of successfully smuggled plutonium - if that were the case - had been assaulting his thought with horrific imagery. Timmis looked him in the eye again. "Oh My Good Lord", repeated Elroy. For the first time, Martin Timmis realised his mentor was not cursing, but pleading. They neither said what they were both thinking. Terrorists going nuclear. No it wasn't mad. Insane, maybe but with the cold reasoning of the fanatic. They also both remembered the case of the convicted fundamentalist who had tried to buy a nuclear bomb. Such madness was no longer confined to the extremes of TV drama and best-selling fiction.

During another pause, in which a temporary sense of futility had descended upon them, Timmis had become pensive.

"You know - Elroy - everything that's happening in your country."

"Mm?" Elroy was broken from his own thoughts.

"All the downsizing", continued the young civil servant, "quite dramatic, isn't it? All those figures on lower energy consumption. You're eliminating traffic jams, power cuts .. and the results for atmospheric pollution .. even the effect on such problems as poverty .. all quite remarkable..."

The big American looked at his English colleague.

"And Africa", continued Timmis, musing half to himself, "all those resources redirected to it. Our government was strong on talking about it but Twigg's the one actually doing it. It's as though she's finding the solution to half the world's problems all at once."

Elroy sensed something else in young Martin's thoughts.

"And?" he queried.

Timmis returned his look, a furrow on his earnest brow.

"Is it vulnerable, do you suppose? America complains the rest of the world won't follow its lead. Look at us here."

Elroy recalled the scenes of ravage and revolt he had seen in London.

"And look at the Chinese", Timmis continued, "and India, and all the rest of Asia. Not to mention Europe. Almost as though they resent being told how to save the planet. It's like a seesaw."

He looked at Elroy with a bashful smile.

"Do you have seesaws?"

Elroy grinned and mimed grasping a handle with his arms outstretched and rocked forward and back in his chair.

Martin's own smile widened, then he became serious again.

"It seems a delicate balance", he shook his head, "as though it could go either way."

His eyes met Elroy's, seeking assurance.

"This, what we suspect," he directed Elroy's attention to the sheets of coded characters, "is it possible this could tip the balance?"

"I don't see how", Elroy shook his head, doubtfully, but the image of a seesaw was a vivid one.

Twelve

"A what?"

"A battery car, Paul."

Paul looked at his salesman.

"Dual power ... I think", added the young man, barely out of his teens.

Paul bristled at this unexpected information; then he felt a little thrill of pleasure overcome his natural annoyance. This was a bit of a bonus, perhaps. An extra car; and a new model, at that. He had only ordered twenty-five.

Bella's head was buzzing as she drove back from Ruth's.

"Just one thing! If there could be just one thing!" she had declared to her friend, as they squatted applying thick waterproof paint to their new 'Save The World' banner on Ruth's kitchen floor. It reminded her of her own words to Elroy as she drove him through London the previous summer, that clouded expression on his face after seeing his scientist friend.

"Just something to ... to *change* everyone!"

'Everyone' encompassed in one sweep, and with Ruth's concurrence, all the populations of Europe and Asia and their '*refusal*', in Bella's vehement condemnation, to adopt the saving, sharing example of her countrymen and women back home. It had seemed such a complete answer - to everything - pollution, congestion, energy consumption, climate change, poverty; even famine and disease, though she had never quite grasped the thread of how Africa had been drawn into the equation, miraculous as it appeared to be. A whole continent was in the process of transformation, somehow controlled at a sufficiently steady pace not to be undermined by sucking in all the same problems now being overcome in the US. The battery cars maybe held the key: oil was not going to be the root of all evil this time.

"Just one thing", she breathed to herself at the wheel, now passing the blackened shopfronts and boarded-up display windows. She checked the time, having arranged to pick Paul up from the showroom. "Just one thing, that *everyone* could share."

"Huh", grunted Gabriel, "if that's where it had *stayed*", as he looked at the Lord with a 'not very preordained is it?' look on his face.

"Senator Jacobson, Dakota", called out the Speaker, "give way to the President."

Speaker Robinson was having difficulty controlling the unruly House.

"Kick their ass!"

"Why are we letting them take advantage!"

"This has gone far enough!"

Senate voices were being raised in anger. Some feathers were evidently ruffled by news from the Middle East. Spain? How dare they! There was not a senator who cared a fig for Spain. It was the principle of the thing. Here was America adopting a new, conciliatory role in world politics, underpinned by the - some still considered dubious - change in economic direction, and did the Muslims respect them for it? Did they goddamned to hell.

"They can see we gone soft!" shouted back Jacobson of Dakota, unwilling to be quelled. Others jeered and murmured. They were a minority but their mood was undeniable. The President rose to her feet.

"The test of our resolve is our ability to resist provocation", she pronounced to the humming assembly. "Besides, why should you be worried by some small group that no-one has heard of?"

So it continued. Like it was acknowledged, you aint never gonna get everyone agreeing in a democracy.

"Twelvers", Timmis informed him, stating a matter of fact.

"Uh?" queried Elroy.

"Twelvers", explained Timmis, "a Shiite sect."

"Yeh?" prompted Elroy, interested.

"They are the only Muslims to believe there could be a kind of 'second coming'."

"That's blasphemy, isn't it?" asked Elroy, from his sketchy understanding of Islam.

"A reincarnation of Muhammed, yes", agreed Timmis, "that's anathema. Muslims can't even depict the Prophet himself in illustrations and they get extremely upset if anyone else does. Remember the row about those cartoons?"

Elroy nodded.

"And they certainly don't admit the possibility of him appearing again."

"Unlike Jesus and Christianity", Elroy commented, "Second Coming."

"Precisely - according to one's belief, I suppose. But the Twelvers", Timmis continued, "believe there's a twelfth imam, last in line from Muhammed, who will surface as a real spiritual leader of all Muslims."

"Well, okay, but that sounds like passive religion", observed Elroy, "not an aggressive takeover."

"Quite", agreed Timmis, "but all sects can have their extremists, their splinter groups."

"This could be them?" asked Elroy.

"Well", considered Timmis, "the code definitely makes several references to the 'Twelve'. 'Conquer for the twelve' was one of them."

Neither man spoke for a few moments. They sat on opposite sides of the clean, teak desk, the computer console between them and neat piles of paper containing endless rows of characters to one side.

"Sir - Elroy - how would they transport it?"

"The plutonium?"

"Yes."

"Have to be something real safe", expounded the American, "heavy. Y'know - lead, preferably - no leakage."

"Radiation?"

"Yuh."

"Insulated? Like a battery?" concluded Timmis.

"Sorta thing", nodded Elroy.

"We could tell Customs to look out for something heavy now", suggested Timmis, "and better inform MI5."

"No!" Elroy reacted sharply. Something about not upsetting apple carts crossed his mind. Not feeding dissent, nor arousing a slumbering discontent, no stirring of a hornet's nest where a new way of life might be exposed as no more than a veneer over demons which had not been slain. Particularly, don't publicise fears of which they could not be certain. He knew he just wanted this - if it was as terrible as they both feared - nipped in the bud, dealt with and hidden away. He was disquieted by his own unease at the idea of informing those who, in a rational world, were the very authorities who should need to know. Was there a fragility he could sense but not identify?

"But, yeh", Elroy assented, "tell Customs." Although he wondered if it was not now too late.

Paul Best also got on the phone to the Customs office at Heathrow.

"Just checking", he said to the officer who answered, "you got twenty-six in your clearance." He did not want to discover he had an illegal import on his hands.

"Yes, sir", came the voice after a pause, "all cleared."

"Okay, fine", replied Paul, "Only I just ordered twenty-five. Nice bonus, eh?"

They both chuckled down the line, each sharing a minor confidence with a stranger.

"One of these new dual-powered cars, too", added Paul. He was standing beside the modified Manchu Met, mobile phone to his ear.

"Dual powered?" queried the Customs man, by way of passing interest.

"Yeh", replied Paul, looking at the open boot containing the large, solid battery, "part-powered by battery." He closed the boot and strolled round to the driver's door, phone still in hand. "Anyway", he finished, "thanks for the confirmation - clearance."

"My pleasure, sir. Hope it works", he rang off with a chuckle. Later, by way of casual conversation over a beer or a coffee, a remark about the battery car at Best Cars reached Gordon Pierce. He had also just received an email from GCHQ, Timmis, and Fitzgibbon, the American guy he had met at the Best Cars showroom. It did not take many minutes for his thoughts to connect. But this was a while after Paul Best had opened the driver's door and sat inside.

Prayer

"Some of them pray for hours", Gabriel grunted. "Hours and *hours.*"

God preserved His silence.

"Chanting, singing... I mean, do they think You are *listening?*"

God shifted slightly. Had He not been God, He might have shifted a little uncomfortably. Being God, he succeeded in keeping the uncomfortableness out of it. Gabriel knew, though, He was uncomfortable.

"I mean", persisted the voice which would not go away (except when it suited him, that is), "What do they think You can *do!*"

"We have been through that", remarked the Lord, quietly.

"Exactly!" retorted the angel, fiercely, glowering at his feet. "All that *time* spent praying. Chanting." His voice was becoming edged with scorn. "*Singing.*"

"Some of them have quite pleasant voices", murmured the Lord, uncharacteristically unsure of what else he should say.

"I mean ..." Gabriel clasped his toes with both hands and began rocking to and fro in mounting fervour "... Think of all the *time*. Think of all their old people they could visit instead of *praying*. Think of all the hungry people they could be cooking meals for. Think of all the poor -"

"Gabriel..." It was another warning shot.

The angel paused and looked up.

"Some of them are poor and hungry themselves", the Lord reminded him.

"Well ..." Gabriel pouted, "... they could be doing *something.* *Anything* instead of *praying.* I mean", he muttered at his toes again, "it's not as if You hear -"

"Gabriel." The warning tone was sharper. Okay, Gabriel, acknowledged to himself: Everywhere, all the time, Watching, Listening. *Supposedly.*

"Joan of Ar -" he began, defiantly.

"Gabriel!" This time the tone commanded a halt. Gabriel spread his arms in a shrug. Give him Splongies. Give him Cryxxites. Give him Tryxxians, anytime. Any of them but humans.

"All I mean is -" he grunted.

God calmly broke in before the angel could continue further.

"Perhaps", observed the Almighty, "perhaps their prayer inspires them to do the things you say they should. It is their motivation. *I* am their motivation. To help others, to consider each other.." Why He wondered, did He feel only partially convinced by His attempt to persuade the archangel?

"As long as they do", muttered Gabriel, glaring rebelliously out beyond his feet, "as long as they don't just do the praying and let You get on with the doing. Huh", he added with a sardonic grunt, "do they think it's that *easy*? Just pray, and you'll do the rest?"

Navigation

Paul examined the digital console on the dashboard which had lit up when he turned the ignition key three-quarters clockwise. He was a bit disappointed. It was an obvious feature the moment he sat in the driver's seat. The array of buttons below the display screen had an unusual configuration: two rows of four round touch keys, one above the other. There was a larger, square key to their right; another, large and round, to their left. The square key was orange-coloured; the large round key was dark green. All the rest were mid-grey, contrasting with the black facia. Paul's initial excitement at seeing something unfamiliar subsided with the realisation it was only a standard in-car navigation device, rather clumsier in layout and appearance than most he had seen.

There was a tap on the side window. He looked round and Isabella was standing outside the car. He experienced the familiar sinking feeling that accompanied her unexpected arrivals at the showroom: the trepidation she was pursuing him for something he had done, or not done, said, or not said. Her expression bordered on the impatient, rather than combative. He felt relieved, pushed the window button and smiled through the opening gap.

"I thought you said you'd be ready", she remarked, also not wanting to stir things up but irritated, nevertheless. He still irritated her by making her feel inconvenienced. The patience of love had not yet been restored, whatever else had.

"I ..er", he shrugged from inside the car, "they sent an extra car. Battery-power. And some navigation system. I thought it looked interesting; but nothing special."

"Well, don't be long." She moved away to take a casual look at other new arrivals, while he turned his attention back to the blank display screen. She didn't want him to think she might take an interest, though she had no interest in anything else there, either.

Paul spotted another, smaller button, in the centre but below the two rows. This one was not a sensor. It was set proud in the facia, inviting a more deliberate press. He prodded it and the display screen lit up. It was a map. Predictable, he thought immediately. Clever, though, as he recognised the image. It was a map pinpointing Best Cars at its centre. Automatic position locator. Well, he grunted, nothing new there after all. He jabbed at the round orange button and a separate window opened at one side of the display screen, showing a set of figures. He realised they were co-ordinates. He was aware that a grid had appeared on the map and when he looked more closely the numbers in the co-ordinates matched the x,y axis of the centre of the map: the location of Best Cars. Hmph, he grunted again. It had looked a fancy piece of equipment at first but it was nothing more than satellite navigation, just less elegant and more chunky than all the versions he had seen.

Typical, he thought. Chinese trying to catch up with the West but still a few steps behind. Better at making cars than the 'extras', he thought. Anyway, he was absorbed enough to try it out. He guessed there must be a way of naming a destination but when he touched the first grey button on the left of the top row, the display of co-ordinates was replaced by a single numeral. He touched it again and a second number took its place. He tried the next button. A number '1' appeared again and repeated touches rotated '2' to '9' through to '0' then back to '1'.

Ah, he was getting it now. He left the first number at '2' and tapped the second to '4'. He repeated the process with all four buttons on the top row until he had generated four random characters. As he tapped them in, a dot - presumably a decimal point - automatically appeared between the second and third numbers. He did the same thing again with the bottom row of four, with the same result. Standard grid reference, he thought to himself: x and y axis. However, the screen display was still centred on the Best Cars' dot of north London.

There was another tap on the door window. He looked up as Bella pointed at her watch. He nodded quickly to indicate he was almost finished. He was like a child really, he knew, or a geek. He understood what the device was. He just wanted to demonstrate to himself that he could make it work. He tried the green button. Nothing. He tried the orange button again. This time the screen instantly cut to a different map section. It showed a number of place names he didn't know, with a couple he maybe recognised. Must include the destination he had punched in. Well, if he found a buyer who wasn't too sophisticated about satellite navigation, maybe they would go for the novelty factor. The car manual probably explained it fully. He looked over his shoulder. Bella was giving him a meaningful stare. Delicate times told him he had better go. He gave a little wave of his hand. Coming now. His brain told him if the orange button was the 'on' button, the green button must be 'off'. Weird Chinese. He pressed the green button and started as if to leave the car.

It was the faintest of judders, the tiniest vibration, which halted his movement at first. Then it was something else. His hands had not left the steering wheel and he was suddenly feeling slightly odd. A touch queezy. He had scarcely time to think about it before he noticed his fingers on the wheel. Or, rather, he noticed them dissolving. There was not even time for the sensation of terror which would have naturally followed before he was aware of everything around him dissolving too, just fading away: the wheel beneath his hands, the dashboard with the navigation screen, his own arms and, as he looked down in stupefaction, his legs and everything else. Blurring, fading, dissolving. But it was really all so quick.

Isabella had turned away to gaze around the showroom again, as much an attempt to suppress her irritation as anything. Try to avoid a row. Impatience was taking over, though. She looked back towards the car a few feet away, ready to up the ante and remonstrate with her husband. No-one heard the sudden choking in her throat. But the whole showroom - staff, customers and even some passers-by outside - heard her piercing shriek. Bella stood rooted to the spot, her expression as wild as her tumble of hair, as her husband and the car evaporated and disappeared before her eyes.

Disappeared

"Should I send for a doctor, Mrs Best?" The voice was anxious, confused, even.

"No! No! No! I don't need a doctor! I don't need a doctor!" Bella screamed at them and broke into another fitful wave of sobs. The hapless team of half-dozen male salesmen stood helplessly around her rocking forward with her head in her hands in the single leather armchair. They were grouped in Paul's small office, partitioned off from the showroom. Of the two female members of his staff, one, his thirty-something secretary-cum-general PA, had gone to the kitchen to make a cup of tea, suspecting in her heart that this very English solution to a crisis was not going to becalm her employer's hysterical American wife. The other woman, younger, prettier and set to make her way in the man's world of car sales, had returned to the showroom as a lone envoy to the clientele.

"Doctor! What can a doctor do!" Isabella took her head out of her hands and stared wildly at the circle of bemused men. "Christ's sake! He just disappeared. Christ!" She shook her head in disbelief, tears slipping down her cheeks. "Jesus Christ!" Her voice sank to a gasp, as she stared blankly into the distance, her mind swimming in recollection.

"Maam. Mrs Best", the senior salesman shrugged weakly, "he's just out giving it a test drive."

"He didn't DRIVE!" she screamed at him, vituperously. He visibly withered in her glare. "He didn't *drive*! He just .. he just ... *went*!"

This time she did not sob. The tears still slid down from her eyes but she simply gazed blankly ahead. None of them could imagine what she was seeing but were unnerved by the shudder and shake of her shoulders. The senior guy wanted to explain about the logistics of the showroom rear doors and how his boss would have driven out to test the car while she was looking at other cars on display; how she would be surprised how little time it took just to drive a car out into the street. How that might well seem like he had just disappeared into thin air. How he had thought the same himself sometimes when his back was turned. In his mind he saw himself saying all this with a bit of a reassuring smile and settling everything back to normal. Something about the way she was staring blankly into space prevented him even opening his mouth.

Teng's face was thin, drawn and angry, his eyes fixed grimly on Gainsborough at his workbench.

"Where is it, Mr Hill?"

Gainsborough shook his head bleakly.

"I don't know", he mumbled, "I don't know." He was peering down at the monitor screen, which was fizzing with dots and lines of interference. He tapped its sides and prodded several button-keys but without result. Teng was standing opposite, watching in fierce silence.

"I'm sure I don't have to tell you, Mr Hill," he began again, with menace. Gainsborough looked up at him and felt he had never been the object of such focused anger, not even that day Emily confronted him with the lipstick. He gamely tried to meet the man's glare. "If our men do not find it...." Teng continued, his voice like cracking ice. Gainsborough fancied he discerned a fear behind the man's own angry eyes, before he turned his attention back to the small control console and its monitor screen.

Mechanic

If it was like anything inside known experience it was like that awful instant of falling asleep, just for a half-second, on the motorway, then coming around in a jerk of realisation, in the next split-second in which reality reconstituted itself into form and shape. Just in time. It was that same juddering sense of familiar things coalescing before his eyes. Just a fraction slower than the motorway experience, so that Paul could actually see his hands rematerialising on the steering wheel, and the car bonnet take shape in the gloom outside. He looked down in the same instant as his knees solidified and the gear stick reappeared at his side.

He could not have known if his trembling was emotional or all the thousand parts of himself regrouping under his skin. Armies of cells falling into line. The experience, if it could be termed that, had been timeless, instantaneous as far as he was aware, with no time yet for him to register the mad impossibility of what had occurred; but in the same instant he was petrified by the notion of what he may have undergone.

Impossible! Yet despite the roaring contradiction in his brain, all his intellect screaming that this could not be so, he had 'woken up', 'arrived' - 'solidified! - at nowhere he could recognise. And he was very definitely not in his own showroom.

He began to shake uncontrollably. He was in a field. The nearest field to Best Cars was at least ten miles away; and that was even supposing you could drive a car straight into it. But this was surely further away than that. It felt remote. He tried to calm himself while his mind raced with all the possible rational explanations: a dream, a nightmare, a road crash from which he was now recovering. None of them linked the timeless shift between his showroom and this field. There was no sound of traffic, no distant rush of motorway noise.

It was getting dark. Early evening in late February. Not even a hint of orange glow from sodium lights. All the characteristics of somewhere deep in the countryside. It looked English enough, from what he could make out: familar-looking trees lining the field, a brick farmhouse in the distance; some horses he now noticed over near the hedge. He was still trembling. He realised it must be shock; when the mind begins to catch up with the body's experience and cannot accept what it means.

He also began to wonder what the hell to do next. Then there was a rap at the window. He shakily reached to lower the window.

"Evening, sir."

The man outside was dressed in overalls, blue overalls like a mechanic not a farmer. He was polite if rather humourless, as though it were a regular but unwelcome part of his daily routine to meet a man in a car in a field at dusk and make the sort of request you might expect from the rescue service.

"If you could just open the boot, sir."

"Er...?" Paul might have felt he was part of a surreal painting or a bizarre comedy sketch: himself, a car, a field, a few animals, the enigma of dusk and a mechanic in blue overalls peering through the window, asking him to open the boot.

"The boot, sir", repeated the mechanic irritably, as he leaned forward a little, looking at Paul while pointing a finger down below the dashboard, barely disguising the implication that he was dealing with an idiot. Even in the gathering darkness, Paul was momentarily transfixed by the deep brown eyes, a mismatch with the untidy strands of sandy hair, still catching the fading evening light and protruding around the edges of the woolly grey beret. He weakly fumbled in front of his knees for the boot catch and tugged.

"Well *done*, sir." The sandy beret-topped head pulled away as the owner of the ironic tongue moved to the back of the car. Paul managed to jerk open the driver's door and stumble out into the crisp late winter air. He could feel the cold dampness rising from the field. It seemed to clear his head a bit.

"There's your problem, sir." Paul peered dumbly into the open boot, beside the mechanic. The large car battery was lit by the boot light.

"Problem?" Paul muttered. 'Problem' struck him as a signally inadequate description of an experience he had still not come to terms with.

"Yes, sir. Battery malfunction", grunted the mechanic and added testily, "obvious, isn't it?"

Paul gazed through the gloom settling around them. Nothing in his present circumstances seemed obvious at all.

"Malfunction?" He repeated the mechanic's word, doubtfully, and thought the man shot a look at him that implied even speaking in reply was wasting his valuable time.

"That's it, sir." The man observed Paul's incomprehension. "Well, I mean, sir", he explained dismissively, "here you are -" he waved an arm at the darkening field and its ghostly borders of trees and hedgerows in charcoal silhouette "got to be something with the battery, eh? That's the trouble with these newfangled things. Otherwise, you wouldn't have ended up here, would you?" He challenged Paul with a look that defied contradiction, to match the thinly-veiled sarcasm.

However, it was beyond Paul to add together an instantaneous transportation, a deserted field (except for horses) and a conveniently available mechanic, let alone come up with 'battery' for an answer.

"So, better fix it, hadn't we, eh sir?" concluded the mechanic, "before it gets even *darker* and *colder*", leaving no doubt as to the irksome nature of his duties. Then he added, unaccountably and to no-one else Paul could see, "No, guv. Getting on with it, guv. Just remarking." And with that, he bent under the boot lid to grasp the bulky battery with both hands.

"Ah", he muttered, suddenly straightening, with a grimace, "frigging connections."

The man reached into a deep trouser pocket in his overalls and withdrew a heavy adjustable spanner. For a moment Paul sensed the vulnerability of anyone alone in a field at nightfall with a strange man wielding a large metal spanner. The man noticed and eyed him sardonically.

"Weapon of choice, sir", turning it in his hand, "tool of the trade." And he bent to inspect the battery.

"Can *you* see these flaming connections, sir?" he snapped after a moment.

Paul bent to look, briefly contemplating the man's unprovoked short temper. Hardly an angel of mercy, he thought to himself. He spotted some fittings at the rear of the battery and pointed.

"There", he mumbled, still enveloped in the fantasy of his situation, absurdly co-operating to disconnect a battery in a field at night, in a car which should not have been there in the first place. He tapped one of the fixings with his finger to indicate its position. "See. Wing nuts."

The mechanic peered and suddenly broke into what Paul could only perceive as a grin of childish delight, momentarily transformed from the surly individual at his side.

"So they are, sir", he grinned, almost cheekily, Paul thought, "so they are. How appropriate."

Paul looked questioningly at him in the gloom.

"Borne on the wing by wing nuts!" the mechanic explained with a crookedly mischievous grin again and Paul was certain he winked in the dark with one of those big brown eyes. "Here we go."

The mechanic dislodged the weighty battery and heaved it up on one shoulder as though it were nothing but a bag of flour. With the other arm he firmly guided Paul back to the driver's door and inside, before marching off into the cloying dusk.

"Getting it fixed ,sir!" The mechanic called back to him, still apparently elevated into good humour by the discovery of wing nuts.

Paul suddenly registered the man was departing with his power source.

"But!" He shouted through the open window. "I can't move now!"

"You and me both, sir!" the mechanic shouted back from the gloom. "Think I want to hang about here? Back as soon as I flaming can!" Then Paul thought he heard him say into the empty night air, "Yes, guv, don't *worry*", but he realised there was no-one else he could have been speaking to and bit his lip to prevent the entire fantasy becoming more surreal.

Paul watched the mechanic stride away in the fading light. Fair enough, he thought; might have been better humoured about it, though. It was only then, as the trembling resumed, he wondered why he could see no breakdown truck. Just a solitary mechanic in a field, who seemed to have known exactly where to find him.

Dissolved

"Who is it?"

"Yeh, yeh. Okay, okay. Okay, hun."

Walt was nodding his head in agitation, the phone clutched to his ear as Olivia watched in concern.

"Yeh, yeh ... hun ... I can't ..." He looked up in confusion at his wife, shaking his head and shrugging his free arm out to his side.

"Here, hun, it's Isabella. I can't make her out." He handed the phone to Olivia, putting his hand over the mouthpiece and hushing his voice. "She's ... I don't know ... hysterical ... Crying."

"Yeh, Bella, love, Livvy. Yeh, yeh ... wait ... hang on .. Whaddya mean? ... *Gone?*" Olivia was shaking her head, frowning as she listened, trying to grab a sense of her friend an ocean away. "Yeh, hun ..no, course I do, course I don't ...no .. it's just .. he can't just ... whaddya say ... *Vaporise?* ... Babe ... *Hun* ...!"

Olivia cast a despairing look at Walt before being drawn back to the phone.

"Gee, hun, love .. I don't know... You got folks there?... Yeh, no, I know hun... Yeh, you and me hun... Hun, if you really need .. Hun, let me talk to Walt ... Yes, honest, I'll call right back."

She clicked the phone off and looked at her husband.

"She wants us to go to her."

"When?" Walt frowned.

"Now." Olivia declared plainly.

"*Now?*"

"Hun, you heard what she said?"

"Paul gone?" checked Walt.

"Disappeared", Olivia nodded, "'dissolved'", she added, helplessly.

"*Dissolved?*" Walt looked at her as if she was mad.

"Hun, I know." Olivia shook her head.

"I always said she was loopy, your friend." Walt tossed his eyes at the ceiling.

"Hun, she's not mad. I don't know if Paul's finally walked out on her and it's ... it's ..broken her .. I mean she's strong but everyone's got their limit. I just think .. I don't think she's got anyone there to ... to *be* with... to be with her." There was a pleading expression. Walt knew her well enough.

"You wanna go?" he asked.

"We can be right back, right back in a coupla days. Heck ... We make like it's the moon. Some people go there and back every day for business." There was a tear in her eye for her friend. Walt took a step to her and held her, hugged her, kissed her forehead.

"*Women*!" He breathed into her hair.

"You'd do it for Elroy?"

"Gee, I guess", he admitted with a smile. "Where is the big guy, anyway?"

"Bella said she'd phoned him, too. No reply. Voicemail."

"Gee, where *is* that fella", Walt grimaced. "Anyways", he pulled back, a hand on each of her shoulders, looking at her fondly, "I'll book the flight."

She drew him back to her in a brief, close embrace.

"Thank you, hun." They kissed.

"I've got it", Gainsborough muttered, eyes fixed on the monitor. "Got it." He looked up at the ever-present Teng, with an expression that mingled relief with apology. The man infuriated him as much as intimidated him. The relief was from the fear of never seeing Vicki again, the terror that the collapse of this stupendous enterprise would forever tear her from him. It allowed him to break into a small smile of triumph, although dour Teng could imagine no reason why the Englishman should smile. This was not a game.

"You may proceed now? You may trace it and control it?" enquired his unamused taskmaster.

"Yes, yes, soon", acknowledged Gainsborough, "just re-establish the coordinates. Someone took local control before I could stop it." He bent to the task of tracking down the car, the monitor now restored to its pattern of map configurations and coordinate bearings.

"I commend you", remarked Teng, with a chill in his voice, "for successfully manoeuvring the product past their import inspections."

Gainsborough appreciated, without much pleasure, the man was complimenting him on the remote precision of materialisation and dematerialisation on the signal from their agent at Heathrow.

"However", croaked his sallow-cheeked guardian crow, "our men are taking steps to retrieve it, should you fail to regain it from here." His eyes pierced Gainsborough from beneath their hoods. "Which will not be forgotten", he added, darkly.

"I've got it .... nearly, got it", muttered Gainsborough, fiercely tweaking the array of knobs and sensor-buttons at his console. He had the new coordinates. His heart pounded for Vicki as he fought to regain control.

The ambitious twenty-something was pleased with the way she had single-handedly attended to various Best Cars customers while her boss's American wife was detaining everyone else with her hysterics in the office. It took a Yank to pull some crazy stunt about vanishing cars just to be the centre of attention. She had never thought much of the woman; looked like she could not bear to throw off the image of her youth - hippy, or whatever it was they called themselves twenty years ago. Sad. Give her due, she wore it well, not like mutton dressed as lamb, but about time she took a look at her hair - Afro perm, I *mean*. And all those wimp men gathered round her without a clue what to do. Just showed she could do all their jobs, all at the same time.

She hadn't noticed the little knot of four men at the far end of the showroom, where Paul had driven off in that car. She began to walk over. She would help them out now, handle all the boss's customers all by herself. She smiled confidently; confident, too, that she had assets besides her sales acumen which enabled her to be all the more persuasive, with the men anyway, if not their jealous partners. She saw that all four of these men were Chinese and talking animatedly in a huddle where Paul's car had been.

She prepared the smile they would turn and see.

"Can I help you, gentlemen?"

Row

"Whaddya mean? Battery car?"

"Car with a battery in the back for power!" glared Gordon Pierce, stretched back in his office chair, hands splayed tight on he desk in front of him, faced once again by Andy defending his corner. "What do you think? Some *toy*?"

"Yeh, I *do* know", retorted Andy, hotly, "like, you think I can open a boot and not see a power battery inside?"

"Depends whether it's the twenty-fifth or twenty-sixth car, I guess", declared Gordon, drily. "You got a blindspot for twenty-six, or something?" Gordon glowered at him from behind his desk.

"Jesus, Gordon. What is this?" Andy slumped into the chair across the desk. "Who's going crazy? Me? You *know* I took all those bloody cars apart. Every one."

"Yeh", muttered Pierce, grimly, "you just couldn't count how many. Remember?"

Andy shook his head miserably. Yes, he remembered his confusion. How could he possibly not count to twenty-five - or twenty-six - and not get it right? Was he going stupid?

"What did you say?" he almost whispered over the desk, "*plutonium?*"

"Shit, I don't know, Andy", groaned Gordon, just as miserable as his colleague. Ever since those other Chinese cars arrived on British soil with dolls - allegedly - stuffed with some deadly metal - uranium? Ha! - the whole order of things had gone topsy-turvy. Cocaine crammed inside flour bags, he could cope with. Heroin compressed into bamboo canes, he had grown to expect. But supposedly sinister Chinese dolls, which turned out to be harmless wood?

And - coincidentally - more Chinese cars, which could not be pinned down to a precise number and, *now*, might or might not include one which was 'dual-powered' and might or might not be linked to - allegedly - smuggled plutonium, which itself might or might not be connected to the phantom uranium which - as it transpired - was *not* smuggled inside the Chinese dolls. Or was it? His calculations had confirmed the probability but the evidence - if ever it existed - had been whisked from his grasp. Gordon sighed a deep, deep sigh and leaned forward on his desk.

"I'm just asking, Andy, was one of the cars dual-powered: battery and petrol? Battery in the back?"

"No", asserted Andy, as forcibly as he could, while the world of sense and order swirled giddily around his head. He could have been riding a fairground waltzer.

"Well", breathed Gordon, still staring over his now-clenched fists on the desk, at Andy, "the client in London says there is."

The two men glared at each other in silence. Andy tried to say something but gulped and could not think of anything. He visualised the line of cars. He tried to see how he could completely ignore one of them and pass on to the next, as though one of them had not been there. He could not imagine it. It was not possible. Was he prone to blackouts and never realised it? Never. He sank lower into the chair and looked away from his boss.

"So", Gordon said, heavily, "we'd better go and check." He did not add, 'despite what you say'; but they both knew what he meant. Gordon felt let down. Andy felt numb.

Sing

The office door burst open with a crash, at the same time as the young salesgirl emitted something between a sob and a scream of terror. She was thrust into the room, held with both arms pinned behind her and a knife flashing at her throat. One of the Chinese men, swarthy in black leather jacket, held her from behind, another gripped her elbow whilst holding the knife. A third, scowling aggressively like the other two, was in front, having pushed open the door. The fourth, slipping around the knot of them in the doorway, was the diminutive Mr Sing.

The sales team all recoiled in alarm. Bella looked up with her tearstained cheeks, framed by her tangle of curls. They all caught their breath in the same reaction of fear and disbelief. The immediate image was of intimidating Chinese men in black, the glint of blades and the fright on the face of the poor girl held hostage at knifepoint in front of them.

"Where is it?" demanded Sing, grimly quiet and fixing his eyes on each one in turn.

"Where's what?" faltered one of the salesmen, regaining some composure after a pause.

"I advise you not to play games with us", responded the tight-lipped Sing, casting a look at the salesgirl. She flinched and whimpered as the Triad with the knife jerked her elbow and held the blade closer to her neck.

"Wha..?" replied her confused colleague, staring fearfully at her and her captors.

"You mean a car?" Bella spoke steadily and calmly. She had recognised the little Chinese man immediately, as the dragon show's innocuous compere. His connection to the cars might be assumed, if not with this vicious turn of character and his posse of thugs.

"I think you know", replied Sing, without expression.

"No, no. Whatever you think; whatever the reason for your behaviour -" the Brooklyn fortitude was percolating back into her veins; fear and distress was being replaced by effrontery and outrage "we know nothing about you. What do you want?"

Belligerence was welling into her expression.

"The car", replied Sing, without reacting to her aggressive tone, "the car which has gone."

Isabella could not prevent a slight gasp escaping her. The vision of the last vestiges of the vehicle containing her husband, evaporating before her eyes, flashed again into her mind. The salesman who had spoken before interjected again.

"Paul - Mr Best - the boss - had taken it for a test drive."

This time Sing's eyebrows raised briefly in irritation.

"Phone him", he demanded.

"We ... can't", faltered the salesman, "he left his phone." And he indicated the mobile phone lying on Paul's desk.

Sing's whole demeanor was suddenly transformed as he broke into a rage.

"I told you don't fool with me!" he shouted. "You steal this car? You don't know what you play with. *You* -" he was addressing Bella. " -you will come with us and tell us where the car is!" He motioned to his heavyweights and two rushed to pull Bella from the armchair, the third still holding the salesgirl at knifepoint. One of the salesmen took the opportunity to lunge at one of the Triads grabbing Bella but leapt back with a cry of pain, blood showing through his slashed shirtsleeve. The Chinaman made a threatening follow-up move with his blade but Sing spoke sharply in Chinese. Then he resumed in English, his tone menacingly cool.

"That is our warning. We will not be misled. And you -" he spoke to Bella, held in the grip of two henchmen, "you will help

us, or...." He let his unfinished sentence speak for itself, except
to add, "I am sure you will tell us where your husband and the
car is, Mrs Best."

He gestured to the third accomplice, holding the girl.

"Leave her. She will be no use. We only need this lady." He
indicated Bella and made a sweeping gesture for their party to
leave. He turned at the door.

"I need hardly tell you what consequences there would be for
this lady, should you be so foolish as to call the police", he
directed at them. His cohort gave Bella a rough shove through
the doorway, wielding his blade, as if to reinforce his point. Then
the men departed, roughly jostling Bella between them, she too
bewildered and frightened to speak. A few minutes later a car
could be heard starting up outside in the rear yard. Slowly, the
group in the office relaxed and the girl became quiet, as they all
began to wonder what to do.

Sulk

"I think not."

"Aw, Boss, that was the hard part. They can manage the rest
themselves." Gabriel adopted his most aggrieved expression.

"I think not", God repeated. "We cannot be sure."

"Yeh", protested the angel, "but like you said about too much
meddling. It'll never stop." It's not as though it's the only planet
in the universe, he thought to himself.

"This is ... This is ..." Even the Inventor of all the vocabularies
in the Cosmos found Himself struggling to find the right words
to appease His truculent archangel. "This is ... an adjustment ...
to restore the path -"

"Railway line?" interjected the sulky angel.

"If you must", sighed the Lord. "We have intervened over one
anomaly -"

"You mean me - I have", Gabriel moodily interrupted again,
still feeling the shivers from that damp, cold field, "despite
interruptions." He risked a further accusing glance up at his
Lord and Master.

The Lord sighed again. Of course he shouldn't nag at the angel while Gabriel was busy on Earth but He had to admit to just the slightest anxiety, which made it difficult to remain completely silent whilst observing the buccaneering angel in full, as it were, flight.

"*We*", He emphasised for the benefit of his Heavenly companion, "must ensure no more anomalies arise."

"Well, the whole thing's way off course, anyway", grumped Gabriel. "I mean , You know, wrong country, for a start. That wasn't the plan; but now, ironically", he snorted, "it's ended up where it was supposed to be in the first place. Only now -"

"Gabriel."

"Well", as he hunched over his feet, "I mean, do You know what's going to happ -?"

"Gabriel." Where patience is never more than a relative virtue throughout His multitudinous flocks, considered the Lord, it was a good job that He Himself embodied Absolute Patience. Especially in present company.

"Well", present company continued to huff at His side, "what I mean is, have *we*", he exaggerated the emphasis, "been wasting our time?"

"Gabriel", came the admonishment again.

"Well -"

"Gabriel."

"But Splong needs -"

"Gabriel." Even absolute patience can wear thin around the edges.

"Okay, Boss."

One reluctant foot over the edge.

"Thank you, Gabriel."

"Yes, Guv."

Gone.

Field

Paul must have dozed off, a natural reaction to shock. He was startled by a tap at the front passenger window and opened his eyes with a jolt. It was the mechanic. It was dark now outside and the face was only partially lit by the man's own torch. The apparition made Paul jump again. He could not make out all the features but lowered the window and recognised the gleam of those deep brown eyes.

"Apologies, sir, unexpected delay." The man spoke gruffly, as though ruffled by whatever had detained him. "I'll hop in the back, sir."

Paul blinked and rubbed his eyes with shaking hands. He was aware he was shaking all over; too much so to wonder why the mechanic should wish to occupy the back seat out of sight.

"What time is it?" he asked in anxiety as the mechanic opened the rear passenger door and stepped inside. He half-turned and thought the man seemed darker than before - darker hair and sallower features - but the light was dim and he felt disoriented and confused.

"Four, sir."

"Four!" repeated Paul in confusion.

"Four in the morning."

"Where am I? Where are we - !" He was once again aware of himself and the car, stationary in the pitch black. Now he remembered the field, too. "Oh my God!"

"Indeed, sir, and mine too", grunted the mechanic from behind him. "Now then, let's get you out of this field."

Paul shivered. The car was cold and he only wore his office suit. If he was of a mind to contemplate the surreal, he might have wondered how a mechanic without a breakdown truck, and sitting in the back seat, expected to extricate the car from a remote field in the middle of the night.

"Let's be off, sir." The mechanic sounded in a hurry now, and as though he expected Paul to do something about it.

Paul blinked ahead at the dark and tried to waken up.

"But", he blurted, "the battery."

"Still being repaired, sir", replied the mechanic, drily, "can't expect miracles."

"Well, we can't move", protested Paul, beginning to turn to the man behind him, while something nagged at his mind about whether a battery could explain his sensation of trauma.

"Dual power, sir. We can manage without it. If you just start her up - there - that console."

In a more composed state Paul might have baulked at being spoken to like a dim child but he was only aware of a gloved finger pointing past his cheek at the navigation device, redirecting his gaze before he had fully turned to address the mechanic. The man was curt in his confidence, in the way of technicians and engineers who know their trade back to front and speak in terms which completely bypass the understanding of ordinary mortals, whilst expecting instant comprehension of their gibberish.

"If you just press that button on the bottom to get her started."

Paul dumbly followed orders and pressed the raised button which had previously activated the screen. A map glowed, centred on the location with its one or two recognisable names, the same as Paul had triggered in his showroom. He continued to touch the other sensor buttons as the mechanic brusquely dictated instructions from behind him. Coordinates appeared. His fingers shook and he knew he should be objecting, even refusing to co-operate but something about the mechanic's tone made him obey like a robot. He touched the orange button on instruction and momentarily recognised the familiarity of the London map with Best Cars at its centre.

"Well *done*, sir", came the voice from behind him. "Now the green button."

Paul hesitated. Something stirred in his memory, of how he came to be in this bizarre location in the first place. He shuddered. He felt fear and panic.

"Now, sir", came the firm bidding.

"But -" Paul could feel sweat on his brow, despite the cold.

"*Now*, sir, if you don't mind." In an involuntary reaction, Paul's finger reached out to jab the button. There followed the faintest judder or vibration again. Paul uttered a low howl and heard the indulgent voice behind him, "It's *okay* sir, soon be there."

Paul was sure he was crying but there was not time for any tears to fall. His hands were disappearing in front of him, the dashboard was fading away, his knees melted into space, the ledge above the dashboard and the outline of the windscreen frame ahead of him both dissolved into the night, and the dark itself became a colourless mist. In fright, he did not know if that was only because his eyes were dissolving, too. He thought he heard the voice behind him fading at the last, as though someone were turning the volume knob to 'mute': "soon be .. th..e..r..........."

Sleep

Elroy had picked up his voicemail messages in early evening, including a recent one from Bella. It was garbled, to put it kindly. Something about Paul disappearing before her eyes. So had he finally run off? Or was it an obscure metaphor for the disintegration of their relationship? He tried to raise her but got no reply, not even a recorded message. He felt sympathy. He liked her, a fellow strong-minded Yank. He had thought Paul was okay, too, to get along with. No telling how marriages are corroding out of view. It made him feel his warmth for Mariana again. She'd had much to tolerate lately, with never a rebuke to him for the hazards of his profession.

He tried phoning Walt, too, but got a voicemail message saying they were travelling and would reply when they could. He left a message about Paul and Bella. That was all he could do. He did not have the Best Cars phone number. He ate at the hotel in Gloucester and turned in for an early night. He assumed British Customs would be acting on the information sent by Timmis and himself.

Gordon Pierce did not want any more embarrassments. His immediate urge was to descend unannounced on Best Cars with a party of officers like the last time. Then he remembered all the detail of the wooden dolls, the vanishing or non-existent 'uranium', the empty kebab house; even the surprise follow-up raid a few days later, just in case they should catch the culprits returning after they thought the coast was clear. All drawing a blank. It was not just the Christmas newsletter, he was lucky it had happened all too quickly for the press and media to latch on. It had been easy to dismiss a couple of belated press enquiries as 'rumour and gossip' a week after the events.

Now, he had phoned Best Cars; was informed Paul Best himself had taken a car for a test drive. Was it a dual-powered vehicle, battery and petrol? There had been a pause before the reply. The Best Cars employee was not sure. When would Mr Best be expected to return? Uncertain response. Perhaps he would drive to see a northern customer and not be back until the next day. Odd, to take a night drive for a business trip, thought Pierce as he put the phone down.

He felt anxious but his confidence had been eroded by the previous fiasco. He needed more to go on than confusion over the car delivery - especially with the sensitivity of the same supplier and client as last time. He worried over the alert from GCHQ but if there was an arms racket they weren't going to risk the same conveyance as last time. And who was supplying this improbable information about plutonium? Yes, the same American guy who had convinced him about the vanishing uranium! He recalled his own calculations about the dolls and his suspicions, bordering on certainty, of what they had contained; but now he doubted that, too: schoolboy weights and measures in a tank of water!

He arrived home late, with Laura already in bed. He disliked disappointing his daughter. He also disliked loose ends but he went to bed himself, nevertheless.

-302The Best Cars salesman had been disconcerted by the phone call from Customs. His next feeling was one of relief and the impulse to blurt out the whole evening's events, from which he was still trembling. Then he remembered Sing's warning. His hand on the phone felt cold. Telling Customs would be like telling the police. What might happen to Mrs Best! He became guarded in his replies, whilst trying to avoid arousing suspicion. He was not sure if even admitting to the car being 'dual-powered' might bring Customs rushing in; he no longer knew what information was safe and which was not.

Perhaps, too, if he suggested Paul might not be back tonight it would prevent Customs coming straightaway. If it was the car they were interested in - just like the Chinese gang - maybe they would stay away tonight if there was no car to see. Suppose the Chinese got wind of Customs arriving in the middle of the night! He felt gingerly at the bandaged wound on his arm. Thankfully, it had been superficial enough for the first aid box to deal with. A knife wound in hospital would bring the police in a flash.

All this had been racing through his mind as he spoke to the Customs man. He put the phone down relieved to believe they could at least try to deal with the Mrs Best situation themselves at the showroom first. That said, none of them knew what to do. They were terrified by the Chinese gang. They discussed contacting the police, regardless, and then shuddered at the thought of being told of a woman's body being found the next day. They risked phoning Isabella's mobile but there was no reply.

Being the senior staff member, he eventually sent the others home, including the girl, who had remained as white as a sheet and still sobbed sporadically. He said he would think about what to do and phone them or see them in the morning. Maybe Paul would return soon and would know where to find a number for the Chinese: the little oriental man was connected with the dragon show.

The salesman unhappily spread himself out on Paul's armchair, hoping against hope the Chinese gang would not harm a woman, and must have dozed off. He, too, was suffering from shock. It was sometime in the early hours of the morning when he was awoken by a sound in the showroom and, when he looked out from the office, saw lights flashing on.

Chinaman

Paul watched dumbfounded and shaking as the man walked over to the light switches and flicked them on. The Chinaman! The Chinaman who had stepped out of the car from the passenger seat behind him! Paul's legs would no longer support him and he sank to the showroom floor beside the car. He could not stop himself squeezing and unclasping his hands and then clutching whole fistfuls of flesh beneath his shirt and trousers as though his body might not be there. He was trembling all over. Somehow it affected him more deeply than being dumped in a remote field.

Here he was, back in his own showroom with the lights full on, as if nothing had ever happened. But it had. It had! He could not be mad and imagining it. And dreams just don't come like this. Or if they do, you wake up and they're gone. Yes, the 'dream' - the terrible, terrifying transportation between showroom, field and back again, that was over. But now the Chinaman! Where was the mechanic? The mechanic who had climbed into the back seat behind him and told him to press the buttons. He had! He had!

Paul could not stop his whole body shaking. He tried wrapping his arms around himself but everything just shook together. He was certain it was the mechanic. It was dark, sure, but he saw enough to recognise him. Hair darker in the night shadows but the voice was the same - and the eyes. And he knew which buttons to press. How would a Chinaman know that? And how did this Chinaman know exactly where the showroom light switches were, to head straight for them?

First the mechanic who seemed to expect him in the middle of nowhere and then, suddenly, no mechanic but a Chinaman in his place! And where *did* he come from? It had all gone dark, everything had faded away, the car, himself, his whole body, *and* the mechanic, surely! And then it had all faded back, like some ghastly effect out of a space movie. Except the Chinaman stepped out from the seat behind him!

"Oh Christ, oh Christ", whimpered Paul by the front wheel of the car.

"Paul - Mr Best - you all right?"

The salesman had spotted the car back in its place and first heard what sounded like small gulps or sobs and then saw his boss, kind of curled up beside the car. He stooped nervously to speak to him. Paul looked up, red-eyed. The salesman, caught between embarrassment at his employer's ignominious disposition and concern for his welfare, helped him to his feet.

"Sorry, Brian, thanks", mumbled Paul, making a feeble gesture to dust himself down. His hands shook violently as he swept them across his clothes.

Whatever his boss's problem, the salesman had to explain right away.

"Paul, they've taken Mrs Best."

"What? Who?" Paul was struggling to get his mind around a further incongruity.

Brian the salesman hastily recounted the evening's events, not pausing to enquire where the owner of Best Cars might have been.

"They want this car."

"*This* car?" Paul looked at the ordinary but extraordinary Manchu Met at his side, for a moment unable to connect his own improbable excursion with any stake anyone else might have in it. Somehow his brain had reached its limit of logical deduction. "But ... but ..."he began to stutter, filling with fear and concern for Bella, "how do we contact them? How do we ...get her *back*?"

Unbidden, his eyes were filling with tears again. It was too much. Much, much too much.

Then he looked up and saw the Chinaman approaching. For a few moments he had forgotten the Chinaman.

Jigsaw

"You have it now?"

The voice was hard. Teng had moved around to Gainsborough's side of the console and was hovering by his shoulder, peering meanly at the screen. Hill hated him scrutinising his work as though the Chinese man had any chance of comprehending it.

"Yes, yes", Gainsborough assured him, trying to keep the irritation out of his voice. The anxiety, too. The car was back at the London destination but he had not got it there himself. Just as he was re-plotting the co-ordinates, someone had taken local control and beaten him to it. Hill was alarmed. The first locally contrived 'jump' was clearly random: someone meddling with controls they did not understand. But the return 'trip', this had been re-plotted with pinpoint accuracy. Who could possibly know what they were doing? Could it be a lucky coincidence? He did not need to calculate the random probability. His forehead felt clammy.

"You can proceed when required?" demanded Teng.

"Yes, yes, of course", concurred Gainsborough, desperate visions of Vicki crowding his mind. He hoped he was right.

Elroy was woken by his phone on the bedside table.

"El, it's Walt. Livvy said I gotta call you, cos of your message."

"Eh?" Elroy heaved himself to examine the bedside clock: three minutes past four. Dark. "Gee, Walt, it's four in the morning."

"Yeh, tell me", came the chuckle in reply, "guess you just curling up with a glass at home eh? We just landed at Heathrow."

"What!" Elroy jerked half out of bed.

"We couldn't reach you to tell you. Livvy's come to help Bella."

"Hey, Walt, I'm here too. Cheltenham."

"You?" came Walt's amazed response.

"Yeh, man, been here a few days. Jest couldn't tell. Too dangerous. Sorry. I'll explain. What's with Isabella?"

"Dunno. Something real bad between her and Paul, I guess. She fell apart on the phone. Livvy had to come."

"I gotta message, too." Elroy sounded bemused. "Didn't think it was a disaster."

"Livvy said Bella went on and on about Paul disappearing with a car. One of the Chinese ones", Walt continued. "No big deal I guess, but you know women."

Elroy did not hear the last part. He had frozen where he sat. Next thing, he was tearing clothes on, with the phone switched to speaker on the table. He could not unscramble anything to make sense but all the awful jigsaw pieces seemed to be gathering in the same place. Maybe there was nothing he could do but he had to be there.

"Walt, you going to Bella?"

"Yeh, man, just collecting bags."

"Showroom or home?"

"Bella said she'd stay at the showroom till Paul came back."

"I'll see you there", shouted Elroy at his phone.

"Yeh?" was the surprised reply.

"Yeh, pal. Soon as I get a cab."

He clicked off his mobile and immediately dialled on the room phone for a local car. Nothing made sense from where he was. Maybe it would in London.

Gordon Pierce woke dripping with sweat. His wife was sound asleep at his side. He had been dreaming but he woke realising it was more than a dream. He had been woken by fear. Battery! Chinese cars! Plutonium! Was it horribly possible! Why had he not made any connections? Was it all that rubbish about the number of cars? That still made no sense. But the London dealer said he had a battery-powered car. GCHQ had warned about looking for heavy insulation for plutonium. But they had *not* checked through any car from China that contained anything other than the usual car batteries, however muddled Andy had been about the number. Now the London guy had apparently driven off in a new car. Why? Nothing added up. But, wasn't that the bitter lesson of his job? Two and two hardly ever make four.

Gordon swung his legs quietly out of bed. Downstairs he made the swiftest of coffees. Only when outside and would not wake the family, did he softly call up three trusted colleagues, who would turn out at no notice in the middle of the night and not betray him afterwards if it all came to nothing. He looked at his watch. Half past four. It would take just over half an hour to get there and meet up. He creaked up the garage door and started the car engine. If his wife woke up now, she would soon go back to sleep. She was used to his job.

Safe

The salesman tensed in terror. Chinese could mean only one thing. He began to back around the car for protection. Paul, still trembling, looked between the Chinaman and his salesman in confusion and felt himself infected by some of Brian's fear. The Chinaman, though, in trim aircraft-blue suit - similar in colour to a mechanic's overalls, had Paul been of a mind to notice - and dark-patterned tie, was no more than brisk and to the point, ignoring or unaware of their unease.

"Now then", he began, with nothing more than a brief, polite smile, "Mr Best", and he added a slight nod of acknowledgment in the direction of the salesman, who had paused halfway into a crouch behind the car boot, "I expect you legard the leturn of Mrs Best as an immediate pliolity."

"Where ... where ... ?" stuttered Paul, being the first words he had managed to utter to the Chinese man since the guy had slipped neatly out of the car to switch the lights on. What he was trying to say was 'where did you come from', while the words he had just heard - 'legard', 'leturn' and 'pliolity' were swimming about in his head like aimless goldfish.

"Where is she indeed", replied the Chinaman to a different question, "you can lewy on me." With that, as 'regard', 'return', priority' and 'rely' were settling on their respective perches (if that is what goldfish do) in Paul's dysfucntioning brain, the man whipped a phone from his inside pocket.

Paul turned in distress to the salesman.

"Brian, I've got to get her back! These people are dangerous, mad!"

They both looked anxiously at the Chinaman, each trying to fit him into the terror gang.

The Chinaman raised a hand to still them as he dialled a number, then a moment later he broke into an animated volley of Chinese. When he had finished, he turned to Paul.

"They come. She is safe." They both thought they then heard him say 'cretins' under his breath but both thought they must have been mistaken in tense and frightening circumstances.

"Coming?" exclaimed the salesman, fearfully, and involuntarily moved a protective hand to his wounded arm.

"Don't wully", dismissed the Chinaman, "they want the car."

Paul and the salesman each took a step away from the vehicle, as though it might do something unpleasant, like give off an electric charge, Paul with better reason to fear than his salesman. Then they both noticed the Chinaman take on a distant look, as if preoccupied elsewhere.

"Yes, boss", he said to no-one.

Paul and the salesman looked at each other then ran their eyes anxiously around the showroom in case someone else had entered.

"Yes, guv." The Chinaman sounded very slightly vexed this time, as he gazed into the middle distance. "It velly *okay*, boss.."

Then he turned again to Paul, as if he had not spoken at all.

"Now, Mr Best", the Chinaman turned to address Paul as though he had spoken to no-one else, "we wait." And then added a particularly emphatic "*Yes, Guv*, velly good."

"Who...?" began Paul, but there was definitely no-one else there besides the three of them and he already wondered if he was going mad. Or else the Chinaman was. The salesman just gawped and frowned; a Chinaman talking to himself was the least of his worries. They had barely time to think of filling the awkward silence, when there was the screech of tyres outside the back of the showroom, followed by slamming of car doors and raised voices. Fists thundered at the rear showroom doors. Brian the salesman started in fright.

"Let them in", the Chinaman said to him, briskly.

"But ...!" Brian was clearly terrified but the Chinaman fixed him with a piercing stare from his deep brown eyes and he walked, as though propelled by another force, to the doors. He opened them and was thrust violently back. The same four Chinese burst through, fronted by Mr Sing, two at his side, the third, behind, gripping Isabella by both her arms. Paul's mind cleared for the first time since he had last seen her. His frame tightened and he leapt forward. He was halted by the front two heavies stepping towards him and he was aware of the flash of blades.

"Bella!" he shouted in worried alarm.

Her head drooped and she did not respond.

"Mr Best", Sing addressed him coolly, ignoring Paul's concern for his wife, "the car." It was a demand. He glanced at the Manchu Met beside the salesman and Brian gestured feebly to it in acknowledgment. Sing opened the driver's door and took a quick look at the dashboard. He seemed to see what he expected and closed the door again. He motioned to the henchman holding Isabella and the man pushed her towards Paul. Now she looked up at him, bleary and unsmiling. He saw she had a cut on her lip and a discoloured swelling on one cheek.

"What!" Paul swivelled angrily in the direction of Sing, all his faculties restored. He half raised an arm but all three thickset Chinese moved towards him, accompanied by a warning, "Mr Best!", from Sing. Paul threw his arms protectively around Bella as she collapsed into them.

"She could only tell what we already knew", shrugged Sing, impassively.

"I just said you'd... you'd ..disappeared", Bella choked, then Paul felt her sobbing into his shoulder.

Sing was turning his attention to the car again, when he noticed the other Chinaman.

"Hey. You", he frowned, "who are you?"

"I phoned you", the man called back, lowering his phone.

"You?" Sing looked puzzled. "What's your name?" Then adding some words in Chinese before the other man replied, giving the distinct impression of making up a name on the spot.

"Mr ... Gee."

Sing looked perplexed, bordering upon suspicious but turned urgently back to the car with an order to one of his henchmen.

"Check the *battery*."

He gave the word a heavy emphasis, as he reached inside the driver's door to release the boot latch. The swarthy accomplice began to raise the lid to look inside but then let it drop at a sudden commotion beyond the far end of the showroom, outside the glazed front doors. A flash and gleam of car headlights in the darkness and more screeching of tyres and brakes. Then shouts and a hammering of fists at the doors. Salesman Brian leapt into action and ran to the doors to shout in reply, instinct telling him this might be their rescue. He ran half back into the showroom an instant later, whilst the Chinese gang were still frozen in alarm.

"They say it's Customs!" He called to Paul, still hugging Bella. "Shall I let them in?"

"Yes!" Paul's head jerked up in instant realisation that relief was at hand.

"No!" commanded Sing, fiercely gesturing his gang to hold their ground. They were too distracted to notice Mr Gee the Chinaman was back on his phone dictating a series of numbers. He broke off to bark at them in the confusion.

"Get in the car!" he ordered. "Quick! Get in the car!"

Sing was about to protest but something in the stranger's tone silenced him.

"*Get in!*" Gee repeated with a shout. "You must get away!" And then added, to neither them nor his phone, "*Yes*, Boss! It'll be *safe!*"

Sing was startled by this address to an unseen accomplice but was further propelled by another battering at the doors and the sight of Brian courageously running to open them. He yelled at his gang to get in the car, taking possession of their trophy. Chinaman Gee appeared to quell his momentary fluster to resume his phone call and the recitation of numbers, as the four men scrambled into the car and slammed the doors.

Gainsborough had taken the phone call quite of the blue. It was just after one o'clock; lunchtime. He was still shadowed by Teng. He had regained control but did not know what to do next. Teng had also taken an urgent call less than half an hour earlier; apparently the car was being collected. Now, suddenly, an unidentified oriental was on the phone to Gainsborough. His tone was quiet but commanding. Gainsborough did not even look to Teng for approval. The co-ordinates were being dictated rapidly down the line. Follow this setting or the car was lost. That was all Gainsborough relayed to Teng. He was being informed there was not time to discuss or delay. Now or never.

The call was briefly interrupted and he thought he heard distant sounds of commotion at the other end of the line. The distant Chinese voice briefly sounded less composed but the numbers finished. He pressed the button.

"Let them in!" yelled Paul over to Brian, who had reached the doors. Then there was a slight rustling in the air near to Paul and Bella, remaining alone by the car, she still held in his arms, the four Chinese hunched inside. She whimpered and trembled; Paul just froze. The car was dissolving in front of them before it vanished.

Footsteps thundered across the showroom; four uniformed men with Brian chasing behind.

"You're under arrest!" shouted Gordon Pierce at Paul and Bella, hugged together beside an empty space in the showroom. Then he looked bewildered. He recognised the showroom owner and his wife. They looked blankly at him. The four Customs men all halted in a group together. Brian pulled up behind them, panting.

"He said", gasped Pierce, indicating Brian, "there were Chinese here. Thugs. With a car."

Paul nodded wearily. He felt emptied inside.

"Right."

"So where are they?" demanded Gordon, feeling something slip away again before he even knew what it was.

"Gone. They've gone", was all Paul could manage.

"Couldn't you stop them, sir? Couldn't you stop them?" breathed Gordon, aware as he spoke it might have been too much to expect of two men and a woman confronted by an armed gang. He was surprised by Paul Best's smile, then the heave of his shoulders, still wrapped around his wife, and the splutters of incongruous laughter that spilled from his lips.

Teng took another call, spoke briefly, gave a short smile of satisfaction and appeared to relax before turning to Gainsborough, who was bent over the console and looked up in response. Teng spoke.

"Good. It is safe."

Map

"Disappeared?"

Gordon Pierce was still turning this way and that, desperately hoping his eyes would suddenly alight on the target of his search and all the pieces would begin falling into place. But the dozen or more small Chinese cars on display all looked distressingly normal. The only abnormality of any description was the space they were all grouped around, from which, he was being implausibly informed, another Chinese car had disappeared a few moments earlier.

"They *drove* it away?" he insisted to Paul.

"No", replied Paul, wearily, his arms still around his wife, one across her shoulders, the other to hold her hand, "disappeared, vanished."

"Evaporated." Bella spoke quietly, raising her reddened eyes for the first time since the Customs team had arrived.

"Sir", began Pierce, controlling his exasperation, but he was interrupted by a beating of hands against the glass door panel out in the showroom and a woman's voice shouting from outside, "Bella! Bella! Are you there?"

Paul gently let go of his wife and strode immediately to the showroom doors, recognising the American accent, and thrust open a door. Walt and Olivia hurried through.

"Oh Paul!" Olivia exclaimed in relief, "You're here! Bella said you'd disappeared!"

"I had", Paul smiled weakly. Just then there were more headlights in the forecourt as a taxi pulled in and the big familiar figure of Elroy Fitzgibbon jumped out, stuffing bank notes into the driver's fist and flinging the door shut behind him. There was a rapid exchange of hugs and handshakes then Olivia saw Bella and rushed with a gasp of dismay to hug her.

"Oh Bella!", she cried as she saw her bruised and cut face, "What happened to you!"

Isabella's eyes welled up again as she haltingly told her friend of her ordeal, Walt and Elroy listening in mounting anger. Paul had let her slip into Olivia's arms and suddenly swung round.

"The Chinaman!"

"Chinaman?" said Pierce, quickly, through pursed lips.

"Yes!" Paul's eyes were darting about the showroom. "In here!"

Pierce followed his eyes and they spotted someone together, at the far end of the display area. They also both realised he was not Chinese. He was strolling casually amongst the cars. He had nondescript sandy-coloured hair and wore a grey-blue jacket with darker trousers. He appeared to be talking on the phone; talking to somebody, anyway. They could hear him from a few metres away.

"Yes, boss ... no, no, guv ... *guv* ... sorted ... well, in a *moment* ..." (Almost exasperation in his voice).

Both Englishmen were too flustered to notice the absence of a phone, Pierce because unexplained events and people were tumbling into each other at a pace he found difficult to assimilate, Paul because all his immediate turmoil was subsumed by indignation at an intruder amongst his cars at an outrageous hour.

"How did *you* get in?" Paul challenged the stranger as they approached him. His voice was hot, his breath short.

"I'm just looking at the cars." replied the young man, nonchalantly but with the impression he was affronted by Paul's aggressive tone.

"It's half past five in the morning!" blustered Paul, incredulously.

"So?" responded the man, looking at his watch, "you sell cars, don't you?"

Before either Paul or Pierce could react to the insolence of the intruder, the man drew a neatly folded sheet of white paper from his inside jacket pocket.

"Here", he said bluntly and held it out to them, "I found this on the floor over there." He indicated the space where the transient Manchu Met had been. He handed it to Gordon. "Seems to be a *map*." There was a hint of sarcasm, suggesting grown adults might not be able to recognise a map when they saw one.

Pierce grabbed it from him, just as Elroy appeared at his side, following them to the sandy-haired man. Paul was still seething at the intruder's evasiveness, thoughts of a police call foremost in his mind as he opened his mouth to remonstrate with him further. He was distracted by a sharp exclamation from Elroy, who was peering over Pierce's shoulder at the sheet of paper.

"Lawd!"

Pierce frowned.

"That symbol!" Elroy took the paper from Gordon's hand and stared at it.

"Yes?" queried Pierce, impatiently.

"It's the scientific symbol for plutonium isn't it?"

"Jesus", Gordon breathed, "is it?" The symbol, 'Pu', was at the centre beside some x,y axis co-ordinates on the primitive sketch map.

"Where is this place?" demanded Elroy. He examined the map bearing. The map itself was no more than a thin black outline divided into a few irregular shapes, like a ground plan for a set of buildings or a group of fields, or both, with the co-ordinates and symbol at its centre. "Where was this paper?" he asked Paul.

"Where the car was, he said", replied Paul, indicating the intruder. "The Chinese. Oh hell! They could have left this map!"

All three rushed over to the empty place. The young man watched without moving. They were unaware of his disdainful air as he saw them stare at the ground.

"You think they left it here?" Pierce asked Elroy, as he pointed at the symbol.

"Don't know, man", muttered Elroy. "Look, man, all we did was intercept messages. I'm guessing everything. But, gee, if you'd told me we'd suddenly find a map, with a plutonium symbol, right where some Tria - Chinese - thugs just been -"

"You said Triads?" broke in Pierce, sharply.

"That's guesswork, too", heaved Elroy, "but, man, it's adding up real bad. Can you find this place?" He pointed at the map.

"Yeh, if it's real", said Pierce.

"Better find out, man", said Elroy. "Lawd", he looked direct into Pierce's eyes, "you better find out."

Trio

Paul and Elroy watched as Pierce and his men drove at speed from the forecourt, Pierce issuing a demand on his phone to the Home Office for a specialist radiation team in protective clothing; a call he had never made in his life and had never expected he would. Then Paul swung to confront the impertinent intruder but was interrupted by yet more screeching of brakes and tyres and a succession of loud thunderings upon the rear doors of the showroom. All five of them jumped. With the Customs men now gone, it could only be foe, not friend. A Chinese voice could be heard shouting:

"Let us in! Or we break the glass!"

Paul and Elroy exchanged nervous looks but a voice behind them spoke.

"Let them in, please, Mr Best."

Paul started, looked, and felt his stomach turn; he felt giddy. It was the Chinaman, who had disappeared!

"Where the bloody he-!" Paul faltered.

"Please, Mr Best."

Paul began to shake again as Elroy looked at him, perplexed, and held out an arm to him but had to watch as, on a second urging from the Chinaman - "Mr *Best*" - Paul took some unsteady steps to open the doors, rattling under the blows. Sing and his three henchmen sprung through and two immediately grabbed Paul. Elroy made to jump to his aid but was halted by the menacing flash of a blade.

"Where is it!" demanded Sing, his dry demeanour completely replaced by a glowering fury.

"What?" Paul could not think and was not even struggling in the grip of the two swarthy Triads.

"The battery!" Sing shouted at him. You take it from the car!"

"I?" Paul began, weakly. "He ..." He indicated the recurring Chinaman but then remembered it was not he who took the battery, it was the mechanic. The mechanic now vanished. He was trapped in a vortex of unreality; there was no way out. He looked helplessly at the fuming Mr Sing and felt hands tighten their grip around his arms and elbows. Elroy was marooned by the fear a knife would be put to Paul if he attempted to help him. Then the unexplained Chinaman spoke from behind them. It was a volley of unintelligible, but clearly short-tempered, Chinese to his fellow-countrymen. Then he finished briefly in English.

"It is here", concluded the Chinaman, with the impatient air of wanting to put a cap on the whole business. "Look, please." And he gestured towards the doors.

Sing was about to challenge the stranger again, who seemed to be interpolating himself randomly into the night's events without any explanation about who he was or where he came from. But the throb of an engine outside halted him. They all heard a truck pull up outside the doors, then manoeuvre, before they saw it back up to the open doorway. It was a breakdown truck with a small crane on the back. A man in blue overalls jumped out of the cab and peered through the doors. He addressed Paul, whose knees were giving way and he would have collapsed to the floor if not held by each arm. The mechanic! Paul looked behind him, nervously, and yes, the Chinaman was still there. Both of them together.

"Here sir. Fixed. Don't say we don't try." The mechanic was deadpan and the brown eyes, briefly meeting Paul's, betrayed a lack of humour that reflected working all through the night. He turned to operate levers at the side of the truck and the crane swung into action. Its grab appeared over the back of the vehicle, holding the heavy battery, which it deposited just inside the showroom doors. The stranger Chinaman gestured to it, with a shrug at Sing and his gang. Paul looked at him as he did so and for a bizarre instant felt he was looking again at the mechanic, so strikingly similar were their eyes. He looked away and tried to straighten his legs. Then he stumbled as his captors released their grip. Sing had stepped smartly to the battery placed on the floor and was examining its surface.

"Good", he declared grimly to Paul as he pulled himself to his feet, "it remains sealed. You are fortunate." His gaze fell on Elroy and Walt, who had crossed the room to see what was happening. "All of you are."

Subconsciously, Paul was staring at the battery. He had only seen it by the car boot light until now. He realised it was not real. It was a convincing dummy, a heavy lead casing with imitation knobs and terminals. It was also sturdily sealed with a lead strap. Then he looked up and found he was staring directly at the mechanic.

"Whe -re?" stuttered Paul, "You were in the car."

"Car, sir?" replied the mechanic, innocently.

"The ... the -" Paul was not sure what he could remember. He thought there was a field. He knew he recognised the mechanic. But from where? Now here he was in his showroom with both the man he was convinced had climbed *into* the back seat of the car and the man who had inexplicably stepped out of it.

Sing was clearly resolved not to allow mysteries, however irritating, to divert him from his course. He motioned to his men.

"Take it", he commanded.

All three took hold and heaved to lift the lead weight. Paul dimly remembered what he had thought was the same object swept lightly onto the mechanic's shoulder. He shook his head at the recollection. He must have been mistaken.

"Yes, guv."

The voice came from behind the group. It was the sandy-haired intruder, overlooked in the fracas.

"Guv?"

The strange Chinaman turned with a look between query and admonishment. The others, English, American and Chinese paused as they sensed a frisson of antagonism between the unidentified pair.

"*Guv*", insisted the intruder with a small glare at the Chinaman.

"Don't wully, guv." This time it was the mechanic, talking to no-one in particular.

"*Wully?*" came the indignant retort from the Chinaman as, this time, he glared at the mechanic, who responded with a mischievous grin. Then the sandy-haired intruder chimed in, addressing the Triad party.

"Better take it, quick. Don't say we don't *tly*." Then added, with a glance at the mechanic, "if you don't mind."

"*Tly*!" The Chinaman swung furiously around at the intruder, as the mechanic sniped from beside his truck, "don't *mind* if we just get in the way, eh?", across at the intruder. The onlooking group momentarily forgot their opposing fears and aggressions as they paused to gape at this incongruous exchange. Sing was the first to collect himself, just as the showroom intruder added, "Safe, gluv, yes, soon."

"*Gluv*?" The Chinaman glared at him again.

-305The Triads were hastened by a gesture and sharp volley of Chinese from Sing and began to stagger out through the showroom rear doors with the heavy lead casing.

"Yes, yes, take it!" The irritated Chinaman urged them, with a Chinese retort of his own to Sing, and then added, "Now, guv, slafe."

"Slafe?" queried the mechanic, with irony.

"*Safe*!" ground out the Chinaman with clenched teeth.

"Yes, bloss." It was the sandy-haired intruder this time and the Chinaman immediately responded with a short, jeering laugh.

"Bloss?" he mocked.

"*Boss*," came the mechanic's voice, although it sounded to the onlookers uncannily like the intruder's. Or was it the Chinaman's? The thought occurred to them all at once, even Sing, despite his preoccupation with ushering his gang out through the doors with the battery. The mechanic issued a burst of encouragement to them as they exited past him and his truck. It made the gang almost drop the battery and Sing snatched for the knife hidden under his belt. The mechanic had spoken entirely in *Chinese*. The others - Paul, Elroy, Walt and now the two women, who had cautiously moved nearer to see what was going on, Bella despite her trauma - watched and listened in growing bewilderment. The sandy-haired intruder called across to Sing as he pulled out his knife.

"Better *glow. Now!*"

"*Glow*?" The mechanic mocked him.

"*Go*", corrected the Chinaman, vehemently. Or *was* it him? The others saw him move his lips but thought the voice actually came from the intruder behind him. Some did, anyway, but those looking at the mechanic thought it was *he* who spoke, though his lips remained entirely still. Sing was replacing his blade and moving to follow his gang who had restored their hold on the 'battery'. He had to pause, if only to share the confusion of the others at the rapid interchange between the trio, who seemed to have acquired some mutual distaste for each other.

"Don't dlop it!" (The Chinaman's voice from the mechanic as the Triads staggered out with the weight).

"*Dlop*?" (The intruder's voice from the Chinaman; the intruder smiling sarcastically, the Chinaman bristling).

"Mind how you glow." (The Chinaman's voice from the direction of the intruder but it was the mechanic's lips which moved).

"*Go*!" (Chinaman, annoyed).

"*Glow.*" (Intruder, sweetly).

"If you don't *mind* .." (Mechanic to the other two, with heavy irony).

"Mind?" (Chinaman's voice, intruder's lips, both glowering at mechanic).

"How?" (Intruder's voice, Chinaman's lips, both still glowering).

"How?" (Mechanic, to no-one).

"Now?" (Chinaman and intruder simultaneously, to no-one).

"Yes -" (Mechanic, a little more sheepishly).

" - boss." (Intruder, also sheepishly).

"Fry away?" (The Chinaman, mildly questioning, mingled with sheepishness).

"Without -?" (Intruder).

" - wings?" (Mechanic).

In a brief pause, in which the three appeared to have momentarily talked each other to a standstill, the Triad gang, urged determinedly by Sing, staggered out into the darkness. The remaining onlookers - Paul, Elroy, Walt, Isabella and Olivia - slowly relaxed whilst passing stunned looks at the improbable ventriloquists. The mechanic broke the short silence, now more subdued than irritable.

"Well then, there you are."

He spread his arms in a gesture that all was completed and began to walk away to the front of his truck.

"You are -" began the intruder, to them.

"Yes -" said the Chinaman, to no-one.

" - boss", added the intruder, this time also to no-one.

"It is -", they heard the mechanic, almost obscured in the dark outside the open showroom doors.

"*Now*", spoke Teng, grimly, as he put his phone back in his pocket, his eyes steeled at Gainsborough, "*now* ..this time .. it is -"

"Safe", the Chinaman assured them, and seemed almost to manage a comforting smile.

"Safe", agreed the intruder, who had slipped a few steps away across the showroom.

"Boss", added the Chinaman.

"Guv", the intruder threw upwards and over his departing shoulder.

"Safe", they thought they heard the mechanic's voice, just before it was drowned by the engine starting up.

Their movement was becoming restored, thawed from being transfixed by their experience and the scene around them. Paul was coming to his senses. He began to want answers. The truck had throbbed off into the winter morning darkness. He turned to speak to the Chinaman, seek some explanations; but the man had gone! Paul looked around, aware the others were doing the same. The diminutive oriental had somehow melted away. Paul and Elroy caught sight of the sandy-haired intruder by the glazed doors at the far end. Too late, he was leaving, too. They both shivered for a second together. Neither of them had seen a door opening but now the man was walking away outside into the sodium-and-black gloom. Paul involuntarily laid a hand on Elroy's arm to steady himself. Elroy felt glad he did, in a moment he needed some reassurance. Neither ever mentioned this to the other. Not ever.

"And now -" Teng's lips had all but disappeared into a single tense line across his mouth, eyes glinting black and hard. " - you will bring it *back*?" He bit on the last word, like the crunching of stone.

Gainsborough nodded gloomily. He was like a blind man, and deaf, too; neither seeing nor hearing what was happening half-way around the world. Only watching co-ordinates appear and reappear on the screen in front of him, changing and rearranging outside his control; the location shifting just when he thought he had pinned it down. Now, though, it seemed to have stabilised. He had to re-establish the co-ordinates, confirm the location. Regain control before something else happened. If only for Vicki, he must do it, if not for himself. He looked up at Teng's taut, angry features.

"Yes. I'll get it back", was all he said.

Part Nine

VISITS

VISITS

Nudging

"Three!"

There was some grunting and testy foraging in the otherwise undisturbed silence.

"I mean ... *three!*"

If toes could complain they might protest at being scapegoats for some maladventure beyond their command.

"I mean ..." A look upwards to check whether the grievance was inducing its deserved sympathy and concern. "I mean .. not in three different *places* ...!" A pause unrewarded with any murmurs of solicitude. "Three .. in the *same* place! Together!"

Crevices of any kind may yield only so much surplus material before there remains nothing but their very nub to yield.

"*Ow!*"

Which is an instance, rare in its way, when even the Greatest Compassion Of All may be singularly wanting.

"I mean, there was I -"

"almost forgetting which one you were", murmured He Who Is Without Malice, softly.

The angel straightened up with a petulant grimace, finger-wiping as he did so.

"Yeh, well." And added under his breath, or so he thought, "might be easy for Some."

"Fortunately", observed the Lord God Almighty, ignoring that little slingshot, "the outcome was satisfactory."

"I mean", grumbled the angel of the Lord, "anyone would get mixed up."

"Anyone .." repeated the selfsame Lord, benignly.

"I mean - do they always have to be spoonfed? ... 'Let's take this thing and drop it over here nice and safe so you can't blow each other up' ... 'Now let's get you back home' ... 'Now you lot take this away before this other lot gets you -'"

"Don't wully", serenely came the Voice That is Never Heard.

Grumpy looked up, sharply, but saw only beneficence and grace.

" - 'Now here's something you thought you lost, only - ha, ha" (spoken without humour) "'it's not the thing you thought it was' ...'And you other lot - guess what I found - take a look at this you dumboes. Do I have to spell it out to you? Yes, obviously I do'!...'So why not go and find it? I've done the rest!'" A pause, engaged in some desultory separating of digits to examine the future potential inbetween. "Three! *Anyone* would get mixed up."

"The path was restored", observed the Lord, quietly.

"Nudging", grunted the ill-humoured angel.

"We adjust only to remove a threat to Our aims and to the path in progress."

"And even that isn't the right one."

Gabriel was not one to let Him forget, vouchsafed the Lord to Himself.

"Wrong country?" added Gabriel, by way of a reminder. "And now the 'great leap forward' back in the *right* country, but too late, and with the *wrong* people!"

"A dislocation", agreed God, with a short sigh (not enough to alter any fates by too much of a margin). Was it the petal? Or the lipstick? Or some other past, for some other future?

"Biscuits and railway lines", was the muttered rejoinder.

"With Our intervention", prompted the Lord.

"Nudging", grunted the angel again, confirming his disquiet, "like the bus."

The Lord raised the metaphorical eyebrow. An invisible action but one recognisable to the archangel.

"The bus that runs over the child", expounded Gabriel. "Why can't that be nudged? Or Joan -"

"Gabriel."

The angel fell quiet. He considered he might have more to say on that some other time, so to speak..

PARADIGM : LOSING

The waves chafed in a fret, as if provoked to their testy ire by some other sway, a potion poured across their backs that they must twist and turn to throw it off yet still it clung, a canker spread upon them all.

"They have grown and they do pain me."

He tenderly caressed her soft skin. The firmness in his hands flenched as his fingers rode along and over the distended knots, which had been but pimples, his pores becoming damp from their emissions, seeping into the torrid air.

"I will tend to them again, my love. The plants and herbs will aid us in our need, as they always do."

"They, too, are diseased", she replied, turning to melt him in her soft gaze, eyes of love and trust but fearful of a changing time. "I think they cannot aid me. Perhaps will only harm."

His head turned at the plaintive cry behind and saw the infant, his son, wrapped in leaves to soothe the sores and twisting his small frame to ease the hurt. She followed his look and clasped his arm at their sorrow for the child. She tried to quell the tear but felt it slipping from her eye and he raised a hand to gently stop it as it fell and had to make as though to scribe a circle round her cheek to meet the tear below, so she would not feel his finger rise and fall over the swollen mound there, another like those upon her back. He felt his own tears rise at this corruption of her flawless skin and felt suddenly he wished to claw it out, to tear and wrench it from her perfect face and hurl it to the ground and stamp on it and destroy it as it came between them. He knew he could not, as it would harm and hurt her sweetness even more. He brushed at his own eye.

"You weep, my love? I shall soon be cured. The air will cure me. Will cure us both."

"No, no, not weep." He fiercely shook his head as he lied to her, as he had never before, to somehow protect her from what, he knew not, and he took a deep breath of the thick heavy air that might indeed have cured her once, before it became so. It caught in his lungs and made him gasp as the sea thrashed its angry tails as if to tell him it already knew.

She made to clasp her arms around him but he started back and tenderly drew her arms from him and held him to her by her hands for he did not want her to feel the strong skin on his back, ruptured in so many places, too, the same as hers.

"My love", he murmured.

"My love", she murmured, too.

They stood under the looming sky that also seemed to hover and wait, holding a smothering mask between them and their dulling sun.

Impossible

"Impossible."

They had listened to Paul's account. And Bella's, too. He, Olivia and Walt wanting to hear the incredible description a second, third, even fourth time. Sitting in the Bests' smart town house lounge, they noticed how Paul's comfortable frame shuddered always when he reached the part where his hands, limbs, the whole car 'dissolved', as he described it. Isabella imperceptibly shook at the same time, as she relived what she had not experienced herself but claimed she witnessed.

"Impossible", repeated Elroy.

Unable to sleep and resorting instead to a cooked breakfast only hours after the incidents of the night, they heard again Paul's faltering tale of how he and the car 'rematerialised' in a field; the mechanic; the return to the showroom. He tried to explain the substitution of the Chinese man for the mechanic but agreed with them that his state of mind after being transported to the field, and back to the showroom, in the same traumatic manner might have dislodged his sense of awareness and reason.

Yet they all knew they had seen both the mechanic and Chinese man in the showroom. The mechanic, they assured themselves, must have slipped out of the car before the return 'journey'; and probably the Chinese man was already in the showroom when Paul and the car returned. It did not square with what Paul said he recalled but at least it made better sense. More sense than the car.

When Olivia quietly suggested that Isabella's own ordeal may have upset her usual rationality she was met with a ferocious retort that she wasn't mad and, anyway, when she watched Paul and the car disappear, hours before the same car containing the Chinese gang 'evaporated', it was long before those thugs abducted and mistreated her. Even Olivia, long-accustomed to her friend's flashes of ire, withered under the fusillade.

Elroy wanted to hear Paul's description of his 'dissolving' and 're-forming' in detail. The whole experience of one's own body melting away and later solidifying. Elroy, even as one disinclined to doubt the veracity of another's story, could not accept it. It bore no connection with scientific fact.

"Impossible", he said again, after a long drawn-out breath.

"Is it really?" asked Walt, from under hooded brows, frowning and trying to visualise for the fourth or fifth time what his wife's friend and her husband had recounted.

Elroy grimaced and shook his head.

"Depends what you mean by 'really'", he replied.

"You mean it's possible?" Walt sought verification.

"No", grunted Elroy, "you know it's not my specialism but, 'sfar as I'm aware, the best anyone's yet done is teleport a few photons."

"Photons?" queried Olivia.

"Smallest particles of light", responded Elroy.

"How small is that?" asked Walt, who dealt with things of physical substance: cars requiring gas, factories demanding energy, and the like.

"Helluva sight smaller than him", Elroy turned his head with a wry smile at the troubled Paul. "And over a few metres, not halfway across England."

"So what are you suggesting it was?" Bella lifted her head to deliver the words in a sharp volley of resentment.

"Hallucination?" Elroy shrugged, uncomfortably.

"*Both* of us?" snapped Bella. "Paul *in* it, me watching?"

"Bella", Olivia tried to soothe her friend, while Paul remained slouched at her side, "you've both been under strain-"

"Livvy!" Isabella's voice was almost a scream before she subsided, sobbing, onto Paul's shoulder.

The other three looked at each other awkwardly. There was a rift. A rift of disbelief. Whatever their two friends had undergone, it had to be something erupting from their own troubled psyches, not from the realms of science fiction. Olivia quietly took charge of clearing the breakfast things into the kitchen and washed them up, while Walt and Elroy drifted in her wake. Then the three of them muttered something through the lounge doorway about taking a walk and slipped out. Paul and Isabella remained huddled together on the sofa, saying nothing.

Plot

The so-called eyewitnesses were, by their own admission, inebriated. It was nearly midnight and the pub in London's East End would have failed in its duty had there been much sobriety by that hour. It was not one of those where parents took their children for a cheap chips-and-something meal, two for the price of one before seven o'clock. Only the ragged scallywags of Dickens' Oliver Twist should have been seen anywhere near it.

The motley, wobbly-legged group of regulars had, some of them said, noticed the three Chinese 'toughs' in one alcove, drinking bottles of what was 'probably' Tiger Beer. It was late by the time they were joined by the two others, Mediterranean-looking, they affirmed. None of them had taken much notice until voices were raised, itself not uncommon in that particular hostelry at that hour of the drinking night. Fists thumping the table had drawn more attention, mainly in protest that woozy heads and befuddled conversations were being unnecessarily aggravated. It was the fight, a ruckus of fists and shouts, which turned every eye; and then it was chiefly to cheer and goad.

The cheering was hushed by the knives. Some said they thought money was the centre of the argument, perhaps in exchange for some goods that were not being supplied. These were only words snatched from the angry voices and then they were drowned by shouts of fear and alarm amongst the onlookers. None were brave or foolish enough to intervene, especially when a splatter of blood shot against one wall, ugly spots splashing on shirts and faces nearby.

This was when the landlord discreetly slipped out of sight to dial 999, as the wounded Spaniard lunged, yelling, towards the door. His companion was seen to rush after him, one arm flailing behind to ward off the slash of blades, the other encumbered by a large leather bag, one handle of which was being pulled back by one of the Chinese. As he reached the door, the second Spaniard took a heavy stab in one shoulder and, with a scream, released the bag, staggering out into the night. All this was pieced together soon afterwards from an incoherent volley of inconsistent accounts, by police officers hurtling to the scene.

The part they discounted as being seriously influenced by a collective alcoholic haze was the jumble of assertions about the car. Before the pursuit had careered down the street, the struggle between the adversaries had converged on a small car parked a few metres from the pub. Dispossessed of their bag and whatever it contained, the onlookers all agreed the Spaniards, despite blood oozing from wounds, appeared intent on claiming the car instead. They were trying to break into the vehicle, whilst fending off their knife-wielding assailants.

Someone said one of the Spaniards screamed, "Is it in here!?", but later acknowledged to the police officer that the accents were thick and so was his head at the time. It was the next bit the police refused to accept, no matter the ten or a dozen who told them *almost* the same story. The car, rocking under the fray, *disappeared*. "Dissolved." "Evaporated." "Melted away." "*Honeshtly* ossifer." "Swear on me life." "And me ol' grandmother's bless 'er soul." "As Godsh me witnesshh." "Would I lie to you?" (That one took some nerve, considering the background of the speaker).

The fact remained, with the combatants fully engaged in their deadly melee, it was open to question who remained to drive away the car and why, indeed, it was now proving so difficult to trace. Nevertheless, growled a senior officer later at the police station, cars get nicked right under people's noses but they certainly don't *dissolve*.

The basic outline - minus the car, since a coincidentally stolen car was just too trivial to report in the circumstances - reached the newspapers and was seen by Elroy and the others, as he and Walt and Olivia prepared to set off to Heathrow. It was also on television. At a press conference, the Metropolitan Police chief superintendent praised the alertness of the pub landlord in making the call and the swiftness with which his officers had arrived. They were fortunate, he said, to have found that this was part of a Chinese Triad gang they had been trailing for some time but had been unable to nail with evidence. They were particularly vicious. The dead Spaniard who had been found in an alleyway had his throat slit and there were other deep stab wounds to his body. His companion was critical in hospital and would only survive with extensive surgery; and even then his chances were not good.

The chief superintendent tried not to compromise his concern for the victims but declared that they themselves were suspected of links with the Spanish Islamists, lately in the news, whose extreme views expounded an Islamic takeover of Iberia, 'by violence' if necessary. He was prepared to concede, in answer to journalists' questions, that the Customs and Excise 'find' leaked a few hours earlier, of 'bomb-detonating equipment' discovered, after a tip-off, 'hidden in quiet countryside', could be part of the same affair.

When interrogated as to why one of his officers had proudly announced that his team had recovered ten million dollars in cash which appeared to have been passed - willingly or otherwise - from the Spaniards to the Triads, the chief superintendent hastily and robustly - rather too robustly to the ears of the more experienced reporters - rebuffed the notion: "slip of the tongue; my men had been in great personal danger; one of those things you say under severe stress; ten *thousand,* not ten *million.* My goodness", he added with a twist of a smile, "you could buy an atomic bomb for that."

A report, a mere hour later, updated the details by announcing that the joint police and Customs operation, which might not have been accomplished but for the call to the pub fight, had resulted in foiling, for the time being at least, a major bomb-plot in Spain. The Islamic extremists, possibly backed by Al Quaeda or a similar terrorist organisation, were suspected of having been supplied with bomb-making equipment, possibly by the captured Chinese Triad gang, but, whether or not this was the case, yet to be determined, detonating materials essential to their programme, had been intercepted, neutralising any campaign of violence in the near future.

"You're talking of conventional explosives, I take it?" asked the TV interviewer, this time supplied with the Police Commissioner himself.

"Yes, of course", replied the policeman, briskly, "the world hasn't gone completely mad, yet."

"Maybe it has", Elroy muttered under his breath.

"What's that?" Walt asked, sharply.

"Er ... mad .. mad enough, eh? Bombs?", Elroy stumbled the words out, wishing he did not have to hide what he knew, even from his best friends.

Calls

Elroy took a call from Gordon Pierce on his mobile. He was on his own in the house, with Paul at work and Walt and Olivia having persuaded Isabella to take them to a local coffee bar.

"You were right, sir, Mr Fitzgibbon." Pierce's voice was crisp and alert, without the tense anxiety of the early hours of the morning; the voice of a man who had caught up with his quarry. "It was a rod of plutonium."

"Good God", exclaimed Elroy, despite himself.

"Encased in a dummy lead battery", continued Pierce's efficient explanation, "in a freshly dug hole in the ground."

"Where - ?" Elroy began in bemusement.

"In a field, sir, bang on those co-ordinates on the map."

"Where -?" stumbled Elroy again.

"Can't tell you more. Sure you understand."

Elroy responded with an unseen nod.

"We've not revealed the nuclear stuff, sir", Pierce seemed to keen to add, "we've only referred to 'high explosives'."

Elroy nodded to himself again. He had been puzzled by the news references to 'conventional' detonating equipment but 'cover up' had seemed a probable explanation.

"International mayhem if the truth came out just now", the Customs man's voice continued. "Security services want to target the Spanish Islamists - you heard about them?"

Elroy refrained from reminding him it was he and Martin Timmis who had passed on the signals information, as Pierce went on.

"But keeping hush about anything nuclear. We've got their plutonium but if those dolls contained the other material, they've got to be found - maybe in Spain already. I don't know quite how we caught up with this, sir, but I know it's been with your help. Thanks."

"Thanks, man", Elroy murmured as the other phone clicked off and left him brooding.

Mr Teng took a call from London, as he stood near to Gainsborough and the Manchu Met. Hill had been applauded for the car's efficient recovery, finally confirming its capabilities. It was now ready. But his sallow-faced companion turned to thunder as he pocketed his phone. It was early evening in Beijing. They were alone in the factory with the customary leather-jacketed guard at hand. Even Hoi Fong had been able to leave straight after office hours for a change, to spend some evening at home before Soo Wong's bedtime and in time to eat the meal Hwee Lo had cooked for him, hot from the wok. Teng's narrow features tightened with fury.

"Did you see what was in this car, Mr Hill?" Teng's lips scarcely parted as he hissed through them.

"The..?" Gainsborough replied, bleakly, pointing to the dashboard.

"No, Mr Hill, in the boot."

"That battery?" Gainsborough had seen the bulky battery and had heard references to 'dual power'. Knowing the car's true character, he had assumed it was part of the subterfuge. He stuck to his job; he did not want to get involved with anything else.

"Did you tell anyone?" The question bore menace.

"Well, no, I -" Gainsborough shrugged. What was this extra complication? All he wanted was to be told his job was complete so he could at last be with his beloved Vicki again.

"Mr Hill, I don't need to tell you -" The pitch was rising in the man's voice, as though to extract a confession. Then his expression altered as something else occurred to him. He breathed softly to himself, "Choi", and looked around at his henchman and beckoned him over. The sinister individual exchanged some word with Teng, whispered in his ear, as if Gainsborough's half dozen words in Cantonese - or whatever they spoke - would have enabled him to eavesdrop.

"Did you see Mr Choi here?" Teng turned to Gainsborough with the question.

Gainsborough looked blank again and shrugged.

"Well, yes, Mr Hoi Fong Choi? It's his factory isn't it?"

"I mean after hours, Mr Hill", Teng pressed him.

"I don't know", Gainsborough sighed wearily at this purpose-less interrogation. Of course he had seen the factory owner often. How could he remember what times of day or night, since he had spent such long hours here himself, to meet the deadline? Teng observed him closely again and then appeared to make his mind up.

"Only one or two people could have known about the battery, Mr Hill, *and* could have informed anyone in London. If not you -"

Teng stared at him again and it occurred to Gainsborough the man was searching for someone else to be a scapegoat for something. There was a flicker of desperation behind his eyes. The Englishman felt tired and hollow. Completing the project had not led to his discharge into Vicki's arms. Instead, he had been pinned to his workbench, while the car had made a couple of disconcerting jumps beyond his control, interfering with communications and causing him a period of panic until he had re-established the co-ordinates. God only knew what had gone wrong and thank the same Lord he had not lost it altogether.

There was another phone call. Hwee Lo picked up Hoi Fong's ringing mobile from the coffee table, as he played and cooed with Soo Wong in the lounge, a last frolic before her bedtime, cuddly toy in one hand, his daughter clasped by the other. He dropped the toy to take the phone. The next instant he almost let go of his daughter and Hwee Lo had to hastily stoop to catch her from his loosening grasp. She saw his hand tremble as it gripped the phone. He was saying, "No ...no... No! Not at all!" Then he added after listening to the other voice, "I was just looking, brother. It is my factory, after all." He was making an attempt to protest, stand his ground, but was forced into defence: "No, no, brother! Surely, you don't think...! What would I do? I know nothing of your ..." He was interrupted and made to listen again. His final words were humbled: "No, no, brother. I thank you. A mistake, indeed. If there is anything I can do..." But the other phone had been clicked off.

Hoi's hand trembled again as he laid the phone back on the table. He looked at his wife as she gazed in concern, their child held to her breast. He reached to touch her face and let his hand stroke downwards to Soo Wong's brow and her smiling chubby cheeks.

"Teng." He was terse and quiet. "He doesn't believe me. We must leave."

"Leave?" Her eyes widened in dismay. "Where?"

"Cousin Wu."

"Oh no, my darling, no."

But he could only nod in grim despair.

Somewhere

"I trust you are ... somewhere?"

Hmmph, thought Gabriel, in mid-pick, who knew what was meant but felt like saying, contrarily, that actually he was right here in Heaven. Obviously.

"Somewhere! One day he will appear somewhere!"

The Twelvers - for, as Martin Timmis had correctly deduced, that is who they were - were at loggerheads amongst themselves. Radical extremists attaching themselves to the 'Twelvers' persuasion had issued anonymous public statements denouncing the West - epitomised by the United States - for seeking to ruin the Muslim economies with its deliberate strategy of slashing demand for oil.

"First they exploit us then they betray us!" was the cry. It was implicitly acknowledged, by these voices, that a planned campaign of violence to destabilise and reclaim 'Islam's Iberia' had been thwarted. Gordon Pierce and Elroy - still in contact - agreed this amounted to confirmation of their suspicions, even without any reference to a nuclear threat, or the loss of ten million dollars for no return. For the time being, it was an expression of impotent outrage that might only offer a temporary respite from danger, for the voices of violence continued to rant.

The moderate arm of the Twelvers - the majority - were responding with their own declaration that violence was not the key. The 'twelfth Imam' was imminent. He would soon appear 'somewhere' in peace: a conviction oft-stated despite decades of non-appearance and disappointment.

"They will be *somewhere*", ground Teng between his teeth. He was sitting in Hoi's office, which he had commandeered to monitor the search, as the routine hum of the factory proceeded normally below. Two days, as his Society henchmen had driven to addresses far and wide: relatives, retired business associates, even old school acquaintances. None had admitted to seeing Hoi Fong or his wife and child, their protestations of ignorance accepted as genuine when stories held firm even as red weals appeared on faces and favourite goats and dogs lay bloodied in the dirt. A group had duly paid a visit to the wizened cousin in his hovel but - Confucious! - no comfortable family could endure more than a few hours in such conditions, let alone hide there. Nonetheless, Teng grimly contemplated, it was close enough to pay a second call. Make certain.

"I will go with you next time. Soon. "

And he motioned two black-vested cohorts to the office door.

Asif Hassan was feeling ever more forcibly that he should be *somewhere* else, a nobler destination than his kebab house. What made him lift those brochures from the backroom shelf? What caused him to take the short walk to the travel agent? 'Why this particular country', he was asked in passing interest, as the booking was made. Asif could supply no reason, just a smile and a shrug. He could only ask himself, why now? Why there?

"I trust ..."

"Yes, guv, honest, guv. Sorted. He's on his way. I'm with him. But is it going to make a diff- ?"

The angel looked up with one of his 'give-me-Splong-any-time' looks, which was met with impassive silence.

In Santander, the port on the north coast of Spain, the tall, kindly Asian walked carefully down the disembarkation gang-way. The bearded figure, somewhere between forty and fifty years of age, bore a venerable aura: that of a saint, perhaps, or in Islam rather, a prophet.

"Well, anyway, sorted."

The Lord wondered where He had heard that one before. but held His silence. If there was never a perfect time, He had to be prepared to adjust circumstances which might otherwise jeopardise the plan. Violent action was the jeopardy; peaceful persuasion the potential antidote. They could do no more.

Sorted

Gainsborough trudged despondently back to the apartment. Since he had retrieved the car and made a few adjustments, it had gone again. This time transported by loader, under the authority of the Government man. He had not seen the factory owner, Mr Choi, for some days. Moreover, he had been informed, obliquely, by a visiting associate, that Mr Teng 'might not return'. He felt no affinity with either of the missing men but it left him rudderless at his workstation, with nothing to do and no-one to refer to. Each day he had to return to a deserted apartment. Vicki's phone number had been dead for weeks and he had no idea where she might be. In his heavy heart, he did not know what to do next. He opened the apartment door and - oh joy! - she was there, in the hallway, flinging her arms around him and smothering him with her kisses!

"Oh, my darling!"

"Oh, my love!"

It was a ferment of passion and lovemaking. His whole world had been restored, black clouds dispersed, only sun above! Then, in the dark illuminated by a single romantic candle, after their panting had subsided and they had furnished themselves with a celebratory drink, she breathed it in his ear. They were to attend the spectacular send-off. He would be an honoured guest, she his partner. He glowed with delight. It had all worked out after all. The unpleasant little Mr Teng had gone but he, Gainsborough Hill, was not abandoned, nor neglected. He had Vicki again and his unique, astonishing contribution was being recognised in his adopted home.

In Beijing, in high circles, there was a buzz everywhere, even with still several days to go. This would be the first visit. It was an opportunity to be seized and relished. For those in the know, it represented something rather more. Something imponderable. This was wholly without precedent.

Gainsborough was thrilled beyond measure. He was lauded in every quarter, Vicki shining at his side. It was like that first week all over again. It transpired, too, that his would be the key role, vital to the occasion. It was magnificent. It did not seem too bold to think that, after all these years of hopes and dreams, he really might play a part in saving the world. In more sober moments, it occurred to him he might be expecting too much but such doubts were quickly erased. This was the *new* world. Eat your heart out, England.

"So", mumbled the picking one, bent to neglected pursuits, "sorted?"

There was no reply. Even He Who could see many futures could only wait upon the moment. The petal? The lipstick? A vase thrown. A decision made. A dislocation? Which future indeed?

Changes

There had been a mistake over their booking. "Cock-up!" as Walt angrily exclaimed, thumping his palm on the check-in desk at Heathrow while the girl hurried away to consult a manager. No, terribly sorry, they just did not have the seats available and, because of the severe contraction in international air travel - "the slow-down, you know" - reduced capacity meant they could only offer seats to Washington.

"Washington!" protested Walt again.

-307"I'm so sorry, sir."

"You better be", he muttered ungraciously and then offered a grudging apology that it was not her fault.

"Ironic, isn't it", smiled Olivia, lightly.

Walt and Elroy looked at her as they walked through to the departure lounge, unimpressed by her amusement.

"Well", she shrugged with another smile, "if it hadn't been for us - you", she aimed her look at Elroy, "we'd be zapping across on the next flight to New York. Only now", she added mischievously, "there aren't nearly as many 'next flights' as there used to be. Think of all the gas we're saving - and all this clean air." She waved her arm breezily above her head. They had to concede her point. They just did not expect to be such victims of their own success!

"Look at it like this", declared Elroy, after they had settled into seats, complete with coffees, "this is what we got. The States: sharing, slowdown, all those reductions in energy consumption and the knock-on effects."

"Brilliant", agreed Olivia.

"Yeh", nodded Elroy, He'd had time to reflect on all those months - well over a year now - since his 'visitation' and the formula, 'Piggyback'; then the seize-ups, the 'Smiling Jesus' phenomena, and all the changes since. Changes, it seemed, for the good of the planet; pervasive in America, if disappointingly meagre elsewhere, except in Africa, powered by the Twigg vision. "And d'ya know, even the young guys - and girls - who only wanted to show off in their big cars, they're even falling in line. For sure." He nodded, enthusiastically, again. "Cos they don't know if it'll pack in - unless it's a dual-powered car, and they aint nearly so sexy!"

They all smiled at that.

"And all this local trading, yeh? And markets? Folks starting to buy local, buy local-grown stuff, instead of things imported - or transported across a dozen states. Even the big guys are falling in line: Wal-Mart's opening outdoor markets in its - empty" (he chuckled) - "car parks, 'cos people aren't going into the stores like they used to. Like, it all saves gas, encourages local trade, saves factory output -"

"for Africa", nodded Olivia, as they smiled.

"Then we got China," Elroy continued more earnestly, "saying America got no right to slow everyone down. So they're burning more oil than ever - *and* coal - and them and the whole of Asia - India and the rest of 'em - all building factories and cars an' all, like crazy. Like, they're saying, this is their chance to take advantage of the States going slow. Like, one half of the world - well, the States - trying to save the planet, the other half trying to wreck it!"

"You can see their point", remarked Walt, "they want the good life."

"Yeh", acknowledged Elroy, "but why don't they do it like we've started in Africa? *Clean* factories, *battery* cars, *controlled* progress, instead of this crazy rush to cover everywhere with tarmac and concrete and fill the whole air with carbon?"

They thought about it in silence, brought up short from having thought about nothing much except work or enjoying London - despite the lingering evidence of looting and unrest in the city.

"And then there's this Spain thing", Elroy started up again, "what's that all about?"

"Spain?" Olivia was the same as the other four. None of them had paid that much attention to inside news pages and had missed most TV and radio news, not bothering to keep up to date with their phones instead. The brief but significant references to Islamic threats from Spain had escaped them.

"Well", explained Elroy, "these crazy guys saying America's betrayed them by not buying their oil."

"Ah! Perfect!" smiled Olivia.

"And", continued Elroy, "the States has gone soft so now Islam can take over."

"The world?" interjected Walt in alarm.

"I dunno, mebbe", grunted Elroy. "This is the lot in Spain - you know, bomb plot - there's a feeling they're making a big noise 'cos their nose was put out of joint. In the old days", he added, "we'd a been in there kicking ass, marines, green berets, or whatever."

"We're not threatening now?" checked Walt.

"No, hell no. Twigg's been saying, 'stay cool. We're showing the new way to take a lead, not going to be provoked'."

"That's good", murmured Olivia.

"Yeh", agreed Elroy, doubtfully, "except they're arguing in the House. There's some don't like seein' the finger put up to Uncle Sam. And now there's this priest."

"Priest?" asked Walt again. "Hey, El, you been *watching* the news or *writing* it?"

"Huh", grinned Elroy, sheepishly, "not priest. Whadda they call them? Imam."

"The Twelfth Imam", murmured Olivia. "I saw a headline somewhere."

"Yeh?" Elroy jerked around to her. "Yeh. Sure."

He had forgotten about what Martin Timmis had told him. "Twelvers", he mused, remembering. "Lord, that's weird."

"What about him?" asked the pragmatic Walt.

"Well", said Elroy, slowly, "reports say he's on a kind of mission, kind of evangelical - Islam, like. He's literally walking through villages in Spain and *apparently* telling them about when their own village was once Muslim - until they were *ordered* to become Christian."

"But that was centuries ago", objected Olivia.

"Powerful thing, history", remarked Elroy. "Look at me. Africa's in my blood. That was centuries ago, too."

Senor

"Mister? Are you God?"

Asif Hassan sat on a large, heavy old white stone under a eucalyptus tree in the centre of the dusty village square. The late afternoon sun was low but the Spring air was already warm, a far cry from London's interminable winter days, dragging on long after the season should have changed. This little square in central Spain, enclosed by its tumble of white and grey, stone and concrete buildings, would be baking hot in a few weeks but, just now, it was an idyll of pale golden sunlight.

He had felt comfortable with the idea of travelling by sea. He did not feel entirely himself inside. He had only travelled by air once, when migrating with his parents from Saudi to England as a child. He did not know if his present mild queasiness might have made him airsick. Sure, the sea could be rough at times. Nonetheless, it was closer to *terra firma* and he savoured the notion of the extra journey time to adjust to his destination and his mission. There was also something special about alighting at the very edge of a country, stepping upon its shores.

He had caught the train from Santander to Madrid, then hurried to the first available connection to Toledo, overwhelmed by the bustling capital. Even Toledo, the gateway to the former Muslim Iberia, daunted him. He lingered by the ancient mosque, converted to a Roman Catholic church many centuries ago, but he could not envisage how to handle even a modestly-sized town. He felt he might begin with villages, initiating contact on an intimate scale. He was filled with a trepidation that vied with the compulsion inside that was driving him on.

He was uncertain. Should he not have experienced a revelation, or seen a sign, like the Prophet Muhammed in a cave with the angel, or Saul, from the other faith, on the road to Damascus, before he catapulted himself into such a venture? It was something compelling him from within. All he could say was he did not feel 'quite himself'. There was a lightness of spirit, a sense of unshakeable confidence and purpose. There had been moments in the journey when it seemed like one of those dreams where you can do the impossible, like jump off a cliff and fly, or perform a virtuoso concert on a musical instrument you have never played. Then you wake up, ruefully acknowledging the reality.

Asif had not 'woken up'. In the very first village, he had paused by the little church, itself a blend of Islamic and Christian origins, and a middle-aged couple walking by had asked if they could help him. It was rather, he had smiled humbly in reply, he wondered if he might be of assistance to *them*. They had not taken it as impertinence or arrogance. They had listened.

He looked up now, disconcerted. The small voice at his side had come from a child, a girl about seven years old, standing by the knee of his flowing white chemise. Rich brown curls were spilling over her head and neck. She wore a faded orange and brown chequered, short-sleeved dress, which perfectly complemented her dark olive skin, colour-toning fashion she was probably unaware of now but would doubtless use to her advantage in years ahead. The hazel eyes stared up at him. The pretty lips were pursed in solemn enquiry.

"No, my dear. I am not God. There is only one God and I am not He."

He was struggling and frowning with his limited Spanish, which had benefited from only marginal enhancement by study during his journey.

"Where is He, then? My Mama says he is here."

Asif regarded the girl and realised he must have looked as grave as she, so he smiled. Then surrendered the linguistic battle and replied in English.

"If you believe in Him, he is here all the time. And, surely, even if you do not."

At this the girl broke into a broad smile, a delight that she could understand and deploy her schoolroom English. Then she became suddenly solemn again.

"Did He see when I trod on that beetle?" she asked, with a little fearful twist of her lip.

Asif looked at the ground and noticed a large, squashed green beetle in the dirt near the child's foot.

"Ah." Asif bent his head forward a little towards the girl. "We cannot know if He has time to see every single thing we do, good or bad." He viewed the dead beetle for a moment and then looked into her earnest eyes. "Should we do something we know to be wrong, even if no-one - not even He - is watching?"

He wanted to take her dirt-stained hand into his and hold it tightly, just for a moment, to fuse a spiritual connection with her innocence but he held back; there was no telling, in this day and age, what the consequences of such familiarity might be. It saddened him. Then he smiled again and it brought the smile back to her face, also.

"What is your name?" he enquired.

"Maria!" came a cry from elsewhere before the girl herself could reply. Two women had emerged from a doorway across the square and were scurrying towards them. The woman who had called out, when the two reached the centre, placed her hands protectively on the girl's shoulders. Then both women relaxed as they recognised the travelling preacher. The girl giggled and clasped her mother's hand on her shoulder.

"Mama!"

The mother smiled at Asif.

"Ah, benos dias, senor", and she bobbed a little curtsey, "you tell my Maria, si?"

Asif marvelled that these villagers knew enough English to help him along, whilst his Spanish was so halting.

"She is a delightful girl", he smiled, "but she -"

He did not know how to phrase it.

" - she thought - you did not tell her -?"

"He says he's not God, Mama", the girl blurted out in Spanish.

"No, no, senor", the mother hastily assured Asif, "I said you are *from* God. Is that not so, senor?"

Was he? He felt he had been given a message to convey, that was all. The news he heard during his journey, of the fanatics in Madrid and their violent plot to strike a blow for Islam in Iberia, had only intensified his resolve. And the people had seemed ready for him in these villages.

"Ah, we know we were all Muslim here long ago", a shop-keeper had informed him, "then the Christians came. We don't know if things would have been better or worse but we are taught to know 'Islam' means 'peace'."

"But the beasts bomb for Islam!" one in a knot of people in the shop had protested, fiercely.

"They are not Islam", Asif had replied, quietly.

"Are they evil?" the speaker had questioned.

"They are ... wrong", Asif had said, carefully.

At first he had taken each opportunity as it arose, in reply to, "Can I help you?", "Do you know your way?", "Are you looking for somewhere?"

"I have come to tell you about the Prophet", he had answered.

They seemed ready to listen, whether it was by the way he spoke to them or the troubles of the world around them. Sometimes it was just one or two, then a small group of six or so. He had only been here a few days, in only a handful of villages so far. But now he seemed to be expected. Word was getting around. He was only partly aware of what they were saying about him. They with their Spanish, he with his phrase-book. They appeared to be looking for something new. Not the bombers. Not, perhaps, the blinkered evangelism of American Christianity, supporting economic reversal, the consequences of which they all feared, in villages and towns seeking to join the thrust forward to modern prosperity. Nor did they admire the materialistic atheism trumpeted from China. Perhaps Islam, still stored in their collective memory, might offer the 'peace' they sought. He did not strive to convert minds; he felt only that he bore an alternative message.

Already he was being invited to larger gatherings. He was conscious his voice stilled all who heard. His board and lodging had ceased to be an issue after the second day; he even found himself facing invidious decisions about which among competing offers to accept. Tomorrow he would be addressing a crowd of a hundred, so he had been told: almost the entire village, excepting the youngest children. If he were not being driven from within, the prospect would terrify him.

"Are you he?" someone else had asked him, with a respectful bow, earlier that day.

"He ..?" Asif had replied, tentatively.

"The Imam", said the man, "they say you are the Twelfth Imam."

"No..no..", replied Asif, troubled by the suggestion and well versed in the faith and the legend. "No, I am a simple Muslim, like ..."

"Like me", a young man interjected eagerly into Asif's thoughtful pause. "But", then he lowered his voice, "I do not say ... it is not to be said too loudly here, you understand?", making the sign of the cross upon himself and glancing nervously at the Mother Mary shrine at the roadside. Asif nodded, as the man continued with a gleam of hope in his eye, "But perhaps not much longer, senor?"

For a moment it made Asif contemplate if it was right; right to preach one faith over another? Was there not only one God? Yet it was surely more right than to seek to change minds by breaking bodies. It reminded him, in sadness, of misguided Mohammed and Abdul, their distorted belief in the 'jihad', and whatever it really was in those dolls.

"Time for tea, Maria", said her mother in Spanish, with a respectful smile at Asif. Her companion smiled, too, with a shy, "gracias, senor."

"It was nice to meet you, Maria", smiled Asif, with the best Spanish accent he could muster. She giggled self-consciously. Then he added in English, because he knew he could not find all the words in Spanish, "Remember, whether He sees you or not, eh?" He glanced at the prone, disfigured beetle. The girl followed his eyes then looked back at him, shuffled a foot in the dust, stuck a finger in her mouth and gave a little coy shake of her head, curls bouncing, and smiled behind her finger.

The women turned back towards the huddle of dwellings across the square, with a parting smile for Asif and the mother reaching for her child's hand.

"What was that about?" he managed to make out mother enquire of daughter, as they headed for their doorway.

Converting

"*Converting* them, is he?" asked Olivia, incredulously.

"Well, he aint gonna convert them in a few days but it's riled
the other lot - the fanatics, who want to take over with bombs.
And the States -"

"Twigg?" put in Walt.

"Yeh. Well, she's okay with it." Elroy had their attention now:
"'Leave them to it', she's saying, 'we're not policing the world
anymore, not getting dragged in'. But there's other voices -"

"Senate?" Walt interjected again.

"*And* The House", affirmed Elroy, "and some media. Saying
suppose Spain goes Islamic again - Iberia - 'cos this imam guy is
apparently one helluva preacher - it'll turn the world upside
down. Islam reaching to the Atlantic. On our doorstep."

"Bit dramatic", remarked Walt, sceptically.

"Yeh, 'course", agreed Elroy, "but in the old days - like, a
whole year-and-a-half ago" - he chuckled, drily - "you only had to
see one little change of colour on the map and we were right in
there, painting it back again. Or tryin' to."

"Somalia", Olivia murmured.

"Cuba", said Walt.

"Afghanistan. Iraq."

They brooded in silence again, over their drinks.

"It's like Jesus", mused Olivia.

They looked at her, questioningly.

"Going through villages", she explained, "converting them."

"Muhammed, you mean", corrected Walt.

"Of course", acknowledged Olivia, "but that's what scares
them. Converting minds."

"Ye-e-h", Elroy nodded, thoughtfully.

"I don't know about Muhammed", Olivia continued, "but they
wanted the crowd to free Barrabas, didn't they? They could
handle him. The criminal. I guess he might have been like a

terrorist now, a bomber if he had the chance. That only destroys objects, breaks bodies. But the prophet - Jesus, Muhammed: he changes minds. They can't handle that, the governments."

"Even though it's the peaceful way?" queried Elroy.

"Peace?" She took hold of Walt's hand, affectionately, as their flight came up on the embarkations screen, "I don't think they see it like that. Do you?"

Arrival

"Paper, madam?"

Olivia smiled in thanks and took a 'Washington Times' from the trolley at the bottom of the embarkation tunnel. Elroy picked a 'New York Herald Tribune'. Walt said he would share; maybe watch a movie. The Virgin Atlantic stewardess was all smiles in her bright red livery, lipstick to match.

"Oh, Jeez!" exclaimed Walt, as they unclipped their seat belts and the aircraft started to level out across the Atlantic. "Not only sent to Washington", as he looked over Olivia's arm at her newspaper, "but on the day of the Chinese visit!"

"Whaddya mean?" asked Elroy, from across the Club Class aisle.

"Wait till we try to get a cab", snorted Walt.

"It's all over the paper", affirmed Olivia, "first full State visit of a Chinese President, not just part of a UN summit, an' all."

"They read in silence for some minutes, Walt wishing he had taken a paper for himself, as he craned to look at the pages of Olivia's.

"Spells it out here", grunted Elroy.

"Yeh?" Walt turned his head the other way, glad to relieve the crick in his neck.

"Twigg wanting to show how 'sharing' works", elaborated Elroy, re-reading the article. "Slowdown doesn't have to mean 'Depression'; 'moderation instead of excess' is how it's put here."

"Excess is what the Chinese *want*," retorted Walt.

"Well, they reckon here", commented Elroy, his eye on the page, "it's a case of one great power - us - showing how it can be done. Here - there's a quote from a professor-type: 'happiness doesn't equal killing the planet'."

"There's a lot of hope", added Olivia, turning a page of her *Washington Times*, "that China will see how not to make the same mistakes as we did: find the right way before doing it wrong first."

"Where's that?" Elroy asked, frowning at his pages.

"Here." She passed her newspaper across Walt to Elroy, jabbing a finger at the page of her 'Post'. "Next to that piece about the oil tankers."

"Tankers?" Elroy scanned the page and spotted the short paragraph about half a dozen oil tankers moored off the Ghanian coast and some dispute about an import licence. He vaguely wondered why it jarred, as he found the long article Olivia referred to.

"Lotta hope everywhere", he agreed as he browsed. "Kinda suggesting America musta got it right to become the world's biggest economy - except all the damage it did - so it oughta be right this time, too."

"Like, we know how to be big so trust us, we know how to make it smaller again?" Walt raised an eyebrow.

"Uh, yeh, guess so", Elroy agreed, dubiously.

"Well, thank the Lord for Twigg, eh?" concluded Olivia.

"The Lord, yeh", nodded Elroy, contemplatively, eyes turning to the azure blue sky outside the cabin window.

They sat back. Walt tried to watch a movie but found it did not capture his attention. Elroy continued to gaze through the window, thoughts elsewhere. Olivia let her paper drop and dozed between the meals and refreshments.

Washington airport was bedlam.

Security was on ostentatious overkill. Passengers were treated as though each individual was more than likely to be carrying a concealed nuclear device. Ribbon tape and temporary barriers were everywhere. They saw one poor guy just ahead, smart, respectable, pounced upon, arms twisted up his back by a couple of Feds, just because a key in his pocket had set off the scanner alarm. He was frogmarched away for, in all probability, a none-too-ceremonious strip-search.

Finally clear of baggage-collection and Immigration, into Arrivals, it was more chaos. Thousands had come to witness the visit, among them innumerable Chinese, doubtless disgorged from Chinatowns in New York and elsewhere. The three of them soon became aware their own arrival must be almost coinciding with that of the Chinese President himself. There was a hubbub of anticipation. A separate area had been cordoned off, with a plush red carpet leading from an evacuated arrival bay. It looked as though the President of The People's Republic was bent on rubbing shoulders with thousands of ordinary travellers and onlookers, making a very public entrance.

"Dunno, man", shrugged a routine airport security guy, in reply to Elroy's question as they stood in an interminable line shuffling through the heavily-controlled Arrivals Hall, "guess he wants to see the people, eh? Commie?" He grinned at that. "Anyways, he's causing mayhem!" They tried to jostle their way outside for a cab but they were just a few among a sea of bobbing heads, looking for the end of a cab line that stretched out of sight.

"Hell", muttered Walt, "we ever gonna get outa here?"

"There's a screen", Olivia remarked.

"Uh?" prompted Elroy.

"In Arrivals", explained Olivia.

They struggled back inside towards a reasonable vantage point to view the giant projection screen which must have been installed for this occasion. It was a CNN TV relay, flicking through pictures of the aircraft arrival apron, the Arrivals Hall complete with red carpet and a huge black limousine parked somewhere outside. They could barely hear the commentary, except to deduce the Presidential arrival was imminent. Joe Kirk and the media mob, TV cameras, photographers, microphones and all, had been awarded privileged positions ranged in rows on the lawn beneath the White House south portico. President Twigg would descend the steps to greet her guest on the especially-erected raised platform of several square metres, which intersected the arc of the driveway curving before the iconic white pillars.

Thousands of onlookers had been filtered through rigorous checks inside the usual security area to stand, rows deep, spread back to fill the expanse of the famous south lawn. They filled the streets to either side, too, which had been closed to traffic, along with the permanently traffic-free Pennsylvania Avenue on the north side of the stately old mansion house. There, out of view of the anticipated arrival, the hordes of onlookers had to be content with more giant relay screens, slung to left and right of the White House entrance.

Back at the airport, rumours of the 'arrival' were rife, rolling like ocean waves through the crowded Arrivals hall. The plane had landed! The Chinese President was already walking down the red carpet! Necks craned. Eyes swung and peered to get a sighting. Then .. had they missed him! No! Impossible! The flight was delayed! He would arrive soon!

Suddenly, the TV commentator could be heard gabbling through a hurried 'update'. It was possible - though impossible! - the cameras had somehow missed the flight arriving. Maybe the President's advisors had been alarmed by the size of the airport crowd. Had he been slipped through a rear exit? They were awaiting confirmation ... pause ... word had been received that the President was already being driven to the White House ... but TV cameras confirmed the large, black limo still stood outside the Arrivals canopy. Was it a decoy after all? People muttered: was this a creepy Chinese game being played on them? Or maybe all a huge security bluff by the FBI to draw a potential assassin to the wrong spot?

Then, unexpectedly, it was apparent from the commentator's confused introduction, a Chinese government spokeswoman was relayed through the CNN news link, direct from Beijing. Even before she opened her mouth, rumours were flying. Had the visit been aborted? Was it all a wily oriental game? Red carpet? Limousine? World's media? But no President?

She was speaking. It was an apology, in an almost flawless American accent. 'Sincere apologies for causing any confusion ... please understand our security concerns .. forgive our caution ... but it is indeed an honour for the President of the People's Republic of China to be welcomed by the President and the People of the United States of America .. in a few moments at the White House'. Hurriedly, the picture cut to the scene in front of the White House, followed by the focus of the world's TV news channels, press and radio commentators.

"Helicopter!" someone muttered in the Airport crowd. Of course. Why risk a limousine through the streets? Remember Kennedy? Disappointing for those with a direct view of the red carpet but an understandable security ploy. The notion was simultaneously echoed by media commentators and the press corps on the steps. Right on cue, a troupe of Chinese mannequin dancers filed from either side of the white pillars and daintily up steps onto the platform, to form a backcloth to the anticipated arrival spot. A bit close for a chopper, observed one or two of the commentators but, hell, they can land these things on a dime! Accompanying trumpeters and drummers struck up a fanfare and melody, while the dancers began their delicate routine, Chinese fans fluttering with their eyelashes. Another fanfare brought the music and dance to a climax, then all were still.

The enormous crowd hushed. Eyes began to look skyward for the helicopter; TV cameras did the same, as the airport crowd quietened, too. There was a stir by the arrival square, which redirected eyes and cameras. It was President Twigg's tall, imposing figure descending between the pillars and then up onto the platform, to stand on a small, upholstered pedestal which was positioned for her in front of the dancers and musicians.

"Phoo!", whistled a TV commentator, involuntarily, "she's too close! She'll get blown off by the rotor blades!"

Many in the crowd must have been thinking the same. There was a rustle of concerned whispers. A few eyes still darted skywards but most remained fixed on their President on her pedestal, at the edge of the square space.

Then it happened. An area at the centre of the empty square began to shimmer. It was as though the air trembled. An array of horizontal and vertical, thin grey lines gradually emerged out of nowhere, vibrating and shaking over an area about four metres long and just less than head-height, like a shoal of pencil-thin eels, quivering in the sunlight. It was a transfixing sight. There were some gasps, one or two solitary cries of fear and astonishment and a single, loud shriek from somewhere deep in the masses. Then the translucent, vibrating pattern began to blur into a dense mist, the eel-like lines coalescing into a single shape.

As the crowd gawped, the TV cameras focused on the blur and hundreds of cameras clicked, the mist began to solidify, acquiring an outline separating it from the space around it. The outline took on an edge, while the mist contained within it hardened and its surface obtained a sheen. There was hardly a sound amongst the gaping thousands; a distant choke here and there, a sob, a gasp. The Presidential security corps, banished as usual to scattered observation points by their wilful commander-in-chief, could only crane necks to seek an invisible assailant amongst the sea of stunned faces.

As they all watched, the shape transformed from mist to metal; it transmuted from an amorphous block into the clear configuration of a car, an automobile, which began to gleam silver in the sunlight. Windows were mutating from blank profiles into glinting glass, wheels materialising into black tyres with silver hubs, doors and handles appearing as if an artist were swiftly painting in the detail. It stood there. The shimmering lessened and ceased. A real car, a small Chinese automobile, stood in what had been an empty space but moments before. Elroy, Walt and Olivia, squeezed among the equally stupefied host before the Airport screen, were all thinking of Paul and Isabella, and now numbly accepting what they saw.

Before the multitude at the White House could muster any voice; before, even, the media commentators could manage anything more than, "By all the -!" or "Holy - !", a Chinese attendant stepped forward from among the musicians. Some TV cameras had picked up shots from the crowd of people collapsing, one was throwing an epileptic fit, another was panicking and thrashing about wildly whilst hemmed in on all sides. Other shots picked out Victoria Twigg, who had remained motionless and imperious upon her pedestal, but for the slightest motion which ran through her body as one camera fixed upon her. Now, all pictures focused upon the car, as the attendant pulled open a rear door, then stood back with a deferential bow. Out stepped the President of The People's Republic of China.

Now the all the throng gasped aloud. A mighty sigh and whooshing cry that swept from its midst to fill the air. The same sound echoed through the Arrivals hall and through countless malls, homes, offices, schools and bars throughout the United

States and beyond. The small, slightly stout figure, in immaculate buttoned-up dark tunic, with sleeked-back, jet-black hair, took a few, short, smiling strides and stretched out a hand to Victoria Twigg. She inclined her head, summoned a smile, and accepted his hand, shakily stepping from the pedestal to greet him.

Perhaps at this point they might have anticipated, at last, a rousing cheer; as might have the assembled media, the hardened hacks, the nervous officials and all who had waited upon, and prepared for, this moment, incredible though its climax was. There was no cheer. Amongst all those crowds, at the event and in front of television screens everywhere, there was total, utter silence.

Silence

The silence had fallen over all America. It fell upon the hundreds, thousands, millions gathered before their television programmes. It fell upon bars, as glasses clattered onto tables, whilst eyes were fixed on screens. It fell upon workplaces, it fell upon restaurants, it fell upon households, it fell upon boardrooms, it fell upon shopping malls and city streets and other usually bustling public places. It fell upon the poor, huddled over outdated TV sets, it fell upon the rich, paralysed before their giant plasma screens. It fell upon the highways, already pacified for lack of automobiles, as those that remained pulled into rest-stops, verges and emergency lanes, just to watch or listen. It fell upon those who neither saw nor heard the phenomenon but were infected all the same.

The silence hung in the air. It hung from the lips of television commentators, who simply ran out of words. It even hung from radios, except for monosyllabic utterances by jocks, presenters, reporters whose own minute-by-minute, second-by-second commentaries had finally rendered them speechless. The silence hung like a drip from a tap, eternally waiting to fall. It hung like a spider on its thread, suspended in mid-fall. It hung across an entire, shocked nation. For some, in silenced, garrulous company, it lasted only seconds; long, long seconds. For others, halted abruptly in the quiet normality of office, shop or home, perhaps minutes. For others, again, already alone, the silence might have been hours, extending the confinement of solitude until that first phone call or tremulous venture out of doors. The silence hung like a velvet cloak across America.

Until the noise began.

Noise

Uproar!

"In the name of the Holy Mother of God -!"

"There's no *way*! No *way*. There's no *way*!"

"How'd he get *in*? How'd he get *in*! We got no *security*?!"

"That's a *spook*! That aint *real*! What's going *on*!"

"They're *coming*! They're *comin*! Gotta get *outa* here! They're coming and we caint even *see* 'em!"

"You got no *right*! You got no *right*! Showing them fake pictures!"

"My ma's nearly *died*!"

"Whole town's goin' crazy!"

"That weren't *real*! *Were* it? Waddya tryin' to *do* to us!"

"I want the cops! I want *protection*!"

"Oh-o-oh, Help me! He-e-lp me!"

"Get him! Shoot him! 'Fore he gets away the way he came!"

"Is it real? Is it *real*? Tell me, tell me! I'm in ma cellar and I aint comin' out till you tell me it's not real!"

"Slimy Chinks!"

"That the new 'Trek' movie? *Cool*!"

"We've been *invaded*!"

"Nuke 'em! *Nuke* 'em! I said we shudda nuked 'em years ago! Now look what they got!"

"You bastards! What you wanna scare the fuckin' shit outa us for!"

"*Please don't swear, sir.*"

"Is that a spaceship! I wanna know! I wanna know!"

"Oh my God! How many *more* are there!"

"That aint no fuckin' car!"

"Please don't swear, sir."

-300"It aint you had the fuckin' shit scared outta ya!"

"It weren't real, were it? It were just one o' them clever tricks? Honest?"

"Madam... I ... I ...."

The phone lines were jammed.

TV call desks, phone-ins, Federal and State offices; cell networks filled up, too. So many people could not get through. Bars and cafes were crammed. Sidewalks, malls, stores, everywhere, ground to a halt. People needed to meet and stop to talk about it. There was alarm, fear, astonishment, disbelief. A car had materialised out of thin air and the Chinese President had stepped out of it. Or so it seemed. But that cannot happen in real life.

The fear had to be dealt with. Fear can lead to panic, and then what? The television and radio networks recognised where their responsibilities lay. They brought in scientists. The event was played again and again and again. And again. And again. People tried to get through to the TV stations just to find out when it would be repeated next. They set their recorders and boxes to save it. There was no telling how many times it was replayed over and over in people's own homes. The scientists all agreed on one thing. It was impossible. This could not have been material teleportation. The most that had been achieved so far was the transfer of a few photons across a few metres in a research lab. Not a car. Not a human being. Not even a fly!

Might it have been an image projected from, say, a satellite? But they could not have projected a whole live, walking, talking President! Was it an optical illusion? Had it all been projected onto a transparent screen, like a speaker's autocue? But the two presidents shook hands. One of them could not have been a projected image! Was there a secret trapdoor through which the car and President had been elevated? How? Behind a puff of smoke? What smoke? The misty effect everyone witnessed? So where did the mist come from? Magicians were pressed into divulging some of their innermost secrets but none matched the 'trick' in front of the White House.

A darker explanation was considered: mass hypnosis. No theatrical, television or clinical hypnotist could support this hypothesis. What would cause it? Some kind of auto-suggestion (*sic*) influencing *everyone*, whether in the crowd at the White House, watching a public TV screen, or in front of their own TV sets at home? Or was it a mass religious experience? It gave evangelists the opportunity to declaim about the power of God but their conclusions were unconvincing and divisive.

The result of all this was a gradual, sickening awareness of a quite different power which confronted all Americans, of all persuasions. After a few days, the continual, desperate attempts to uncover a rational, or even relatively sane, explanation led remorselessly in only one direction. China, somehow, impossibly, had actually done it. Even then, no-one dared to spell it out: no politician, no academic nor military analyst. What clinched it was the departure. After three days of ceremony and private conference, the President of the People's Republic chose to leave the way he came.

This time the crowds were heavily restricted, for fear of mass hysteria or organised violent action. Public screens were only erected under stiff security, onlookers limited and sectioned by barriers. Nevertheless, one way or another, everyone who wanted to witness it, did so. And that was pretty near everyone, excepting the sick, the decrepit and the infants in prams: in America and in many countries across the world. The event was identical but in reverse, the car beginning to 'melt' as soon as the door closed on the President. But this time, as the square lay empty in front of the White House and the troupe of Chinese dancers and musicians paraded off, there was no silence. This time the uproar began right there and then.

"First the Muslims mock us in Spain! Now China gives us the finger! Would the President care to tell us who's going to make a fool of America next!"

Predictably, it was Senator Jacobson of Dakota who led the assault. President Twigg managed to deflect this lunge with the haughty suggestion that the senator might not understand that successful diplomacy was not always conducted with full frontal attacks. However, it was not a fortunate choice of phrase and 'full frontal' provoked some sardonic ripples of amusement through the house. Besides, Senator Jacobson was not about to drop his baton in mid-charge.

"And now they have this .. device! If it's real -"

"It's *real*! " a voice called out in support.

"they've invented something we thought you only saw in the movies! It's unbelievable! And are they about to share the technology with us? No! They wave it in our faces! Our scientists say it's not possible? But we've all *seen* it!" Jacobson did a body-turn to sweep his eyes around the chamber. "And whether we want to believe it or not, they've *got* it. *And* ..." he added with venom and a stab of his finger, "... How are *we* gonna *get* it!"

"Gee, Jerry, it makes me feel kinda stupid."

"Yeh, Amy?" Jerry Corrie rolled his eyes at Al behind the control room window, to indicate this might not be a surprise to anyone who knew Amy, but he was nonetheless attentive. He stayed at the top because he was crack at measuring changes in the popular mood.

"Yeah, Jerry, buying all them twisted beans at the market."

"Wa-a-all, Amy honey", drawled Chattanooga Two-Two-Two's dangdest host, with a wink at Al, "they're good for yuh, aint they? They're organic, aint they? All the best things are a bit bent, eh?"

A thousand smiles in a thousand kitchens but fewer automobiles were testament to Jerry Corrie's finger on the pulse of *double-entendre*.

"Yeah, Jerry", responded Amy, straight as a die and the only one not to see the fun, "but they don't seem no tastier'n the straight ones we useda have. An' there's me sharing my washer, an all, and my ol' Sly his car", she rattled on before our host could famously cut her off, "an' I caint see them Chinese doin' that, eh? An' I guess they have *straight* beans, eh, Jerry?"

A thousand silent nods somehow transmitted themselves, unseen, to Jerry Corrie, who nodded sagely in unison.

"Guess you be darn right there, Amy. Straight beans and no sharin'. I guess I seen that maself."

So had the thousand and more. Coincidentally, the Beijing government had bent over backwards to facilitate Western TV broadcasting of China's affluent lifestyles, while the two presidents conferred in Washington.

"I mean, Jerry", came another caller, "look at their stores! Jest like ours useda be! Full o' stuff!"

Chinese society was being presented as a carbon copy of America, writ large. Bolder, brasher, more materialistic. Significantly, every Chinese seemed to possess the latest gadgets and electronic wizardry for home, car and office. And there were cars everywhere, cramming the streets, gleaming, modern, plush. It was the galloping materialism and consumption which America had been assiduously turning its back on for the past year and more. A sniff was directed at the very notion of neighbourhood trading and local markets: facets of a primitive economy China was only too delighted to leave in its past. It brandished possessions from its own modern factories, from all around Asia, from the world; although, notably, not from the United States. There was not a bent bean to be seen. No-one shared a goddamned thing. And now they had *this*.

Part Ten

CRETINS

CRETINS

Resurrection

"**A**re You going to tell them about the Resurrection?"

Gabriel was not doing anything in particular. He was not picking at anything in the foot division. He did not even smell of anything especially unGabriel-ish. The last Splong mission was some time past. He was sitting with his knees up in front of him, elbows resting on them, chin on hands, staring bleakly into the eternity which stretched before them. There were times when God almost wished he did not have an angel. He felt at these times He could well manage without one, even to the extent of taking on all those trips He presently delegated for various, not necessarily Holy, reasons. Times when to be an angel-less Deity would be a mite less troublesome, a considerable release from the persistent tap-tap-tapping of the little hammer of doubt at the otherwise impervious conscience of the Supreme Being. Or, if not entirely non-existent, at least to be far away on some excursion of winged wondrousness. Times when He would prefer him to be anywhere but here, beside Him in the exposed vacuum of Heaven. There were times when this was how He felt about the good, loyal, not entirely subservient but ultimately reliable and altogether rather too perspicacious archangel Gabriel. There were times like that. And this was one of them.

"Eh? Are You?" Gabriel still stared ahead, motionless, only his chin moving in rhythm with his mouth as he spoke, lost in thought. "Going to tell them?"

"It seemed -" began the Lord, slowly.

" - like a good idea at the time", intercepted Gabriel, immobility unaltered below the chin. He recalled the stone, the empty cave, the gasps of wonder, the awed responses to his flawless impersonation.

"Christianity -" the Lord resumed.

" - I thought You'd preordained it all", Gabriel butted in again.

"I -" The Almighty was sounding like a cornered Immortal like He had rarely been before (except over the Joan Of Arc thing).

"I mean", chimed in the relentless one, mouth just moving enough to allow the words to escape over knuckles and twitching chin. "I mean, that wasn't preordained was it, the lad and the stone?"

"No..." replied the Lord cautiously.

"Well, then, why do it? Christianity was all set up already. Just let it carry on."

"Not necessarily", the Lord responded, still in a tone unwilling to be drawn any further. Gabriel did not look quite himself, as though carefully reviewing something he had never really turned over in his mind before and not being comfortable with what he found. "It would not necessarily have acquired the power to swell through generations, and centuries, and then millennia, without that particular event. I am sure you know this", the Lord added, as if to remind Gabriel that it was a bit late to start querying it all now.

"So You're not going to tell them." It was a detached kind of summary, chin and knuckles moving in unison, eyes expressionless, demeanour suggesting that there was a drawbridge raised up between them and the human race, to remain there forever, for better or for worse.

"What are their religions without myths?" stated the Good Lord, levelly, "And what is belief without myth? Perhaps I would that it were not so. But ..." His voice tailed away into His thoughts again. But He had preordained pragmatism, the defiance of fact denying belief, believing only what could be seen, touched, heard, smelled; unless it were inexplicable. The unexplained. The power of myth. Legend, belief. Cause, effect. A stone, an empty cave. A figure seen, reported, written about, borne through time into history, to be part of the present. Legend become fact, at any rate to those who believed. If He had preordained that faith in *fact* should be so strong that it would deny belief, then *legend* must acquire the strength of fact to resist and retaliate. So legend becomes belief, and that belief becomes fact. Then it's my fact versus your fact. Quits. End of argument. Stalemate. No-one wins, no-one loses. Everyone believes what they want to. And what they believe is the Truth.

"So the ones who *don't* believe in it", struck in Gabriel, moodily, "think they are just as right as -"

" - as the ones who do", murmured the Lord, picking up the angel's words, in harmony.

"So what's the point in them believing in anything, believing in *You*, if they never know who's right?"

"And who is wrong", enjoined the Good Lord once more.

"*Everybody's* right", grunted Gabriel, sardonically. "So whose side are we on?"

Side

"You know what he said, Renee?"

Victoria Twigg was standing in the lounge of the 'Victoria Twigg' suite in Cheyenne's classiest hotel in Wyoming; the suite renamed to celebrate her surprise electoral triumph to succeed to the Presidency. 'Classiest': a three-star rating was the best the State's principal city could offer and 'suite' was really only two guest-rooms cordoned off together; but Victoria did not mind. It felt like home and she chose to stay just out of town, with the privacy and views that went with it. After her transition from Congresswoman Twigg, she had been - still was - their 'golden woman', shining a brilliant light upon one of the Union's least regarded political partners.

Here she was again, fulfilling one of those ill-considered post-election promises, proclaimed in the exultation of victory, to attend a charity fundraising dinner organised by her election team. Yet she knew she did not mind; she acknowledged an inner warmth to be back in the cradle of her political nascence.

She gazed across to the mountains and cast her mind back over those heady three years at the country's helm, nearly half of them dominated by the 'new way', triggered by the unsolved 'seize-ups' and the extraordinary phenomenon of the 'smiling

Jesus'; and her own visitation from 'my angel'. Now she was well into the next round of primaries for the Presidential election.

She was reminded of John F. Kennedy all those decades ago. She, like him, had been heralded as a breath of fresh air, a new beginning. The difference was she really *had* come from 'nowhere', in American Presidential parlance, swept on a wave of popular support. JFK's radical image belied his carefully-underplayed origins in wealthy plutocracy and liberal conserva-tism and had been slow to emerge from that heritage. Her zeal sprung from her roots; Kennedy's had been acquired in spite of his. Yet, had he not been assassinated, his late conversion to such causes as civil rights and the relief of poverty might already have sealed his electoral fate.

Twigg was minded of the many analyses published since then, that John Kennedy would have struggled to retain his Presiden-cy, if not failed to gain a second term altogether. Her mind swept the popular downtown blocks and streets, visualising her new America blossoming there; one in which the marketplace and home were gaining ascendancy over the pressured office and the diminishing throb of traffic.

But now the horns of reaction were beginning to emerge from the body-politic once more, seeking to impale the shoots of change before they could become established as the new landscape. Much of what Kennedy planted successfully re-sisted attempts to uproot it, yet how much more withered in the heat of retaliation from those whose world of materialistic ag-gression had been threatened? Now, her own fragile alliance with the media was being undermined by reversion to its natural conservative allegiances. China's advancement was being bran-dished across TV channels as its claim to be the next superpower, reinforced by images of glittering technology and accelerating prosperity, in contrast with America's reversion to a humbler ideal.

The message was a question, loud and clear: what future for the USA if it continues upon this path, whilst China and the East march defiantly into the next era of materialism? Twigg's America might have won the argument by standing its ground, might have won eventual acknowledgement that a future based on the mis-takes of the past would be a future bleak indeed; that whatever the allure of beating the West at its own game, it was a new era now, an era in which the interests of the planet and all who occupied it had to be put first.

But now there was this. This preposterous, incredible, impossible invention, which all America, and much of the rest of the world, had witnessed and with which America was being taunted. The Chinese President, stiff and courteous, had resolutely declined to indicate any point at which this breakthrough might be shared. "Still developing ... not fully tested" (despite his own immaculate transportation) .. "when our scientists are ready."

"When might that be?" she had pressed, controlling her indignation and dismay.

"Aah", was the inscrutable response, and nothing more. No inclination to share with the world, amid a hint of bitterness at the 'sharing' ethic which the United States was trying to spread to every shore. Twigg could scarcely contemplate the implications of such technology residing solely in the hands of their oriental would-be usurpers. Moreover, these new pretenders to world domination were refusing to accept even the slightest element of America's urge to adopt 'a new way'. She turned to her faithful aide, her confidante and, when, needed, rock of support.

"He said, 'Where's your God now? Is He not on *our* side?' Outrageous, Renee. They let Christianity take a foothold in their atheist state and then, when is suits, claim it for their own."

"Ma-am", Renee Fleck nodded in acquiescence, not knowing what to say but understanding her brave, noble, lonely President needed her support.

"Whose side *would* He be on?" Twigg mused as she watched the morning sun glint on windows. "How does He choose? *Does* he choose? How *can* He choose?"

"We're not at war with them", Renee reminded her, quietly.

"Not yet", Twigg grimaced at her.

Renee observed her President's expression harden as her head turned to the window again. The voice that floated back to her was more the Twigg decisive self.

"Take me for a drive, Renee."

"The big car or the other one?" Fleck asked.

"The other one", Twigg replied, with a slight smile as she turned again to her. Fleck nodded. The nondescript dark grey

Ford was always to hand, flown or driven to each Presidential destination so Victoria Twigg could take to the streets unnoticed and see life as it is, like any ordinary mortal.

Shack

"Oh my darling", lamented Hwee Lo, tears in her eyes, "they must still be seeking us somewhere." It had become too much to bear. Three days in the spartan shanty hut. Cousin Wu had quickly overcome his astonishment and consternation at their desperate arrival at his door and devoted all his energy to returning all those many, many favours. His exquisite talent for combining the simple roots, shoots, husks and berries of the countryside into delicious meals was a consolation, but it was their only one. His home was nothing more than a wooden hut in a dusty grove of sparse fig trees, other shacks scattered about. The solitary bed was an ancient netted hammock slung from four stout bamboo poles driven into the mud floor and took up a quarter of the available space. The only ornament was an incongruously large - almost life-size - colour portrait on wood, of Chairman Mao-tse-Tung, by the door. It was said Wu's father hung it there to delude Revolutionary search squads about his allegiance.

"But he avoided them anyway", Hoi Fong had told her, "by hiding in his safe hole."

"Hole?" The concept sounded dreadful to her.

"Yes, yes, a hole, a burrow, beneath the floor. A proper place to hide from Mao's men."

Cousin Wu's father, Lo Linh Wu, had been a suspected imperialist - Emperor's supporter - during the Maoist revolution and had escaped the communist pogroms by excavating his dugout beneath the mud floor, sending his son to relatives for safety.

"He stayed there nearly two months, only coming out sometimes at night." Hwee Lo had trembled as her husband had added, "If the Society comes close we can hide there."

The shack was bleak and bare. Hwee Lo had only been there once before, on a courtesy visit, soon after their marriage, and she'd had no desire to go again. Wu gave up his hammock for her and Soo Wong but the three nights had been interminable hours of rocking and swaying whilst trying to soothe the fretful child. Hoi Fong slept not at all, laid on sacks next to Wu on the dry mud floor. The classic Mao portrait, which was known to bear an unseemly resemblance to the current President of the Society, mocked Hoi. There was no water, except for what Cousin Wu fetched in an old wooden bucket from the well a hundred metres away. Hoi Fong dared not accompany him to double the supply, for fear of being seen.

Their clothes were already grimy, the pores of their skin clogged with dust. Hoi and Hwee Lo had done their best to occupy Soo Wong with games invented from sticks and pebbles on the floor. The child chafed to go outside; they could not risk it. When they had heard Teng's men approach and they had scuttled into the tiny pit under the floor, a space little more than two metres square and less than head height, it was all they could do to keep Soo Wong quiet and themselves, too, from coughing in the airless, pitch black, earthen cell.

When they heard the boots clumping over their heads, on the mud-covered, concealed trapdoor, Hoi feared he would suffocate his own daughter with the hand held over her mouth for silence. After a few, unending moments, they had departed, with a disgruntled voice distantly muttering, "somewhere." As the frightened family clambered out of the pit, Hoi Fong grimly wondered how long they could remain safe.

Things

In downtown Cheyenne, the marketplace was almost empty. Closer inspection revealed some handfuls of browsers wandering between the stalls, a few of which sported a semi-permanent structure of half-brick, half-wood-and-metal, confidently challenging the downtown stores, many of which had been crippled by the slowdown. The marketplace had sprung up to fill unused parking lots and street spaces, cheek by jowl with the variety of electrical, clothing, home furnishing and other outlets. Some had done better than others during the slowdown. Clothing was the kind of specialist industry unlikely to be replicated on a small scale so those stores - in particular, 'western fashion' - had continued to attract bouyant trade. Electrical goods were superficially quiet but, while the retail arm of the business was in the doldrums, manufacturing remained healthy, the products now bound for Africa.

Food supermarkets suffered the most. They had already been suspected of paying no more than lip-service to concerns about excessive transportation pollution and exploiting developing economies. Now they were widely shunned in favour of produce from local and inter-State growers and markets. Except where imports were essential to sustenance, America was rediscovering its ability to feed itself, and its people prepared to forgo exotic fare only obtained from overseas, unless evidence could be produced that it had been secured at a price which justly reflected its true value. That, at any rate, was the remarkable transformation in progress up to now.

"There's no-one about", observed Victoria Twigg, frowning through the rear door window of the car; "mid-morning", she added, implying it would usually be a busy time for shoppers.

"There are, ma-am", Renee corrected her, looking out of her side, behind the driver, "hundreds ... see."

The President turned her head to peer past her personal assistant.

"Gawd!" she exclaimed, more in the vernacular of Miami street girl than mistress of the White House.

There were indeed hundreds of people. Could have been a thousand or more, since the lines from the doors of the food, clothing and electrical retailers appeared to merge and overlap before disappearing out of site behind the arc of buildings. One or two market stallholders could be seen looking forlornly across at the endless column of missed sales.

"What's going on?" breathed Twigg, gazing uncomprehendingly at the shuffling lines of people, who were displaying signs of impatience, jostling together; some raise voices could be heard, muffled by the bullet-proof glass of the car windows. Renee shrugged, unable to suggest an answer.

"I've heard about this, Ma-am", the driver volunteered from in front, as he slid the car inconspicuously into a gap between the few parked vehicles ranged down the street. "Some folks I know. Sayin' they want things in the stores again. 'Why should the goddam Chinese have everything?' 'Sick of sharing'."

"I heard something like this", Renee muttered, her eyes fixed, too, on the people moving restlessly in their lines, some banging palms and fists on the shops' display windows. "Talk of Americans being 'shamed' by the Chinks."

Twigg looked at her, sharply.

"I know, ma-am." Renee averted her eyes, apologetically. "I guessed it was just somethin' or nothin'; a bit of talk; sayin' the stores would sell the stuff here if people wanted it. They couldn't, could they?" She looked at her President again. "Folks have changed, they don't shop like that any more."

"Don't they?" Victoria Twigg was staring at the scene from their stationary car. Her grim tone clouded by a sadness in her eyes. "Come on, Renee."

"Ma-am! Madam President!" Renee started with alarm, as Victoria Twigg swung open her door to step out. The driver, too, reacted by leaping out of the car.

"Madam President! It's not safe! We don't have security!"

He was as troubled as Fleck by the President's insistence on making such excursions without any security cover, declaring she should be allowed to use anonymity alone for concealment. Privately, she felt hurt she could not walk freely among the people who elected her.

"Not all of them did", Press Secretary Will Jerome had once dared to remind her.

Victoria Twigg had drawn a scarf over her head and was marching determinedly towards the lines of people outside the stores. The driver and Renee Fleck scurried along the sidewalk to accompany her, one on each side, aware they would helpless if any danger arose. They could see a small grocery supermarket had opened its doors, revealing shelves stocked with provisions where hitherto they would have been empty or punctuated with long, bare spaces. People were thrusting themselves forward to gain entry, some pointing excitedly at what they could see on display.

"Ask them what's happening", the President urged Renee, as they approached to within a few metres of the line.

"Ma-am?" Renee queried her, nervous about drawing attention to their trio. Twigg prompted her with a finger pointed at the nearest in the line. Maybe it was that imperious gesture, maybe the scarf was simply an ineffective disguise. Probably, it was merely the unavoidably recognisable posture of the proud leader of the nation, seen, televised, photographed on so many hundreds and thousands of occasions that the proverbial blind man would probably spot her in a crowded room with the lights switched off. In short, whether or not she realised it, President Victoria Twigg was as instantly recognisable to most Americans as their own mothers. No headscarf, probably not even a beard and moustache, could mask that haughty bearing, the sensual sweep and curves of her body, the leonine swing of her limbs as she moved.

"Hey!" A man's voice called from the line, as the group of three caught his eye." *Jeeeeez! ... Hey!* ... it's ..it's ... *Twigg*!"

"*Wha -?*" exclaimed a woman near him, then another from further down the line. Twigg's driver grabbed her arm to pull her back to the car. Renee Fleck jumped protectively in front of her President, although her basic training in martial arts, for the White House, did little to boost her own confidence, faced by hundreds of fellow citizens.

"No!" Victoria Twigg snapped, fiercely, shaking her arm free and adopted a familiar relaxed pose for the gaping shoppers.

"*Jeeeez*!" The first man uttered again in astonishment, "Victoria! ... I mean, *President*?"

She nodded and smiled. Her bosom felt a warmth. It seemed so long since she had been close to ordinary Americans, way back in the early campaigning days for the Presidency, 'on the stomp' around the towns and counties of Wyoming: meeting, shaking hands, laughing, conversing, cajoling, rubbing shoulders; until 'security' began to envelope her, because she was a 'target'. It separated her, cordoned her off; ordinary people became throngs, memories, nurtured exchanges in her brain, a substitute for genuine contact.

"Hey, what you doin' here, Victoria?" shouted a man half-hidden the other side of the line.

"Is it really you?" a woman closest to her asked, wide-eyed.

Twigg nodded again and smiled. The driver and Fleck shifted uneasily either side of her, casting glances this way and that.

Fleck unobtrusively reached for her security cellphone, thinking to tap the emergency-call digit while the phone was concealed in her bag. Twigg saw her out the corner of her eye, guessed her intention and jab a finger in a sharp gesture to prevent her. She wanted to speak to them, not be hustled away. These were people she had only seen on television in the last three years, or in deep crowds as she was swept through them in a limo flanked by FBI outriders.

"I -" she began.

"Hey! ... Ma-am President!" called the first man again. "You aint gonna stand for this, eh? Those Chinks!"

"Chinese!" A woman yelled from deep in the line.

"Who they goddam think they are!" another shout.

"We gonna look stoopid?"

"We want -!"

There was a short pause at that cry.

"*Things*!" A woman suddenly shouted.

"*Yeh*!"

"*Yeh*!"

"Like ... *here*!" A woman who had called out already waved an arm at the open shop doors at the head of the line. "We aint gonna let the goddam Chinese have everything!"

The woman who had gazed in awe at her inadequately disguised President from almost beside her, spoke softly from in front of the rest of them..

"Are we, Victoria?"

Twigg looked at her, dismay rising in her throat.

"You won't let them, will you?" The woman, a small, sweet-faced middle-aged motherly type pleaded with her, "we are Americans, Madam President, we are the best. Aren't we?"

Twigg nodded. She tried to smile through her unease.

"We don't take shit from no-one, do we?"

Twigg recoiled inwardly at the unexpected profanity from one so moderate in appearance. She remained immobile but it was like stepping on a mine concealed in a field of lilies. It was the voice within.

"Yeh. No shit!" A man nearby picked up and it became a refrain rippling through the crowd.

"No shit ...!"

"We'll show 'em, eh President!"

"We got stores better'n theirs, eh?"

"They think they gonna take over the goddam world?"

Twigg tried not to flinch under the gathering verbal on-slaught. She drew herself up.

"What about -" She half-turned to indicate the deserted market stalls behind her. She knew her voice sounded weaker than it should. They sensed it.

"We don' want no more of that!" shouted a man. "Where's that got us?"

"Yeh! The Chinks are laughing at us!"

"We got no respect no more! We want *things*!"

"*Things*!" someone else cried.

"*Things*!" became a refrain to replace "*no shit*!"

The crowd started to heave and surge as the front of the line tipped through the shop doorway but it seemed as though it was bursting sideways, threatening to envelope the President and her two aides.

"Ma-am!" This time the driver was having none of it, no shrugging-off by the President. His supreme duty to protect the First Citizen kicked in. He was dragging her back towards the car, all six-foot-one-and-a quarter of her, a full two inches taller than himself. Renee Fleck wanted to grasp her phone again but impulse brought both hands to grab the President's other side, to half-pull, half-push in the same direction as the driver.

"You'll do for us, Victoria!" A voice rose up from the bustling line.

"Yeh!" cried another and prompted cheering and waving from among them.

Twigg angrily shook and pulled her arm to free herself from her two attendants and they half-let-go but she knew as well as they did she could do or say no more. Her answers were not what her people wanted to hear. They associated distress and vehemence at subordination by their tormentors from across the world with America's 'new way'. She recognised that. Her heart sank inside. On another day, in another time, she might have exulted in American pride and the resolution she saw played out in that store line; a determination never to be outdone. She somehow maintained her bearing as Fleck opened the car door for her and permitted a persuasive hand on her arm as she sank into the seat. She watched the crowd milling into the store for their 'things' as the car took her away. She had wanted her countrymen and women to lead the world along a new path. The path looked tangled with briars now. She wondered if even she could clear a way through.

Debate

"Humiliated!"

It was not just Jacobson of Dakota, it was even Cissy Mandeman from Twigg's 'own' State of Wyoming. Other senators were taking up the cry. Senate was bristling with anger and indignation, resentment and humiliation.

"We gonna let them just walk all over us?" (Senator Wells of Ohio, who had long been a loyal supporter, now speaking with the uprising).

"What next?" (Senator Ignatious Grant of Illinois, who had been chafing at the first opportunity to attack the President without being derisively shouted down).

"They gonna start telling *us* where we get our oil? They gonna send *their* troops to protect *democracy*?"

A huge guffaw from the assembled senators at this notion of China protecting freedom.

"They gonna just snatch *all* our power away? We just gonna let go of being the greatest country in the world, just like *that*?"

Grant snapped his fingers in the air as he spoke and the cries of "No!" rang almost in unison around the house, before he added his *coup de grace*:

"While we *share* our beans and tomatoes?"

The rest was a barely-controlled uproar, the Speaker valiantly attempting to persuade voices to be heard individually, arguments to be aired but, as they were almost all singing from the same hymn sheet, it mattered little. Those who contemplated more deeply and remained loyal to the President's cause found it impossible to carry their thoughts further than a sentence or two before being drowned out.

"And Spain!" was a cry that emerged from the hubbub, and "Muslims!"; "Kick ass!" "They aint following a *man*! They got their *prophet*! Kick ass before they take it over!" And these strident calls from anti-Islamic Jacobson and others - popularly kindling the fears bred from nine-eleven onwards - began to be echoed by another: "Africa!" "Are we watching our backs?" "They gonna take *that* from under our feet?"

For Victoria Twigg, her eventual exit from the Chamber was little better than a retreat. Her habitually haughty and assured declarations had been received in a murmuring half-silence before voices erupted again and again to retaliate after each of her responses.

"You have little choice, Ma-am", said Press Secretary Will Jerome, evenly, as he and Renee Fleck sat with the President in the Oval Office afterwards. She raised a weary eyebrow to him. Where now the triumph of political evangelism, her absolute power to persuade? She knew he was right. The voices of disaffection in Congress would quickly infect the population at large who, as she had seen outside the Cheyenne stores, were only too ready to be led back the way they had come. Then the virus would sweep out of control, dashing aside anyone standing in its way, including herself.

"Ma-am." Renee spoke quietly to the President she had grown to respect above all others in her years of service. "Do you *want* a second term?"

The question was loaded like a nuclear missile, albeit spoken in tones of reverence and warmth.

Was that it? Power at any price? Would defeat be humiliation or a noble stand? She did not know why but her mind was suddenly filled with the image of the handsome young stranger, the visitor who glowed and whose glow had filled and inspired her. Had he started it all? Where was he now? Her 'angel'. She sighed aloud. Jerome and Renee exchanged glances at that sigh. They knew as they had known with all Presidents, even one as principled as this. Surviving to fight another day was what it would always come down to; fighting to survive. Whatever it took.

Hotel

Elroy carefully emptied the couple of drawers he had used and placed the contents in his case. Underwear, socks, three or four shirts he'd not even unfolded to hang up. He moved around the bed towards the wardrobe, glancing through the ninth floor window as he did so, at the panoramic view of the city. The elegant shape of the White House gleamed distantly in the sunlight. An involuntary vision of the materialising car leapt unbidden into his mind. He paused at the vista before him, the memory of that extraordinary event painting itself over his vision. He wished he had been there, not watching, crowded and jostled, in front of the airport plasma screen. It was momentous enough to see it in those circumstances; it must have been awesome to stand amongst the White House crowds.

All three of them had stayed in the hotel that night. The furore which immediately followed the Chinese President's 'arrival' made booking transfer flights to New York impossible unless they had been prepared to wait and queue till the next day. Not only did half the visitors seem to want to do the same thing, Washington was engulfed in a kind of panic. On the one hand, an undercurrent of fear gripped the city, as though a whole invasion of materialising cars were about to occur and swallow them up; on the other hand an irrational security blanket was hurled over everyone and everything, particularly all transport terminals and the airport itself.

No-one appeared prepared to analyse how smothering people's travel requirements had any bearing on the phenomenon they had witnessed. If anyone else - or indeed whole armies - were likely to arrive or depart in the manner of their esteemed visitor, the technology would clearly allow them to do so as they pleased, and no amount of cordon tape and breast-beating security police would prevent them.

Elroy, Walt and Olivia had, like the rest of America, and most of the rest of the world, talked of nothing else from that moment on. They knew, though, they were different. They had been told of its existence already and had been inclined to disbelieve. The first thing Olivia did, once they had secured their two hotel rooms, was phone Isabella. Bella and Paul had watched it, of course, repeated countless times on television in the UK, as everywhere else.

"Bella, Bella, what can I say?"

There was a moment's silence.   Then her friend's voice sounded uncharacteristically fragile.

"We tried to tell you, Livvy."

"I know, I know, just ..." Olivia knew no words to repair the schism of doubt she had inserted between herself and her best friend.

"I know, Livvy, hun. It's impossible. I knew you couldn't accept it from me. I tried and I cried." Bella's voice trembled over the call. "I nearly stopped believing it myself. Thought I'd gone crazy. *And* Paul. Until .. until .. ."

"Yeh, honey", Olivia shook her head sympathetically, "you okay?"

She heard a relieved sigh.

"I guess ... I guess .." Then there came a throaty Bella chuckle. "I guess I feel one hundred and one per cent now." She laughed again, a laugh gurgling with humour that made Olivia smile. "I mean - I saw it first, didn't I?" They felt each other relax as they spoke some more, the bond of long friendship resealing itself.

"Speak soon, honey", smiled Olivia.

Isabella had talked more warmly of Paul than for as long as Olivia could recall. She said he was coming out of himself again; even expressing annoyance that the car - *his* sales stock - had disappeared without anyone paying for it!

"Do ya think it's the same car?" Walt asked Elroy later, as the three of them sat over coffee in the hotel restaurant lounge.

"Dunno", mused the big guy. "Could be the same prototype; could be one of many. I just caint think who on earth..." His voice tailed off.

"On earth?" Olivia prompted him.

"Coulda invented it", he continued.

"The Chinese..." Walt murmured.

"The Chinese had it at Paul's showroom", Olivia added to their collective thoughts. "Or one like it."

"Yes, but..." Elroy leaned forward, index fingers supporting his chin. "Who?" The other two watched him as he pondered.

Then he leaned back suddenly, drawing in his breath and gazed at the soft peach glow from the concealed lights illuminating the ceiling. "No-o-o.." The breath was exhaled with the elongated exclamation. And then they saw his eyes widen. "Gainsborough Hill...!"

"Who?" queried Walt.

"The scientist?" Olivia remembered what Isabella had told her of Elroy's strange attitude as she drove him back from his visit to the lab in London.

"Yuh", Elroy nodded and then shook his head slowly in disbelief. He had told them nothing of the incident with the formula, or the bizarre connection with the birthday card, or the man's wild eyes of triumph and his shouted, then fervent, hiss of 'Yes-s-s!' Now Elroy told them all of that, what little was known to him. Particularly, coincidentally, that the car with the birthday card was one of Paul Best's Chinese 'Mets'.

"Ya not saying that's the connection?" puzzled Walt.

"Dunno, man. But he had a formula. *I* had a formula. We both had it *provided*. I mean, man, I knew *parts* of mine already and he'd been working on his for years. We both found missing links that we sure would never have found ourselves if we'd lived to a hundred-and-fifty. And he mentioned transport. Just 'transport'. Then he had those eyes. Man, I never seen eyes go like that. Outa this world."

"So's teleportation", remarked Olivia, quietly.

"But you said *you* had a *visit*, man", Walt reminded Elroy, though he still found it hard to conceptualise his own friend's tale of the revelation in his study at home.

"And he had that birthday card", wondered Elroy.

"Well", said Olivia, firmly, with her woman's eye for pragmatic explanations, "it had to be discovered sometime."

"Yeh?" Elroy raised a sceptical eye.

"Well, you said then only photons have been teleported", she reminded him. "Once there was only a spark, now electricity does all this." She swept an arm in gesture around the restaurant lounge, taking in lights, plasma screen, hot coffee in cups, phones, air conditioning. "So he - someone - invented it before anyone thought it was possible."

Elroy shook his head.

"That's it", he allowed himself a slight, wry, grin, "it's *not* possible. Not *yet.*"

"From photons to ... cars?" Walt quizzed him. After all, he and millions of others had *seen* it.

"But if it was", Olivia reflected, "It could be the answer."

"To -?" Walt looked at his wife, as she turned it over in her mind.

"To ...", she weighed, "well ... everything."

"Everything?" puzzled Elroy, at her ambitious declaration.

"Well, think about it", continued Olivia, "no fuel, no gas, no pollution. No aircraft. Not even roads, tarmac, all that production and more pollution. No congestion. No road crashes. No wasted metal. No car factories -"

"Cars? This was a car", Walt reminded her.

"Doesn't have to be", said Elroy. "That was just a box to put it in. Could become something you hold or on your belt -"

"Beam me up, Scotty!" joshed Walt, with a grin.

They all chuckled.

"But it's more than that." Elroy became contemplative again. "Think of it. If it was used worldwide - no reason why not; everything else is - no more competition for oil, or even to make batteries or hydrogen cells -"

"And *they* need factories, energy", remarked Walt.

"Yeh", continued Elroy, a fervent gleam in his eyes, "real worldwide drop in pollution. Good Lord, we'd be tearing up all that tarmac and planting forests again! I mean, surely, surely, it'd be such a revolution, like .. like .. all jumping centuries ahead together, overcoming so many problems all at once. D'ya think -?" He looked at the other two. "D'ya think it'd bring us all together? Like they say an alien threat would?"

"Only this'd not be a *threat*!" The ringing twang of the other side of the Bridge. Isabella had called back in the middle of their conversation, suddenly waking in the early hours of the morning in London, struck with the same thoughts, as if woken by a dream. Olivia had passed her phone to Elroy, seeing how her Brooklyn friend desired to be part of their deliberations. Bella was sitting bolt upright in bed, Paul sound asleep beside her, glowing with the fire of triumph, could they but see her; she who had devoted so much energy and passion to saving their future.

"Elroy! It'd be a gigantic discovery! Change whole of human life. Whole planet! For all of us to share! It would be ... momentous ..fantastic! Even more than what *you* did!"

Elroy shook his head again with a smile as he handed the phone back to Olivia, the excited New York tones, unsubdued by a decade in London, ringing in his ears. It remained a smile of disbelief.

"It's still not *possible*", he insisted with another shake of his head at his empty coffee cup on the table. "And I don't get it: Gainsborough... Chinese ...Triads -"

"Triads?" exclaimed Walt in astonishment.

Elroy sighed.

"Part of my secret research. GCHQ. I'll tell ya another time. Think we traced 'em and that coulda been the gang, in the showroom. But why were they in that car? Don't get it." He shook his head.

"The scientist", Olivia interjected, thoughtfully, "you said he had that Chinese girlfriend." She looked queringly at Elroy. "At the party."

"And then they both disappeared", added Elroy, acknowledging her train of thought. "But why Triads?" He shook his head again. He knew more than the rest of them but it made even less sense.

He grinned again, ruefully, at them and cast a wry eye to the ceiling.

"Who plans all this, eh? Do ya know? Makes sense, does it?"

Elroy found himself shaking his head in recollection at this conversation, as he took trousers and jacket from the wardrobe. It had suited him to stay in Washington for a few days, using the city office as his base. He had not spent time there for a year and was expected to maintain personal contact occasionally, even though he could achieve less than when on home territory in New York. Walt and Olivia had caught a flight late the next day when some order had been restored to Washington life. Elroy had made another fond and apologetic phone call to Mariana. He sensed there was less forbearance this time and assured her it was the last delay.

He cast an eye around the room and opened and closed drawers and wardrobe doors to check he was leaving nothing behind. His hand rested on the Bible a moment before he restored it to its bedside cabinet. He had flicked through some familiar passages each evening. He stood for a few seconds, pondering. Is any of this planned? By anyone? He picked up his case and left the room.

Exist

"Who *me*?"

God marvelled at how Gabriel could effect such an air of innocent surprise, as though Heaven might be positively teeming with other angels, any more than it was self-evidently not teeming with souls. It was not as though Gabriel even spoke the words; it was just the look on his face. Then that changed, to something more contentious.

"I thought You said -"

The angel was checked by an aura of Divine Disapproval.

" - nudging?" he probed, doggedly.

"We -" began The Lord.

" - have to help the ones ..." nodded the angel in a 'yeh-yeh-tell-me' fashion, "who have been..."

"...drawn in", sighed the Lord, ignoring the insubordinate tone.

"by our -" and the angel's voice halted again, succeeded by a further 'yeh-yeh' nod and grunt. And then muttered into his feet, "not as if they even think you exist; most of them."

Did it make a difference, God sometimes wondered? He existed anyway, whether they said He did or not. His existence did not depend on the tragedies, or otherwise, of living things. Splongies asphyxiated in agony, Tryxxians and humans drowned, in their different ways. It had all been there in that single dot of matter before the Beginning of Everything. You either created a universe or You did not. It either all began and continued or it did not. You existed whether they thought You did or not, whether they blamed You, thanked You or ignored You. You could not fiddle and meddle, manage and manipulate, to spare the occasional life (or the occasional million), or to divert the course of suffering. It had to work both ways. No-one asked You to curtail their joy, extinguish their ecstasy, did they? 'Please God, I'm too happy, do something about it'... 'Please God, my life is charmed and trouble-free, can't You rain tragedy upon me?' Only the echoing refrain ... 'Please God, my loved ones have been torn from me, please bring them ba ...'

So when it came to occasional 'nudging' and repairing the consequences for those unwittingly sucked into the eddying pool of dislocation, it did not matter if, to them, He did not exist. They might pick and choose over their beliefs and allegiances, He could not. He could determine their fate, by intervening or otherwise, but He could not pretend they did not exist.

"It does not matter", He murmured aloud, "if to them I do, or do not, exist", and then added, "when, by Our intervention, they have become Our responsibility."

He considered this might be more than a hint on its own but found that an additional meaningful look in the direction of his trusted angel and servant was required as well.

"Aw, Boss. *Now?* I've only just come back!"

Refuge

There was a rumble of heavy, all-terrain tyres over the scrub. They heard it from inside the shack.

"Quick, quick! Down!" Cousin Wu frantically ushered them through the camouflaged trapdoor and they scrambled, Hwee Lo clutching Soo Wong, into the unlit pit. Wu hastily shut the trapdoor and swept the dust over it and heaved an old bamboo chest on top, then hurried to busy himself at the small stove over a kettle for some tea. Footsteps strode swiftly outside.

"Oh my dear, oh my dear", wept Hwee Lo in the dark, holding the dozing Soo Wong in her arms, "What did we do for this?"

"You, you did nothing my love, my sweet one", he whispered. Tears were in his eyes, too. "Even I - they suspect me of tampering with their affairs - yet I know nothing of them but they can do dreadful things even when there is nothing to tell. He could hear a thin voice, crackling its command just as the flimsy door was thrown open. "Hush! Hush!"

"In! In! They must be *somewhere*!"

Terrified to his soul, Hoi Fong silently thanked his foresight for asking policeman Cousin Fo to collect and hide their car, though the subterfuge might be of no avail now. They had walked the two miles to Cousin Wu's, to seek refuge and whatever meagre hospitality he might share. Cousin Wu, whom they so lightly entertained in the comfort of their splendid home, with never a thought that they might one day in desperation depend upon him, in his lowly circumstances, to do the same for them. Hoi and Hwee Lo clutched each other in their dungeon. They could hear the muffled voice of Teng from above.

"So", Teng leered at Wu, whose arm was held in a tight half-nelson by one of the two thugs with the sinister Society man, "they are not here? There is nowhere for them to hide." He cast a contemptuous look around the sparsely-furnished shack with its single, worn hammock, old bamboo chair, a stool and an ancient little paraffin stove. "And no self-respecting factory owner would bring his wife and child to such a disgusting place, even if they were desperate. Eh?" And he dug a short ebony stick he was carrying, into Wu's ribs. Wu let out a sharp cry of pain and Hoi winced below the trapdoor, clutching his wife even more tightly.

"And perhaps that's what I am supposed to think, eh?" Teng dug again, harder, and again the sharp cry, followed by an involuntary sob. Wu's thin, innocent features were contorted with fear and pain. "But it is said your old father hid himself here somehow - for many weeks after the Revolution - and how could he do that?" Teng glanced at the Mao portrait by the door. "Where could he hide here? But you wouldn't tell me that, would you?" Another vicious prod, another cry. Hoi felt he could not bear much more, distraught to have brought such calamity upon his poor, humble cousin.

"You would be brave, wouldn't you?" Teng was continuing, "if it meant protecting your honourable" - he spat the word - "cousin? But how brave can you be, *Cousin* Wu?"

He motioned to the henchman, who suddenly forced Wu's bent arm upwards, higher up his back and the poor man yelled in agony, feeling his arm about to break.

"No! No!" Hoi shouted from beneath the trapdoor, and began to thump on the wooden panel above his head. Hwee Lo pulled at him in alarm but it was too late to retract.

"Hah!" Teng's eyes gleamed as he swung to look at the old chest, from where the muffled exclamation appeared to come. He pointed to it as the second accomplice leapt to drag the chest from its position, revealing the earth beneath vibrating from Hoi beating fists. The swarthy man scuffed at the loose earth with his hands and revealed the wooden trapdoor.

"Hah!" exclaimed Teng again, as his sidekick pulled at the metal ring and lifted the trap. Hoi's head appeared, as he still shouted "No!", staring wildly through the opening until his eyes fell upon Cousin Wu, lifted half off his feet and squirming in pain.

"No!" cried Hoi again, hauling himself out of the refuge, whereupon the henchman who had lifted the trapdoor grabbed him and heaved him to his feet, to force his arm into a half-nelson like his cousin Wu.

"So!" Teng allowed himself a small, triumphant smile, ignoring Hwee Lo as she pulled herself, Soo Wong in one arm, out of the hole. "So, Brother Hoi, I must assume you have something you have not told me, or you would not have committed yourself and your dear family to such an ordeal." He cast a disdainful look at the small square hole in the floor and the gloom beneath. "Would you?"

Hoi felt himself trembling with fear. This was the other side of the Society. Behind the cold smiles lay the baleful hatred of resistance and betrayal. But how could he betray them with ignorance? He knew nothing so what could he tell them?

"As you know, brother", sniped Teng, "we have many ways of finding out. But not here. We have a place we can go - where we have the means to assist your memory, should it fail you." Hoi shuddered, a terror passing through him. The Society did not take ignorance for an answer. A deep sob welled inside, a premonition of a life for ever changed by disablement, or worse, all because he had no tale to tell. "Dear me, cousin", Teng was turning again to Wu and at the same time looked at the Mao portrait by the door, "did you think our esteemed Chairman would protect you? He only protects true children of the Revolution, not *traitors*." He took a swipe at the painted wooded board, as he spoke, rapping his stick against the figure's midriff.

Disconcertingly, the picture responded with a hollow, "Oooph!" And one of the arms which had been in pose by its side lifted to clasp the point where the stick had struck. Then the figure proceeded to step out of the picture, still with a hand to his middle and grimacing from the blow. Or at least, he appeared to. But the portrait was hanging by the door. The onlookers - captors and victims - all watched dumbfounded and then could not be sure that the figure - Chairman Mao himself - had not instantaneously arrived through the door. They all looked at the picture, and thought they saw the Chairman in the process of stepping from it but, when they blinked, the portrait remained intact. Yet the same figure was now amongst them. But was he? They were confused, frightened. They looked at the doorway, where he now stood. Perhaps, truly, that is where he came. They looked at the picture; it was still the Mao portrait except, though they scarcely noticed in their confusion, one arm was now bent up to clasp the midriff.

Then they looked at the new figure among them And they looked again. It was not quite the image of Chairman Mao. It was - and now Teng himself shook with trepidation - it ... he ... had transmuted into that near-likeness, the President of the Society, a reclusive, secretive figure scarcely ever seen. This President was grim.

"A sharp blow, brother", he said, "but not so sharp as your deceit, eh, brother Teng?"

Teng's jaw already gaped wide open in disbelief. Now his lower lip quivered, too.

"Bro - Mr Chairman - Your Excellen - Brother -"

The usually icy Teng blustered and stumbled. He was gripped by a fantasy in which a portrait of the esteemed Founder of the Revolution had inexplicably delivered its own likeness - but no, his own Society President, long-compared to the venerated Chairman - in flesh and blood before him, and accusing him of what?

"Yes, brother", the gravelly President continued, his short, stout frame facing Teng square-on, "your deceit. And the item you have lost -"

"Me?" blurted Teng.

"Yes, Brother, and which you try to claim has been stolen *here* while you know - you know - it has been captured in England."

"England? The seal was intact. The whole battery had been switched -" faltered Teng. "The contents had gone!"

"Pah! The seal! The battery!" snorted the President. "A fabrication in collusion with that traitor Sing, eh? So you can seek to cast the blame upon our poor brother, here." He clapped a hand upon Hoi's shoulder, who by now had been released by his stupefied captor. "And you would have employed all manner of means to extract a confession which you knew - you knew - he could not have supplied."

"Brother, I -" Teng felt his knees shake, while the shack and its occupants swam around him. He heard the President's words continue through a daze.

"I - we, the Society - will give you one opportunity, in view of your hitherto unblemished loyalty, to escape your deserved retribution. You will leave Beijing, never to return."

"Leave? Brother, I -" Teng's whole face was twitching in dismay.

"Yes, boss."

Teng's expression became briefly flabbergasted. Hoi looked at the President in bewilderment, too.

"*Yes,* boss." The President was staring straight at Teng, who could not fathom why admonishment had suddenly changed to a term of respect.

"In a *minute*, boss!" The President's brow had furrowed, his eyes screwed up in frustration, while he appeared to look right through Teng now, at some unseen object beyond. "I *know* two .. at the same time? ... yes .. but when I've *planned* it, boss.. eh?"

The others in the shack all followed the President's glance upwards at the bamboo roof of the shack, which was plain and empty of all adornment, almost expecting to see someone reply. But the President's eyes dropped sharply again, as he frowned at the dusty floor.

"Isn't it time we just left them to-?"

Then he looked up suddenly again, staring straight through the dumbstruck Teng.

"No .. okay, boss.. I'll be there."

The figure of authority before them had been partially transformed to one of compliance, without any noticeable change in the stout demeanour. Hoi and Hwee Lo looked at each other, perplexed. Teng's two sidekicks, still standing by, exchanged confused glances. Teng just stood, transfixed, star-

ing at his erstwhile oppressor. The President muttered something under his breath, that sounded like, "Just wasting our
time." Then his bearing altered again, stiffening in restored
self-command. When he spoke, he addressed Teng directly once
more, resuming the judgement he had been delivering to his
'brother'.

"You will go to Qinghal to spend the rest of your days there."
The President's voice continued sternly, impervious to the reaction he was eliciting in the quaking Teng, who was doubly shaken
by the strange metamorphosis taking place in front of him.

"No ... I .." Teng was reaching forward in supplication, the
horror of banishment to the outback impelling him.

"Yes, Brother", the President responded stonily, "or the Society
will .." He allowed himself a pause in which it could only be
imagined what the Society would do. It was evidently not beyond
Teng's imagination, as his slight frame crumpled whilst the
President gestured the henchmen towards him.

"You have family there", avowed the President, allowing
consideration that his 'brother' would not be cast into isolation.
Teng nodded dully in acquiescence, remembering all the despised peasants he had long since abandoned. "You will be taken
to a flight now."

"My things?" Teng looked up, hopefully, as though discovering a means of delay.

"They have already been packed for you", stated the President, flatly, "your flight leaves soon. I hope for your sake,
Brother, that we shall not meet again." The meaning was
transparent, as the henchmen, having recovered their senses
and completed their deft switch of allegiance to their new
master, began to usher Teng through the door. As he passed
the President, he was momentarily transfixed by the deep
brown eyes, as his persecutor added, "Remember, Brother, the
Society has eyes in many places, should you attempt to return
..." Again he let silence speak the volumes it implied, watching
as Teng shuffled outside to the limousine which had conveyed
him there, held by the men who had until now been in his own
command.

The President turned to Hoi Fong and Hwee Lo, his brown
eyes twinkling disarmingly.

"Now", he declared, with an extra twinkle for Soo Wong in her mother's arms, "you may collect your possessions; and perhaps take your noble cousin with you for some rest."

Cousin Wu grimaced wanly, still flexing his sprained arm and shoulder to ease the ache.

"But -" Hoi glanced anxiously through the door at the departing black car.

"He will never return. They will speak of this to no-one", the President assured him and allowed himself a sly wink, somewhat out of character with the severe persona presented to the humbled Teng.

"I will leave you now, in a manner of speaking." He winked, twinkled and walked through the door. "I should not be seen here."

Assuredly, once outside with their bags of belongings, there was no sign of the President but they could hear an argumentative voice in the clearing. It came from a little wizened old man with a grey goatee beard, stomping around and striking the hard earth with his gnarled walking staff.

"I mean", he was saying, "*You* said ... *You* said ...we can't keep interfering! ...Yeh, I know ...because of *us* ...but, I mean, even *so*, all this rushing about -!"

The old man paused to listen, then continued stomping and banging his stick.

"Yes, but this lot don't even *believe* in You... I mean, not as if they even *pray* -" Then he appeared to mutter to himself, "as if it made any difference", but he mustn't have covered the phone mouthpiece because his voice changed from argumentative to contrite: "Yes, okay ..okay ..guv .. they're *all* Your childr- yes, guv." Then he turned around almost to face them and they could see the wide-eyed, ingenuous expression on his face, as he spread his arms in gesticulation to his unseen listener,

"Inventive? Boss? I mean! ..." Then contrite again: "Yes, guv." Then sounding under pressure once more: "*Yes, guv...*on my way ...*now.*"

They shuffled in mild embarrassment as this overheard conversation ended with the old man muttering to himself again, "*Inventive?* ...got to keep the interest up somehow." And Hoi thought he might have added the word, "cretins", but he couldn't be sure. Then the man looked up and saw them, the three adults and a child held in mother's arms. He beamed as they approached and a pair of brown eyes sparkled kindly at them. Hoi started in surprise, so similar was that look to the one with which the President had left them a short time before.

"Confucious!" Hoi exclaimed softly, despite himself.

The old man heard him and grinned a yellow toothy grin.

"Ah, quite, my dear boy. But it is finished now, you may go home."

"But -?" queried Hoi.

"Yes, yes, he has left", nodded the old man, vigorously, "I am here to look over you until you have safely gone."

He reached to touch Hwee Lo's hand as she gently lowered Soo Wong to the ground and she felt a warmth and comfort which matched the look in his eyes. They set off to walk home. Hoi Fong only then wondered why he had not seen a phone in the old man's hand, nor any other device by which he was communicating. Then they heard him again, his voice slowly receding as they headed off at the child's toddling pace. Hoi wondered at such an ancient possessing the latest in micro-technology.

"*Yes,* guv ... Boss... just finished." Then, although Hoi could only just make it out, as the old man, looking but not speaking in the likeness of China's revered sage, muttered again: "As You can see, anyway."

Hoi had drifted a few paces behind whilst listening. Hwee Lo had been more preoccupied with Soo Wong, holding her hand so she would not trip over loose stones and tufts. Now she turned and reached back her other hand to beckon her husband.

"My darling."

Hoi dropped his puzzled frown, smiled and quickened a few paces to reach and grasp her hand. He thought he might have heard the old man's last few words before they were out of earshot but he must have misheard as they made no real sense.

"Is it worth it? Cretins."

Hearts

The three frigates escorting three troop carriers had passed through the Suez Canal into the Mediterranean almost without comment, just some cheerful flag-waving - with a touch of irony - from Egyptians watching the passage. It was seen as all part of the continuing American withdrawal from previous flashpoints in the Middle East. Remarkable, commented international observers, how unrest in that troubled region had simmered down the moment the USA had begun its departure. Not in recorded history had a domineering nation such as the United States attempted pacification by candid retreat. Even the British Empire of the Nineteenth and Twentieth Centuries had crumbled under pressure of rebellion, reluctantly contracting its dominion to within its own island shores. The small convoy cruising east to west through the Med was one of a number witnessed in recent months. There would be more flags and cheering - without the irony - through the Straits of Gibraltar, before the open ocean and home.

President Twigg was attended by half a dozen senior advisors in the Oval Office. She retained her proud posture and the politicians sitting around - all men - still quivered or tingled to one degree or another, in her company. But she felt hollow and there was melancholy in her eyes.

"Hearts and minds, Madam President", said one, "hearts and minds."

"Remember Cuba", urged another.

"Which we lost."

"And Vietnam."

She nodded. She had already given the authority in principle. It was not too late to reverse the order in practise. But she would not, she knew it. A knife was being turned in her core. Who was she betraying? Only herself? Or a planet? She had woken in the night, perspiring, Renee's words writhing like snakes in her dream: "second term". She had bitten the apple.

"I gotta washer, Jerry!"

"Well aint you just the cute'n purdy one", drawled our Two-Two host, taking a swig from the can before crushing it in one big, lanky hand and tossing it in the 'Marlboro: 100x20 packs' cardboard box that served as the studio litter bin in a corner. A couple of other cans, obviously distracted by callers in their flight, lay on the floor at its side.

"Brand new! Works just fine!"

It was all they wanted to tell him today. And yesterday. And, as it would turn out, tomorrow and many days to follow. Going to the stores again. Buying new things. No more goddamned sharing, eh? To hell with the Chinese. F**k them. The delay bleep did not always catch that one but no-one cared, not even in deep south America. They grinned. They knew big Jerry Corrie would be grinning too. Like as not the pastors and the preachers would be hiding their faces with their hands as well. Wipe the slinky smiles off of those slit-eyed Chinese faces. We'll show 'em. No-one puts one over old Uncle Sam. Least of all, the Chinese.

It seemed suddenly no-one remembered they had supposed to have been showing the Chinese, and all the rest of the world, a 'new way'.

"Go for it!"

The big hand achieved the mightiest of thumps on the tabletop. *Smash*, more like. Abe, Tom and the others were each massaging their palms with fingers under the table, as though kinetic energy had transferred the smarting to their own. Big Max Drummond flinched not a jot, as ever. No-one knew if he privately and tenderly applied balming cream after they had all departed. But probably he did not.

"*Make* 'em!"

He almost smiled, with a face which had never been designed to accomplish such a contortion, even from birth.

"Get 'em out there. Beat the other fuckers before they get started!"

"Yes, Max", Abe nodded, agreeing for the rest of them, to a proposal which, as ever, he had put to Drummond himself, to witness it instantly appropriated as the big chief's own. "Excellent idea, Max."

"Good, Abe", Drummond nodded gruffly. "Need an ideas guy like me to see off the rest of the fuckers, don't we?"

"Yes, Max", they all nodded, agreeing in unison, silently thanking the brain of Abe for keeping them all in business and in jobs. So it was gasoline alley again! Cars with good old petrol internal combustion engines. Cheaper to make, easier to sell, more 'ooomph' for the driver. American motorists would be happy again. No more compromise. No stupid batteries taking up space. To hell with seize-ups. Lightning don't strike twice. Well, certainly not four times. Anyway, they had been secretly testing conventional gasoline automobiles for months and none had faulted. Nasty phenomenon it had been but it had gone now, whatever it was.

There was a knock on the cabin door.

"Come in."

The twenty-eight year-old major looked up to greet his second-in-command entering his private quarters. Two was a crowd in his small office with bunk and toilet cubicle. His visitor, a few years younger than himself, smiled as he entered. He had short, sandy hair - though not quite short enough in the opinion of his senior officer - poking out from around the edges of his garrison cap.

"Good to see you."

The major rose from his chair behind the desk, smiling in return and stretching out a hand as his new Number Two clicked the door shut behind him.

A seaman was patrolling the same gangway below decks a few minutes later, the distant hum floating up from the ship's engine room. He noticed a light from under the Marine commander's door as he passed, similar spillages of light shining beneath other doors on either side of the narrow, dark steel passage. Only after a few more steps did he subconsciously note the extra brightness from under the commander's door. He stopped to turn and look back. The light did appear to be stronger than from other door sills. Actually, he frowned, looking more intently, it *was* very bright. Hm, these troops bringing their own lights on board; can't they see properly? He smiled to himself but his smile faded as the light noticeably brightened as he watched, and seemed to spread up the door opposite. He observed, puzzled.

Now the light was spilling through the gaps between the door and frame. His cheeks flushed with concern. The whole door was beginning to glow, diffusing the light through solid grey metal, tinting it with peach-yellow luminance. Then it began to shimmer and pulse. The midshipman's eyes widened, his jaw dropped. He looked up and down the gangway for support but there was no-one. He heard some sounds like banging or scuffling from behind the door and then what sounded like a choking cry. A stifled shout sprang from his own throat as he ran down the gangway. He dared not intervene alone. Lord knew what trouble he might be in if he intruded on their guests' commanding officer at an inopportune moment. Best that two share the responsibility! He disappeared around a corner, still looking.

By the time he returned, a few moments later, with a fellow seaman, they were too late to see the Marines' second-in-command slip out of the door, shutting it behind him, and head off up the gangway. They were in time to hear, though, the sounds of banging and breaking from inside the cabin. They did not wait to knock when they heard the single scream from within and burst through the door. They were confronted by the Marines' major dishevelled and wild-eyed, a laptop and desk ornaments scattered on the floor at his feet, along with the broken remains of some coffee mugs. The desk was in disarray, the items swept off it and some books had been knocked from the bookshelf behind the desk. The officer's cap lay in a corner, his hair was tousled and half his shirt buttons undone and his tie hanging loose as if he had been tearing at them.

He stood staring at the two shipmen as they moved to each grab an arm to steady him and he screeched and writhed to resist. They struggled to grip him tighter and hold him as he bucked and yelled a volley of incoherent gibberish. They led and lifted him out and down the passage, his arms and legs waving and flailing, they calling for help as they went.

Victoria Twigg suppressed a sigh as the group of 'grey suits' departed. It was not just the operation in Spain. She had also agreed a new bill to rush through Congress, modifying the Clean Air Act and withdrawing all restrictions on automobile manufacturing, along with factory production for everything else that mattered. There was to be a rush for re-growth. China was no longer just a challenge but a rampaging threat. If the US ambassador in Beijing could not immediately obtain the secret of the 'teleporter' by diplomatic persuasion, or the FBI, CIA and the rest of the covert operators flush it out by other means, the United States in the meantime would resume its position at the vanguard of global progress, come what may.

Oil was still plentiful, why cut ourselves off from it, she had been urged. The planet has plenty of life in it, why strangle the life out of America in a dubious cause? No-one in the rest of the world is taking any notice of our attempts to find a 'new way', instead we are being left behind. We'll be the primitives of the West, trailing in the wake of the new super powers of the East. It's not too late if we change now. It was a noble idea but too far ahead of its time. Let the factories use the fuels and technologies they know best. Let's get the economy back to what it was. And the dollar!

We're not polluting our environment. Lawd, look how big it is, we aint gonna run out of air! But we sure might run out of clout! Anyways, what use is breathing clean air if we're being strangled by China. And Africa: let's go for it. We can build it up twice as fast if we do it how we know best. Yeh, sure Madam President, sure we'll be developing these other methods in the background: the *next* generation can take them on board.

Victoria Twigg nodded, blankly. The next *generation*? What hope for the next *term*? The apple tasted truly sour.

Minds

The small convoy did not head out into the ocean after Gibraltar, it turned right, to starboard. The commander in the leading frigate was worried. They were running late. The unscheduled docking in Gibraltar, while the rest of the group waited at anchor offshore, had seriously upset his calculations. There had been no choice in the end. Keeping the Marines' major on board was unsettling his own troops and the ship's crew almost to the point of panic. They were all trained to deal with real, definable threat, whether missiles at sea or in the deadly ferocity of hand-to-hand combat. But when they had a major whom they could hear perpetually screaming he had seen visions, that God had abandoned them, they were all 'doomed', there was nowhere to hide him away.

They had tried the medical room but his wild hollering could be heard all down adjoining gangways. They had tried the secure cells for their own offenders or captured enemy but still his cries carried. In any case, he so unnerved any crew or marine compelled to guard him that their reports of his crazy rantings were giving rise to an almost mutinous atmosphere in parts of the ship. He had to go before he undermined the whole operation. They rejoined the rest of the convoy nearly three hours behind schedule. They would be forced to proceed in daylight. He had queried the wisdom of this with superior command but was reminded the Spanish government was turning a blind eye in order to resolve the situation without further international embarrassment. So he was to go ahead as ordered.

They cleared the Straits not long before first light would break their cover. Then, after the 'Rock' had slipped into the paling darkness behind them, with the lights of Cadiz passing to starboard, he had ordered the forty-five degree turn, keeping the coastal outline parallel, instead of receding into ocean gloom. He checked the positions of the other ships. Three troop carriers, each with two hundred marines and infantrymen on board, would be very definite overkill but they were on their homeward route anyway and who knew what they might expect.

They were good men. Some rumblings when they were told their return to the US was being interrupted by a mission on the way but, well, it would be a change from sitting for endless days in the baking desert waiting for nothing to happen. He only planned to use troops from one ship. That new captain would lead the mission, the one who had abruptly turned up at embarkation, papers signed from high command. Fortunately, he had been briefed by his own senior officer just before the man was 'taken ill'. Desert conditions could lead to delayed repercussions in even the toughest men. The new officer then lost no time in informing the brigade on board and they had taken to him instantly. Most of the men were sure they had been under his command before but could not remember when. "It's his eyes", one of them said, "just kind of hold you."

Elroy's seating companion in Club Class snorted.

"Huh! Typical newspapers. Always behind with the news!"

"Hmm?" Elroy turned from watching the ground fall away, to offer a polite response.

"TV had it before we left", grunted his neighbour, "*and* radio."

"What's that?" enquired Elroy, not wishing to point out that newspapers needed time to go to press, even in this age of lightning communication, and were therefore always at a disadvantage over breaking news.

"Spain invasion", came the glib reply.

"What?" Elroy was suddenly attentive.

"Some of our ships spotted off the Spanish coast", was the clipped explanation, clearly expecting Elroy to know it already, as well as the papers.

"Ours?"

"Yuh", confirmed his companion, gruffly. "About time too. *Muslims* -" he spat the word "kick ass!"

Elroy shook his head, gravely, and turned to the window again. American ships? Spain? Muslims? An invasion of a friendly country was wholly improbable, even to eliminate terrorists in Madrid or anywhere else. He remembered what Olivia had said: 'hearts and minds' are what the Establishment fear. He shook his head again, eyes unfocused on the clear blue sky above ruffs of cloud. He could only wait to see if there was any more news when they landed in New York.

"Do you pray, sir?"

The young captain looked at the even younger marine staring up at him in the dawn light in the bows of the amphibious assault vehicle. The frigate commander's worst fears were being realised as he watched the party of eight craft head for the shoreline. He fervently hoped no news had leaked of their arrival in these waters. Television would have a field day if they knew.

"Why would I pray?" The captain cocked his head to one side to enquire. The marine's naturally fair face was leathered and creased by a year in the desert sun and wind-blown sand but his eyes retained their freshness, sky blue against tan.

"Well, with a name like yours, sir, I would have thought .."

The young fighting man clutching his machine gun looked a little abashed, as though his suggestion was stepping over the bounds of acceptable presumption. Lieutenant Gabriel observed him for a moment. A number of his companions nearest to him, huddled in the gently rolling craft, were listening with interest.

"Does it make a difference?" he asked his questioner, glancing, too, at the others around him.

"Sir?" the marine frowned.

"If I pray. If *you* pray. Does it make a difference?"

"Sir?" The marine was confused now, at this challenge to the basis of his faith.

"I mean", the captain pressed him, not waiting for further response, "who do you pray to?"

"Well, God, sir. Of course." The marine was blushing indignantly beneath his tan.

"And is He listening?"

"Sir!" The marine was torn between the offence taken and maintaining respect for his officer.

"Why would He be listening?" The captain was pressing him with insistence. "How do you know He's not too busy? What would you pray to Him here, right now?"

The marine bucked at the challenge.

"Well, I, sir - if you don't mind, sir - I'd pray for our success - for our lives." He was hot and indignant, the first streaks of sunlight raking the top of his helmet and catching a flash of his burnished cheek.

"And what about the other lives?" The commander leaned forward to look intently into the young man's face. The marine was taken aback by the deep brown eyes so close to his own.

"The others, sir?"

"The enemy."

"Well, they're the enemy, sir."

"And what if they pray, too?"

"If they? ... If they? ..."

The marine fumbled for more words and looked around at his companions for support. They shuffled in their uncertainty and remained dumb.

"If our mission was wrong - *if*", Lieutenant Gabriel emphasised, to counter any suspicion he might be suggesting it *was*, "then would praying to God make it right?" He waited briefly before going on. "Do you have children, soldier?"

The marine was momentarily taken aback.

"I gotta daughter, sir." He smiled bashfully. "Two years old."

Lieutenant Gabriel smiled with him, then became serious.

"And if she was going to be run over by a bus -"

"Sir!" The heat of distress flushed suddenly into the marine's face.

"If -" his commanding officer looked keenly at him, "tomorrow she was going to be unlucky enough to step into the road just as a bus was coming -" he struck a palm with the other fist, *smack*, which made the marine start, "could you pray to change the bus timetable, or your daughter's steps? If they pray - the enemy -" The captain held his stare into the junior soldier's eyes, "if we both pray - if we *all* pray - will it change anything? And if it does, whose side is He on?"

"Who, sir ...?"

The marine looked like he wished he had never started this exchange, yet he needed it to reach its conclusion, for his soul, perhaps.

"God."

"Sir?"

All the marines within earshot were listening as best they could, above the splash of waves against the hull and the dull throb of the motors behind.

"Whose side do you suppose He is on?"

The marine knew the answer to that. And recovered his confidence at last.

"Ours, sir! America! *Ours*, sir!"

There was a small cheer at that, from the others around him, a kind of relief that a temporary element of doubt had been firmly removed. Their commander looked at them intently, then spoke with a low intensity that carried to each of them while he fixed his eyes mainly upon his young interrogator.

"And if we both pray. Them and us. And we both believe we are right. And they believe He is on their side, just as we believe He is on ours. Who is right? And how does He choose?"

He stood upright again and steadied himself against the handrail as the craft bounced on the breaking waves at the beach. His men had gone completely quiet. Was it his eyes? Was it what he said? Was it how he spoke? Was it that they had never considered this notion in their lives before? He shouted his order, the landing ramp dropped open, splashing onto the surf, and they were pounding across it almost before it hit the sand, minds wholly trained on the mission ahead.

Capture

"Senor! Senor!"

Asif smiled. He had only just emerged from the doorway of the whitewashed lodgings into the brilliant early-morning sunlight of the village square. Another square, another sunlit morning, another generously-provided overnight stay, by humble hosts who had little to share, yet shared everything they had. His gentle walkabout had become a whistle-stop tour, sped from village to village by locals eager to be the next to hear his 'message'. He would be politely bustled into a car or onto the back of a moped at the conclusion of one meeting and transported along bumpy roads and through dusty streets to the next gathering awaiting him.

He was awed but delighted. It was not to him a doctrinaire mission; he only wished to correct a false impression, lay down the roots of true knowledge, counteract the forces of evil and violence claiming the name of Islam. Whenever it began to feel too much, or he tired and wondered if he could summon the strength and will to continue, that inner compulsion lifted him, the element within he could not define, which drove him on.

"Senor!"

Always the children spotted him first and ran to him, smiling and laughing. Sometimes they called him 'God' and he had to gently chide them, telling them he just had things to say about God, that was all. They tugged at his long, flowing white chemise, causing him to look down through his wiry grey-black beard and twinkle at them with his eyes. Before they became too bold, and threatened to playfully spin and twist him this way and that, parents would call from doorways or from the shade of olive trees: "Manuel!" "Rosa!" "Jose!" And they would tumble away from him, giggling and tripping over one another and casting backward looks in fun as they ran to where they had been called.

He held their clutching hands this morning, his long fingers twisting about theirs, three of them holding on, another three laughing and prancing around. He could see the sea, glinting at the bottom of the steep hill, a narrow cobbled track leading downwards and out of sight towards the shore. He had not expected to reach the coast so quickly. He had missed out many villages and towns along the way but the course of his progress had been determined by who wanted him next and where they took him. To him it was not important; every place was new, every one as valuable to him as another.

His Spanish was improving and he picked up excited comments about their 'Muslim past' and vows to convert to Islam again. It made him reflect upon what drove him here; then he would remember the forces of violence, recall sadly the blind vehemence of Mohammed and Abdul, shudder at the evil that called itself 'Islam'. He remembered he was not driven to convert nations, only to see the understanding in people's eyes. He could not know if others saw it differently. He stood and looked. Although he had not come as a tourist, the view from the village square was magical. A crystal blue sea spread below, glittering in the sun, nothing to break the rippling swell but the cluster of grey ships out towards the skyline.

There was a commotion out of sight where the cobbled track wound away down the hill. A knot of children came scrambling and scurrying round the bend past the dusty olive trees and up towards the square as fast as they could run, casting frightened looks behind them. Asif was still sitting in the square, smiling and talking with some locals. Almost as the breathless children hurtled into the square, rushing to cower behind mothers' aprons or in darkened doorways, a platoon of soldiers rounded the corner up the hill and came yomping up towards the square.

Alarmed villagers leapt off stone benches at the sight of the solid formation of green-grey jacketed foot soldiers, five-abreast, heavy automatic rifles held akimbo in front of them, jogged relentlessly up the short hill. Asif drew himself up slowly from his wooden bench on the broad stone slabs marking the centre of the square. The three women and two elderly men who had been chatting with him, in their mixtures of broken English and measured Spanish, had already scattered in consternation at the incongruous intrusion upon their ordered lives.

"Americanos!"

The exclamation rippled around the village square. Asif found himself standing alone in an empty space in the sunlight, as the troop of soldiers pulled up at the far side behind the raised arm of their commanding officer. The leader appeared to spot Asif immediately and beckoned the first row of five soldiers towards him.

Just as he did so there was a rumble and screech of tyres as a van the size of a small delivery truck hove into the square, a satellite dish wobbling on its roof. It braked to a halt thirty metres from Asif and the advancing marines. A woman jumped out of the passenger door, while the wide side door slid open, to reveal a television cameraman scrambling out, humping his camera to his shoulder and already focusing on the confrontational scene unfolding in the square. Another man followed out of the side of the van and handed the woman a microphone. She was dressed in shirt and dungarees but oozed a sophisticated confidence, with smart good looks in a tanned and elegant face, rich black curls framing her head.

She turned immediately to face the camera, with the backdrop of the tall Asian and the advancing soldiers behind her. She had not even opened her mouth before the next line of marines at the edge of the square swivelled to face her at fifty metres, guns pointing. But there was a sharp order from their commander which made them lower their weapons. The local onlookers, cowering at the perimeter, could see the confusion in the soldiers' faces.

"Our information was correct!" The words exploded from the female reporter's mouth in Spanish. "The American ships are a landing party! You see the troops behind me!"

Another man had emerged from the side of the van, holding a clipboard.

"English! English!" He called to the reporter. "CNN!"

"We welcome viewers in America and around the world!" she declared, hastily converting to English. Some observers in the square could see through the open side door of the van to a technician working at a control panel, as he gave a thumbs up sign to the man with the clipboard, who grinned and repeated the gesture the reporter. Meanwhile the line of five marines had reached Asif, who had remained standing motionless, except to look briefly to one side at the television crew. The troop commander had left the main party of soldiers at the edge of the square and followed the small group to Asif.

"Hold him!" he barked, and two marines each grabbed an arm, while the other three swiftly ranged themselves behind Asif. He looked questioningly at the commanding officer without making any attempt to resist. The man looked more gentle than the rasp of his voice and Asif noticed the wisps of sandy hair framed by the green olive-washed helmet. But there was something else as the officer returned his stare. It was not just the deep brown eyes, so striking even from several paces. Asif quivered. He felt a strange bond. It was as though he might be looking at a brother, a kindred spirit or even, he felt momentarily giddy inside, himself. Looking at himself. For a fleeting moment he felt the officer was experiencing the same sensation. The brown eyes blinked, then looked away to his men.

"This is the imam who has been preaching Islam in Spain", the reporter was barely containing her excitement beneath her professional delivery, "while politicians in the United States have been protesting that the Spanish Government had been allowing parts of the country to turn to Muslims and extremists-"

"No! No!" Asif heard this commentary and turned to dispute it, still in the grip of the soldiers. "Islam means peace!"

The soldiers each pushed him roughly to silence him but the commander raised a staying hand then suddenly turned towards the brigade still waiting at the edge of the square and beckoned and ordered them over to him. Within a few moments the whole troop were clustered together, with Asif a solitary figure held at their front, the commander at his side. Tall and composed though he was, Asif Hassan looked a threatened, vulnerable figure in the grip of the invading force sent to capture him. In that instant he realised his campaign of peace was over. He did not feel fear, only regret, and once again caught up in the forces of violence. First it was Mohammed, Abdul, the Spaniards and the Chinese gang; now it was the American army. His regret was for the words of peace once more being drowned by cries of aggression.

The young commander at his side was barking orders to his men, to prepare to take their captive to the ships. The soft brown eyes took on a hard glare as the officer strode from left to right to prepare the brigade to march. It was all over, Asif sadly realised. Whatever consequences there might have been to his actions, that he could not have foretold and that might have inflamed the ire of nations, he only knew what he had seen. He had seen a light in people's eyes, an understanding of an alternative view, a delight in enlightenment.

He let his eyes fall to take in the bright, white, sun-scorched pebbles at his feet. Then he lifted his head in quiet pride to face whatever would become of him next. He was startled as his eyes met those of the officer, who had turned to face him. For a moment, again, it was like seeing a reflection of his soul. Then the officer abruptly turned away and called to the television crew. They thought they were being challenged and began to back off but he called them over, issuing an order as if to his own men.

"Here! TV crew. Here!"

They hesitated.

"Now! Here!"

The cameraman was first to move, never one to miss a picture opportunity. The reporter ran with him, and then the producer with the clipboard.

"Here!" commanded the officer and directed the cameraman to focus face-on to Asif, himself and the brigade ranged around and behind them. The reporter was about to resume her commentary but the officer silenced her with a gesture and instead faced the camera himself.

"We have come!" he declared confidently to the lens. What millions saw on their television screens was a good-looking young captain standing beside a tall, bearded Asian man in an imam's cloth, surrounded by a platoon of marines and gripped tightly by two of them. It was a scene of successful capture.

"We have come to take this voice away from Spain, a voice preaching to change the established order, infect minds, breed revolution, incite violence."

"No!" Asif turned his head to look at him and then winced at the restraining grip on his arm.

"Renee. Quick! Tell the President she needs to be watching CNN!"

Will Jerome was sitting in his Press Secretary's office keeping a weather eye on CNN rolling news; all the more keenly in the early hours of this morning, aware as he was of the unwelcome dawn sighting of the convoy and reports reaching overnight TV News in the States. He was thankful the East Coast would mainly be asleep but further west people would still be up and viewing and news quickly spreads. He would not normally take it on himself to keep watch at this hour, he would leave it to routine monitoring. But he was all nerves this night in Washington, as the sun began to set the Spanish coastline aglow. Then there he was, the platoon commander, outrageously addressing the television camera - a camera from a Spanish TV channel which had somehow identified the convoy's position from the half-light report of a couple of hours earlier.

"But she's only just gone to bed, J."

Renee Fleck was conscious of the pressures keeping her President awake until well after midnight these days.

"Get her up, Renee. Chrissake! This is not what we wanted! She needs to see it! It's supposed to be *covert*!"

Renee reluctantly rang the alarm in the President's suite upstairs in the White House and touched the remote button to switch on the TV set there, where it would already be on CNN.

Victoria Twigg had not even closed her eyes, staring at the darkened ceiling, turning thoughts over in her head, and in a moment had swung her feet to the floor from the couch where she had lain down and was now sitting upright, staring at the wide plasma screen in the corner.

"We are cleansing this infection."

Twigg gaped in wonder at this insubordinately bold captain delivering an unauthorised oration with his captive at his side. What was he doing? He was talking like the leader of a nation, not the commander of an expeditionary platoon.

"Cutting it out before it spreads across this whole nation and turns the *hearts* and *minds* of this European people against us and our God."

What was he talking about! How dare he! Who gave him this command! Victoria Twigg was about to hit the 'call' buttons to both Jerome and Renee simultaneously, to demand the officer's arrest on the spot before he got completely out of control. She had never heard a *general* talk like this, never mind a mere captain! But her fingers never reached the buttons.

"Is this what you want? Madam President?"

She stiffened in shock. Who? Her? Was he addressing her? How could he know she was watching? Why was he singling her out from the millions of ordinary American citizens watching at the same time? Her eyes were drawn hypnotically to the screen. The captain was looking directly into the camera; looking directly out of the television screen; looking at anyone who was watching; looking at *her*.

"Is this how you wish it to be, Madam President?"

If millions were watching, as indeed they might well be, across the still wakeful half of America, and other parts of the world, too, then they were all at her side as the treasonable marine addressed the screen, looking at them all; addressing, they must all assume, *her*.

"Is this your answer? To silence the tongue that speaks a different creed? Snatch it out before too many have heard? Like the street bully who strikes with fists and knives to still words and thoughts he does not understand and does not want others to heed? Is *that* your answer?"

Victoria Twigg could say nothing. Could say nothing to a television screen but could have said nothing anyway. She stood, staring at the television pictures of the captain, the imam and the body of troops surrounding them in the golden morning light of the Spanish village above the sea. Her eyes were drawn towards the captain, his eyes piercing the screen, light sandy hair catching the sun beneath his helmet and the silver wings of the insignia pinned to his collar. The TV cameraman seemed to understand something, instinctively. He slowly zoomed in on the young commander so he was filling most of the frame; just the uniforms of some of his men seen to one side and behind, the imam's shoulder next to him.

Victoria Twigg let out a stifled choke, alone in her Presidential chamber. She reached behind her to summon Renee Fleck on the desk intercom, before sinking to her knees in front of the screen. The eyes were looking directly at hers and - it must have been the brilliant morning light all around him - the young man appeared to glow. She stared, transfixed, at the screen, and emitted something between a quiet sob and a low sigh as the feeling she thought she would not experience again stirred deep inside her.

"My angel", she softly breathed, hypnotised by what she felt and what she saw.

"Madam President!"

Renee Fleck burst into the room, closely followed by Will Jerome.

There was no immediate reaction from the President, then she slowly raised her deep, brooding eyes to them, as she knelt before the television. The CNN newsreader was providing an impromptu commentary over the pictures to fill in the silence, as the insolent captain was giving the impression of waiting for an answer from an unseen President, while astonished viewers waited for him to be summarily dragged away.

"Madam President?" Will Jerome spoke tentatively, unsure what to make of the proud leader kneeling almost at his feet.

"My angel", Victoria Twigg breathed again and her two subordinates saw the glint of a tear in her eyes as she remained motionless, staring at the screen, seeing the deep brown eyes and the golden glow through her own watery haze. Had it all come to this moment? All those years in the gutter, the years in Baltimore, the independence of giving herself to charity, then turning to serve her fellow countrymen and women through the State and, finally, the Presidency? Had all those years led to this one defining moment? One choice? She was aware of Renee Fleck out of a corner of a misty eye. She could hear the echo of her insistent reminder again: "second term?"

The unwavering brown eyes of the captain were still fixed on the screen, fixed on *hers*, gripping her inside. The artful cameraman had widened the shot a little to show the full figure of the silent, dignified imam, standing at the captain's side, not knowing quite where to look. In that one moment Victoria Twigg was quite, quite certain. She was not sure she knew why but she was sure she knew.

"Let him go." The words were soft but controlled, her eyes still on the screen.

"Ma-am?" Will Jerome half raised a hand, as if to pass it across his President's eyes, to break the trance, dispel a calamity.

"Ma-am?" Renee Fleck leaned towards her President, wanting to impart her anxiety, bring her back to reality before it was too late. "Ma-am?"

Victoria Twigg raised her eyes just enough to look at each of them in turn, then turned back to the screen. They saw her expression harden and heard her voice assume its imperious edge once more, though her eyes remained soft and moist, fixed on those of the young captain, still staring through the television camera to her own.

"Let him *go*."

Elroy's attention was caught by a TV screen showing rolling news in the JFK airport arrivals hall. He could not hear any sound above the hubbub of passengers and loudspeaker announcements but he could see a tall, white-attired figure standing in brilliant sunlight and a knot of green-grey-jacketed soldiers marching away from him down a path towards a shimmering blue sea.

"Mr Fitzgibbon?"

Elroy looked to his side. A smart, dark-uniformed chauffeur was standing with hand outstretched to take his luggage trolley.

"Er..", began Elroy.

"Your car, sir."

"Oh.. Thank you .." stumbled Elroy, "I didn't recognise -"

"I'm new, sir", the chauffeur smiled, showing his ID card, "but they told me how to recognise *you.*" He said it deferentially and Elroy smiled in acknowledgement. Despite this cosmopolitan age, the description, 'tall, black, well-built, close-cropped, slightly greying, on his own' would not give rise to much confusion at JFK Arrivals in the dead hours of the night.

"Thank you", Elroy smiled again, letting go of his trolley. "Very welcome. I don't think they've ever sent a car for me before."

"Ah, sir, I only take the orders but I've heard you've been important in England."

Elroy nodded a little doubtfully. Had he? He, Timmis, Customs, all of them, seemed to be just *behind* the chase from start to whenever it might yet finish. They reached the large black limousine outside in the darkness, lit by airport lights, as the chauffeur briskly opened a rear door to let him in.

Elroy was dimly struck by the rapidity with which a large, second man appeared out of nowhere to lift his luggage into the boot, while the chauffeur appeared to quicken his pace to reach the driver's door and hustle himself in. His assistant lurched around to heave himself in beside Elroy - not, as might have been expected, beside the driver - and then vigorously slammed the door on them both. It was so quick, as Elroy became aware he could not move across the back seat for a third man who was already sitting there, the two sandwiching Elroy between them.

"Good morning, Mr Fitzgibbon."

Elroy swung around with a start at the familiarity of the syrupy voice. Slick Hair!

"I'm afraid you have rather kept us waiting", his unwelcome companion proceeded. "Still, no problem. Still time."

"Time?" Elroy's mind was racing. Unfamiliar 'chauffeur'? No wonder! So they had caught up with him at last! What about Mariana and the children? He was not allowed further speculation.

"Time, Mr Fitzgibbon, for Africa."

"*Africa?*"

"Where's the captain?"

The sergeant looked around the platoon squatting on the benches lining the hull of the amphibious assault vehicle, as it bobbed on the surf at the beach head.

"Sir."

The young marine who had been in the bows with the captain when arriving spoke up.

"Marine?"

-310"He's gone, sir."

"*Gone?*"

"Sir, he went over there." The marine pointed to a headland jutting out in to the beach a few hundred metres away.

"What are you saying, marine?"

The sergeant looked like thunder, looked like he wanted to apportion blame.

"He said don't expect him back, sir?" The marine was trembling beneath his brave exterior. "He ordered me not to say anything till you asked."

"Marine!" bellowed the sergeant above the chopping surf, "did you think I wouldn't *notice*? What was he doing?"

The marine bit his lip.

"He was just walking away, sir. Turned to tell me... And .."

"*And*, marine?"

"I saw him picking up stones, sir."

"*Stones*?"

"Rocks, sir ..small rocks."

"Desertion, eh?" sneered the sergeant, who had little time for the intellectually opinionated officer class, "couldn't face getting his orders wrong." It was already assumed among the company that the whole debacle had been in direct contravention of the President's wishes and the officer in charge was the obvious scapegoat. "Well, he'll sure have to face the court martial one day. Worse, after desertion, and after he's found his own way back." The sergeant spat into the froth over the side and ordered the craft to pull away to the waiting ship offshore.

As the men were filing back to their berths below decks, the fleet commander was receiving an odd call from the hovering helicopter which had flown in to provide air cover while the troops had been marching back to the shore.

"Can't make it out, sir", rasped the co-pilot's voice over the radio, "was there a landing signal to guide you in?"

"Signal?" The commander frowned, peering towards the shoreline.

"On the beach. Guess it's something and nothing, sir. Looks planned that's all. Thought it might be a codeword for you."

"Stones, you say?" puzzled the commander.

"Yup. Looks like it from up here." The chopper was hovering above the beach hidden beyond the headland. "Tell you what it is: 'suif'"

"Suif?" The commander was bordering upon irritation, wanting to get away.

"Yup", came the co-pilot, "s ... u... i... f.. and then there's other stones on the sand ..looks like a formation but doesn't make sense."

"You don't *say*", called the commander, sardonically. "No, no signal expected. Kids playing with stones."

"Look too big and heavy for kids, sir. Need superman to lift some of those. Hang on, sir, might be looking wrong way up."

The helicopter circled around to face tail-on to the sea.

"Ah.. Yeh, sir.. Got it, I think. You expecting us to pick up this message for you from the air? Here .. C .. R oh, it's a 't' in the middle, looked like an 'f' the other way up..and not a 'u' an 'n' ... yeh, sir .. Got it ... 'C..r..e..t..i..n..s'"

"Cretins?" The commander screwed up his brow and grimaced.

"Yeh, sir, that a codeword you know? Us guys are the only ones who'd see it - up here. Someone musta known we'd spot it. Don't make no sense, eh?"

"No it doesn't, officer", the fleet commander snapped back. "You're stood down. We're headed home."

"Okay sir", the co-pilot's voice crackled back. "Don't make no sense, eh?"

The helicopter wheeled around as it lifted to fly back to the waiting carrier in the Med. The fleet commander heard him repeat the word of stones once more, almost audibly shaking his head.

"Cretins."

Bus

"I mean -"

The Good Lord Almighty in His infinite wisdom needed only to employ a small, finite part of it - of His infinite wisdom, that is - to discern that He was not about to be given an easy ride into the deeper recesses of the archangel's ruminations. There was an almost imperceptible Deific sigh. Not sufficient to inject discord and disruption into otherwise reliably preordained cosmic expectations; just a slight ripple across the Universe, a shudder enough to dislodge a few malevolent intentions and displace some innocent aspirations. There are no winners where there are no losers. God's Own Universe is like that.

"I mean ... it wouldn't make any difference. Would it?"

They had a pact. An agreement, if you like; part of the deal. God can read minds, foresee the future, tell what someone is about to say. Not with Gabriel. It would have made their coexistence pointless, where One knew the whole of any conversation before it even began. So the other would see no purpose in starting one at all or, indeed, in offering a response to one began by the Other. Heaven, already quiet, would be altogether stilled. God occasionally considered this might be a not unwelcome proposition. However - sigh - One had to accommodate a garrulous archangel or have to do everything Oneself. In which case, One had to wait with bated breath, as it were, for what might be coming next.

"Would it?"

The archangel raised a look from his toe region to repeat the riddle. He regarded the Lord closely, as if dealing with One who had not been paying attention quite as One might.

"If they prayed. It wouldn't make any difference."

"I -" began the Lord.

"About whose side You're on." Gabriel was getting into his stride, hands dropped to idle beside ankles, while he focused on an unseen spot ahead of him, eyes staring in fierce concentration. "Or about the bus."

"The bus?"

"Yes", replied the eager angel, "the bus running over the child. There's no point in them praying because it will anyway."

If the Lord could wither, in the way any of his multitudinous flocks might, He would have at least blenched a bit under the angelic gaze turned upon Him. As it was He did not, but He might have.

"But You could change it anyway!" The angel abruptly blurted out. "Couldn't You?"

The Lord composed Himself under this unexpected (due to their pact) offensive. This was a variation on an old theme. He felt sure the angel must know it.

"You mean", He responded calmly, "I could change bus timetables? Or -" before Gabriel could interject again "cause the bus to leave a little earlier, or a little later? Thus missing the child?"

"*Yes!*" declared the angel with vehemence.

"With *all* the children who are run over by buses?" the Lord pressed him.

"Well, some of them at least", replied the angel with a peevish shrug.

"How do you know I didn't?" The Lord regarded him, levelly.

"What? -" the angel shrugged again, at this riposte.

"What about all the children who are *not* run over by buses", God persisted.

"Well, I'm not counting the ones on the beach or sitting watching television."

"Why not?" God regarded Gabriel, "How do you know if they had not crossed the road to get to the beach five minutes earlier they would not have been run over? Or if there wasn't a different television programme on, that they didn't like, they would not have switched it off, gone outside and got run over?"

"I'm not talking about *them*", muttered the angel, sullenly, "I'm talking about the ones who *are* run over."

This was one of those times when God felt Gabriel was very much like a child himself, stubbornly refusing to concede the argument. Like a child, too, he just carried on, regardless.

"You could make a minor adjustment and they would be saved, too", came the complaint.

"So the bus leaves earlier", returned the Lord, "and a different child is run over?"

"They're not all queuing up on the roadside", retorted the angel, "just jumping out at buses all the time!"

"That's not the point", responded the Good Lord, quietly, "and well you know it. Every change causes another change, and untold more besides. Which is why", he added, as the archangel pondered for a moment in silence, "it is all -"

"preordained", Gabriel cut in, moodily.

"Precisely", affirmed the Lord, " so we - *I* - cannot change individual events here and there because of all the other incidents, some tragic, some joyous, which would occur as a result. Millions of consequences. All diverging from their predestined paths. As you know very well. And", He added for emphasis, as though the archangel did not know already, "I would simply never stop changing events, second by second, all around the world - Earth - the Universe, constantly balancing and counterbalancing each and every change. And even *then*", He felt bound to add to enforce the point, "there would be calamity as well as jubilation."

"The bus leaving earlier -" grumbled the angel.

"Precisely."

"to save *one* child", muttered the angel.

"Indeed", accorded the Lord.

There was a moment's - as it were - quiet, as the angel brooded on this, before his thoughts surfaced again.

"But", he suggested, stubbornly, "You could go back to the beginning and change it all from there, instead."

"The *beginning*?" queried the Lord, Who thought He had pretty much explained it all by now.

"Yeh", grouched, the angel. "Tweak it a bit."

"Tweak it?" This was becoming a concept too far, even in Heaven.

"*It*", affirmed the angel, emphatically, as though it were obvious.

"Tweak the Big Bang?" questioned the Good Lord, incredulously.

"It would save someone, somewhere", grumped the angel and lowered his eyes as he added, "maybe even Joan of Arc."

"*Gabriel.*" Unmeteorologically forecast clouds gathered inexplicably somewhere over Earth - and Splong, come to that, and other planets where clouds, or an approximation to them, were a climatic feature - "it *cannot* be changed."

The clouds hovered, rumbling.

"Except?"

Gabriel raised his eyebrows, sensing the loophole.

"Except", conceded the Lord, clouds lifting beyond the computations of cosmic science, "when they exercise their own self-will."

"Self-determination", nodded Gabriel.

"But -", added the Lord.

"Even that -" granted the angel, reluctantly.

"Only moves them from one predetermined path to another." The Lord wondered how many times through Eternity He would have to repeat this.

"Biscuits and railway lines", grunted the angel, casting eyes to his feet again. It was almost time to give in. But not quite.

"So what's the point in them praying?"

It seemed, in the uncomfortable silence which Heaven had just become, that the obvious answer would be the easiest and the best. But that answer would not do for an angel who knew almost as much as he did Himself. So He could not say, 'They pray for their souls', in a Heaven empty but for the two of them.

Gabriel continued before the Lord Himself came up with an alternative response.

"Some of them pray for about the whole of their lives, don't they? And some just pray to get You on their side."

God maintained His troubled silence.

"But", added the angel, with an air of finality, "it doesn't even change a bus."

He looked at the silent, beneficent, omnipotent Deity.

"Does it?"

PARADIGM : DESCENT

She tried to hold him. Her fingers gently slipped and felt around his tender torso, seeking places where he would not flinch when she touched him, caressing so gently as so deeply she cared for him, her heart rent at his whimpers when her straying finger caught a tender place distended on his infant frame and a sob caught in her throat, the finger moistened by the slow wet puss it found there. She wished, too, to reach her arm to caress the hunter at her side, as they stood together on their rock, she holding the child, but he raised a hand to stay her, knowing she would only feel the fissures on his own skin, which she could anyway see with her eyes.

She set the infant on the rock, but holding him so he would not fall.

"See how he wants to come to you", she faltered, her eyes red with tears, "see how he yearns to step to his father and clutch him, yet he cannot."

They watched their child strive to move tiny feet, red and mauve with yellowed lumps, seeking to match his will with motion but stumble and totter in his mother's clasp.

"And yet I do not wish for him to reach me", the hunter sadly said, "look what he would touch." The boils and lumps, with their seeping ruptures, beckoned yet repelled and warned to any who came near. He pressed at the dried, limp leaves which covered some, the worst, but too many if he were not to be wholly shrouded.

"He is sick. He will not take my milk and it is bad and he will not eat food", she lamented.

"*Food*?" His eyes were wild in their despair. "The beasts are sick, the fowl, as are we. How can we eat? But only roots and berries, which should be our *cure*! And so ..."

He cast a helpless look at her, her perfect sheen split and punctured with unsightly mounds, binding and bursting to have their way, her face breaking with seams not there before.

"The land has left us!" he cried in despair. "The sky -!"

He quivered as they marked their sky, swirling in angry clouds of black and amber, curling itself around the air. The sea throbbed beneath, savage in its lair, and cuffing and crashing at all who dared it.

"The sea", her voice was quiet, "Is it changed. What is it?"

"A thing we know not of", he replied, his dull gaze fixed on the mired waters before them, while a fish, its eyes bulged, was beat lifelessly and distorted against their rock. "A thing ... somewhere ..."

She looked, too, they both looked. He reached to carefully take her swollen hand, as she lifted the child once more to her breast, her useless breast.

"The thing", she whispered to the ugly sea, "will it come?"

And the sea twisted and tossed its prey, the fish, and cast its ochre claws upon their rock, slipping back to leave its trail to stain their feet as it slunk away, to wait.

Waiter

"Perhaps you would like to see the car?"

"Yeah, sure, if we can do that. 'Course, I'm really here for our scientists ..."

It stuck in the craw of the United States ambassador to Beijing to feign obsequiousness to the little Chinaman at his side. The People's Republic Minister for Science and Technology, or however they termed it. What did it matter? They possessed a secret they had to be persuaded to share. Somehow. It was his job to try the diplomatic approach. It was not his style to be obsequious, especially not to wily little Orientals. He was a big man; ex-army. By no means stupid; maybe not so subtle either. He had fought in Vietnam. He'd had enough of the slit-eyed little bastards then. Okay, they weren't Chinese but they're all the same, aren't they?

Some thought it bold, others foolish, when President Twigg had given him the post. Truth was, she had to put him somewhere, for the politics of neutralising your opponents. You were unlikely to match the Chinese for guile so maybe a bit of bluff soldier talk would have more impact. So here he was, kow-towing with exaggerated *politesse* to this sly Mandarin who now held the power of worlds in his grasp.

The doors were held open for them where the car stood in a courtyard without road access, within the confines of the Government palace. It looked incongruous, as though it had been airlifted in, a modest Manchu Met overlooked by the ancient walls of dynastic history. The driver, actually a quantum physicist, was already inside. The Minister took the front seat beside him, consigning the ambassador to the rear, much to his frustration. He leaned forward to squint between the two front seats.

"Of course", he declared with ill-concealed anxiety, "we don't need to *go* anywhere. It's just our scientists who need -"

"Not far", chuckled the Minister, amused at the big American's hesitancy, "just a short trip, to show-" and then his tone became unexpectedly savage "how it does not pay to attempt to impose your will on us before you know what you may be denied."

The ambassador was ruffled but quelled his annoyance. It was his job to be a diplomat; not a role which rested easily upon his broad military shoulder.

"We are trying to show the world how to progress without destroying the planet", recited the ambassador of a mantra he found difficult to swallow, much less convince others.

"You force it on us", the Minister ground between his teeth, only half turning his head from the front, "and now you want to take Africa, too!"

"That is not why I'm here", muttered the ambassador, "it is this car, you *know*, It is something we all need to share."

"Hah, so!" came the stiff reply. "Like your selfish 'new way'."

"Sir, I am ready."

The 'driver' had been tapping at the buttons on the control panel set into the dashboard.

"Good. Let us go." The Minister relaxed his grim expression as he turned back to face the front.

"We don't need to *go* anywhere", the ambassador urged again, anxiety returning to break the diplomatic ice. He had seen the television pictures like everyone else.

"Not far, not far; just to show you." The Minister was infused with *bonhomie* once more and uttered a cheerful, "Go!" from the front seat.

The 'driver' pressed the green button. The ambassador gripped the armrests on either side of him. There was a crackle and fizz and flashes and lines of interference traversed the display screen.

Gainsborough had been having the time of his life. 'Feted' was an understatement. He was taken everywhere with Vicki as his companion and partner. Banquets, ceremonies, receptions; a continuous flow of celebration of the People's Republic's glorious achievement, all due to his 'genius'. He felt like the flavour of the century. It had all, finally, come good. Now it was time to share the *secret* with his Far Eastern hosts and benefactors. He had set his soul with theirs, they were his future. If a pang of doubt invaded his conscience, as to what they might intend to do with their 'miracle', he felt assured it would have been deployed no more wisely in the West. Just look at the record of the British and Americans when it came to technological discoveries in the past. Competition, aggression, possession; those had been the bywords.

He had taken precautions. Principally, the formula was cached in his brain. His safeguard against a fatal pinprick of amnesia was to store it twice more: once on a memory stick, once in his laptop. He had brought both with him, more secure on his person than in the apartment safe. He was not so naive as to believe he held the only keys. He sat at the restaurant table opposite two Beijing government officials from the Science Ministry. He was fulfilling his duty to hand over the formula. After all, he reconciled it to himself, where would the world be if Eddison and Bell had revealed only *what* they had achieved, not *how*.

It had been his choice to meet at the restaurant, not a private office in a guarded building. This was too public for any strong-garm stuff, should the 'deal', which would be worth a luxurious future to him, turn unexpectedly sour. They were surrounded by tables of other diners in the red and gold glow of one of Beijing's classiest eating houses. A waiter came to the table to take their orders.

"Thank you, gentlemen", he bowed deferentially as he repeated what they had recited from their menus, "fried chicken with bamboo shoots and black bean sauce, sweet and sour special pork, and our speciality of the day, lobster with fresh wild mushrooms and green peppers. And", he turned to Gainsborough, "do you believe in God, sir?"

Gainsborough blinked and recoiled, screwing up his face in puzzlement at the waiter, who was addressing them all in almost perfect English, in deference to the esteemed 'miracle' inventor. The man continued unabashed, neat white napkin over one black-sleeved arm.

"Well, sir, we have Christianity in China now, it's official, isn't it? Religion. Do you believe, sir?"

"Well, I -" Gainsborough was ruffled by this unconventional approach from an ordinary waiter. His two Government companions cast uneasy glances at each other, then with annoyance at the waiter.

"Well, God, sir", the waiter was intent upon proceeding, "that's impossible, isn't it? Something up there", he raised a forefinger to the ceiling, "in charge of the whole universe?"

"Waiter", broke in one of Gainsborough's companions, testily, "we have ordered -"

"Sir?" The waiter swung to the man who had spoken. "You, sir. Do *you* believe?"

"*Look!*" There was overt anger now in the Government man's demeanour.

Gainsborough was staring at the waiter's back, nonplussed at his behaviour, trying to engage them in entirely inappropriate conversation. He noticed a couple of lumps on the man's back, underneath his smart black jacket. They seemed to move as the waiter turned abruptly to him again.

"But you, sir, you believe in the impossible?"

Gainsborough frowned again.

"I think you do. Perhaps you believe because you are one, sir, who has *achieved* the impossible? Perhaps?"

Gainsborough and the other two men began to stare at the waiter. Something was happening to him. He took up his theme again, fixing Gainsborough with his eyes now, as though lecturing him.

"So you of all people, sir, if you have achieved the impossible, would *believe* the impossible? Yes?"

The Government men looked embarrassed and annoyed on behalf of their guest but, however either intended to rebuke the presumptuous waiter, the words stuck in their throats. They were gawping. The waiter was changing colour; and they, too, saw the lumps on his back, lightly pulsating and pushing from inside his jacket. They and Gainsborough were becoming mesmerised by the shimmering change to the waiter.

"So if there *were* a God - an impossible God - gentlemen - whose side would He be on?"

All three at the table were now gazing in stupefaction at the waiter, whose black suit was fading to white, white tinted with a shimmering gold. As he swung to address them in turn, they each had a view of his back. The lumps had sprung through the back of his jacket as it was transforming to white-gold. The lumps were little shoots of white.

"If you had invented the impossible, sir", the waiter seemed to be towering over Gainsborough now, "and the God who had created the impossible universe looked down - as it were - and saw you holding the impossible in your hands -"

Gainsborough felt himself shudder. The waiter was now clothed all in a white robe, no longer a conventional suit, which shone with a gold light. He was aware of twin gasps escaping from the mouths of his companions, and gasped himself as the waiter swung to them, his back to Gainsborough. The white shoots had become two neat, small, white feathered wings, sprouting through slits in his jacket. And they were growing.

"Gentlemen - and perhaps because you saw it was so impossible , sir -" he turned again to Gainsborough before addressing them all, "so impossible that you had to keep it to yourselves - gentlemen - perhaps now you would like to change your orders to the impossible - we serve all impossibilities here, sirs, but we like to think we serve them for everyone, not just for the few."

Gainsborough shot a hasty glance to other tables. They were drawing no attention from them; no-one else seemed to be aware of anything unusual. He did not know whether he was scared or awed. He tingled through his whole body. His table companions gaped in silence at the waiter, who had grown - surely, grown! - he must be fully seven feet tall now, towering over them in glowing white and gold. The wings, like the white wings of an angel, were spreading across his back and above his shoulders. His voice beat at them like a drum.

"Dishes to *share* - gentlemen - are you ready to order again? We like to think *our* flavours may be enjoyed by all - gentlemen? - sir? - we like to think that's not impossible - gentlemen -"

Gainsborough and the other two men were gulping in disbelief, their heads beginning to crane back to look at the huge apparition, its enormous white wings spreading out, behind and above him, ready to curl around and envelop them all.

"that *all* may be allowed to enjoy what we create - sir? - gentlemen? - your new orders now? - but if you believe the impossible can be given - sir? - do you believe it can be taken away? Did you say you believe in God, sir?"

"I -" Gainsborough stuttered.

"Gentlemen? No. Impossible, gentlemen? Those Christians, what do *they* know? What do *they* believe? Do they believe in the impossible? Do you, sir?"

Gainsborough could only stare. He felt swamped by this white-gold, winged phantasm of a waiter.

"Do you believe in the impossible, sir? I think you do, sir. But will you remember? Will you remember what you believe? Or believe what you remember? Can you remember the impossible if it is no longer there? Your order, gentlemen?"

They could only cower beneath the winged wraith of white and gold.

"No? Not ready to order? Perhaps I should leave your menus and return in a few moments. And your laptop, sir."

"Wha -?" Gainsborough clutched at his laptop computer, which he had wedged between his feet.

"*Thank* you, sir."

Gainsborough was aware of lamely yielding up the neat, grey case, despite himself.

"And the stick in your pocket, sir."

"Wha -?" Was all Gainsborough could utter again, as he fished the hidden memory stick from his inside jacket pocket and handed it to the awesome figure.

"*Thank* you, sir."

The waiter, who appeared to float beside them now, held the two precious objects, one in either hand and, as he did so, they slowly turned from grey to a glowing gold.

"Sometimes we see the impossible, even though we do not believe it - gentlemen? - and sometimes we refuse to believe the impossible because we *cannot* see it - gentlemen? - and sometimes we will remember the impossible, even though it *was* impossible - gentlemen? - and sometimes we will *not* remember the impossible even though *we* invented it - sir?"

This last, stabbing query was directed at Gainsborough through what he now saw were deep, brown eyes that contrasted starkly with the vibrating white and gold encasing the whole figure of the waiter. He felt the laptop and the disk being placed back in his hands and saw them fade from gold to grey again.

"You will not remember, sir. Whose side would He be on - gentlemen? - those who held the impossible in their hands, or those who did not? Is it impossible to believe - gentlemen? - is it belief in the impossible that leads you to hold it to yourselves and expect Him to be on your side? Or expect not to believe in

Him at all? Or expect to believe the impossible will be on *your* side? Why?"

He addressed Gainsborough again, and then the two Government men.

"Sir - you will believe but you will not remember. Gentlemen - you will remember but not believe. Please order when you are ready, sir, gentlemen. We have a range of dishes on our menu, enough for the widest tastes. Try one of our impossibilities, gentlemen, and see if you believe."

Then, impossibly, the winged apparition rose slowly and gracefully towards the ceiling, radiating a golden glow all around. But the other diners saw nothing except a black-jacketed waiter, with a white napkin over his arm, leave the table with the two Chinese men and the Englishman, with menus under his arm. Gainsborough and his companions watched the waiter courteously bow and leave them, too, and when they looked upwards again there was nothing but the white-frescoed ceiling to be seen. They all three heard an echo, though, and no-one else did.

"You will not remember the impossible..."

Gainsborough broke into a sweat. He felt muddled in his brain. His fingers clutched at the laptop lid to open it. He didn't know why but something was dreadfully wrong. He hit the boot-up button, waiting with trembling hands. His memory was swimming. The two orientals regarded him with slowly recovering composure. Gainsborough's shaking fingers typed his password. They watched his eyes widen in distress as he frenziedly retyped. It was a cry of horror.

"No-o!"

Gainsborough could scarcely insert the memory stick with his frantically shaking hands and then punch a succession of keys. Nothing appeared again.

"No! No! No!"

His voice was loud enough in its anguish for nearby diners to look across in surprise. His companions were observing him with mounting concern. Gainsborough screwed his fists to his temples, trying to remember. His fingers hit the keys again, his eyes flicking wildly from side to side. He started to sing under his breath.

"Ha - a - ppy B-irt - day ..to you.."

One of his companions leaned forward, frowning, but recoiled with a start as Gainsborough jerked backwards, his eyes darting in every direction as he frantically tried to recall. But it had gone. It was not in the computer. It was not on the stick. He could - could *not* - retrieve it from his memory. It had gone. The precious, unique, extraordinary - impossible - formula had *gone*! He was about to shut the laptop, drained and desolate, when he noticed a flicker on the screen. The flicker was forming itself into letters, and as they lined up into a word, they also rotated, like a barrel, first appearing in English then rolling over into Chinese characters. Gainsborough dumbly stared as the word became clear, in shining gold letters. In English he read the single word:

'Cretins'.

He could not react. He was numb. His companions realised he was looking at something on the screen and one of them took hold and swivelled the laptop so they could read it, too. The word rolled over and over, revealing itself alternately in English and Chinese. They both frowned, affronted, as they read it, grimacing at Gainsborough as they did so:

'Cretins'.

The ambassador and the Minister had waited in the car while the driver attempted to restore the screen to normal view. They had not moved anywhere, to the ambassador's intense relief and the Minister's worried annoyance. The driver had even, despite being a quantum physicist who should have known it would not reveal the solution, opened the bonnet to peer into the car engine.

"What is it?" hissed the Minister as the driver climbed back into the car.

"I don't know", he shrugged, equally worried. He tried a combination of buttons again, and again pressed the green button. The American grabbed at the armrests once more. The Minister stared, willing the display screen. Suddenly, the car gave a slight shudder and the screen flickered. All three stared at it, the ambassador leaning forward, his hands still gripping the armrests for safety. An image like a barrel on a gambling machine appeared, divided into blocks, each block a letter. It revolved like a barrel, as it did so appearing as English letters then Chinese characters, in turn, coloured in gold. The Minister flushed. The quantum physicist driver shook. The ambassador just looked, relaxing his safety grip, still leaning forward, now in amazement. They sat in silence watching the word revolve between English and Chinese:

'Cretins'.

Part Eleven

DIFFERENCE

DIFFERENCE

Turning

"An African safari?"

"Yeah, honey, sure."

"Oh hun! What a wonderful surprise! The children, too!"

"Sure, honey, sure. Making up for things, yeah?"

"That's right, Mr Fitzgibbon. Keep that smile in your voice, like she can hear it."

I mean -"

"House arrest? Really! Do you think it will bring it back?"

"But you still betray us, Mr Hill."

"You were there. You saw it was nothing to do with me. I keep telling you I'm a scientist not an illusionist. How long are you going to keep me stuck in this place while you wait for me to tell what I don't know? And where's Vicki?"

"Your young lady *escort ...* will not wish to be associated with a *failure.* And in such humble - no, degrading - quarters. Such a pity we had to move you here. However, when you regain your memory of the formula, you will surely enjoy your former comforts. And *she* also. In the meantime ..."

"*I mean -*"

"Africa?"

"Yup. That's what El says, Livvy, hun."

"And he wants you to go?"

"Us. Making up the party, or something. And keeping Mariana company when he's working."

"Work? Not a holiday?"

"Bit of both, I guess. New research, he says. Hey, Livvy. Africa! Think. Animals. Jungle. Basic instinct!"

"Walt! Keep your hands to yourself. I'm wiping the dishes!"

"*Where?*"

"Africa!"

"Joking."

"No joke. *Paul*.... Olivia says she wants me - *us* - someone to be with when Elroy's with his family. And -we're their *friends* - love -"

"'Love'?"

"*Love* ... spare places on the safari, Paul. It's .. it's ...a chance-"

"Chance?"

"It's ... it's ... The first time we can get away since that *thing*... and be together."

"*Guv -?*"

"*Mmm...?*"

"That *thang*. Sure that *thang* sure doggone seems to ha' *disappeared*, eh Jessica?"

"Oooh, Jerry. You so right. But where, Jerry, where's it gone? I's so afeared!"

"Why that *thang...* sure could *materialise* - a'most *anywhere*. Eh, ma sweet Jessica?"

"Ooh, yeh, Jerry, sure you're right. Sure your right. It makes ma flesh creep jest ta think."

"So ya better look behind ya, *sharp*, eh sweet *Jessica* ma *girl*!"

"Ooooh-ooooh, *Jerry*! Help ma *SOU-OUL*."

"*'Thing'* or call it whatever you like."

"Aw gee, come on, Will. When was smart-tongued Will Jerome ever stuck for words!"

"Yeh, Will! You gotta problem? You call it what you goddam like. We're just the crap press, eh? We only use words to earn a dime."

"The *thing* ... gentlemen ... may either be seriously damaged, badly compromised, or - or no longer *exists*."

"Yeah? The ambassador say that?"

"The ambassador, gentlemen, was there. You weren't."

"Yeh, with his high velocity brain, eh?"

"Bam, bam! 'If it's got one thought in its head' -"

"'which is one more than mine' -"

"Ha ha ha." "Ha ha ha."

"'shoot it'."

"Ha ha ha." "Ha ha ha."

"so shoot it!"

"Ha ha ha ha ha ha."

"The ambassador, gentlemen, is well-schooled in modern technology."

"Got a chip in his green beret, eh Will?"

"Or just on his shoulder?"

"Ha ha ha ha ha ha."

"Look -"

"Yes, Mr Hill?"

"we'll need a miracle. "I'm a scientist. I don't do miracles."

"You pray, don't you, Mr Hill? Maybe you should."

" I mean ... let's face it ..."

"Do you pray, Renee?"

"Ma'am?"

"Why should He hear *our* prayers, Renee?"

"Madam President?"

"Why should we expect Him to take *our* side? ...Why not *theirs*?"

"Is that why you let him go, Ma'am?"

'THE PRESIDENT OFFERS NO *EXPLANATION* WHY SHE LET HIM GO!'

"You seen *The Times*, Will?"

"Sure I have, Renee."

'TWIGG BARK LOSES BITE!'

"And *The Post*?"

"Yup. Can't you get her to say something, Renee?"

"She just says -"

"You know ... Boss ... "

"My angel."

"Ma-am?"

"Mmm ...?"

"I mean ... You not appearing isn't really working, is it?"

"Get the fuck *in* there!"

Thump!

"Max?"

Bam!

"Kick *ass*!"

"Would Senator Jacobson care to elucidate?"

"Show them whose side He's *on*, Mr Speaker!"

"We've already got a strong line exporting to Africa, Max."

"Good on yer, Abe. So fucking double it!"

"Good ol' fashioned gas."

"Who's this?"

"Tom, sir."

"Gas?"

"Cheap, hot 'n nasty, Max, sir!"

"Well aint you the clever guy, eh? Fuck them all! And show me when you done it! Or you're wet behind your Mammy's ears!"

Crack!

"Yes, Max."

"Muslims!" Islam!" "China!"

"Senator"... "Congressman" ... "One at a time, please!"

"Let's show em, eh!"

"Yeah, Jerry ...right on!"

"I move to support our trade, Mr Speaker!"

"Hear! Hear!"

"Whatever it takes!"

"We're all with that, Senator!"

"Yeah, Jerry, let's kick ass!"

"Keep China off the rest of Africa!"

"Thank you, Congressman."

"And Mr Speaker, kick Islam where it hurts!"

"Yeah, yeah, Congresswoman!"

"We all gonna kick ass for America?"

"Yeah, Jerry. Them Chinks!"

"Them Muslims!"

"Hey Jerry!"

"Yeah, ma friend?"

"I gotta new arms contract to Africa, Jerry. Keep them coons tooled up, eh?"

"Wa'all, man, Ya aint offending no-one if ya keeping 'ol Uncle Sam busy, eh?"

"The President will explain the new arms export policy at her next briefing."

"Gee, thanks, Will. The President gotta new line in confessin' she's losing it?"

"Second term, Ma'am."

"Renee?"

"You want it, Ma'am?"

"We'll sell the oil to the highest bidder. The next tankers?"

"Loading right now."

"And they can fight each other for it if that's what they goddamned want."

"And Fitzgibbon will 'adjust' the sales data?"

"You think he gotta choice?"

"The Americans must bow to Allah!"

"Allah and the imam defeated the President!"

"I mean ... don't You think?"

"I ..."

"Guv ...?"

"I'm tired. I don't feel well."

"Senor! You don't leave us? Please?"

"They use my name. They take my name in vain with our God. Allah. I feel ashamed. I am not well."

"Senor. Don't go. You have done so much for us here. You make us feel there is hope."

"I'm sorry. I cannot stay. They are using me. I wanted to deny their violence. Now they use me in their war of words. And perhaps worse."

"Senor, senor!"

"Child. Yes I shall miss you all. Keep our God in your hearts. Do not let them taint your soul."

"Goodbye senor. Adios. We shall remember your words."

"Farewell, adios to you all. I am sad to leave you."

"I mean ... I've been here ..."

"Mmm ...?"

".. And there ..."

"Africa, Ma'am. Take it."

"Yes?"

"Or the Chinese will."

"Because they're as bad as us, eh?"

"Ma'am?"

"My darling, you feel safe now?"

"Yes, my love. Thank you."

"Or thank whoever it was, yes?"

"Yes. And for our little Soo Wong. I am so relieved."

"I've done this ..."

"Mmm ..?"

"... And that ..."

"Indeed."

"But has it made any difference?"

*"*Ah'm sick to ma gut of a' this sharing, Jerry."

"I aint doin' it no more, Jerry."

"I aint seen ma sister in Illinois for near six months, for sharing an' no car an' no flights that aint costin' the earth."

"Let's get us a new President, eh, Jerry? One that aint droppin' her pants a' the time. An' droppin' America in it, too!"

"You'd like to be tha one giving a helping hand, eh?"

"Whaddya mean, Jerry?"

"Giving *America* a helping hand, ma friend. Whaddya *think* I mean?"

"Heh, heh, Jerry. *You* shud be President."

"Yeh."

"Yeh."

"Heh, heh, heh."

"Africa, Ma'am. Go for it."

"Is that where all this has led us?"

*"*Ma'am?"

"Is that all? Africa?"

"Second term, Ma'am."

"I mean ... You've been putting it off."

"I beg your pardon?"

"My darling, it's so funny."

"My love?"

"I've been putting off going out?"

"Yes?"

"To the shops, since we came back."

"Nervous, my love?"

"Perhaps."

"We're safe now."

"I know. And now - yesterday - you ate those last rice biscuits. With vodka, my love! You never eat biscuits with vodka. So funny. Whatever made you do that?"

"I don't know, my darling. Perhaps so unexpectedly feeling free of danger."

"Perhaps. But I shall have to go out after all. You like them so much."

"Thank you my love. You are so thoughtful. And you are safe now."

"But I shall take our masks."

"Of course. Naturally."

"Walt! I can't believe she's reversed the Clean Air Act!"

"Yeh, I know."

"And the aviation gas tax!"

"Ye-eh."

"Just so we can swamp Africa with industry!"

"And pollution, Livvy!"

"Yeah, Bella, I know, I know."

"What was the point, Livvy? What was the goddam point of it all? *Everything*!"

"Walt, darling, don't just shrug."

"Olivia, honey, what can we do?"

"I don't think I even *want* to go to Africa, now, Walt."

"We gotta go. For El, okay? Maybe he can do something, you know?"

"By himself?"

"He done the rest by himself. And some help from us, okay?"

"Okay, hun, we'll go."

"Putting off appearing, I mean."

"And the car, Paul. All that we went through!"

"The car?"

"What was it all for? I thought maybe it was connected somehow. You know, like Olivia said, the answer to everything."

"Oh yeh?"

"We have to believe in something, Paul!"

"Well, it's gone, now, love."

"It's gone for sure, Ma'am. They don't have it."

"For sure?"

"What the ambassador said. And the other reports. The inventor locked up."

"You say."

"Our contacts, Ma'am, you know they're reliable."

"So what you're saying is ..."

"If they don't have it."

"Maybe it never *was* ."

"We saw it Ma'am. Smoke and mirrors?"

"So?"

"So they'll want Africa real bad instead."

"So we -"

" - go for it, Ma'am."

"And fucking *win*!"

"Yes, Max."

Crash!

"Hey Jerry!"

"Yuh, ma friend?"

"Got new wheels, Jerry!"

"Vroom, vroom, eh?"

"Yeh, Jerry!"

"No more goddam sharing, eh?"

"Sure thang, Jerry!"

"Good on yer, ma friend."

"Well done, Mr Fitzgibbon. Welcome back. Your family and your friends. A safari party and no mistake. Excellent cover."

"If that's how you want it."

"And you, Mr Fitzgibbon. You, too, remember? You're one of us, aren't you?"

"Putting it off?"

"Yes, Guv.... For most of eternity."

"I think perhaps you may be exaggerating."

"Well, for their part of it, anyway."

"Do we have much choice, Ma'am? Think of it. Russia diverting gas to China. Europe forced into trade treaties with Asia just to get some gas. China wanting Africa's oil - and anyone else's it can lay its hands on. All the East and most of the rest of the industrialising world cosying up to China and India instead of us. What's left but Africa?"

"So go for it?"

"You said it, Ma'am."

"My angel."

"Excuse me, Ma'am?"

"Forget it."

"Thank you, Ma'am."

"I mean ... Is it our fault?"

"Mmm ...?"

"It's messed up? Is it our fault?"

"We .."

" ... Nudged?"

"Mmm .."

"You're telling me I won't see her again."

"Mr Hill -"

"Is that all she was! Just a pawn in your game!"

"Our game, Mr Hill?"

"*Someone's* game."

"We don't play your games, Mr Hill."

"Well, it's gone. God knows, I'd bring it back if I could. It was my life. It was my life, don't you understand? It wasn't a game. Emily could tell you that."

"Emily, Mr Hill?"

"Never mind. Another life. Gone."

"Nor can you go, Mr Hill. You understand? We would not know if you had taken it with you. In your head. You see, you have to stay. Until ..."

"Life imprisonment?"

"You will be looked after. Perhaps that will aid your memory."

"Am I supposed to thank you?"

"Thank you again, my love. For making us safe."

"I did nothing, my darling. I wish I knew what had happened."

"I am sure he rescued us because of you, my love."

"Or perhaps our Soo Wong."

"*Now it'll be like the bus.*"

"Bus?"

"*The bus and the child. Too late, or too early. Wrong place, right time. Whatever.*"

"*I said then ...*"

"Boss?"

"*Appearing wasn't really necessary.*"

"*And now?*"

"I think I'll take her to the shops."

"In her pram?"

"Yes and perhaps let her walk a little."

"Walk? Traffic? The people."

"In my hand, darling. Safe. She loves the lights and the sounds and ground under her feet. A little excitement to compare with her quiet life here."

"Take good care, my darling."

"Of course, my love. And thank you again."

"And now ... is it? ... necessary?"

"Perhaps We may still make a difference."

"You said -"

" - Mmm ... change attitudes."

"Nudging."

"In a manner of speaking."

Part Twelve

APPEARING

APPEARING

PARADIGM : DECAY

At length he found her, crying. Soft, slight tears slid as twin stains from her eyelids over her cheeks, tracing a sinuous course between pustules erupted above the still firm line of her jaw. She had stepped from their rock and sat out of sight, below the brim of the gully, seated on the tumbled boulders scourged by the boiling sea. She lifted her head as he approached, their babe, blighted, cradled in her arms, restlessly asleep as its mother stared across the gruel.

"It is come." She spoke quietly, as she reached for his hand and wanted to draw it to her sutured face, yet held it off, knowing what he would touch.

He looked down at the seething waves, of maudling green and grey and black, chaffing and churning at the rock's edge, scything through gaps and funnels between the boulders onto slates of dark sand obscured below; its rancorous retreats marked by taints that clung and clove to rock, a claim for its return.

"It is come", she said again, a fragile sadness in her. As he stood, seeing her radiance dulled and raked, he felt the anger rise within him, the rage of the hunter, himself ravaged so he could no longer pursue and prey. But for what? What remained if he could but leap and run and kill again?

"The sky has defiled the air so the fowl they fall and die and we cannot eat!" He shook his palsied arms above as the mask that was once their sky drew thick and dark across the shadowed sun, it glooming sombre red yet hurling a torrid heat into their fetid air.

"And the air has cursed the land so our beasts are diseased and so are we!" he cried again and his soul beat and burned as he saw his woman and his child and he could do no more and they could only waste and wait. She pressed his hand in hers and now drew it to her, for it could not harm them to be close but the rage still tore within him at what he could not do and what the sky and the air had wrought for them and the birds and beasts lay dying and the fish which stank upon their shores. And with his hand upon her ravished cheek he felt her warm tear slip over his skin to drip and spill into the moiling waters below.

Fish

"You know when they were fish?"

Gabriel was gazing out across the blankness of Heaven, chin on hands again, elbows on knees.

"They?" came the mild response, despite Himself.

"Yeh, fish."

The angel's lips parted just as much as his cupped hands would allow.

"Fish?"

The Lord might have admitted a touch of exasperation to enter his voice had such a sentiment been at all admissible in The Everlastingly Patient One, which of course it was not.

"Yeh." Gabriel cast a sideways glance at his Lord and Master. "Them. Down there." At times like this, in what he perceived as trying and unrewarding circumstances, he found it quite difficult to actually name the principal inhabitants of Earth.

"Mmm?" The Lord responded, as if feigned indifference might induce silence. As if.

"Them. You know. When they were still in the sea. Millions of - their - years ago. As You preordained it. Didn't You? Swimming about, just fish, in the water, You know -"

"Yes." Eternal patience can take a bit of maintaining at times, even when You are God. "I do know."

"Well, then." Gabriel leaned forward to jab at something less than attractive in a crevice, which had caught his eye. It had not gone unnoticed, either, by The One Who Is Unfortunate Enough To See Everything. "Couldn't You just have left them?"

"Left them?" The response sounded a little faint.

"Yeh." The angel gave a short, vigourous nod of the head as he sat up again. "Left them ..." He bent forward once more, his attention diverted by a job apparently not quite done.

"Yes ...?" The Lord could not help but enquire.

"As fish", declared His archangel, straightening up. "You know. Left them as fish. Swimming about. As preordained."

There was no immediate response to this suggestion and Gabriel turned to look up at the Lord. He was met with an evasive turn away from his enquiring eyes. Gabriel suddenly broke into a surprised grin, eyes widening in amusement.

"Oh!" he chortled, "don't tell me!" His grin was spreading with delight, eyes sparkling mischievously. "Railway lines?"

The Lord, had He not been the Lord - which of course He was - might have shuffled slightly, so of course He did not.

"Oh!" gasped the grinning angel, "You mean it .. all that -" he gestured vaguely down below Heaven "was all because of a -" and he emitted a brief, slightly hysterical giggle - "a *biscuit*?"

"Fish", replied the Good Lord, stoically, "as you well know, don't eat biscuits."

"Not those little flaky things?"

There was a brief pause across the Cosmos. One of those hiccups in Time, which scientists scattered throughout a myriad galaxies, in their separate lives, their discrete epochs, universally concurred were infinitesimal fragmentations in the tapestry of the Universe, the tiniest moments in which expanding Time halted, e'er so briefly, to catch up with itself, but were in fact God catching the Deific Breath over something Gabriel said. Such are the misconceptions of mere mortal physics. Or mere Splongian, for that matter.

"Flaky things?"

"Yeh. You Know."

If the Good Lord Of All Creation had to concede that, among his multitudinous inventions contained within the Beginning Of All Things, were little flaky things for fish to eat, he was disinclined to do so for his loyal archangel.

"Do I?"

"Yeh. So are You saying that all *that* down there is only there because a fish ate a bis - a little flaky thing - when You didn't preordain it? Is that it?"

The concept of a fish, prior to acquiring the superior intelligence of an organism which it was not otherwise preordained to become, exercising the self-will - self-determination - however involuntary, accorded to that organism before it had actually evolved into it, was one the Lord was unwilling to entertain when it was all in the past (so to speak) anyway.

"Does it matter?" He breathed, in a supremely measured tone.

"Well, it would have been a sight less trouble."

Safari

The head had not been severed cleanly. Hacked off, more like. Several rough strokes of a machete, or a small axe, maybe. Whatever, it was a woman; or, rather, it had belonged to a woman. Elroy stood a couple of metres away, where he had pulled up short in horror. He was looking down at the ghastly object, its dark, coagulated blood rimming the torn neck below the strangely placid face; a face topped by matted black, crimped curls, almost the colour of the blotted skin. He jerked his head away to one side, squeezing his eyes shut for a moment whilst clenching his jaw to quell the ball of vomit he felt rising in his throat.

This apparition lying in the tufted savannah grass was its own explanation for the decapitated, skirted and bloused torso they had stumbled past in the glade a minute earlier. He could not overcome the compulsion to turn again and look.

"El!"

The shout was from Walt, striding breathlessly through the glade to join him. Elroy swung around.

"Walt, man! Don't look!"

His warning was too late. His friend lurched to a halt beside him.

"Jesus Christ!" Walt breathed and stared for a few seconds before wheeling to look away. "Jesus Christ", he repeated more softly, staring at an empty quarter of the coarse, stumpy earth.

"Man." Elroy's voice was husky as he reached out a hand to clutch at his companion's shoulder.

"You can help, sir?"

The voice came from his side, a couple of feet away. The small black, khaki-clad safari guide was looking up at him with a kind of tragic anxiety, elephant rifle slung downwards over his shoulder.

"Wha -?"

"Sir. Can you, sir?"

"I -" Elroy began to mumble.

"Help, sir. Can you? You see this ..."

He gestured with an air of helplessness at the sightless head, eyes already half eaten out of their reddened sockets. "Sir, you big man, sir. Important man, sir. American. And African." The man's eyes widened in hopeful recognition of their common ancestry. A brother from afar. "You can help us?"

Elroy's shoulders slumped in despair, and with revulsion at what they witnessed.

"More, sir."

The guide stepped past them, tugging at Elroy's cotton shirt-sleeve so he had to stumble along with him, Walt reluctantly following. In a few steps past some skinny trees they were upon more results of the slaughter. Another head, a man's, then other bodies with heads attached but limbs torn from sockets or missing altogether, likely to be those scattered amongst the grass and trees. Neither Elroy nor Walt felt like counting but it looked like about a dozen dead; then they realised probably a few more, as the infants had at first been obscured in the undergrowth. The guide swung to face them both and gestured around him at the sickly scene, which bore the look of a load of dismembered shop dummies dumped from a passing truck.

"How can we stop this?" the guide pleaded and they could see his eyes were glistening. "They go mad. But you can help us?"

He stood there in the glade, surrounded by bodies, like a farmer after a fox had been at his chickens, arms held out from his side in the gesture of impotence. Elroy could only stare numbly back at him..

"Man, I ..."

"Walt! Elroy!" Women's voices.

"No!"

"No! No!"

Elroy and Walt wheeled around together.

"Go back, hun!" shouted Walt

"Mariana, no!" Elroy choked a cry at the wife he could not yet make out through the trees. "Bella! No! Stay there! Paul! Don't see this!"

In a wild moment of panic he saw how the guide's 'special detour' was a desperate ploy to both shock them and enlist their aid. But shock his family and friends!

"Honey, stay back!" was Walt's frantic shout again. "Livvy!"

Elroy did not condemn the motive but silently cursed the guide for what he had visited upon their party. Despite the strain of maintaining the appearance of a normal safari holiday, the group of family and friends had at least been enjoying the forays into the bush, the Fitzgibbon children in particular crying out in delight at the lions, elephants, monkeys and giraffe roaming free in their natural habitat. Enjoying it, until this moment.

"Pa-a-a!"

The scream forced Elroy to whirl around just as his eight-year-old son flung himself into his arms, shaking and sobbing.

"Pa! It's got no head!"

Elroy hugged the boy and tried to cover his eyes but it was too late.

"Aaagh! Pa! Pa!"

Young Joseph screamed and sobbed into his father's midriff, clutching his arms around him with all his might, a vision of the sightless head overprinting the torso in his mind. Elroy stared back to the edge of the clearing, where Walt was struggling to prevent Olivia from coming any further but she, too, had already stumbled past the headless body and was fiercely breaking towards Elroy, his boy and the guide, compelled to see what else lay before them.

"Mariana!" yelled Elroy, just glimpsing his wife chasing through the grove of trees before the clearing. "Stop! Stay there! Catch Coral!"

But that was too late, also. The six-year-old was racing after her brother and shrieked as she reached the dead body, her mother rushing just behind. In bare moments, there was a huddle of trembling, sobbing children clasped by their quaking parents and the other adults throwing their arms around each

other and the family. The three guides watched sadly, though
their sadness might have been more for the broken bodies of
their own kith and kin than for the visiting tourists. They knew
nothing of LOTUS, of the facade of the safari party, of the big
black American's departures for superficially routine visits to oil
refineries, of his clandestine hours in anonymous offices to
manipulate data and devise misdirecting systems programs; but
they knew of new jealousies in their own corner of their own
continent and hoped these new people might offer deliverance.

Isabella suddenly pulled herself clear of the others.

"Is this *us*?" she demanded, staring around wildly at the rest
of them. "Is this our doing? Is this America?" Her curls were
shaking about her head and cheeks, which were flushed and hot
with her distress and outrage. "Is this *Twigg* ... and her '*go* for
it. Let's give Africa what it needs'! Is this what it needs Do they
need *us*? Oh, Elroy ... Elroy ... Was this all you did it for?"

She was sobbing into her forearm, wiping it abandonly across
her perspiring brow.

"Bella ..Bella .." Olivia moved to stretch an arm to console her
but it was Paul who stepped first to her side and she flung her
head onto to his shoulder, tears running down her cheeks, both
arms around his neck.

"Love, love." Paul clasped her to him, one hand on her shaking head, the other pulling her to him around her waist. It was
all he could say, as she wept. Olivia was crying, too, quietly, Walt
squeezing a hand in both of his. The two children were weeping
in shock, unable to comprehend anything of the horrific sight
they had confronted. Mariana held an arm around each.

Elroy took Walt a step to one side.

Walt could see his friend was still trembling and realised he
was, too.

"Man, I dunno what I can do. I can't do *anything*. They
brought us here to ... to.."

"Shock us?"

"Yeh .. no.. not just that. He wants me - us - to help. Help
what? Stop this slaughter? They don't know, man, they don't
know I'm not their *saviour*, I'm part of the cause."

The big man's shoulders were heaving. Walt faced him and
took hold of an arm with each hand, looking him in the eye.

"El. You're not responsible .. for this!"

"No? And I'm not twisting their oil figures? Corrupting their industry? Creating illegitimate wealth? For whom? They don't know, do they? They see it and they want some of it. They see there's no rules any more so they do *this*!"

He gestured blankly behind him towards where the carnage lay around.

"Elroy, man, you aint causing any savagery. Africa's been like this for decades. What you're doing, it aint that."

"This aint savagery any more, Walt , it's .. it's ... pure greed ... killing just to keep a share of the action."

"Women and children?" Walt was searching for a way to puncture his friend's irrational sense of guilt.

"It's always women and children, Walt. You tell me when they don't get hurt for ...for ...avarice."

The word was spat out. Walt had scarcely heard it spoken before. Terminology from antiquity; yet it suddenly seemed right up to date. He repeated it to himself in silence.

Avarice.

Helicopter

"We better get everyone back", Elroy muttered, dumbly. "Get them outa here." The group of family and friends were still huddled in the blighted clearing, their three guides hovering just apart, a waning expectation clouding their eyes. The devastated safari party appeared to hold no promise of change.

"Come on guys."

"Let's go!"

Isabella had to raise her voice beside Elroy's, above the thundering helicopter in the background, which they were now aware of, as it began to swoop so low as to force all their eyes, including the children's, away from the glade and skywards.

"There." The army Chief of Staff paused to point and direct her attention to an area below. "Madam President."

"Oh God", whispered Victoria Twigg, and her knuckles tightened on the armrests.

"One of many, Ma'am." The Chief affected an air of troubled resignation, prompted by a determination to forestall any last-minute reversals of policy. Even at this height, the scene revealed enough of what she had been warned to expect. She frowned and caught her breath, clutching the leather rest more tightly.

"That's why we're here, Ma'am."

"Fifty thousand?" She looked directly at him, challenging without undermining him.

"Just to start with, Ma'am. We'll need more."

"This is because of us?" she muttered half to herself but he heard above the roar of the military engine.

"No, Ma'am, if you mean your policy, no. I admire you for it." He grinned a firm, approving smile at her. "And you know, Ma'am, I'm not political. This is just personal."

"Take us lower", she ordered quietly and stared, appalled, at the scene below as they drew very low, close enough to make out disarranged bodies and limbs and the little knot of people, some children, huddled nearby. As she watched, wind from the chopper blades was flattening the grass, exposing corpses in stark relief.

"You can't account for their jealousies, Madam President", the Chief raised his voice above the engine roar, "Africa has always been like this. Show them an opportunity and they fight each other for it."

"It wasn't to be like that", she declared bitterly, "there should be opportunity for all."

Victoria Twigg sighed and screwed her eyes tight against the weariness creeping in. They must have crossed ten countries in the last two days. Or was it eleven? Or twelve? In this vast and beautiful continent. Its beauty was still evident from the air. Transition from jungle to veldt, to enormous stretches of open water, to pockets of desert, great pythons of rivers snaking between plain and forest; the speed with which flight executed the changing view made it all the more breathtaking. The industrial stampede into which 'Autos for Africa' had been transformed, against her deepest misgivings, appeared scarcely more than a few additional pinpricks upon the landscape. But she had reckoned without the tragic feuds this race might spawn.

"Once we've got it under control", the Chief was continuing confidently, "it will all calm down. They just need some order." He spoke into his intercom to indicate they had seen enough and ordered the pilot to pull the machine away. Isabella was glaring fiercely at the helicopter and its tailplane insignia, 'United States of America', as it began to rise from above them, so close they could see faces peering from the windows. One face was familiar. It looked directly at Isabella. As she looked, Victoria Twigg felt as though a laser blazed back at her beneath a shock of dark curls blown by the wind. Isabella stared at the face of dark olive skin framed by luxuriant drapes of silky black hair. She felt a jolt of recognition, improbable though it seemed, as they stood amongst dismembered bodies in the African savannah.

"Is she in that?" she intuitively shouted skywards and half raised a clenched fist. "Coming to see what she's doing to Africa! Can you see *this*?" She was railing at the lumbering helicopter as it moved upwards into the blue. "Is this how we save the world?" Isabella suddenly sank to her knees, hot and flushed, still tearstained cheeks, then looked plaintively up at Elroy Fitzgibbon, standing helplessly by; his good friends Walt and Olivia to one side, his desolate family to the other. "Elroy, what happened?"

And then she lifted herself to her feet and threw her arms once more around her husband, the car salesman from England who might have everything to gain from this new world but who never expected to see heads shorn from bodies and children lying dead and twisted in the dust.

"Oh, Paul."

He stood and limply put his arms around her, too, then hugged her and felt himself shake. Again.

Victoria Twigg bit a lip as the horrible scene receded. The 'Race for Africa' would be guarded, protected and enforced in the only way Uncle Sam ever seemed to know. The fifty thousand troops, some yet to arrive, were dotted about the spread-eagled map of Africa like little clusters of pebbles to start a dam. They would never be enough. Soon there would have to be a hundred thousand, then fifty thousand more. Perhaps two hundred thousand and more again. Withdrawals from the Middle East and

Europe made them available. Moreover, military recruitment was spiralling upwards with enthusiasm for the 'Twigg Plan'.

She grimaced. Ingenuous young men and women were pouring into recruitment centres. This was not an invasion, not an incursion for a remote and uncertain cause in some ill-defined foreign field. This was America at last making a welcome contribution to world development. Black Americans, especially, were captivated by the cause: going back to the land of their forbears, to protect it from itself; whilst their adopted home, the United States, lifted it out of the darkness of poverty and despair. The irony that they would be using the same weapons as their feuding cousins, supplied by US arms dealers jumping on this bandwagon, would escape them all.

Victoria Twigg felt sick. Was it just too many helicopter flights? Was it just too much for this President of the wonderful, paradoxical, preposterous United States of America? She looked around in her seat and met Renee Fleck's smile behind her. Second term? Who wants it?

"Jacobson can't match you on this, ma'am", spoke Renee, confidently.

The President turned away to hide her disquiet. She would smile and encourage her troops. And then again more. She sank back into her seat as her bird flew her through the African sky. Renee Fleck smiled behind her. She knew it was hard but she really would like to see this President back again.

Walt gripped Elroy's arm as the deafening roar of the helicopter was fading.

"Man, you can't help this. Africa's always been like this."

His friend shook his arm free, glaring back in guilt.

"But have *we* always been here? Have *I*?"

"El." Walt spoke quietly, grasping him gently by the arm again, "you can get out?"

"Me? Can I?" It was a desperate challenge, not a question. "Why do you think we're all here? Why do you think Mariana and the ... kids...?" He was choking on his words as he looked across to where his family and the others were now numbly stumbling towards the jeeps. "They got me, Walt. Me, her, the kids."

Walt knew. He tried to think what he could say. All he could think of was that day they trudged through Manhattan; that winter's day, with his friend warning of 'bugs' in their shoes and coats, and of the incipient threat of being tied to a sinister, clandestine organisation such as LOTUS. One that no-one officially knew about, which didn't officially exist, while making half the wheels of the world go around. And once you were stuck in the spokes ...

"Man." He gave Walt a saddened, defeated, resigned look. "Man. They got me. I gotta do their stuff. I got no choice."

Bella was looking again at the disappearing aircraft, eyes wet, face distrorted.

"Is this it?" She shouted at the sky. "Vietnam... Iraq ... Afghanistan ... !"

She pulled her arms from Paul to stare upwards, her jaw set in grim contempt. Then she raised her hands in front of her and brought them heavily together in a slow, repeating, handclap.

Shopping

"Take care, my love. Remember she can run a little now."

Hwee Lo smiled affectionately at her husband and brushed a slender finger across his cheek as he sat on his bamboo chair with Saturday morning cup of green tea.

"Of course, my darling, you know I shall be most attentive to our loved one. And you must have your rice biscuits."

Her eyes were twinkling and he touched her hand with his, looking up from the Beijing People's Daily, and smiled at her. Then he could not suppress a slight frown.

"You'll take your masks", he reminded her, anxiously. "You know: the fumes."

"Of course, my love", she laughed lightly. "And I am taking her reins."

She was lifting Soo Wong into her arms, to set out to the car.

"And you know where to park?" he added in concern.

"Of course, of course, my dear, don't *worry.*"

He relaxed his frown and smiled again. It was different now the weight of The Society had been lifted from them, the threat removed. The loan would be repaid when improving sales allowed, yet he still could not quite shake off the sense of foreboding which had haunted him for so many months.

"Give Daddy a kiss." Hwee Lo lowered the little girl so her lips could meet her father's cheek and deposit an infant peck. Hoi Fong chuckled and clutched a chubby hand.

"See you later", he smiled, as his lovely wife turned to the door, child in her arms. He gave a little wave, then let his eyes fall back to the 'Daily' and all those problems, a world away, over Africa, America and Beijing.

God

There was an echo in the Cosmos. It bounced and rippled amongst the most distant stars and planets at the very edge of nothingness. It sprang and swelled between the clusters of long-created matter expanding into infinity. Had it been coloured, this Echo, it might have seemed like fiery nebulae exploding in a thousand hues across the wastes of empty space. It rolled and grew, the Echo, gathering its vibrating sound, folding and revolving over and over until it was a multitude of overlapping echoes, as it spilled and tumbled through the invisible portals of Heaven itself.

And it leapt around the ears of the archangel Gabriel, as he sat, picking, alone. Alone in Heaven. For the Lord God Almighty, Who is everywhere all the Time, was not there. And the Echo, as it surrounded and enveloped the sole, solitary angel, was, Gabriel realised, his own words rebounding back to him. Back from the furthest reaches of God's Own Universe, an Echo reverberating and colliding in wave upon wave ...

'YOU ... NOT ... APPEARING ...
     ... NOT ... APPEARING ...
        ... NOT ... APPEARING ...
           ... APPEARING ...
            .... APPEARING ....
'ISN'T ... REALLY ... WORKING ...
         ... REALLY ... WORKING ...

... REALLY ... WORKING ...

           ... WORKING ...

                  ... WORKING ......

'IS ... IT ...

      ... IS ... IT ...

           ... IS ... IT ...

                ... IT ...

                    ... IT .... IT .....?'

Gabriel looked around and, certainly, it was true, for the first time he had ever known,

GOD

Had

GONE.

Chicken

Homer Hughes counted his chickens. At least, he liked to think he did but even his familiarity with all forty-five thousand, six hundred and fifty-three of them (at the last count) did not guarantee he could confirm the exact number at a glance. All cooped up, four to a cage, in parallel rows a hundred metres long, even his canny eye could be deceived. And today, his confidence was minutely undermined. Could it be six hundred and fifty-four? Whilst he employed the barest handful of staff to maintain a generally automated process, Homer kept a personal tally of all the births, of which there were many hatchings daily, and all the deaths, of which there were not a few - natural, that is, if death by crushing under your fellows' feet or asphyxiation by the same could be called 'natural'. And today there seemed to be an extra one, alive. Must have been conveyed from the hatchery to the laying house without his tally. Surely not. HH strode the length of the aisles again. There was one big critter, more the size of a cockerel than a hen. It was halfway down Row Six. H stared at it. It stared back.

"This one laid?" Homer called to Pete.

"Nope, Boss. Big critter, all meat and no eggs!"

Pete knew his chickens, did Pete.

"Hnk!" snorted Homer, "how long's it been here?"

"Dunno, Boss." Pete took off his greasy cap and rubbed his brow with the brim, frowning a puzzled frown. "Only jest noticed it. It's jest kinda ... *appeared*."

"Well", snapped H, "if it aint layin' and it's big 'n' lazy, it'll fetch a good price. It can *appear* on the line."

"Bit soon, eh, Boss? Afore its time." Pete knew his chickens and their accorded life-span, too.

"The *line*", emphasised Homer, firmly, "afore it's gone all to fat 'n' no meat. Lazy critter."

"Sure, Boss."

Pete put a tag on the cage and marked it 'big un'.

The hen continued to stare, its head still, not bobbing about, except it cocked it to one side in a wondering kind of way, almost pleading in a way, as though it might, unlike all the others, know what was coming next.

"Hnk", snorted HH again, "Hnk. Just appearing !" as he stalked off. He wouldn't know a wondering, pleading look even if it *was* staring him in the face. And, anyway, an oversize chicken, that was all meat and no eggs, was in no position to wonder and plead. It was for the chop.

Progress

"Whaddya say?" Elroy shouted above the din.

"Such a goddam *noise*! I can't hear myself speak!" Isabella bawled at the big, black American as they emerged onto the township street from their hotel.

"Yuh", Elroy agreed, almost soundlessly amidst the racket of traffic and construction machinery outside.

"The new Africa!" mouthed Bella, sardonically, as they stepped past a car-sized generator throbbing electric power into the half-built edifice of steel girders and concrete at their side. She choked in a cloud of dust that drifted from the guts of the erection, incompletely stencilled against the azure sky. "Sonofabitch", she spluttered.

Elroy grunted sympathetically and looked back to see Olivia hurrying to catch up with them and side-stepping a giant yellow earthmover that lumbered down the street. It sported a dusty stars-and-stripes motif on its flank, beneath which someone had clumsily scrawled in thin black paint, 'Jacobson for President'.

"What the hell!" she exclaimed, at either the gigantic vehicle, its graffitied inscription, the bedlam, or all three.

Bella swore, too, at the handwritten words, Elroy shrugged, almost in embarrassment it seemed to the two women.

"Walt? Paul?" Elroy enquired.

"Coming", Olivia affirmed. "And Mariana's sorting your kids." She laid a friendly hand on Isabella's bare arm in the warm morning sun and pulled her confidentially to her.

"You and Paul are closer, aren't you?" she smiled, while having to press her lips nearly to her friend's ear so as not to shout for everyone around to hear.

Isabella allowed herself a self-conscious smile in response and gave her friend's hand a light squeeze.

"Yeah, Livvy, I guess."

"Since the ... The *thing*?"

"Yeah, I guess", Bella nodded thoughtfully.

"Brought you closer?"

"Uh-uh." The Brooklyn expat nodded again.

"It must have been ... we never ... Bella, you know, we didn't, we couldn't really *believe* you, until Washington -" Olivia still found it hard to look her great friend in the eye and admit to the mistrust of those days and weeks, face to face.

"I know, Livvy. Couldn't blame you, you know." She gave an extra squeeze.

Olivia smiled and nodded, pensively.

"It must have been ... so ... traumatic."

"It was impossible, hun, wasn't it?" Isabella regarded her friend, coolly, knowing that what she had seen at close hand, her husband experienced and half the rest of the world had witnessed from a multitude of view points, was nevertheless beyond the boundaries of belief.

"That's what Elroy says", returned Olivia, and they both glanced back, where the big man was hovering to wait for the others. "Says it must have been a fluke, some kind of scientific accident; which is why it seems to have collapsed or whatever."

"But it coulda made a difference, eh?", said Bella. They had moved away from the construction site and the heaviest of the traffic and no longer had to shout to be heard.

"But I am pleased for you, hun. Both of you." Olivia looked at her, earnestly. "And Paul's got over it, now?"

Isabella inclined her head in acknowledgement but then burst into a familiar vehemence.

"I just *wish* Paul would see what all this *means.*"

She swept an arm to gesture at dust, steel girders, concrete walls, thundering vehicles and machines, the congress of buildings, tarmac and traffic which signalled the chaotic advance of industrialisation over what they had anticipated to be a quaint and quiet untouched corner of this huge land. And such mutation had stalked them at every turn, as they were conveyed from place to place, each hitherto a steadily developing community in a gradually urbanising landscape, now suddenly a cacophony of the screech, whine and metallic thunder of progress. Their only escape had been on the safaris themselves - and look what they had discovered there!

"But he thinks it's part of *his* future", Bella continued despairingly. "He's even talking of getting in on exports to Africa."

Olivia listened, disappointed that her closest pal of the old New York days could still not be at ease with herself.

"Any change on children?" she asked gently, wondering how an addition to their relationship might refocus Bella and Paul upon each other.

"Hey, no", Bella let out a broad chuckle that hinted at a regret, "that's way off the radar. You know what I went through."

Olivia nodded. She had passed many a long transatlantic phone call consoling her friend over the miscarriages.

"What about you and Walt?" Bella shot her a grin. "It's five - hey, six - years, isn't it? Aint it time you pulled the stopper out?"

Olivia poked Bella's arm in a jovial rebuke. As if on cue, there was a shout and Walt and Paul were on their way towards them, with Elroy gathering up Mariana and the two children behind.

Walt threw an affectionate arm around Olivia and she could lower her voice to him.

"Walt, hun, I really don't want to go on this safari. I don't think any of us does."

"Livvy, I know." Walt hugged at her shoulder. "But Elroy, ya know - he *needs* us. Mariana -"

"Yea, I know, hun, and the children. But they must be terrified."

"Yeah." Walt shrugged, helplessly. "Its just El, ya know, like a business gesture .. Can't pull out of it now. That - ya know - what we saw - that won't happen again."

The grip of LOTUS meant dissembling to friends and dearest ones alike; evading the whole truth, peddling white lies and sometimes darker ones. He hated it; and knew Elroy did, too. But what choice was there?

"Anyways", he added, looking across the street, where their convoy of three jeeps had pulled up to wait for them, "I think they replaced that guide."

She peered at the vehicles as they walked across to them. There was no sign of the little guide who had gambled on taking them to see the carnage in the clearing, hoping the Americans might find some succour for him and his people. A false hope, thought Walt, and now he had gone. Taken? Where? Who knows what might become of him, if it hadn't already. LOTUS would stamp on a solitary African guide like an ant in the dust. Some safari holiday, he pondered sombrely.

"So we aint going nowhere we're not supposed to", he reassured Olivia, without a smile, as the party boarded their transport and were driven away .

Several hundred miles, and by now three or four countries distant, President Twigg, too, had little stomach for further excursions across this troubled continent. Rallying her troops was becoming clouded by dark horizons and wasted life. Bitterly, she tried, and failed, to reconcile it with the vision that had inspired her.

The Chief of Staff sensed something in her mood.

"Just one more flight, Ma'am", he encouraged, as they drove across the uneven tarmac to Big Bird Marine One under the dazzling blue sky. "They'll appreciate it, Ma'am, and wouldn't want to be the only division left out."

She nodded and managed a smile. Presidential duty must override her personal inclinations. Renee Fleck, stepping out at her side, touched her elbow and smiled.

"Just one last flight, Ma'am."

And her eyes, as she spoke, said the same as they had been saying for weeks and more now: 'second term'.

Victoria Twigg returned her smile, but she felt her heart sink, sink deep into the soul of the ghost of Africa.

PARADIGM : CONDEMNED

He turned her to him. He still had the strength in his arms to hold her and enfold her to his bosom. Yet his hands flinched to touch the weals and boils and his skin blenched as her welts pressed against him and the ooze was such he did not know if it was from him or from her and it mingling with his own and his sweat and the tears from them both. And there was their child, crumpled on his bed of leaves, which stuck to the softness of him and caused him to whimper and cry when they were pulled free, yet also soothed him whilst they remained, yet also must be poisoning him, for they were poisoned as was everything in their land.

And their land was their rock, and the forest and the plain and the sea and the sky. And he wanted to shout again and to curse and to raise his fist to them all, and his knife, and avenge him and her and their son for what was done. But he could only hold her to him, her soft, weeping body, and clutch her and recall the golden days; his hair lank now, and hers, burned, twisted and limp. And when he looked up, the forest was lost in a haze, the plain was cracked and bare, their rock black and fouled by the ugly smears of the sea. And he did now raise a fist in silent rage and despair and there was the sky, torrid and alive, glowering in its conquest of all around, and the sun, its mortal blood-red arc licking across the smoke of the sky to reach the threshing waves, which jumped and kicked at its flickering touch and danced red and black in its embrace. And they all danced, all three, to their new song, their refrain for the days to be.

"It is come", she whispered, in her sadness. And he felt her breast heave against his, "We must let it come."

And it fired him to one more challenge, he, the hunter, who defied death's peril to bring life. Now it must change.

"No!" he at last cried, his head to the sky, the air, the sea, each in turn, his eyes aflame, his fist held high, "No! No! No!"

Proceeding

Off to the shops. Along busy streets. Mother and daughter.

Child seat in the back. All the safety harnesses and straps in place. Everything correct.

Happily.

"There, my sweet one." A loving smile as the last buckle is given a final tug. Safe.

The child, Soo Wong, beams a grin in return. Going somewhere! In the motor car! Always fun!

"And we have our masks, my darling." Hwee Lo checks in her handbag that the smog protectors have not been forgotten.. She smiles again. Smog nor nothing will mar a carefree day.

"And all because your father ate his biscuit with vodka", her mother chuckles.

Soo Wong chuckles, too, all strapped in, as if she might understand about the unexplained consumption of biscuits with vodka.

"And for no reason!" Hwee Lo chirps happily along. Hah, she muses to herself, no reason. And she chuckles again out loud, whilst thinking to herself, why should anything have a reason? At such a time when one is relaxed, burdens are lifted. She smiles and chuckles some more at the wheel. In the back, Soo Wong chuckles, too. Just for pleasure. Off to somewhere! The shops! As the car threads its way through the busy streets and the 'insufferable' - but not today! - traffic.

Upside down, the large chicken is motionless; except for the turn of its black, beady eye. It is hung by its claws from the steel rail. One among hundreds, all moving in line, for the chop. It has passed through the stunner unscathed, as some do; particularly a big, robust one, such as this. Or perhaps it wriggled in just such a manner as to evade it. Unlike most of the others, though. Most of the others are inert, spared the horror to come by the electric stunner's mercy, as they pass along the steel conveyer rail towards the blade. A few twitch a little. Perhaps they are conscious, or partially so, where the stunner has not quite done its job. But the large chicken is fully awake, fully aware.

Now it moves its head, twisting it upwards from facing the feather-strewn, bloodstained, sawdust floor. Its head cranes around, staring with its beady eye. It sees the long line of inverted chickens, behind and before. Behind, as they pass through the stunner; before, as they approach the blade, not so very far away now.

Then, while looking, upside down, at all it surveys, the large chicken squawks. Not a squawk of terror; nor of dumb ignorance. It is a command for attention. It is such, that someone must come, even as the chicken approaches the blade. A piercing, terrible, compelling command.

"Squw...eee...aar...aar...aaaah...aaAAAGH...AAWKK!"

Someone must come.

Skyscrapers

It was no use. The children were trembling with every step, each clinging to their mother's hands, Mariana herself breathing deeply to stifle an impulse to sob at the slightest rustle or crack of dried scrub. Elroy attempted to stride out with the guides, demonstrating the challenge of new sights, wild animals grazing on the plain, a vista to enthral. The children only whimpered, Joseph pleading to be taken home - not 'home' to the safari hotel - right back home to New York State. Isabella moved ahead of Paul to catch up with Elroy, Walt and the guides. She pulled at the big man's short shirt sleeve.

"El. It's no good. Can't we go back?"

Her eyes were pleading but there was also the redness of anger behind them.

"El", she emphasised, turning him to face her, "whatever this is all about, why we have to do this, it's no good. Look at your children." She gestured back to Mariana, plodding reluctantly with Olivia for company, the boy and girl stumbling and simpering, each with a hand in their mother's. "And the rest of us, El, we're sick to our stomachs. Aren't you?"

She challenged with her look and he turned his eyes away, guilt swimming in them.

"We don't know what we're going to see next. It's like being in a horror movie." Her eyes were watering now. El had got to know her well enough over the last eighteen months to recognise that blaze of distress mixed with ire. He was wrestling to find words to respond with but he got no further. Under their feet, the ground suddenly vibrated and shook.

"Aah!"... "Ohh!" There were three or four cries of concern from amongst them. The whole party shifted their feet, gaping at the ground as if expecting it to split and open beneath them.

"Earthquake!" reacted Walt.

"No! No, sir! Not earthquake!" called their chief guide, clearly alarmed. "We have no earthquake here!"

"Run for the jeeps!" cried Elroy. But then there was something else.

"Look!" faltered Olivia. She pointed ahead at the grove of trees. There was a kind of grey mist *appearing*, like thin smoke from nowhere, amongst the foliage. They all stopped in their tracks. Then they started at the distinct sound of a vehicle horn; then another swiftly afterwards, and the incongruous, gathering noise of traffic, right there in the middle of nowhere in the heart of the African jungle.

Up in the air, hundreds of miles away, helicopter Marine One, made an unexpected tight turn, throwing its occupants sideways in their seats. Renee Fleck lunged a steadying hand forward to her President's shoulder, in case it was needed.

"What's that?" barked the Chief to the pilot.

"Don't know, sir", came the instant reply. "Something ahead ... I think."

The military man was disconcerted by the uncertainty in the pilot's voice. Their lives - their Presidency - depended on him. He craned to look anxiously out of the window.

"Look, Ma'am!" Renee was peering, too.

"I don't believe this, sir!" The pilot's voice revealed genuine anxiety now, although he was holding the aircraft steady again. "Do you see?"

President Twigg was looking, also. All three gasped and they could hear an exclamation from the pilot through the intercom as well. Ahead and below were forest and mountain, ranged in magnificent troughs and folds, mile up on mile. There was also something else. More than one; in fact, growing and increasing in number as they looked, sprouting out of the terrain below and some of them appearing as though they might grow swiftly enough to block the helicopter's path.

"Skyscrapers!"

All three exclaimed it together. Impossibly, the concrete and glass buildings, in ones and twos and threes, were looming out of the vista of mountains and jungle, and growing taller in front of their eyes. The pilot brought the helicopter to a halting hover, unsure which route to thread between the tops of the upsurging towers, forming their own forest ahead and around them. For a moment they could only gape in disbelief.

Road

"The jeeps!" shouted Elroy again, gesturing to marshal the party and head them back along the path through scrub and thickets their guides had negotiated. The guides themselves seemed to have lost control, confronted by a freakish menace beyond their experience. They were jigging and juddering in panic, staring this way and that for an escape route but the peril was everywhere about them all. No it was not an earthquake, surely, but the ground rumbled and shook, vibrating to the thunder and roar of what sounded like machines.

"This way! This way!" Elroy was urging the party to follow him, crossing the open patch of scrub between clumps of wiry trees and making for the gap through denser foliage that lay between them and their transport. They all recoiled and pulled up short in shock. The children both screamed in fear. The guides yelped in a fright which would not have been induced by an attacking lion. The rest of the party emitted varying startled cries and exclamations. Bella clutched at Paul, Walt threw an arm around Olivia, Elroy swung around to see that Mariana had tight hold of the children, each shuddering in her arms. The crash just ahead of them had been thunderous, deafening, even above the roar of engines. The violent smash and crack of breaking branches was all around them and the tearing wrench and screech of whole trees torn up by their roots.

All of them stared wildly about. Smoke and dust was billowing through the trees and curling around their feet. For an instant they feared they were being enveloped in a forest fire!

"Oh Walt!" screamed Olivia, clutching her husband and wheeling around to seek the source of their danger.

"Livvy! Livvy!" Isabella plunged towards her friend, dragging Paul with her, seeking safety in close contact, then turning to grab hold of Mariana's arm to bring her and the children into their huddle of comfort. Elroy began to plunge to protect his family.

"Here!" yelled Walt to them all, swivelling to drag them back to the trees behind but they were halted again. The noise came from every direction. Like rabbits in headlights, they froze. Then there was a crescendo of screeches of metal, roar of engines and smashing of trees and branches. The whole group swung around again in time to see a glint of steel tracks, before two giant earthmovers lurched into view through the trees, towering in a blur of smoke, dust and flying branches, leaves and scattering clumps of earth and scrub. Trees toppled and splintered under the onslaught. The huge vehicles, all yellow and black metal, steel tracks at shoulder height, lumbered heedlessly at the group, who flung themselves to either side, the children dragged with Mariana and Elroy, the metal giants just missing them all and continuing to flatten everything else in their path, a broad swathe of destruction in their wake.

"Now!" yelled Elroy, as the blind earthmovers passed on, but as they began to struggle through the tangled debris of jungle, making for the jeeps again, they were thrust back this time by a choking cloud of black smoke and the asphyxiating heat and stench of tar, as a huge tarmac road unrolled in front of them, steaming and hissing over the newly-cleared track, endlessly unfolding like a thick black carpet or a gigantic yaw, ten feet high, of treacly black, filling the destroyed tract of jungle with a four-lane gleaming hot highway before their eyes.

Flown

"Something's gotten hold of us!"

The strain in the pilot's voice was breaking through the discipline of his training. He could not maintain his calm any more than he could control his aircraft. The helicopter was being pulled downwards, down amongst the bristling forest of towers that was rapidly replacing the forest of trees below.

"Goddamn it man! Take us *up*!" yelled the Chief of Staff, gripping his armrests and bracing himself for impact. Victoria Twigg's knuckles were white around the rests, too, and Renee Fleck's behind her. They both tensed and stared at the walls of concrete and glass surrounding them.

"I can't! We're being dragged down!" exclaimed the pilot.

"Get control, man! Get control!" The Chief was screaming, whether in fear of his life or fear of what it would be worth if he was responsible for losing a President.

"I can't, sir! I can't!" The pilot was heaving at the control stick in despair. "Something else has!"

"*What?*"

"It's still flying, sir! It's not falling. It's like .. It's like .." The pilot was struggling with words as he wrestled with the controls. "It's like we're being *flown*!"

The craft was swooping in and out of the maze of high-rise towers, then sweeping upwards and above them, revealing an overhead view of mile upon mile of skyscrapers, rooftops, snaking roads and streams of traffic in a smoky haze, stretching as far as the eye could see, obliterating all but the highest mountains from view. Then the same force snatched them downwards again to weave and plunge amongst the walls, just above crowded streets full of vehicles and people, factories and fires, the smoke of exhaust fumes and untold, unexplained disasters spiralling up and around them.

As the helicopter swung upwards and downwards, to and fro, like a toy under remote control, Victoria Twigg was forgetting her fear, feeling herself filling instead with dismay, then alarm, then guilt, then despair. Whether, spread before and beneath her, this was a dream, a nightmare, a vision, or some cold, hard reality no-one had told her about, it was the horrible truth that was appearing as Africa. Her Africa. 'Autos for Africa' it was to be. But not this.

Beggar

"It's just a beggar, my sweet."

The child totters forwards, pulling against the reins.

"No, no. A beggar. Don't go."

The mother, Hwee Lo, holds back on the reins. She does not wish to exert control; wants to allow her daughter a sense of some independence; but cannot let her run to touch the dowdy man in ragged old brown clothing, who has appeared with his wooden begging bowl by the shopfront.

"No, my darling." She stands firm, halting Soo Wong as the smiling child attempts to trot right up to the old man. Old? A beggar is such he can be of any age. Sitting there, one leg in crumpled trouser, stretched out from beneath the old brown coat, the other tucked under him somewhere, for him to sit upon. Gnarled fingers protrude from the stained coat cuffs, one upon the extended knee, the other hanging loosely at his side. The begging bowl lays just beyond his foot. He wears an old brown cap, something like a skull cap on his head, but not so, perhaps an aged and battered Chinese traditional head covering, some relic from a rural past. Tangled hair sticks out from under the cap and over his ears. He has a ragged beard and moustache, neither quite grey nor quite brown; they hide much of his mouth and cheeks, which, where visible, are a yellowish brown and might not be very clean.

He looks upwards at the people around him, such bustle and throng in the city street, by the shop corner and amid the throb and roar of traffic a few metres away. Hwee Lo catches his eye, quite inadvertently, as she checks that her child has not gone too close, held tight at the length of her reins. The reins are only a metre in length. She, her daughter and the beggar are so close. The eyes are sharp; a mixture of hues you could not tell; and black; and kind.

Hwee Lo cannot stand so close to a beggar. She must pull back. Yet, for a moment, her eyes remain on his as she speaks.

"No, a beggar, my darling, he might be dirty. Come away."

The child is still smiling as she has to step backwards on her reins, away from the strange man. He will be moved soon. A pair of policemen, in the distance, are walking towards them along the sidewalk.

"Hwee Lo!"

The mother swivels around.

"Li Mang!"

She greets her friend with pleasure. They hug and grin.

"How long it is!"

"So many months!"

"How are you!"

The traffic roar is so loud, they have to raise their voices to be heard. Soo Wong peers about at the sights and sounds. Such excitement! Whilst her mother chatters away, reins in hand.

Olivia

The jungle is disappearing.

"Which way! Which way?"

Elroy pulls at the arm of one of the guides, all three of whom are shaking in fright, the steam and smell of the new tarmac road catching in their throats. The guides stare wildly about, wanting to seek the direction back to their jeeps, through the pall of smoke and savaged jungle. It is a jungle not just shattered but melting away.

"Come *on*!" rages Elroy, grabbing the guide's other arm. But the bewildered African is panicking. There is nothing familiar for him to determine their direction. And there is less and less. A further violent cacophony of clashes and rumbles heralds another pair of giant earthmovers, as a swathe of jungle collapses beneath them, thundering by on their other side, another carpet of tarmac highway unrolling in their wake.

The group are suddenly stranded on an island of broken foliage and churned earth between two new gleaming black roads. Then their island of leftover jungle itself begins to smooth and flatten into concrete and paving, trees simply disappearing on every side, as city buildings rise in their place, surging upwards towards the sky. It is sky whose hue is changing, too, from shimmering blue to a dull steel grey, clouded in city haze.

"Elroy! Where are we! What *is* this!"

It is Olivia in tears. Cool, calm Livvy, shaking and wild-eyed.

"I *dunno*! I *dunno*!" cries Elroy above the din of traffic which has begun to flow up and down the twin highways, car horns blaring, wagons and trucks thundering, exhaust fumes choking them.

The guides are falling to their knees, clasping hands in front of faces in desperate prayer, muttering and mumbling in supplication. As they all stare about, there is a new jungle appearing, a jungle of concrete and glass, a man-made chaos of construction; huge and gaudy advertising posters adorn buildings and roadside hoardings. There are flashing cola signs and massive burgers draped half-a-block wide. Trams and buses lurch into view and hurtle away again. And there are people; more and more people. The little, terrified safari group are completely surrounded. The sights and sounds, and dust and dirt, and bedlam and madness of the city hem them in. The jungle has gone.

A scuffle breaks out just across the new road and Bella and Olivia both shriek as they see the flash of a blade and a smart-suited African slumps to the sidewalk, oozing blood. Mariana spreads her hands across the children's eyes before they can see the sight and herself lets out a cry of distress. Throngs of people hurry this way and that through the city streets they can see across the tarmac road. The noise of traffic, horns and voices is drowning them. They hear shots, followed by police and ambulance sirens and, mesmerised as they stand, they see the flashing blue lights of emergency and distress.

Then Olivia glances up at something that catches her eye.

"No, no!" she cries, pulling herself away from Walt's protective arms. High up on one of the nearest tower blocks they can see a figure; a man or maybe a woman, too high up to tell. The figure is hovering on the edge. A small crowd begins to form, staring upwards from the street below. They can hear shouting. Is it from the group? Or from the figure on the building? Or from both? Can it be anger, or fear, or despair?

"Oh no!", Mariana stifles a sob and clutches the children more tightly.

The figure seems to waver, sway atop the building. The movement induces a silence in the gathering crowd, a silence evident beyond the sounds of traffic. Then the figure makes a more pronounced move, leaning forward, bending at the ankles, as though in a breeze. Then silently it falls. It plummets to the ground. They do not hear the impact but they are aware of a gasp from the crowd.

"Oh no!" cries Olivia and rushes to cross the tarmac road, driven to help, too late to prevent the tragedy.

"Livvy!" screams Walt as she speeds from his grasp.

"Livvy, no!" Elroy yells in panic as she flings herself across the road, disregarding the stream of vehicles as she attempts to rush and thread her way through.

"Livvy! Livvy!" Isabella thrusts herself after her friend, aghast at what she is doing. It is in vain, as Bella stops at the roadside, cut off by wheels and blaring horns, and witnesses pale-gold Olivia stop and turn in the middle of the road, just in time to see the thundering truck before it smacks right into her.

Image

For an instant, suspended in time, much of the world - or the world that was watching television, which was indeed much of it - stood still. Perhaps it was as brief as those subliminal adverts that had been banned in most countries for stamping images upon the brain's subconscious. If so, it was indeed stamped, indelibly, even though it was too brief to be recorded and held and proved for posterity.

Everyone saw it, inserted into whichever television programme they were watching at the time, in whichever country, in what-ever language, on whatever media. No-one could tell at the time, nor remember afterwards, whether it had been a flash, a micro-second, a blip; but it was so compelling, every viewer - in millions - recalled it in its minutest detail and could speak of scarcely anything else for days afterwards.

It had appeared. It had simply *appeared*.

It was an overwhelming image of skyscrapers, tower blocks, black roads, roaring traffic, choking industry, war, crime, pestilence, genocide, rape, massacre, conflict; a land covered in concrete and glass, tarmac and smoke; a land that had once been mainly green and yellow and grey and blue; a land not without guilt; nor without destruction and despair; not without anger and hate; a land of beauty but a beauty marred; a land of the human soul. It was a land that had clamoured for change; still clamoured. But for this? This was a land smothered in change. A land lost. A land they knew as Africa.

And then the image was gone. Normal service was resumed and that suspended moment of time had passed. Afterwards, all that remained, amongst people everywhere, in streets, assemblies and studios, was conversation, reflection and debate. Much debate.

Trinity

"LIVVY!"

"LIVVY! NO-O!"

Walt charges up to the kerb at Isabella's side as the truck smashes into Olivia. They can only just make it out through the torrent of vehicles passing in front of them. They both are trying to put a foot into the road but it will be instant death. The traffic seems to be moving ever faster, nose to tail: there is no way through.

"Livvy! Livvy! Livvy!" Walt's arms flail wildly about his head in distraction. His beloved wife is only metres away, though he cannot see for the traffic and cannot move to her aid. Bella is twisting this way and that to seek a way through. The fumes are darker, the atmosphere becoming more dense. They dimly hear a desperate voice shouting behind. It is Elroy crashing towards them.

"LOOK OUT!"

They both spin around and then duck and swerve in horror.
"Aaagh!"

They scream in unison as a decapitated head, with torn
bloodied neck, flies through the smog at them, narrowly missing
and thumping to the ground at their side. As Elroy breathlessly
reaches them, they are aware of the huddled group behind him
also screaming as another head whirls at them, as they scatter
in terror, Mariana screeching and dragging the children clear.
Paul and the guides fling themselves apart, too, on the concrete
island between the teeming carriageways. Then suddenly the
smoky air is punctured with body parts everywhere. They dodge
and duck to avoid being hit with dismembered, bleeding arms,
legs, hands, feet and whole torsos. They hear the screams of the
dead, too, retching the air about them. There are gunshots
above and around them, machine gun fire, screams of humans
being deprived of life. For these ghastly moments, even Walt
cannot think to rescue or succour his dear Olivia. It is all he or
any of them can do, in the heavy, black swirling air, to avoid the
rain of horror about them.

Walt's eyes stare wildly about, as one severed arm, its
shoulder stump ragged and dripping blood, appears from the
gloom and crashes towards Isabella's head.

"Bella!" He yells.

But it is too late.

Echo .... Echo ....

Pete has gone cold. He has been on the line, watching the
blade, when he hears the chicken's squawk. Homer Hughes is
there, too; counting. He feels a bristling at the nape of his neck.
He is unused to the sensation. The sound shoots through both of
them like an electric bolt. It seems to have filled the whole shed.
They turn and hurry to the spot. *Slice. Slice.* The blade swishes
with its mechanical regularity. *Swish, slice.* A head drops into
the sawdust basket. *Swish, slice, head. Swish, slice, head.* The
large chicken is five away from the blade as they approach; now
four, now three, now two, now ...

The conveyor line halts with a loud clang. Homer Hughes and
Pete his foreman stop short and they are in front of the chicken,

the chicken which just appeared, confronting it. Or is *it* confronting *them*? Upside down, its head twists up to look at them, each in turn, with its beady black eye; fixed on each in turn.

Echo ... Echo ... 'You not appearing' ...

"Bella!"

Walt cries out in a mixture of horror and confusion. Elroy, too, sees the severed arm hurtle down at her and slam into her upturned head, as she recoils in fear and disgust. But there is no sound of impact; the limb passes right through her head and out the other side, landing on the ground behind her. Mesmerised, she wipes bleakly at her face and looks for the blood on her arm but there is none. Distracted, Elroy fails to notice a leg sweeping his way and tries to leap aside too late. The limb strikes his midriff but without impact, too, as it sweeps through him without a sound. There are louder cries from the group and they can see them, adults and children, too slow to avoid the rain of bloodied body parts but their screams merge with shouts of confusion, as dismembered limbs and torsos rain at them and pass through without impact.

Then there is a cry from behind the three at the edge of the roaring highway.

"Walt!"

He turns to peer through the dust and fumes and the momentary gaps in the traffic. There is a figure there; standing, walking. Walking towards them. Olivia.

"Olivia!" he shouts in disbelief and joy.

Olivia walks towards them. Through the traffic. Walks *straight through* the traffic towards them.

Echo .... Echo .... 'Not ... Appearing .... Appearing .... Appearing' ....

The child's eyes are darting around. Delight at the sights and sounds. She is not afraid of the noise. The atmosphere excites her. It is full of colour and movement. She wears her mask and no-one can see her smile. But they can see her bright eyes, if they look, full of fun and wonder and challenge

beneath her shock of black hair. Everything is of interest: the
feet passing; the buzz of voices; the bags people carry, just at
head height; the things people drop, bright and enticing -
litter or merely mislaid? The beggar watches. He starts to
raise an arm, perhaps about to speak. Hwee Lo chatters away,
delightedly, hand loose upon the reins. The policemen approach
from behind the beggar. Whoever he is, he makes the street
untidy, menacing even, according to the official line. A bus is
coming.

Echo .... 'Appearing' ....

"*Olivia!*"
"*Walt!*"
They fly into each other's arms at the roadside, body parts
railing around them. Drawn by the shrieks from the rest of the
group, and the children's piercing cries, they rush to rejoin them
at the centre of the long traffic island. They clutch at each other
in a shaking huddle, still engulfed in the noise of gunfire and
battle, the screams of the dying, the gory human cascade, the
smoke, dust, fumes and the roar and bedlam of traffic hurtling
on either side. They begin to gaze distractedly at the litter of
limbs, heads and torsos around their feet on the blood-spattered
concrete.
"My God!" Elroy breathes. "My dear God!"
The others are trembling. The guides, all three, are still on
their knees, hands held in prayerful supplication to whichever
god might provide the most immediate release from this mad
terror.
"My God." Elroy, the big man, is shaking as much as any of
them, clinging to Mariana and the children, Joseph hanging like
a limpet to his knee. "My God", he breathes again, looking up
and at the rest of them, "it's ... it's ... not ... not *real!*"
"El?" Isabella looks at him, trembling too, holding tight to
Paul.
Elroy gazes about them in bewilderment.
"See?" He pokes a tentative foot at the nearest severed leg
and watches it visibly pass through as though through a ghost.
"It's ... it's like it's *virtual ...* like a *hallucination!*"

"All of us?" stutters Walt, his arms still clasped around Olivia. "All of us hallucinating?"

.... *'Appearing'* ....

"Get it working", says Homer, bluntly, to Pete at his side, while still fixed by the beady stare of the chicken. "What's broke?"

"Dunno", replies Pete, he, too, rooted to the spot by the chicken's eye flicking from his to Homer's and back again. The chicken does not flap its wings or twitch at all, just stares. It is hung by its claws on the stalled steel rail, one swish away from the blade. For this instant, does it reach into any part of Homer Hughes that is not concerned with the rearing, laying and dispatch of an endless succession of chickens, day by day, week by week, year on end?

"Fix it," declares the motionless HH, unchanged, unmoved, even if it might be suggested he were to be so.

"Sure", accedes Pete, still without stirring.

The chicken blinks once, at each of them. Pete quivers and shouts down the line.

"Start it up!"

The steel rail jerks and rolls. The chicken lets its head down, its neck straight as it is conveyed into position.

Swish.

The blade swings and strikes as the two men watch. And, as they watch, there is a mighty crash and clang as the blade strikes the steel bar behind, raising a yellow spark in the empty space in the line of inverted poultry, for the chicken has disappeared, vanished before their eyes.

... *'Appearing'* .... Echo .... Echo ...

The bus approaches, just one vehicle in the continuous, heavy swirl of traffic. Something dropped has blown or bobbed off the sidewalk into the road. It is bright, red and yellow, it rolls about. The child's eyes gleam wider and she darts forward, reins easily tugged free from the relaxed grip. The beggar's arm, somehow anticipating, rises more urgently; he leans forward, he is about to cry out, but suddenly there is an arm on his, forcing it down.

"Here, you!"

The policeman's strong, gloved hand grips the beggar's arm, while his colleague wraps an arm around his neck and they drag him to his feet. It is all in an instant, just the time it takes for the mother to realise she no longer holds her child's reins and to see them trail behind her towards the road. Just the instant it takes for the bus to reach that same point in the road and for the child to dash over the kerb to reach for the bright thing rolling around in the path of the bus. Just as the beggar who tried to prevent it is hauled away.

"NO! .. NO-O-O!"

The frantic mother, Hwee Lo, screams and rushes to the edge of the road as she hears the sound of the impact even above the traffic noise and the screech of brakes from the bus and sees her child flung forward and to one side, to lie almost at her feet.

"Soo Wong! No, no, no!"

She begins to sob. It is all too late.

"No .. No ... No!"

'Appearing .... ing .... ing .... ing .....'

Remarkably, as unbelievably as the experience itself, while the helicopter weaves and swerves amongst the skyscrapers and swoops low over the swarming streets, the pilot still wrestling in vain with the controls, the infinite view of concrete and tarmac jungle, stretching in every direction as far as they can see, replacing all vestiges of the natural landscape, begins to melt away. It is dissolving, evaporating. The skyscrapers shrink into misty, transparent shapes, the streets and hubbub of vehicles and people blur; and, as they watch, it all melts back into trees, rivers and mountains, a landscape just dotted here and there with modern development, as before.

"I've got her back!"

The pilot's voice breathes relief, breaking the silent astonishment of the President, the Chief and Fleck.

"Take us up", the Chief snaps, unable to quell the tremble in his voice.

"I am, sir, I am", the pilot responds, now in command of his craft but now shaking, too, like the others.

Victoria Twigg notices her knuckles still tight and white on the armrests and relaxes her grip. She feels Renee Fleck's hand clutch at her shoulder from behind. It feels like a hand needing as much comfort as it might provide. Twigg tries to collect her thoughts. There is nothing rational there; except, all she knows, somehow, in some unexplained way, she has just been shown another Africa.

'You ..... Appearing ......' .... Echo.........

As they stand around, clutching each other and trembling and shaking on the traffic island in the bedlam, trying to comprehend the 'hallucination', it all starts to fade away. The heads, the limbs, the bodies are all dissolving into the ground. The ground itself, the concrete, blends once more into the browns and greens and yellows of the natural earth. They look around them, unable to take it in. The noise of the traffic is subsiding and diminishing, the horns becoming quieter, the roar fading to a rumble. As they watch, the highway is evaporating, and the vehicles with it; beyond, the buildings are dissolving into the air, including the one from which the figure has jumped.

As they stand, the landscape of scrub and trees materialises to wrap itself around them once more and they sink, almost as one, to the now natural earth at their feet, nothing but the sounds of the birds and the occasional crackle of twigs to be heard. And all else that can be heard, as they scoop the brown earth in their fingers, and pluck absently at stems of dry grass and scrub, is the sound of their own whimpers and broken sobs.

The two men, the boss Homer Hughes and his foreman, Pete, stand staring at the empty gap in the line. And slowly turn their heads to watch it as it passes along, to be followed by the next suspended feathered body with waiting neck.

Swish, slice, head.

The two men stand for some minutes, unable to speak or move, as the line passes on, unendingly, before them. No-one knows what they may be thinking or, even, praying.

An ambulance clatters to a halt. A bus driver, shaken, hovers in anguish. A crowd is also hovering, watching, then passing on. Two policemen stand, each with a hand holding an empty old brown coat. They will dispose of it somewhere, unable or unwilling to confront a superior officer with the account of how the coat's occupant, a beggar, disappeared - just vanished into thin air - as they were arresting him. They feel stupid but they are also trembling.

A woman, the mother, weeps, weeps, weeps at the edge of the road, the body of a child in her arms.

PARADIGM   :   LAST DAY

She had swept their babe up to her breast, from its bed of soothing leaves, fearful of his intent. The fierce look in his eye, as he stared in wild rage between the sky, the sea and she, holding their son. The sky mocked him with the power of life and death, the sea taunted and the torrid air was filled with the howl and wail of the diseased and dying. He shall not be so quelled! He, the giver and taker of life, the hunter and provider; he shall decide! He shall not be shorn from his dominion!

He faced them, the woman and his son, as the air was sucking life from all it touched. The passion rose within him. He lunged, a fire in his eyes. She recoiled but he reached to snatch the babe from her arms, too frail even against his enfeebled grip. He raised their ailing babe above his head, his hands clasped around its neck.

"They shall not have you!" he cried in his agony of despair. They shall not take you, to hold and curse you until they deem it is your time! You are not for them! We are not for them!"

His fingers tightened about the throat. She screamed and flailed at him, her blistered fingers clutching and beating at his chest, tears flowing down her cheeks. But still he held the infant aloft, his fingers tightening the more, it kicking as it choked, high above his head, as he raged and stood against her vain assault; as the child became limp, while he railed and wept in his torment. Then with a great cry of anguish he hurled his child down, down onto the rocks by the swarming sea, for the waves to lap and roll the lifeless form in its smothering foam.

"No! No! No!" she cried in frenzy, her weakening fists beating at his chest. Then she made to pitch down to the rocks if it was not yet too late. But he seized her now, grasping her, too, about her neck.

"Nor shall they have you!" he cried. "They take the birds, the fish, the beasts, but neither he nor you!" He cast his eye to the limp form of their child tossed on the rocks below, as his hands enclosed about her throat. His eyes were blinded with the tears of agony and grief. He could only feel her struggle in his grip, only hear the sounds of her voice, the sounds stumbling from her tortured lips, the lips of beauty he had kissed and loved, in the golden face he had caressed and adored; he could no longer see the cruel ferment on her skin, the scars and fissures wrought by the air; his eyes were only filled with his own tears, as he could only hear her fading cries beneath the turmoil of the sea below and the howls in the air and then felt her tears, too, fall across his hands around her neck, as her struggle ceased and with a tormented sob he cast her, too, to the rocks beneath, pounded in the foam. She lay beside her own child, the waves still lapping and snatching at them both, and he saw their deep, sightless eyes only staring at the boiling sky above.

And the sky fumed in its rage, the air smoked and curled, the sea foamed, deprived of its prey, as he sank to his knees on their rock, their sullied rock, their life, and wept. The sound of his weeping mingled with the sounds of the dying around, the moaning in the air and the thrashing of the sea, and he wept and wept until he could weep no more.

Worship

"A *chicken*?"

God, being God, as clearly was the case, did not feel an obligation to reply; particularly as it was a question He would rather his trusty aide had not asked. It had not seemed unreasonable - while it was in the natural order of things He Himself had ordained, for many among His species on Earth to prey upon one another - that He should experience one such circumstance at first hand. He could have chosen from a myriad examples: the beetle about to be stamped, the torture victim, the stag at bay, the mouse with the cat, the innocent at execution.

"So did it make a difference?" grumped the picking one, with a sharp jab, undeterred by absence of a reply.

No, sighed the Lord God to Himself, the chicken had not been to make a difference. It had not been to change the order of things; they had been through all that, time and again in Heaven. It was not even to understand, He understood it all. He had created it, hadn't He? It was to be there, to experience what He had created. To be on the receiving end of the dark side, where there could be no resistance, where the order of things was its own justification; but where there might not be the want of care. A want of care. He had felt the want of care.

"And You didn't stop the bus." The voice of the angel might almost have been an accusing one, had it dared.

No, the Lord sighed again. The beggar had not been there to stop the bus with his thin arm. The beggar had been there to make just one attempt, just that time, to divert an outcome to spare one victim of the consequence of a dislocation in a chain of events not of its doing. Just that time. The beggar was there to offer a choice; to be heeded or suppressed. Another echo through time.

"You knew they would get You."

There was a silence in Heaven. No, He did not *know* that the beggar's good intention would be thwarted. Not until the choice had been made. One choice. More than one future.

"And the rest of it. Do You think they actually noticed?" There was some grudging admiration now. Gabriel reckoned he had achieved quite a lot himself recently, done everything expected of him, and more. But when it came to appearing, the third in this trinity, as an entire continent - *and* making sure the rest of the world saw it - he had to hand it to the Guv. And no wings! It certainly beat setting up a bit of instant molecular transportation; though he still grinned when he recalled his little pigtailed Chinese girl.

"Noticed", brooded the Almighty.

"Well, the last time they actually thought it was You - some of them - it didn't exactly helps things much. Made them worse, if you ask me" (something God was not about to do). "So *this* time ..." Gabriel considered he had made his point by not elaborating further and the silence hung upon them once more.

What more could He do, God pondered, but provide a sign? If influencing attitudes and behaviour were not enough, what else but to provide a contemporary equivalent of parting the waters or speaking from a mountain top? Then it was up to them to respond, to choose. Which future indeed?

"Hmph", grunted the angel. Then, after a pause, added, "How long have they got?"

Another silence, deeper now, and longer. A brooding silence in Heaven. A silence that hung.

"They'll still worship You, you know", he grunted again after a while, "some of them."

Worship! Why? There were times when God wanted someone else to provide answers for a change, when even the loyal and perceptive archangel, who had been at His side for most of Eternity, could not help. Had He, the Lord God Almighty, *expected* to be worshipped? Had he *demanded* it? What would be the point of it? Who else amongst the multitudes in the Cosmos considered it appropriate to *worship* Him, to kiss the hem of his metaphorical garment, or bow to his imagined knee? He sighed once more. All he expected was reasonable behaviour one to another. Reasonable care.

"And half of *them* just think it lets them off the hook, anyway", grumbled the same archangel, still at his side.

"Mmm?" The mild enquiry.

"Worship."

Water

Perhaps the whole world had hallucinated. It was a theory, anyway, improbable though it might be. Not eighteen months since scientists in the US, the United Kingdom and China had been puzzling how numerous mechanical devices, from cars to washing machines, had unaccountably stuttered to a halt - and found no answers - than they were now charged with determining how the world's television programmes had been infiltrated with alarming, horrific images of what purported to be the African continent. All of it.

Yet, although indelibly marked upon the consciousness of millions, those images had come and gone in a flash. Suspended long enough to be viewed, absorbed and remembered, in all their disturbing graphic detail. Too brief, though, to be recorded and captured to be analysed. Or were they? Technology was capable of capturing images in milliseconds. How come these pictures and sounds had not 'stuck' on any recording medium across the entire globe?

For everyone, it was a virtual event; images via television, internet, cell phone and all manner of electronic receivers. For everyone except a small safari party of Americans and English, with their African guides who, it was rumoured, experienced the event itself; along with, allegedly, the American President, whilst touring her troops on the continent in her helicopter.

"But why us?" murmured Bella. "Why ...." and she paused to look up with a sense of realisation at Elroy " .... You?"

Elroy returned her look then turned away, his eyes elsewhere.

"I think ..." He turned back to her, sombrely. "I think we've been shown the future."

Bella looked at him, questioningly.

"*A* future", he measured his words, "one possible future - or probable, maybe."

"If we don't get it right?" she queried. Then she added, hesitantly, "Do you mean this was a ... vision? Like what you saw?"

"I don't know, Bella." He shook his head. "Bigger. Much bigger. Not the same at all." He had a distant look in his eyes and his voice dropped to a whisper. "This might have been the first time ... He's come."

The group had at last returned to the jeeps, through the disconcertingly peaceful scrub.

Walt regarded his friend, quizzicaly. He'd overheard a snatch of the conversation.

"That's visions, isn't it? Where only one or two actually see it and have to spread the ... word ... to the others?"

In all these months, Walt Brown still found it almost impossible to come to grips with this archaic concept: visions. His big friend dropped to his haunches, sifting the dry brown dust through his fingers, brooding at the ground. Mariana was ushering the two children, now very quiet, into one of the jeeps. The rest of the party began to follow suit.

"Well, man", Walt spoke down to the hunched Elroy, encouragingly, "it aint gonna get any harder - easier now - the oil's running out and, anyway, look at what's happening: folks - corporations, whole governments - getting serious about pollution, saving energy an' all. Even if sharing's collapsed and the bad old days coming back, it aint gonna last for ever -"

"You don't get it", Elroy interrupted him, with a glance upwards.

"Eh?"

"It's not gonna be oil anymore."

"What?" Walt frowned.

"See this?" Elroy raised a hand full of dry brown dust and let it sift through his fingers to the ground. "Half the world's gonna be like this soon. More than half. It's water, man."

Elroy rose to his feet and stared grimly at his friend.

"Water. The 'new oil' they're calling it."

"Well, that lets you off, man." Walt placed a hand on Elroy's shoulder and tried to speak brightly.

"Does it?" Elroy's eyes were penetrating Walt so he had to momentarily lower his own, "Do you think they don't know this?"

"They?"

"LOTUS. And all them. It's gonna be water now. Fiddling figures, cheating supplies -"

"Again?"

"Yup. Again." Elroy's shoulders slumped and he turned away. "I told you, they got me, man."

Walt followed his friend's eyes to the seated Mariana in the nearest jeep, an arm around each child in the back seat.

"For water?" Walt gazed bleakly at him. He had never for one moment considered this.

"For water", Elroy nodded, staring vacantly across the scrub and through the spindly trees.

Walt saw there was moisture beneath his friend's eyelids and did not know what to say. El spoke for him, turning to look at him so his eyes shone in the sun. It was not the sadness Walt expected to see. There was anguish, anger, despair playing across a face which twisted in unfamiliar bitterness as the words were ground out.

"There's always gonna be *something*, Walt." The big hands were clenched into fists as if ready to strike the unseen foe. "*Always!*"

Preordain

"Of course, you *could* say ..."

God considered he really would rather not, especially as, for once, it seemed to be a more generalised 'you' than a direct reference to Himself.

Los Angeles. 9am. Warm sunshine.

"What we saw, Renee. Was it the future?"

"Ma'am? They're still saying it was a hallucination, aren't they?"

"They? They weren't there, were they? We were."

"Ma'am."

"The people out there. Is that what they want? That future?"

"They tried one way, ma'am: you showed them."

"Sharing."

"Yes, ma'am."

"Now they want to go back? To the old way?"

"You showed them, ma'am. A new future. Back to prosperity."

"I didn't know the price, Renee."

Somewhere beyond the hotel window, the crowd would be gathering for the next campaign rally. Did she have the resolve? Was there not another way?

"Second term, ma'am."

"My angel...."

"Ma'am?"

"You *could* say", persisted the one who was fresh - although quite the opposite, actually - back from a brief vacation on Splong, "you *could* say - if You can hear me from over there - it was never going to make a difference anyway."

God resisted any response other than the almost imperceptible raising of a metaphorical eyebrow but it did not deter the pungently picking and loquacious one.

"Because You'd preordained it all."

"It?"

"Yeh. Everything we've done - the nudging - You preordained it. Preordained *everything*." Gabriel was becoming animated, as his brow furrowed with the dual intensity of gathering matter and gathering his thoughts. "*Everything*. Including what wasn't preordained."

"Gabriel", observed the Lord, with the supreme patience only accorded to The Supremely Patient One, "how could I preordain anything that was not preordained?"

"Because You forgot", replied the angel, simply.

"Forgot?" Supreme Patience can feel its supremacy challenged on occasion.

Same time. London. 5pm. Warm, cloudy.

"Chilli sauce, sir?"

Asif Hassan smiled a twinkling smile. It was good to welcome back a familiar customer after an absence.

"No - thanks", grimaced Paul, but with a smile, too.

"You have been away, sir? You look brown."

Paul nearly said, 'so do you' but thought better of it. Besides, he liked the man.

"Not seen you in a while, either", he remarked, eyeing the two kebabs to check they were not receiving a surreptitious sprinkling of killer sauce.

"Ah, yes", nodded Asif, a trifle gravely, thought Paul, "I was away, too. A journey."

"Hm", acknowledged Paul, wondering if it was one of those trips to Mecca, or whatever. "Well, I hope it was good - and the kebabs", he added with a chuckle.

"It was, sir - but not as good as the kebabs." But the riposte had lost some of the twinkle.

"Well, thanks, see you." Paul exchanged cash for packages and stepped outside. His step bore a lightness to it. A touch sombre, at times, these Asians, he thought. Then he smiled in anticipation. He was getting home early from work. He managed it much more often nowadays. He so looked forward to home and Isabella. It was almost like when they met. Had it been the 'car'? Or Africa, that had brought them close again? His not to reason why. He turned key in ignition, still smiling.

"Yeh, Guv, our nudging. Forgot You'd preordained it at The Beginning Of All Things. Ouch!" Gabriel was in danger of becoming overexcited as his exposition unfolded and the netherest parts of him were bearing the brunt. "So it was always going to end up like this. As preordained in the first place. So - wow! Ouch! - when You said about us making a difference, nudging and all that, You were only saying what You'd already preordained You'd say! Only You forgot. I mean it *was* a long time ago - if You know what I mea -"

"Gabriel." It was a sharper interruption than was customary for the Lord. "I do not forget."

"Joan of Arc?"

"Gabriel!"

The angel was subdued into silence. But only briefly.

"So, well, that's the point isn't it? If *we've* only being doing what You'd preordained us to do, the future they'll end up with is the future that was preordained - *You* preordained - in the first place. So it's not exactly a surprise."

He leaned back on his elbows, staring out at Heaven, a satisfied look on his face.

Same time. London 5pm, warm, cloudy. New York, 12 Noon. Hot

"Yes, he'll be home soon. It's cool, Livvy, it's like love again!"

"I'm so pleased for you, Bella!"

"And he keeps getting home early now. Instead of late, with excuses."

"I guess he's making the excuses at work now."

"I guess!"

There is laughter between friends, across the ocean. Then a pause.

"Livvy, it seems like nothing worked out in the end."

"It might, hun. Maybe it's not too late. You know, lessons learned, maybe."

"You think?"

"The President ..."

"Huh. Aint it all about votes?"

"Dunno .. But, listen, Bella, got some *news* for you!"

"Yeh?"

"Yeh .. Hey .. No, wait .. The other phone's goin'. Bella, hun, I'll call you back."

"The news?"

"I'll call."

"Of course, we could have a go all over again, only first You'd have to remember what You'd preordained in The Beginning so we made sure we did something different, You know, I mean, I supp -"

"Gabriel." It was a softer command this time, but no less constraining. The angel was quiet.

"They still have a choice", murmured the Lord. "They always have a choice, whether we -"

"nudge?" Gabriel interjected, helpfully.

" or not. There are always alternative futures."

Same time. Kashmir. 11pm. Warm. Overcast. New York. 12 Noon. Hot

"Livvy?"

"El? Hi! How are you?"

"Okay. I'm okay. Walt there?"

"No, sorry, El. He's out. Work."

"Oh, yuh. I was forgetting the time."

"Where are you?"

"Oh, away, ya know."

"You okay, El?"

"Yuh. Yuh. Fine. Hey, Olivia, will ya tell Mariana everything's fine. Ya know. And the kids."

"You tell them, El? Mariana'll be home."

"Yeh. No. Gotta be careful with calls."

"El. You okay, El?"

"Yeh. Fine. Cool. Livvy, tell Walt. Tell Walt, will ya? Tell him ... it's like I said."

0"What do you mean, El? Hey, El?"

"Gotta go, Livvy. Ya know. Be seeing ya. Tell Mariana, won't you ..."

There is a catch in the throat across oceans and continents.

"El?"

"Biscuits and railway lines?"

"If you put it like that", came the guarded Divine response.

Gabriel was contemplating the notion of a choice between alternative futures being exercised on Earth.

"Yeh, well, let's face it ..."   he concluded, in a 'need-I-say-more-what-hope-is-there?' kind of way.

Same time. Beijing outskirts. 1am. Humid

"My darling."

"Oh my love, my love."

Tears. Always tears, now. Tears and emptiness.

"Please ... It was not you ... There was nothing you ..."

And silences, with words which cannot fill them.

"My love ... how could I .. how could it be ... I ..."

And more tears.

"Come. Let me hold you. We have each other. I have you. We have ... we have memories. Now we must have hope."

"I thought .. I thought we had been saved ..."

And more, more tears.

"Now we must save ourselves."

Later. New York. 6.30pm. Still hot

"Oh, Walt, I forgot .. I was going to tell Bella."

"You only told *me* yesterday!"

"Well, thank your lucky stars I remembered!"

"Hey, stand still while I catch you!"

"You think I can't still run away from you!"

"Hey ... Hun ... You better take care on the running!"

"I'm not an invalid, Walt!"

"Not yet!"

"Walt! Walt! Keep your hands off."

"You said you're not an invalid!"

"That doesn't mean you ... Ooh ...oooh ... Walt ...mmm!"

Passers-by - and maybe 'burger' Joan was one of them - might well have noticed that irrational giggling and other preludes to baudy lovemaking were once again rampant from behind the Brown closed doors.

"But Walt, seriously ... Ooh, hold me like that ... Ooh, yes ... You know, after all this time ... and what we've seen - do you *want* to bring a baby into this world?"

"Hun, Livvy, don't you want to?"

"Of course ... of *course* .. you know, when we began to think we couldn't .. but, you know ... what we've seen ..."

"Wouldn't that just be giving in, hun? Don't you think maybe we can still make a difference?"

"Just us?"

"Not just us. Anyone who cares. And our child."

"Child? ... Oh, Walt, what a wonderful word."

"I couldn't reach El. Line dead. You said he sounded ... strange."

"Yeh, hun. Like he was going to choke. Where is he?"

"Don't know, hun."

"Really?"

"Yeh, really. He's ... In deep."

"Oh, Walt."

"Yeh...."

"Hold me."

"I love you, babe."

"Babe?"

"You're always my babe."

"You'll have two, soon."

"You gonna tell Bella?"

"Tomorrow. Hold me tighter."

"Love you."

"Love you."

He lay on their rock. He watched them half floating in the lapping waves. There was nothing left. No life in them, nor in him. No tears. They had gone, too. Only emptiness. Nothing more. Only the swirling cloak around them. That was all the sky, the air, the sea had now become. A cloak to smother all else that might have striven to live. A hollow conquest, in which nothing else remained. Nothing but a stain. He, he was that stain. A stain upon their rock. A stain upon the memory of their world. He had nothing more to give and there was nothing left to take. He could only wait. In the end, he and they would be gone. Not even a stain would remain.

Maybe

The aisles of Wal-Mart were kind of bustling and kind of not. The management, right up to Board level, couldn't work it out. It was like the aisles themselves weren't sure. Not the foodstuffs. They were always busy. Folks had to eat. It was 'houseware', 'electricals', goods like that: vacs, irons, dvd players, and so on. There had been that big rush – what the media had dubbed the 'stampede for things' – but it had been short-lived. As if folks had second thoughts; or even – 'Heaven forbid!' they had exclaimed in the boardrooms – folks discovered they did not *need* the 'things' anymore. So in 'houseware', and electricals', trade had dwindled again. Then another little surge. Then falling back again. Like a tide of uncertainty, ebbing and flowing.

"Hey, Rita!"

Rita turned her eyes from the serried rows of cans and saw the smile beaming at her.

"How y'all?" exclaimed Abigail, "We're making a habit of this!"

Rita smiled, too. There must be some unwritten routine that took people to the same store, same time, same day, even the same aisle!

"I'm jus' fine, Abigail. And you?"

"Gee, yes, thanks."

"I passed your place a few days ago", remarked Rita, "you sure had a few folks around. Some barbecue!"

"Yeh", grinned Abigail, passing an eye along the soups and chowders on the opposite shelves, "our Joel's birthday. Lotsa friends and relations."

"Some barbecue", repeated Rita, in friendly awe, "could see the glow from the sidewalk."

"The fence", chuckled Abigail.

"Fence?"

"Yeh, Rita, you know: blown down. Liked it better that way."

"So you still never put it back up?" queried Rita.

"Nope. On the barbecue!"

"Whole fence?" Rita considered there had been enough fence to feed a bush fire, not a barbecue.

"Lotsa barbecues!" explained Abigail, cheerfully. "Been another hot summer, eh? Lotsa barbecues and lotsa fence to burn!"

Rita shook her head in silent admiration.

"So that's it? You gonna just keep it open with the folks next door?"

"Yep." Abigail dropped 'Uncle Ben's Clam Chowder' into the half-full trolley. "Easier than carrying their vac up and down both drives and back again."

Rita paused in the aisle.

"Sharing it, you mean?"

"Sure thing, Rita." Then Abigail allowed a little frown to cloud her brow. "Don't tell me you aint sharing any more. I mean, shucks, Rita, I thought–"

"Yes", broke in her friend, "Yes we are, I just thought, I thought, maybe, a lotta folks were thinking it's stupid now."

"Stupid?"

"Yeh, sure, you know, now it's all changed."

"Changed? I aint changed, Rita." Abigail decided on another can of 'Uncle Ben's' and looked emphatically at her friend. "Anyways, we all like going around to each others'. As well as we don't need *one each* of everything. *That* changed." She smiled again and looked to Rita like someone who knows everything is just fine, as she added, "We aint choking each other. We just aint going back to the old ways."

"We're the same", murmured Rita.

"Our old vac's broke", Abigail carried on, "We don't need a new one, Cherry's is swell, and she's put a big recycling box where her busted washer used to be. Just swell."

She was checking the shelves again for anything she might have missed.

"Recycling box", repeated Rita, half to herself, "Gee..."

Another voice chimed in behind them.

"Why, 'mornin' Abigail, ma'am."

Both women looked round.

"Hey, Sylvester", smiled Abigail at the big young man, "how y'all?"

"Just fine, ma'am." And he smiled a polite nod to Rita, too, who smiled in return.

"Hey, you looked weighed down, Sylvester", chortled Abigail, eyeing the long, heavy box the boy was struggling to prevent from slipping off the shopping trolley it was straddling.

"Latest vac", he grinned proudly.

"Oh yeh?" said Abigail, with a raised eyebrow.

"Yeh. Holly wants a new one. Says we can't keep borrowing from the other folks."

"Sharing, you mean?" Abigail eyed him.

"Yeh", the thirty-something shrugged, "Yeh, you know ..."

"You don't *like* other folks?" enquired Abigail.

"Well, hey, of course Abigail. We just couldn't -"

"You lend things, too?" she asked.

"Well, sure ..."

"You don't like other folks coming around to borrow your things?"

"Yeh, sure I do." Sylvester was beginning to sound a little sheepish for a big strong young guy. "I go fishing with Bess's Hank when she comes to watch our TV with Holly."

"So what do you want a new vac for?"

Abigail was adopting a motherly tone with this young man who was no relation but needed a bit of soft interrogation, she could see.

"Well ... Holly..."

"Well, your Holly", began Abigail, and she broke off. Then she took up again. "You don't mind sharing your things?" She did not wait for a repeated confirmation. "And I guess other folks don't mind sharing with you? We all got accustomed to it, aint we?"

Again, he did not attempt to respond but pretended to square up the big box perched awkwardly on the trolley.

"And *all* you folks *like* being together, like ... like ... sharing's just *part* of it. And maybe ..."

It was like a little lecture in the middle of aisle number twenty-four - '*Canned Vegetables*' - such that some other people with laden trolleys were turning back and going the other way. There was this big, good-looking guy, stopped with an empty trolley, except for a big, long box straddled awkwardly across it, and two women kind of squaring up to him. Well, one was, while the other looked on, not knowing if she should say anything but thinking she'd better not, better just leave her friend to it.

"And maybe", Abigail continued, "maybe you might just not go fishing no more and your Holly might not get to see her friend, *and* -" Abigail laid a palm firmly on the cardboard box - "theres *one* vac'll stay in the cupboard most of the time, *or* -" she looked the young Sylvester in the eye "there's *two* vacs only gonna be *half*-used and a guy sitting at home while a lotta fish havin' a peaceful life."

She smiled broadly at him. She was not out to make him uncomfortable. Well, she was, but she had just achieved that, she could tell; so she was just able to finish it with a smile.

"Hey, shucks, Abigail, what'll Holly say?"

"Sylvester. You take the money back to her and say you're taking her out to buy a new dress. *I* know what she'll say."

He grinned. All three grinned, as he swung the trolley around to return the smart new vacuum cleaner to its shelf, an arm across the top to stop it slipping as he went.

"Gee", smiled Rita, "I guess you told him."

"Hope his Holly sees it the same", observed Abigail, wryly.

They pushed their trolleys up the aisle towards the next.

"I'd heard of *some* other folks still sharing", remarked Rita, "but not everyone."

"Plenty around us", replied Abigail. "We just kinda don't *need* one of everything. And we got used to sharing, seeing folks, helping out, fetching things, taking them back."

"I guess it musta been like that in the old days", added Rita, as they rounded the top of the aisle, "what did they call it? 'Community'?"

"Yeh", breezed Abigail, "*and* we only use things when we need them, not get the vac out for every speck of dust, like there's nothing else to do! Clean, sure, but my kitchen aint an operating theatre. And the bills, Rita - same as yours? - electricity right down, all these things we used to fetch out of the cupboard or switch on every minute of the day. And gas for the car. Can't remember when I last filled up."

The energy of her enthusiasm was in danger of sweeping all other trolleys before her, leaving scattered shoppers in her wake. Rita smiled and caught her arm to slow her down.

"Oh yeh, sure", grinned Abigail, throttling back on her Wal-Mart Speedster, "but - cars - we're trying to sell our other two -

the Chevy and the Mustang - same as a lot of other folks but, heck, no-one wants to buy them!"

"Not everyone, though," Rita was pondering, "only a few sharing? Pockets here and there, like your neighbourhood?"

"I guess", shrugged Abigail.

"And it's no good", added Rita, as they had paused halfway down '*Flour - Rice - Pasta*', if the Chinese and all the others just keep making more stuff, using up energy, polluting."

"My Ed", declared Abigail, "says they followed us up to the top of the hill -"

Her friend looked queringly at her.

" -things, goods, *materialism*? All that. And maybe they'll follow us down again." She examined a pack of '*pure white rice*' disdainfully and put it back. "If that's where we're heading."

Rita was thoughtful in the middle of the aisle.

"Abigail. Will you vote?"

"Sure thing."

"Who do you reckon? Mind me asking?"

"Dunno yet", stated Abigail, "Ya know, it's not about 'parties' now, is it?"

"No?"

"No." She picked the rice off the shelf again and held it out. "Think of all the *energy* and *power* they use to take all the good stuff *outa* this, and leave us with just the rubbish to eat!" She put it back, this time taking a pack of '*wholegrain rice*' instead. "No, it's about who's gonna get it right. Yeh? Right for America. *Us*. *And* the World."

"Saving the planet?" asked Rita, thinking it would take more than some packs of rice, but add it to everything else and, heck, her Cal might even like this, as she dropped a pack into her trolley.

"The planet?" nodded Abigail. "Heck of a big deal. My vote? It's whoever gets it right. If *any* of them really try."

Rita gazed thoughtfully at the shelves.

"Everyone - every country - all folks sharing; sharing more, using less?" she mused.

"Sure."

"Could that be the answer?", Rita asked.

"Answer?" Abigail was moving on again, revving up. "What answer?"

"This - what we've been saying: using less, sharing more. Sharing."

"The answer to what?" Abigail's mind was half on what time it was and what she still had to buy.

"Well, you know, saving .. us ..the world." Rita smiled, a little embarrassed at expressing what might be considered grandiose thoughts, on the way from '*Flour-Rice-Pasta*' to '*Deodorants*'. "The answer to everything."

"Aw, come on", chortled Abigail, grabbing her arm to steer her round the corner. "What planet are *you* on?"

Cosmos

It might have been a beautiful morning in Heaven. If Heaven had mornings. Or afternoons. Or evenings. Or days or nights. Or dark or light. Hot or cold, wet or dry. Or ... anything. Thus, if it had been anywhere else but Heaven, it might have been 'beautiful'; instead of being just 'Heaven'.

"So, anyway, Guv. Where now?"

Good question.

Gabriel was gazing across all the Cosmos, or as much of it as could be observed from Heaven which, in some ways, was all of it. It presented countless opportunities, challenges, (and as recent experience demonstrated) frustrations. The concept of 'where now', much like 'where next' along with 'future', 'present' and 'past', had little relevance, of course, for God, Who was everywhere all the time (as it were) and all that. But humour the archangel, humour him.

"Where do you suggest?"

Gabriel thought for a moment, then brightened, maybe with a particular recollection or an occasion fondly remembered.

"How about Number Five?"

This was the problem with being God. All these parallel universes. Sometimes He had difficulty remembering which one He was in. Yes, yes, He was everywhere in each one all the time, past, present and future. But – really! – to be focused on each part of every one simultaneously: all the galaxies, all the species, in *every* universe; it would be enough to drive any Deity dotty (well, let's not exaggerate). So He was only truly 'in' one at any point in time (and let's not start arguing about the different definitions of 'time' in each separate parallel universe. Nor about the concept, 'parallel', come to think of it) And then there were all the space-time dislocations to deal with.

"Five?" prompted the Good Lord Almighty, unwilling to indicate He could not remember which one that was.

"Yeh. You know."

Gabriel was not much help when he identified the universes by numbers: 8, 14, 9, 2, 463, 93, and so on. 'How about Number 5?' was more like a quiz question. So... thought God ...which one is that? It was both a help and a hindrance that they were all so similar. A help that many of the same galaxies were in all of them and so were many of the same, or at least passably similar, species. There were a few notable exceptions. In one, the missing link was still missing on Earth and the equivalent of the Pope was a giant amphibious ant (and much less difficult).

Generally, though, Earth was one of those planets which presented problems in all the universes, just not identically in each one. So it did not make a huge difference where they went 'next' but if Number Five was the universe where the Splongies were odourless then He was all for that.

It was a blessing, He considered, that no species, however advanced, in any galaxy, had discovered the 'wormholes' (strange 'intelligent' definition cropping up in several universes) connecting *their* universe to any other. Nor were they ever likely to if the future went according to its predestined path(s). There again, what with the gift of self-determination and all, He could never be quite certain.

"Mmm, yes", declared the Wisest One, as though He really did know, and not wishing to suggest an ambivalence which might set Gabriel off on the wrong foot (oh dear, yes, *that* seemed to be pretty much the same in *every* universe), "Number Five."

It was not as though He could be precisely certain which one they were in now. 16? Or 61? However. "On condition –" He added.

"Uh-oh", groaned Gabriel. Always loading things with conditions, the Great Determiner (not a term he used to the Almighty personally).

"On condition", continued God, "that you don't make such a fuss again if there are matters (bad choice of word) to be determined on ... Earth.

Actually, Gabriel could not always remember which versions of which galaxy, which solar systems, which species were presented in each and every universe. He just had this slightly uplifting feeling that Number Five was generally a better bet than the one they had just been 'in' (it was 61, actually). Only snag, he could not quite recall which version of *Earth* it was.

"Gabriel?" It was the Good Lord Almighty, Supreme Being, Creator Of All things, and so on and so forth, interrupting the angel's thoughts this time. "Earth? Fuss?"

"Okay Boss", shrugged Gabriel, but quietly decided to take a pair of wings, just in case; and resumed picking.